Jennifer,

Plowshares in
the Palatinate

So glad you asked ... ("When is
the next book coming ??")
Here it is! Enjoy!
Love,
Phyllis

Plowshares in the Palatinate

A Novel

Phyllis Harrison

iUniverse, Inc.
New York   Bloomington

Plowshares in the Palatinate

A Novel

iUniverse books may be ordered through booksellers or by contacting:

iUniverse
1663 Liberty Drive
Bloomington, IN 47403
www.iuniverse.com
1-800-Authors (1-800-288-4677)

Because of the dynamic nature of the Internet, any Web addresses or links contained in this book may have changed since publication and may no longer be valid. This is a work of fiction. All of the characters, names, incidents, organizations, and dialogue in this novel are either the products of the author's imagination or are used fictitiously.

ISBN: 978--14401-5217-7(pbk)
ISBN: 978-1-4401-5218-4(ebk)

Printed in the United States of America
iUniverse rev. date: 7/17/2009

For my father, who gave me a love of history and story-telling, my mother who left a legacy with this nearly-forgotten story to tell, Barry for his advice and technical expertise, and Joan, genealogical researcher extraordinaire.

For Frank and Jayne who listened to my stories, and for Glenn and Lynn who wouldn't let me quit.

For adventurers and dreamers everywhere who will not give up on their aspirations, and finally, for all of our kin who have lived for a time in the Rhine River Valley: Those who were born there, those who only sojourned there, and those who are there still.

Amsterdam, Netherlands, December 1640

Hendrick leaned on the table, his greasy gray and brown-streaked head of hair supported by his gnarled hands and tobacco-stained fingers, trails of crumbs leading down from his beard, across the table to the loaf of dark bread and block of moldy gold and green cheese in front of him. A knife protruded from the center of the pungent pale moon, having been plunged into its heart.

Gilles couldn't avoid seeing Hendrick sitting there as soon as he came out of the bedroom and he didn't need to observe any more to know that his father-in-law had probably been awake for some time already on this winter morning, drinking ale for his breakfast and drinking a good quantity of it. Gilles refused to let this be a concern to him, even

1

if he *was* certain that the cheese was a surrogate for his *own* heart, the old Dutchman's wishful thinking being evident. Hendrick must have derived at least a small measure of satisfaction from burying the knife in his morning meal if he couldn't bury it in his new son-in-law. Gilles would not grant him the favor of his time *or* energy in thinking about it though; he had more immediate and pressing challenges with the very rocky start of his week-old marriage to Hendrick's eldest daughter and life's other unending daily challenges. He could not allow his energies to be diverted to needless worry and empty threats from an old man.

Survival in a foreign country after his escape from a French prison would have kept anyone busy enough, but in addition to this, Gilles had to be constantly on his guard, avoiding the bounty hunters who occasionally showed up, poking around the city in the hopes of seizing Gilles or some other fugitive, taking him back to France for yet another try at execution, by burning or hanging, either method being equally acceptable to *les chasseurs*.

Gilles knew that it was nothing personal. The King's two-legged hounds were simply on the trail of the substantial reward offered for the return of a teenage Huguenot, not much of a prize in and of himself, but one from a substantial family. Executing this Protestant rebel should certainly be sufficient to permanently dissuade the rest of the city of Rouen, if not the entire province, from further flirtations with Protestantism. The spectacle of it would most definitely make a lasting impression, underscoring graphically the penalties for forsaking the Catholic Church. Such an execution would also provide some excellent public entertainment as well.

"Awake *at last*, are you? You left us to handle the inn alone and supper was a disaster!" Hendrick slurred his words, reproaching his daughter, Elsje, who had come into the room just behind her bridegroom. "Two customers *left* because there was no food and I had to pay the kitchen help *extra* to stay late and keep serving ale."

Elsje ignored her father completely and set two plates down, one for herself and one for Gilles, reaching right across her father's place, under his very nose to retrieve the bread. She didn't sit down though: She never sat down during mealtimes because she was always too busy. Elsje went over to retrieve the butter from the preparation table for Gilles. She had already learned, and already accepted, that her new husband didn't care very much for Dutch food, the Dutch ale and hard Amsterdam cheeses included. Gilles much preferred the French food and wine that he had been accustomed to for the whole of his life, all nineteen or so years of it, but it was not always possible to find it in Amsterdam, not even in the growing French section of the city, even if one had enough money for such luxuries.

When he thought that perhaps Elsje couldn't hear him, when he thought that she was *just* far enough away to be out of earshot, Hendrick said blearily to Gilles, "But you *promised* me."

Hendrick had underestimated his daughter's sensory abilities though, and Elsje *did* hear the remark. The peace that had settled over the house for the past few hours vanished as quickly as daylight on a December afternoon. Elsje's temper rose and she turned on her father, scolding him loudly.

"How *could* you? If you *ever, ever,* interfere in our marriage again, we will *leave* here and be gone *forever* from this house! Then you will have to pay someone *every day* to do *all* of the work that I do around here! You can find someone else to run your damned inn!"

Gilles' hopes rose when he heard this, and he fervently hoped that she meant what she said. He wondered if it was worth provoking the old man, purposely starting some mischief with him, so that Gilles could hold Elsje to her threat of moving out. Gilles was painfully aware that he was sitting at the old man's table, in the old man's family apartments, on the top floor of the three-story inn that was owned by Hendrick. While Gilles *was* grateful for the refuge, it pained him to remember all that he had left behind so unwillingly in France: his home, his family, his wealth, and even his beliefs about the eternal realities of the world, his religion. Gilles didn't know if it would ever be possible to return to his home and bring his wife there with him. Wordlessly Gilles took the bread and butter that Elsje offered him and he stuffed it into his mouth, as much to stop himself from saying anything that might worsen the situation, as to keep both father and daughter from *expecting* any reply.

Elsje poured some ale for Gilles from Hendrick's cracked and dirty old white pitcher, emptying it to the last drop.

Somebody would have to go and get some more.

They would have to go all the way down to the first floor of the house for a refill, down from the family's private living quarters on the top floor, the third floor, past the second floor where they rented out rooms for sleeping, some rooms being private little chambers no bigger than a human squirrel's nest for the more prosperous travelers who demanded privacy and one great big room with comparatively vast floor space, crowded at night with the snoring and wheezing bodies of many frugal travelers, all packed in together and more like a great litter of animals than men. Whoever went to refill the pitcher would have to go all the way down to the family's tavern and dining business on the main floor, the first floor, to fill the pitcher up again from the keg and it would take them more than a few minutes.

Gilles hoped that it wouldn't be Elsje who went downstairs, although sending the woman to fetch it was the obvious course of action. He was fairly certain that his being left alone with Hendrick without any witnesses would end very badly, one way or the other. Gilles would have to do without for now, without ale and without asking for more.

There was silence for too short a time before the old man unwisely chose to speak again. His better judgment must have been impaired by the ale that he had been consuming as the greater portion of his breakfast this morning. Even so, he should have surmised the outcome.

"It is not seemly that you two mate like wild animals with your younger sister in the next room. This, this...*Frenchman*... has excessive appetites! I don't even recognize my own child since you have been under *his* influence. The papists *all* have peculiar appetites and I fear for your soul, Daughter..."

Elsje, primed for a fight now, rounded on her father.

"*Oho*, do not worry yourself about *my* soul! You will not have to worry about me *at all* if we move out, only about how *you* are going to run an inn without me when you can't even feed *yourself!* I will not hear *one* more word against my husband! *Not one!* What happens behind our bedroom door is our concern!"

"He doesn't even have the courage to stand up and defend himself. The French are *all* cowards."

Hendrick nonchalantly tore another piece of bread from the loaf as he said this, not looking directly at Gilles, but then again, he probably was confident that there would be no challenge, no reprisal from Gilles for the verbal barb.

Gilles could control himself no longer though. He pushed back his chair and he was going to hit Hendrick, just *one* time. He had been aching to strike back at the old man for months now, retaliating for all of the slanders, all of the snide little comments, the sabotage, even the investigator that Hendrick had hired to follow Gilles around to look for some reason *other* than just Gilles' refugee status to put an end to the friendship between the young couple that had steadily grown into something more, until somehow, and Gilles himself wasn't even quite sure how it had happened, he and Elsje had become husband and wife. Gilles looked briefly at the cheese knife, more to make sure that it was still there and out of Hendrick's reach, but Elsje saw the glance and she grabbed her husband's arm.

"Nee! You will *kill* him, Gilles!"

"A *violent* man he is too; he will probably beat you every day and then one day he will *kill* you! He will be the end of you!" Hendrick admonished her, the effects of the alcohol now quite noticeable in his speech.

It took every ounce of mental determination that he had, but Gilles forcefully seized control of himself and slowly eased himself back down into his chair, Elsje's strong restraining hand still on his arm and his heart pounding angrily in his chest, beating in protest against the cage of his ribs. Elsje had so far, for the most part, maintained her outward composure but her face burned red now with inner rage. She snapped her head back, but being unsuccessful at clearing a lock of her hair from her eyelashes, she impatiently brushed it aside with her fingers before she spoke to her father again.

"How shall we resolve this, Father, *hmm*? Do you want the winner of a fight to have say over *all* that the family does here? Or perhaps just to have say over what *I* do?"

Gilles was still angry too, but for the moment he was content to be a spectator, as always he was in complete awe of the force and magnitude of his wife's temper. He wasn't going to say anything more, not a single word lest she turn on him, too. If he had learned anything at all about his new wife, he knew that Elsje might not be close to being finished with unleashing her full fury on her father yet.

"I make up my *own* mind! How *dare* you even *think* to tell my husband when he can lie with me! We should have moved out after the wedding and lived in the French Quarter!"

Elsje planted herself in front of her father with her hands on her hips, just waiting for his response, daring him to say another word. She had no fear of him at all, and often, Gilles thought now, with an equal mixture of approbation and dismay, she had no *respect* for her father, either. It had *not* been that way with his father back in France; France was a civilized country where children respected their elders as well as their betters.

Gilles waited patiently for Elsje and her father to resolve the issue. While he waited, he daydreamed a little about what it might be like to have his fist connect with Hendrick's face just *once*, and then he indulged himself by thinking about hitting him a *few* times, bloodying his face completely. It was a very tempting idea after all of the insults that he had endured for so many months, after all the old man had put him through, on top of Gilles' already difficult, miserable, and fearful life that was only starting to get a little bit better now that he no longer lived and worked in a stable run by a Jewish man and no longer had to beg for his food on the streets as his physical survival had required after he made his way to the sanctuary of Amsterdam.

One day Gilles had decided that he was not going to live like a rabbit any longer. He had summoned the courage to ask for Elsje, and although Hendrick might have wanted to deny the request at the time, Dutch women were frequently allowed some say in the matter of their marriages, also a new concept to Gilles, and it was *Elsje* who had accepted the proposal on the condition that she would not have to change anything else besides her marital status. Before the ceremony, Gilles had swallowed the insults from her father so as not to jeopardize the alliance. Marrying a Dutch woman opened doors, both to a safe haven and to economic opportunity, but Gilles *was* genuinely fond of

Elsje, and her plain but good cooking was a bonus. If Gilles found Elsje a little frightening and intimidating at times, he also found her *infinitely* more interesting than her younger sister, Tryntje, who seemed to be spoiled and with limited intellectual abilities. Gilles was fairly certain that his inquisitive young sister-in-law must be awake in her curtained bed just a few feet away from them and listening to everything that transpired this morning.

Gilles had to wonder how he was ever going to sit at this table again and be civil to old Hendrick. He guessed that somehow, he would *have* to find a way: Even if there was no Elsje to battle over, Gilles had given Hendrick some of his money to invest in Dutch West India ventures.

This time the old man had really gone too far, though: He had insulted Gilles' country, his people, his religion, *and* his honor, all in the space of a few minutes. Non, Hendrick had already said too much that he would never be able to take back, even if he hadn't been such a stubborn old ox of a man who was not even slightly acquainted with the concept of apologies.

Hendrick apparently still had enough presence of mind, or perhaps hard experience, to know that saying anything more to Elsje would be a very bad idea. Elsje sat down at the table and the three of them started to silently eat their food, more tearing at it with their teeth and forcing it down their dry throats rather than savoring, or relishing the taste of it. There they remained in stony silence, a strange and silent party, with each one refusing to leave the room and not one of them speaking aloud.

There was a great deal more that Gilles *wanted* to say and someday he would say it to Hendrick's face; only in the last twenty four hours had he managed to sort out the misunderstanding that started following their wedding celebration and lasted nearly all of the first week of their marriage. Perhaps it had been Hendrick's fault, or perhaps it had been

Gilles'. It didn't really matter now, but it was a very inauspicious way to begin a lifelong relationship.

If Gilles had his old life back, his parents would have chosen his wife for him without consulting him on the matter, a completely respectful and obedient wife no doubt, and he would *not* have had to worry about whether he had made a good choice in a spouse or in-laws, although his best friend Jean Durie, his friend who had survived the prisons with him and accompanied Gilles on his journey away from his enchanted and blessed past, through their horrific ordeal to the uncertain present, had assured Gilles that marrying Elsje had been a good move, at least under the present circumstances. Jean had known Elsje and Hendrick for years through his ties with the merchants and traders of Amsterdam and moreover, Gilles trusted Jean's judgment, which was usually every bit as reliable as his formidable and nearly clairvoyant business sense.

Hendrick did not eat much more than a few bites of bread, just enough to re-establish his territory. Outnumbered though, he left his remaining food on the plate, scraped back his chair and tottered off-balance across the room to the staircase. Gilles heard him descending the stairs, traveling at an arthritic pace all the way down to the first floor.

The large open room that comprised most of the family's crowded little living space had two curtained beds just a few feet away from the table, one for Hendrick and one for Tryntje. Hendrick's three other children, two small daughters and a son, had been living with their deceased mother's cousin ever since Hendrick's wife had succumbed to the great epidemic that had ravaged Amsterdam ten years earlier. Only the small enclosed bedroom that used to be Hendrick's, now claimed by Gilles and Elsje, was separate and relatively private, although sound and lamplight carried effortlessly through the cracks in the thin plank walls.

"I do not need my wife to defend me!" Gilles whispered to Elsje, very much aware that their conversation was probably not private. "You *must* let me fight my own fights, *especially* with your father."

"Nee." Elsje looked him straight in the eye and said calmly, "Whoever wins such a fight, it makes no difference; *I* am the loser. I will not allow you to fight with him."

Gilles strongest inclination was to take Elsje across his knee, to discipline her and to make her understand that *he* was now her husband and master, and as such, the unquestionable authority in the family, at least where *she* was concerned, but another part of him, the stronger part on this day at least, unfortunately realized that she was right. He chafed at her use of the word *"allow"* but he did see that there was no good solution that readily presented itself; Elsje's was probably the *least* unfavorable of his few options.

"Elsje, would you *really* consider moving out with me? We could live in the French section and nothing would change, only where we sleep at night."

"I am needed here most of the time, very early and very late, and it costs us nothing to live here," Elsje replied, taking another bite of her cheese, "besides, it is *my* home too and I will not leave it."

"…except perhaps our marriage." Gilles touched the back of her hand. "It might cost us our *marriage*."

He was a bit taken aback now to realize that he really did feel some affection for his new wife. That was a peculiarly *Italian* kind of a thought, considering that they had been married for such a short and tumultuous time. Gilles' mother had once assured him that close feelings would probably come to a marriage over time, but she had imparted this bit of advice to Gilles on the eve of a marriage that had never taken place. She had been most clear on this point, that finance and social position were the greatest priorities, if not the *only* considerations in a marriage, taking precedence over every other measure of compatibility, including ages, health, and interests, just as long as the intended spouse had no sympathies with the Protestants. If Madame Montroville ever found out, she would be horrified at the thought of her oldest surviving son marrying a *Reformee,* a follower of these anarchist rebels, especially a woman who was so completely beneath them. There had been very solid and objective reasons, financial included, for Gilles' marrying a Protestant woman now that he made his home in the Netherlands: Elsje was nothing like any of the young women he had known in France, and not at all like Marie, the thirteen year old girl that he had been betrothed to at home in Rouen.

Gilles' life would have been *so* different now if his home country of France was not so caught up in the insanity that swept across that great and ancient land. The accusers and prosecutors who perpetuated the trials and scheduled the executions of the treasonous Huguenots had wound their poisonous way around to the Montroville's door, sniffing at the family's ancestral land holdings. It was a fact that the Huguenots had broken with the one *true* church, the Catholic Church, defying King Louis XIII and Cardinal Richelieu, but the moral battles weren't *always* about stamping out the growing spiritual rebellion; frequently they had much more to do with the real estate that could be auctioned off after seizure of a criminal's property to cover the expenses of the trial and maybe contribute a little toward the cost of the decades-long war that was rapidly bankrupting the country and half of Europe as well. Sometimes the land wasn't sold off though: Sometimes it just made a nice addition to the King's current holdings without the expense and bother of purchasing it from the previous owners.

Gilles had never had any interest in joining up with the Huguenots, and he didn't have the *vaguest* idea as to what these fanatics were about, but in the end that had made no difference: He still had to flee for his life, leaving his family and home far behind him. Elsje had not only stanched his aching loneliness and filled his stomach with her good cooking, she was also the daughter of a man with excellent trade connections, not just in the city, but around the world, a man who could help Gilles' future prospects greatly just by *being* his father-in-law. The plain and simple first floor dining room of Hendrick's inn was the daily gathering place for the rich and powerful, with many members of both the East and West India Companies coming in for a hot meal or an ale or two. Gilles' family was well known in the shipping and trade business and Gilles and Hendrick had many common interests. They *should* have gotten along very well, and at first they did.

Elsje managed to relax a little and she found a smile for Gilles. "You and I will move out before I allow anything to come between us. We must be honest with each other though, and you must tell me *everything*, instead of putting me through what you did this past week. No more secrets! No more lies! Is it agreed?"

"Agreed."

Gilles decided that he would tell his wife everything from now on, but that it wasn't necessary to burden her with all of the misery that he dragged with him from his past. He would lock those parts away, relegating them to some closed-up place. His privileged childhood, his trial, imprisonment, and his personal relationships with Marie in France and Hannah in Amsterdam could all be left there. It was not necessary to mention any of those things to Elsje.

Elsje put out her hand to shake his in a businessman's agreement. Gilles shook her hand, still marveling at the feeling of a woman's soft flesh and tiny bones connecting with his in a gentleman's handshake. Although he had lived in the city for some time, Gilles still couldn't get used to the Amsterdam women shaking hands with men, frequently with complete *strangers*, although he was careful to honor the custom whenever a hand was offered to him. He shook his wife's hand first before he pulled Elsje over onto his lap.

"Father just can't get used to having another man around the house," Elsje explained as she put one arm around Gilles' neck. "*Please try to get along with him, Gilles. For me.*"

"*I* get along with him very well; it is *he* who can't get along with me!"

"Hmm. Well, you can help us out here at the inn for a few weeks until your work at Msr. Ste Germaine's gets busier. Things will be better by then."

Elsje stood over her father later on that day, lecturing him loudly for the better part of fifteen minutes, until Hendrick came around to accepting her suggestions that he should make some needed repairs around the inn while business was so slow. With Gilles' help, Hendrick repaired some of the fencing that corralled the few chickens and lone cow residing in a shed on a corner of the inn's back lot. Gilles held the boards in place for Hendrick, wondering at each blow of the hammer if the old man might look to his son-in-law's fingers and hands for revenge, but Elsje found enough excuses to check up on them frequently, so that any minor irritations did not have the time to smolder and then burst into flames of open anger. The shaky truce held, at least for the next few weeks.

The sea trade from the Caribbean, Africa, Spain, Portugal and the silk routes was still active but business from the more northerly ports was still slow or nonexistent, the ferocious storms during the winter months threatening every vessel and foolish captain that sailed against the odds. This break in business gave Elsje plenty of time to clean the inn and their living quarters thoroughly without the interruption of customers. The two hired kitchen servants were given a few weeks off and Hendrick's inn was even closed all day on Sundays for a time, not just during the morning hours for church services. Elsje's younger sister Tryntje helped with the cleaning too, that is, when she hadn't disappeared on some very urgent errand that she had suddenly remembered.

They were the very picture of family unity and peaceful coexistence when they attended church on Sunday, the Reformed church of course, and Elsje never failed to wear the pearls that Gilles had given her as a wedding present. The sight of the pearls no longer bothered him quite so much because every Sunday night Gilles got to take them off her when they retired to their bedroom. This act gave him great satisfaction, almost as much as the physical being with his wife that always followed.

The pearl necklace had originally been purchased as a wedding present for Marie, his fiancée in France, although Gilles had never bothered to mention this fact to Elsje or to anyone else. The string of pearls was one of the few things that Gilles brought with him from his past life, that other lifetime, although their transport had been unintentional. After Gilles had escaped his death sentence and went into exile, Marie had been handed over to Gilles' younger brother Charles. The heiress to the powerful Junot family's fortune was Charles' reward for being the more compliant and obedient son, the son who would tell his father only what the senior Msr. Montroville wished to hear, whether it was the truth or not, the son that had *not* been accused of heresy and collaboration with the Reformees.

But that was then and this was now. That was far away and in truth, life was not so very difficult here and Gilles knew it; Gillaume Ste Germaine was a generous employer, but he could be a very demanding one, so Gilles decided to take advantage of this lull in the yearly business cycle and give himself a small reward for his hard work. Ste Germaine had given Gilles the wedding gift of a fine horse and for some time his employer had been urging Gilles to take Elsje to his country house for the day. Gilles convinced Elsje to go only once, during the month of January, but he was able to sample a little taste of what his old life used to be and indulge himself in some creature comforts.

Elsje had not wanted to leave the inn for any period time but Gilles appealed to her curiosity, at last getting her out to Ste Germaine's country home, grander than any house she had ever set eyes on, where she sampled delicate cakes and drank *tea*, the new beverage that everyone in Amsterdam had to try. The beverage was served in an ornate Chinese porcelain theiere, poured into individual portions in a cup and then consumed from the matching saucer that completed the fussy ensemble. On that rare warm day just after the Christmas season, Gilles left Elsje in the house to be waited on by the house servants until he returned from riding, discovering then that a part of his soul that he thought he had lost forever was restored to him once again when he was on the back of a good horse.

Ste Germaine seemed fond of Elsje too, and at times Gilles could almost forget that his employer's tastes ran to men and not to women at all, although Ste Germaine did appraise women in much the same way that he did horses; that one being too stocky, the other not refined enough, the bone structure of that one being very good. It was the same with the paintings by the Dutch masters that Ste Germaine hung on all of the walls of his eating establishment: good composition, the paint too heavy on that one, excellent colors on this one.

Elsje couldn't sit still for very long at Msr. Ste Germaine's country house though, not even to be waited on like she was a Bourbon or a Habsburg, and so Gilles only went to the country house a few more times, and then always without Elsje as she had no inborn or cultivated capacity for relaxation. Within a matter of weeks though, Gilles had resumed his duties and his very long days of work at Ste Germaine's eating establishment; he was too busy most of the time to pursue childish country pleasures.

Msr. Ste Germaine had no lack of confidence in Gilles but he modified and revised the actions of *all* of his employees more frequently than Pope Urban revised the Catholic Church's hymns and prayers. He was *so* exacting that he did not even trust the warehouses to deliver their own goods, but the owners of the storage buildings always sent word to him first whenever they believed they had laid hands on an excellent batch of wine, superior cognac, or some other commodity that might fetch them a premium price from a very discriminating customer.

Gilles was not in the least surprised to find that the Scottish musician, MacEwen, who had wandered in looking for a meal a few months earlier, was still there. The wanderer had virtually taken up residence at Ste Germaine's and was staying on for more than the proposed "few weeks", even when there *was* no business and no audience for him. MacEwen made himself scarce when he wasn't eating, ostensibly to conduct other business, but the traveler from the northern isles remained aloof, a mystery to all of them, even as Msr. Ste Germaine made every effort to get to know him intimately better.

Msr. LaRue, Ste Germaine's long-time associate, returned to the establishment after having gone missing for several weeks and another duty that Gilles took on, without express request from his employer, was to keep the two rivals, LaRue and MacEwen, apart and to keep Msr. LaRue away from Ste Germaine's cook as well, as the two of them had frequently exchanged uncivil words. Gilles also intervened when necessary to keep MacEwen from fleecing the occasional customer with his bets and games of chance at cards in the tobacco salon. While Gilles tried to keep Msr. Ste Germaine's mind focused on his *work* and not on his amorous intentions toward LaRue *or* MacEwen, it made for a very challenging as well as a very tiring day for Gilles, even without the added responsibility of Gilles' regular assigned daily duties. There were his mundane chores, checking stores of food and spirits and there were the not so mundane chores, this week having to clear a blockage in the dining room chimney flue, occasioned by a stork that was off schedule and attempting to build an early nest there. Gilles had to get the ladder out, climb up on the roof, shoo the bird away, and then dismantle the nest every few days.

Gilles and Elsje both worked very hard and very late at their respective places of business, but they had been blessed so far with excellent health and the energy of the young so Gilles was taken by surprise late one night when he found Elsje already in bed asleep. He kissed her cheek after he climbed into bed with her.

"You are in bed early but the inn is still open. Are you feeling all right?"

"Just tired," Elsje replied. She smiled but she didn't open her eyes.

"You are tired a lot lately, no? I have never seen you this tired."

"Yes, business …" she murmured.

"You aren't sick?" Gilles asked. The plague usually started later, in the spring months.

"Nee. Maybe there is *another* reason." she smiled again in her half sleep.

"*Is* there another reason?" Gilles asked her.

"Ja." Elsje sighed and then she was sound asleep.

Gilles let her rest. He pushed her hair back from her face and he smiled in the dark. Children were a sign from God, the blessing of a union, his mother used to say. It was a peculiar thought, to think of *being* a father since he didn't feel much older than a child himself, but he hoped that it would help to ease the loneliness that he still sometimes felt. Gilles had been lucky to have such a good wife *and* his best friend in Amsterdam with him, but they had not completely filled the place in his heart of the large family that Gilles had left behind. Now that Gilles was starting a new family of his own, growing an entirely new branch on the family tree, the new lineage might fill his house as well as the pages of history someday. He *was* bitter that his fortune was gone, the fortune that he had been born to inherit, disappointed also that he would not be able to take his son to the fields, vineyards, ancient apple orchards, shipyards and great landholdings that his family had in Normandie. Gilles realized that he had looked forward to one day showing his child all of the family holdings and telling him the history of those places, the orchards, the fields, the great old oak trees and the hills. He would have introduced the newest generation of the family at a christening in the great cathedral of Rouen to the fine old families in the region that had been the Montroville's neighbors, allies, and adversaries for centuries past.

Gilles blamed the French King and Cardinal Richelieu for his financial and emotional losses as well as his father: It seemed to Gilles that with his father's *and* his fiancé's great wealth and political connections, the situation might have been remedied somehow, at least enough for him to safely return home, but that hadn't happened. Maybe Gilles would write to his father, telling him the news, and maybe old Hendrick would make more of an effort as well to get along with Gilles now that there was a child with their common blood to consider.

Taken as a whole, Gilles' life was not so bad. He was no longer hungry every day, no longer cold or sleeping in a barn, no longer shoveling out horse stalls for a pittance. All in all, Gilles did not have reason to complain. Things had been better in his past but he was thankful for the way his life was going now, comfortable in his skin, and only a little bit apprehensive about the increased responsibility of having a child. Gilles fell asleep with his cheek on Elsje's head.

As usual, Elsje woke up before Gilles and she was already downstairs at work in the kitchen when Gilles opened his eyes. It was early yet so Gilles took the time this morning to have some tea and bread before he went off to his work, sitting at a corner of the kitchen preparation table. Gilles preferred eating the kitchen when he took a meal in the inn, leaving the tables in the dining room to the paying patrons. There *was* the added bonus of it being warmer in the little kitchen when the fire was going, and it was also far away from Hendrick who stayed all day long in the dining room, at his little table by the fireplace, talking with his guests and calling out orders to Elsje and Tryntje as they passed by him, bringing food out from the kitchen to the customers. Elsje took a moment to pour Gilles some tea when she returned from the dining room to the kitchen. He waited until Elsje had finished pouring the hot water from the kettle and when she turned to go, he caught her by her other arm.

"Do you remember talking to me when I came in last night?"

"Nee," she said apologetically, "I must have been *too* tired."

"I asked you if there was a reason that you were so tired and you said there was." Gilles caught her eyes with his to keep her from racing away, back to her work.

"Of *course* I'm more tired, we are *busy* now!"

Elsje wasn't petulant with him though, as his wife could sometimes be; she winked at him, pulled her arm away and went out into the dining room still carrying the tea water.

Gilles put down his knife, left the table and followed her out there, calling over his shoulder to the two kitchen maids, "Leave the food; I'll be back to finish."

Elsje was waiting to hear an order from a man at a table when Gilles caught up with her.

"A word in private, Elsje!"

She frowned at his interruption of business but she excused herself from the customer and followed Gilles to the corner of the room farthest away from Hendrick.

"I have to go to work and we *don't* have much time to talk. Are we having a child?"

Elsje blushed at the bluntness of his query. "I *think* so. I can't talk now, we are *busy* this morning!"

She pulled away from him and returned to the customer as Gilles looked after her. She glanced back at her husband and smiled briefly before she went on with her duties, taking the requests back into the kitchen. Gilles followed after her, not exactly sure of what was expected from him now.

Perhaps there was nothing for him to do. In France, Gilles couldn't recall the men speaking of such things, except in reference to some scandal or as confirmation of the continuation of a family line or a business alliance. The Netherlanders were odd people though, with different customs, and although Gilles tried to the utmost of his ability to do the right thing to make his wife and father-in-law happy, his friend Jean, older, and more experienced with the ways of the Dutch, frequently had to advise Gilles on what was socially acceptable or expected of him here. Often though, Jean's best advice to Gilles was not to concern himself with the lowlanders' idiosyncrasies.

Elsje filled a plate with bread and butter and maneuvered around Gilles on her way back out to the dining room. Gilles decided that his only course of action at the moment was to finish his breakfast so he took his seat at the kitchen table again and resumed eating, the noise of the pounding butter churn a background in his thoughts. If Elsje had nothing that she needed to talk with him about, then perhaps it was none of his business, only a woman's concern. Gilles believed that it was going to be a good year with trade starting up again so soon after the doldrums of Christmas and it would be a *very* good year to have a child.

Good fortune did not continue, though. The fevers came early that year and with most of the town falling ill, Gilles was worried to the point of distraction about losing Elsje as well as the child that she carried, during both his waking and his sleeping hours. Hendrick put forth the theory that it was the *Jews* of Amsterdam who had infected everyone with an evil spell because one of their kind had been beaten by some drunken sailors on a Friday night as he returned home from worship at the synagogue. The perpetrators of the assault were caught right away and given public lashings in the town square, the Dam, but apparently the Jews did not see fit to reverse their curse as the fevers continued.

Gilles had his doubts about this though, but not because he had any special love or fear of the *Juden*. He had lived among them and they had kept him hidden and safe when he had first fled to Amsterdam. He *was* grateful to them but he also carried within him an enlightenment, an understanding that only comes from having lived in close quarters with them and truly knowing a people, the good and the bad of them, the myths reinforced or exploded, the mortality and humanity of them, although it might be of a different flavor. His discovery that his best friend Jean Durie had been the bastard child of one of the Amsterdam Jews didn't impact greatly his opinion of his friend *or* the Jews: Jean was unique, one of a kind in the world. Gilles had known Jean and already formed his opinion before he had discovered Jean's secret. Gilles seriously doubted that *any* single man or any group of men had the power to call a plague down from the heavens and visit it upon a city. After the misery he had suffered in his own life, Gilles didn't believe in much of anything anymore, not even the validity of most of the witchcraft charges that were occasionally leveled at troublesome old women.

Grietje, one of Hendrick's kitchen maids, asserted that it was a Portuguese trade ship, coming from the orient with a load of sick sailors that had brought the illness into the port. No matter how it began, soon a season that had started with the promise of so much prosperity foundered as sailors took to sleeping on their ships to avoid contact with the sick population, lying on the open decks even in the damp and bitter cold of the early spring nights, withholding their wages from the alehouses and prostitutes, as well as from the ship repair and provisioning businesses.

On his way to work at Ste Germaine's one day, Gilles noted that some discarded bodies had started to appear at the docks, dumped there by shipmates who had neither the desire nor the conscience to do anything more with them than to leave them behind as they sailed away, spent lives and used bodies piled up with all of the other refuse that had been left behind from the ships. One body lay rotting for a full day near the entrance to one of the major loading docks and the local officials were livid.

At first the townspeople, Gilles and Elsje included, tried to continue to go about their business, pretending that nothing was unusual, that nothing was out of the ordinary, but with no abatement in the epidemic, the wealthier citizens started to abandon their city dwellings, leaving an armed servant or two behind to guard homes and businesses as they took refuge in their country homes, taking supplies of grain, chickens, and cows with them to provision their families for as long as it might take for the misery to pass. Gilles arrived at work one day to discover that Ste Germaine was in the process of closing his business too, with plans to stay at his country house until the pestilence was over. Gilles was more concerned at first with this interruption of his income but then he wondered if he shouldn't take Elsje out of the city too, thinking that they might seek sanctuary with Ste Germaine for a time. Gilles raced home to ask her if she would go but Elsje refused to leave the inn even though there was scant business coming in the door.

No one in Gilles' family had shown signs of the illness yet but he wondered if there would be any medical help available in the city if they needed it. Elsje had once told him that she didn't place much faith in her family's usual doctor, although they occasionally called on him when Elsje's remedies failed to bring results. Amsterdam's physicians, renowned throughout the world for their skill in healing and enlightened surgical procedures as well as their low infant mortality, were helpless in the face of this illness that overwhelmed them, both in terms of the sheer numbers of sick people and their inability to save their patients. Soon most of the populace just stopped calling on the professional chiurgeons as it was obviously wasted money.

One English-trained physician tried to bleed some of the bad humor from the sick with leeches and his vacuum cups. He bled his healthy patients as a precaution, too, but when most of his patients died, the sick as well as the healthy, it was rumored that the doctor was spreading the sickness. The physician despaired of his lost patients and his lost practice and hanged himself before the illness got the chance to take him too, jumping down toward the waters of the Prinsengracht with one end of a rope secured around his neck and the other tied to a bridge support. A few of the doctors even admitted their impotence in the face of this formidable foe and helplessly referred their sick patients to an African woman who was said to have had great success with herbal potions and incantations. When news spread throughout the city that the magic woman had died of the sickness, true panic set in. Because there was almost no commerce at the inn, Hendrick sent the two kitchen girls home to their families for the duration, promising to send for them afterwards, as long as he survived.

Occasionally, when supplies ran low or when he couldn't stand to be cooped up with the family any longer, Gilles went out on the streets to try and find some flour or some other staples to buy. They had plenty of milk and eggs, having the chickens and cow as well as a supply of dried peas and beans, but Hendrick ran out of his tobacco and this made the long vigil even more difficult, both for Hendrick and for the rest of the family who noted his shortened temper. The markets had little to buy, the perpetually busy areas of commerce now being nearly deserted, but everywhere people were busy digging in the sandy dirt. In the churchyards, in their backyards, in the countryside, by the sides of the road, small and great trenches opened and were quickly sealed up again after receiving the deposited souls. People marked these spots, if they had the time or the inclination to do so before they themselves died, and the barren and suspect-shaped patches of dirt were given wide berth as the sites *themselves* were said to have infected unsuspecting people as they walked by. Frequently the lonely graves were not marked at all, and only the freshly turned soil indicated the terminus of a life that had once been a father, a mother, or someone's child, each plot indicating solely by its dimensions whether or not the denizen had the opportunity to reach adulthood. Some parents buried all of their children within days of each other, only to follow those burials with their own parents and then, finally, with each other. It was as if their sole purpose for being born was to bury the family that they had accumulated during their short lives.

On some of these forays, Gilles would go by Jean Durie's home and call up to his friend's bedroom window, just to inquire as to his friend's health. Jean always assured Gilles that he was well and sent his best wishes for good health to the Hendricks family. Gilles frequently noted on his way home that whole city blocks appeared to have been emptied of the living, those residents who had the wherewithal having fled to the countryside, a few who tried to live on their ships out in the harbor, and those who had died. Black ribbons and wreaths were on most of the doors in the city and farm and domestic animals left to their own survival roamed the streets, foraging through the garbage and sniffing at the dead bodies that had been made ready at the edge of the street for the daily body collection. Chickens, cattle, pigs, and even dogs scavenged along the streets and in the untended yards, munching on the new lily and tulip shoots that were just starting to come up or pushing their way through a hedge here and a gate there to gain entrance into the neighboring yards in search of food.

Gilles thought about grabbing one of these animals, and he decided that he would do it if his family was hungry enough. He wasn't sure what he would tell Elsje and Hendrick about how he had come by the animal, but it would likely *not* be the truth. Most of the grocery businesses had closed and now famine followed closely on the heels of the pestilence. The grocers and merchants had all died, fled, or were too frightened to have any contact with the populace at large. As food became scarce for the remnant of survivors in the city, the roaming animals vanished, either having been taken for food or kept safely locked inside their master's homes to keep them from being purloined. Gilles had to wonder if the thieves they caught and other prisoners in the jails feared for their lives as well: There were *no* guarantees that the jailers would remain healthy enough to care for them and not abandon the prisoners to death by starvation behind the locked bars.

Sometimes Gilles looked out over the city at night and he could see lamplight in the upper windows illuminating exhausted and emotionally spent mothers who stayed up all night with their sick children. There would surely be those who swore in later years that they had survived only because their mother had simply *refused* to let her child die. Before contact with the outside world had been cut off, Gilles had heard the gossip that many more infants were being born deaf or blind. The orphanage was already over capacity with a greater than average number of children, both those who were healthy orphans and those with sensory impairments.

Gilles didn't know what he would do if he lost Elsje and so he silently prayed. *Seigneur, prends pitié, Seigneur, prends pitié.*

Elsje still wanted to go to church every Sunday but neither Gilles nor Hendrick would let her go, convincing her that even if the church was still holding services, it was not safe for her there and God would excuse her absence for a time. It was only when Gilles pointed out that she would be putting her baby at risk too, that Elsje was convinced not to go. Gilles had not married her in a fit of passion, but Elsje *was* more than just his pass key to local privileges: Gilles was concerned for her safety and for the child and he couldn't envision continuing his life here in Amsterdam by marrying Tryntje. Although many of the men in the city probably harbored a few secret thoughts about the young beauty, Gilles had never had any desire to share Tryntje's bed. Gilles could do nothing more than wait out the storm, spending all of his waking hours, and many of his dreaming hours, silently saying the rosary and the Lord's Prayer, in secret as he knew that his Protestant family would not approve but he hoped that the incantations would persuade the heavens to spare them since Gilles had *already* lost an entire family and his previous life.

There was no time that could be pinpointed when people could say that the suffering had finally ended. They watched and waited as a few ships trickled in, still with a gnawing need to trade in spite of the death that overshadowed the port, lying in wait there. Gilles couldn't know this, but the shipping business continued although it was conducted for a time at a distance, with goods unloaded from the ships stacked on the docks and the captains warily watching from up on deck while the tradesmen counted the goods, carted them away, and left boxes with money for payment, the coins having been first soaked in vinegar at the request of the ships' captains. It *was* fortunate that the epidemic was not the plague, as that malady had been known to ravage whole cities for a full *year* or even longer. Gradually, though, trade saved Amsterdam as the sailors began to leave the ships while they were in port, tentatively at first to get only the food and water that they needed for the barest level of sustenance on their voyages, and then, little by little, some brave or foolish souls left the ships to sleep in the relative comfort of the inns when they could no longer stand the hard and cold dampness of the ship's decks.

Gilles, Elsje, Hendrick and Tryntje weathered the storm as best they could, cutting back drastically on the amount of food that they cooked and consumed, filling the hours of boredom as best they could. They lived for one entire week on a soup that Elsje made from her supply of dried beans. She always made enough to send a little extra over to share with her cousin Vroutje and the other Hendricks children, admonishing Gilles to leave it on their doorstep and call out to them to come and get it after he was gone.

One day a sailor came to the inn's door looking for food and Elsje was so overjoyed to see him and so anxious to have news of the outside world, that she let him in, fed him, and didn't charge him anything at all. It may have been more her fear of contaminated coins than her generous mood that led her to refuse payment but the seaman brought the good news that a few of the trading stalls had reopened in the Dam, at least one church was conducting regular services, and the illness had abated in some of the nearby ports. They rejoiced at this good news but

Gilles wondered how long it would take for his life to revert to the way it had been before.

It was nearly mid summer before daily life arrived at a *new* normal, although many things in the city had been changed forever, and laughter was still in short supply. Some of the new babies were still-born, deaf, or blind, but a good number of them appeared to be quite healthy. The new infants were mostly named for their dead relatives, and defective or not, with resources gradually improving, they were generally cared for more lovingly and more fiercely than their older brothers and sisters who had been born during "normal" times; it was a little difficult, a little strange, to get used to saying "*Little* Evert" instead of "Old Evert", and "*Baby* Roeloff" instead of "the senior Roeloff". Gilles didn't broach the subject with Elsje, but an entire generation of afflicted and defective children had been born, and he didn't dare name his fears out loud or speculate on the health of their coming child, as giving voice to these concerns might bring it to terrible reality. He didn't know what he would do if their child was born blind or deaf but it was out of his hands now and in God's.

Hendrick's inn and business survived that terrible year, as did Ste Germaine's, but many others did not. The Dutch had proved without a doubt once again that no one could pinch a florin flatter than they could, nor squeeze more out of it when it came to running a business or a household in the most economically efficient way. During the panic, MacEwen, the Scottish stranger that had taken up temporary residence at Ste Germaine's, disappeared from the city at the height of the sickness. With Ste Germaine's permission, he had been staying upstairs in the rooms over the business as a caretaker of sorts in his employer's absence, claiming that he had business that kept him in the city anyway, although if there *was* any other commerce that MacEwen attended to, Gilles never discovered what it might be. Gilles had passed by occasionally to see to his employer's business and inquire as to the state of MacEwen's health, which appeared to be good at last check, but he just vanished one day, never to return.

Upon his return to the city and his business, Ste Germaine went to much trouble and expense to try to find out what had happened to the Scotsman, but he never did learn with certainty what MacEwen's fate had been. A visitor from Leiden brought news to Ste Germaine's that a man matching MacEwen's description had been found dead in the countryside just outside the city and was buried in an unmarked grave there. Ste Germaine grieved for the lost MacEwen but his attention was soon turned to other concerns when it was discovered that a large sum of money was missing from the hiding place in a secret compartment under the stairs. Gilles suspected that It had not been a random thief after MacEwen's sudden disappearance but that the "caretaker" had escaped with the money, whether he lived long enough to enjoy it or not.

It could also have been stolen by the cuckolded Msr. LaRue, though, if he had returned during the pestilence without Gilles' knowledge, and evicted the Scottish intruder before taking advantage of the chaos in the city and Ste Germaine's absence to remove the funds for his own use. Being unable to ascertain whether MacEwen, LaRue, or a random burglar took it, Ste Germaine decided just to keep his money in a safer place from that point on.

The black ribbons still hung on the doors in Amsterdam but they became faded and tattered under the strengthening sun and ever-warmer days of approaching summer, flapping and fraying in the brisk spring winds. Eventually these announcements of deaths were taken down, door by door, and occasionally new wreaths for the birth of a child were put up in their places, but the new graves that were the more palpable reminders of the event continued for some months to grow a different shade of greenery than the grassy meadows and older interments. These sites were a sore and constant reminder of the city's losses.

Gilles took care to cover his mouth and nose as he passed by these places and, when no one was looking, to cross himself as well. He had not had anything to do with the Catholic Church since he had left France but after the epidemic, he found his thoughts turning to it more and more these days. He wondered about all the graves that were not in holy ground and about all of the souls who had never received any last rites. He hoped that God and the devil would take care of all of them, and that the spirits of the dead would not stay by the graves to greet passersby at night, particularly when he had to travel by these spots in the dark on his way back home from working late at night at Msr. Ste Germaine's.

In the early part of the summer, everyday life was still muted, still quieter than it had been before, but little bits of children's laughter were heard again in the streets, accompanied by the healthy cries of new babies. The merchants returned to the Dam, the women to the markets, and the men to the taverns. Elsje still appeared to be healthy and she grew larger and rounder as the months passed. Gilles was amazed, curious, and sometimes repelled by her new body all at the same time, although he certainly was not going to tell his wife this.

Gilles didn't mention that he still worried about the child's health and Elsje's chances of surviving childbirth. Perhaps God waited and schemed to take vengeance on Elsje and the child for Gilles' sins. The priests in France had always been very clear and certain about this, that God had all of eternity to wait for his revenge, to come back and pay the wages of sin at the worst possible moment. The priests of Gilles' youth had assured him that God might forgive a great deal after confession, almost anything, except for abandoning the Catholic Church or missing sacraments.

"Do not punish them for my transgressions!" Gilles prayed silently as he watched Elsje, smiling and humming as she worked, but he could not shake off these fears. If he lost Elsje and then was left with a blind child, he felt he would have little choice but to leave it in the city orphanage that was already filled to the brim with such children and he didn't know how he might comfort Elsje if their first child did not survive.

Gilles wondered if it might be wise to reserve a part of his heart and not give it completely over to a wife or children. He thought of the intense pain that still lingered over the loss of his own older brother and of Ste Germaine's lost wife and child. He thought also of all the tiny graves that he had to walk by every day on his way to and from work.

Later that night, when he and Elsje were in bed, he gingerly put his hand on her stomach. He only wanted to be sure that the child was still alive and not already dead. A great rolling movement in her stomach was followed by a sturdy bump to his hand.

"Ha ha!" Elsje laughed out loud. "He just kicked your hand off! He's a strong one!"

Gilles had not previously thought much of the child as anything but a lump that would later become a howling baby, without gender or characteristics, but now the thought occurred to him that it would be a little *boy* or a little *girl*, a blond or a redhead, thin or chubby, looking like his mother or father or perhaps like Elsje.

"Are you *so* sure it's a boy?" he asked her, but he too, was certain that it *must* be a son.

"Absolutely! We will call him Yellas, after you. Yellas Yellasen."

"Ah! And not the French, Gilles Gillessen?" he teased his wife. "He *has* to have some middle names, too."

"Why? Aren't *two* names enough?" she asked. "No one but *royalty* needs more than one name, unless you are from Zeeland, over where Claes Martenszen is from."

"My family *always* has more than two names," Gilles said, "to honor our ancestors. Why don't you have any *more* than one or two names? Is there a legal limit?"

"All right then, how about Jean Hendrick Gilles Yellasen or Jean Gilles Hendrick Yellasen, after your father *and* mine."

Gilles groaned. "That's *too many* 'Gilles'! Too many 'Hendricks'! How will we keep everyone straight?"

"What do *you* want to name him then, Pieter Stuyvesant Gillessen?" Elsje teased him.

"Why not Gilles Jean Montroville?"

"Now that *would* be confusing and I see that you would leave *my* father out completely! He wouldn't like that, and with Jean Durie being your friend and no one here knowing that Jean is your father's name as well, would people not wonder who the father of my child might be?"

"You wanted to name him for *my* father and my father's name is Jean," Gilles said defensively. "Maybe we could name him Jean-Paul or Jean-Louis."

Gilles *had* thought more to honor his best friend with the naming of his son rather than his father, but Elsje didn't need to know that.

"Agh! They will think he is a little *Frenchman*!" Elsje made a face.

"And what is wrong with that?"

Gilles' reply was to tickle his wife and they both rolled over each other laughing. Elsje's weight on top of Gilles' caused one of the hemp ropes supporting the straw-filled mattress to snap and they both laughed even harder, tears starting down Elsje's face in uncontrollable fits of laughter.

"Hendrick Cornelius Barent Teunis Gillessen!" She offered, purposely leaving off *both* the Gilles *and* the Montroville name.

"Francois Rene Louis Pierre de Montroville!" Gilles fired back.

"Next you will say you want him baptized in the Catholic Church too!"

Elsje was still laughing heartily but Gilles was not: He had not given a thought to this very important matter before this moment. He *did* want his child baptized in the Catholic Church for if the child's life ended prematurely, he wanted to know that he had done all that he could for the infant's soul.

He did not say anything more but Elsje appeared not to notice his silence. She snuggled down into his arms, closed her eyes and sighed contentedly as she fell asleep. Gilles was not sleepy though, and he looked down at her peaceful face, still streaked with tears of merriment. He wanted his child baptized by a priest but where could he find one in Amsterdam, no ordinary priest, but one who would also do it discretely, with regard to Gilles' delicate legal situation?

There were Catholic churches in the city, of course, the Dutch being fiercely liberal in that they allowed *everyone* to share their freedoms and their city with them, even those under whose auspices they had suffered so much, the very men who would deny them the *same* liberties if they were in control of the country. These renegade churches were frequently conspicuous only because they had missing bell towers that were allowed only for houses of worship that were of the Protestant persuasion, the *right* Protestant persuasion. There were services of many kinds that were held in the attics of private homes, too. Perhaps Gilles could somehow explain to Elsje that a Catholic baptism was important to him or, as head of his new family, he might just *insist* on having it done for his son.

If she objected to it though, he didn't know what he would do. He fell asleep as he pondered this, dreaming of churches and priests, a blond-haired son and his own older brother, no longer dead as he had been these several years past, but hale and hearty, now grown to full manhood, standing over their bed and smiling down at Gilles as he slept.

As things returned to normal at work, or at least what was normal for Ste Germaine's, Gilles wondered more and more each day *why* he was still employed there and what it was that he *did* each day to earn his pay. He lived in constant fear that Msr. Ste Germaine would call him over and say to him, "You do nothing here, really; I do not need to pay you to stand around, and I have to fix everything that you do, so just go away and don't come back."

Gilles stayed on, though, day by day his worries at work adding to his worries at home, not knowing if they were founded or unfounded. He had felt no security, no peace, since he had left France, and so he assuaged his fears and salved his mind by investing every stuiver that he could put his hands on with the West India Company and with private investors that Hendrick or Jean Durie had recommended to him. Each investment was a climax of sorts, a short-term relief that bought him a little feeling of security for a few more days until the next bout of fear threatened to overtake him. Gilles still gave Hendrick small sums of money to invest for him in the fur trade and other schemes, just to salvage a little of what was left of their battered relationship, but he no longer trusted his father-in-law to handle the bulk of his investments. He no longer needed Hendrick though: In Amsterdam there were investments and business wagers with good odds on nearly every street corner.

Boredom was not the source of Gilles' growing discontent as there was always more than enough entertainment in watching the customers; Ste Germaine also kept him very busy but now there was also the remodeling project that had started after the busier summer season was past, in the early autumn of the year.

As he had impatiently paced his country home and waited for the pandemic in the city to subside, Ste Germaine had plenty of time to think about it and stew over each facet of the planned renaissance of his business. During his exile in the country, he had come to the conclusion that what his business *really* needed was a complete overhaul. He had planned, made notes and sketches, and then waited impatiently for the to illness leave the city and then he waited for the end of the summer, when he would be flush with cash, when closing his doors during the slower autumn season would not have as great an impact on his finances. Unlike Hendrick's inn where local working men and even women drank all year round, Ste Germaine's business *always* had fewer customers during the slow season as the local residents had never made up the majority of his clientele. They did not have much of a taste for fine French food, not yet, but Ste Germaine was determined that this was about to change. He vowed that he would teach the Amsterdammers to *love* French cuisine, even if it took him the next five years to accomplish this goal. After all, it was *he* who had come up with the novel idea of having a place where a man of refined tastes could go just to eat, to restore his soul, no mere tavern or roadhouse, but a place that would serve lobster, mussels, beef, and venison as well as the finest tarts and cakes in existence: petit choux with rosewater icing, benioles, pate feuilletee, bergamot genoise soaked in cognac, and etageres des pastries.

Ste Germaine started the renovation by insisting that the exposed ceiling beams be covered, then plastering and liming the ceiling although it was at great and needless expense. After he had asked for everyone's opinion, including Gilles, customers, friends, acquaintances, business associates and even craftsmen, Ste Germaine went ahead with his plans, following through with very few if any of the suggestions, but he *had* asked.

New leaded glass casement windows with fleur-de-lys beveled glass jewels were installed, having been created just for Ste Germaine by the city's finest glassmakers. Excellent wood paneling and a new parquetry floor boasting three *different* kinds of wood in the dining room, and marble in the foyer, went in next. New draperies and wall sconces were purchased as well as a fine crystal chandelier and all new china and silver settings for the tables. For the crowning touch, a chef was imported all the way from France to show Ste Germaine's regular cook how to make some new recipes.

The cook sullenly listened for two days before he started showing up late, leaving early, sampling the sherry in between cooking lessons, and being rude in general to the visiting chef. The guest chef was probably infuriated, that is if he understood *all* of the cook's mutterings, both aloud and under the cook's breath, and he would have had to have been completely obtuse to have missed them all, but he maintained his composure, even cooking alone for Ste Germaine one day when the regular chef had gone missing altogether. Gilles thought that the compensation for the French chef's time and aggravation must have been *very* worth his while for him to put up with such daily abuse, even though he only had to endure it for a week's time. Ste Germaine alternated between standing over the workmen in the dining room as they put in the new floor and standing over the battling chefs in the kitchen. Whichever room Ste Germaine happened to be in at the time, he always sent Gilles to oversee the operations in the *other* room and to report back to him.

"Go and see if the cook is listening, Gilles."

"Go make sure the workmen are not taking a break, Gilles."

"Go make sure the chef tells cook about desserts, Gilles."

Ste Germaine was quite visibly annoyed whenever the workmen stopped to eat, take a break, or even to relieve themselves. He drove them mercilessly, by daylight and by lamplight to finish in the seven days that he had allotted for them to finish the great undertaking, threatening to reduce their pay or to not to pay them *at all* if his reopening was delayed by as much as a day. The contractor doing the flooring work had negotiated a daily half hour dinner break for his workers to ensure that Ste Germaine would not stand over them as they ate, and perhaps the man wondered if Ste Germaine would soon inquire as to whether they could chew a *little* bit faster and thus return to work a *little* bit sooner.

On the sixth day, Gilles took advantage of the workmen's brief dinner break to escape the chaos and dust, protesting that he needed to stop in at the chandlers and make sure the new candles were suitable and would be ready for the grand reopening. With Ste Germaine's grudging blessing and admonition *not* to be late in returning, Gilles went to the chandlers first and then stopped in to see his friend Jean on the way home.

Jean had set up his tiny accounting office, no more than a desk and two chairs really, in his small apartment and he worked from there, having secured enough customers in the time he had been in the city to start his own business.

"Gilles! What a delightful surprise! Sit down! What brings you here today?" Jean looked up from a large black ledger book.

"I'm checking to see if you have had supper recently with any more beautiful women," Gilles said mischievously as he sat down in the chair opposite Jean.

"Oh, the one from last week? Her father is one of the East India Captains, a *Marrano* who worked his way up through the ranks from cabin boy. Do you know that he actually left us *all alone* with some pretext of business at the docks? She *was* very easy to look at but so uncultured! She had no table manners at all. It's a good thing he returned when he did or I would have had to abandon her there in Ste Germaine's dining room with her fingers still sifting through the ratatouille."

Gilles grinned at him. "Was she *really* that bad?"

"So what brings you here?" Jean asked again with a smirk that answered Gilles' question.

"Do I need an excuse?" Gilles asked. "I just had to get away for a time."

"You generally have something you need whenever you come to visit me. Isn't Ste Germaine done yet with whatever it is that he is doing to his place? It's a *terrible* mess."

Gilles was not at all put off by Jean's friendly jab. "He's still working on it. He is driving everyone crazy, including me. The cooks are experimenting on anyone who is hanging around so I felt it *safer* to leave and get my dinner elsewhere. I'm afraid they will poison someone."

Jean laughed heartily. "Well said! I hear that the French chef has some very *unusual* dishes but what can you expect from someone from the *south* of France? Well, we can go out now and get some *real* food together; I'm ready for a break. How is Elsje doing? It must be getting close to her time for the baby to come."

"She is well," Gilles said as he straightened his lace cuffs.

"So it's about Elsje then? The reason that you came to see me?"

Gilles took his hand off his cuff and looked at his friend in amazement. He shouldn't have been surprised though; Jean never failed to astonish him with his quick grasp of situations and leaps of logic, all infused with an intuition that led him frequently to an uncanny and accurate assessment of any matter.

Jean raised a hand to silence any objections from Gilles. "I can read your *very* thoughts, Gilles! *Anyone* could with an open face like yours, but I can do it *better* than most, having known you for so very long. You want to ask me something, so go ahead."

Gilles had to ask himself *why* he was asking this favor of a Jew who had almost died at the hands of the Catholics in France and aside from being his best friend, the only obvious answer was that Jean seemed to have personal and business connections for just about anything that anyone could ever need. Jean didn't allow Gilles to proceed with his verbal request though, and with Jean's having interrupted the carefully planned and practiced speech, Gilles was unable to get his bearings until after his friend began speaking again.

"It's all right, Gilles. Don't make it more difficult than it is! I will be *happy* to be your child's godfather. I have been wondering if you would ask me and I would consider it an *honor*."

Jean closed the account book he had been working on and leaned back in his chair, folding his soft hands together but still looking thoughtfully at the ledger as if trying to solve a lingering problem. He looked back up at Gilles after a few moments of silence and his absentminded smile faded slightly. "There's *more*? The Protestants *do* have godfathers, don't they?"

"Yes, and that would be good, *too*. You know a lot of people..." Gilles began. "I don't know if you *can* or *will* help me..."

"*Will* help you? What is it? Are you raising an army to invade France?"

It was Gilles' turn to smile. "Non. I want a priest. I want my child baptized in the Catholic Church." There, he had said it out loud.

Jean's smiling face grew serious as he looked at his friend. "I heard you right? Where will you find a priest here who will not have sympathies with the authorities in France? You're not exactly in *good* standing with the church! Elsje wants this for the child too?"

"Well, I haven't talked to her about it yet..."

"There are those priests here who *might* do it, but not all of them practice the sacraments openly, Gilles. They might be stoned to death on the streets or have their houses set afire by the victims of their predecessors, the Reformees here not having the patience to wait for God's justice in the afterlife. The Netherlanders aren't especially noted for their short memories and they have suffered *grievously* at the hands of the Spaniards."

"Let's go have some dinner now," Gilles said, changing the subject. "I can't be away from Ste Germaine's for long."

He stood up. He never should have asked Jean. He just hadn't thought it through enough before he came here. Jean shrugged, stood up, retrieved his jacket and opened the door for his friend. There was uncomfortable silence between the two as they walked up the street but after a time, Gilles thought that perhaps Jean was not thinking about the request but was more preoccupied with some business concern.

Jean took Gilles to a tavern nearby where they could get some tavern food along with their ales. Jean sat in silence, looking at his nails, and Gilles, being Jean's equal only when it came to accounts work, was about to offer his professional help and opinion on whatever problem it was that had so preoccupied his friend when Jean finally spoke to Gilles once more.

"If you *really* want this, Gilles, then I will see what I can do for you. You need to talk with Elsje first, though."

"What if she says 'Non'?" Gilles asked, a queasy feeling seeping into his stomach.

"I don't know, Gilles, but you can't just do something like that without telling her."

They fell silent again as the proprietor brought out their drinks and their food, a stew that had been waiting for customers in the iron pot all morning, or maybe even a few days longer.

Jean waited for the man to leave before he leaned across the table and said to Gilles, "You would have to go by the name "*Yellas Jansen*" and you couldn't just go to *any* priest. Your particular situation makes it *more* complicated than it would be for a Netherlander."

"Maybe it's just too much," Gilles said. "Maybe I should just forget about it."

"It would take some thought and some planning, but it *could* be done. I would think very carefully about this and if you really feel that you *must* do it, you will have to tell Elsje."

"What would you do? I mean if it was you, Jean, in this situation, what would *you* do?"

"I am not you, Gilles. For myself, I am finished with the Catholic Church forever."

"You are a heathen," Gilles replied, but he said it with an affectionate smile.

"It's not the first time I have been called that."

Jean returned the smile but Gilles heard the note of bitterness in his voice. Jean was right of course: It really made no difference at all if a child was baptized or not, but if Gilles had complete freedom of choice with no other political or personal safety considerations at all, then he would make the choice to have his child baptized. The sacrament offered protection from illness and the promise of heaven for his son, especially when another epidemic swept through, as it surely would, if not this year, then next. *Having a choice* was the meaning of freedom to Gilles, to leave outside constraints behind and to make your own decision. Shouldn't he avail himself of an opportunity that might be denied to others if he considered himself now to be truly a free man?

After they had finished their dinner, Jean said to him teasingly, "Can't you ever just simply *live* your life, without complicating it?" but he clapped Gilles on the arm affectionately before he returned to his accounting books.

The frenzy of Ste Germaine's alterations to his establishment with only one more day left to go before business resumed soon drove all other thoughts out of Gilles' mind. More than once Gilles thought of God creating the world in seven days and the parallels with Ste Germaine and his grandiose project. Would Ste Germaine never rest? He was recreating his entire world as he wanted it. Did he believe he would have total domination over all of creation?

Perhaps.

The construction was nearing completion and all of the right touches had to be finished for the grand reopening. There was a minor argument over the quality of some wood trim and a major argument over a replaced floor board which ended up being replaced yet a *second* time, set down in place three times in all, with much grumbling from the workers and an angry glare at Ste Germaine from their foreman. At last the workmen declared that the work was completed, secured their money and took their leave, even as *every* person who worked for Ste Germaine in any capacity at all was put to work, even the cook and Gilles who were herded in with the maids who dumped the chamber pots, cleaned the floors and washed the dishes, all of them put to work scrubbing, dusting, and polishing everything. The new draperies were hung and the portraits that had been removed from the walls were put back into place with the exception of the portrait of Ste Germaine with his wife and child. Ste Germaine replaced it with an elegant new painting of a prosperous young couple and their four children standing beside a fine country house that was surrounded by fields, large oak trees and grazing horses. Gilles thought that the house looked a great deal like Ste Germaine's country home and the patriarch looked rather like Ste Germaine, but he did not recognize the woman although there *was* something very familiar-looking about her. The painting smelled of oil for many months afterwards but it was a happy picture to look at while one dined on sumptuous feasts, or while one supervised others who waited on those who dined. Carved vases of imported Italian Ferrara marble were unwrapped and set out on new carved wooden pedestals as a last finishing touch. The overall efforts of the renovation were well worthwhile and when every last task was completed, Gilles affirmed, under his breath of course, "What Ste Germaine wants, Ste Germaine gets!"

Customers thronged in at the reopening that started precisely on schedule. Ste Germaine had already sent word to most of his regular customers to tell them what day and even what *time* they were expected to come. He did this for two reasons: One was so that he could be certain that they *did* come, as promised, and the other reason was so that he could plan a balance of customers in order of importance for seating and cooking purposes. Just this *one* time, Ste Germaine could have a *perfect* week, without too many very important customers needing his best seats all at once or too many lesser customers taking up all of the good seats for too long while his best patrons had to wait impatiently at the door for an open table. Because Ste Germaine was such a well-known and respected man in the city, most of his guests did come when he told them to, except for a few who *insisted* on coming when they felt like it, throwing Ste Germaine into alternating panic and annoyance.

Being the complete manager in the extreme that Ste Germaine was, he had every detail planned, both inside and out. He had hired an army of young boys that he sent out into the city dressed up as French court pages in velvet and satin outfits, carrying scrolls with the news of the grand reopening. Ste Germaine carefully taught them *what* to say and *how* to say it, even how to stand and how to hold their hands as they delivered their message. The young boys, recruited from the ranks of a nearby school, were not mere street urchins or uncultured apprentices, and had been mercilessly drilled for an *entire* day before they were at last released to their respective lists of customers. They went to every important customer and business establishment across the city inviting people to come, telling the would-be patrons to inform Ste Germaine's head waiter of the name of their personal page for a reduction in the price of the dinner and a small additional bonus to be paid later to the boy. After the first two weeks of gathering names, there would be a lottery drawing for a painting commissioned from Rembrandt Van Rijn's group. Ste Germaine did things in his usual big way even though he really didn't need to be concerned about his clientele coming back: His biggest problem was generally where to seat everyone when they all lingered for too long over their authentic and superb French dinners.

Ste Germaine was very pleased when they survived the first night of the reopening and none of his patrons went away angry, although the sudden discovery that his headwaiter was illiterate and unable to write down the names of the customers *or* their pages bogged down the progress of seating until Gilles stepped into the breach, helping the man with the names when he wasn't busy running to the kitchen to check on a dinner, inquiring as to an important patron's comfort, and if necessary, retrieving more wine from the cave, the man-made earthen warehouse structure on the lot behind the building.

The guests had all come to anticipate such spectacles from Ste Germaine and indeed, to be a part of such a momentous event, they correctly and almost happily anticipated a wait for their seats and their food. Gilles learned much during this time about expectations, diplomacy, creativity, hard work, and even cooking. While Ste Germaine would not allow Gilles be seen waiting on the tables or clearing them, stirring a sauce out of sight in the kitchen while tables were finishing up was another matter entirely.

Gilles was struggling with seating arrangements on the second night and doing his best to avoid having Ste Germaine take charge in front of everyone, making Gilles look the fool again, when a familiar-looking woman walked in. She was dressed in finery and at first Gilles could not place her. He knew her from somewhere else a long time ago, but where? Was it France? Jean Durie's office?

It was the *clothes* that were different, as well as the location, and Gilles stood across the room, looking at her standing in the line of customers as she and her escort waited to be seated. Gilles did not recognize her companion, he was certain of that. At last he recalled the dark mole on her cheek. She was the haughty Jewish girl who had tossed him his dinner every night from the back stoep of her tavern, just up the street from Jacob Van Zeelandt's stable when Gilles had first come to Amsterdam, and had been living in the cold and drafty hayloft there, hiding in the Jewish quarter from the French bounty hunters, living every waking and sleeping moment in fear for his life.

Gilles' conscious decision to live the rest of his life as a completely free man, without fear, for however much time he had left, had been a momentous decision that had completely changed his life. Without that determination, Gilles might still be cold, alone, and poor, cowering in the miserable stable like the animal that he had become for a time. Now *she* had walked in the door and she brought it all back to him now, the terror, the hunger, *and* the humiliation. Gilles drew in a sharp breath at the sight of the woman and fear rose up in his chest, making it feel tight against his crisp white shirt.

What if she asked *out loud* what a stable boy was doing here, working in the dining room? Gilles had never told his current employer what he had been forced to do to survive those first few miserable months. Gilles looked at her once again as she stood by the door and he wondered what she was doing on the French side of town, or more to the point, in the *non-Jewish* part of town.

As he observed her, Gilles could plainly see that she and her companion were nervous, as well they should be: They were frightened to be here among all of the Christians but nonetheless, they wanted this experience and they wanted it badly enough to venture in to where some of the more affluent Spanish and Portuguese Jews might be welcomed, as they would be able to blend in well enough, but where they, the common German type of Jews, Ashkenazim, would not. They surely would not have been admitted inside the front door if their identity had been guessed. The couple must have received an invitation through some page's error and then seized the opportunity to avail themselves of the unique and certain to be wonderful experience, hoping to pass for those in the throng that did not give a moment's thought to walking through Ste Germaine's very ornate carved oak and polished brass front doors.

Gilles gathered up his courage and approached them. In an icy voice, with as heavy a Normandy accent as Gilles dared put on without his coworkers noticing, he asked, "Madame et Monsieur sont ici pour le soir ou seulement pour le repas?"

Just as Gilles had expected, they did not understand what he said.

He repeated his question in Nederlands, with an affected accent in that language also, hoping that he had said few enough words to the girl in the past, when he had begged her for his food in the shadows of the dark alley where she threw her leftovers out to him like a stray dog. Gilles hoped that she would not recognize him *or* his voice and if so, *he* had the advantage now: He had learned enough of the Jewish languages in Amsterdam to comprehend any conversation between the woman and her companion if they dared to speak those words aloud here in public.

Apparently both the heavy accent and Gilles' greatly changed appearance, both in dress and in his choice of facial hair, was successful in obscuring her memory of Gilles. Before he had worn his dirty and matted long hair pulled back with an old leather tie. His beard had been a scraggly full one but today his well-groomed coiffure was held neatly in place with blue silk ribbon and it framed a more fleshed-out face sporting a neatly trimmed moustache and goatee. No doubt her fear and overwhelmed senses played a part in preserving his anonymity on this night as well.

The woman's companion straightened himself up, invitation in his hand, and said in a self-important voice, with his own linguistic affectations, a poor and pathetic, even somewhat comical attempt at sounding like the educated class in Amsterdam, *"Just the meal."*

Gilles tried not to smirk openly at the man's attempt at bravado and now he could see that they were both shaking slightly. The girl looked as though she might faint and seemed to be seeking an escape as her eyes flitted briefly back toward the door. The crowd pressing in behind them would not allow for an easy exit, even if she was determined to turn and run, but her companion was not going to give up so easily.

Perhaps he wanted to impress her. Perhaps he wanted the woman and all of the opportunities that were before him, even those not intended for his kind. Gilles was quite certain that the man was not her husband yet and he marveled that the girl was out alone with him: This was not so rare among the Protestants in the Netherlands, as long as they were family friends or already betrothed, but it was highly unusual for the Jews, who generally walked along, women with women and men with men, even after they were married, or with the women following back a few paces behind the men.

Gilles wanted to pay the girl back in kind, to embarrass her for all of the times she had spit on him, had ground his spirit into the dirt with the heel of her shoe and generally looked down on him as a lower form of life. He remembered the time that she fed his supper to a dog when he was too tired and too sick to retrieve it one night, and then the next day she charged him for it anyway and then compensated him with a rotten old potato after he protested and before she would give him his meal for the day. A plan took shape, forming without conscious intent in the back of his mind.

Gilles approached them, swept a low bow that was among his very best ever, and said, "Madame is *most* lovely tonight! Come, I will give you my *best* table!"

He did, too. He gave them an excellent seat which made them even *more* uncomfortable in the glare of the spotlight, the center stage of the dining room. They clung to their cloaks, refusing to give them to Gilles for safekeeping as all of the other patrons did. Gilles ordered an excellent bottle of wine for them and when they questioned if it was an additional cost, he told them that it was paid for. They looked at each other and Gilles heard them quietly speak to each other in their own language, questioning if this had been included with the invitation.

After the wine was served and their order taken, it became clear to Gilles that they had no capacity for drink at all, which was not surprising given what Gilles knew of many of the Jews, and soon they were giggling away while the other patrons looked at them in surprise and annoyance. The couple grew steadily less conscious of their surroundings with each sip and eventually even Ste Germaine noticed the spectacle and came over to speak privately to Gilles.

"Who *are* those people, Gilles? We need to get them out of here!"

"Oui, Monsieur," Gilles replied.

"Who invited them? One of the pages?" Ste Germaine mumbled something else over his shoulder and was off to bother the cook in the kitchen.

Gilles ordered a mince pie for the couple, knowing full well that it was made with pork and lard, a salade, and large glasses of brandy for them. The mince pie garnished with fragile shavings of lemon peel was more of a Netherlands dish than the kind of thing Ste Germaine generally liked to serve in his establishment but Ste Germaine had added a few local specialty items to the menu, upgraded and refined from the usual recipes of course, just for the opening few weeks, a concession to the locals, some incentive to entice the Netherlanders to try the food in his establishment, to compare his new versions to their old standards.

"Monsieur!" the waiter whispered urgently to Gilles, "We *cannot* bring their dessert now! We have not cleared their supper plates away yet!"

"Never mind," Gilles said, "just put the dessert and brandy down on the table anyway, ask if they have finished their dinner yet, and then just take the plates away from them. They *won't* know the difference."

The waiter hesitated for a moment but seeing no modification in Gilles' unusual and overtly rude instructions, he reluctantly moved forward to carry them out. After all, Gilles was second in command only to Ste Germaine himself.

Indeed, the couple did *not* know the difference, although a few of the regular patrons gave the headwaiter some questioning looks when they observed this breach of serving etiquette and the many half-eaten dishes piled up and strewn across the table, hazards just waiting to connect with the diner's elbows or slide off by themselves onto the new floor. The couple puzzled over the salade, something that they were not at all familiar with, and then continued on with their raucous dining, two crows among a great flock of canaries.

"What are you *doing* to my dining room?" the headwaiter whispered anxiously to Gilles. "This is a *gracious* place and you are destroying the ambiance!"

It was then that Jean Durie made his way inside the front door and into the crowded vestibule of Ste Germaine's. Gilles had been just about ready to physically throw the couple out, but now it was he who was uncomfortable. Would Jean take it as a personal insult that Gilles had mistreated the Jewish couple, even if the couple did not even realize that they were being treated badly? With Jean's close ties to the Jewish quarter, it was a certainty that Jean knew who she was if he did not know her personally. Being ever diplomatic and sociable, of course he would greet them, just as he always greeted everyone that he knew, and very soon he would know that something was amiss.

The head waiter tried to take control of the situation and Gilles briefly considered a retreat to the kitchen to check on the cooking himself, leaving the eviction process entirely up to some underling, but Ste Germaine was still in there with the cook and Gilles didn't want to come face to face with his employer at the moment. Gilles stood his ground and hoped that the chaos would settle out around him. At the epicenter of the storm, the two diners dined on, still blissfully unaware of the disapprobation that swirled around them, the other patrons and the servers all taking mental notes of the many faux pas of the couple, the staff frantically, if silently, trying to restore the equilibrium in the room.

The two had tasted everything and stuffed themselves without leaving much of anything on the dishes. She scraped the plate with her knife a few times, licking it off and then running her finger through the meat sauce again and again, loudly sucking the juice from her fingers, which brought even more stares and glares from other diners. By this time the waiters had managed to get just a few of the empty plates away from them and remove them from the table.

"If Ste Germaine knew they were Jews," Gilles thought, *"he might throw out the chairs and table as well as the new dishes."*

Jean Durie seemed not to have noticed the furor yet. From his position by the front door he was surveying the far reaches of the dining room, definitely searching for someone.

"Bon soir, Jean. Can I help you find someone?" Gilles asked.

"I don't see him, Gilles, and I don't think you know him. He's a French ship's captain who is new on the Netherlands trade route."

Jean's eye was now caught by the activity and he had definitely noticed the scene in the center of the dining room. His eye fixed on the girl. It was difficult for *anyone* to miss the couple's antics, even in the general noise of the crowded dining room. The girl's companion ate greedily with one hand while his other hand migrated openly from his lap to his companion's thigh. Gilles waited for Jean to say something aloud regarding the situation but he saw only hesitation on his friend's face. Jean must have known the girl and Gilles waited for him to go over and talk to her, but he didn't.

"Will you have a good table opening up soon?" Jean asked Gilles, as he pulled his eyes away from the rollicking couple.

"Of *course*, Jean, you have special privileges with the manager!"

Gilles flashed him a smile that he hoped was casual but his attention and thoughts were still fixed on the table with the two insouciant diners. The waiters were now trying to remove the rest of the dinner plates but the two patrons were now noticeably drunk and had begun to playfully throw the salade at each other. Most of the seated diners were eyeing them now, some surreptitiously and others openly, and the volume level of the dining room had quieted appreciably. The girl didn't seem to care that she had petite fours in her hair or the man that he had something white clinging to his mustache and beard.

Gilles wondered briefly how much his gift of the drink had exacerbated the situation. *"But if you don't know how to act, drunk or sober..."* Gilles thought, coming to his own defense.

If Ste Germaine came out and saw this now he would most certainly be stricken with apoplexy. It was now time for someone to remove the discordant diners from the room and to remove them quickly; understanding this too, the head waiter sent a junior server over to remove the last of the dishes. This task was not easily accomplished as the man seized the brandy glass and clutched it to his chest while the woman held fast to the plate with the mince pie, although neither one of them seemed to be consuming any more food, only playing with it.

The head waiter went over to the table, bringing a firmer hand to the eviction process.

"Madame et Monsieur, thank you for coming here to enjoy our supper presentation. May we show you to a more comfortable chair in which to finish your brandy? Or perhaps the smoking salon?"

The man growled at the head waiter, much like bear with a fish that had suddenly come under challenge from an interloping beast.

"Subtlety and good manners are just wasted on them," Gilles thought derisively.

Realizing that they did not speak French, the request was repeated by the head waiter in Nederlands with perhaps not as polished a presentation, or as friendly a meaning, as it had been originally when put out there in the earlier French version.

"We paid for it and we're staying!" the Jewish man snarled.

Seeing no alternative, the head waiter withdrew quickly to diffuse the situation and it was Gilles' turn to step in. He knew that he was in large part responsible for the unhappy current situation and now he had to either succeed in remedying it or fail in front of a room full of Amsterdam's finest citizens. He just hoped that Ste Germaine would not investigate the incident later and then fire him.

Gilles approached the table, bowed low and smiled the most charming smile he could manage for the woman.

"Mademoiselle." Gilles looked into her eyes.

She looked back at him with a glazed and inebriated look but the puzzlement there told Gilles that she was registering *some* familiarity and was now trying to remember who Gilles was.

He continued in a very low voice so that only the two diners could hear his voice. "Mademoiselle et Monsieur, thank you *so much* for coming to our establishment tonight. It is so good of you to have made the trip all the way across town to try our hospitality when you have your *own* place, over there."

Fear briefly registered in her eyes and something akin passed over her companion's face. Gilles knew that they comprehended his meaning, that he had made it clear enough to them. He continued, "...and now it is time for you to leave before the owner returns. He is more...ah, *discriminating* than I am, as to which friends he has personally invited into his establishment."

The hint was taken and the woman even managed half a smile at being allowed a gracious exit as her companion clumsily helped her on with her cape.

"I trust that you have had a pleasant evening. Bon soir!" Gilles called after them, more for the benefit of the rest of the room, and he bowed low again as they hurried out the door.

Ste Germaine was at his elbow before Gilles could rise from his bow.

"The head waiter *told* me! *Well done*, Gilles! I *knew* that you were management material when I hired...Oh Mon Dieu! *What now?*"

Gilles looked in the direction of Ste Germaine's stare and saw two ragged men standing at the door, clad in what looked like dead animal skins. They had great dusty woven baskets harnessed to their backs, packs that were stuffed with their ragged personal possessions, the items overflowing at the top and poking out through great jagged holes in the sides.

"You make a fine establishment and the very *dregs* of society come to it! Handle this for me too, Gilles!"

It was a command, not a request, and Ste Germaine ran off at a trot to distract some important guest from looking over at the next floorshow of the night that was just beginning at the front door.

"Jesus Christ didn't have to perform *this* many miracles a day," Gilles muttered to himself as he put one foot in front of the other and walked toward the men, wondering how he was going to "handle it" as Ste Germaine had ordered.

The two vagrants were indeed wearing animal skins and they appeared to be father and son, although there was a great variation in skin coloring between the two men. The shorter father scratched his beard and his stomach as he looked curiously around the room. The son, who appeared to have some colonial savage bloodlines as well as a few of his attending parent's features, was as tall as Gilles and stood sniffing the air in much the same way a horse would when wolves had recently been around the pasture.

"May I help you?" Gilles asked, wondering if *they* spoke French.

Gilles was caught off guard when the older man answered him in excellent French.

"We have business here in the city and I was told that you have the *best* French food in all of Amsterdam. I don't speak Nederlands," the man added with an apologetic smile.

"Do you have business with a Frenchman here?" Gilles asked, hopeful that he might escort the men outside and then give them directions to somewhere very far away.

"Actually it's a *Netherlander* we've come to see, but I understand we'll be able to communicate with each other all right."

The older man pulled at his unkempt beard, picked a nit out of it and tossed the bug to the marble floor, squashing it with his boot before he looked past Gilles, out into the dining room, interest and curiosity settling in on his visage.

Gilles was just not going to seat them; Ste Germaine would be *beside* himself and would fire Gilles if he did that.

"Monsieur, we are *so* busy tonight that I would not like to have you wait such a long time for your food. I am sure that you are *very* hungry, so perhaps I could help you to quickly find some good food *and* the businessman you seek. I know many, many people in the city," Gilles cajoled, smiling as friendly a smile as he could put on his face, but he did not step out of the way.

The young savage looked Gilles over, perhaps wondering if he could take him down quickly in a physical contest. Gilles ignored the young man's posturing and focused his complete attention on the unkempt father, who was certainly the more civilized of the two ruffians.

"His name is Hendrick and he runs a tavern," the older vagrant replied. "The blessed Netherlanders don't *use* last names so I guess it will take me most of the day to find him tomorrow! There certainly are a *lot* more taverns in this city now than there used to be."

The seated customers had started to notice the men and now many of them were openly staring. The level of talking had decreased markedly once again so Gilles decided on a more direct course of action.

"Ahh, I *can* help you! Come with me!"

He took the two men by the elbows and walked them outside, nodding a signal to the headwaiter to take over and fill up any empty tables as quickly as possible before they could return. Under Gilles' firm grip, the young man's arm was as strong and hard as the trunk of a tree and the father's was just *slightly* less so. Gilles could plainly see that he was no match physically for either one of them alone, let alone the pair. To get rid of the men, Gilles would need to use every ounce of diplomacy that he might harbor anywhere in his being, all that he had been born with and all that he had learned during his entire life. Gilles devised a quick plan: He would ask a few questions, invent a destination, and then send them to the far side of the city where they would probably get lost.

"We are *hungry* and have money to pay," the older man said, the complaint carrying with it an edge in his voice. The young man looked to the older man, probably for direction as to their next course of action.

"Of *course* you are!" Gilles flashed them a wide smile. "But *first* allow me to help you to find your contact here. It would be *wonderful* if you could find this tavern you seek tonight and stay there. You would be fed quickly, rested, and *all ready* to conduct business in the morning, eh? Eh?"

Gilles shook their muscled arms slightly in encouragement of a positive response but none was forthcoming. The older man didn't answer him and the younger man just looked back at Gilles with unblinking black eyes. Unperturbed, Gilles continued his friendly repartee, mostly a monologue with himself, because the two men were not responding, at least not in the way that Gilles had hoped they would, while he steered them further and further away from Ste Germaine's front door.

"There are a good *many* Hendricks here, that is true. You say he runs a tavern? *Half* of the tavern keepers in the city are named Hendrick! Is this about Dutch West India business?"

"Non, we don't deal with those *big* companies! We have a trapping agreement with Hendrick Hendricks, as he calls himself, and his French son-in-law."

Gilles laughed out loud in surprise and let go of the men's arms. "You are looking for my *father-in-law*, Hendrick! There are no others that would *have* a French son-in-law!"

The older man smiled an uncertain smile back in spite of Gilles' self-deprecating remark. This was indeed Gilles' lucky night for solving problems for Ste Germaine.

"If I may suggest though, Monsieur, just be careful to refer to his business as an 'inn', and not as a 'tavern', as Monsieur Hendricks is just a *little* bit sensitive about that term. Some travelers *do* stay there, but it's true that his main business is ale and bier. "

Gilles took the older man's arm up again to lead the way. The man still hesitated, wanting to go back to Ste Germaine's, Gilles could tell, but he would not let him turn around. If he could lead the older man, Gilles was sure that the son would follow like an unbroken colt behind a mare in harness.

"We are *very* hungry and would like to eat *first*," the man said.

"Oui, oui, of *course* you would! And Hendrick's daughter, my wife Elsje, is the *best* cook in *all* of Amsterdam."

"Can she cook Normandie French food?" the man asked hopefully.

"Normandie?" Gilles asked in surprise. The scruffy man was from his *own* region in France. Well of course, Gilles should have surmised this from his accent. Who *was* he? Did Gilles' family know him? The ruffian would *surely* have heard of Gilles' family. "Her cooking is the best on three continents and you never have to wait for it." Gilles replied, avoiding the direct question of French cuisine.

"So you work for another man, in his tavern?" the older man asked, puzzled.

"I just try to find seating for people, and that's *all* I do," Gilles said modestly.

"But..." the older man looked back over his shoulder at Ste Germaine's and tried to slow his steps as Gilles continued to pull at his arm and talk him along, across the heart of the city.

"Now you *must* tell me all about this new venture! It's Van Corlaer's venture, or Van Curler, as some call him, is that right? I have to go back to work after I get you settled at Hendrick's, but when I return, you will tell me *all* about it, oui? Hendrick can put you up for the night, feed you, talk as much business as you want tonight, or just let you sleep now if you are too tired to talk this evening."

The man kept walking beside him, the son still shadowing them and Gilles kept talking. "Allow me to introduce myself. I'm Gilles Mon... uh, you just call me Gilles, since we are *already* trade partners, n'est-ce pas? Now what is your name and where did you come from in France? So you live in the colonies now? Do you live in Rensselaerwyck, Van Corlaer's uncle's patroonship?"

Gilles had almost given the man his real name, something that he had avoided scrupulously for the past year, as it was best to hang on to his anonymity if he was going to keep his life. He had been caught off guard, lulled temporarily into complacency by the Normandie accent and his lifelong habit of giving his full name whenever he was asked, particularly when it was in his own language, and always announcing it with great pride.

Gilles kept up his fast pace, in step and in talk, all the while thinking that Ste Germaine had better *not* be angry with him for leaving the dining room while they were so busy: Gilles' absence was for a *very* good cause.

"My name is Thomas Pelletier and this is my son, Francois. We left our home in Little River, New France, three months ago to come here."

"All that way? Just to see us? And which ship did you come over on?"

Gilles was relieved when Hendrick's inn finally came into sight. He had been talking and they had been walking for about fifteen minutes in a rather circuitous route, but he wanted to make sure that the two men wouldn't be able to find their way back to Ste Germaine's.

"Ah, there it is! Let me assure you, Msr. Pelletier, Hendrick will take *very* good care of you while you are here."

Gilles hustled them inside the inn and even there, in the more earthy and provincial surroundings of Hendrick's inn where they were accustomed to patrons of *every* sort and from every country in the known world, pirates, drunks, Moors *and* the occasional prostitute, Gilles' two guests in their costumes created a sensation.

Upon seeing Gilles at home early with two savages at his side and probably expecting trouble, Hendrick stood up and stepped out from behind his usual table, perhaps prepared to run into the kitchen where he kept his rusty old matchlock. Gilles hadn't had occasion to find out if the firearm even worked but it *was* occasionally useful in persuading troublesome patrons to leave when it was pointed directly at them. Gilles quickly set his father-in-law's mind at ease and made introductions, running out the door again before he could say much more than "Elsje can translate until I get home!" Gilles hurried back to Ste Germaine's to resolve the next crisis that was probably already waiting for him there.

The rest of the evening at his work passed without any worse incident than a waiter's dropping a plate of *canard a l'orange*, although Gilles couldn't stop thinking about the two very strange events of the evening. Ste Germaine was *so* pleased with Gilles for taking care of the two nuisance parties that he gave Gilles a bonus for the night of ten guilders. As always, Gilles supervised the clean up of the dining room and the kitchen before he left, and he was rather hoping that the two beggars he had left in Hendrick's care would be gone, or at least fast asleep before he arrived there. When Gilles started for home at last, the position of the moon in the sky told him that it was at least midnight, if not past. It had been a very, very, long night and he only hoped that the other nights of Ste Germaine's grand reopening would not be nearly as taxing to his body or to his wits. Gilles needed to keep his job, just as long as he could be assured of keeping his sanity too: His investments alone were not enough to support a family yet although he hoped that the day would eventually come when they would.

Hendrick's inn was quiet when Gilles arrived there and even the usual drunks had already left, but the three business partners, the two savages and Hendrick, were still sitting at a table in the dining room along with Elsje, the glow of light from the table's lamp lighting their faces but leaving the rest of the room half hidden in dark, flickering shadows. Elsje, very far along in her pregnancy now, was happy to be taking some of her enormous weight off her feet for a change, and was seated at her father's table, trying to translate. It seemed that lately, whenever Gilles saw her sitting down, Elsje had her tired head propped up on her hands as her dark-circled eyes occasionally flickered shut before springing open again, usually just after her head dropped from its resting place on her closed fists.

Tonight Elsje seemed to have more energy than usual though. Perhaps it was a better night's sleep the night before or maybe it was the interesting visitors who kept her so alert. Gilles could see that the men had made extensive use of ink and paper drawings to communicate with each other. He could hear the voices of Tryntje and the two other women who were still cleaning up in the kitchen but the low level of noise told Gilles that they were probably almost finished for the night.

"Did you men find much to talk about? It is *late*, our guests must be tired!" Gilles repeated this in French for Thomas' benefit.

"Monsieur Hendrick Hendricks is a *most* interesting man, a man of great ideas!" Thomas smiled across the table at his new-found friend. Gilles translated for Hendrick who grinned his gap-toothed smile in return at his guest.

"We will *both* become rich from our partnership," Hendrick declared.

Gilles started to translate but Thomas held up his hand to signal complete comprehension. The two older men were working their way through a bottle of wine which probably did as much, or maybe even more than Elsje's linguistic skills to facilitate communication and understanding. Gilles was quite certain that it was not their first bottle either and Thomas did not seem to mind at all that Hendrick, being a Dutchman, had no discernable taste or palate for *good* wine. But of course Thomas *would* be polite, and the only reason that Gilles ever drank from Hendrick's supply of vinegary wine was that it was only *slightly* preferable to the miserable Dutch ale.

Gilles brought a chair over to join them and Elsje heaved herself up onto her feet to fetch a mug for Gilles' wine. Gilles wondered if

Elsje shouldn't get some sleep as she would have to be up again very soon, fixing breakfast in a few more hours, but he didn't say so. Elsje was strong-willed enough to go to bed when she was ready and she had been *very* snappish of late. She did seem to be walking a little bit faster into the kitchen, with a little more spring in her step and she returned quickly with a mug for her husband.

Gilles had been trying for weeks now to sell Hendrick on the idea that the French, and other refined people including the Dutch West India Company men, preferred *glasses* of their favorite beverage, that the wine just tasted *better* than it did in the mugs and steins, but it was all to no avail. Hendrick wouldn't make the investment and Gilles certainly wasn't going to pay for it out of his own pocket. Gilles sighed in resignation and took a sip of his wine from the heavy pottery.

The two kitchen maids left for the night after Hendrick bid them a safe trip home and soon after, Gilles watched Tryntje come out of the kitchen and stand in the shadows at the dining room door, drying her hands on her apron. Francois stood up and gestured to Thomas who nodded at his son before Francois made his way out to the back to relieve himself, the savage obviously already acquainted with the route.

"I've been looking at that all night. What is it?"

Hendrick leaned forward and pointed to a pouch that hung around Thomas' neck. The little bag was made of leather but the outside had colorful designs on it. Thomas lifted the pouch from around his neck and opened it by loosening the leather strings. Inside were colorful stones and long, sharp, teeth from some large animal, perhaps a bear. Thomas handed a tooth and one of the large, dark red stones to Hendrick. Gilles leaned forward with interest and wondered if the stone might be an unpolished ruby.

"Are there *many* such rocks like this where you come from?" Gilles asked Thomas.

"Ah oui, more than you can *count*," Thomas assured him. "They are *everywhere,* in the bigger rocks and sometimes even lying on the ground, too. Some are as large as a man's *head*."

If this was true, then perhaps there *was* a fortune lying around in the new world, just waiting to be claimed, rubies, diamonds, gold, and more.

Gilles' seat faced the back door and now he appeared to be the only one at the table who was aware that Francois had returned from using the privy only to find his way back to the table blocked by Tryntje. Even in the darkness across the room, Gilles could see that she smiled coyly up at the young man.

There was nothing shy about Tryntje: She was as forward as a young woman could be, in the brashness of her youth and beauty, and her behavior toward Gilles had been a contributing factor early on to the difficulties between Gilles and Hendrick. Hendrick had been convinced that it was *Gilles'* behavior and not Tryntje's that needed modification, and that Gilles lacked the proper respect for them, encouraging and eliciting inappropriate behavior from his daughters.

Gilles was just going to pretend that he didn't see it. Elsje was probably too tired to take notice and Hendrick was still busy examining the decorative work on the pouch that had been around Thomas' neck. Gilles could not believe that Tryntje would be so bold as to flirt with a *savage,* especially when her father was in the very same room.

Hendrick asked Thomas about the tooth, what animal it was from and why he carried these things around with him in the pouch.

"It's from a bear," was the reply, "for good luck, and for medicinal protection."

Gilles converted the French response to Nederlands, with a little help on the words from Elsje as Gilles had still not completely mastered all of the subtleties of Nederlands, and the New World words and concepts were strange enough for anyone to comprehend and manage, even in their native language. Hendrick set the red rock and the sharp tooth down on the table. He ran his finger over the raised design on the little bag as Thomas held it up for Hendrick to examine.

"What is this design made with? It's not some kind of thick thread?" Hendrick asked about the specifics of the pouch decoration through Gilles.

"It's from the back and tail of an animal, very sharp hairs, maybe like bald feathers with sharp points, a little like sewing needles, but they bend just a little to work them into the hide. We call the animal a *porcupine*. It's like a very large hedgehog. The women dye the quills with juice from berries and plants and make very fine designs from it. See, it's much stiffer and thicker than thread." Thomas ran his thumb nail over it to demonstrate the thickness and difference in texture to Hendrick.

Gilles was not sure if he was translating in a way that was satisfactory, in a way that made sense, or conveyed *all* of the meaning of the words even though he translated every word as he heard it and as he understood the meaning.

He had to see this for himself. The *quills*, as Thomas called them, were not like the quills one would get from a goose, and they were much heavier than those found on the little *herisson*, the hedgehogs Gilles observed sometimes out in the fields. They were almost like fine rounded slivers of wood, stiff, and yet slightly flexible at the same time; not dull but shiny blue, red, green, yellow and ivory. The little cylindrical rods were the length of a sewing needle or shorter, and the plain ones that had not been dyed were an ivory color. Thomas explained that every one of them had a sharp black tip but these were tucked inside the little bag. It was very pretty, fine enough to make the most expert Dutch seamstress or tailor from the guild envious of the workmanship, and Elsje stirred herself to move closer so that she could touch it too.

Gilles marveled at the precision of it and he *also* marveled that the others at the table had not yet noticed the interaction between Tryntje and Francois, which had progressed now to the physical. The savage was touching Tryntje's sleeve, curiously feeling the printed fabric even as Hendrick examined the little bag with the quill work. Gilles saw Tryntje running her hand over the design on Francois' dirty leather sleeve, a design that had been magnificently tooled by some aborigine, then embroidered with heavy thread in an intricate floral design. Remembering his own experience with Hendrick's daughters before he married Elsje, Gilles wondered idly if Hendrick would be rude enough shoot a guest and trading partner while the guest's father was seated in the inn or if Hendrick would just throw both of them out into the street.

Gilles was just *not* going to get involved this time: It generally didn't work out very well for him when he did, although there was the time when he had interceded on Elsje's behalf late one night when she was having difficulty with some drunken pirates. It was on that night that Gilles felt he had finally proven himself, to Hendrick *and* to Elsje, at least enough to be considered husband material. Non, this time Gilles was going to ignore the situation and leave it all up to her father to defend Tryntje's honor if that was his choice.

Francois was touching her hair now, examining the color and rolling the textured gold between his fingers as he had felt her sleeve a few minutes earlier, and Tryntje was smiling broadly up at him now. Gilles turned his body just *slightly* to the left so that he would not have to look directly at the two of them together, although he could still observe them quite clearly out of the corner of his eye.

"It's been a long evening and after your very long journey, you must be ready for sleep," Hendrick said to Thomas.

"Oui, I'm afraid I am," Thomas replied with a nod and a tired smile.

Francois must have heard this, and understanding what they said, he moved Tryntje aside by her elbows, but not without a final parting smile for her. Gilles pulled Elsje to her feet and she lit a second lamp for their guests to take up with them before she led the way over to the stairs. Francois gestured back at the stone and the large tooth that Hendrick had left on the table, but Thomas shook his head at his son who, although he looked puzzled, obeyed his father and left the souvenirs of his homeland behind as he followed the others up the stairs.

Gilles, Hendrick, Elsje and Tryntje returned to the family's apartments on the third floor after showing the Pelletiers to a private room on the second floor, one usually let out to travelers who paid a little bit more for a room that boasted a door and some privacy, although the room was barely long and wide enough to accommodate a single narrow bed and *one* man, let alone two. Gilles wasn't sure if the Pelletiers had paid Hendrick anything for the room but he definitely saw the logic in Hendrick's just giving them the chamber for the night even if no money had changed hands: It was too late at night for any paying guests of honest purport to come asking for a private room and besides, putting the two men in the great sleeping room would frighten the others and probably disrupt the peace when the strangers were discovered the next morning, rough though the communal sleepers generally were. Thomas and Francois would have to decide who was going to get the narrow bed with the lumpy straw mattress and who was going to sleep on the narrow floor space in the tiny room.

Gilles took his pants off, sat on the edge of his bed and flexed his tired and aching feet before he swung them up and pushed them under the covers. The entire evening had been one long, bizarre nightmare tonight. He thought about the Jewish girl coming to his place of work, Ste Germaine's hysterics, the savages from New France, and Tryntje's complete lack of discrimination or decorum when it came to *any* male, especially an unpredictable savage. These strange events were almost too much for Gilles to endure in a single day and he felt as though his energies had been completely spent.

Elsje slipped her overdress off, no longer having to untie any laces since she could not get anything laced over the expanse of her enormous stomach and abdomen. She went over to use the new chamber pot in the corner, something that Gilles had professed to be a gift to her, but Elsje suspected that it was *he* who wanted the comfort of the modern convenience. She had protested of course, that she had no need of such a thing, but it *did* make it a great deal easier for her. Having had a great deal of difficulty these past few weeks when she tried to use the oversized ceramic bowl, barely six inches from the floor, she shifted her increasing weight as best she could to successfully make the jar and not hit the floor, all the while holding fast to the nearby chest to keep her balance. Gilles had the chair delivered one day, an oak throne with a hinged seat that lifted up, revealing a wooden perch with a circular cut out. Below that was a shelf that held the chamber pot. There was barely enough space in the tiny bedroom for *another* piece of furniture, considering that there was already a wardrobe, two chests, a bed and the old cradle in there now, with just enough room left to close the door. The wooden indoor privy chair was a luxury, and not very bad looking; indeed, one could mistake it for a very nice hall chair if the purpose of the thing had not been known.

At last, her bladder emptied and her mission accomplished, she climbed into bed for the night. Gilles was just about asleep when Elsje got up again.

"Where are you going? You are so tired!" he called after her.

"I have to use the chamber pot."

"Didn't you just go before you got into bed?"

"My body won't hold any water! All I do is *go*!" Elsje snapped at him. "I am *so* sick and *so* tired of going all the time that I am tempted to save myself the time and just sit there *all day*! Then there are other times when I *run* to the chamber pot and the baby moves so I no longer *have* to go and it's a wasted trip!"

Gilles could see that Elsje was very tired and in a very bad mood. He knew enough not to talk to her when she was in one of these states and now he wondered just how much *longer* this misery was going to last. He didn't know if he could take many more weeks of her bad temperament and for now he was most grateful for the long hours of work that kept him at Msr. Ste Germaine's and away from her for most of the day and night.

"I don't *really* want to know all these things," Gilles mumbled, rolling over.

Elsje completed what she needed to do and with a tired sigh, she crawled back into bed.

Gilles was nearly asleep a second time when Elsje got up yet again.

"*Again*, Elsje?" he asked, before his mind cleared enough to keep his mouth closed.

"Now I have cramps! The chowder was only from *yesterday* but it must have gone bad. I hope I haven't poisoned any of our customers with it. I'll throw the rest out in the morning. *Ow*! It feels as though someone has me cinched around the middle with an iron band and I can't breathe!"

Gilles hoped that she wasn't going to vomit or have the intestinal flux in the chamber pot: He would probably have to be the one to get up and dump it outside in the middle of the night so he could sleep without the unpleasant smell lingering on in the small enclosed room.

Gilles heard no sound from the area of the chamber pot, though, and was thinking that he might *finally* be able to go to sleep but by now he was wide awake and not sure if he could fall asleep, in spite of the late hour and his physical and mental exhaustion.

Elsje climbed back into bed but she didn't stay there for very long before she was up again. This time Gilles heard a gush of water pouring into the chamber pot.

"Gilles! Wake up! I think the baby comes!"

Gilles threw back the covers and was pulling on his pants before Elsje's next words.

"Get Tryntje out of bed and then go get Cousin Vroutje!" she ordered.

Gilles asked no questions and wasted no time. Stuffing his shirt into his pants and his feet into his boots as he went, he shook Tryntje partially awake, and then for good measure he dragged her out of her bed by the arm to be *certain* that she was awake enough to stay with Elsje while he was gone. Gilles was down the stairs, two at a time, and out the door before another minute had passed, running across the back lots, the lot owners, their neighbors, be damned if it upset them and their barking dogs tonight, to get to Cousin Vroutje's house as soon as he could. Gilles banged on the door of Vroutje's house, not wanting to go inside at first, but then realizing that he was probably waking several of her neighbors with this noise, he pushed his way inside. Nearly tripping over something large in a heap on the floor near the door, he made his way around it and called up the stairs to Vroutje. He heard movement up there and very soon Vroutje climbed down the stairs to him, a little stiffly and arthritically, but as quickly as she could manage, pulling a coat on over her under dress as she went. Not waiting until she reached the bottom of the stairs, Gilles fired his story out at her, that Elsje told him the baby was coming *now*, but Vroutje just smiled and shook her head at him.

"We have time, Gilles, relax!" she said. "And don't wake Heintje." She put a finger up to her lips and pointed over at the bundle on the floor that now shifted slightly and then fell motionless again with a sigh.

Gilles hurried Cousin Vroutje as much as he could, impatiently waiting for her to go back up the stairs and put her overdress on before she came back down and pulled her cloak around her stooped old shoulders. Gilles repeated that the baby was coming *now*, although Cousin Vroutje kept assuring him that there really was no need to hurry, that the first baby never came quickly, disregarding both calendars and timepieces. Vroutje was experienced at delivering babies as she had helped all of the women in the family and more than a few of her neighbors during childbirth. She was prepared for the event, having kept a small bag full of necessary items at the ready by the front door for a few weeks now.

Gilles ventured to ask her if they shouldn't send for a midwife, too, but Cousin Vroutje just shook her head, smiling at him again in a patronizing way, and telling him once more that they would have plenty of time, perhaps *days*, to send for one later if a midwife was needed.

As he stood there in Vroutje's kitchen, Gilles suddenly realized that

Elsje's time *had* come after these many months of waiting, and now he would have a child or lose one, keep Elsje or lose her too.

It was fortunate that Gilles did not have to worry himself with this for very long as the baby didn't tarry. Even though it was Elsje's first, the boy arrived just before the sun did, much to Cousin Vroutje's surprise. Gilles' expectations for long days of waiting while Elsje labored, and warnings about how long it might take and how difficult it would be, were quickly forgotten. The child seemed healthy enough, with his sight and his hearing fully functional as Cousin Vroutje demonstrated for Gilles. In spite of her exhaustion from the labor, Elsje might have attempted to rise to make breakfast for everyone at the inn if she had not been so completely overruled by Cousin Vroutje, Gilles, *and* Hendrick. Gilles sent word to his employer of his news and Ste Germaine generously gave Gilles the entire day off "to catch up on his sleep" before he had to return to work the following day.

Gilles wondered now if his life would ever be the same again and although he had months to prepare for the change in family status, he was still in a state of disbelief. It was one thing to get accustomed to a wife with a larger stomach but quite another to get used to having a baby around.

Whose small child was this? Was this really *his*? He was too young to have a child.

News of the birth spread quickly around the inn as the kitchen staff arrived first and then the earliest patrons, everyone noting Elsje's absence and the unusual level of chatter and happy noise in the kitchen. Elsje and the baby slept while Vroutje stayed for a few hours, helping Tryntje with breakfast preparations for the inn's customers. Hendrick went from table to table, giving everyone the news of his first grandson with a free ale.

In the great room of the apartment, just outside Elsje's bedroom door, Gilles slept at the table with his head down on his folded arms. He had refused both Tryntje's and Hendrick's offer of *their* beds, preferring to stay as near to Elsje as he could, just in case she needed something. A knock at the apartment's door woke him from a groggy sleep and to Gilles' surprise, Thomas and Francois Pelletier stood on the stairs.

"May we see the child?" Thomas asked Gilles.

It was a little unusual that men would ask such a thing but it didn't seem a completely unreasonable request, although they might have waited a few more days for Elsje to recover. In his exhausted state, Gilles said *"Oui"* before he thought too much about it, but he did have the presence of mind to first see if Elsje was awake and if she would allow it.

Elsje was awake and she had heard the voices; she might not have let strange men into their bedroom at all under the circumstances but Gilles had already told them that they could see her. Gilles whispered to her that it could not do any harm to let them just *see* the baby for a few minutes. Elsje nodded but she held her baby tightly to her as Gilles beckoned and the men entered the bedroom. In spite of the pleasant camaraderie that they had all shared the night before, the strange men seen for the first time in the light of day made Elsje visibly uncomfortable this morning.

Possibly sensing this, Thomas explained, "It is our custom to celebrate the arrival of children just as soon as they are born, and *not* to wait until there is a baptism. Although we have seen many wonderful things on our journey, it has been a lonely time for us, being away from our family at home. We hadn't realized how much we missed our people and our village until your wonderful news reached us this morning."

Gilles smiled his understanding of the words as well as the sentiment and translated for his wife as Elsje relaxed just a little. Francois pulled something out of the pouch and removed something else that hung around his neck. For the first time to Gilles' knowledge, Francois spoke aloud. He spoke in full sentences, in simple French, not quite as good as his father's speech, but comprehensible, and here and there some unfamiliar words in the savage's language were sprinkled in.

"He is a fine strong dzidziz. He is a n'namoun, a son, oui? These stones will give the child protection."

He handed Gilles a stone that looked like a large diamond, about the size of Gilles' thumbnail, and another red stone that was held fast in a web of leather string. In spite of the present circumstances, all Gilles could think about for the moment was when he might be able to get the stones over to the diamond merchants to see how much they were worth. He had to wonder what *other* kinds of jewels might be secreted away in the men's neck pouches. Gilles thanked Francois and Elsje did too, but Gilles could tell that her thoughts were only on her child and how safe the baby might or might not be in the company of these strangers.

Francois looked down into the baby's eyes for a few minutes without speaking, but then he looked up at Elsje and said, "Call him 'Kelozid nspiwi niwaskok', '*Speaks with all of the Spirits*'".

Gilles translated for Elsje who still held her baby very tightly.

She replied tersely, "Thank you, but we have already decided on a *Christian* name."

Gilles was fairly certain that in addition to her resentment at someone *else's* deciding her child's name, she didn't like the sound of the offered name at all, it being a little too close to "talking with angels" which children were purported to do as they prepared to die during serious illnesses.

Sensing Elsje and Gilles' discomfiture, Thomas interceded on his son's behalf.

"It is generally the custom among us for a name to be given after the child is much older and has earned himself a name, but Francois has inherited some of his mother's ...ah...*talents*. He sees something in the child that merits a name right now, although it is generally an *elder* in the village that bestows the name."

Thomas smiled at Francois, perhaps to reassure his son that it was all right for him to make his offering of the name, and that the Europeans had not taken great offense at anything he had said to them, at least not so far. Thomas seemed to sense Elsje's continuing malaise and he tried once again to put her at ease.

"Madame Elsje, the name means that there are *many* that the boy will speak with, all here, and all of the *others* as well."

Thomas' explanation was failed by his inability to find even the French words that he needed to explain what he was trying to communicate. Gilles could make no sense of it at all and was unable to make a satisfactory translation for his wife.

Thomas tried one last time. "I can only say that it is a good omen for the boy's future and for a long life, and not a bad omen in *any* way."

He finally gave up and left that summary as his final effort to communicate the name's meaning.

Gilles translated this for Elsje who seemed to relax only slightly. Her eyes begged Gilles to get rid of them and though she was docile now, it would probably only be a short time before she recovered her usual presence of mind, lost her patience *and* her temper and was blatantly rude to her husband's trading partners. Gilles nodded understanding and acquiescence.

Francois spoke a few more words in his native language, something that sounded like a prayer or a blessing and Thomas said a French Catholic prayer that Gilles remembered from his own childhood before the two visitors crossed themselves. Now feeling somewhat uncomfortable with the guests himself, Gilles politely brought the visit to an end, pleading that his wife and child needed to rest as he ushered the men out of the living quarters, escorting them over to the stairs and thanking them for coming.

Thomas and Francois resumed their trade discussions with Hendrick downstairs in the dining room and Gilles, at Elsje's insistence, went down to translate. After seeing that the kitchen was organized as much as possible and some very basic food was prepared for the inn's guests, Cousin Vroutje checked on Elsje one more time before she left with a promise to return after she fed her own flock their midday dinners. Gilles went up the stairs several times to see if Elsje needed anything but Elsje just kept sending him back down again to check on the dining room for her and to tell Tryntje not to forget this or that.

After his fifth trip up the stairs, Elsje was irate with him.

"You *can't* stay here to watch us sleep all day and you wake me up every time you come into the room! Go talk with my father, go check the kitchen, go look after our business!"

Gilles decided that he would *not* go back upstairs again and that his wife could probably make it down the stairs herself if she needed him for anything.

Gilles returned to the business discussions, a more comfortable milieu for him anyway as he had absolutely no idea as to what was expected of new fathers and he really hadn't expected to *be* one, at least not this early in his life. As the Amsterdam agents for Van Curler's new trade venture, this was the perfect opportunity for Hendrick and Gilles to go over their business plans with the Pelletiers. Gilles had harbored some concern that Hendrick might go ahead and sign both names to an agreement without him, but with all of the parties there except for Van Curler, and especially with Gilles doing all of the translating,

Gilles had a little more confidence is securing a good outcome. He had already decided though, that he would leave nothing completely up to Hendrick, and would ask Jean Durie about every detail of the plan *first* before he put anything in writing.

It sounded simple and straightforward enough: The savages in the new world would supply the furs, trapping and tanning them, then bringing them down the Mauritius, Hudson's River, to the tip of Mana-hat-a Island to New Amsterdam, where they would be shipped across the ocean for eventual sale in old Amsterdam. Hendrick and Gilles would make the arrangements to sell the fur pelts, either to a few ready purchasers in the Netherlands, or if necessary, they would go out and find their own customers. The savages really had the hard part; Gilles and Hendrick only had to work out was which transatlantic ships would have room for the cargo and what monetary agreement could be made to ensure that transportation was affordable and that the captains understood the importance of delivering cargo that arrived in good condition. Even if the pelts were not all snapped up by one merchant or the tailors and guilds, they would still command a good price and make a nice profit on the open market, if necessary by selling them piece by piece in the Dam. The latter was by no means the preferred course of action though: It would complicate things and create new expenses. Gilles and Hendrick would have to find a vendor as well as an acceptable storage space, probably a warehouse, and that would take more chunks out of any potential profit.

An additional pitfall would be the necessity of concealing the source of the pelts. Young Arendt Van Curler had not apprised his powerful great uncle, Kiliaen Van Rensselaer, of this little side venture of his, and Gilles knew, although no one said this aloud, that it was an unmistakable conflict of interest. Van Rensselaer was not only a diamond and pearl merchant; he owned several of the warehouses in

Amsterdam and had already spent a small fortune over in the colony in trying to restrict any free Indian commerce, although he had trade contracts in place with the Maqua, adversaries of the Abnaki, as these benefited him and gave him a virtual monopoly on the trade north of the Esopus. It would be disastrous for this undertaking, and perhaps for Gilles' and Hendrick's livelihoods too, if Van Curler's participation in the venture came to light: At the very least Van Curler would lose his position as the administrator of the Rensselaerwyck colony.

Hendrick wanted to draw up the papers and sign them right away but Gilles said that he needed a little time to draft the papers, after he had a little more sleep. In actuality, Gilles had enough of his mental facilities intact to know that he wanted to talk with Jean Durie *first*. The four partners celebrated their accord though and traded stories for the rest of the day. The men from across the ocean provided such wonderful entertainment that Hendrick refused to accept any payment at all for their room, food, or drink even though they offered several times to pay. Gilles translated the tales and Hendrick barely moved from his seat all day, except to call out for Tryntje to bring him more ale or more tobacco and occasionally, to get up and use the facilities outside since Tryntje couldn't do that for him. Many of the patrons at the inn joined them at the closest nearby tables, eating and drinking more than enough to bring in a good profit for the day as the Amsterdammers sat there enthralled, listening to the raconteurs and staring at the exotic strangers who had come from the New World, more than offsetting any loss of income Hendrick may have incurred from not charging the Pelletiers for anything. Mevrouw Onderdonk had to send someone around to see where her husband, Conradt, had spent the entire morning and he reluctantly left for home with a vow to return just as soon as he could slip away from his wife again. Johanna Schuyler, having heard the commotion inside as she passed by with a newly purchased baby pig from the market, came into the inn, bringing the grunting animal along with her. They stayed there until the pig started squealing, but fortunately she left before it made a mess on the floor, as Gilles was expecting would happen at any moment. Hendrick didn't say anything at all about it and it was fortunate for Johanna that Elsje wasn't there to see it.

Thomas Pelletier was a skillful and practiced story teller and with the slightest of prompts and the least of questions, he readily told tales, starting with one about the great empire of the Huron tribe of savages, Huronia, a place that existed far to the north of New Amsterdam and the west of New France. With Francois' encouragement, additions, and embellishments, Thomas told of the great Mohawk tribe, or *Maqua*, as Gilles had heard them called, the most powerful of the Iroquois confederation of tribes, now driving Thomas and Francois' tribe, the Sokoki Abnaki, to the east as surely as they had driven out the *pziko*, the great wooly beasts bigger than dwellings that used to roam the open spaces, old paths and trails of the dawn land not so very long ago. Thomas told several gruesome tales of the Maqua's ferocity and cannibalism, with many exclamations of horror from even the least civilized of the men in the Dutch audience.

"What are the *Wilden*, the wild men, near the New Amsterdam settlement like?" Hendrick asked, avoiding Francois' eyes, "Are they *all* like the Maqua?"

Although Thomas was somewhat vague on this subject, it being an area much to the south of where they lived and having peoples with whom he was not very well acquainted, he did mention the names of some of the ones that Hendrick *had* heard of, the Wappingers, the Lenni Lenape, and the Esopus people among them. Thomas assured Hendrick that it was quite true what he had heard: That there were *thousands* of Wilden *nations*, each one with their own language and customs, many, many more nations than were known in *all* of the rest of the known world. There was great disbelief that this could be a fact, but the audience politely listened on, although more than a few of them shook their heads and smiled and winked at each other at this declaration.

Francois broke his silence long enough to tell a story, although he was not quite as good a story teller as his father. He told of the *Ancient People*, the ones called the Arankakx, who had once lived in the great mountains that split the sky.

"I never heard of them," Hendrick interjected. "And I know I've heard of *all* of them."

The "Tree People" as Francois also called them, were believed to have been formed by the creator from the trees, and they lived their lives enlisting the help of their "relatives", the trees, the plants, and all manner of growing things, to make all kinds of magical powders and potions to heal and prolong the lives of their fellow creatures. In truth, Francois explained, they were a very strange and ancient race, almost all of them gone now, the few remaining with this bloodline intermarrying and living with the Mahicans, the Wabanaki, and even with the Oneida who were allied with the ferocious Mohawk. The strange details of this very peculiar story fascinated many in the audience, Gilles included, whose basic knowledge and understanding of the wild people on the new continent was buried in a flood of new information that the young man provided.

"I get it!" Louckes Van Der Heyden exclaimed. "It's a fairy tale, right?"

Francois looked uncomfortable and confused. He looked over at his father for help while Gilles asked Thomas, "C'est une fable, n'est-ce pas?"

"Non, non! It is believed to be as true as you or I stand here, and my wife, Francois' mother, is descended from these *very* people."

"Why did you come so far across the sea?" Gilles asked them, "Just to meet us?"

Thomas replied that the idea had come to him during one of Arendt Van Curler's regular trading expeditions into the wilderness. Van Curler had already made a preliminary agreement to trade with Thomas' people when he mentioned Hendrick, the man in the Netherlands who sat at his table in far-off Amsterdam all day, talking and dreaming of the distant land. Thomas couldn't comprehend the mentality of the Dutch traders at Fort Orange who had only offered to trade ale for his furs, and even then only at their own low price, thinking that there were no other options and no other markets that would be available to the Pelletiers, but Thomas *could* empathize with one solitary man's hopes and dreams even though that man might be a world away and of a different nationality. Van Curler happened to mention Hendrick's French son-in-law too, and in Thomas' mind, that sealed the deal: He reasoned that a business proposition with Gilles, another Frenchman like himself but with ties to New France in the north, and with Hendrick, a Netherlander with ties to New Amsterdam to the south of Fort Orange, would give them two *additional* outlets for their goods, and through those two seaports they could send the pelts out to the European markets, even if Quebec and New Amsterdam were a little bit farther away than Fort Orange. The higher selling price in Europe would hopefully make transporting the goods over the additional distance worth their while and the only difficulty was in moving the cargo safely down the North River, Hudson's River, through Mohawk territory.

The New Amsterdam port at the tip of Ma-na-hat-a Island *was* preferable but alternatively, sending the skins up Pitonbowk,

Champlain's Lake, and out along the Sainte Laurent River, just *might* be profitable enough to make that somewhat longer route workable as well. Although this area was already packed full of trappers and French ships, *those* pelts were destined for the saturated French markets and not for the Netherlands.

Thomas added that he had already given some thought to making a journey back home to France someday before he died. There had been good profits from trade in recent years and with improving travel conditions on the great winged ships due to more familiarity with the direct sea routes, visiting the other continent was becoming more common. Thomas had also secretly harbored a desire to show his son the great civilization across the ocean into which he had been born, the other great cities and the world of the Europeans.

When Francois had a dream that they had traveled across a great sea, Thomas knew with certainty that it was time for them to move these thoughts and plans from a wish to reality and they set out on their journey. It was decided that they would personally meet with Hendrick and Gilles first. Thomas explained that handing over the pelts to Van Curler would have been easy enough but this was *not* the Abnaki way: They never liked to deal with strangers and if you met a man once, then he was no longer a stranger. If Dutchmen could travel to New Amsterdam, then the Pelletiers reasoned that the people of Ndakinna could go find the man who dreamed the day away at the tavern table, in the far-off land across the sea. They would then travel on to France before returning to their home in the great and ancient mountains of the new world.

Gilles listened attentively to all of this but he said nothing. He was not going to inform them that he had *no* ties to New France's markets and in fact, that he would scrupulously *avoid* any dealings with the French in Quebec, in case someone there discovered his identity and sent word back to the French authorities as to where the fugitive Gilles Montroville could be found. Gilles would just have to talk Thomas into conducting *all* of his trade with New Amsterdam and abandoning the northern trade route up Champlain's Lake. He could explain that it was just not practical, due to recently imposed French tariffs, for them to transport the furs up the longer distances to the French colonial ports for shipment to Europe and still make a profit, even if it *was* friendlier territory for the Abnaki and French coureurs de bois.

"What is it like where you live?" Hendrick asked the travelers.

Thomas told them a little bit about his home in the mountains to the north of Fort Orange and Rensselaerwyck, the Patroonship holdings of the Amsterdam pearl merchant and Van Corlaer's uncle, Kiliaen Van Rensselaer, then some about the Dutch settlement at Beverwyck. He finished by telling about the long journey they took to reach the Netherlands, of how they had sold a few of their pelts and traded a few strings of wampum along the way. The trip had been quite an adventure and well worth their time in terms of their future income, too.

Gilles could see that Thomas was one of the most affable men that he had ever met, and he could also tell that the man was no fool; either by accident or more probably by design, Thomas was here now and he would certainly find out, if he hadn't known it before, what price his New Netherland furs would fetch in the Dutch market.

Perhaps this had been the real reason for his coming all the way from the other continent. Now Hendrick's promised profit margins for the venture would vanish like chimney smoke on a windy day when the Pelletiers demanded, as they surely would, compensation that was more in keeping with the current prices on the world commodity markets. The numbers might have to be reworked to keep this trade agreement in place and only now did Gilles understand why Thomas Pelletier had insisted on renegotiating the agreement every year, although it was a known fact that the savages tended to keep prices and terms fixed *forever*, no matter how the demand for goods fluctuated. In the past this re-pricing had frequently led to misunderstandings, sometimes with violent consequences, like when the West India Company traders tried to break the bad news that they were no longer interested in buying up all of the clay pots that the Maqua could fire in a summer.

"We have already formed a trading company with Thomas and Francois," Hendrick announced to his audience of locals. "Their furs will be sent south to New Amsterdam down the North River; you might have heard it called the *Mauritius* or *Hudson's River*. Alliances will be made with friendly Wilden settlements along the way, and the unfriendly ones will be avoided by taking alternate routes, even if they have to go as far east as the Quinnihticut River, the long tidal river."

Hendrick made as eloquent a sales pitch to the assembled men as Gilles had ever heard the old man make, and the old tavern trader told the gathered assembly who were so reverent in their rapt attention, in no uncertain terms, that this might be their very *last* chance to get in on the big profits early by signing up to invest with him right now. He even called Tryntje to bring over paper, pen, and ink to sign up all of the new investors.

"The Quinnihticut is *too* far to the east," one man in the audience objected. "That just *doesn't* sound reasonable to me."

"Exactly how much profit are we talking about, and how much of an investment is needed?" a second demanded.

"What about the difficulties we hear about with the Wilden in New Amsterdam?" a third Dutchman asked Gilles to ask Thomas. "We may not have *any* wilderness trade at all if it gets any worse over there."

Hendrick looked uncomfortable but Gilles asked Thomas the last question anyway, wanting to know more about the situation himself.

Thomas replied, "I expect they will clear up the difficulties in New Amsterdam very soon as their raison d'etre *is* trade! Imagine! Governor General Kieft told the Lenni Lenape and *all* the representatives of other Native nations that they were now *Dutch* subjects, and as such, subject to all Dutch laws including paying taxes to the Netherlands, to their new rulers! I'm sure he will very soon realize that this is folly, a ridiculous notion! Why is it that the *first* thing that the Europeans *always* do in a new place is attempt to collect taxes? Even *before* they build their houses?! It is *not* the Netherlander's land to collect on, even the English say as much, demanding payment, too, because *they* lay claim to it as well! The land belongs to the Almighty and we pay Him our tributes. We won't pay Governor General Kieft, although he might believe that he *is* God."

After a fairly thorough translation of this small speech, a few in the audience tittered at Thomas' gibe aimed at the pompous governor, even though in truth, most of them saw nothing at all amiss in Kieft's demand for taxes as he *was* the local administrator for the Netherlands and the West India Company, and there *were* expenses associated with running the new colony. Certainly the tax burden shouldn't fall on the average citizens of the Netherlands, most of whom realized no benefits at all from the New Amsterdam colony since they were not investors or stock holders in the company.

It was at this moment that Gilles realized how difficult it was to look for concurrence between parties without having the same reference points, let alone the same allegiances. Many of those assembled frowned in outright disagreement with Thomas' statement and now Hendrick gave Gilles a hard look as well, perhaps thinking that his son-in-law was *not* helping him very much in recruiting new investors to their venture.

Here was the perfect opportunity for Hendrick to scoop up new capital and a healthy percentage in commission on each investment: He had a captive audience, a representative from across the sea, a real live Wilden man in front of them who was quite impressive in his glorious savagery, but at the same time looking tame enough to work with, trainable anyway, and the opportunity was being *completely* lost, mainly due to his less than helpful son-in-law.

"Well, that *minor* point will be settled in no time at all, as Msr. Pelletier says, and trade will continue to grow, isn't that right, Gilles?" Hendrick asked enthusiastically.

"We hope so!" Gilles said to Hendrick.

Thomas did not say anything at all.

"If there *are* agreements, treaties with the Wilden, won't there be a *lot* of people along the way to be splitting our profits with?" another man asked.

"We don't know how many there will be until we get the exact route established and that is Thomas' job," Hendrick replied. "I *do* know that there will be plenty of profit for all of our investors, though."

Gilles knew that Hendrick couldn't brag *too* much about the profits of the venture while *les sauvages* were there or Thomas would certainly want to raise the asking price of his furs to realize a greater share for himself.

Gilles was grateful that the door to the inn opened just then and Jean Durie pushed his way inside, his arms full of gifts, and suddenly Gilles remembered that his wife had given birth to a son a few hours earlier. Jean handed Gilles a small chest of money for the new child and set several bottles of good French wine down on the table.

"I hope I brought enough! Jean joked, looking around at the large group.

"Tryntje! Bring more mugs!" Hendrick bellowed at his harried-looking younger daughter. She glared at her father but then she went to get them.

Gilles introduced Jean to the Pelletiers. It still amused Gilles greatly that the young savage's name was *Francois* as the young man did not have a face that anyone would put with such a Gallic name. Gilles enjoyed even more watching Jean's face when the savages spoke to him in French. At last Gilles was able to give his scratchy throat and failing voice a rest from the strain of translating all morning long in the smoke-filled room, and soon Jean was engrossed in conversation with the Pelletiers, sometimes getting so excited about the subject of their conversations that he forgot to translate from the French for the gathered Amsterdam guests. Increasing requests for it escalated to the point where a translation was loudly demanded by the entire crowd.

At first they talked only about trade, but soon Jean's conversation with the visitors turned to filling in the details regarding some of the objects of curiosity in his personal art collection. Jean collected items from around the world, from the silk route, Africa, and China as well as the new world. He urged Gilles to go get his wampum belt to show to the visitors.

"The Netherlanders call it Zeewant," Jean informed those present who did not already know this. "I gave it to Gilles as a gift."

The crowd ooohed and ahhhed over the mere *description* of the item and begged to see it until Gilles finally acquiesced and tiptoed up to his bedroom, past Elsje and the baby who were sleeping peacefully in their bed. In truth he *was* glad to have an excuse to go up and check on them and was equally glad that Elsje was sound asleep. He noticed with relief that Elsje had almost completely devoured the food that had been brought up to her and placed on the chest beside the bed. It looked to Gilles like Elsje was going to be fine, just as soon as she got some rest. Gilles retrieved the purple and white clamshell beadwork belt from his trunk as quietly as he could, wincing at each clicking and squeaking noise that was made when he opened the trunk, when the belt's beads tapped against the sides of the chest and when it clicked as it swung back on itself, the shell beads noisily contacting other ones in the weaving. Elsje stirred a little at the noise when Gilles eased the lid of the trunk closed, but thankfully she did not wake up.

Gilles tiptoed back out of the bedroom and brought the wampum belt down the stairs, the gathered crowd all admiring the beauty of the polished shell beads and the precision of the work, but Gilles observed that Thomas and Francois were uncomfortable as soon as their eyes rested upon the object. The two guests of honor had a brief and subdued conversation in the savage language as the audience of Dutchmen commented on the picture patterns of dark purple and white, pointing out this or that and speculating as to the meaning of the design.

Most of the assembly of local guests tried to be polite and tried *not* to seem like they were listening intently, but those closest to the foreign visitors even crept a little closer, all the while trying to give the perception that they were not interested at all as they strained their ears to listen in on the conversation of strange grunts, growls, and hissing noises, reaching European ears that had never been tuned to accept these alien sounds as a human language.

Always quick to sense a shift in the wind, a change of mood, Jean Durie was more direct with the foreign guests. "Is there a problem?" Jean asked them. It was *his* understanding that the intricately designed shell tapestries were somewhat commonplace across the ocean, although his gift to Gilles was certainly the most beautiful and elaborate one he had ever seen.

"Where did you get this?" Thomas asked Jean.

"I traded for it. A man on a ship needed some money for a place to stay and some food, so I bought it from him."

There was some more discussion among the two men of New France.

"What is it?" Jean asked them again.

Thomas replied, "Such things are considered not *only* written records but also *legal* documents among our people. We do not understand how something like this came into *private* possession. Was the seller one of you or one of us?"

Gilles had to suppress a smile when Thomas referred to himself as one of the savages but he found the concept of economic and legal uses for common sea shells, although wonderfully set in an artistic presentation, intriguing to say the least.

"I was given to understand that they are used as decoration or as money, and although it appears to be a very handsome design, I did not know that such things had any other uses," Jean replied honestly. "As I recall, the man who sold it to me looked to be a Moor sailing on a French ship, but I don't know how he came into possession of it."

"It is all right," Thomas said. "It is just a curiosity that you have it at all."

Gilles thought that Thomas and his son did not seem "all right" with his having it, but Thomas spoke a few words in the savage language to Francois who bared his teeth at Jean in an attempt at a friendly smile. The young man suddenly stood up at the table and offered his hand for Jean to shake. The gesture was awkward, but Jean shook his hand anyway, as did Gilles. Francois' "smile" faded from his face even before he abruptly sat down again and returned to stony silence.

"Is your son always so stoic?" Jean asked Thomas, taking a sip of his wine, possibly trying to change the conversation away from the sensitive subject of the wampum belt to something a little more light-hearted.

"He is *these* days," Thomas sighed. "He wanted to marry a girl but she did not accept his proposal. He is *so* broken-hearted that I thought the voyage might be a good distraction for him, another good reason to come. He used to be at the heart of any celebration with all of his jokes and usual good humor."

"Ah," Jean replied. "So there is no negotiating with the girl's father?"

"It is not done that way among us," Thomas replied.

It seemed to Gilles that a look of mutual sympathy and understanding passed between the two lonely men, Jean and Francois, unobserved by anyone else. Gilles tried to picture Francois regaling guests with a series of hilarious jokes but the picture just would not come into his head, except as a jest itself.

The day of Gilles' eldest son's birth passed gradually from the present into the past and only from time to time did Gilles' attention stray from the extraordinary company and other-worldly conversation in the dining room. He remembered occasionally, but not without a great deal of disbelief each time, that Elsje was upstairs with their new infant son. Cousin Vroutje had returned late in the afternoon with a wreath to put on the door of the inn announcing the birth of a boy and she brought a paternity bonnet for Gilles to wear so that all of Amsterdam would know that he was now a father. Gilles thanked her graciously of course, but he had no intention of wearing the silly thing, not even to humor Cousin Vroutje or his wife, or to honor any ridiculous Lowland custom.

After suppertime, Gilles removed himself from the circle of men downstairs that had now grown to include many members of both the East and West India Companies. He hadn't had any sleep at all during the day to compensate for losing so much the night before. Gilles had to get up in the morning to go to work at Ste Germaine's and it would surely be a very long day. He had been nodding off at Hendrick's table for the previous half hour and the stories were now interspersed with short and strange dreams that Gilles had, mainly about the new continent. He no longer was entirely certain of what he had heard presented as fact and what had been dreamed by him. He decided that it was time to go up to his bed although Gilles didn't really want to leave the ebullient company and fantastic, if not quite believable, tales.

Gilles retrieved his wampum belt and picked up a lighted lamp from one of the empty tables on the far side of the room before walking wearily up the stairs, calls of congratulations following him out of the room. As quietly as he could, he tiptoed into the bedroom but Elsje didn't move at all; she slept soundly with the child at her side in his cradle. Gilles carefully set the wampum belt and the lamp down on the top of the chest, before leaning against the door and removing his boots and pants. After getting his bearings, there being so little floor space visible now with the addition of the infant's cradle to the room, Gilles extinguished the light. He had a pretty good idea of how light a sleeper Elsje was, but he had *no* idea about the baby. Gilles made his way slowly over to the foot of the bed, crawled up into his spot, and lowered himself, as quietly and as gently as possible, down onto the mattress before working his way under the warm coverings. Elsje stirred slightly in her sleep after he settled in and a short distance away from Gilles, the child made soft noises in the darkness. It was *very* strange to hear the sound of the new little creature nearby. Before he fell asleep, Gilles thought about his new responsibilities as a father. He smelled the smoke drifting over from the extinguished oil lamp and he thought briefly of France and the fires that he had escaped there, the fires that were constructed to consume Huguenots, witches, or people like himself who had been caught up in the wide French dragnets. He thought once again about how he wanted to have his son baptized in the Catholic Church. Gilles was *so* tired that he did not even wake up fully during the three times that night that Elsje got up to feed the crying baby and change the blood-soaked cloths beneath her.

Very soon, the next morning in fact, Elsje insisted upon returning to the kitchen to do the cooking. On Thursday, his usual day off from Ste Germaine's, Gilles went to Jean Durie's apartment to confirm and solidify his trade plans. Jean had some very good suggestions as to what should be in the contract, as well as which local buyers or warehouses Gilles should approach. It was a very good thing that Gilles had a little time before the first pelts arrived from New Netherland: Hendrick had not taken a very active role in working out the details but this was all right as it left Gilles in control to make most of the decisions and he was not going to let the opportunity slip through his hands. Jean took a personal interest in the new business, even signing on for a small share and offering to do a little research himself. That afternoon Gilles drew up the final agreement and after the Pelletiers signed all of the copies, they left the city to continue on to their next destination, France. They planned to visit with their family in Normandy and with their woodworking cousins, a dynasty of them as Thomas explained it, living in Paris. Gilles would have *gladly* given a few coins to see the looks on their faces when the Paris Pelletiers made the acquaintance of their cousins from across the sea.

A week later, on the following Thursday, just when Gilles started to entertain thoughts of sleeping late and catching up on his sleep, he was informed by Elsje that from now on he would be the sole caretaker of his new son on his days off. Gilles was greatly incensed at having this burden put on him. Not only was Thursday his one and *only* day off during the week, but it was his wife who insisted on working in her father's business when it was not necessary. It was apparent that she expected Gilles to gladly suffer the humiliation of carrying a wet infant around with him all day.

Gilles' family had been an important one in France and his mother had had very little to do with her children at all after their birth, from feeding and care by wet nurses to education by priests and tutors for the boys and by a governess for the girls. Gilles kept his composure after Elsje's announcement, for just long enough to ask Elsje, as calmly as he could manage, if she might not consider hiring a servant to care for the baby. Young girls were always available for just stuivers a day but Elsje had already made up her mind. She retorted that the men in Amsterdam took care of their *own* children and did not entrust the care of family members to strangers.

Gilles thought about suggesting Tryntje as a caretaker but immediately thought better of that idea before this idea could make its way from his head to his mouth, Tryntje being the *least* responsible person Gilles knew. He wondered if Elsje's younger sister Jennetje was too young to be pressed into this service yet. The fourteen year old already had a better head on her shoulders and was much more dependable than Tryntje. Elsje just handed the child over to Gilles and told him to take good care of *her* son, otherwise he would have to answer to her later, and then she stalked off, back into her kitchen, her kingdom, her domain.

Gilles spent the first hour hiding in the backyard with the baby, wondering if he could stay there on *all* of his days off for the next ten years. Boredom overtook him, though, and Gilles ventured out into the streets with the baby in his arms. He would just take the infant with him to a tavern and drink all day. The women in Amsterdam often did so, just as long as he didn't forget to pick the child up from the chair next to him when he was through with his pitcher of ale or bottle of wine. He hoped the child wouldn't cry all the time and he hoped that his Thursdays wouldn't be completely miserable. He didn't get very far, though, before people on the street began stopping him to get a better look at the new arrival. To Gilles' chagrin, many of the admirers called the baby "Elsje's child", but he soon discovered that having to watch the infant brought with the responsibility and a few drawbacks, certain opportunities and bonuses as well. Street vendors in the Dam gave Gilles free food and little gifts as congratulatory offerings. Gilles stuffed his pockets full with them and munched on a free apple as he turned up the street toward Jean Durie's home. He could go and pay his devoirs and besides, Jean hadn't had a *really* good look at Little Gilles yet, just a perfunctory one the day after he was born. Gilles thought that he might just stop for a moment there before continuing on to spend the rest of the day at a nearby tavern. Maybe he could even get a free meal and bottle of wine out of it with new baby in his arms.

"He's a fine healthy boy," Jean said when he saw the child. "You *will* have your hands full with him later if he is anything at all like *you*."

Jean even held the child for a few minutes and Gilles was greatly surprised that his friend took any interest in the infant at all. He wondered now if Jean might be able to make room in his life once again for another woman and perhaps someday, a family of his own.

Before their trial in France, Jean had been planning his own wedding, having lost his heart to a young woman there, but the legal difficulties and public airing of his inauspicious beginnings, as well as his subsequent conviction on charges of heresy and treason, destroyed any chance he had of a future life with her.

"You have given up on the idea of another baptism?" Jean looked up from the child's face to Gilles'.

Gilles sighed. "I can't explain *why*, but I just want him baptized in The Church. There will be the baptism with the family in the Reformed

Church this Sunday, of course, but..." Gilles' voice trailed off. "Maybe it's only superstition..."

"You need to do what makes *you* comfortable, Gilles. If this is truly what you want, I will do what I can to help you. Does it have to be inside a Catholic Church and on a Sunday, Gilles? That would be *very* difficult to do. I can't see Hendrick standing up with us, either."

Gilles thought about it for a moment. "Non. A priest, holy water, prayers, that would be enough."

"What about Elsje?"

"Elsje?"

"You need to tell her so that she can come with you."

"I suppose..." Gilles didn't see how he could tell Elsje.

"She *has* to know, Gilles." Jean gave his friend a sharp look. "You *must* tell her."

Gradually the uproar over Gilles' change of familial status died down and in truth, he was greatly relieved when everyone stopped making such a fuss over it. Jean Durie and Tryntje were the godparents at the official baptism, the one that was performed in the Protestant Church, and it was the appointment of Jean Durie to this position, the man he had trusted with his own life on more than one occasion, that eased Gilles' mind. Elsje had originally wanted Hendrick to be the godfather but they had come to an agreement and compromise after Gilles raised objections to naming Tryntje the child's godmother. Gilles could not see his young sister-in-law taking responsibility for anything, including her own behavior, let alone something as important as raising a child, his child and his oldest *son*, but just as Gilles trusted Jean Durie with his own soul, he trusted him with his newborn son's, regardless of who the child's godmother was.

Elsje insisted that they should name their son after Gilles' father,

94

naming him Jean Gillessen, but Gilles informed her that in *his* family, the first son was *always* named after the father, and not after a grandfather. Gilles refused to bestow the honor upon his father, mostly because Gilles was still angry with the old patriarch, and he would not be moved at all on this point. If his own father would let him rot in exile and then just hand over Gilles' fortune and his intended bride to his brother in order to secure the family fortunes, then Gilles was not going to honor the man by naming his first-born, his primogenital child and heir, for the old Frenchman.

Gilles didn't tell Elsje any of this though; he simply put his foot down and said that he would not go to the church unless his son carried the name he wanted. To Gilles' amazement, Elsje finally capitulated an hour before the baptism and their son was baptized *Gilles Jean Hendrick Gillessen* after they informed the befuddled predikant of the divergence from tradition and all of the names. Gilles didn't mind the inclusion of "Jean" as the infant's middle name; he would tell Jean Durie later that little Gilles carried the name of his father's best friend, and not Gilles' father.

After the ceremony, Jean found a private moment to whisper to Gilles that he had been able to make arrangements for the "other" baptism on the following Thursday. He asked Gilles directly if he had discussed the matter with Elsje but Gilles only mumbled in reply that he had not yet had the opportunity.

Gilles had looked for a chance to talk to Elsje but she was always busy, socializing with family and friends on the day of the baptism in her church and then busy with work and childcare afterwards. Gilles didn't know how he might even *begin* such a conversation, if and when they might *finally* find a few minutes alone. Elsje was usually asleep when he returned from his work and already with her customers when Gilles rushed off to Ste Germaine's every morning. He knew better than to interrupt her cooking to tell her: He had made that mistake only once and when the bread burned, he never forgot it, or rather Elsje wouldn't *let* him forget it. To complicate matters, the two kitchen servants and Tryntje were always in the kitchen with Elsje. It would have taken far too long to go through all of the reasons why it was important to him and why his child *should* be baptized in the Catholic Church. Gilles wasn't even sure if he could find the right words, in French *or* in Nederlands, to explain it to her. They had never had a discussion about religion in general or about the tradition that Gilles had been raised in.

When he woke up that morning and realized that it was already Thursday and he had not *yet* spoken to his wife on the subject, Gilles made a final decision not to tell Elsje at all. She had let him sleep, as she always did on his days off, and because everyone was already downstairs working, or in Hendrick's case, watching everyone else work, Gilles got out of bed and quickly and quietly searched the apartment, wondering what on earth Elsje could have done with the baby's christening dress. He couldn't find it and he couldn't very well ask Elsje or she would certainly want to know why he needed it. God would just have to understand if the baby was not wearing the baptism outfit. The ceremony was far more important than the clothing, Gilles rationalized. It was *not* how it should have been done, but this was *not* France, he reminded himself yet again, as it seemed he had occasion to do nearly every day since he had left there

Gilles felt a little better when he suddenly remembered that he still had his father's rosary. He pulled it out of the bottom of the trunk and put it on over his head, making sure that it was completely hidden under his shirt before he went down the stairs to get his breakfast and his son. He told Elsje that he was going to take the baby all around the city and that he might not make it back to her before noon. He stood there patiently and allowed Elsje to berate, scold, and lecture him about the consequences of letting the child get too hungry, too wet, and too upset in between feedings and changing. When she had finished, Gilles humbly agreed with her on every point and then set off with Little Gilles in his arms, more nervous about his mission than concerned with anything that Elsje had to say.

The Dutch authorities were not so much a worry to Gilles even though they were known to occasionally harass Catholics. It was the reaction of his fellow townspeople that Gilles feared more if they were to find out where he was going and what he was doing. It had to be done today, though, or he might not find another opportunity or the will to go through with it another time.

When Gilles arrived at Jean Durie's home, Jean was ready and waiting for his friend, even wearing his best clothes for the occasion.

"Are you ready, Gilles?"

To Gilles' great relief, Jean didn't ask about Elsje. Knowing Gilles so well, he probably had surmised from the beginning that Gilles wasn't going to tell her. Gilles nodded. His throat felt dry but he was ready. They walked silently through the dew-soaked morning streets that were already busy with traders and young boys scampering around, delivering messages and running errands. The two men made their way to their own business that morning, the business of saving a tiny soul. If Jean had any personal opinion on the matter, he kept it completely to himself. Although he didn't know this with absolute certainty, Gilles surmised that the incongruous facts of Jean's life had made the simple effort of living his life full of challenges at times. Knowing of his friend's past difficulties with the law as it concerned religion, Gilles had to wonder *why* Jean would help him at all with this matter unless it was due to his friendship and exceptional generosity of spirit.

As they walked on, Jean told Gilles that he had asked around, but in spite of diligent inquiries, none could say why the priest was not still practicing his faith in France, when he had arrived on this distant shore, or what made him hide now among the Protestants who had escaped France's own version of the inquisition to seek refuge in the Netherlands. There were, of course, *many* reasons why a priest might choose to leave his country, but this man seemed to keep no company but his own and Jean confided to Gilles that there *was* a peculiar sense of familiarity about the man, as if he had known him in a dream, but Jean was absolutely convinced that he had never seen the man's face before.

They passed by a printer's shop and young Resolved Walrond leaned against the doorframe, his ink-blackened apron staining the undersides of his forearms as he stood with his sleeves rolled up, his arms folded across his chest.

"Just enjoying this fine autumn weather, Walrond?" Jean asked him.

"Ja, too pretty to waste inside," the young man grinned at them. "Winter comes too soon and I'll have plenty of time *then* to be inside."

"And the boss is away in the Dam getting more ink and paper?"

"Ja, just taking a break until he returns," Walrond responded with good humor.

"Printing up any more pamphlets for the seditionists?" Jean asked him with a grin.

"Nee, only Bibles today..."

They walked on toward the French section of the city until Jean came to a halt in front of a farrier's shop. He held the door open for Gilles to go inside, gripping it hard with both hands to hold it fast against the wind that had now started to pick up. Gilles smelled leather and grease along with the smoky smell of the great forge that took up one entire stone-paved corner of the edifice. In spite of the smoke, it reminded Gilles of Jacob's stable, and he wondered why they were stopping here first. An older man with thinning gray hair, a smooth face and bright green eyes stopped his work and looked up from hammering out a metal stirrup. After straightening his back out completely with the aid of his curled fists, his torn and stained old leather apron crackling softly as he did so, the man wiped his blackened hands on a nearby cloth that was every bit as dirty as his hands before he embraced Jean in the French way, a kiss on each cheek that was a perfunctory, polished, and professional expression with no affection in it, only polite acknowledgement. His arms were bands of flesh-colored steel, their only human characteristics being a layer of fine reddish hair on his forearms and protruding blue veins.

"You've come then?" he asked, looking at Gilles and then back at Jean.

"Oui. This is Gilles Montroville, the child's father."

Gilles was uncomfortable hearing his real name being spoken aloud but he supposed that God required it for the ceremony and with this Catholic priest being surrounded by a city *full* of Protestants, the lone man was certainly in no position to be much of a threat to them. Even if he meant Gilles harm, after they left this place, the priest would probably have no idea as to where he might find Gilles again. Gilles quickly rationalized all these things while the man's eyes, hawk like, shot over to Gilles' face and lingered there for a time before they returned to Jean's face, appearing to comb over all of Jean's facial features next, as if the man was memorizing something.

"Ou est la mere?" the priest asked, breaking the awkward silence.

"There is only me," Gilles replied, hoping that the man would think that he was just one of the many widowers in the city whose wives had died in childbirth and hoping, too, that Jean wouldn't think too much less of him for having skirted the truth, and doing so with a priest.

"Call me Father Victor. Eh bien, I guess we should get on with it."

The priest's hoarse voice sounded familiar somehow to Gilles but as was the case with Jean, he had no recollection at all of the man's face or of his mannerisms or gestures. Gilles tried very hard, but at this moment, he could not recall who it was that the man sounded like. Gilles recalled that priests always used aliases, and now he wondered if it was the same thing as the savages in the new world, choosing their names at a certain time, or a conjunction of events during their lives. It was a given that the priests would take a Saint's name to try and live up to, and Gilles' friend Claude had taken the name Brother Francis at the time of his final vows, but now Gilles wondered if it might not *also* be an attempt to obscure the true identity of the man in the priest's robes. At the moment it served both purposes.

Father Victor hung a sign outside declaring that the business was closed and then he barred the front door. "I just hope the owner doesn't come back early," he smiled a bit nervously at Jean. "He went to Rotterdam and shouldn't be back until later on today."

"I have taken care of it," Jean told him with a replying grin. "He won't be back until tomorrow."

Father Victor gave Jean a puzzled look but said nothing more, leading them to the back of the building, opposite the forge. Even across the great open shop, Gilles could still feel the heat radiating from the coals that glowed red in the fire pit. Father Victor untied his leather apron and pulled it off over his head, tossing it onto a work table. He bent down and moved a small but heavy stack of onion shoes and some shoeing tools from in front of a battered and worn old cupboard. When he had succeeded in excavating the lower right hand side door, he opened it, pushing a tangle of old harnesses aside. He reached way in the back to pull out a water basin, and behind that, a Franciscan cloak and a rosary of the type worn by priests, with great large beads the size and color of cured olives, the string of prayer beads leading down to and culminating in an elaborately carved wooden and silver crucifix. Father Victor brushed cobwebs and dust from the cloak and put it on, then completed his habit by kissing the rosary, then putting it around his neck as he quietly hummed a barely audible, soft and tuneless prayer to himself. Gilles remembered his own rosary now and stroked it under his shirt with his left hand as he held onto his tiny son with his right. Gilles noted that the man had no church robes, only the cloak.

"Are you *really* a priest?" Gilles asked him, before he thought better of asking it. The question seemed completely stupid before it had even left Gilles' lips: After all, Gilles had a priest's robe at home and he was not a priest. He had used the robe in his escape from France and it had served well the purpose for which it had been needed. Gilles had buried the robe under his other belongings and he hoped that if Elsje wasn't the nosy kind, then she was at the least the busy kind, too busy to go through his old things. Still, Gilles supposed that he should dispose of it somewhere and do it soon; he had just about forgotten about it, along with a few other searing reminders of that terrible time. Gilles life was just one of the thousands that had been turned upside down and perhaps nothing on earth would ever again be as it had been before. Perhaps nothing was as it *seemed* to be as well, not a Dutchman named Jansen and not a priest named Father Victor.

Father Victor, unperturbed by the query, replied, "I am *indeed* a priest, or at least, I was once a member of the order. The mortals who now claim the Church as their exclusive kingdom will no longer give their blessing to me unless I redeem my so-called sins by offering my soul to the fires in repentance. I can't very well do God's work on earth if I'm dead, now can I?"

"For what?" Gilles asked, his own voice a little hoarse from the smoke in the air that had drifted over toward them from the fire pit. He wondered what this priest's crime had been. Had it been rape? Theft? Murder? "What was your crime, if I may ask?" Gilles asked again meekly.

It may have been bad timing to quibble over whether the priest was a good one or bad one, especially after Jean had gone to so much trouble to find a man of the cloth, but Gilles wanted a *good* priest for his son. He didn't want one of the bad priests. It was important to him.

"You are worried that I might not be devout enough?" There was no confrontation in the priest's tone, but perhaps there was some amusement.

"If you have committed great sins..." Gilles stammered.

He didn't know how to finish the sentence in a satisfactory way and he held his son a little tighter to his chest. He had sought a priest out and now he didn't know exactly why, but he was very uncertain about this one. Perhaps it was simply that they were in a smith's shop and not in a real church, and it *was* Jean Durie who had brought them here, to this place and to this man.

Gilles was very ill at ease now but the priest seemed not at all put off by Gilles' concerns.

"It is my personal belief that only God in heaven may judge our sins. I answer no longer to *any* man and perhaps *this* is my chief sin, but I will tell you this, and *only* because I choose to: The crime for which they seek to burn me was performing a marriage. I performed the sacrament for a Reformee girl and a Catholic boy, the scion of an old family in France. The couple asked me if I would perform the ceremony, and I did. They were of age, they both wanted it and I did not know that the parents were not only still alive, they were persons of quality in that province! The young people presented themselves to me as bonded-out orphans, in a hurry to be wed as their masters opposed their entering into a legal marriage. I had to decide which was the *greater* sin, fornication, or going against the master's wishes. If there had been a bastard child born later of such a union...Well, the truth only came to light later when a marriage was arranged by the boy's parents and he had enough courage to tell his father that he had a child on the way with his present wife and he would not renounce her or commit the sin of adultery."

The priest ended his story there and Gilles wanted desperately to ask what had happened to the couple but instead he asked, "Just the *one* marriage ceremony? And they would burn you for that?"

Gilles didn't know why it should surprise him. After all, he himself had not committed *any* crime. Did the thousands who had left France already, the hundreds that continued to flee the country every day, did they *all* believe themselves to be blameless? Gilles thought that his situation and Jean's had been unique and the idea that they were not alone in being falsely accused by The Church was not only discomfiting, it left him with a peculiarly disoriented and helpless feeling, much like being adrift in a storm at sea without any working sails or rudder. Gilles had always believed without question that *no* country was the equal of France in any way, that her laws were just and merciful, and that it was only in his case, his and Jean Durie's, that one of France's judges had made a terrible mistake.

The priest cleared his throat. "Well, there were *several* marriages before that one, of *lesser* importance to the authorities. And some last rites I administered to those that the church felt should be denied. They did find an unmarked grave in the churchyard and they wanted to refuse sanctuary to the dead. They wanted me to ...ah, *evict* her. Her wish had been to be buried next to her husband and when I went to give her last rites, she begged me with her dying breath to be placed next to him. I gave her my word and I *keep* my word. The Church should not come between families: This is my belief."

The priest stopped recounting the charges and looked at Gilles again. "*Their* list of charges against me, true and not true, is too long to recite and I make my confession to no one any longer except God. I will tell you only this: *I* sleep well at night. It took me a great deal of introspection and prayer, as well as a few *years* to remember that my calling was from God, that I serve Him and *only* Him, in whatever way I feel that He wants me to serve. I came to the conclusion that excommunication from The Church is not the worst thing that can happen to a man."

Gilles thought that it was a pity to waste the man's excellent sermon on only two listeners, three, if one counted Little Gilles who had no comprehension of the words yet. Gilles had heard rumors about some of the priests in Rouen doing such things, following their own conscience and not obeying the church authorities. Were these things happening across France, perhaps across the entire world? Were there others like Father Victor? Much as Gilles wanted to know more, he held his tongue so he would not be tempted to ask any more foolish questions like the one that he had already asked, the one that still hung in the air like an unpleasant odor.

"There are priests who have actual congregations here, ones that *have* the church's blessing. You might prefer that *they* perform the sacrament for you and that is fine with me. I am merely a vessel and God sends people to me," Father Victor concluded.

There was not really enough time for Gilles to fully think over whether he wanted this particular priest to perform the ceremony although he felt that blindly following what one perceived to be God's wishes was a misguided and cowardly approach to life, even for a priest.

Gilles nodded his assent and said to Father Victor, "I want it done now."

The priest bent over and pulled a pitcher of water out from under some burlap bags next to the cupboard. He poured some of the water into the basin and said to Gilles, "This is *indeed* Holy Water, although I have had the devil of a time keeping my employer from drinking it or watering his horse with it."

The priest started with his prayers in a quiet voice, almost a whisper, not a loud proclamation meant to be heard by as many rows in the cathedral as possible, but the ceremony was almost exactly as Gilles remembered it from the many years he had witnessed it in France with only very minor variations. If he closed his eyes, which he did twice, Gilles saw in his mind's eye the great cathedral and he heard the muted crowds behind him, the multitudes who had come to celebrate a new life with him, even his *grandmere*, long since gone from this world, but looking down with a smile from one of the upper galleries. Gilles saw the angels looking down on the ceremony from the faux balcony, a decorative affectation in the architecture, inaccessible to mere men, but there for the heavenly hosts to occupy as they pleased. Gilles saw one of the wingtips from a brilliantly glowing white angel brush the baby's face. They used to say that when this happened and the child smiled from the touch of the angel's feathers, that it was an omen that the child's life would be especially blessed. Children had never smiled during the ceremony, not to Gilles' recollection, but he had heard a great many of them cry.

When Gilles opened his eyes again, he thought he saw his son smiling up at him but he could not be sure. He *believed* that it was a good sign. Gilles saw the faces of his mother and sisters when he closed his eyes once more, but he shut out those of his father, his brother, and Marie. He would not share this moment with them, not in person, not even in his daydreams.

The exiled priest was efficient and well acquainted with the ritual. He completed the ceremony swiftly. There was no incense, no organ music, no lavish vestments, no bells, no reading of passages in Latin, no mass, not even any crosses except for the ones that the priest and Gilles wore and the signs that the priest made in the air, but the *essence*, the blessing part of the ceremony, it *was* there.

Gilles watched the priest's hands as they finished the rite and he thought back to the soft, jeweled hands of the priests at home. This priest had hands that were stained with dye, covered with burns, cuts, and scars, both old and new, and cropping up on his palms at the base of his fingers were small hills of yellow calluses. His old blue veins stood out on the back of his unadorned and naked hands and they contrasted sharply with the delicate pink and unblemished skin of Gilles' brand new son. Gilles believed that he could now see the same magic and power that he had always seen, and felt to the very core of his being, whenever he looked at a priest's hands.

Jean was named the child's godfather, should anything happen to Gilles, and the child was baptized Gilles Jean de Montroville, as Gilles whispered to the priest who nodded and got it exactly right on the first try. *Petit Gilles* started to whimper from the cool water on his head until he found a fist full of fingers to suck on, just before the priest handed the baby back to Gilles.

"God entrusts the care of His child to you, his earthly father. Know that the child has been blessed and *will* be protected by God the Father, the Son, and the Holy Spirit. We do not often have the privity to God's mind, but sometimes He chooses to reveal it to us, showing us that we have indeed made the right decisions in our lives. I am honored to have performed this baptism, this act of love, for you, Gilles Montroville. Go with God's blessing."

Gilles nodded his thanks and Jean gave the priest a pouch of coins. Gilles was a little abashed that he had forgotten to bring the money, but then Jean *always* thought of everything. Gilles made a mental note to reimburse Jean later as the priest removed his cloak and his cross, stowing them away again in the spider webs beneath the cabinet. Perhaps not wanting to throw it out into the gutter, Father Victor sprinkled the holy water from the basin around the outside of the forge so as not to extinguish the fire but to evaporate the sacred liquid up into the heavens. He put the pitcher and basin back in the cabinet when he was finished.

"Come Gilles, we need to go now, your son will be getting hungry," Jean said as he led the way to the door.

Father Victor transformed once again into a smith at his forge, removed the crossbar from the door and Gilles took his son back outside into the world of men, away from the world of the sacred and into the world of the profane, without even a backward glance at the farrier.

"How did you find this priest? From the friend of a friend?" Gilles asked Jean as they walked up the street. He was a little curious about this but something else about the man, lingered on in his mind, nagging at him but refusing to come fully out into the light.

"Eh? Oh, it was from a fortuitous meeting, Gilles, although I frequently find that just thinking about getting something will bring me the solution I seek. I was walking in the Dam, wondering how I was going to help you, when who do I see but the captain who brought us safely into Amsterdam! He takes passengers back and forth to England now since they lie in wait for him with a noose at the ready in France.

He asked me how things were for us and why I looked so preoccupied. I had trusted him with my life once before and felt that I could again, so I told him what I was looking for. He told me of this man, this priest who was in exile here. It took some doing to track him down but the captain mentioned that the priest had worked as a smith before joining the monastery. I asked around and tried all of the different smith and farrier shops until I found a man who spoke French. The most difficult part was communicating to him that I knew *what* he had been, delicately of course, that I needed his help, and that he could trust me. It was good to find out that his employer travels a little and is easily distracted by a pretty face, too. The priest seems to be a good man but he does have a strange way of staring at us, n'est-ce pas?"

Elsje wondered aloud why the boy's head was damp when Gilles brought him home.

"I guess I had him bundled up too warmly," Gilles said, hoping she would believe this.

"*Don't* do that, he will take a chill and get sick!" Elsje exclaimed. "Never mind, *I* will take the child for the rest of the day to keep an eye on him in case he has fever, go on! You're no help to me at all!" She shooed Gilles away.

Gilles and Jean had a quiet bottle of wine together at the inn, a silent and subdued celebration, not at all like the one that there would have been in France, involving *all* of Normandy, if not all of France, if Marie Junot of the Normandie Junots had been the mother of Gilles' eldest son. Elsje looked over at them in obvious and open disapproval of Gilles' and Jean's drinking so much wine so early in the day and without any good reason for it.

That night, Gilles dreamed of the baptism again. He handed Little Gilles over to the priest and the priest baptized him in the marble font at the center of the great cathedral in Rouen, with throngs of people looking on and celebrating the Montroville family heir's baptism into the Catholic Church. The priest set the baby down on the font, saying that *more* cleansing was needed due to his father's many sins. He reached into a place underneath the font that Gilles had never noticed before and pulled out another ewer of holy water. As he poured it over the child, Gilles saw that it was not water but blood that flowed from the vessel, over the priest's hands, over Little Gilles, over everything.

Gilles woke in a terrified sweat, brought on by the horror of the dream, and he wondered what spoiled food had caused his feverish mind to come up with the idea for the terrible dream. He listened fearfully to the noises around him but beyond his own pounding heart, all he heard was the regular breathing of his wife and child. When the sweat had evaporated enough to cool Gilles down, he finally relaxed enough to turn his shaken mind back toward sleep. As he was drifting off though, he thought once again of the priest's hands, and he was now certain that he *had* seen those hands once before: They had been wrapped around a bloody knife in the predawn hours at a prison in Rouen.

Jean thought that he was crazy of course. He assured Gilles that the man who had helped them escape from prison had been taller and had a different, harsher voice.

"You told me yourself that he seemed familiar," Gilles exclaimed, "and given what we had been through at the time, *of course* our memories would not be clear!"

"There were rumors about a priest who had liberated a French prison while rescuing his brother, but *even* if the story was true, although I've never thought it very probable, I doubt the tale was about *our* deliverer. This man, this Father Victor who baptized young Gilles, doesn't seem the efficient kind of killer who could dispatch a prison guard with a single pass of a knife. Don't you remember, Gilles? Our dark angel also threatened to cut *my* throat! I just don't think it possible that this gentle Amsterdam *forgeron* could do violence to any of God's creatures."

Sensing defeat, or at least reluctance in the extreme on Jean's part to even consider this idée fixe of his, Gilles finally let it go, not because Jean had persuaded him that he was wrong, but because he didn't want to argue with his best friend. Besides, Gilles was reasonably sure that he would never see the blacksmith again unless they crossed paths in the marketplace.

Gilles had too many other things to think about taking up all of his time and energies now. There had not been a baby in Elsje's family for ten years, and being unaccustomed to having one around, no one except Gilles seemed to know what to call him. Aside from a variety of unoriginal endearments used by the rest of the world, Elsje complained that "Little Gilles" seemed far too formal. The child soon acquired a nickname, though, one that would stick with him until the day he died.

"He looks so *serious* all the time, is it gas? Can he have worms already? Does he *never* laugh?" Mynert Pieterse asked Elsje. "He looks like old Nicholas De Bruin, *always* so grim!"

Mynert's wife Jackomyntje laughingly agreed, adding, "He's a *beautiful* boy, Elsje, but just *look* at that serious face! You should call him 'Bruinje'. It's a good thing he can't talk; he might have a very *long* list of complaints all at the ready for you! Do you carry the worries of the world around with you so soon Bruinje?"

It was soon forgotten who had given it to him or how he had come by the moniker, and to Gilles' great annoyance, a good many of their neighbors forgot completely what the infant's real name was. Gilles disliked nicknames on principal, *especially* for his oldest son, but the appellation stuck and would not go away, even though Gilles made a point of correcting each person who used the despicable name in front of him. Even when the boy was no longer so serious, even when he started to smile and laugh, *still* they called him Bruinje. Soon even Elsje started using the name, although Gilles tried for a very long time to swim against the tide, always referring to his son as "the younger Gilles". Bruinje was healthy and plump and grew rapidly into a child who was every bit as charming as he was serious and contemplative, but it soon became obvious that he was also incredibly stubborn.

"He has his mother's personality," Gilles lamented to himself one Thursday morning as he held his sleeping son and looked down into the infant's peaceful face after a very long and mostly sleepless night. The battle over who should watch Bruinje on Gilles' day off had resumed briefly after Gilles took his son to be baptized by the priest. Gilles revisited the subject, having no further need of time alone with the child and hoping to win the battle during the second round but Elsje refused to discuss the matter any further.

Some people in the city, Elsje's father included, felt that these arguments were proof conclusive that Gilles had no control over his wife and that she needed to have a firmer hand and perhaps a firm rod applied to her as well, especially when stories of these squabbles over Bruinje's upbringing leaked out into the public domain.

Old Hendrick had no concerns or doubts about his daughter's capabilities and he had a definite opinion as to whose responsibility it should be to watch the boy on Gilles' day off: The new grandfather frequently suggested that his more competent older daughter could certainly handle all of her duties at the inn *and* keep an eye on one very small child as well if Tryntje would only do her full share of the kitchen work. Gilles had the distinct feeling that this rare show of support for him was not so much a vote of confidence from Hendrick as it was a reluctance to have his first grandchild subjected to Gilles' Gallic influences.

There was no question at all in Gilles' mind that childcare was women's work and that females were uniquely suited for it, as God had rightly intended, since they were the ones who bore the children and fed them at the breast. If Elsje wanted to abandon her divinely decreed duties, then Old Hendrick should watch the child himself since the old man did nothing at all every day except sit around the inn, drinking his ale and smoking his pipe as he talked with traders who came in from the far reaches of the world. Gilles volunteered to educate his son later on, when the boy was old enough to learn about accounts and commerce, feeling that he was being *more* than generous with this offer of his most valuable time and considerable talents.

Elsje reminded Gilles that it was not unusual for men in the Netherlands to care for their children, especially when it was only for *one* day a week; he could see that for himself on the streets every day. The last time the argument surfaced, it followed along its usual lines, but this time Gilles replied with a caustic remark about the masculinity of the men in the Netherlands which unleashed a storm of anger from both Elsje and Hendrick that lasted for days.

In the end it was simply easier for Gilles not to argue with Elsje anymore and it probably appeared to all outsiders to be just another battle that Gilles had lost. In truth though, Gilles had not put up very much of a fight: He didn't want to admit it, not even to himself perhaps, but he was becoming accustomed to having his son around and he even began to enjoy it a little after his pride recovered and after he noticed that Elsje was right about Amsterdam men, even highly respected businessmen, who often had their children with them during the day. Bruinje was a very good listener to all of Gilles' complaints, even about Elsje and Hendrick, and Gilles was careful to tell Bruinje only in French, just in case anyone overheard him or if the child suddenly started to speak in full sentences, repeating all of Gilles' words like the great colorful birds that could be seen sometimes in the Dam, riding on the shoulders of their seafaring masters.

Bruinje was a great conversation opener and he facilitated Gilles' acceptance into Amsterdam's trade and business circles with greater speed and ease than had a full year of drinking their putrid ale with them. Gilles would start the day by buying Bruinje a brightly colored fruit or vegetable from the market, preferably something less messy, like an apple or a pepper as opposed to berries, and Bruinje occupied himself with the object for hours, feeling it, chewing on it, shaking or banging it on something while Gilles made the rounds, visiting Jean Durie, the taverns, or the merchants in the Dam on those Thursdays.

Having earned a little of her good will, Gilles convinced Elsje to let Tryntje clean up the inn at night, ostensibly to help her learn the responsibilities of the business, but in truth Gilles only wanted to spend a little more time with his wife on Thursdays and if he could, at other times during the week too on those rare occasions when Ste Germaine's establishment closed a little bit earlier. If he could have asked for anything more out of life, it would have been just to have a little more time alone with Elsje, away from the cares of their work.

The autumn days grew shorter and colder as the brown, red and gold leaves rained down on the city with each icy gust of wind coming in from the Zuider Zee. Gilles was readying himself for his second winter in Amsterdam when a letter arrived from his father in France informing Gilles that his brother would be a father soon also, putting Gilles into a depressed and belligerent mood. He wondered angrily why every time there was something happy and good coming into his life, that providence seemed to send him some miserable reminder of all that he had lost. Perhaps what happened in France no longer mattered, Gilles told himself. He was more at home in the Netherlands than he had ever been in the country of his birth. Amsterdam was far away from his father's heavy-handed control and daily lectures on how to conduct himself and his business, far from Charles, the younger brother who had vied with him for the meager bits of their parents' attentions and who, it seemed, had finally won out in the end. Not inconsequentially, Gilles reminded himself, he *was* far from the fires and gallows of France. Quite possibly the Montrovilles no longer even gave their lost son much thought. They had gone on with their lives, giving Gilles' birthrights and his betrothed to Charles. When Gilles thought long enough about the definition of kinsmen, of what truly defined a family, more and more these days he came to the conclusion that those people in France were his family no longer. His family all lived here, in the city of the Amstel. Amsterdam was open and free and accepting of everyone who entered her port, no matter who they were, no matter where they had been before or what circumstances they had come from, just as long as they obeyed the law or at least did not break it frequently or in an open and flagrant way. Here in this port city it was always exciting, filled with exotic people, busy trade opportunities, and mysterious new commodities to sample. The air was full of the sweet smell of spices, exotic fruits, and the most unusual foods, with scents that swept across the city from the Dam, the East India House, and the neighborhoods where the new immigrants had settled in with their mystic and aromatic cooking pots, bringing new olfactory experiences to everyone with each change of the wind direction. In truth, if Gilles could have just kept his *new* life in Amsterdam and somehow still had his old home, his inheritance and his lands in France too, just to visit them sometimes, his life would have been absolute perfection.

Jean Montroville's great trade ships still came into the port in Amsterdam where they regularly left letters and money for *Yellas Jansen* at the West India Company offices. Gilles retrieved these, discarding the former and investing the latter. It was a joke to Gilles that he had changed his name *not at all*, except to take the Dutch *version* of his name, calling himself Jean's son Gilles, and the authorities either did not take notice or perhaps they just didn't care. Rounding up all of the political refugees in the Netherlands would have been an impossible task anyway. Gilles no longer needed the money due to his improved financial circumstances but it was too much trouble to send the coins back to France; converting them to Guilders required a changing fee, netting Gilles *less* money just for the privilege of carrying Dutch coins around in his pocket, so he just invested all of it with the Westindische Compagnie just as soon as it arrived. The French money was invested at full value and Gilles thought that someday he might send all of the money back to his father by turning over his holdings in the WIC.

Jean had urged him to write something in reply, just to let his father know that he was doing well, but Gilles had nothing to say except that he was alive and well, was married and had a child. Perhaps if he had read his father's letters, he might have had something to say in response, but he could no longer bring himself to open and read them. The months went by at a steady pace and soon Gilles realized that he had been living in Amsterdam for *three* winters now, and still he had not succeeded in writing a single letter to his family. His father's letters were less frequent now, but Gilles still occasionally received them. He no longer bothered to tell himself that he should write to his family; he was fairly certain of what his father's letters said because they had *all* been the same, news of Charles and Marie, best wishes for Gilles' health and happiness, and requests to let them know that he was receiving the money that was being sent to him. Gilles didn't recall *any* inquiries regarding Gilles' health or his well-being.

The winter of 1642-1643 was not as severe as the previous year when the canals had frozen solid, sending everyone to their old storage chests to find old mittens and skates. This was unfortunate because the first furs sent over from the Pelletiers arrived just in time for the onset of winter and had immediately found ready markets. The warmer weather slowed sales and cut into prices a little bit but still it was a success. Ste Germaine's establishment remained busy all of the time now, even throughout the winter and when Gilles couldn't stay on top of the fur trade business every day, he enlisted Jean Durie's help although Gilles still kept his own books. At fourteen months old, Bruinje kept everyone occupied, usually in trying to discover where the boy had gone. He was an accomplished walker now and frequently wandered off to wherever his curiosity took him. Elsje finally had to tie him with a rope to the heavy kitchen table and she kept both eyes on him as she cooked. She tried to get Bruinje to talk with her to pass the time and to distract the boy but he only responded with nonsense sounds. His total vocabulary was still no more than a few words although other children of his age were not only speaking many words, they were starting to form sentences and questions. Bruinje would babble back to Elsje for a short time but would soon tire of the game and turn his attention and concentration to something more interesting, like trying to untie the rope that held him fast to the kitchen table or dragging the entire table across the floor, with food still on it, to wherever it was that he wanted to go.

Although Elsje was unaccustomed to asking for help from anyone, she turned to Gilles for help at home. She was pregnant again but this time she was not as robustly healthy as before, having a debilitating sickness with her condition that she had not experienced when she carried Bruinje. Gilles helped her for most of the day on Thursdays, even serving the food occasionally when they were very busy, all the time angrily wondering why they could not just hire a girl to watch Bruinje or why Hendrick could not get up from his table to help them a little more since it was *his* business that they were tending.

It was during that winter that word reached Amsterdam of Cardinal Richelieu's death in France and virtually every soul in the French quarter openly rejoiced at the news. Special pastries in clever shapes reminiscent of France were sold in the shops and crowds mobbed Ste Germaine's, some of the patrons spending their very last coins for celebratory dinners. Every night for two weeks afterwards, the streets were full of drunken French expatriates who had become inebriated from toasting the news a few too many times, testing the patience of the Amsterdam constables as well as the capacity of the jail. Gilles was not alone in believing that with Richelieu's death, soon all of France's troubles would be over and peace and prosperity, as well as reason and rationality, would quickly return to his homeland now that the old devil in his red robes was dead and gone.

"This *is* good news, eh, Gilles?" Ste Germaine asked when he heard the news. "Sanity can now make her return to France. I might even make a trip back myself, just for a brief visit."

Gilles doubted his employer would *ever* leave the running of his business to someone else for even a single day but it was a nice fantasy for both men, Ste Germaine anticipating his return to his homeland and Gilles anticipating his employer's absence for an extended period of time. Repatriating themselves, for a short time or a lifetime, was a fantasy in which many of the French refugees were indulging.

"We will eat *Coquilles Saint Jacques* and drink *Calvados* until we burst!" one man from Normandie declared.

"Ah the *food*, it is *always* the food that we miss the most," Ste Germaine observed with a faraway look in his eyes. "How well I remember the taste of my mother's simple fish stew! I *must* see if I can replicate that dish for our dinners. You might go to France too, Gilles, when we are not so busy, of course. You could take your family and introduce your wife and son to the rest of your family there."

Gilles did not want to discuss any plans to return to France with Ste Germaine so he replied, "Elsje is not feeling up to a trip now; anyway, the King still lives. It may be that nothing *at all* has changed there. For myself, I will wait and see what news follows."

At first Gilles did not know why he didn't feel like celebrating until the realization came to him that no matter what France's turns of fortune, he could not go home again. He doubted that he could even go back alone, even if it was safe to do so, and he could not envision what his family would say to him when they were introduced to Elsje.

Quite simply, they would be appalled and horrified.

They would not see her as a good-hearted and strong woman with a pleasing face and healthy embonpoint; they would see her as a fat commoner with no family wealth or political connections, nothing French about her, in short, a woman with no redeeming qualities whatsoever. Gilles was irritated when other people asked him if he had plans to return and even more irritable when they *insisted* on sharing their future plans with him, especially when he was not in the least bit interested. Further increasing Gilles' irascibility, Elsje was always in a bad humor these days making it very difficult for Gilles to face going home to her *at all*. He sought refuge at his work but when Ste Germaine berated Gilles in front of customers for a relatively minor mishap involving a roast duckling one day during mid day dinner, Gilles left his work in disgust and despair, going to the docks to sit alone there in the cold, dark prelude to a winter night.

He sat there for some time but his anger did not cool with the cold temperatures: It was fueled to even greater heights when he noticed that one of his father's larger ships had just arrived in Amsterdam and was moored in the outer harbor. A small boat was ferrying a group of passengers from his father's vessel in to the docks, and it was approaching him very swiftly. Gilles got up to leave but he realized too late that there were several people seated in the bow, people that he recognized from his home city of Rouen and they appeared to be staring right at him from their seats in the boat, pointing at him and talking among themselves. One of the passengers, Jacques Pierre, even called out across the water, "Gilles Montroville! Is it *really* you?"

Gilles said nothing and slowly turned away. Pierre was believed to have Protestant sympathies and he might not have been the most dangerous person in the world to have spotted him but perhaps Gilles could simply pretend that he was *not* Gilles Montroville at all, just someone who happened to look like Gilles, as long as he did not speak or acknowledge the man.

"But *of course* it is you! No one *really* believed that story that you had died in the fire! How *are* you? You look very well!" Pierre called out to him as the boat pulled up and he was helped onto the quay by one of the oarsman.

Seeing no way out of the situation, Gilles answered him.

"Je suis bien, Jacques, merci. Do my father's ships carry human cargo now?"

"If there is room for people and we have the money to pay, the ships are still the fastest way out of France! We are on our way to the Palatinate in the German state but we didn't tell anyone that, of course. Officially we are here on a visit but we came to get my sister before we continue on our way. She has been living in Amsterdam and we will go on from here."

"I didn't know that you *had* a sister," Gilles replied, wondering if he knew her, had possibly even seen her everyday in the streets of Amsterdam. He didn't ask her name, though. Gilles had thought once to go to the Palatine region but he had put that dream aside when he married Elsje. His life circumstances had improved sufficiently when he was hired by Ste Germaine so that he no longer looked beyond the Netherlands for his future.

"And what about *your* sister? Who knew that she would ever go so far from home?" Jacques smiled at him but Gilles wasn't taking the bait: He hadn't read any of the letters from his father so how would he know what his sisters were doing or who they had been married off to?

Moreover, he didn't care what any of them were doing now and so he changed the subject.

"What are you going there for, Jacques? Aren't things better now in Rouen? The Rhine River Valley has been ruined by war and plague, hasn't it? Why not stay in France now?"

Gilles almost added *"now that Richelieu is gone"* but he stopped himself in time. Gilles wondered uneasily if there was anyone else on board the ship who might be a greater threat to him, in essence, if there was still a large reward being offered for him. Gilles needed to get away from the man and the other disembarking passengers as well as the ship's crew so he looked around for a means of escape, a quick excuse to go.

"Things are *still* not good in France, Gilles, but the war may be coming to an end; there are many leaving for the farmland in the German states now. All we desire now is to live in peace, with enough food to eat and a warm shelter. Difficulties can *greatly* change your point of view, your perspective on life and your values, n'est-ce pas?"

His wife and children had been helped out of the boat onto the dock and they took their places next to Jacques Pierre. The three children were the remaining survivors of the spotted fever and all of them looked too much like their mother, unhealthy, with gray shadows falling on their pale, pinched faces, sunken black eyes glittering back at Gilles from their dark sockets. The youngest one was deaf, too. Gilles wondered how the lives of his countrymen had been during the past few years but if they had suffered any shortages of food, it had not decreased Pierre's girth at all.

Gilles nodded to the man in understanding of the difficult years that had just passed but he noted that there was no mention of God or divine freedom, two themes that were usually so much in evidence and to be expected in the Huguenot speeches, especially from those going to the Rhine River Valley, in search of their God who apparently resided there, further up the river.

"I have friends who write and tell me that I should be able to get enough cash crops in to get another horse within a year. The houses are already built, just *waiting* for us and the taxes and tithes are low! Ah! I have something here that I *must* show you, Gilles!"

Gilles edged slowly away from the man, searching for an excuse to make his exit as Pierre dug through a leather shoulder bag. He pulled out a small mass of earthy-smelling roots partly bound in burlap. He thrust it in Gilles' face.

"Look, Gilles, *grapevines!*"

This was the last thing that Gilles might have expected to come out of the bag and he looked at the magical bundle with genuine interest. Growing grapevines and making wine was the one thing, the *only* thing that Gilles had enthusiastically shared with his father. It was a kind of family madness with the Montrovilles, an insanity that drove Gilles' father to attempt over and over again to try and grow different varieties of grapes in the soil of Normandy, experimenting in that place where it was not suitable at all, ridiculous to even make the attempt, due in large part to the climate and in small part to the soil. Gilles couldn't tear his eyes away though, and he *had* to look. The exquisitely formed tiny roots probably wouldn't make it through the first winter but Gilles didn't tell Jacques Pierre that; after all, many of the *families* probably wouldn't make it through the first year, either.

What could Jacques Pierre know of grapes and vineyards? His family had always been weavers and traders in cloth. It was unlikely that Jacques would know anything at all of growing *any* crops, especially when it came to cultivating the noble grape.

"Don't let them go moldy, they will be no good and infect the other vines," Gilles said anyway, knowing as he said it that his advice was completely wasted on the man. It was the very *least* Pierre would need to know to keep them going, but really, what did it matter? They would probably all be dead from starvation long before Jacques had to worry about mold on the vines.

"Oui, oui, I *know* that! I had a friend bring them to me from the south of France before I left and I am going to start my own vineyards when we get there. The Rhineland is *perfect*! It's very warm there and not too wet, with excellent soil and plenty of sun! They already have vineyards started that are turning out magnificent wine, but no *French* grapes, no French grapes at all! After a few years of farming, my vines will start to bear fruit and these vines will make my fortune in ten years' time."

"If we live that long," his sour wife interjected, but Jacques Pierre was a man drunk on the dreams of wine without having ingested any.

"I...I wish you well, Jacques, but I must go now."

Almost reluctantly now, Gilles turned away and went up the dark street. It was time for him to go back and see what peace he could make with his employer, what treaty he could forge with Ste Germaine.

Perhaps Gilles would be fired from his job for having left the dining room.

No, Ste Germaine hadn't let the cook go yet and the cook *regularly* stormed out, on the average about once a month in a fit of temper, even occasionally coming to blows with Msr. LaRue, although it *was* true that the cook might be harder to replace than Gilles. If Ste Germaine took a hard line with him, Gilles would probably have to plead with him to get his job back because Gilles had a wife and a child to take care of with another baby on the way. Gilles might have to listen to long lectures on the proper serving of poultry, but Gilles needed the money from this job and there were no other jobs in the city, at least none that paid as well and had such good working conditions. Gilles didn't know if he could tolerate being idle while Elsje worked and he wasn't going to work for Hendrick even though Hendrick had once offered him the position. That proposition had been offered a long time ago, and probably Hendrick would think better of making such an offer now.

As Gilles made his way back through the streets, wagons rolled by loaded with goods coming from the Waag, the weighing house for imports, from the ships, and from the warehouses. Everything was closing down for the night. Once Gilles had taken the time out to wonder about the cargo on the wagons, their originations, and their destinations. That had been long ago though, a few years ago when he had first come here, when he was still just a child. His life had taken on a hard, fixed, and permanent quality since that time and it was not a good or comfortable feeling to him.

Unbidden, the tendrils of the tiny bits of grapevine wound through his thoughts and Gilles thought about his own transplantation and how his new life had taken root in this new country. When the grapes matured, if they survived at all of course, they would have to be different than they were in France. Even though they were of the same ancient stock, they would be similar but would not be the same, never exactly the same. There was no reason why the wine could not be as good, maybe even *better*, depending upon the soil in which it was planted, the sunshine, the temperatures, and the prevailing winds and weather. Gilles had no idea what the soil was like on the arable land up the Rhine River. Perhaps no one knew or had ever talked much about it in front of him, or if they had, maybe the conversation had not seemed very important to him at the time.

Gilles thought about his future now and the years that stretched ahead of him, working for Ste Germaine with his fussy, demanding ways. He thought about still doing this kind of work as a very *old* man, still groveling, still trying to please the newly rich young gentry with their brand new and greatly expanded expectations of what personal service should be, just so they would find the experience satisfactory enough to return to the place and subject Gilles to it all over again. There was nothing to be done about it, though: Gilles simply had to accept this humiliation as a requirement of his work, the worst part of his job description, and just do what was required of him.

When Gilles arrived back at St Germaine's, he didn't bother to find his employer; he just took up his usual position inside the front door. Ste Germaine passed by him a few minutes later but he said nothing to Gilles about his extended absence, probably because there were customers seated nearby. Gilles knew that his employer *had* to have noticed, though, since nothing ever escaped Ste Germaine's detection. After another half an hour, when the diners had left, Ste Germaine did stop to speak to him on his next pass through the dining room.

"Are you *still* sulking, Gilles? *Stop it!* We have supper to serve! You must be cheerful, *cheerful!* And while you are being cheerful, go throw Descartes out. He ties up my tables for *days* but he never orders much food, *non!* He just sits there all day, spouting his nonsense and dreaming about marrying into royalty! Crazy old man!"

Some of Ste Germaine's other employees overheard this directive and dutifully plastered their practiced smiles back onto their faces as they continued with their work. At this moment it came to Gilles with great clarity, that aside from the volatile cook he had no true friends here unless one counted Ste Germaine himself. Perhaps this was because they were all *required* to be pleasant and happy all of the time and just as soon as their work was done, they removed their emotive uniforms and escaped from their requisite contentment out into the world of real feelings where they could be angry or sad or anything else that they might choose to be, in their other, real lives.

Gilles thought again of grapevines, thought of the leaves bent under the drumming and cleansing rains that were as necessary for the plant's health and survival as taking in the quiet, but occasionally burning, energy of the sun. Then Gilles thought of the leaves that never got any sun, the leaves that started out as all the other leaves had, only to turn white from lack of sustenance and nourishment and die under the weight of heavy rocks or the dying old vines where they had started life, but had *never* emerged, had never reached maturity or blossomed, just another mistake of His that had gone unnoticed and uncorrected by God. Gilles sighed, put a smile on his face, and went over to throw the less profitable patrons out onto the street, in as graceful and as pleasant a manner as he could of course, with the smile on his face that Msr. Ste Germaine required.

When he was in bed that night, Gilles lay staring up into the dark. It didn't *have* to be winter still; spring was not *really* so far away, and if he listened closely enough and inhaled deeply enough, he could reach the memory of springs past. He really could be back in France. The birds that he heard now were not the usual night birds of Amsterdam: They were the spring songbirds that were found only in the morning meadows of Rouen, searching among the fallen apple blossom's perfumed flakes for their breakfast. Nearby the moist earth parted slightly to show new grapevines with pale but vigorous green shoots coming up through the legs of the thick old brown and gray vines, verdant new vines with much *more* vitality than any he could actually recall having seen at any time in his life.

"Elsje…" Gilles said.

"What is it?" she asked, rolling over once more, still trying to find a comfortable position.

"Elsje, have you never thought to have a bigger garden in the back?"

"We have no time for that! It's cheaper to buy the vegetables than to find someone to tend them," she said flatly. "Tryntje's no help at all, as you well know; besides, the Marranos would just come and steal the vegetables at night."

"What about grapevines? They take care of themselves and they require very little tending everyday."

"And what would we do with *them*? Make a bottle of wine from the six bunches of grapes we got each year? You try to think up *more* work for me to do!" Elsje grumbled, adjusting the bedcovers and rolling over once again. "The *one* cow and few chickens we have keep us busy enough!"

Out in the adjoining room Bruinje gave a cough and they both fell silent, listening for a moment to see if he was awake or might be coming down with something. He slept outside his parents' bedroom now, in a small bed in the great room next to his Grandfather Hendrick's curtained bed, and both the old man and the young boy enjoyed each other's company by day and by night, although Elsje frequently said that such closeness would spoil the child and discourage him from becoming independent.

After a few more moments, when there was no more noise coming from Bruinje, Gilles turned over, defeated again. It wasn't *exactly* the garden that he wanted...

"If it makes you happy then, put in a garden, but *you* will have to tend it." Elsje moved closer to him and planted a kiss on his ear.

Gilles grunted. He thought now about going back to Ste Germaine's in the morning. It was *only* about thirty more years until he died, maybe as many as fifty if he lived to the age of his Grandpere; thirty more years of Ste Germaine, of the snotty young rich dandies, of keeping the peace between crazy LaRue and the cook. Gilles sighed and rolled over, kicking at the tangled bedclothes, then pushing his feet back into the warmth, looking for refuge in the other world, the world of dreams, at least for a few hours, until he had to return to being awake.

He awoke feeling tired and out of sorts. It was very early, so early, in fact, that even Elsje was not awake yet. His body ached and he didn't know why; perhaps *this* was what old age felt like. He was not yet even twenty-five years old but he felt that life, his life, might be far too long and boring. Perhaps death might not be such a bad adventure. Did one really go to heaven? Was it a place that needed exploration upon arrival? He looked over at Elsje, still sleeping, and he was glad that he had a life with her, but he dreaded the thought of going in to his work.

Maybe things would be better today though; Ste Germaine was not *really* so bad an employer. Gilles should be grateful that he had such a good position and his own little business on the side. He didn't have to do any difficult manual labor, didn't have to get very dirty, didn't even have to listen to his father's lectures every day, but still, he had to listen to Ste Germaine's litany of complaints all day long, or worse, endure his scrutinizing stares without any verbal cue as to *exactly* what it was that Ste Germaine was staring at, what he had found lacking. There was not much chance that Gilles would ever again set a foot on the deck of a ship or feel the rushing seas under his feet again.

Perhaps this was all that there was, all that there ever would be, and he should just accept that this was his lot in life now that he had reached maturity. He could almost hear his father sternly telling him that this was *so*, and also telling Gilles that he should give thanks to the Almighty that he had paying work at all.

Gilles had to admit that even working at Jacob's stable had not *really* been too bad, since he had to put up with only a small number of rude men and Jacob had not been a very demanding employer. Gilles liked horses and sometimes boredom had been his chief adversary in that previous job. It had probably been a good thing in the beginning that Gilles couldn't understand very much of what the Jewish men had been saying about him. Later on he had learned enough of the four languages that were spoken there so he could communicate with any variety of Jew that came in, Sephardic or Ashkenazi. Gilles' time there had mostly been his own, just as long as he was around to take care of customer's horses and the work got done.

He tried to put a name to what it was that bothered him most about his present situation and he concluded that aside from a bit of *ennui*, it was having no sense of real accomplishment in his life, nothing to make a name for himself besides having produced a son to live beyond his mortality. Gilles was losing any self-confidence that he had in himself, any faith in a better future, and Ste Germaine's exacting ways were undermining the confidence that he had gained from surviving the prison in France and then discovering that he could make his own way in the world, that he could succeed as well as, or better than, many grown men facing similar circumstances. Today Gilles was the master nowhere, not at work and not even at home since he lived under his father-in-law's roof.

Gilles berated himself for not insisting that they move out after the marriage ceremony but now that he and Elsje were entrenched at Hendrick's inn, it would be that much more difficult to justify the separation. Even though Gilles might use the excuse of his growing family and needing more space, Hendrick would probably find *some* reason to keep Elsje and Bruinje living there. Gilles thought of the spacious rooms of his home in France, of the entire wing of the manor house that would have been his and his alone, for the use of his family, his wife and children, and then he thought of the tiny attic space that the five of them now shared, eight people on Sundays, it being in essence a three-story rabbit burrow. Gilles had to remind himself, as Jean often did, albeit much to Gilles' irritation, that he had once been a different person, living a different life. That life still existed for *someone* living somewhere else, but it was no longer his. Even with all of the money that he was accumulating and investing weekly, Gilles was, in a sense, still a beggar, still dependent on too many others for too many things.

The simple truth was that Gilles envied Jacques Pierre and he wished that *he* could be getting on a boat to go somewhere, to a new beginning again and to a different future as well. The idea of ending up in a place with only fields and horses and grapevines was not unappealing to Gilles, either. He did not think that he was cut out for living his life out in a city.

All too soon, though, Gilles had to bring his mind and his body back to Ste Germaine's, back to the cook arguing with a waiter, back to Ste Germaine berating a cleaning boy, and back to the newly rich patrons, each one trying to outdo the next with how rude they could be to each member of the staff and how many complaints they could relay to Ste Germaine in one sitting. This day was no different, no better and no worse, and from time to time Gilles salved his mind with thoughts of country houses and fields of grazing horses. He heard cool streams of water gurgling by newly cut fields of oats as great wooden-wheeled carts loaded with fragrant hay rolled by him going to a barn somewhere far in the distance. He felt the warm sun on his back and his face as he bit into a pea pod that had been freshly plucked from the vine and scanned a field bursting with ripe vegetables to be savored by him at his leisure, a great variety and abundance of fresh meat, both wild and domesticated, still on the hoof, grazing in the adjoining fields, ready to be harvested and roasted over an **open fire.** He saw the cool shade underneath great grape arbors and innumerable clusters of tiny green grapes, each grape still no bigger than the head of a pin, but with the future promise of bending the vine's frames under the weight of the mature fruit and heavily laden vines. With such bounty, what else could one possibly need?

Perhaps he needed a little money to buy the first year's seed, to get farm implements, and occasionally to pay for the repair of an item, a little cloth for new clothing when the old wore out completely, but his investments *had* provided Gilles with a small cushion of savings. Gilles could see Bruinje running in the fields, becoming bigger and stronger with each passing year, and his new little brother joining him in his daily adventures. Gilles saw both of them growing up, strong and healthy youths riding on their own galloping horses, just as Gilles and his best friend Claude used to do so many years ago. Gilles would join his sons on horseback and he would teach them to be great horsemen. They would live in a community of other French people and Bruinje would learn to speak the language fluently, to speak as magnificently as great orators of the past, a modern-day French Demosthenes or Cicero, not just making a few grunts and noises that sounded suspiciously to Gilles' trained ear like *Nederlands* sounds. These dreams consumed his entire day until all of the meals, all of the time, all of the complaints, and all of the boredom had passed and once more it was late, time to go home to Elsje again. How many years could he pass in this manner? All of them?

Gilles climbed into his bed and was almost asleep, but he woke enough to curl up around Elsje when she came in. He quickly drifted back to sleep again though, to France this time. The scent of the apple blossoms overpowered him and a storm of petals came down over his head as he passed under the trees in the orchard, the disintegrating blooms blowing over the fields, the water, and over everything else, creating a blanket of warm white and pink snow. Under the shade of a twisted old oak tree, two men were sorting apples, selling some that were less bruised and had fewer wormholes in them, and making cider with all the rest. Gilles could hear the sounds of a great press working in the building behind the men. One of the men offered Gilles an apple from the pile that was for sale. Gilles didn't know where he was now and so he asked the men, "What is this place?"

The men smiled at Gilles and one of them answered him, but his reply was not in French. In a peculiar German accent the man said, "We have apples here, *too*, you know."

Gilles woke with a start and shook his head at the strange dream. His stomach rumbled loudly once, and he decided that he was hungry enough and rested enough to get up for the day even if it was a little early yet. He poked one foot out from the covers before he remembered that today was Thursday, his day off, so Giles pulled his foot back in, pushed his head down into the pillow once more, and tried to go back to sleep, hoping as he did so that the dream was not the augury of an approaching fever.

A few minutes later he was conscious of Elsje getting up and then scolding Tryntje outside in the big room, but Gilles stayed in bed with his eyes closed a little while longer until they had gone down the stairs to their work. If his father in law was awake, and he probably was, no doubt Hendrick would have something to say if Gilles didn't go downstairs soon after Elsje.

"See how lazy your French husband is?"

It was very cold in the bedroom this morning and when Gilles did get up he rushed to put his clothes on so that he could hurry down and warm himself by the kitchen fire. Elsje would have had enough time to have it roaring by now. He thought that some warm tea would be nice, too, even though Hendrick was certain to tell him that it was an *afternoon* drink and it took too much time away from her work for Elsje to prepare it for him in the morning. Gilles put on his woolen stockings as quickly as he could, but they did little to insulate his feet from the chill of the cold wooden floor. He pulled his icy pants on next and then tucked his shirt in, noting as he did so that it smelled strongly of smoke from the fire he had tended at Ste Germaine's the day before.

It made no difference today; it was his day off and no reasonable person demanded a clean shirt *every* day, no one except Ste Germaine. The time and expense in laundry alone probably consumed half of Ste Germaine's employee's wages and *all* of their wives' goodwill.

Gilles jammed his feet into his cold boots, the frozen leather chilling his feet even more, numbing his heels in addition to his toes. He even put his outside cloak on before he tiptoed out, past where Bruinje was still sleeping, and descended the two flights of stairs to the kitchen in search of warmth and some tea.

Gilles helped himself to a slice of bread and some nearly frozen butter that he chiseled out of the kitchen butter dish. He washed that down with some pale tea that he hastily prepared himself, not bothering to ask Elsje to fix him some. The tea was too light to have much taste to it but Gilles held the warm cup in his hands to warm them while he warmed his insides, sip by sip.

After Elsje had the fires in the kitchen and dining room blazing and the food preparation for the day had been started, she went back up the stairs to wake Bruinje and get him dressed. She brought him down into the warm kitchen and Gilles tied one of Elsje's aprons around the child's neck before he fed the boy his breakfast and then cleaned him up with a cloth dipped in some icy water from the kitchen pitcher. Gilles took Bruinje back up the stairs to get his outside clothes, including some warmer wool socks. It was tempting to stay inside by the fires all day but if Gilles stayed in the kitchen, Elsje would find *something* to scold him about, and if he stayed in the dining room, Hendrick would start to pester him again about buying a replacement teapot. Theirs had started to develop holes in it and it was Hendrick's claim that Gilles drank most of the tea, so *he* should be the one to buy the new teapot. If this was true, then Gilles reasoned that Hendrick wouldn't know that the teapot *had* any holes. Hendrick had never mentioned nor complained about the use of it by the customers who sometimes asked for tea, and other than keeping this as a ready additional complaint regarding his son-in-law, Gilles didn't know why Hendrick didn't just have Elsje go buy a new one and be done with it.

It didn't really matter: Gilles could always find a warm and friendly hearthside somewhere else for the day, somewhere where lectures were not an integral part of the ambience. He bundled Bruinje up against the brisk winds, stuck the child's hat and mittens on him and ventured out into the morning cold, passing the anchored ships near the Dam on his way over to Jean Durie's.

Gilles hadn't realized it fully before this moment, but recently he *must* have been giving some unconscious thought to just going off to sea again one day.

Maybe he had been dreaming about it.

He could run away in the spring, get on a ship, and just disappear into the morning fog. Hendrick and Ste Germaine would have no idea where he was or whether he was alive or dead. He felt a pang of regret when he thought of leaving Jean and Elsje, but Gilles still thought about going, even thought about it half seriously.

He could go to India. They certainly wouldn't look for him there, but he didn't like what he heard about India: It was too hot and too uncivilized.

He might go to the Virginia Colony in the New World; that might be better than India although he had heard that it, too, was hot and uncivilized, even though some very important English families were going over there. It had great trade opportunities and even greater tidal rivers for shipping out timber and tobacco from deep within the territory. They *did* speak English in the Virginia colony, a language that Gilles knew, and Gilles knew a little bit, although not a great deal, about the tar that was so necessary to the shipping industry and was one of the southern colony's major exports.

The wonderful wild horses that had been left stranded on the nearby Virginia Islands by Spanish shipwrecks were already the stuff of legends: They were magnificent horses, fast horses, and Gilles could probably find a way to get several of these fine animals at no cost as well as some land if he settled over there. Gilles had heard, too, that there were some French people who lived among them, a few Huguenots and some other stray miscreants who had originally escaped to England from France and then followed the British colonists across the ocean. Perhaps a fellow Frenchman who had already found success there would need a good man who was fluent in the language of accounts, with excellent business acumen, as well as a talent for getting along with all kinds of men, not to mention one with language abilities in English, Latin *and* French. It could certainly be a fortuitous match and *their* lucky day when Gilles presented himself for service. Together they could find wealth and success in the new land.

Bruinje pulled on his father's hat, shifting his weight against Gilles' shoulder and Gilles was suddenly reminded that he was not alone in his travels this morning. The child snuggled his cold face into Gilles' neck for warmth and the realization only came to Gilles at that moment that he could not leave his son behind, much as he wanted to leave his problems and everyone else behind on this shore.

They came to the last ship in the line at the quay, and Gilles noticed that the little vessel was being loaded with farming supplies and a string of bleating goats all tied together in a long line. The stubborn goats were being pulled very slowly and laboriously up the planks by one of the younger boat hands.

"Buh, buh!" Bruinje cried in excitement, pointing at the goats as the animals at first balked and resisted the lead, but then after being pulled forward by their four-legged general, the herd suddenly surged up the plank and onto the boat, trampling the lad who previously hadn't been able to get them to budge at all. The tethered goats raced around the deck in a single frantic group, snagging the sheets and tie lines and tripping up another boy on the main deck until some other sailors came swarming up from below the deck to help round them up.

"They don't *only* use goats for cheese there!" the herd boy yelled menacingly at the goats, a parting shot at the animals to assuage the assault on his body and his pride.

When he had stopped laughing, Gilles yelled over to one of the men, "Ho there! Are you going up the river to the Palatinate?"

"We *are*! Are you a passenger? We leave at noon, whether you are back in time or not."

"Will you be making another trip very soon?" Gilles asked.

"Ja, we will! Another boat leaves next week, but then no more until we find enough passengers or goods to fill the next boat."

"What day are you leaving? Can I just come aboard and pay then?" Gilles was only half joking with them.

"We will *make* the room for you and anyone else who wants to come! Five guilders apiece, children two. On Tuesday we leave from here again."

"Why so much? If there's no demand for the passage, why charge so high a fare?"

"There is nothing to bring back in trade! They don't *buy* anything and they don't pay on time either, *that's* why," the man growled.

So another ship was leaving again next week. Gilles bid the man good day and moved on, taking this bit of information away with him. He held it to his chest and peeked at it from time to time like a lucky hand of cards and then put it away again for safekeeping. Gilles kept his feet going, walking on toward Jean Durie's although he was in a mental fog, thinking about the fortunate goats that would get to go to a different place, up the river to a new life, grazing in the valley of the Rijn like free men of great means, while Gilles had to stay behind and continue working like a tethered mule in a treadmill yoke for Msr. Ste Germaine.

Jean did not provide a pleasant diversion for Gilles today either: He mentioned news he received from France that Gilles' younger sister, Elysabet, had married an English trader, affiliated somehow with the *Merchant Taylor's* School. Gilles had no idea what the Merchant Taylor's School was, nor did he care. He wasn't going to ask, or Jean would certainly go on and on, telling Gilles *all* of the details, but Jean seemed greatly interested and excited by this bit of information. Perhaps this was what Jacques Pierre had been babbling about when he had mentioned something about one of Gilles' sisters.

"How could they have met and been betrothed?" Jean wondered aloud. "Aren't you going to write to your sister, send your congratulations and a gift? Perhaps you can secure some trade contacts in England and the English colonies through your sister's new husband!"

Gilles mumbled something about not knowing where to send a letter, that it might not be safe to send one, and that he might do it in the future, but Jean, always quick to seize an opportunity, had already started moving his quill pen quickly across an expanse of open paper, making a list of suitable wedding gifts, a rough draft of a congratulatory letter, and a mental list of discrete ways that Gilles might find to make inquiries about his sister's husband, what his chief interests might be, his political and family ties, and possible connections to both the New England and Virginia Colonies. Gilles escaped from Jean by feigning a headache and remembering an imagined errand.

If it had not involved his family, Gilles *might* have been interested, as trade interests had been his profession and his chief interest before circumstances forced him to go to work for Ste Germaine, but he wanted to hear no more today about the Montrovilles.

When he walked through the door and in to his work the next morning, Ste Germaine immediately shrieked at him.

"Gilles! *Where* have you been? You're *late*! We are expecting *important* people from Leiden here today and we *must* be ready for them! I have told you *twice* already this week!"

In response, Gilles revisited his thoughts of leaving on the next ship out and he smiled a secretive smile.

He could just get on the ship and go. He wouldn't *need* to bring that much with him; just a few provisions and an extra shirt.

But he knew that he couldn't go: He could only fantasize and dream. As the day continued, though, the dream kept resurfacing, bobbing up to the top of his consciousness like loose cork fragments in a wine bottle and each time that the vision *did* come back to him, he could see it more clearly each time. Simply to be on a ship again would be *such* joy; the sea breezes and salt smell, the sun flickering over the waves like a school of silver fleshed fish, traveling over the water at great speeds, onward to a new adventure, to newly plowed fields and magnificent vineyards, and when he *finally* arrived there, riding across open fields on horseback all day long.

People grumbled around him, customers were rude, but all

morning Gilles clung to his thoughts of the place far away from all of the mundane and miserable things around him. He thought of freshly made cheese, velvet blue grapes and hot crusty baked bread with slabs of fresh butter melting over the sides, all eaten while sitting on a fence, watching his horses grazing nearby. He passed the afternoon in the same way until even his coworkers started to wonder at his peaceful state of mind.

"It's a *woman*," one of the waiters whispered to another, "I've *seen* that look before!"

Under Ste Germaine's relentless barrage of demands all day, his employees were all angry and sullen, even with the smiles still stuck fast on their faces, the waiters, cook, servants, *all* of them, all except for Gilles. The important visitors came and Ste Germaine's minions performed as trained, attaining a small measure of relief only after it was all over. Gilles ended his day by thinking still about wild rivers full of salmon and fruit trees with apples and pears as big as his fist, the fruit without blemish, weighing down the branches of the trees almost to the ground. Even as he climbed into bed with Elsje that night his heart was still in that other place, the place that he had never set his eyes on in his waking life. These comforting thoughts tried to fade on their own during the night but Gilles would not let them go: He clung to them and pulled them back to him, reeling them in, over and over, until the new day's first light when he got out of his warm bed and made his way past the mental traps that had been set for him, first by Hendrick, and then by Ste Germaine. He started his morning routine at work, checking the wine and food stores and making notes as to what he needed to buy. Ste Germaine caught up with him at the door to the cave, and would not let Gilles leave the wine cellar.

"Gilles, a word with you, please. I want to thank you for your level head yesterday. I don't know why everyone else was *so* disagreeable!

Your calmness smoothed the way greatly and made a great difference to our special guests *and* to me."

Ste Germaine reached for Gilles' hand and deposited a purse with heavy coins in it. Guilt washed over Gilles as he thought about his daydreams the day before that consisted mainly of *leaving* Ste Germaine, leaving his establishment, and leaving Amsterdam.

"I was only doing my job," Gilles mumbled. A woodcut he had once seen long ago, of Judas greedily clutching his bag of coins, surfaced briefly in his mind as he spoke these words.

"Non, I *knew* that I had not been mistaken in hiring you and perhaps I don't tell you this often *enough*, but you contribute greatly to the success of my establishment," Ste Germaine declared as he patted Gilles' arm fondly.

Gilles squirmed under the compliment, but he didn't know why he should: It wasn't as if Gilles didn't deserve hundreds of compliments at times when they were not forthcoming from his employer. Not knowing what to say, he just nodded at Ste Germaine and thanked him.

Later that night, Gilles took the coins home and threw them on the chest in the bedroom.

He wasn't going anywhere, not really.

There would be good days and bad days but he was stuck here in Amsterdam. He started to undress but Elsje, although she was not done with her chores downstairs yet, had come up into the bedroom. She said nothing for a few minutes as she stood with her hands on her hips, watching him undress for a time before she shouted at him.

"What is it?" she screamed.

Gilles looked up at her in surprise. *"What?"* he asked. "What is what?"

"You have been *pouting* all week like a spoiled child! Did my father say something to you again? You are *just* too sensitive! Don't take everything he says the wrong way!"

"Nee," Gilles shook his head at her and smiled. "He has said nothing to me."

The smile on his face seemed to make Elsje even angrier. She stamped her foot before she spoke again. "*What* is it then? Is it Msr. Ste Germaine?"

"Nee, Ste Germaine gave me extra money for doing an *especially* good job this week. Take it and buy yourself something."

Gilles swept his hand grandly and beneficently in the direction of the coins on top of the chest. He tossed his pants over a chest, climbed into bed and prepared to go to sleep.

She was only distracted for a moment. Gilles could feel her eyes stray over to the money and then back to him again before they narrowed, just as they always did when she was angry.

"Now I *know* that you are sick! You aren't investing it all!"

"Let's go to the Palatinate." Gilles said. It was worth tossing it out to see her reaction.

She walked around to the bottom of the bed, in front of him, to search his eyes with hers.

"I have heard of no cases of fever yet this year," she said in a slightly quieter tone.

Gilles smiled a wry smile at her. "I'm not sick, it's a *joke*," he said to her.

"I don't understand it then," Elsje replied. "The German states have been completely destroyed in the war! There is nothing but misery there, the travelers *always* say this when they come here to beg for food and for jobs."

"It's just a joke, I didn't mean it," Gilles mumbled, pulling the covers up to his chin.

"I think you *did* mean it. There are crazy people who *are* going there, *French* people. They claim it's too crowded here, there aren't enough good jobs for all the newcomers who want to work, they want *land* because they lost theirs in France, and they don't like their children learning the Nederlands language and ways. But you have *enough* work at Ste Germaine's, ja?"

"It's just a thought I've had, but that's *all* it is, Elsje. Just forget it."

"My father told me that you would want to go back to the sea. He *told* me you would leave me eventually," she hissed, a faint hint of fear creeping into her voice.

Gilles pushed the covers back and sat up in bed. "I'm *not* leaving and keep your father *out* of this! It's never anything but *trouble* when he's involved!"

"Shhh!" Elsje rolled her eyes at the door and seemed to be listening for her father.

"I don't care if he does hear us!" Gilles raised his voice again. "What is between us is between us! He would *sleep* between us in our bed if he could!"

"Shhhh!" Elsje pleaded again with her voice as well as with her eyes.

"We aren't discussing anything, anyway. There is nothing to discuss."

Gilles lay back down in the bed and rolled over to face the wall, away from her. Elsje waited a few moments more but with nothing in the air but silence, she finally left the room to go finish cleaning up the tavern's supper dishes downstairs.

On this night, Elsje had too much on her mind to take part in the nightly ritual of rumor exchanges between her sister and the two kitchen maids; she used her time in the dishpan to think. Elsje made sure that every one of the dishes was cleaned, scrubbed out with sand when necessary, dried, put away, and ready for the morning, not allowing Tryntje to leave the worst kettles to soak until the next day as she sometimes did, but still the other women had already gone to their beds before Elsje. She wiped down the washing pans after she dumped the wash water outside and made sure that all the doors were closed securely. She checked to make certain that the fires had burned down enough so they wouldn't be a safety hazard while the family slept, filling up the buckets of water by the fireplaces, just in case there was a fire that started from some small exploding ember during the night. Satisfied that the inn was secure, ready for the night and for the next morning, Elsje finally picked up the lamp and climbed the stairs. She looked in on Bruinje before she went into the little bedroom and closed the door behind her, shutting out all of her other responsibilities, closing herself in with her husband and her worries.

Gilles appeared to be sleeping quite peacefully but the unborn child roiled in Elsje's stomach, tossing and turning as Elsje herself might be doing, if she had been in bed already. A sick feeling came over her, not the pregnancy sickness that was finally beginning to subside a little bit after all of these weeks, but nausea coming from the fear that she might lose Gilles now. Initially she had worried about losing him to the plague or to another woman, but after a couple of years of marriage, she had come to believe that she could hold her own on both of these fronts, being the *hardnekkig* woman that she was. She just wasn't sure if she could prevail against his dreams, though.

After many years of verbal sparring with everyone and anyone, no matter their age, level of education, or social status, Elsje had become *very* adept at debate and with her strong and fixed opinions, she was justifiably confident that she could win any argument. She was fairly certain that she could win enough verbal jousts with him to keep

Gilles here in Amsterdam for just one more day, each and *every* day, but how long would it be until he stopped arguing with her and just disappeared?

How many battles until he capitulated and stayed but stopped talking with her and sharing the thoughts of his heart?

She did not see a final victory for herself, not in the end, nor could she think for even a moment about leaving her father and the inn, especially not for the desolation of the Palatinate. She rubbed her stomach, rubbing it briskly from side to side. *"It's all right, it's all right,"* she silently told the little one. *"It will be all right, go to sleep now."*

Elsje took a deep breath and did what her mother had taught her to do so many years ago when crises and demands threatened to overwhelm her: She reviewed the goodness in her life and she counted up all of the things for which she gave thanks.

She had her family, the inn, her fellow townspeople, and the members of her church. Her life was as good as life could be and yet with all of these things that so many people in the world craved, but would never have, or *worse*, what they had a taste of briefly only to lose these blessings to war, sickness, or simple misfortune, still *all* of these things would not be as sweet without Gilles to share them with her. It was not just the comfortable familiarity of him; there was *more* to it than that. There was something different about him that had always been there, ever since the first time she had set eyes on him.

Gilles had been sitting with Jean Durie at the table against the wall, wearing simple clothing and no hat, but his dark eyes had followed her, rested on her in a way that was not like the other men, who were obviously always more interested in what she might look like without her clothing on. No, it was more of a look of great interest, or curiosity, and then some unnamed emotion, something between passion and recognition, that came over her, or perhaps it had come from somewhere inside her. For just a moment, something akin to a warm spring sea wind seemed to pass completely through her.

She had brushed these silly and childish thoughts aside right away of course, because when she looked at him once again with a more critical eye, Gilles had seemed *very* young and really *not* very special at all, just another stranger in her father's inn who was in need of a warm meal and a stein of ale and so she had put these thoughts about him out of her mind before they had a chance to take hold there.

It just *wasn't* fair to have to make choices between which parts of her good life she could keep and which parts she would have to give up. She cursed Gilles for upsetting her world. Why couldn't he just happily join her in the bounty of their lives together? In balance, was he *worth* giving up all of the other wonderful things she had?

Maybe it would have been better if she had never met him at all.

She shook her head "nee" at this last thought, though, thinking of Bruinje sleeping soundly in the next room as she took off her overdress, and thinking too, of her unborn child. She worked her dress up over her widening waist and climbed into bed, hoping as she did so that it was a healthy child she carried in spite of her ongoing sickness.

"You will be all right. We will be all right," she told the child firmly.

It was a promise, an admonition, and a prayer.

Gilles got up every day for the next week and went off to work, going through each day as he always had before. To all outward appearances the days had settled back into normality after his temporary imbalance of temperament. On his next day off, though, he told Elsje that he had some unfinished business to take care of at his work and would she watch Bruinje for just a few hours this morning? He truly *meant* to go and ask Ste Germaine about the red wine supply that was getting low in the more expensive price range, something that he knew he should have taken care of before taking his day off. If Ste Germaine ran out before Gilles returned to work on the following day, Gilles would certainly hear about this failure, this shortcoming on his part, probably for months to come. Gilles thought that he might just stop somewhere for a quiet cup of morning tea first, somewhere far away from the inn, or more to the point, away from Hendrick and Elsje.

Because he didn't usually stop anywhere on his way to work, he had no idea what establishments were open or what refreshment they served. The tavern that he stopped at this morning, a rundown little place, didn't have any tea. They didn't even seem to know what tea *was*. When Gilles tried to explain that tea was a drink made from little ground up dried black and brown leaves floating or sinking in a cup of hot water, the man gave Gilles a peculiar look. Gilles realized that the proprietor was getting annoyed after Gilles insisted that surely by now everyone in Amsterdam, and indeed everyone in the civilized world, *must* know what tea was. Not wanting to anger the man further by getting up and walking out without ordering anything, Gilles settled on some wine, which they *did* have, and some cheese and bread to go with it.

Gilles was having a second mug of the wine and slicing some of the dryer parts off the cheese when a sailor from one of his father's ships walked into the tavern. Gilles had always tried to stay safely hidden, just in case someone recognized him and might be tempted to turn Gilles in. It was impossible to escape in time and when the man hailed him, Gilles saw no alternate course of action but to invite him over to share his table. The mariner's two main distinguishing characteristics were a weathered, deeply-lined face and an inexhaustible mental library of stories. A gossip as bad as any old woman, Gilles thought at first that it was too bad the tattle-tale couldn't have found Gilles in a better setting, such as at Ste Germaine's, it being much more elegant than the seedy little tavern, but then Gilles decided that it was a *good* thing to be in this out-of-the-way place: He didn't want anyone from France to know where he was all the time or to observe the humiliation that he had to put up with each day at his place of work.

The sailor spent nearly every moment of his time talking when his mouth wasn't completely full of food and drink, and sometimes even when it was full, spraying crumbs and saliva across the table as he related to Gilles all of the things that he had experienced or even *thought* about on his last journey, ever since his feet had last touched land and ever since he had last met up with anyone who would listen or even pretend to listen to his thoughts, observations, and experiences.

Gilles mused to himself that the man must be without a woman, because if he had a wife or a lover waiting somewhere, he wouldn't be nearly so talkative to complete strangers about anything and everything, including things that Gilles felt were rather too personal to be shared with mere drinking acquaintances, including a woman the sailor had occasion to be entertained by on his last trip to Morocco and the resulting eruptions and pustules on his private person after the encounter.

Gilles didn't mind though: He was only half listening to the man babble on and he was enjoying just sitting and drinking, with nothing more urgent requiring coherent thoughts or a return to his feet any time soon. It was still early in the day so Gilles wasn't going to worry about it. Gilles bought the man a hot meal and one for himself, making certain that the seaman knew he had plenty of money in his pocket so he could relay that news to anyone who might ask. The two men ate, or rather Gilles ate, while the man talked in between a gobble of food here and a gobble there, and then talked some more, mostly about a nasty bout of lice he had recently which resulted in his having to shave his head and then take the extreme measure of subjecting himself to immersion in a *full* bath of water. The sailor then proceeded to catch Gilles up on the news and gossip from France and their home province

At first it was general news but then the seaman brought out all of the information on Gilles' sister's marriage, presented with his audience, the high-born brother of the bride uppermost in his mind. The details were laid out as carefully as new church clothes arranged for the first time across the foot of a bed as Gilles washed his anger down with more wine. He attempted to continue looking interested in the tales because he *didn't* want word to get back to France that he was unhappy, bitter, or jealous.

Seeing this as encouragement, though, the sailor talked even more; he told Gilles about how the city had been shocked to learn that the King had seized fully a third of Jean Montroville's best orchard and grazing lands, and about the troubles that different families from Rouen had endured since Gilles left. The sailor also had tales to tell about some of the Protestants and their sympathizers who had escaped to other countries, including the Palatinate and the not-quite-believable stories of their successes that had come back from that region. Gilles was actually quite interested in this news, much more so than in any news about his family or the latest storms at sea.

"But I have not asked about *you* yet, Msr. Montroville!" the sailor slurred at the start of the fourth bottle of wine, the thought perhaps having just occurred to him. "How are things with you? I hear you married a *barmaid!* Could this be so? Eh?" He grinned a suggestive grin and winked at Gilles.

"My father-in-law owns an inn and my wife has always helped her father to run it," Gilles said coolly. "The women do so here in Amsterdam, you know. In fact, the women, as well as the men, are *very* good at business, usually quite successful. My wife mainly oversees all of their servants, as she is very particular about how she wants things done: Of course they wanted me to run it for them when I married her, but I had another position already and it was quite impossible for me to do both. I have to deal with some *very* important merchants, people who have wide connections in world commerce."

What Gilles said was mostly true. Important people *did* come into Ste Germaine's every day. Gilles drained his drink again, hoping that he had sufficiently clarified that bit of commerage in the mariner's wine-soaked brain and that he had squelched some of the rumors regarding his fall from grace. Gilles found it all *very* embarrassing to hear that these tales were told about him at home, and he could only *imagine* how enraged his father must be when they reached his ears and he had to deal with the public humiliation. Certainly by now Jean Montroville was not just *insisting* that his son was dead, but probably also *wishing* that it was true, rather than having to believe that Gilles had married a *serveuse*.

But how could they have heard these things? Who would know so much about him that they could send this news back to Rouen? Jacques Pierre had hinted at the same thing, that there had been gossip that Gilles was still alive, and Gilles had thought at the time that it was some nicety of conversation, not that there could *really* be any stories, whether they were based in fact or not. Jacques Pierre could not have been the one to spread any of these tales either: He had not returned to France but had gone on up the Rhine River in the other direction.

Gilles' own father had put the rumor out into circulation that Gilles was dead, killed in a gunpowder explosion on one of his ships. The idea that there was someone who could be informing on him, watching him even *now*, gave Gilles a peculiar sensation, an eerie sensation, as if something was slowly creeping up his neck, advancing toward his hairline.

The first time Gilles had traveled to Amsterdam, a few years earlier, it had been for the purpose of solving the mystery of who might be stealing cargo from his father's ships. He had never found out who it was, and to his knowledge, his father never had either, but Gilles had experienced the same sensation then: that someone watched him, that someone knew his every move and that someone wanted to do him harm. This malaise had turned out not to have been a complete figment of his imagination: Although an assault that left him unconscious was taken by others to be a poor attempt at a robbery, no one could explain why money was left undisturbed in Gilles' pocket. It *was* true that the pocket was a hidden one, but it would have been an inexperienced thief indeed who would *not* have searched the linings of Gilles' waistcoat or inside his hat and shoes.

Perhaps not even registering Gilles' remonstrance regarding his new wife's social status but flitting back to the previous subject and pouring himself another full measure of the wine, the sailor chattered on.

"I dream about going the Palatinate sometimes," the man mused aloud. "I hear about how *good* the land is there, but I love the sea too much. A river, no matter how big, is *not* for me. Perhaps one day, when I am an old man..." he turned his mental sails in that direction and floated off briefly.

Gilles forgot temporarily about his self-consciousness regarding his wife and the complete change of subject caught him off guard. He knew and understood that love of the sea too, and this induced feelings of camaraderie with the seaman and *oui*, even perhaps some jealousy. Gilles wished now that he could go back to the ship with the sailor, or better still, trade places with the mariner, just for a single day. That was a thought to ponder: a trade of souls, a chance to escape and glory in the sea, in the adventure and the precipice of the unknown.

It was wicked and dangerous, fearsome and wonderful. Gilles then had the thought that his father had *never* approved of this secret passion of his, this love of adventure. Jean Montroville had tried to stamp it out of him, to kill it or at the least to bury it alive, but he could no more accomplish this than he could change the color of his son's eyes.

They were halfway through the fourth bottle of wine when Jean Durie walked into the tavern. He hesitated at the door, adjusting his eyes for just a few moments before he scanned the room and then strode over to the table.

"Ah, *there* you are!" Jean hailed Gilles in Nederlands as he pulled a chair up to the table.

"Were you looking for me?" Gilles asked, pouring himself a refill and gesturing to the barman to bring another mug for Jean.

"Bonjour, you are a friend of Msr. Montroville?" the sailor enquired. "You *do* look familiar..."

Jean ignored the man, acting as if there was no one occupying the other seat at all. He replied to Gilles in Nederlands again, giving no indication so far that he knew a word of French.

"You're not so hard to find: It's a small city, everyone *always* knows where everyone else is," Jean said.

"I should get back to the ship now anyway..." the sailor mumbled as he hoisted his body up from the table, lurched one step forward, and then finally centered his ballast and righted himself. He pushed his hanging shirttail back into the top of his trousers and reached for his woolen coat that had been sliding on a glacially slow but certain path down from his chair to the filthy floor. "The captain didn't know if we would sail *late* today or leave tomorrow at next tide. He had to replace or repair some sails after the storm. Did I tell you about the storm?" he asked.

"Oui, you did," Gilles said as he took another sip of wine.

Jean said nothing at all but sat with his eyes on Gilles, his arms folded across his chest, a disapproving frown on his face. The sailor pushed one arm into one of his coat sleeves and then succeeded in getting the other sleeve on while navigating across the room in a zigzag pattern to the door. He left the tavern, forgetting to leave any money, forgetting to say goodbye to Gilles, probably forgetting everything, Gilles thought, even the small fragment of their conversation that Gilles hoped he *might* remember and take along with him, the part about Gilles' being happy and successful and *not* married to a barmaid.

"Is this becoming a habit with you?" Jean asked, speaking in French at last. He took a sip of the wine and winced at the bitter taste, but his face had dropped the expression of disapproval that had been there since his arrival.

Gilles was still enough in control of his faculties to notice that Jean was making a great effort to look nonchalant. "What, drinking wine? Of course! I *still* can't stand the Netherland ale and their bier is even *worse*. Their wine isn't much better, but it's the most tolerable drink they have here." Gilles took another deep draught from his drink although he knew that he didn't need any more. He was already suspended in the ether just above the table, just above reality.

"I *meant* your sudden disappearances, Gilles! Ste Germaine told me about last week, and today it seems that you are drinking away your entire day off. Elsje's worried." Jean was raising his glass, drinking with him, but he was still broaching a less than comfortable subject.

Gilles dismissed Jean, and Elsje as well, with a wave of his hand and then he topped off his mug with the last of the bottle. "I have *one* bottle of wine with an old acquaintance, on the one day I have off during the week, and now I am among the *missing*? Really, what is there for Elsje to worry about?" Gilles put a smile on his face, just for Jean, but it wasn't playing as a friendly smile, and Gilles didn't care any more. He had no need of a guardian.

"You have *responsibilities*, you know, two and a half responsibilities, to be exact. What will your son think of you?" Jean queried.

"Bruinje? He never thinks about me at all and his mother only wonders where I am when her father needs help or when she wants my pay for a new dress. I could die *today* and no one would miss me, no one at all."

"Gilles, you need to stop feeling so sorry for yourself. Your life is not really so bad. I wish *I* could find myself a woman half as good as Elsje."

Without answering Jean, Gilles took a last sip from his drink and pushed his chair back from the table. He stood up and turned to go out to find the outhouse. He had been out there a bottle ago but remembering *how* he got there and how he got back again did not come easily to him now. Behind him he saw Jean throw some money on the table and follow him out the door into the pale afternoon sunshine. Gilles found the place and latched the door behind him once he was inside the fetid, dark little closet that was perched on the cold ground behind the tavern. He yanked at his pant laces. Gilles could hear Jean waiting for him outside.

It took Gilles a very long time to finish and he marveled at the capacity of the human bladder. He had enough time to let his eyes adjust to the darkness inside, to consider a spider just to the side of the other two holes, to wonder how the insect could *still* be alive in the cold, and to hear a bird land on the roof and sing its song before a flitter and the hum of wings announced that it had taken off again. Gilles lost his balance once and had to grab one of the wall timbers for support while trying to put his clothing back in order. It took him *so* long that he had nearly forgotten about Jean when he stepped outside again into the bracing fresh air.

"Are you making sure that I didn't fall in? Or don't escape? You want my family? Take them! I'll just disappear. You can just tell them I fell into the hole in the shithouse and my body was never recovered."

Gilles pushed past Jean, shoving him aside with his shoulder as he headed back in the direction of the tavern door but Jean grabbed his arm and would not let it go.

"Jean, you don't want me to hit you, do you?" Gilles groaned. "I don't *want* to have to hit you. I'm much *bigger* than you are and you *know* I'd probably hurt you. "

"Gilles! You are too much of a gentleman for that, but just *listen* to yourself! It is obvious to me that you need to make a change in your life and the change that is needed most urgently right now is in your *thinking.*"

Jean didn't loosen at all the firm grip he had on Gilles' arm but instead he took a chance and a step forward, then another, as he led Gilles away from the tavern and out to the street.

Jean had once again calculated correctly and Gilles offered no resistance; he was less in a fighting mood today than in a self-pitying mood. Several curious people smiled and nodded in greeting to them, perhaps noting the smell of the alcohol and thinking that they had *both* been on an early outing together.

"All right then, take me home, Jean," Gilles mumbled amiably. "My day off is just about over, anyway. If you take me home now though, *you* will have to talk to Elsje. I'm not talking to her today; facing her and her father tomorrow will be bad enough."

"Fair enough, Gilles, I'll talk to Elsje for you."

It wasn't quite suppertime yet. Gilles was able to make his way up the stairs and into the bedroom under his own power with Jean following behind him and Elsje trailing Jean. Gilles flopped down on the bed, hitting it rather harder than he thought he might, not remembering at all navigating through the customers in the dining room or around Elsje in the kitchen on his way to the stairs. He fell asleep quickly, though, before Jean even had his second boot off, drooling as he snored loudly into the pillow, but even this did not wake him up.

Elsje shook her head in disbelief, leaving Jean to the task of putting her husband to bed in the adjoining bedroom while she stirred a little pot of stew on the warming stove that sat on the preparation table in the great room. She didn't usually bother bringing food up to their apartment during the week: It was extravagance, really, to go to all the trouble. The bricks had to be placed on the preparation table and the little hot stove, no bigger than a roasting pan but twice as heavy, was filled with hot coals and carefully brought up the stairs from the kitchen and set on top of the bricks. A very small pot of food could be brought up and placed on top of the warmer to be kept hot for the family. On ordinary days, all of the meals were simply dished up from the large pot in the kitchen and the family ate downstairs, either in the kitchen or in the main dining room of the inn, depending on how many customers were taking up the seats.

On Sundays and holidays though, when Elsje's younger brother and two sisters came over from Cousin Vroutje's, Elsje wanted something different. She wanted a family meal in their *own* living quarters without having to run plates up and down the stairs before the food got cold. She insisted on keeping the dining table on the third floor and making use of the warming stove, although they could surely have used the living space to much better advantage. Hendrick thought that it was a lot of bother and that she should just serve *all* of the family's meals in the inn's private back dining room on the main floor. The inn was closed to the public on Sundays anyway, at least until all of the church services were over, but Elsje insisted that their home was their home, plain and simple though it may be, and she wanted the family all together in their own private space.

Elsje had had something else in mind for tonight, though, something special for her husband, but it wasn't working out as she had planned and she had already replaced the coals in the warming stove twice today.

After Gilles was settled into his bed, Jean came out of the bedroom and shut the door behind him, even though it was unlikely that *anything* could disturb Gilles' repose. Elsje knew that the action was more to shield Gilles, and consequently, to shield her as well, from any other prying eyes in the household, her father's or her younger sister's in particular. Elsje didn't look at Jean directly when he came out of the room, but she spoke to him as she continued to stir the stew.

"I don't know *what* to do. What is happening, Jean? Is he turning into a drunk? Has he gone mad? They say women go mad while they carry a child but I carry the child and *he* is the one who is acting strangely! Was he like this before and I just didn't see it?"

She put the heavy wooden spoon down on the table. Her eyes still didn't meet Jean's though; she looked off into the distance.

Jean glanced back in the direction of Gilles' bedroom and shook his head. "Nee, it's not like the Gilles I know. He might be having some difficulty adjusting to his new responsibilities."

"What responsibilities? Children? All *he* has to do is go to Ste Germaine's every day, which is *not* a very hard job at all! I *thought* that he was responsible enough or I would not have agreed to marry him. Perhaps he was just too young. Perhaps *I'm* not what he needs or wants."

Elsje jammed a hand into her apron pocket, searching for a handkerchief that was not where it should have been. She sniffed and rubbed her nose with the back of her hand before she picked up the wooden spoon and began stirring again.

"It's not you. You are a good wife to him, Elsje, and he's lucky to have you." Jean took a step closer to her and put a halting hand on her shoulder.

Elsje said nothing for a few moments but then she put the spoon down again, her hands forming fists at her side. She began to speak slowly but once she started, the recitation of the day's tribulations gained momentum until everything spilled out.

"Oh Jean, it has been a bad day from the *moment* I got up! I asked Father to take Bruinje out until bedtime to give me some time alone with Gilles, to talk. I even wore this new dress but I didn't know where Gilles was all day so that's when I sent you to find him. God in Heaven only knows *how* the inn is surviving! I have Tryntje running things and closing up with Father on some nights but I need to go back down now and make sure that she hasn't *already* locked the door and put the lamps out! Father has gone out with Bruinje so there is no one there to watch her! She burned the dinner I made for our guests and we didn't have enough earth apples left to make more of the same, so now it's no longer stew, it's *soup! Only soup* for our customers! I even cut my finger with the big kitchen knife and Bruinje was fussy all morning with more teeth coming."

Elsje held up a bandaged finger and then suddenly stopped speaking although there was probably more that she had intended to say. She inhaled deeply, ending that with a catch in her voice, a sound that was close to a sob.

Jean gripped her shoulder a little tighter, for once in his life not seeming to know what he should say or do, whether to remove his hand, a small and ineffective gesture of comfort really, or to offer *more* words in the hopes that they would make Elsje feel better. He appeared to decide on the latter course of action and put as much emphasis and clarity as he could behind each of his words when he addressed her again.

"Elsje, the inn will take care of itself for now. You need to make sure that you are all right, even if you can't sort things out with Gilles right away, although I'm sure that you will both do that very soon. I can talk to him for you if you want me to."

"I am fine! I'm not the one out drinking, *I'm* here, *I'm* cooking, and *I'm* working! What else can I do?"

Tears of frustration, anger, and fatigue started to well up in her eyes although Elsje clamped her mouth shut after she spoke, still refusing to break down and cry.

"*Regardless* of how he chooses to conduct himself, you need to take care of yourself and your children, both of them."

"Ja, I do."

She straightened her back with her hands and drew in a deep breath, letting it out slowly, reinforcing some inner dyke. She pressed her lips together and pushed back a wisp of hair before she spoke again.

"Maybe I'm just getting weak. I don't know *what* is wrong with me lately. I'm happy, then sad, and sometimes I'm even afraid. Maybe it's old age."

Her chin quivered then and Jean, noticing this, pushed aside his own reticence and put his arms around her, pulling her head onto his shoulder and resting his head on hers.

"You're *not* old and you're definitely *not* weak! It will all look so much better tomorrow, Elsje. You just need a little more rest and more help and understanding from Gilles."

The words that he had meant to soothe her had the opposite effect and a flood of tears followed, her shoulders quietly shaking as she buried her face in Jean's shoulder.

Elsje had never cried, not at all since her mother's death. At that time the ten year old girl had put her tears away with her toys and accepted the full terms of her new responsibilities in life, without attempted negotiation or complaint, vowing to fix everything, never to cry again, and *not* to be a burden to her father or to anyone else, in case they should decide to send her away too, or put her in the orphan's home. It took a little time for the years of unspent tears to finish and Jean stayed with his arms around her, waiting patiently for her sobs to die down as he pulled his handkerchief out of his pocket and handed it to her. It was a square of lace-edged saffron yellow silk that *exactly* matched the material in his shirt, so ridiculously impractical that Elsje almost laughed when she saw it, in spite of herself and her present misery.

"I'm sorry, I'm so sorry," Elsje apologized. "I don't need to bother anyone else with this. Father says that it's all my fault for marrying Gilles and that I deserve it."

"I'm hardly a *stranger* to the family, Elsje! I've known you since you were a little girl when I would bring little cadeaux for you and your sister when I came into town. Nee, it's *not* your fault. The problem is with Gilles; I can see how his actions would try your patience."

Elsje had herself fully back under control now. She dabbed at her eyes with Jean's zakdoek, but not wanting to ruin such a lovely thing, she handed it back to Jean and then used the corner of her apron to blow her nose. She took a few more breaths and straightened up, looking Jean in the eye at last. She even managed a small smile in repayment for his kindness.

"Thank you. I am better now."

Jean kept one arm around her, rubbing her upper arm as if she was still a small child and not a grown woman. "Elsje, I can't say *exactly* what is wrong with him, but if you want, my offer still stands: I will talk with him for you."

"Would you? I would talk to him myself but I don't know where to start. He doesn't *listen* to me!"

"I think he does listen, but ..."

Elsje put her hand up to her stomach suddenly.

"Are you all right?" Jean asked, putting a tentative hand to her stomach.

"It's all right. I just get these sharp pains sometimes. Thank you for asking. Thank you for *caring*." Elsje put her hand over Jean's and smiled up at him.

Convinced that she had calmed down enough now, Jean took her face in his hands and kissed her gently on both cheeks, in such a typically French expression of parental concern, that he felt compelled to make her feel a little more at her ease by following it with a kiss on her lips in the Dutch fashion. Jean kissed her mouth a second time, reinforcing the first peck on her lips, but this time Elsje reacted unexpectedly, responding with passion to his kiss.

Jean didn't back away though; he returned the kiss, his right hand traveling from her cheek to her neck and his left hand moving down her shoulder and arm to her waist, around to the small of her back, pulling her closer to him. Their allegiances conflicted with their mutual needs of the moment but there was no stopping, not for either of them until the sound of a step at the top of the stairs, just outside the living quarter's door, forced them to quickly separate.

The door opened just as Elsje picked up the wooden spoon and stirred the stew again, straightening her bodice and then her cap with her left hand. Jean straightened his jacket with both hands and Tryntje started to speak even before she stepped into the room.

"I give up! You just can't make *anyone* happy! Some of the West India Company men came in, not *even* an hour off the boat from New Amsterdam, and *all* they do is complain! I had their ale before they even sat down and they complain! I gave them our *best* seats and even move heavy tables, *just for them*, and they complain! Not fast enough, not good enough! I *hate* this business! They should be grateful to be back in civilization!"

"I'll come down and straighten it out," Elsje replied, putting the big spoon down and wiping her hands on her apron. Her face had nearly returned to its normal color except for a little red blotchiness on her cheeks. She tucked some loose hair back under her cap.

"I have to go now, anyway," Jean volunteered.

"No, stay and have some supper with us, Msr. Durie," Elsje gestured toward the table.

"Do you really have to leave now, Jean?" Tryntje smiled at him, her complaints forgotten for the moment.

"Yes, I must go now, but thank you. I will come for supper another time."

Jean picked up his hat and cloak, flashed a bland smile in the direction of both sisters, and then he left.

"Where is Gilles? I thought I saw Jean bring Gilles home." Tryntje stuck her finger into the little pot of stew and quickly put it into her mouth, as much to cool it off as to taste it.

"He's sleeping!" Elsje snapped. She shoved her sister roughly away from the stove. "Do I *always* have to go down and fix *everything* for you? Who is taking care of our customers?"

"You don't have to *yell* at me. The customers are all fine; I left the other girls there and I just needed a little break. I *hate* this inn and I wish we could have a *normal* life. I wish we lived in a house that *wasn't* our business so we could leave it sometimes for an hour or two, and I wish our friends *weren't* our customers so we could have disagreements with them sometimes if we wanted to. We *always* have to be nice *so we don't lose their business!*" Tryntje finished her complaint with a fairly good imitation and mockery of their father's frequent admonition.

"You talk nonsense, Kathrijn Hendricks! We are lucky to *have* the inn and all that Father has provided for us. How would you support yourself if not for the inn? Answer me that!"

Elsje glared at her sister, probably not *really* expecting an answer. Somewhat satisfied that there was no immediate emergency downstairs, though, Elsje picked up the spoon again and stirred furiously.

"Ahh, I'd have a rich husband and a great house in the best section of the city and my home would be *filled* with servants and lovely things to look at, paintings and tapestries and art from Cathay, with all of the chocolate I could drink and all of the marzipan I could eat. It's an embarrassment to work as we do, like animals, like scurrying sheep jumping all the time to obey the orders of each new master who comes in the door! It's *no wonder* that we can't find anyone decent to marry us. Who would want to marry a scrub woman anyway?"

Tryntje shook her head in disappointment at her lot in life as she dipped her finger into the stew once again.

Elsje wasn't sympathetic to Tryntje's complaints though; she stopped just short of slapping her sister but she did grab her sister's wrist and pushed her toward the door as she scolded her once again. "You *said* you could manage and it hasn't *even* been a half hour without me! Now get back down there!"

Tryntje calmly sucked the last of the stew from her finger before she answered her sister. "No one needs anything right now. They can just wait a few minutes while I take a short break. I'm *tired* of doing all the hard work. I do all the laundry, the sewing, *and* the cleaning, and all *you* have to do is cook and smile at people! Of course I can serve food and smile, too. My hands are red and cracked and *always* bleeding from doing the laundry every day! My back is breaking, and you just have a sore face from *smiling*. I should have been born first."

"*Who* burned the dinner I made? I keep this place together and the customers coming in the door! You are no cook, and you can't even manage for this *short* time without me! You are *useless*, Tryntje!" Elsje slammed the spoon down on the table and reached around with both arms to retie her loose apron strings. "I can see now that I will *just* have to do *everything* myself! Get out of my way!"

"I can manage, and it's been closer to an *hour*, not a half hour."

Tryntje seemed not at all flustered by her sister's agitated state and far from setting her feet into motion to quickly obey her sister, she stepped right in front of Elsje, turning her back to her older sister and deliberately blocking Elsje's way before she opened the door in her own good time to return downstairs. "Well, maybe that cute merchant who just set up shop in the Dam will come in again tonight. I guess it's *good* to be the one in charge sometimes," Tryntje tossed over her shoulder as she left.

"He's *married!*" Elsje yelled after her sister, although she knew that it probably made no difference at all to Tryntje. Elsje wondered how many girls like Tryntje had been flirting with her husband during the day today, in whatever tavern Gilles had spent the day in. Elsje was left alone with that miserable and tormenting thought and left alone, too, with what had passed between herself and her husband's best friend. She still tasted Jean on her lips and now she wondered if Gilles was still asleep. How could he sleep through all this uproar? Perhaps he had been awake the whole time, listening to *everything* that went on in the adjoining room. As quietly as she could manage, Elsje cracked open the creaky old wooden bedroom door, as pockmarked and battered as a survivor of the pox, and looked in on Gilles. The light from the main room fell on his face and Elsje could see that he was still sleeping soundly; his responsibilities, the world, and all of his concerns completely forgotten.

"My lord protector," Elsje thought, but as well as anger, she felt relief that he was still sound asleep. She didn't know what she might say to him if Gilles had overheard any of the exchange between herself and Jean Durie. Elsje counted herself as fortunate that her sister had come in when she did; uncomfortable, but lucky. Her strength of will appeared to be gone as well as any moral strength of character. What was happening to her and to the entire family?

As she stood looking in at Gilles, Elsje heard her father coming up the stairs. She quickly stepped into the bedroom and closed the door behind her, shutting herself in with Gilles. Without enough light to make use of the looking glass on the wall, she straightened her hair and cap as best she could and then splashed some water from the wash bowl onto her face, hoping that the cool water would tone down any remaining brightness in her cheeks. What she didn't need now were any questions or pointed comments from her father.

"Elsje!" Hendrick called from the room outside. "Elsje, where *are* you? The boy is hungry! He wants his mother!"

Elsje took a deep breath and left the bedroom, shutting Gilles in behind her. Bruinje ran into Elsje at the topmost speed that his short legs would carry him forward. He buried his face in her skirts before Elsje took a tearful Bruinje up onto her hip.

"He's been crying for you the *whole* time we were out!" Hendrick exclaimed.

Elsje kissed the chubby little tearstained face, the face that looked so much like Gilles' today, as much to comfort herself as the child, and wiped Bruinje's face with her apron which was still damp from her own tears, before she set the little boy back down on the floor. Bruinje cried out in anguish and threw his arms around his mother's leg, clinging to Elsje as she dragged him over to the little warming stove.

"Where is Gilles?" Hendrick asked as his eyes lingered for a moment on Elsje's face.

"He's asleep, he's tired," Elsje said, hoping that this would be the end of it and that nothing in her voice invited further questions from her father.

Hendrick mumbled something about not understanding how anyone who did nothing all day, every day, could be *tired*, but Elsje ignored him. She calmly admonished Bruinje to be patient, that Mother was getting him his dinner, as she dished up a little of the stew from the pot. Silently she mashed a broken slice of bread into it before she tested the temperature of her son's supper with her finger.

Bruinje whined impatiently for his mother to finish what she was doing and then to pick him up again but she did not: Elsje filled a second dish of the stew, this one for her father, and pulling a whimpering Bruinje along behind her as he had now firmly attached himself to her skirts, Elsje managed to bring both bowls over to the table without spilling the hot contents of the two bowls on the floor or over Bruinje. Triumphantly she set the full bowls down, took Bruinje by one shoulder, knelt down and looked into his eyes.

"Now Bruinje, you will eat your dinner with your grandfather and *no more crying*. You are getting *too* spoiled, and besides, I'm not going *anywhere*. You will be a *good* boy or you won't get any supper at all and I will put you to bed right now!"

Her speech seemed to have been understood by the child because Bruinje did stop crying immediately, but he still sniffed vigorously at regular intervals even after he crept silently over to Hendrick's knee. Climbing up on his grandfather's lap, he ate hungrily from his dish with his fingers although he never took his large and shining eyes from his mother's face.

"There, there, Bruinje, come to Opa! Mother must be tired, too. She hasn't done anything all day, *either.*"

Hendrick held his grandson on his lap with his left hand and ate his stew with his right.

"He should be sitting in his *own* chair and eating there, *with a spoon,*" Elsje observed sternly, ignoring her father's barb. "Has he had a nap today? Did you feed him anything *at all* while you were out?" she asked as she brought bread and butter to her father from the preparation table.

"He's already eaten at Vroutje's but he still wants more. He's going to be a great, tall, strong, boy, just like his vader, ja?" Hendrick consulted Bruinje on this matter. "Just as long as you grow up to work hard *like a Nederlander* and *not* be lazy like the Frenchmen!"

Elsje let the insults go again and said nothing in reply to this slander of her husband as she retrieved her father's nearly-empty bowl to fill it again. For no particular reason at all, she suddenly thought about Hendrickje Conradt who had killed her own child and then drowned herself in the canal a few years earlier. Elsje thought about going to visit her mother's grave later and then taking a walk, maybe all the way to Haarlem and back, just to have some time alone to *think*, but she soon rejected all of these thoughts, both the reasonable and the unreasonable ones. She *couldn't* leave the inn tonight; it would be irresponsible and everyone would certainly wonder where she went, especially with Gilles at home and Tryntje left in charge.

Elsje went down to the kitchen to get some warm water to bathe Bruinje and also to get away from her father for a few minutes, but there was no refuge there, either. The kitchen girls and Tryntje were unusually silent when she entered the room, and it seemed to Elsje that they all looked at her in a strange and uncomfortable way, following her with their eyes as she filled the wash basin with hot water from the kettle and then added a little cold water from the kitchen pitcher to cool it down. As she went back up the stairs with the full basin, Elsje resolved that she was *not* going to be making another trip downstairs tonight for anything. She couldn't stand having anyone look at her in that pitying way. Whatever Elsje might need, she could well do without it until the morning came.

Elsje set the wash water down on the table next to Hendrick and pulled a soft rag out of the little cupboard. Bruinje had finished eating and was only playing with his remaining stew now. Elsje picked him up from her father's knee and sat Bruinje on his own chair, washing his face and chin before moving on to his hands, arms, legs, and the rest of him.

Bruinje howled at the touch of the cloth and pushed Elsje's hand away. "Koud! Koud!" he cried.

"Stop that!" Elsje ordered. "*Be still* while Mother washes you!"

"Fwa, fwa!" Bruinje cried, grabbing at the cloth.

"We'll have no more arguments and *no more* baby talk!" Elsje scolded him. "You be quiet while I finish bathing you and then you go right to sleep or *I* switch your bottom for you!"

Bruinje bit his lip but his eyes filled with tears, making Elsje wonder if she had been rougher than usual as she washed him tonight and making her feel even more miserable than she had been already.

"Mother *is* tired tonight," she said to Bruinje, by way of an explanation and an apology.

Elsje put Bruinje down in his bed, lit another lamp from the one she left behind with Hendrick and took it with her into the bedroom after bidding her father good night. Even though she was hungry and had eaten nothing since midday dinner except for occasional samplings of the stew, she thought she might wait in the darkness of the bedroom for her father to go downstairs or go to sleep; when he did, she could slip out to get something to eat and eat it in peace, without sharp comments or stares from him. What Elsje wanted, more than anything else right now, food included, was to be left alone and there was no place for her to go other than the bedroom, even though Gilles' loud snores made it difficult for her to think and impossible for her to sleep.

Elsje decided that she would not worry about leaving Tryntje and her father the task of closing the inn tonight: She would take Jean Durie's advice on that. She just hoped that Tryntje wouldn't burn the place down with them in it. Elsje *had* hoped that Jean could talk to Gilles on her behalf but now she worried about what else Jean might say to her husband. She removed her overdress, noting that her stomach was already beginning to get very large, in fact larger by the day.

Jean must have felt the child pressing against him as they embraced. She felt the blood rise to her cheeks again as she blew out the lamp. After making her way over to the bed in the darkness, she heaved Gilles over from the middle to his own side next to the wall. He grunted as she did so, but he didn't wake up, and his snores almost immediately resumed the same cadence and rhythm as before. After Elsje crawled in next to him, she lay very still, listening for Hendrick to leave the apartment as she stared up at the ceiling. A beam of light intruded from one side of the ill-fitting bedroom door, illuminating a curling cloud of smoke that had come from the just-extinguished lamp.

Elsje didn't know why she had acted so disgracefully earlier with Jean but what confused her even more was Jean Durie's conduct. She had known him for a good many years and he had never given her the *slightest* indication that he had feelings for her that were anything other than paternal, even though there was only a slight five years difference between them. Jean had never responded to any of Tryntje's many overtures, even with all of the encouragement, nee, outright teasing invitations that Elsje's younger sister had extended to him on so *many* occasions. He had always been more like an uncle in spite of his young age, an old man trapped in a young man's body, a kindly if somewhat boring gentleman who brought the little girls pretty hair ribbons whenever he came into town but then quickly got down to business and directed all of his attention to talking trade with her father.

It suddenly occurred to Elsje that her actions had graver implications than merely the emotional complications that had previously preoccupied her thoughts: She had kissed a Jew and it was against the law in Amsterdam for a Jewish man to have relations with a Christian woman. Elsje was not sure if it was against the law for her to kiss Jean Durie though. Which actions specifically comprised "relations"? Was there a stopping point before which it was shameful but not a crime? Was it a crime for her not to resist? With his mixed parentage, would Jean even be considered Jewish by an Amsterdam court of law? Could Elsje be locked up away from her family, giving birth to her child in prison due solely to a few minutes of emotional confusion and weakness?

Elsje had never given the law a moment's thought before since it had nothing to do with her: She had always believed devoutly that if one's conduct was respectable, then there was no need to be concerned with the written laws because the lawmakers and judges were all learned men, reasonable, moderate, and for the most part, temperate men, with just a few glaring exceptions. Elsje was too busy to concern herself with what the prostitutes in the city did every day; that was *their* business.

Did Jean expect more from Elsje now, perhaps for them to carry on an affair? What would she say to Jean if he came back to see her tomorrow while Gilles was away at work?

Elsje didn't know what was wrong with Gilles lately and now she wondered if she could ever be able to get her husband and her life back as they had been before. Perhaps having children *had* changed everything or maybe Elsje had never really known Gilles, or for that matter, Jean Durie. Just when she needed Jean and his diplomatic abilities the most, she was not at all sure that she could put her trust in her greatest advocate and in Gilles' best friend.

To make matters even worse, Elsje wasn't sure if she completely trusted herself. She craved the sympathy of someone who showed concern for *her*, even more than she craved the cooked eggs that she had been eating all day long, every day, for these last few weeks. If only she and Gilles could have some time alone together, away from their work, without her father and Jean Durie around, together they might be able to sort out their difficulties. She had tried to the utmost of her ability to create that time together today but that hadn't worked out as planned.

Regardless of what was to be in the future, tomorrow would come anyway, and it would be no easier for lack of sleep, she sternly told herself as she cut off all further lines of thought. She willed herself to listen to her own breathing and go to sleep in spite of her anxieties and in spite of her aching stomach. It might have been hunger pangs that she felt, but when she thought about eating, she was not sure if she could keep anything in her stomach so she decided that she wouldn't even try. At last she fell into a state where she was aware of all of the sounds around her but not awake, her eyes closed in a kind of sleep that was not restful and did not rejuvenate her.

Gilles woke up much earlier than usual, and was very much pleased to find that he had only some minor lingering discomfort from his consumption of all the wine the day before. He managed to get himself dressed for work in the dark without too much difficulty, other than having a slight lack of balance that he needed to counteract. He tiptoed out so as not to wake Elsje, as much to let her get a little more needed sleep as to avoid a morning argument, and then he set out for work, only stopping briefly in the kitchen downstairs to down some water directly from the pitcher and then finding some of Elsje's bread to take with him for his breakfast. Gilles didn't bother lighting a candle from the fire; he just pushed aside the shutter on the little window over the table, getting enough useful light for his purposes from the half moon that was just sinking down behind the trees. He found the knife and got out the loaf of bread.

While he was cutting a slice from the loaf, he saw that the teapot had been left on the table. He pushed it aside to make more room for the bread, discovering in the process that there was still some tea left in it. He was still very thirsty and hot tea would have been wonderful this morning, but it was certainly left over from the night before. He poured the cold tea into a mug, leaves and all, to take with him on the road. If it wasn't enjoyable, at least it would wash down the bread.

Tryntje must have closed up last night: Elsje would never have left so much as a crumb behind on the table, let alone an entire pot of tea and she wasn't going to be happy when she found it there after she got up later on. Where had Elsje been last night?

Gilles had a vague memory of coming back to the inn but he couldn't remember anything more after that. He thought he might have passed her in the kitchen with the others when Jean came up the stairs with him and led him to his bed. He vaguely remembered Jean promising to say something for him to Elsje and now Gilles wondered if Jean had been able to smooth things over with his overly demanding wife, at least regarding yesterday's missteps. She could be *so* unreasonable sometimes, but with Jean on his side, maybe Elsje would let yesterday's little excursion pass completely without comment. All Gilles wanted was *one* day to himself a week, and he didn't think that was so very much to ask. Gilles had to smile in spite of himself; Jean was *so* adept at diplomacy that he just might smooth things over, even with Elsje.

Gilles thought he heard footsteps at the top of the stairs but it was only the cold and maybe the wind that was making the old building creak. He negotiated his way out of the inn, even with his hands full with the tea and the bread, and then he pushed the door shut again with his elbow after he was outside. He rebuked himself just a little as he ate and walked up the street: He really shouldn't have spent the *whole* day yesterday drinking, wasting all of his precious time off with that jabbering sailor. Jean was right, Gilles just needed to just face the fact that his life was not as he had known it, not as he had *hoped* it would turn out, but it was not such a bad life: After all, the world was jammed full of people who were poor, alone, hungry, or sick.

Many of the unfortunates, like old Botte, the French aristocrat turned vagrant who had been murdered in the streets of Amsterdam, sheltered themselves under trees or bridges *every* night and even during the day when there was inclement weather. On rare occasions these creatures could be seen bathing themselves or washing their clothing in the canals if they still had enough self pride and food in their bellies to think about grooming during their daily quest for survival. They bore their children outside like farm animals and raised the ones that survived under the open skies, in the sunshine and in the rain, in the summer's warmth and in the bitter winter cold. The offspring that lived were bonded out as servants as soon as possible if the opportunity presented itself, but such opportunities were rare and it was not unusual for the parents to sell their children outright for a few stuivers if they were fortunate enough to come across a buyer for the sole commodity that they could produce as well as anyone else. These other human-like creatures that shared the space of the city with Gilles usually expired outside and were frequently buried in mass graves. Only occasionally were they put in numbered graves, if any public institution cared enough to take the time to label their final residence in that way, finding only at the very *end* of their time on earth, a permanent and secure place for their bodies, but only after their souls had already moved on to whatever reward or punishment might be in store for them.

Similarly, Gilles knew that the world had a good number of people who had plenty to eat and *any* comfort imaginable, but were bound in marriage and in misery to partners that they detested, even abhorred. Those bedeviled by marriage's legal bonds might occasionally tolerate an infrequent mutual intimacy born of animal need, in order to avoid spending money on a prostitute or the entanglements of an affair, but any child born of such a union, one that mixed the two bad bloods, more frequently than not paid the price, living with the revulsion of both parents and living up to the fears of both. It was usually the case that each half of a yoked pair united with the other in only *one* activity: the separate but equally zealous daily spiritual communion, offering up to the heavens the shared silent prayer for deliverance from their misery, and requesting relief by *any* means at all to rescue them from their mutual torment. The monstrance of their life was closed and dark, not revealing anything at all to outsiders, let alone showcasing something that was supposed to be joyous, or at the least consecrated and sacred. In spite of their unfaltering commitment in the Netherlands to having divorce rights available to all, it was still a hotly contested right, sometimes to the point of violence incited by those whose religious beliefs did not permit what they considered to be a sin against God, this reneging on the divine marriage vows. Gilles had been here long enough to observe that it was a solution rarely undertaken and seized upon by the Dutch populace, even in the most drastic of circumstances.

On the whole, Gilles was happy with Elsje, and Amsterdam was incontestably the most humanitarian, pleasant, and comfortable city on the face of the earth. Gilles told himself that he should *at least* feel a little guilt at his complete lack of gratitude to the Almighty, luck, or whatever force it was that had preserved his life thus far and brought him to live here, giving him everything that he had now, in sharp contrast to so many needy and miserable others. What Gilles just *couldn't* get beyond, though, was the discrepancy between what he had now, at this juncture of time and place in his life, and what he had *once* had, not only the material things that made life so comfortable and so pleasant, but the freedom that he had known then to sail off and travel to new places from time to time as well.

Gilles had considered telling Elsje something about his mind's journey that he had traveled along recently, to tell to her what it was that was lacking in his life, what he achingly longed for, in point of fact, what *she* was missing in life too, but he doubted that she would understand it, even if he could find all of the right words and the amount of time that it would take to adequately explain it to her, even if she would listen long enough and be able to comprehend what he was trying to tell her.

Perhaps she was better off not knowing.

Elsje had probably never known much beyond the inn's kitchen door in her thin slice of the world. Even when a vast variety of God's creation came to *her*, as it often did in the form of sailors, travelers, and fortune-seekers, Gilles didn't believe that Elsje ever saw anything very interesting in them or their lives; to her they were just another task to be completed, another problem to be solved. Unlike the madmen over in the Dam who played the day away with their array of little glass lenses that they used for many different purposes, Elsje looked at life through only one kind of lens that examined only everyday objects, bringing familiar people and things closer to her so she could see them in greater detail.

Gilles, on the other hand, preferred to focus his attention on whatever was at the periphery of his experience, his mental telescope scouring the horizon to bring very distant and heretofore unknown objects closer to him for his examination.

If Gilles had been born a Netherlander, he might have been able to secure a better job at one of the India Companies, a job that could provide him with greater opportunities and possibly adventure too. As it was, without having a great deal of money to buy more shares in the company, he could only be a minor stockholder, not a full member, and would probably be stuck at Ste Germaine's for the rest of his life unless some sudden stroke of luck befell him. Marrying Elsje had helped his social standing and prospects greatly, but not as much as he had been hoping for as he affixed his signature to the marriage contract. Even the WIC's young apprentices, some of them under the age of ten, yes even their *bonded servants*, were seeing more travel and living more adventurous lives than Gilles.

Gilles sighed. Before he knew it, his feet had already carried him right up to Ste Germaine's door this morning and there was no more time for day dreaming. As he walked inside though, he resolved to make the best of things and to keep his eyes open, looking for opportunities to advance himself and maybe even to do some traveling. Thinking back to the illness that had swept through the city such a short time before, Gilles was reminded that life could be shorter than one assumed. He would waste no more of his time or energy on self-pity.

Elsje had been awake when he left for work but the time wasn't right yet for saying what she was going to say to her husband and so she pretended to be still asleep. She waited until she heard him descending the stairs and only then did she pull herself up to a sitting position at the edge of the warm bed. She was still not feeling well in the mornings, and this was doubly true this morning, perhaps because she had eaten so little the night before. Trying to ignore the sour burning in her stomach for the moment, she picked up her shoes, no easy task lately with the bulk of her stomach in the way, and pulled the top cover off the bed to wrap around her before she crept down the cold stairway in her stocking feet. Pausing in the stairwell, she shivered and listened until she was sure that she heard him leave the kitchen and then quit the inn entirely. After hearing the distinctive squeak and thump of the front door in the dining room closing, she crossed through the downstairs rooms and opened the upper half of the door a crack to better see him as she stood at the door and watched him go. Already this morning she was more tired than she was cold and hungry. Her life's energy was constantly being drained from her by the growing weight of the child she carried, her perpetual sickness, and her worries about her marriage.

Before Bruinje was born, Elsje had felt energized, and even being so heavy with the boy, she felt as if she could walk or even *run* as she had when she was a child, much longer and miles farther than she *ever* could before, at least up until the very end of her pregnancy when the weight of him was more than she could manage. She had never been sick for a day, not even a minute, when she carried Bruinje.

Elsje knew already that this next child was very different: Bruinje was a healthy, outgoing, concentrated bundle of energy but the child that was now in her belly seemed somehow sad and heavy, even morose, and Elsje worried that all the sickness and worry she carried with her had already affected the child's health and personality. In her darkest moments Elsje worried that the child would not be quite all right when it was time for the birth, but she always pushed these thoughts out of her mind quickly, even before she felt the movement inside her start up again. After all, there was nothing that could be done right now except to wait patiently unless you put any confidence in the charms and enchantments that the fortunetellers sold in the Dam. For the time being, Elsje would be patient with her coming child and patient, too, in selecting the time to speak with Gilles about his behavior the day before. It was not a time to allow her anger to burst out: For the moment she needed to hold it in check so that she could choose the best time and place to have a discussion with Gilles and get him to talk to her.

Jean Durie was also on Elsje's mind this morning. Would he stop by Ste Germaine's to intercede on her behalf, as he had promised? If he did this, would he also open up his soul to Gilles, making a confession of what had passed between Elsje and him the day before?

Elsje should have told her husband first, not to lie about it, but just to be certain that there were only the facts with no embellishments, although Jean Durie was nothing if not factual. Who knew what men shared with their friends about women? None of what she ever overheard in the inn's dining room was good. Unfortunately there was no time for any discussions with her husband early this morning or on any other morning: It would have made Gilles late for Msr. Ste Germaine's and Gilles had frequently told her how exacting and demanding Msr. Ste Germaine was, especially concerning punctuality.

Elsje imagined many things happening on this day as a consequence of Jean's talking to Gilles, most of them bad, and she wondered if Gilles might arrive home during the day, angry and wanting to confront her. Would Gilles chastise her or beat her? She had heard that the French men were like that in matters of honor, emotional and volatile. Although he was very proud, as all of the French were, she had never seen any indication of violent behavior in Gilles before, not even to avenge obvious slights, but then again, she had never seen any indication of drunkenness in him either, at least not until recently. Nee, his conduct on his day off was *not* acceptable and Elsje would not tolerate it or allow it to continue. She had every right to be angry with her husband and to *demand* more civilized behavior from Gilles.

Elsje knew that Gilles disliked confrontations, though, and it was not in his nature to initiate one. Perhaps if Jean *did* say something to Gilles about their brief encounter, Gilles would value his friendship over his marriage and wouldn't bother to talk to Elsje at all. He might just go away, maybe even leaving the city without saying a word to her, going on to some unknown destination, and the last glimpse that Elsje would ever have of her husband would be what she had seen of his back this morning as he vanished into the dark streets of Amsterdam.

Under other circumstances, a woman might look to secure a new relationship with the other man, for him to make it right for her, to take care of her, but in this case, not only was it *not* what Elsje wanted, the law of the land made it impossible. If she lost Gilles, she would be all alone with one child and another on the way, both of the children orphans, or at least bastards, in the eyes of the law.

Elsje would not give in to fear, though. She dismissed the sudden urge that she had to run after Gilles as feeble-minded, an artifact of her present condition, insecure and with child, and she decided she would hold her ground. It was just *not* going to happen that way; she would not stand for it.

Gilles may not have known this, but Elsje wasn't completely in the dark as to the source of Gilles' discontentment: She knew well enough that Gilles craved the adventure of traveling and she knew, too, that he had a destination in mind, in fact had had one in mind for some time now. If Elsje had been born into a different life, if she had been completely free to chose, she would have liked to see a *little* something of the world herself, just as long as she could always come right back home afterwards. She would have enjoyed going with Gilles to see the places that she had heard about in France, and perhaps see Leiden and some of the other great cities and towns in the Netherlands.

Gilles didn't want to go to France or Leiden though; he wanted to go to the Palatinate. Thinking about going anywhere was a complete waste of time. Who would run the inn if Elsje and Gilles went away? What would they do when they got there, run another inn or travel on to another place? Would they travel until they died and were buried in some strange place with no one to tend their graves or would they come home to Amsterdam sometime in the future? What would become of the little ones with Cousin Vroutje and what kind of lives would their own children have? Did Gilles have so much money put aside that he could even half seriously consider the wanton extravagance of moving them or did he intend to leave his family behind in Amsterdam as sailors and soldiers did?

Elsje didn't know the answers to any of these questions. She sighed and as she saw the steam of her breath in the air, she realized now that she was still just standing stupidly at the open front door, letting all of the cold air in, although Gilles had already gone on into his day. She closed the upper door and latched it as she wondered how many more mornings there would be like this one in the years to come. Would Gilles be constantly drinking away his unhappiness as she looked on, a spectator to her husband's life and misery? As she thought about the future, she suddenly had a vision of herself becoming very old at the inn, a gray old woman, her spine twisted with arthritis, bending over a large cooking pot, never having had even a single day off to venture as far as the next town to see what it might be like, how it might be similar or how it might be different from her city. For a brief moment she felt that she understood Gilles but then the feeling evaporated and was gone from her. Why couldn't he just *share* her life and all of the good things they had here? Why couldn't he be satisfied with things the way they were?

A movement outside the window caught her eye and Elsje saw smoke in a wind gust being blown back down to the ground from the chimney next door. A storm would be coming in off the sea soon. It might be best to go out to the market early today, *before* the cold rains started. Elsje put her shoes down on the floor and slipped them on. They were like blocks of ice pressed up against the soles of her feet. She could scarcely feel her toes as they were *already* numb with the cold in spite of the heavy woolen stockings that she always slept in during the wintertime. Back in the kitchen she threw off the blanket and replaced it with her long scarf and heavy wool-lined cloak. Reaching into the pewter mug on the shelf where she kept the kitchen money, she pulled out five guilders and stuffed them into the cloak's pocket. Elsje cut herself a slice of bread from the loaf Gilles had left out on the table, breaking off a moldy blue-green edge and tossing it into the fireplace. She didn't bother putting away the knife and the bread as she always did, just today deciding that she would leave them out. She would be back before very long. Grabbing up her market basket, she turned toward the door again, thinking momentarily about hurrying to catch up with Gilles, to inform him that Jean Durie had acted inappropriately toward her, which *was* partially true. Gilles would certainly have to defend and comfort his wife if she confessed such a thing to him.

If she said nothing *at all* to Gilles though, in time Elsje might be able to forget about the way Jean Durie had kissed her and the way he had touched her.

There were no other witnesses. If Jean *did* say anything to Gilles, Elsje might deny that there had ever been any impropriety between them at all. She might just insist that Jean had an overactive imagination. Such an assertion, if she could convince Gilles of it, would avoid trouble with her husband as well as with the authorities, although it would make Jean Durie look like a madman and probably put an end to the family's long friendship with him. Surely Jean wouldn't bring trouble down on himself and Elsje, too, just to ease a troubled conscience. In fact, maybe there was nothing to tell Gilles about at all. Maybe the incident was just something trivial that had passed swiftly between them, an insignificant occurrence that had already been completely forgotten by Jean Durie.

Elsje didn't even remember having left the house or closing the door behind her but she found herself walking up the street with her shopping basket. Her feet took her in the direction of the square and not toward Ste Germaine's. She nibbled on the slice of bread she brought with her even though she wasn't conscious of being hungry; she had only brought the bread with her to ease the pain in her stomach. The food was all right in her mouth but she found that when she tried to swallow, she just didn't feel like it. When she finally did move the food down her throat with a conscious effort, she developed hiccups, painful spasms that would not stop. She suppressed them as best she could as she walked on.

Elsje turned to walk by the ships, just to go somewhere different today and to have a little extra time to think. They must have heard her hiccups because some rough-looking sailors looked up from their work and called out to her, making crude noises and remarks to each other that were meant to be loud enough for her to hear. She remembered now that she had left the house without her overdress on and she wondered if the men had observed this and took her for a drunken prostitute finishing up a long night of working and drinking. She pulled her cloak more tightly around her as she walked on. It was insulting but it was also just a *little* bit amusing too, that they would act this way toward her when she was *so* large with her coming child. Elsje suddenly realized then that they would probably *not* be able to see much of her expanding shape under the heavy cloak. Was she suddenly so attractive to all men now, to loose sailors and to Jean Durie and to every other man on the face of the earth? This was an extraordinary thought for Elsje to be having, although it occurred to her now that it must have been a familiar one to her sister Tryntje every day, an integral part of her sister's flirtatious and glamorous makeup, her every day reality. It was Tryntje who was the pretty one, and Elsje was not accustomed to being cast in this role.

One battered and patched old ship was tied up at the dock and many people were gathered on the upper deck this morning, whole families, and although Elsje couldn't identify the language they spoke, there was no mistaking the chattering excitement as well as the tension in the air as they prepared to leave the port for a new life somewhere else, just as soon as the tide came in. Perhaps they were Puritans going back to England or up the river into the hinterlands of the German states. The ship looked far too small and too dilapidated to safely make it across any great expanse of ocean. Two young children played at one couple's feet and Elsje watched as the man pulled his wife over to him and then kissed her. She tried to remove her eyes from them but found that she could not: They surely couldn't know at this moment what their future held, prosperity or death, but it was obvious to anyone who observed them that they had their hope and reassurance in each other. Elsje smiled at this and kept walking.

The wharfs were growing more active as the day advanced on Amsterdam and the night retreated. A slave crew made up entirely of Wilden men unloaded hogsheads of tobacco that had been ferried over on a launch from the New Belgium vessel anchored in the outer harbor. Their master leaned against a piling and lazily snapped a small whip at them in rhythmic time. All of the savages, to a man, appeared to be quite sick with something, coughing and spitting constantly as they tried to keep going to avoid a taste of the overseer's whip. Elsje pulled the neck of her cloak up to shield the lower part of her face as she wondered what sickness it was that they had, what the land was like where the dark men had been born, and what their everyday lives had comprised before they were taken into slavery, before they were taken sick. If they had any way of knowing what the future held for them, they might have taken more opportunity for pleasure in their past or perhaps they might have chosen death over slavery and life itself.

The master must not have been Dutch because slaves were not usually treated so badly here: They were an expensive commodity and like a good horse, they were an investment that was usually well-maintained, occasionally better than some of the family members. If food was in short supply, a horse or a slave was *needed* to keep a farm or a business going, but a little hunger was not such a bad thing for a man or his wife to endure. Elsje looked at the taskmaster and decided that he was probably trying to get the cargo shipment offloaded before the crew died, before he had to buy or hire any more men to finish the job.

She walked on, passing a hurrying sailor with long, brightly colored red, yellow, and blue feathers in his hat. Where did the bird live who *gave* those feathers? Were there many such birds there? Were there as many as there were pigeons here, all flying around in great colorful flocks searching for food in some other strange and distant city?

It was so early that most of the vendors were not at their stalls in the Dam yet and the merchants who were wealthy enough to own the shops that stood side by side, ringing the square, certainly had no urgency to open up, at least not for a few more hours. Wrapped in dirty ragged blankets, a few of the street merchants ignored the local ordinance and slept on the ground next to their covered stands and some other empty tables waited patiently for their proprietors to return from wherever they had gone for the night. Only a handful of the traders had already arrived at their little businesses this morning to set out their goods and their wares. There was nothing edible out yct, mostly just wooden shoes, tools, woolen goods, and kitchen utensils. One man unloaded farm implements from a dog cart as the two great furry beasts sat patiently waiting for their master to finish.

Elsje took in more this morning than she had taken notice of in the past ten years. Knowing that he had grown up in the countryside far from the city markets, she could see why the Dam would be such a draw, such a fascination to Gilles. The walk in the morning air had calmed her fears for the moment but as the sky turned slowly from ink to azure, she knew that it was time for her to get back to where she was needed, back to sort out all of the business of the day at the inn. Her personal difficulties with her husband and with Jean Durie would simply have to wait until after the inn's problems were solved.

Elsje heard the sound of a mill working in the distance. The grinding and thumping sound clearly carried over to her across the water this morning and because of this, she was now certain that rain would be coming soon, although it was early yet and there was not the usual noisy clamor of commerce to drown out the distant noise. Without any sustained wind besides occasional small gusts to move the long and heavy arms of the windmills, the mill must be working with the help of oxen this morning. It did seem to be very slow and rhythmic, a resting heartbeat resounding through the body of the Netherlands.

Flour!

She almost forgot that she had to get some more flour for baking today since she had used the last of it, except for some starter, to make dumplings for the soup yesterday. There would not be any bread for tomorrow's meals either, if she didn't get the flour and start the bread today. It would have been a terrible oversight on her part to run out of the *one* thing she needed for every meal but there was no time to stop for it right now; she would have to send Tryntje out for the flour later. Elsje only took one more minute, one for herself, to stop at the churchyard and say a quick prayer over her mother's grave. She asked God and her mother for help with Gilles, hoping that between them, the departed woman and the deity could intervene to help their earthbound daughter with her marital difficulties; it couldn't hurt to ask.

Often Elsje wished that she might have remembered more about her mother but sometimes that was a *good* thing: Since she couldn't recall very much, Elsje could imagine her mother in any way that she pleased, even remembering her differently at different times, sternly telling Elsje what she should do, being light-hearted, young and playful, or very old and very, very wise. Elsje told her mother that she would come back for another visit very soon and then she scurried back along the return path to the inn.

She arrived at home to find blazing fires in the hearths of both the dining room and the kitchen, something that was usually her job, and her father sitting at the kitchen table bouncing a wailing Bruinje on his knee as one of the two hired kitchen girls worked around him, starting the midday meal preparations for the patrons. Tryntje was nowhere in sight, of course.

"We didn't know where you went and his teeth are bothering him again! What was *so* important that you left so early? You didn't start the fires and you don't even have anything in your basket!" Hendrick fired accusations at Elsje above the noise of Bruinje's sobs.

"He slept well enough through the night and I thought he'd sleep *later* than this. You could have given him some bread crust or a bit of wet cloth to chew on," Elsje retorted, pulling over what was left of the bread and getting a block of cheese from the cupboard. She wondered angrily why not a *single* other person in the household had thought yet to do this *simple* thing for poor Bruinje. Hendrick grumbled loudly that the boy was virtually *an orphan* with a father who was always off drinking and a mother who never took proper care of him.

Elsje took off her cloak and hung it up, telling herself as she did so, *not* to reply to her father; it would only start trouble, but Hendrick shook his head and frowned at her, obviously an unspoken comment on the disgraceful and indecent state of her undress.

Tryntje came down the stairs to the kitchen at last, rubbing her eyes and yawning, sleepily walking over to the kitchen table.

"Go and see if we have customers in the dining room, I thought I just heard someone come in," Elsje urged her sister. "I need to slice what is left of this bread and then get dressed."

"They can wait for a few minutes," Tryntje mumbled as she picked up a piece of the sliced bread and sauntered over to the fire, turning around to warm her backside.

"Do I have to do *everything* here?" Elsje screamed, throwing the bread knife down on the table and striding back into the dining room, ignoring her father's calls after her that she wasn't properly dressed. She didn't care. She had just about had enough of *everything* already this morning, and that included her father.

As it turned out, there was no one in the dining room. It had only been the sound of a chunk of peat falling, settling into the fireplace grate. Elsje suppressed the overwhelming urge that she had to scream out loud in frustration, the calmness that she had gained from her morning walk already having dissipated into the atmosphere like overcharged air before an approaching thunderstorm, but instead of opening her mouth, she clenched her fists, digging her fingernails into her palms. She took several deep breaths to calm herself before she returned to the kitchen.

One of the girls, certainly not Tryntje who was still munching on the bread and rubbing her backside before the fire, had filled a pitcher of ale from one of the corner kegs and brought in the morning's milk from the cow along with some eggs. Elsje grabbed the last of Tryntje's bread from her sister's hands, threw it into the fire, shoved her sister toward the table, and ordered her to start cooking the eggs as Elsje poured a mug of ale for herself to settle her stomach. Ignoring her father's disapproving glare, Elsje drank it down in three gulps. She also poured a glass for Bruinje this morning to ease the pain of his teething but Bruinje was in such a bad temper, kicking, screaming and crying, that Elsje left it on the far side of the table where he wouldn't knock it over. She did dip a cloth in the ale but when Bruinje refused to take it from her, she threw it down on the table in front of her howling son. She needed to get the cooking going now or it wouldn't be done in time for her early customers who *surely* would be walking in at any moment now. She didn't have the time to pick Bruinje up now; he would simply have to recover his temperament on his own.

Hendrick responded to the tumult by removing himself to the dining room and Elsje swore once again, as she had every single day for the previous three weeks that *this* would be the day she hired a girl to watch Bruinje so she could get all of her work done. Her father might complain about the expense, but hiring some street child to watch Bruinje would be cheap enough, just *stuivers* a day, and Elsje accomplished very little when she had to spend most of her time with Bruinje on her hip or trying to keep him out of the fire. Already this morning Elsje was *so* tired that her overwhelming inclination was to just sit down and cry, and this before the morning sun had fully cleared the horizon yet.

Even though Friday nights before the Saturday market were usually busier, the cold rain that started in the afternoon hurt business at the inn, keeping away all but the regular drinking customers and just a few others who only sought a sheltered place to sleep for the night. It was still very early in the spring, though, not late summer or early fall when the bulk of the crops came in and the market was overflowing with produce as well as with customers. Hendrick, Tryntje, and Bruinje were in bed asleep and the kitchen help had left hours earlier but Elsje stayed downstairs reorganizing the cooking utensils and dishes while she waited for Gilles to come home. The fears that had nearly overwhelmed her early that morning returned with nightfall's darkness and she worried just a little that he might not come home at all. She moved quickly away from those thoughts though, back to her project, and told herself that *of course* he would be late; Msr. Ste Germaine's establishment was *always* very busy these days, even on stormy nights. She rearranged another cupboard and reminded herself that it was still early yet; it only felt much later because of the dark and rainy night and because business had been so slow all day. Elsje thought fleetingly of the embracing couple she had seen on the ship this morning, wondered where they were now and if all was well with them tonight.

She had just about convinced herself that her worries about her husband were unfounded but she was still relieved, and even jumped a little at the sound, when she finally heard Gilles' step at the front door. He was soaked from the rain, through his cloak and his clothes right down to his skin but he had not been drinking, at least not as far as Elsje could detect. He did not seem greatly different in spirit tonight either, so Elsje supposed that Jean Durie had not said anything to him today, good or bad. Elsje told Gilles to spread his cloak over the chair before the fire so it might have a chance to dry out a little before he put it back on again in the morning. Closing the door to the last cupboard that she had been working on, she took up the lamp and followed her husband up the stairs, holding the lamp high so he could see the steps in front of him. She waited patiently until after he had changed into a dry shirt and climbed into bed; only then did she speak to him and say what was on her mind.

"Husband, let's talk."

"About what?"

Gilles knew it was coming, he just hadn't known *when*. She hadn't said anything to him yet about drinking on his day off and his not taking Bruinje. A few minutes earlier, he had been surprised to find her still awake and in what *seemed* to be a good mood, but he should have known that Elsje would not forget about his little excursion the day before. Here it was, a lecture at the very least, possibly a full-fledged fight if he wasn't quick enough with the apologies and the promises. He *hated* it when she started these things so late at night: He didn't feel like arguing with her and truly, *all* he wanted was sleep when he returned home from very long days at Msr. Ste Germaine's.

"The Palatinate. If you *really* want to go, I will go with you," Elsje said.

Her statement took him aback and Gilles made sure that his ears had heard correctly before he smiled and shook his head, not believing the veracity of his hearing. He closed his eyes and didn't say a word in reply: It was obviously some kind of a trap.

"Talk to me!" Elsje exclaimed impatiently.

Gilles' eyes were closed but he still knew what she was doing. She was standing there the way she always did, with her hands on her hips, her eyes glaring down at him.

"What? I'm *tired*, Elsje. We can play tomorrow," he mumbled.

"I mean it!" Elsje walked over to the armoire, pulled all of their clothes out, and threw them into a heap on the floor, *his* clothes first and then her dresses on the top of the pile.

"You have gone mad," Gilles said in a calm voice, after he rolled over and opened one eye to see what she was doing. He had detected not even a soupcon of insanity in her *before* tonight; bad temper, yes, but not insanity.

"I am *not* mad. I am perfectly serious. Where will we go and what will we do there? *You* are the husband, the head of the family. You just tell me and we will do it."

She had a set to her jaw that seemed like anger, or determination at the very least, and Gilles couldn't tell if she was about to lose her temper or not, but he didn't want to risk it this late at night. He had to get up in the morning and it had already been a late night. All he wanted right now was his own warm bed so of course he was going to say whatever was needed to make her happy.

"All right, we will go up the river through the German states and become farmers, live that life without working late into the night and dealing with belligerent drunks who urinate and vomit everywhere and on everything. It will be hard work from sunrise to sunset but after that, our time will be our own and our profits will be ours to keep."

Gilles took one more look at the pile of clothes and then looked back at her to see if Elsje had her objections to his proposal all ready and lined up for him.

"All right then, when will we leave?" she asked instead, calmly taking her cap off and setting it on the stand next to the washbowl, apparently having decided that it would do for another day's wearing before she washed it out.

"Tomorrow. I'll just tell Ste Germaine that I'm leaving. You can put our things into a seaman's chest and we'll be gone on the next ship going in that direction."

Gilles rolled over onto his back on the pillows, looking up at the flickering shadows from the lamp as they rolled in waves across the ceiling. This fantasy was beginning to be somewhat entertaining.

"That's not practical. I need to give instructions to Tryntje, tell my father and cousin Vroutje, get some supplies, as well as pack, and we need to secure passage on a ship; they don't go up there every day, you know. A week should be about right."

She pulled off her overdress and threw it on the top of the pile of clothes before she took her hair pins out, shook her hair loose and started to brush it. Gilles was afraid to say anything more and he couldn't think of anything to say anyway, so he just watched her until she was through brushing her hair and tying it back up into her night cap. She blew out the lamp before she walked over in the dark and sat down on the edge of the bed. Gilles heard her leave her shoes where she left them every night, where she would step into them right away in the morning. She lowered herself down onto the pillow next to Gilles and tucked her feet in under the covers.

"I'll have to explain to the little ones at Vroutje's and I wonder where I can find a good woman to help me have the baby there..." Elsje's voice continued as if there had been no break in her conversation at all.

Gilles snorted. "It's *almost* as if you were serious."

"I am *quite* serious. You arrange for the trip and talk to Msr. Ste Germaine; I will make the other arrangements. I have never left Amsterdam before but I can find someone who might help me plan, perhaps Mevrouw Van Tassel who has done some traveling. Do you bring all of your pots and pans with you or do you buy them there? What about your horse at Msr. Ste Germaine's country house?"

Gilles rolled up on his elbow in the dark. "*Don't* tease me, Elsje. If you say to me *one* more time that we are going, I will hold you to it."

"We will go and live our lives there if that is *really* what you want, or we will stay here, be happy, and talk *no more* of idle wishes, Gilles," Elsje replied firmly.

"I *know* people there, Elsje. I'm *good* at farming and I know a *lot* about vineyards. Could you stand to have a husband who has dirty hands and nails all the time and smells of sweat and manure?" Gilles could hear the eager tone in his own voice and he hated the sound of it: It was *too* much like begging.

Elsje sniffed in derision. "Hard working men have *never* bothered me. *You* are the one who is so concerned over not having your hair curled every week and the latest fashion in hats."

Both of them stared up toward the dark ceiling in silence for a time, planning and dreaming, thinking both of the good things that might happen as well as the bad, but both of them had secret wishes that a new life might fulfill and both of them had things that they wanted very much to leave behind, although neither one dared to share those thoughts yet with the other.

"Would you do that for *me*?" Gilles asked after a few minutes, in a voice softer than any Elsje had ever heard him use before. "Are you still awake?"

"I'm awake. Only for you, Gilles," she replied.

He slipped his arm beneath her and pulled her over to him. "Come over here and warm me up, then. I'm still chilled to my bones from the rain."

The next morning Gilles woke early and rolled over to Elsje again, starting a perfect day in the perfect way. Afterwards he kissed her all over her face and when he was assured that she was in a good mood, he pinned her down and tickled her for good measure. In spite of her queasy stomach, Elsje laughed until she scolded him, saying that by now she would certainly have customers waiting for her downstairs and *he* would be late for Msr. Ste Germaine's this morning if he didn't get going.

"Does it matter now?" Gilles asked with a grin before he kissed her loudly on both cheeks and then her lips.

Elsje sighed with contentment. She was almost looking forward to moving, now that a final decision had been made, but she *still* couldn't rid herself of the fear that accompanied their decision. She didn't know how she could leave her father and the inn, or even how she would *tell* Hendrick that she was going. How could she just leave her home, her city, her life, and everything that she had ever known? Her father depended on her so much!

There were just too many questions; she *hated* all the unanswered questions. Elsje always liked having all the answers, all the time. Maybe she *was* crazy to go along with her husband's wild ideas.

Gilles whispered in her ear, "It will be good, you'll see. We'll be happy, the four of us!"

He didn't stay in bed this morning though; he kissed and patted Elsje's stomach before he rolled right over her and out of the bed, landing on his feet on the floor like a cat. He danced across the room with a spring in his step that Elsje hadn't seen for a very, very, long time, across to the pile of clothes she had left on the floor the night before and he dug down through them to find his clothes for work today. Elsje pulled herself out of bed too, put her shoes and overdress on and started down the stairs to start the morning fires up before Gilles had finished dressing. She was still walking along in this odd dream, even if she *was* headed to the most familiar place in the world to her, the hearth in her kitchen. Surely when she died her ghost would remain here from habitude, tending the fire, as so many hours of her life had already been spent in doing it. After raking up the red coals hiding in the gray ashes of the previous night's fire, she started a new blaze by feeding a small, dry piece of kindling to the hungry embers, then nurtured the little flames with larger and larger pieces of wood as the fire grew in size and warmth. Gilles came down the stairs at last, now in clean clothes, straightening his sleeves and his doublet before he picked up his still-damp casaque from the chair and threw it over his shoulders.

"Take some bread with you, Gilles," Elsje urged him. "I need to finish the old loaf up."

"I'm not hungry just now; I'll get something when I get there," Gilles said and he kissed her goodbye.

Elsje didn't stay behind in the kitchen this morning though, as she usually did when they woke up together. She walked him to the front door and Gilles kissed her again, a *real* kiss goodbye that they both lingered over.

"Elsje, it *will* be good for us," Gilles said again, kissing her on both cheeks and then playfully swatting her derriere as he turned and left for his work.

Judging from all the stars left behind in the dark night sky, now fading to light in the east, the spring day looked like it was going to be bright and clear after the hard rains of the day and the night before. With the promise of a glorious red sunrise that was just beginning, Elsje hoped that it was God himself who was out there giving his colorful blessing to their plans. After she closed the door and walked back into the kitchen, she sliced the last of the old bread, buttering one slice and taking a few bites, which her stomach accepted grudgingly, before she checked the fire again. It was coming along nicely now and was just about ready for a pot of water.

They had promised each other that they would do it, that they would make the move to the Palatinate but promises meant naught if nothing was ever done about it. The first step had to be taken now and then another step to set the changes into motion, to end the inertia. Elsje left her half-eaten bread on the table and marched up the stairs, ignoring the gravity that pulled at her heavy stomach with each step on the way up and the tightening sensation she had in her belly when she finally reached the top. She remembered feeling this sensation before, when she was pregnant with Bruinje, as if someone tightened a corset around her, not really uncomfortable, just peculiarly associated with pregnancy. She didn't stop to take stock of her senses or to wonder at the cause of it as she sometimes did, but forged on through the tightness in her midsection to sweep open the curtains around Tryntje's bed and shake her sleeping sister to consciousness. Elsje would pull her out by the feet, if necessary, as she used to do when Tryntje was a child and would not wake up.

"Opstaan, Tryntje! Opstaan! We have much to do today!"

"You seem terribly happy this morning. Have you declared a truce with your husband?" Hendrick called over to her.

Elsje's father sat on the edge of his bed across the room, running his hands through his thinning gray hair as he did in the mornings, a fast and squirrel-like substitute for any more prolonged grooming. *"Just in the same way the rats do..."* Gilles had teased Elsje once about her father's morning habits.

"We were never at war," Elsje replied, "but we *have* decided that we are moving to the Palatinate."

It just came out of her mouth. Well, it was done now. There would be no more worrying about how to break the news diplomatically.

"Don't be *stupid*. Only your crazy husband could think up something like that," Hendrick replied. "Doesn't he know that they have been at war for twenty five years, that all that is left up there is a pile of rubble along the river, and that they survive only by eating their own recently deceased?"

Elsje bit down on her lip and said nothing in reply but made a mental note to herself that the comments from her father were just *one more* good reason for them to leave Amsterdam. The continuing battle between the two men was too taxing for her, even when she *wasn't* pregnant. She didn't have the energy for the additional peacekeeping work that was required all of the time.

Tryntje said nothing at all, trying very hard to avoid being pulled into the family fight and perhaps becoming her father's next target. Finding no more battles to be fought here, the old man said no more, turned and went down the stairs, still grumbling incoherently to himself, probably about Gilles. Elsje put her father out of her mind and pushed ahead with her own agenda for the day.

"We have *much* to do, Tryntje. Gilles and I plan to leave within the week. I will tell you everything that you will need to do every day and you will have to have everyone help you as much as ever they possibly can. It will be up to you to take care of Father and the inn."

For the first time in Elsje's memory, Tryntje had no ready retort, no sarcastic reply ready for her older sister. In silence, Tryntje put on her overdress, put her hair up under her cap and compliantly followed Elsje down the stairs.

Perhaps Tryntje thought that Elsje had lost her mind too, or maybe she believed that Elsje would tell her more as long as she didn't *ask* any more; questioning her older sister too often elicited only acerbic replies from Elsje.

Gilles and Elsje were unable to leave within the week due to the many requisite preparations that used up the time very quickly. Gilles ordered five chests to be constructed by the timmerman for shipping their belongings. He didn't know what specifications he needed so he told the craftsman to just make them the way all of the other voyagers ordered them, with the exception of one that was to have a secret locking drawer in it. The containers were delivered to the house and then hauled up to the living quarters, one by one, using a rope that was threaded around the large pulley that was located on the outside wall just above the top floor. Each one of the chests was maneuvered inside through the open windows that had only been opened rarely in the past few years, during unusually warm spells in the summer months.

Hendrick worried that the device had not been maintained and that the pulley and rope might not support the weight of even a *single* empty chest although they had, within the past few years, been able to bring up the clothes wardrobe that Gilles insisted on buying for his, and of course Elsje's, clothing. Several of the inn's patrons took their mugs of bier outside the first floor tavern and watched the proceedings with great interest; a few had even placed wagers as to whether the rope would hold the chests or give way, sending the new chests crashing to pieces on the paving stones below. The ropes and pulleys held though, and the winner of the bets, a red-faced man with a very large and bulbous nose, promptly spent all of his winnings on another round of drinks for everyone.

The trunks stood open next to the wall in the main room, wedged in between the dining table and the sleeping area, their fragrant new wood smell on the inside and the wax and oil finish on the outside reminding everyone every day that change was literally in the air. Hendrick observed acidly to Elsje, in front of Gilles of course, that no one that *he* knew needed *five* chests for *anything* and it was a great waste of good money but Elsje found that she had more possessions than she realized and her few dresses took up far more room than she would have believed possible. The chests were packed with clothes, dishes, linens and farm implements, then they were unpacked and repacked as priorities shifted and changed, as news of what they would need to bring along with them reached their ears, and as new ideas occurred to them. Elsje asked Gilles for money to buy some new linens, trenchers and other wooden dishes, utensils, and necessities since she did not want to take things from her father's household. She wasn't sure if she would be able to buy anything they needed once they arrived there, so she spent a little time each day out shopping for these necessities, and much more time worrying over what she had already bought or would need to buy before they left.

Elsje set aside one of the new chests to leave behind, to pack up things that they would not take with them right away, things that they would send for later when they were more settled into their new home. The first item packed in the Amsterdam chest was Jean Durie's vase, the wedding gift. It had been a beautiful sentiment at the time and it *still* was, but Elsje didn't want to think of Jean Durie now, not for a while anyway. She owed it to Gilles and her marriage to put Jean out of her mind and to make a fresh start with her husband. Satisfied that this was the best course of action, not to leave it behind completely *or* to take it with her, she would leave fate to decide if the pretty little Italian vase was to make it out to them later in one piece or not. Elsje looked around to see what else might be packed away to make more room in the little apartment for her father and sister.

When Gilles had first moved in with them after the wedding, Elsje had given Gilles one of the family's old chests to keep his clothes in. She couldn't have known at the time that her husband would have so many clothes or that the big wardrobe he had ordered that seemed like such a frivolity at the time would be necessary to keep all of *his* clothing inside. Elsje's family had never owned anything like it and they were all fascinated with the drawers on one side and the wooden pegs to hang their clothes up on the other. There were many pegs, and it held many outfits but Gilles assured Elsje that there were plenty of families in the world who owned more than one of these pieces to hold all of their clothing, frequently one entire wardrobe for *each* member of the family. Hendrick had acidly asked Gilles if anyone *besides* royalty owned them and to Gilles' credit, he had not returned verbal fire, not even after the old man had declared that it was something good Christian people *didn't* need. A few of Gilles' unused and nearly forgotten things had been left in the battered old chest after the arrival of the great wardrobe, things that had probably not seen the light of day since just after their wedding. The old trunk hadn't been opened at all in some months now and its primary use was as a table to place the lamp on at night while they undressed. Elsje undertook to sort through Gilles' belongings for him during the afternoon lull in business since he probably was not going to get the chance to complete this task before they left.

Although they had been married for some time now, she had never gone through his things before and it felt a little strange, even though the chest was a familiar one that had been in Elsje's family for many years. Elsje felt like she was going through a stranger's things, perhaps as a thief or the legatee of a deceased loved one would, even though she told herself that it was a silly sentiment to have: They were her *husband's* things, sitting there in her family's trunk, in her own bedroom, in her own house. She had cleaned his underwear, slept next to him and had intimate relations with him, so it was ridiculous for her to be self-conscious about performing this task.

There was a stale, musty smell, of old sweat perhaps, and she hoped that everything hadn't gotten damp with black mildew spots on the lighter items.

Not that it mattered very much now, beyond simply rotting the material: Gilles wore mainly dark clothing, except for his white shirts, and the objects that he had stored in the chest probably couldn't rot. She hadn't set eyes on it in quite some time and now she admired Gilles' wampum belt that lay on the top of the pile. She held it up to the window's light and ran her hand over the fine purple and white beaded designs, feeling the rough coldness of it. It *was* beautiful and it *would* have been nice to take it along with them, but every inch of space and every pound of provision was critical so they could not drag everything with them, not this time. Elsje carried it over to the "for storage and shipment later" trunk, and folding the heavy shell weaving end over end around itself, she set it down carefully next to Jean Durie's vase.

Dress clothes and the fine clothes that Gilles wore to work at Ste Germaine's would not be needed and would be left behind for now, too, with the exception of one outfit for each of them for church, but the strange-looking garments from Gilles' other life, the ones that he had worn after he escaped France and lived in a stable for a time, would be *very* useful as farm clothes. Elsje held them up and looked at the strange cut and style and the unusual dark wool fabric. The fine stitches were much better than any she had ever managed to master and now Elsje thought about her sister. Tryntje had long ago become the seamstress in the family, making all of their clothes for them, except those that Cousin Vroutje made for the younger children. Perhaps Elsje hadn't given Tryntje enough credit over the years for her contributions to the household; Tryntje *did* do all of the sewing, laundry, and a good deal of the cleaning, too. Elsje would miss her sister and her skills, and now she wondered how she would manage in a strange new place without Tryntje's help in the new land, especially with the new baby coming. Elsje also wondered how her sister would do here when she was on her own.

Elsje puzzled over the brown robe that looked almost like a Catholic priest's robe to her, but not being at all familiar with such things as they were unknown in Amsterdam, she decided that it was just some ugly type of cloak in a style that had once been popular among the gentry in France, a cloak that was no longer in fashion.

Gilles and his obsession with clothing! He was *every bit* as bad as Tryntje! It was made of wool though, and it looked warm, so Elsje put it in the trunk to take with them: Warmth was warmth, and ugly or not, they might need it there if the winters were bitterly cold. An unwashed stain on the front looked like blood but Elsje assured herself that it was not that; it was probably wine or some kind of food. If it wouldn't wash out, the garment could be cut it up into pieces for new clothing or at the very least, serve them well as a blanket.

As she lifted the wool robe out, her eyes fell on the rosary that lay underneath the fabric. She was taken aback by the sight of it. Gingerly she touched it and then picked it up, holding it as if it would burn her fingers or cry out of its own accord at the touch of a Protestant. She had heard of such things but had never actually *seen* one, let alone put her hand on one. She had never talked with Gilles very much about what had been in his life before he came to Amsterdam and he had never volunteered anything about it, even when she commented on the merits or shortcomings of a particular sermon on their way home from church, on her mother's place in the afterlife, on her childhood memories, or even when she sometimes thoughtlessly made disparaging comments about the Catholic Spaniards that still occupied her country, the soldiers who were occasionally seen lounging on the street corners of Amsterdam, looking for some mischief to engage in to pass their deployment time. Now Elsje felt almost betrayed, like she had been living with a deceitful stranger. Gilles was her husband though, and she didn't like feeling this way about him, so she pushed these thoughts, as quickly as she could, far away, into the back of her mind.

Elsje edged around her discomfort, trying to think back, to remember what he had said to her when she tried sharing her feelings on the subject with him occasionally. He had not said much of *anything* to her. His reply had been mainly silence, as she supposed all men responded to such conversation. She had to wonder at this moment if she was going off alone into the wilderness with an idol-worshiper, one that she had not only shared a bed with but also one for whom she had born a child and was now about to bear another.

She didn't like the uneasy feeling that came over her now and the discomfort of these thoughts was too much for her to tolerate, even for a few moments. Elsje decided then and there that the horrible beaded thing that she held in her hand no longer had anything to do with Gilles; it was simply some old family memento or keepsake belonging to the distant past, an antique of the same genre as the rusted old sword of his grandfather's that Hendrick kept under his bed, a relic from some distant ancestor that had escaped its own time and traveled into the future like an unwanted old relative that was going to outlive everyone, a missive from the days and times when men were uncivilized, when there had been hand to hand fighting in the bloodstained streets of old Amsterdam. As such, this small religious relic, as welcome in her house as the grisly old bones or ancient gray hair of a long-deceased saint, most certainly was no longer needed.

For just a few moments she was greatly tempted, but she decided finally *not* to throw it out with the rest of the trash down the privy hole. She would leave it behind in the box of items to be sent for later and let Gilles deal with it then. Elsje just hoped that her father would not take it upon himself to go through the chest while they were gone as she could just imagine what his reaction would be and what he would have to say about it. She had never mentioned it to Gilles before, but the Catholics had killed Hendrick's grandparents, both of them on one terrible day before Elsje was born. Maybe she could ask Gilles to have a lock installed on the chest and close it up before they left, but would Gilles want to know the reason *why* she would request such a thing? The prayer beads were very like the things the Arab people held in their hands as they walked around the Dam, obscenely fingering the beads, rolling them around, mumbling prayers, the Bedouins always in search of their god in a place where Elsje was very sure that He *wasn't* to be found. She slid the beads in between the folds of one of Gilles' old white shirts and put both items away in the chest to be left behind. It was *almost* as if she had never laid eyes on the thing.

A long and sharp knife, a weapon that she had never seen before, was in the bottom of the chest. It had an Amsterdam maker's mark at the base of the handle but the clean condition of it proved that it had not been used for anything by her husband recently; perhaps all it had ever been used for was slicing apples after a purchase in the market. Elsje decided that it was probably something that appealed to young men, a souvenir of sorts, and that it might be useful for *something* if they brought it with them, trimming apple trees or something else. Although there might be bears, boars and other wild beasts there, the weapon would probably not be very useful against such creatures if they were to attack at close quarters. As farmers living among other good God-fearing and law abiding people, far removed from the miseries of "civilized" Europe, they would probably not have any need of it at all, just as long as they built good strong fences. She would ask Gilles later if he wanted to take it with them.

Elsje would certainly take her precious spice box with her though; she would not leave that behind and she wondered what kinds of things she would be cooking there. Vegetables, of course, and she *had* heard that there was a plentiful supply of salmon in the Rijn River. Would they have any lamb, pork, or beef there? She hoped so, but she didn't know. Perhaps they ate goat! She had never tasted any, but had heard that it was a delicacy in the less civilized places in the world. Elsje would put the spice box in last, just before they left, so that it would be on the top and ready for her to use in her cooking once they got there.

Elsje's thoughts returned to her sister. Perhaps putting Tryntje in full charge of the inn would settle her down. Maybe it would be a *good* thing for her. A husband like Gilles might be found for her in the next few years, one who did not object to his wife working at the inn. Tryntje was too young to marry right now, not yet being twenty five years of age. Pieter Stuyvesant had not been around the inn lately, having been far away in the Brazil Colonies, the Orange Tree Colonies, far to the south of New Amsterdam across the ocean, but since there were no women at all there, unless one counted the female animals or the savages that inhabited that wild place, he would still be a good marriage prospect in a few years if he did not steadfastly *insist* on having a wife of higher social status than Tryntje, one who could further his own political ambitions. After all, Stuyvesant was fast becoming an old man and he had not yet taken a wife. It could work out very well if Tryntje turned out to be his choice: Pieter Stuyvesant could continue his career in the colonies and Tryntje could stay safely behind in Amsterdam running the inn. From a distance, Tryntje could probably put up with his sour moods and demanding temperament, especially if she only saw him once every few years.

There were several Dutch India Company men, both from the WIC, the Westindische Compagnie, and the VOC, the Verenighde Oostindische Compagnie, who frequented Hendrick's inn regularly and it was obvious to Elsje that they had been coming in as much for Tryntje's friendly company as they had for the food and drink. Elsje knew, as her father did, that these men were *not* good marriage prospects. They had plenty of money and very good futures ahead of them, but they did not come into the taverns looking for *wives*. If they considered marriage at all, they looked for more cultured and cultivated showpieces to improve their connections and future prospects in the company organizations. Elsje had decided long ago that this reality was just as well: These women would *only* have their husband's undivided attention and affection for as long as their youthful looks, family money, and influential company contacts lasted. Tryntje would have to make her own decisions without her big sister around to advise her. Elsje had tried to mother all of her siblings, but as close as they could be at times, Tryntje had never wanted to hear what Elsje had to say, dismissing her older sister's opinions as insignificant. Tryntje probably believed that Elsje knew nothing about the world outside but maybe that was about to change.

Elsje rechecked the items in the chests nearly every day. She went about her daily work in a state of disbelief, knowing somewhere in the back of her mind that she would be leaving the city soon, but not really assimilating the belief in this reality yet. Her pregnancies had been like that, a sort of denial that a living child would soon join their family, a tiny individual with a mind of its own arriving into their midst via the strange distension and distortion of her stomach. In an interesting way though, having children had *opened* Elsje's mind and given to her a heretofore missing belief in future possibilities. She supposed that most other people, especially the dreamer that she had taken for a husband, already had this capacity that she lacked, this ability to envision the future as different, perhaps even better, and so she was more than a little surprised when she asked Gilles halfway through the week if he had given his notice yet to Msr. Ste Germaine and he told her that he had not. Elsje expected that he would have already told *everyone* that he knew, if only to collect on the free round of drinks that would surely follow the announcement of such news.

Gilles told Jean Durie the news on Thursday when he stopped in on his day off with Bruinje to visit with his friend.

"Which is the best ship to take?" Gilles asked. "Is there a best captain?"

"You are *serious*? You *can't* go, Gilles, whatever the difficulty at home is, you must *not* leave her! You must *stay* and work out your difficulties with Elsje."

"But Elsje is going with me, of course!"

"Ah," Jean said, calming down a little, "*Of course* she is. This is true, then? I would *never* have expected her to ever willingly leave her father or the inn."

Gilles saw the uncomfortable look on Jean's face before he got up and poked at the smoking log in the fireplace that was threatening to extinguish itself.

"I know that you will miss me greatly, and I will miss you too, Jean, but I have been thinking about this for quite some time. I don't know why she is suddenly so agreeable, but I will take advantage of her change of heart and do it quickly before Elsje can change her mind."

"Well then, there is nothing for me to do except to wish you *bonne chance* and a good future but are you *sure* that you want to do this, Gilles? Elsje has one small child and another one on the way." Jean nodded in the direction of Bruinje who was now attempting to climb to the top of a tall leather-upholstered chair across the room. "You aren't a lone pioneer, only risking your own life. It's very hard for women and children and many of them don't survive. Shouldn't you wait until *after* she has had the baby, leaving them here in safety until you get settled there?"

"I won't be the only one with my family there, Jean," Gilles grinned at him.

"Non, I suppose not, but life there is not in *any* way easy. The country has been nearly destroyed by war and there are all kinds of hazards there."

"And I am safe *here*? The French mercenaries still prowl the city with the Spaniards and even if there was *not* a price on my head, with the plague coming as often as the soldiers, the countryside seems *by far* a safer place for us than Amsterdam."

"Yes, well, that may be true in our *particular* case," Jean admitted. "You *would* be leaving a good position with Ste Germaine, though. You would *never* find another as good."

"A gilded cage it is! Non, I *must* work for myself. I have come to that conclusion."

"Gilles, there is something else that you may not have considered: They don't tolerate Papists in some of those settlements as readily as they do here. You would have to be *very, very,* careful to follow *all* of their ways. A slip of the tongue could make things *very* uncomfortable, even dangerous for you."

Gilles had expected Jean to be a little sad that they were leaving but he had *not* expected such a complete lack of support. There were not even any congratulations extended from his best friend. He held his tongue though, and let Jean finish what he had to say. Living with Hendrick these past few years had at least taught Gilles the virtues and occasional benefits of patience.

"The new child will not need a priest?" Jean asked, nodding his head in Bruinje's direction again. "For baptism?"

"Non," Gilles answered immediately, although a small part of him was not completely convinced. "I'm no longer a Catholic, you can ask The Church about that."

"Gilles, even though the Church would not claim you, you may forever be a part of that Church in the eyes of *others*, even if you renounce it publicly and embrace a new church. There are those that believe baptism to be an irrevocable contract, as the Marranos escaping the inquisition in Spain well know."

"I guess I'll have to find out for myself then," Gilles replied.

"I blame the *English* and their putting up with their insane King Henry for this entire debacle! After all, if it had not been for his excessive appetites when it came to women and his complete lack of self-control and discretion, *none* of us would be in this mess today! Imagine being forced under threat of beheading to switch from being Catholic one day to Anglican the next, then back to Catholic and then Protestant *again*, all in the space of one generation! That generation must have been at the very least, greatly confused, and it left the survivors of that time and place without *any* moral compass whatsoever. It's no wonder the Puritans were able to shut down all the theaters and even after these hundred years since the bloated old ox died, the world continues faith-based torture and killings! It might not have turned out *quite* so badly if he hadn't married his brother's Spanish Catholic widow and then divorced and deposed her."

Jean shuffled through some papers on his desk, apparently looking for some particular item. His usually tidy office space was filling up with work and he was busier than he had ever been before. He moved two ledger books to the side, nearly upsetting a bottle of ink and continued to sift through a new pile, cursing softly in French under his breath.

Gilles had opened his mouth to reply, but knowing that no one would know more about religious intolerance than Jean with his mixed parentage and difficult heritage, Jean who had suffered at *everyone's* hands, Gilles shut it again without addressing this particular issue. He took a breath before he attempted to steer the conversation in another direction.

"Well, enough pontificating!" Jean declared, speaking again before Gilles had the opportunity. "You *know* all this, I'm sure. Each country deals with the issue in their *own* way, Spain and France reinforcing Catholicism by force, England in essence doing the same thing, supporting Protestantism, and the Netherlands and the Rhineland trying to ignore the whole mess. Just watch what you say around your neighbors."

"Are you saying that you think I should *not* go?" Gilles asked.

He attempted to control his voice but he was growing irritable with Jean. He was beginning to think that he should *not* have told anyone, Jean included, until just before they boarded the ship to leave.

"Not at all! If that is what you *truly* want to do," Jean said with an expression of satisfaction on his face as he held up the document that he had been seeking for the past few minutes. "I'm simply telling you to be very careful and to make *as few enemies as possible*. What did Ste Germaine say when you told him?" Jean asked. "I'll wager a bottle of cognac that he *wasn't* pleased."

"I haven't told Ste Germaine yet. I will tell him soon." Gilles squirmed at the question.

Jean looked up at him. "I would hope *so*! He has come to rely on you and it will be difficult for him to replace you, especially on short notice. So you haven't booked passage yet?"

"Well, as I said, I don't know which captain is best," Gilles said.

Jean set down his paper. "You haven't told Ste Germaine and you haven't booked passage. Are you *really* going or is this just some wild idea, some *possibility* in the distant future? I misunderstood you to say that you were going *soon*."

"We really *are* going soon," Gilles said with determination in his voice but he felt foolish now that Jean had pointed out this discrepancy between his words and his actions.

"If you *are* serious, and I have to wonder if you really are, Gilles, I can book a passage for you for next Monday. I am handling some of the accounting for that particular venture and I happen to know that they have some room left for a few more people that could be had at a *very* good price, or at least they did a few days ago. Now I ask you, should I do this for you or not? Take some time to *seriously* consider this move. Another ship will go at another time if you want to wait. The country will *probably* still be there next year." With a more kindly expression on his face Jean concluded, "I sense hesitation in you now, and the Gilles that I know would not hesitate for a *moment* to do something that he truly wanted to do. And of course I *will* miss you, all of you, very much if you go."

"I would be grateful if you could get us on the ship, Jean."

It took Gilles some effort to say it: He was irritated that Jean did not take him seriously, but he was also more than a little annoyed with himself.

Jean was right, of course: If any other man had told Gilles the foolish things that he had just been telling Jean, that he was leaving civilization soon but had not told his employer, had not booked passage, had not done much of *anything* to realize this objective, then he would have laughed out loud or suffered from the effort not to do so. Gilles had wanted to go to the German frontier for a very long time and yet there was something inside that him held back, something that grabbed at his heels and slowed his steps in that direction. He could not explain this irrationality because he had no idea what it might be; whatever it was that slowed his progress, the revelation of the thing would not come to him, not in the logical determinations or soul searching of the day, nor in the dreams and expansive intuitions, the knowledge of all things known and unknown, that sometimes came to Gilles suddenly in the middle of the night. He still wanted to go and it made sense for him to do it if he wished to be a farmer and a vintner, but as it happened sometimes in the course of his dreams, his feet would not take the action to obey the wishes of his heart.

Perhaps it was simply that he had started to settle down, that he had become *so* comfortable in Amsterdam or set in his ways that it was hard to muster the willpower and initiate the momentum to leave. Possibly it was some character defect that he had been born with, or a lack of resolve after his ordeal in France, his being too tired all the time, or simply a lazy acceptance of the passable life that he had made for himself here, even though Gilles did not want to admit to any of these things. He sincerely hoped that he still had the force of will to go forward to new places, to reclaim the fortune that he swore he would recoup after fate had taken it away from him. It was time now for Gilles to take the leap of faith, to do it *before* he was an old man, before he had a dozen children and was unable to uproot them all to take a single great chance on a new and better life. He wasn't going to be like the other sheep in the world; Gilles believed to the depths of his soul that he was born to be a land *owner*, not a tenant farmer or a tradesman and he hoped he would never be satisfied enough to drop this aspiration.

Jean spoke softly when he spoke again. "Eh bien, Gilles, perhaps it *is* a divine hand that guides you to do the right thing at the right time, or perhaps momentary insanity that has overtaken you for the moment. Either way, I wish you the very best of luck but promise me one thing: Promise me that you will take very good care of Elsje, and that you will talk to her. She needs you much more than you know."

"Of course, we take care of each other," Gilles replied, happy that Jean had asked nothing more difficult from him and wondering why his friend bothered wasting his breath to ask.

"And another thing Gilles: buy *plenty* of wooden shoes. Leather is no good there; it will only rot with the work in the fields, even with plenty of goose grease."

Gilles grinned at this bit of advice but Jean was serious about this, too.

"I wanted to ask you something else, Jean.

"What is that, Gilles?"

"I was hoping that you could take over the Amsterdam fur trade business for me. Keep half of my share for your trouble. It's all been set into place but I don't know who else I could trust it to."

"What about Hendrick?"

"He's the only other partner for the moment but I can't rely on him to work out any problems. He just doesn't have our background or perspective."

"I can do that for you, Gilles but when and how will I get your profits to you?"

"I won't need any for at least a year. I'll get in contact with you if and when I need it; otherwise, invest anything I earn with the West India Company."

"All right, I'd be happy to do that for you."

Gilles picked up Bruinje from the leather chair that the boy had been repeatedly climbing up and sliding down on before he made an excuse about more errands that he had to do, but in truth, Gilles just wanted to be alone with his thoughts now. Maybe he had only come to get Jean's blessing anyway, and feeling that he had secured it, although in a half-hearted kind of way, Gilles had everything that he needed in order to follow his heart and leave Amsterdam. Gilles had only one thought in mind as he left Jean's: that things had been set into motion and now there was no turning back.

He would tell Elsje about the date being set, tell Ste Germaine that he was leaving, and then he would have no choice but to follow through. Their future path was set out before them and Gilles would reject failure from this point on, only accepting success in his life.

He felt a little shaky and just wished that Jean had been *a little* more encouraging, a little more enthusiastic.

Jean had not said anything further as Gilles took his leave. He just sat there looking into the fire with his elbows propped up on the desk, his hands folded in front of his chin, perhaps pondering some accounting problem; no doubt Jean was feeling some sadness too, with his best friend leaving Amsterdam soon, and knowing that they might never see each other again.

As he returned to the inn, Gilles bolstered his courage and resolve by reviewing the list of reasons why they were going. He remembered all of the usual ones that he had been reciting for months and then he thought of his home in France, how it had been the center of social as well as business gatherings, the big parties and the small ones. Gilles hadn't realized until this moment how much he hated the cramped little table upstairs in Hendrick's tiny third floor apartment; he didn't dare to invite anyone to his home for a quiet dinner away from the crowds downstairs in the tavern room, even if there *had* been anyone there to cook for them and serve Gilles and his guests a real dinner. Elsje was forever busy cooking for the rabble, the masses coming in the door looking for anything warm to fill their bellies, just as long as it accompanied some ale or bier. It was not in any sense *Gilles'* house: It was Hendrick's house, and everyone there was always busy running Hendrick's business. Although it was true that Gilles would be leaving behind the very people that he wanted to invite, he still wanted to live in his own house and have something that was more his, something other than the crowded and miserable quarters that was and always had been the abode of Hendrick's family.

Non, he was *sure* that he was doing the right thing. He needed to make the move for his sanity, even if it meant moving halfway across civilization for it. He needed to be his own employer, to farm and have vineyards and horses again, to be out of the city and away from the beggars and the open sewers, to breathe fresh air during the day. He needed a way to get his wife out of the tavern business and on to the sole and much more important business of being his wife. He also needed French people around him and around his son so that the child would grow up knowing the language and the ways of the French, not those of the Netherlanders. Gilles' list grew longer and his reassurances to himself firmer as he turned the final corner to home and he was at last smiling in absolute certainty of the decision he had made when he walked through the door of the inn with Bruinje clinging to Gilles' neck, riding astride his back. Elsje was clearing the last table from midday dinner and only a few patrons were left drinking ale at the other tables. It might have been something in Gilles' face that made her stand up and look expectantly at him as she straightened her cap.

"We have a sailing date," he said to her. She smiled a broad, if somewhat nervous, smile back at her husband. They were really going.

Cousin Vroutje tried to talk them out of it. Gilles thought he might see Elsje cry for the first time while she was breaking the news to the three little ones. Her younger brother and two sisters had lived with cousin Vroutje ever since the death of Elsje's mother, but Elsje had seen them every Sunday when they went to church together and then gathered together at Hendrick's table for Sabbath dinner. She promised them that she would come back to visit Amsterdam someday and eventually she was going to send for them to come and live with her. Elsje assured them that she would need a lot of help with the chores, caring for the new baby, cooking, sewing and working alongside Gilles in the fields. Hendrick might have wanted his young son, thirteen year old Heintje, to stay in Amsterdam so he could eventually take over management of the family inn but Vroutje insisted that Heintje was still a few years too young for that. The boy was not too young to help Gilles farm for a few years first, though.

With a definite departure date now, Gilles had worked up his courage to tell Ste Germaine that he was leaving. It was an uncomfortable moment even though Gilles told Ste Germaine of his gratitude for all that his employer had done for him before he broke the news and Gilles emphasized that he needed to do this for himself and not because of anything Ste Germaine had done or had not done. Ste Germaine at first tried to dissuade Gilles from leaving by offering him a better title and more money but in the end he, too, understood that Gilles had made up his mind and that there was nothing he could say to change it. He wished Gilles well in an obligatory sort of way, and told Gilles that his old position would always be open for him at any time in the future if things did not work out as hoped in the German state.

Gilles had the distinct feeling that his employer was expecting him back in a few weeks, especially when he asked Ste Germaine's permission to sell the horse that had been a wedding gift to him. Ste Germaine told Gilles that he would be happy to *loan* him any money he needed and keep his horse for him until Gilles returned. Gilles decided that he didn't really need any money from Ste Germaine and so he just thanked him for stabling the animal.

Everyone at the inn was still awake when Gilles returned that night as it had been a very late night at both Ste Germaine's and the inn. Hendrick was just sending the last drunk out the door when Gilles walked in, wanting to tell Elsje the news. Gilles pulled Elsje over to him, kissed her, and said in a low voice in her ear, "It is done. I told him."

"Ah, *another* drunk with a yearning for my beautiful daughter," Hendrick said to Gilles as he passed by him on his way up the stairs.

Gilles let his anger toward Hendrick drain away tonight. He let it go with the knowledge that he would be leaving next Monday and after that, Hendrick would be just a bad memory. It was likely that Gilles would never see the old man again. Someday news would reach them of Hendrick's death as they lived their new lives far away on the banks of the Rhine. Of course Elsje would cry when she got the news, Gilles would console her, and that would be the end of it. Hendrick had no power to ruin their plans or their future now. It would all be *so* much better when Gilles got Elsje away from here and at last they would have the life that they should have had from the very beginning of their marriage. Elsje would no longer be a barmaid, only Gilles' wife, and he would be the man of the house, with his word carrying the full weight of his authority. His children would learn the French language and the French ways, growing up in the beautiful wine country on the river and when the time came, Gilles' children would marry French spouses and someday they too would own great tracts of land. These thoughts warmed Gilles inside like a freshly-poured cup of India tea.

Elsje seemed to be happy about the decision now, too, and her morning sickness was becoming less severe, either because of the ginger tea that one of the Dutch East India wives had recommended, or maybe because her pregnancy had progressed to where it was not bothering her quite as much. Ale still bothered her stomach though, and Gilles was in *such* good spirits that he joked with her that it must be a *girl* child she carried who cared nothing for any drink stronger than milk or weak tea. No matter, when they moved to the Palatinate, they would *all* drink the good wine that would be plentiful there and it would improve everyone's health, Elsje's included.

It still did not seem quite real to Gilles as they set off through the morning mists for the docks on the following Monday morning, at the appointed boarding time that Jean Durie had given them. It seemed rather late in the day to be starting out on the journey but that was all right; it took some time to get everyone together even though they had been making preparations for weeks. Cousin Vroutje accompanied them with the little ones, teary-eyed, holding a lace handkerchief to her nose with her right hand while keeping a firm grasp on little Corretje with her left one. Jennetje, having just turned sixteen and nearly as tall as Vroutje now, had a similar iron grip around Heintje's wrist as she walked a few steps behind Vroutje and Corretje.

Hendrick had refused to come at all, saying that *someone* needed to watch the inn, presumably since Elsje had abandoned it, and had muttered under his breath something to the effect that they would be back on the next ship *anyway* when they saw what kind of hell it was that they were walking into there. Elsje had pleaded with her father that she did not want to part in this way. Visits back would be infrequent, if they happened at all, and with his advanced age, Gilles knew she was thinking that she might never see her father again. She had initially screamed at Hendrick and scolded him, but in the end, she had simply kissed his cheek and said, "I will miss you, Father."

Hendrick coolly wiped the kiss off his cheek with his hand and went back to the bowl of walnuts that he had been cracking with a small wooden mallet on his table in the dining room. The two kitchen girls who had insisted that they could handle all of the business this morning wished Elsje a loving goodbye and waved farewell to her and Gilles at the front door of the inn.

Tryntje was more than eager for *any* opportunity to leave her work, especially to accompany the entourage to the docks. She couldn't contain her pleasure at their parting, since she would no longer have Elsje around to tell her what to do and how to do it. Tryntje wore a dress that Elsje felt was inappropriate for daily wear, in fact, rather inappropriate for wearing out in public at all. Judging by their comments and calls to her, Tryntje's revealing outfit was greatly relished by the majority of the sailors and workmen they passed on the streets on their way to the docks. Elsje even stopped once to pull her sister's neckline up higher and to scold her, much to one sailor's amusement. Tryntje's response though, was only a smirk at her sister. She let Elsje win this last battle that they would ever fight and realizing the emptiness of this small victory no doubt annoyed Elsje much more than anything else Tryntje could have said or done.

On their way to the ship, they saw Claes Martenszen, the nephew of Jacob Van Zeelandt, the Jewish man whose stable Gilles had worked in when he first came to live in Amsterdam. Having come far from his days of hanging around the waterfront with the pickpockets and thieves, Claes had now become quite respectable, mingling with the more sophisticated brigands of the West India Company. He had ingratiated himself with his betters and was now entrusted with a good deal of responsibility which was quite surprising considering his humble beginnings. Although he had gained the respect of many men in Amsterdam, Gilles still did not trust him. After the robbery attempt on an earlier business trip to Amsterdam, before he sought refuge here, Gilles had been beaten until he was unconscious and his thoughts had been muddled for a time afterwards. He couldn't be *absolutely* certain, but Gilles remained convinced that it was Claes' face that he had seen in the alleyway just before everything went dark. Now that they were leaving the city, Gilles supposed that his suspicions about Claes no longer mattered.

"What are you doing, still hanging around the docks?" Gilles needled him. "Don't you have any work to do?"

"I do," Claes replied. "It's boring work, waiting for a ship to come in so I can deliver my message and take possession of some cargo, but it *is* honest work and the pay's not too bad. There was no work at all, none that paid enough to live on anyway, in Oud-Vossemeer where I'm from. I *won't* go back there although I'm not sure if I want to stay in Amsterdam, either."

"Maybe you'll go to New Amsterdam. There are opportunities there," Gilles suggested.

"Maybe," Claes replied politely, but he didn't appear to be

enthusiastic about the suggestion. "Just as long as we go forward with certainty and faith that things will work out."

"Yes, that's true," Gilles agreed, casting a glance at Claes' ring with the cross on it. Gilles wondered if it was Claes' recent conversion to Christianity and his newly-found faith that had taken him to these places so far from where a man born into the Jewish faith might *reasonably* have been expected to go in his lifetime. "Take care of yourself then, and good luck to you, Claes," Gilles said.

"Dank u," Claes said, "and Gilles, I never thanked you for, well, for introducing me to the *right* people." Claes offered Gilles his hand and there was nothing weak or uncertain in the hearty hand shake that followed.

"It was nothing," Gilles replied and it was the truth that he spoke: It had been Claes who had made his *own* way and made his own future.

"You're not going too, are you Jennetje?" Claes asked Elsje's younger sister.

The girl blushed and stammered, "Nee, I'm staying here." She had a shy smile for him.

"Well, have a good life then, Gilles, since I may never see you again."

"Probably not," Gilles replied. "You have a good life as well, Claes."

Jean Durie joined the group at the docks with a basket full of salted meat, dried fruits, Spanish figs, apples, and wine for the trip. He embraced Gilles, kissing him on both cheeks before he turned to embrace and kiss Elsje too. "Take care of yourself and our Gilles," he said.

"I will," she replied, giving him a smile to accompany her good-bye kiss.

Final embraces and kisses were exchanged all around and Elsje made her way uncertainly up the plank, hitching her skirts up and trying to watch each one of her steps although the size of her stomach made it difficult for her to see her feet, and her greatly increased weight made her uncharacteristically clumsy. Gilles was next, balancing Bruinje on one side and a bundle of clothes on the other. Elsje had insisted on bringing the changes of clothing on board in addition to the full chests that had been hoisted up onto the ship. Bruinje was too fascinated with all that went on to be very much trouble at all today.

The morning mists were not heavy this morning but they were not lifting either, even with the breeze picking up slightly and quietly swirling the cold, damp air around them. Gilles' spirits were lifting though, as they paused on the deck to wave good-bye to the small group still gathered in the mists just beyond the walkway below them.

The little ship had been in port for a whole day now, with most of the passengers who had started their journey before Amsterdam continuing on with them. The majority of the travelers had stayed on board the vessel as there were few that could afford the luxury of getting off the boat and taking a room in the city for the night. All of the passengers and crew were now accounted for and they had already taken on supplies to feed and water the passengers and sailors. A few new travelers from Amsterdam joined the others who had originated with the ship, somewhere in France.

Gilles had taken this opportunity of the layover time in port to look the ship over. He couldn't talk his way on board before she sailed although he tried, the crew perhaps being suspicious that he would attempt to stow away, but he could make a few observations and inferences about the vessel: She was barely two decks, an upper and a lower, and no more than fifty tons at the outside, a cobbled together wreck of an old ship that might have been originally built to carry three dozen French soldiers between outposts or just munitions from port to port, or maybe she had even begun her life as a very small trader, hauling goods up and down the French coast or local rivers. Now that her better days, her more glorious days, were far behind her and now that she appeared to have more tar than wood left on her sides, Gilles noted that the previous name of the ship had been clumsily painted over and now the newly named *Edelweiss* carried only Protestant cargo, back and forth, up and down the Rhine river, although during the present time in history, it was a lot more forth than it was back.

He said nothing aloud to his crew, but the French captain on the deck of the small ship eyed Gilles' party with interest. The Frenchman was to be expected, many of them having already fled Amsterdam after discovering that there was just *too much* freedom here and that they would rather be back among their own kind where they lived more by tradition's boundaries and society's prescribed behaviors than by their own inexact judgment, escaping from the moral snares of the overly-tolerant Dutch flatlanders. The Frenchman's wife was obviously a Netherlander, though, and that was a little bit of a surprise. Although unions between the French and Dutch were not completely unheard of, it was unexpected considering what the captain knew about this *particular* Frenchman. Generally the French were not inclined to take wives here unless the women were very rich widows and the men were very lonely. The Dutch women were too often saucy, much too freethinking and overly independent, all of them. The term "strong-willed" didn't even *begin* to describe this breed of women, at least insofar as the French men were concerned.

The captain had already given Jean Durie his word that he would take them, on the condition that they were the last to board, just before sailing time. If he had been given more time to think about it, Captain Durret might not have agreed to take them on his vessel at all, knowing that there was probably a very substantial reward offered for the young man by the French King. He had surmised this, although it was not stated, but he believed that it was probably so for a man like Jean Durie to take an interest in securing passage for someone. These days it was nearly impossible to tell who was a fugitive and who was not, and the sorely-needed money for the ship's repairs that Jean Durie had pressed into his hand the week before had sealed the bargain, locking Durret into the agreement unless he wanted word to circulate among every person who had anything at all to do with the sea or the river, that he was an untrustworthy pirate of a captain who went back on his word and took money without delivering on a bargain.

The captain was not a greatly religious man, except sometimes when there were exceptionally rough waters, and he was generally sympathetic to the Reformees who all seemed to be harmless enough; he was to this one as well, especially when he saw how young Msr. Jansen was and that he had a sweet young pregnant wife and a small child. It would be the best course of action to stay as far away from the young man as possible, feign ignorance if anyone questioned him, quickly put as much distance as fast as he could between his ship and the port of Amsterdam, and hope for the best. The captain nodded to Gilles in greeting from the deck.

"Jansen."

"Captain," Gilles answered him.

The captain looked out to the little group that had come to wish them *bon voyage* and he made a small motion of acknowledgement to Jean Durie, more of a salute, really, than a greeting, and Jean Durie nodded his head in the captain's direction.

Gilles observed none of this though: He was busy worrying that with all of the new things Elsje had bought, the captain would refuse to take the extra weight on board but either the captain did not notice the excess baggage or more likely, he was concerned with other matters, for he gave no sign that he objected to the four trunks. It was not until a few days later that Gilles would notice their wealth of goods and that no one else on board had as much, not even the two very *large* families with a dozen children each.

As soon as Gilles' family was on board, and even as they made their way over to the hatchway, the planks were pulled up, the lines were brought in, and one sail was let out, just to get them moving off in the right direction, as one very strong sailor manned the tiller. It was a very slow and delicate process, making their way safely between all of the other ships, with so many vessels being packed in *so* tightly together in the harbor that there was no chance at all of gaining any speed without risking a collision. The last thing Gilles saw as they were shepherded across the deck toward the hold was a pitiful view of Cousin Vroutje alternately wiping her eyes and her nose and scolding the two younger children.

"Tryntje is so young!" Elsje called over her shoulder to Gilles as she led the way. "However will she manage?"

Gilles patted her on the back. "She has the servants and your father. She *knows* how to run the inn: You showed her how. They will be all right."

"I hope she remembers to clean up well after Father today. The nutshells make such a mess and will attract the mice and rats if she doesn't get them all up."

Elsje hesitated slightly at the top of the steps, turning back toward her family and with a final wave, which they probably couldn't see from their vantage point, she bid them goodbye before she started down the hatch. Gilles descended with Bruinje after her, into the darkness and the smell of old fish and unwashed humans. It was much worse than Gilles had expected but he forged on behind Elsje. In the dim light below Gilles could make out narrow bunks, more like shelves than beds, lining the walls of the little boat. There were still three empty berths and they chose one of them for themselves. A grandmotherly woman with gray hair looked Elsje over and leaned over from her bunk next to theirs.

"Bonjour, bienvenue!" she addressed Elsje.

Elsje smiled as Gilles replied for his wife, "Merci! My wife doesn't speak much French."

"I hadn't thought about *that*! We will all have to speak *French* now!" Elsje whispered to Gilles with panic evident on her face, even in the darkness of the hold. "How *will* I manage?"

"You know enough to get by. All you need to know *now* are the words for laundry, cooking, and husband, anyway."

Gilles tried to reassure her with teasing and a smile. His attempt at good humor was lost though, in a sudden wave of nausea that swept over Elsje just then.

"I need…some air," Elsje panted and she began to gasp for breath.

"Can you go over by the ladder and get some?" he asked her.

The smell *was* overwhelming, even for a man with a good strong stomach who was *used* to the worst the seafaring trade could offer in the way of endurance tests. It was the smell of dead fish, old chamber pots, rotting food, sweaty bodies and perhaps a whiff of some previous livestock cargo. Gilles had nearly forgotten about the smell in the holds of ships and he hadn't thought to mention it to Elsje.

"I need… more!" she cried as she fled from their berth toward the light and the air.

Elsje ran to the stairs, leaving Bruinje behind with Gilles. Gilles scooped up his son and followed his wife back up onto the deck. She dashed to the rail behind the capstan and by panting and swallowing in quick succession she managed to retain the contents of her stomach.

"Hey! What are you doing up here?" the tiller man cried out.

225

"One moment, please! My wife is sick!" Gilles said.

"*So?* Go below, out of the way and get sick there!" he shouted back.

"ONE moment!" Gilles snarled at him. "Are you all right?" Gilles asked Elsje.

"Do I *look* all right?" Elsje snapped at him between breaths. She did calm herself a little but then Bruinje began to kick and scream for Gilles to put him down.

"Passengers aren't *allowed* up on the decks! Get below *now!*" the sailor shouted again.

Gilles wondered if Elsje was going to be sick for the entire trip. That possibility had *never* occurred to him. She couldn't stay here by the rail for the entire journey.

"Where are our things?" Elsje asked Gilles. Her face had taken on more of a white tinge than a green one and Gilles could not decide if it was a change for the better or the worse.

"I left them downstairs. I was concerned about you," he replied with some effort as he tightened his grip on a whining and kicking Bruinje.

"Never mind *me*, do something useful! Watch our son and our things!"

"All passengers must go below," the captain affirmed. He had seen and heard the exchange and walked the short length of the deck over to them.

"Please, can my wife stay here?" Gilles asked. "She'll stay out of the way."

"*She* can stay for a very short time if she needs to, if she stays clear, but *you* must go below." The captain wasn't going to let the man stay on deck, plainly visible to all passing eyes.

"Go on, Gilles. I will be better soon," Elsje urged him. She turned away from him, back to the rail, but her face was turning pinker now. That she could be angry and think of their belongings was a *good* sign to Gilles. Seeing that she was not in the way and that they would probably not trouble her if he took Bruinje away and went back down below, Gilles decided to return beneath the main deck, at least for a time.

"I'll be back to check on you," he assured Elsje before he left her there.

Gilles dragged Bruinje back down the stairs and his eyes had to adjust all over again to the dark hold. The crude series of low bunks, perhaps two dozen in all, was a clumsy attempt at a minimum standard of comfort, put together by carpenters who were hopefully more skilled at fashioning masts and spars than they were furniture. These wooden attempts at passenger comfort had been affixed to the walls using the guidelines of a few old gun ports, mostly patched over with mismatched wood and then tarred shut. Beneath each bunk was just enough room for a few personal belongings. The gun ports spoke of a more exciting past, even if their original purpose had been mainly to dissuade the thieves that prowled the coastlines. Each family shared one bunk for a sleeping space although the berths looked like they were made for a single person, not an entire *family*. Once they were under way, leaving Amsterdam, members of the two large families spread out over the two extra bunks.

Gilles' trunks, along with the few others, a *very* few others, were set off to one side, over in the stern next to barrels of food stuffs, probably dried and salted fish along with what looked to Gilles like baled canvass that was covering some flax or other similar material that was going up the river. There were perhaps a dozen families and a few lone men, and as his eyes became accustomed to the dim light, Gilles saw a large patch on the other side of the boat that appeared to have been the result of a collision with something large and very solid, probably another ship that had been in better condition and was made of sturdier stuff than their own. He noted a pattern of wormholes near the waterline and the smell of the pitch and tallow that had been used to recently repair them. Gilles was a little concerned about the little ship sinking or capsizing; after all, they could die just as easily on a large river as they could in the ocean and this poor craft looked none too seaworthy. The older woman on the next bunk spoke to Gilles again.

"Does the boy want to sleep? He can share my space. There is only me here."

From the longing way that she looked at Bruinje, Gilles wondered if she might have some grandchildren somewhere, or had lost a child.

"Merci, but I think that sleep is the *last* thing on his mind. He wants to go and explore."

"He needs a toy! I may have something here for him."

The woman went through the belongings that were piled on her space with her and pulled out a ball of yarn. She pulled the strand going to the knitting needles between her hands and it separated with a pop.

"Comment t'appele tu?" she asked Bruinje as she handed him the ball of yarn.

Bruinje just smiled up at her.

"What is the boy's name?" the woman asked Gilles.

"We call him Bruinje," Gilles answered. He briefly considered telling the woman that his son's given name was *Gilles Jean* but by now it was a lost cause: Bruinje had only answered to his nickname for the longest time now.

"I'm Claire Montserrat."

"I'm pleased to meet you. I'm Gilles...uh, Jansen."

"It's a Neerlandais name, but you are not Neerlandais?" the woman pried.

"Non."

Gilles broke eye contact with her and he fastened his eyes on Bruinje. The less *anyone* knew about him and his past, the better, even if they *were* other refugees who might have a history similar to his own. His fervent hope was to put that part of his life behind him, so that neither he nor his wife and children would ever have to deal with greedy bounty hunters again and if he told no one his name or *anything* about his past, then there would be no one that he had to concern himself about. It no longer mattered who he had been once, anyway. As of today he was reborn; he was *Gilles Jansen*, German farmer and vintner.

Bruinje was fascinated by the texture of the fuzzy ball of yarn and immediately put it into his mouth. Elsje had never had any time to sit and knit. Every one of the scarves, hats and mittens that the family owned seemed to originate from Cousin Vroutje.

"The child is hungry and his mother cannot feed him any longer," the woman declared, "*and* she has another child on the way. How did *that* happen?" She looked suspiciously at Gilles.

Gilles was confused by her meaning at first but then he understood the accusation: Elsje must not have been able to nurse Bruinje properly or her current pregnancy would not have happened.

Gilles briefly considered telling the nosy woman that it happened in the *usual* way, starting with a kiss, and then their taking off their clothing. He held back a smile that the woman apparently took as embarrassment that his wife was *unable* to nurse the child for a sufficient period of time.

"There, there, it's all right," she soothed Gilles. "They aren't *always* sickly if they can't nurse long enough. *Sometimes* they grow up all right."

Her attempt at reassurance had the opposite effect on Gilles and he looked at his son with concern. Bruinje was a fine, fat, healthy toddler and the boy enjoyed food so much, *any* kind of adult food, that Gilles could not picture him as being anything *other* than healthy. He thought back to his son's Catholic baptism and Gilles thought that the blessing and the protection of the sacrament had succeeded in working the magic for which it had been intended.

As if reading Gilles' mind, the woman inquired further, "He *has* been properly baptized in The Church, yes?"

Gilles caught his tongue before he replied and then reminded himself that she was a *Reformee*, a Protestant. Gilles had heard somewhere that the Huguenots referred to *their* church in this way too, as the only true church, in the same way that the Catholics had *always* referred to theirs. With so many *Only One True Churches*, it was all too confusing. Jean had been right about that: Gilles would need to be very careful in his choice of words, in answering her and in any conversation from now on and he felt that he had to find some escape from the woman before he blurted out something that could be dangerous. In their new home he would keep to his own house and his own fields until he knew who he could trust, who he could relax with and who might become a friend of his.

"Mais oui!" Gilles replied and left it at that, although he *did* think of how much he would have *liked* to add, "…baptized in a couple of *different* churches."

The odd thought occurred to Gilles that even though he was back among French people, his own people, his wife who couldn't even speak their language would be more at home with them than he ever would be, due to the difference in their religious perspectives. Perhaps he *was* a secret Catholic.

Gilles didn't know anymore what he was: He no longer observed the sacraments or feast and fast days. He even ate meat on Fridays when it was available. The Catholic Church, his church and the church of his fathers all the way back to Roman times, had tried to burn him at the stake when he had committed *no* crimes against it, none at all. Gilles could no longer make sense of *any* of it so he chose to disregard it, not to think about it, just to try to get along with everyone, and to avoid the subject altogether.

"Does he speak French or Neerlandais? Parle-tu le Français?" the woman asked Bruinje.

"Can you watch him for me for a moment? I need to go and check on my wife. She's not feeling well. Have some of our food!"

Without waiting for any indication of assent, Gilles thrust Bruinje *and* the basket of goods from Jean Durie at her, relieved to get away from the woman and to get a break from Bruinje. How *did* Elsje stand it all day? It was one thing to take the child out around town and let him run around for a day but quite *another* thing to have him confined with you all day.

Claire looked delighted with both gifts and pulled Bruinje onto her lap. Bruinje looked like he was about to wail aloud at being separated from his father and being handed over to a stranger but Elsje had often enough enlisted the aid of Hendrick, the kitchen help, and even inn patrons to care for the boy so that now Bruinje's lip trembled for only a few seconds before he composed himself, curiously regarded his new caretaker with his wide blue eyes and then reached up to grab her black hair ribbon.

"Viens ici, mon petit! Que tu es *beau!*" she cooed. "You are such a *big* boy, too! Can you count yet? Can you say Maman ou Papa?"

Gilles found a much-improved Elsje at the rail when he reached her on the deck. They had cleared the outer harbor and were making for open water now.

"Where is Bruinje, Gilles?"

"He's fine, he's with the woman we met when we got on board. She's nice enough and won't harm the child, I'm sure. She's not a gypsy and besides, she *can't* steal him: there is too much water around us for her to escape with our child. She'll watch our things, too."

Elsje drew several more measured deep breaths before she said, "Go back to Bruinje, Gilles. I'll be back down there *soon*. I just couldn't take the smell."

She reached into the bag that hung from her belt by the purse strings and pulled out a dried oval slice of something that was pale yellow. She put it into her mouth.

"What *is* that?" Gilles asked.

"Dried ginger. Ginger tea would be much better but it will work this way too, I hope." She chewed thoughtfully and drew a lot of air into her mouth. "It's spicy," she told Gilles. "It's what I've been taking for the sickness. Now you go back down; I'll be all right. I'll join you very soon. I promise."

She smiled weakly at him.

Gilles made his way back down the steps for the third time, to find Claire singing children's songs to Bruinje and the other passengers listening to her intently, some even humming along with the sweet berceuse. Gilles smiled, believing that Bruinje had probably never heard any French children's songs before. Elsje hadn't even had much time to sing him *Dutch* lullabies, whatever *they* might be like. It was already a very good thing, living among these people.

"He doesn't speak much, does he?" Claire probed.

"His mind is all right," Gilles said defensively, "He's just more interested in what's going on than he is in *talking* about it."

A forgotten memory surfaced in Gilles' mind, of a time long ago when he and his friend Claude along with Robert LaGrange from the next estate, followed another young boy around. Their quarry was a deaf mute, the son of two of Gilles' father's servants, and the hunters delighted in sneaking up on him silently, as close as they could, and then throwing stones to see if they could hit him before he ran away. Pierre hit him right on the forehead one time and the injured boy let out a roar like a wounded animal. The deaf-mute boy had developed his other senses, though, senses *so* keen that he seemed to sense it whenever his attackers were nearby so the game was to see how close they could get to him before they started throwing the stones. Gilles' father had whipped him with a buggy whip, whipped him until his bottom bled right through his trousers when he discovered that his son had been bullying the boy, taking part in the torture.

Gilles' mother had been even *less* inclined to mercy but her remedy was not physical punishment: It was to patiently explain to Gilles that the boy was *also* a child of God's and as such, was not to be harmed, but protected. This lecture took place in her chamber, as all of her other lectures did, and it lasted the better part of an hour while eight year old Gilles had been forced to stand *perfectly* still. Even when he thought it was over, his mother insisted that Gilles go to his knees and beg for God's forgiveness, saying three Hail Marys aloud, slowly and clearly, while his mother worked on her embroidery. When Gilles *at last* thought that he was done, his mother informed him that he would come to her chamber for the next nine days to say Novenas *and* three Hail Marys on each day. Gilles was never allowed to play with Robert after that and he didn't see his friend Claude for a month, either. Gilles thought at the time that the punishment had been an overly harsh one, but it had made enough of an impression on him that Gilles never strayed into that behavioral territory again.

Gilles looked at his beautiful son and it pained him to think that this might be his son's future. There was nothing wrong with Bruinje's mind or hearing but why didn't he talk more?

Perhaps he only speaks with spirits, and not with people, Gilles thought angrily, remembering the name that the savage, Francois Pelletier, had given him and the peculiarly unenlightening and unsatisfactory explanation given by the aborigine's sire. Gilles tried to coax Bruinje back over to him but Bruinje crowed in protest and hung onto the yarn tightly.

"I'm not taking your yarn! You can keep it and come back to me!" Gilles said. Bruinje looked at his father briefly and then went back to putting the yarn in his mouth again.

"Stay there, then!" Gilles laughed.

Elsje was looking much better and even enjoying the sea air a little when Gilles climbed up onto the deck for the third time. Gilles took a moment to look around, taking in the expanse of open water and the sea air. He had not thought of it consciously before, but somewhere in the back of his mind, he must have given *some* thought to the river. Just beyond their final destination, if one continued upstream towards Switzerland, German territory came to an end on the western bank of the river and France began, was *so* close in fact, that one could almost taste it on the wind. Gilles' home city of Rouen was much further to the west so it was unlikely that Gilles would run into anyone he knew, unless it was someone in the Huguenot group, another fugitive like himself.

"You *love* this," Elsje accused him as the ship suddenly listed to one side. She just narrowly avoided being thrown from her feet as she grasped the rail firmly with both hands. "You love the boat *and* the water, you *even* love the traveling."

Gilles didn't try to deny it. "The air has a different smell and I want to see the people and the places on the shore as we pass by, all the birds and the schools of fish, too. A ship, any ship, no matter how simple, is home to me."

Elsje shook her head in disbelief. "I can see *plenty* of pigeons or starlings in Amsterdam anytime I want and the *only* fish I want to see are the good-tasting ones on my table, although I'm not so much in the mood for any of them today. I can't *wait* to feel the solid earth under my feet again and for all this motion and dizziness to *stop*! Will it be much like Amsterdam there?"

Gilles took a moment before he replied, gathering his thoughts and taking in what might be the last expanse of open water that he would ever see in his lifetime. He hoped that what he said might comfort his worried and ailing wife.

"I can't say exactly *what* it will be like, but I hear that Mannheim, across the river from the settlement, is a regular port of call. I know that we will *make* a good life together there."

He put one hand on top of hers and with the other hand he patted his pouch full of gold coins that, with luck, would be the magic seeds that would take root and mature into a great fortune someday. He had carefully calculated how much he would need, many times, and he was certain that they had money enough to buy a little land, get a farm and vineyards started, and survive for the first two years, even if there was very little income in the first year. They were assuredly far and away better prepared than anyone else on the ship, and possibly *more* prepared than anyone who had ever ventured up the river to live in the Palatinate. *Ah oui, money in the pocket gives a man a great deal of confidence in the future*, Gilles thought.

The journey up the river lasted for several weeks, even with favorable winds and tides and a modicum of good luck, but it took all of the captain's skill to avoid the many hazards lurking silently beneath the surface of the rolling waters, including sandbars in the middle and submerged tree carcasses at the perimeter of the river. The sailors, if they could be called such, grumbled constantly about the lack of wind and the excessive time that it was taking to reach their destination. Gilles saw them as little more than impatient farm boys steering a barge, even if the barge had square barque sails stuck on it. At times the young crew seemed to forget that people and not cattle were the cargo she carried. Gilles would have bet most of the money in his pouch, and quite safely too, that none of them had ever been on a ship out on the open sea; he could plainly see in just the few minutes that he spent with Elsje on the upper deck that even he knew more about the operation of the sails than most of the ship's mates. Elsje's sickness was gone for as long as she was in the fresh air but each time she returned below, her sickness came on again, although not as seriously as it had during the first few minutes of the first day. She stayed out of the crew's way and for their part, perhaps to avoid complaints from all of the other passengers if she was to be taken sick below and foul further the already-stale air, the sailors tolerated her presence on the deck while Bruinje spent much of his time with Claire who was a delightful grandmotherly companion to him. Claire stopped asking Gilles questions, probably because she never received any satisfactory answers, and just prattled on about herself. She was joining her daughter, son-in-law, and grandchildren in the Palatinate after the recent death of her husband, who had made her promise to sell all of their things and join her daughter when he was gone from the earth. She told Gilles that Bruinje brought to mind her youngest grandson whom she had never seen, although by now he would certainly be much bigger than Bruinje.

As Gilles stood on the deck with Elsje during one of his many trips up to check on her, the captain joined them and remarked that the land they passed now did not look very much like the Netherlands. Elsje agreed.

"There is ...difference," she said in her halting French. She spoke to Gilles in Nederlands. "There are forests and hills, the river banks are higher and there are fields and farms clinging to the sides of the mountains."

The captain understood enough of what she said.

"Oui, not just dikes, levees and tulipes everywhere!" he laughed. "Have you enjoyed seeing the great cliffs and the castles we have passed?"

After Gilles translated, Elsje said that she could not *avoid* seeing them and remarked that the great stone fortresses and the land crowded in on her, the overhanging hills loomed large over her, making her feel uncomfortable and more than a little anxious, although she couldn't say exactly *why* they made her feel this way.

Gilles was certain that she would get used to her beautiful new home in time. He looked over the spring green hills and remembered the sea of colorful flowers he had seen as they passed through the last of the Netherlands, the fields of bright early printemps flowers just starting to bloom. Waves of wind had rolled across the open meadows of the little islands and made wide patterns in the flowers as they bent over, first this way and then that, reversing course and miraculously bending over in a different direction each time without breaking the long, graceful stems in half. Gilles thought that if he just tried hard enough, he might be able to read a secret message in the flowers, written by God's hand with the wind, some divine pattern or sign that would tell him, in no uncertain terms, that what he was doing was the right thing. He was now the unquestioned authority, the head of the family and so he would not allow himself quarter for any open display of doubt but Gilles did understand that he had asked his wife to do an insane thing, to throw away a perfectly good life for the sake of going off to a great unknown, and unbelievably, she had agreed to do it, for him.

Gilles didn't worry so much about himself and what he would find there, but he worried about Elsje. He didn't know what he would do if she didn't start to feel better soon or if she wasn't happy in their new life. There would be much work to do and no Tryntje or kitchen help, no one there to take any of the burden from her if her health failed her, no one except for Gilles, and their new neighbors.

Every night the ship tied up at havens along the river, where the local authorities extorted heavy fees from the captain in exchange for declaring that it was secure from the river pirates, local highwaymen, and the navigational hazards scattered along the waterway. The ship took on fresh water and bread where any was available and when they were fortunate enough to find any. Gilles and Elsje took accommodations off the boat for the night, although Elsje didn't think any of these way houses merited the title of "inn". They were simple places where simple people lived, not so *very* different from where Elsje and her family lived, to Gilles' way of thinking. Mostly these places were only private homes that offered only the most basic of amenities to travelers. Gilles did not really want to spend the money on this small luxury even though the poor people of the region asked little enough in payment, but Elsje's stomach sickness and a hoarse cough that Bruinje had developed convinced Gilles that the minor expense would be money well spent to keep his family alive until they reached their new home. Gilles would have preferred to keep the money and sleep on the ship if he had been traveling alone but he wouldn't ask his wife and child to do this when he had the money in hand and they were not feeling well.

Although she protested to the contrary, Gilles knew that Elsje looked forward to these stops as she found the hosts' hospitality was more akin to what she had been used to in the Netherlands, at least more so than the strange food and nasal language of her French companions during the day. The other voyagers, having very little money if they had any at all, stayed on the ship at night, and if they were resentful of the Jansen family's better sleeping accommodations, they said nothing, although many of the children had developed the same cough that Bruinje had. Gilles told himself that he would make up for the loss in his funds later on, somehow. His sense of malaise increased daily as they went up the river, seeing no evidence of prosperity laid out before them, but Gilles continued to tell himself that it didn't matter: They were going to be farmers and would do well enough, no matter what their neighbor's fortunes.

Elsje despaired that they would *ever* arrive at their destination and she told Gilles that they seemed to be sailing forever deeper into the countryside, to the very ends of the earth, and she suspected they had already gone too far and would be nearing India soon. Not very long after she made the comment though, the captain called down the hatch to the passengers that the journey was nearly at an end and they would arrive at their destination before the sun went down. He instructed them to gather up all of their belongings and prepare for their arrival, informing them as well that they had arrived fifteen days *before* they thought they had, owing to the fact that they followed the *old* calendar in this part of the world and so were fifteen days behind the Netherlands.

Gilles had been keeping a tally of the passing days, making a knot each day in a small string he carried with him. He had been impatient to get there too, although he didn't tell Elsje that. He wondered how the captains and crews could keep their sanity, always gaining and then losing days, on top of all of their other concerns, water hazards and river bandits being chief among them. *But,* he reasoned, it probably didn't matter very much to the crew *what* the date was: It was always the same trip and the weather only mattered to the farmers on the riverbanks who worried, as Gilles did, that the planting season was rapidly coming to an end.

The little vessel had discharged a few passengers in towns and cities along the way, getting a little lighter, a little faster, but not very much less crowded with each passing day until the remnant of the original passengers, only the ones going on to the Huguenot settlement of Nouvelle Rochelle, were left on board. They sailed past the ruined port of Mannheim, laid out on the larboard side and quite visible from the top deck. Some of the passengers, upon hearing this news and not being satisfied with a limited view of it through the cracks by the old gun ports, tried to elbow their way up to the top of the stairs, pushing and jostling each other to get a glimpse of what would be the closest thing to a real town that existed near their final destination. Only a few were successful in seeing the full panorama of it, including Richard DeMare, being well over six feet tall and towering above all of the other passengers. It was probably the only time during the entire voyage that he had been able to stand fully upright without his head connecting painfully with the beams supporting the deck overhead and he was able to see well enough from the second step down from the top, generously calling down to the others below and describing what lay before him, the great fortifications that had not held back the invaders, the vestiges of great and tall buildings that were no longer habitable by men. The passengers murmured that they hoped to find flour to buy, seed and tools there, too, even though Gilles had to wonder if any of them even *had* the money to buy these things. Unlike the rest of the trip that had passed so slowly, the ruined river port passed by them far too quickly for anyone's satisfaction and so the voyeurs retreated below deck again to wait impatiently with everyone else. Georges LePard was so pleased with the advent of his better future, that he danced a galliard with his wife in the middle of the trunks and the bunks.

Untrained ears could not hear it, especially above the excited chatter of the passengers, but Gilles heard it: the sounds that were familiar to him, the changes in speed, direction, and the water beneath them. He knew it so well by now that he could almost calculate *exactly* the remaining distance to anchor drop, even given the variation in timing due to the current of the river as opposed to a seaport, variations in depth of the water, and an inexperienced crew; he could see it all clearly in his mind's eye. Gilles heard the confirming clanks of the parrels, the movement of the braces and the noise the ropes made as they traveled swiftly over the deck, the whoosh of the dropping sails as they were taken in, and shouted commands before the boat slowed, dropped anchor, and at last came to a rolling, bobbing halt.

Only then were the passengers allowed to climb up out of the hold. Most had already grabbed up their bundles and were pushing forward, emerging out onto the deck for the very first glimpse of their new lives ahead of them, as well as their first glimpse of full daylight in a very long time. The travelers stampeding up onto the deck had tilted the little boat heavily to the settlement side, prompting the captain to shout at them that they needed to move back or they would all *surely* drown before they *ever* set a foot on dry land again. The young sailors pushed the group back roughly with the long poles they used for maneuvering the vessel, and enough of the travelers were forced to comply so that a few of the passengers could safely begin offloading while the boat was in a more upright position. Gilles and Bruinje were still stuck below in the melee with the last of the passengers and as he made his way over to the hatch, he lost his footing, grabbing for the ladder to steady himself so that he would not fall over on top of Bruinje.

Encumbered by a small child and the bundle of clothing, Gilles was one of the last to exit from below the main deck. He followed the line of people up the steep steps, his left arm around Bruinje and his left hand clinging to the bundle of clothes, while his right hand sought out whatever anchor he could find nearby to steady him, hoping all the while that the creaking, water-rotted stairs would hold the weight of both of them. He joined up with Elsje who was already on the top deck at the plank, waiting for him.

Having his whole family together in one place at last, for perhaps the first time in days, Gilles relaxed a little and took a quick look around him. He observed, with some surprise, that the land was flatter here than it had been for much of the journey and almost completely devoid of civilization except for grazing animals of indeterminate species in the distance and the little settlement's scattered rough buildings, thin smoke curling up lazily from most of the smoke holes or wooden chimneys on this warm afternoon. The river was very wide here but just under the surface of the waters, Gilles observed that the current was still quite swift. In the far, far, distance great mountains unlike anything Gilles could have ever imagined glittered in alternating light and dark patches under spring's melting ice and snows. Being so far away, the peaks might have been taken by the casual observer for an unusual cloudbank, were it not for the reflection of light, the running water on the rocks so many miles away. In the foreground one small, low green hill stood welcoming them and any monotony in the scene was broken up with sprinklings here and there of stony outcrops and copses of shrubs. Looking back down the river, from whence they had come, Gilles could see just the smoke rising from the cook fires of Mannheim. Their new home, Nouvelle Rochelle, was no more than a fly speck on a map, a small Huguenot enclave comprised mainly of a handful of French Protestant families clinging for dear life to the riverbank.

On the northernmost edge of the settlement, where the ship had passed while the passengers were still down below, a lone farmhouse was set far back from the river. A tiny plot of cleared land ringed the house, perhaps trying to prevent the encroachment from the rear of the great dark pine forest that stretched behind it, maybe as far west as France and as far north as the Netherlands. Gilles could see from the many leftover stumps all around the area that the woods had been trimmed back from the river by the settlers but the trees still refused to be conquered completely, growing behind the settlement lands in every direction, on this shore of the river and on the opposite shore as well. There would certainly be bears and wolves in those woods and Gilles would have to remember to tell Elsje that she needed to keep a close watch on herself as well as Bruinje. In front of this evergreen backdrop Gilles observed what he believed to be chestnuts, black poplars, willows and gray alder and in front of those were the pastures and fenced planting fields, a paler green landscape, a few deciduous trees and bushes scattered here and there, interspersed with clumps of coppice forest and thickets of wild tangles of brush. Finally, on the very banks of the river, were the houses of the settlement.

The air was much warmer here than he thought it would be, with a sweet fragrance in the air that reminded Gilles of almonds and figs. It was a great land, a fantastic land, even more beautiful than it had been in Gilles' dreams, although he saw no cider mills. It was a place of overwhelming beauty and peace with no visible evidence of war here at all. This was an enchanted land where Gilles was quite certain that his family would soon happily settle down. In this moment he knew that he had found *his* place, the one place in all of God's creation where beauty and reality resonated together in harmony, a place that was familiar to him although he had never set eyes on it before, the place where he believed that he was meant to be, to live until the last of his days.

Gilles had to admit that his first glimpse of the settlement was not *entirely* promising: For one thing, there wasn't nearly as much to it as he had hoped there would be. It was not simply the missing cider mill from his dreams, but all of it, even the new buildings and even from a distance, looked to be a little run down and in need of repairs. The houses did not face a center green, a main street, or even the church, but instead they lined up expectantly facing the river, as if waiting for something, perhaps prosperity, to come sailing in very soon. The settlement had not been established so very long ago but the more recently built houses, judging by their lighter color of wood exteriors and straighter lines to their roofs without sagging centers, had been built at a greater distance from the river than the earlier ones, probably due to the floods of recent years reconfiguring the shoreline of the Rhine. This year there had not been as much snow in the mountains though, so there was not enough water in the river to flood the land. The captain had mentioned something to that effect, that the low water had slowed their ship's expected progress over the final days of their journey.

With their new home finally fixed in their sights, some of Gilles' fellow travelers murmured their first impressions to each other, but most did not say very much, perhaps because there was not so much the feeling of arriving at a destination or of coming to a new home, as the feeling of having arrived in exile. The captain had refused to stop at Mannheim, even to discharge passengers, saying that it was not a safe place, but Gilles had the feeling that it was more the captain's desire to finish the journey and be done with it than for any concerns regarding their personal safety. Gilles had been one of those passengers requesting debarkation there and he was more than a little fache now that he would have go to all the trouble of finding a way to double back, locating a suitable inn for the night, and *then* returning to Nouvelle Rochelle to retrieve his family. Gilles had already made up his mind that his wife and child were safer here in the settlement. Besides, he could travel much faster on his own and he would have more immediate success at securing a place to stay for the night if Elsje wasn't there to argue with any prospective hotelkeeper. She could be difficult in the *extreme* at times.

Gilles would most likely be blamed for finding the wrong place, of course, but it was easier to endure that than to try and find other places to stay that were more to his wife's liking. Elsje might even enjoy exploring Nouvelle Rochelle a little bit and meeting some of their new neighbors while Gilles was gone. Gilles would have to find a way to get across the river to Mannheim and then back again, and it didn't look like this could be accomplished before dark.

As the line of passengers continued to move slowly off the ship, Gilles took advantage of the delay in disembarking and looked around to see more details of life on the shore. The houses themselves looked nothing at all like the houses in the Netherlands: Some were single-storied clay and wood buildings, similar to those favored during the reign of the Tudors in England, but with oddly-slanted half timbers showing through on the exterior. The rough walls, wattle and daub no doubt, squinted out from underneath thatched straw roofs. Other structures had rough weathered plank sides, presumably covering a wood frame or maybe even timbers, the uniformly dimensioned little cabins topped by battered wooden boards, secured not with nails, but only the weight of flimsy poles thrown haphazardly on top of the slabs to hold the roofing material down.

Gilles took heart a little more when he saw that the fields behind the houses were already showing tiny bits of pale green coming up, crops tagging along behind the houses in long, crooked rows. Trellis works next to some of the houses even held the promise of future grapes; from the great distance and Gilles' poor vantage point, it was difficult to tell with any certainty, but he judged none of the vines to be much thicker than the width of a finger yet. A few cattle, sheep, goats, hogs, and chickens could be seen wandering among the houses.

Gilles' eyes swept down the length of his new home town, beginning downstream, from whence they had come, with the lone German farmhouse and barn, standing shyly off to one side. Going upstream from the farm, along the line of rough dwellings and across a swampy section of the shoreline, his eyes came to rest on the small graveyard. Next to it, there was what must have been the church although it lacked any kind of ornamentation to distinguish it as such, except for the simple cross affixed to the peak of the roof. Gilles decided that the very last dwelling, being a little larger and more prosperous looking than the others, as well as being on the far side of the church, must surely be the minister's house. It was appropriate that the clergyman's home and the church would be the furthest upstream, closest to Switzerland and France, where the tenets of the Calvinists' religion had been formed.

In fact, the settlement was bracketed by the two vastly different and diverse houses, the first one a solid old farmhouse with a stone foundation that looked to have been there for many generations, probably inhabited by an old German farmer if Gilles had to make a guess, and the other a newer residence without any farm outbuildings to speak of, surely inhabited by a man much more interested in the affairs of faith than with concerns of the stomach. Perhaps it was a continuum too, from the old people and old religion of the land, stretching out along time and space into a new future with the church spearheading the change and all kinds of people following the church, flooding into the land in between to settle along the river valley.

A very long and rickety dock jutted out into the river, floating and jumping on the current. It would surely have to be replaced soon if this was their *only* access to the river, but after looking around, Gilles saw no other, better place for a ship to tie up. The vessel had already dropped anchors, perhaps to keep it from smashing into the landing and taking out the flimsy quay completely, and two of the young sailors leapt stag-like, from the boat to the dock with lines in hand, securing the vessel just enough to allow the passengers to disembark. After the ship had been lashed to the bobbing landing, it *still* rocked ferociously, like a trapped animal, squeaking and squealing as the wood of the dock rubbed up against the ship's port side. The passengers were pulled off the vessel one by one and with each new body that landed on the walkway, the floating platform danced even more vigorously. The passengers were offloaded first, Gilles, Elsje, and Bruinje being the last of these, and the belongings that had not been carried off by the passengers were unloaded by the sailors, quickly and none too carefully, dumped unceremoniously onto the boards, leaving the owners to attempt the removal of the items themselves or to plead for help from the people on the shore. The crew might have kept the cargo for themselves if they thought it had any value and if the weight of it wouldn't slow their progress in getting away from this place, but it was fairly obvious that they viewed the baggage as mere passenger droppings.

A few of the inhabitants of Nouvelle Rochelle, perhaps those anticipating the arrival of someone they knew, wandered down to the riverbank to see the newcomers, but there were no throngs of people at the water's edge as there usually were in Amsterdam: There were no boys or men loitering there, looking for a way to make some quick money by carrying or carting baggage, no vendors offering food or drink, and there were no well-dressed women casually happening by the dock to offer a smile and friendly hand to any lonely man with a little money in his pocket. Most of the travelers had so few possessions that it was not a great burden at all to carry their meager belongings across the dock on their backs, even though a good many of Gilles' fellow passengers were in a weakened condition after the voyage and after whatever ordeals they had managed to survive before they started out on their long journey. For some of them, the cost of their passage took the very last of their money and the last of their courage as well, but they had risked it all, every bit of what they had, on this chance for a new future. The new arrivals lifted their weary heads now to look around and see where fate had landed them.

A dark haired woman, presumably Claire's daughter from their mutual reactions on spying each other, arrived at the waterside within a few minutes of their docking, wiping flour-covered hands on her apron, and then hugging her after Claire managed to make her way across the wobbling pier to the terra firma of the shore. The younger woman sniffed once, certainly from the emotion of the moment, and pulled back a lock of loose brown hair, securing it with one dough-covered finger behind her ear.

"They said you were finally here but I couldn't believe it!" she exclaimed,

"I am!" Claire responded, with tears of her own.

Gilles and Elsje had no one to greet them. Their four trunks sat out on the end of the dock where they had been stacked in haphazard piles of two trunks each. The chests nearly blocked the way completely between the boat and the land but it made no difference now; the other passengers were all on land with their belongings and the last of the crew was clambering back onto their vessel.

A young man coming from the land ran lightly and quickly to the end of the landing, not coming to help Gilles as he had at first surmised, but pushing past Gilles and his family, the boy reached right over the chests, handing a dirty sack and some coins to the Eidelweiss' captain.

"Nothing else, just letters," he said, tossing the last lashing rope up to the ship's hands.

The captain nodded to him as the anchors were pulled up and then the ship turned and was off again, just as quickly as it had come, without even a "goodbye" or a "good luck" wished to the people they had shared their life with of late, just gone, already a memory fading quickly in the distance, rushing with the current back down the river.

Gilles approached Claire and her daughter and being uncertain of how greetings worked here without introductions, he saluted the younger woman by tipping his plumed hat to her.

"Bonjour Madame, and please pardon my forwardness. My name is Gilles Jansen and this is my wife Elsje. We need someone to take us and our things across the river, over to Mannheim. Is there anyone here who can perform such a service for us?"

The younger woman's eyes flickered briefly but that was her only facial response besides her verbal reply. "We have no men or boats to spare. They are busy in the fields or fishing and won't be inclined to carry heavy trunks around when their long day is done. No one will bother your things unless you have brought robbers and thieves with you from the boat. We don't have much, but we are good Christians here, not *voleurs*. That path over there will take you towards Mannheim."

In spite of her lack of help, Gilles thanked her and said to Elsje, "You are tired and need some time to rest. You stay here with Bruinje and the chests and I will go into Mannheim to find us a place to stay for the night. I won't be very long and I will be back to get you."

Claire jumped into the conversation. "Mais *non*! You *can't* stay out here in the hot sun! Elsje, you come along with me to my daughter's house and rest. She will not mind if you stay there until your husband returns."

The daughter tightened her mouth and said nothing.

Gilles had noticed the woman's malaise and he tried to find a graceful way to refuse Claire's offer but before he could think of a credulous objection, Claire, seemingly oblivious to her daughter's lack of enthusiasm, grabbed Elsje's elbow and *insisted* that Elsje come along with them. There seemed to be no choice but for Elsje and Gilles to accept the older woman's extended invitation.

Gilles kissed Elsje on either cheek and said, "Go with Claire, Elsje. I will *go* directly and I will *be back* directly."

"How will you find us?" Elsje objected.

"Where is the house, Suzanne?" Claire asked. "Which one is it?"

"Third house to the right," Suzanne mumbled, gesturing.

Elsje was too tired to do otherwise, although Gilles knew that she would have preferred sitting on the dock all night to going where she was not wanted.

"Come back soon," she pleaded, and her eyes also asked Gilles not to tarry long there.

"I will," he promised and he set off at a very fast pace down the worn path that meandered alongside the riverbank.

Elsje grabbed Bruinje's hand and prepared to follow Claire.

"But you have not been properly introduced!" Claire suddenly exclaimed, as if they had not just completed a grueling journey in the dark hold of a stinking ship but were both guests at a party where any lapse in manners would have had dire social consequences. "I am *so* excited and *so* tired all at once that I *completely* forget my manners! Let me present to you my daughter, Suzanne LaFleur. Suzanne, allow me to introduce Elsje and Bruinje Jansen."

"Elsje Hendricks and Bruinje Gillessen," Elsje corrected, and she was not disappointed to see the anticipated look of confusion that crossed Suzanne's face. The French were always baffled by the completely logical Dutch naming customs, giving all new babies, boys *or* girls, their father's surname if one should ever be needed, and keeping that same name until they died, whether they married or not. If any further differentiation was needed, they could always give their home city, as in *Elsje Hendricks Van Amsterdam*. Two Elsjes from Amsterdam, of no relation but with fathers named Hendrick, would be referred to as *Elsje the senior* and *Elsje the junior* since it was highly unlikely that they would be of the same age. Even the slow-witted English understood this custom although occasionally it happened that they mistook a *John Smith the senior* and a *John Smith the junior*, of no relation to each other, for father and son.

Once, a drunken French patron at the inn had very rudely *insisted* that if Elsje did not have her husband's family name, then Elsje must not be legally married to Gilles but must have born his bastard child out of wedlock. He had made this assertion just moments before Elsje threw the man out into the street herself without any help whatsoever from her father or anyone else. It wasn't such a difficult feat though: He had been a small man, very drunk, and not very strong as Elsje had told Gilles later. Elsje had fumed for the rest of the night, even *obsessed* over the rude remark for several days afterwards. It made no sense to her at all for a woman to stop honoring her father simply because she might marry.

What was a woman to do, change her name *every* time one husband died and she took a new one? Elsje knew some women who had buried four husbands but they always had just the *one* name.

Even the Scots who were great friends of the French, distant cousins it was said, followed more the Netherlands naming custom. Remembering the insult, but suppressing the devilish smile that promised to find a place on her lips, Elsje again upset the French woman's protocol by thrusting her right hand forward and offering it to her.

As Elsje knew she would be, Suzanne was even *more* perplexed by this action, looking as though she was not quite sure if she was expected to kiss Elsje's hand or to shake it. Suzanne resolved the dilemma by just ignoring the offering completely, turning away, and leading them wordlessly up the path from the river to one of the poorer-looking ramshackle wooden houses.

In another time and place, the dwelling might have been mistaken for a romantic vine-covered cottage, possibly even a gentleman's rustic country fishing retreat on the river, but here in this place it looked just like what it was, a cabin, a dilapidated and shoddy excuse for a dwelling. After shooing a few chickens away from the front door, they stepped inside the dark little structure and Elsje could not at first determine why her footing was so uncertain. Perhaps it was simply that she had spent so much time on the boat or possibly her sickness had returned, affecting her balance and disorienting her. Maybe it was the weight of the growing child that was more difficult to compensate for since the last time her feet had touched land. Slowing her steps to the slightest forward movement until her eyes had adjusted a little bit more she noticed first that the single room where the family lived was only illuminated by firelight and an opening in the roof. Elsje soon realized that the floor of the little house was not made of wood or tile but was comprised entirely of dirt. Elsje started to take in a little more of the interior as she made her way slowly over to the table, until her eyes rested upon an incomplete set of fine China dishes, luminous white in the dark of the room, stacked on what had once been a beautifully carved oak side table. The top of the fixture slanted so much from the uneven floor that the dishes threatened to slide off to one side and then onto the floor completely. Elsje saw that the legs of the piece had sunk down into the dirt so far on one side that it gave the impression of being a peculiarly deformed and very oddly-shaped indoor tree growing up out of the ground.

It was impossible at first to determine the dimensions of the room as the walls of the house were the last features of the interior to come into focus, rounded logs still mostly covered with bark and where this covering had fallen away, uniformly smudged a brownish sooty gray, without any decoration or ornament of any kind to break up the expanse of bleak and dingy backdrop that blended into the rest of the dark interior. There was no real chimney to the house, only the square opening high in the wall at the other end of the single room, directly over the fire that was burning on the far end of the interior space, an end that was not so very far away given the diminutive dimensions of the structure. The length of the entire house was probably no more than the height of three men on each of the four sides. A narrow stone hearth was set into the dirt floor although Elsje was not at all sure if this was a necessary precaution in a house that already had a dirt floor. The iron spit stretched across the fire, from forked holder to forked holder, each of the two vertical support pieces having been forced down into the dirt and partially swallowed up by the earth. Hanging from hooks on the spit were two black iron pots with steaming contents. Someone had plastered irregularly shaped and sized broken bricks and stones into clay that had been smeared onto the wooden wall behind the fire, a crude attempt to protect the wooden walls from the flames, the heat, and occasional sparks. Elsje looked up to the exposed wooden rafters and wooden slab roof of the house, seeing some daylight through the roof before remembering her manners, removing her eyes and placing them on her hostess.

Suzanne gestured to several broken chairs around the small table. "Seat yourself."

She went over to the fire where the two iron pots hung from their hooks on the crossbar and steamed away over the low flames. The picture brought to Elsje's mind something she had heard about but had never seen, a wilderness campsite, and she imagined that someone had then gone to the trouble of surrounding it with walls and a roof. Suzanne removed one of the pots from its hook with a thick bundle of blue cloth that served as a potholder. Even from across the room, the cloth looked a great deal like Elsje's blue silk dress material.

"Would you like some tea? I have some left that I have been saving for company. I *guess* this is company," Suzanne said with an unenthusiastic shrug.

Claire and Elsje accepted the offer and now Elsje wondered if her French vocabulary was up to the task of another hour or so of conversation in that language. She hoped that would be *all* that she would have to manage before Gilles came back for her and Bruinje.

"Would your son like some milk?" Suzanne asked Elsje.

Elsje nodded. "Oui, merci."

"Where are the boys?" Claire asked as Suzanne poured some milk from a bucket into a crudely made wooden cup and handed it to Bruinje. Neither the cup *nor* the milk looked very clean as there were clumps of cream in there as well as some small bits of grass and other brown specks that Elsje took to be dirt or perhaps slivers of wood from the decomposing old bucket. Elsje was torn between refusing her son nourishment and risking his health; she had always strained all of the milk at home through a cheese cloth, both the milk she bought and even the milk from her *own* cow, even though she thoroughly cleaned the bucket *and* the cow each and every time. She always separated the cream first, then shook it to get an even consistency before she gave it to Bruinje.

Suzanne tossed her head to indicate the back of the house. "They are out helping in the fields. We were hoping to start planting some pommes de terre soon but we weren't sure if it was too early in the season yet. It was *very* cold here last night and this morning was bitter cold."

Suzanne sliced some bread and gave pieces of it to Elsje and Claire. No butter or jam was offered for the bread, nothing at all to help make the dark and coarse loaf more palatable. Bruinje ate pieces of the bread that Elsje fed to him while he played at her feet in the dirt, making trails with his hands and scooping it up into little piles, extricating stones and piling them up on top of each other. Elsje wanted very much to remove her son from the floor, or to be more exact, the ground that was sheltered by the walls of the house, and scold him for getting so dirty, but she wondered if this action would greatly offend Suzanne. Poor Bruinje did need *some* diversion to pass the time. He had spent *so* much time confined below deck on the miserable little boat and this was the first change of scenery the child had had in a very long time. Elsje decided that there was nothing she could do right now except to relax and to make the best of things until Gilles returned. Claire bustled around, playing hostess for her daughter who seemed very listless, having neither the inclination nor the energy to remember company manners as she shoved the bread dough that she had been working on into a bucket and pushed it into a corner near the fire.

"Where do you keep your cups, *Chere*? Do you have a spoon?" Claire asked her daughter and then she said to Elsje, "You are tired, eh? I know you have much to think about."

"I was tired and pregnant, too, when *I* first came here, when I first set my eyes upon this place." Suzanne murmured, casting a glance at the door.

"How many children?" Elsje asked, at last hoping that she might have found a good subject for discussion to take some of the unfamiliarity and strangeness out of the room.

"Just two left," Suzanne's voice contained unconcealed bitterness.

Elsje didn't know what to say next to dispel the cloud that had settled even more darkly over them all. Claire attempted to make the conversation more cheerful.

"Well, you will have *many more* healthy children now that I am here to help you with your chores and to care for them." She reached over and patted her daughter's hand but Suzanne pulled hers away from her mother's touch.

"I don't *have* any energy left for my husband any more. None of us have any strength for *anything* beyond survival. We just toil here while we wait to *die* so we can at least get a *rest* and collect whatever our damned reward might be for our goddamned virtuous lives."

"Don't *say* such things! You don't *mean* that! You are *so* tired, *Ma Petite*! I am here to help you now and things will be better very soon, you'll see."

But Claire's optimism only seemed to make her daughter all the more despairing and all the more irritable.

"It doesn't *matter* anymore! Just sit and eat, Maman."

The brief spark of anger that lit up Suzanne's face was soon gone and the tired resignation seeped back into her face. The work of registering her own emotion seemed to require too much effort and was too hard to sustain, even for a few seconds, and Suzanne's visage very quickly returned to the defeated and lifeless mask that it had been before.

Bruinje went over to Elsje for more bread and Elsje attempted to pull Bruinje up onto her lap but the chair creaked and wobbled noticeably.

"I'm not sure that chair will hold you both," Suzanne said, getting up. "Sit over here in my husband's chair."

They exchanged places and as they did so, Elsje observed that the chair was held together with small strands of rope and messy splotches of what looked like homemade glue at the joints.

Suzanne was aware that Elsje had noticed the repair and she commented on it.

"My husband is *no* carpenter. No one here is. We are all just a bunch of formerly rich idiots with high ideals and silly dreams about what life *should* be. All we had to do was to bend our knees just a *little* and kiss whatever needed kissing just a *little,* and we might have been able to keep our old lives."

Claire gasped in shock but Elsje could see that Suzanne was not contrite at all about her harsh statement or her beliefs.

"I'm sorry Maman; I guess I need to go get some air. Please, help yourselves."

The words were all there, they were all correct, but Suzanne's tone radiated no warmth. She swept her hand grandly over the rough bread slices and the watery tea before she got to her feet and wandered out of the cottage, still carrying her blue potholder in her right hand, leaving the hewn wood door wide open behind her.

"I am *so* sorry for my daughter's rudeness," Claire said to Elsje.

"But her life has been *so* hard lately. She lost her last *three* babies. The devil has surely tried her soul."

Elsje understood the general meaning of what Claire said, even if she did not catch all of the French words. She nodded sympathetically.

Bruinje thrashed around in Elsje's arms and she knew from his actions that he was very tired and would soon be going to sleep.

"Is there a place where I can put my son down for a nap?" Elsje asked Claire.

"Go ahead and use their bed, I'm sure they won't need it for a few hours yet."

Elsje rocked Bruinje and hummed a song to him, something that she didn't often have the time to do. Bruinje fought off the approaching state of sleep but the long journey had worn him out thoroughly and very soon the battle was lost as he closed his eyes in sleep, two of his fingers curled into his mouth. Elsje carried him over to the grand wooden bed that nearly touched the chairs at the table, taking up nearly a quarter of the dwelling, and in spite of the very dirty featherbed and countrepoint, she put her son down there to sleep. She wouldn't worry about the dirt just now; she would bathe Bruinje later.

Elsje wondered if *all* of the French people were so dirty. Gilles was not; he was *quite* fastidious in fact. Perhaps Claire's assessment of Suzanne was correct in that the younger woman had been completely overcome with *something*, sadness or exhaustion or both, and this accounted for her state of mind as well as the state of her house.

Elsje walked from the bed back over to Claire who was quietly contemplating the fine china saucer that she had been drinking from.

"It's a funny thing to see this here, this *magnifique* French china so far away in this distant place, isn't it?" Claire asked.

Elsje didn't know what to say and so she said nothing at all.

"I'd never tried tea myself until now and I'm not sure if I like it. It's like a thin soup that smells like summer hay. Someone gave Suzanne some of it when she lived in France and told her how to make it. She never *could* get me to try it there. It's a wonder the hot water doesn't get into the crack here and break the cup *completely* to pieces. Maybe that's what happened to all of the other saucers in the set, though; I know she used to have more."

Elsje looked outside the open front door and out toward the river. Apparently Claire had not yet noticed the advancing coolness of the afternoon. Elsje had to wonder if they would be warm enough in their beds tonight, *wherever* they slept, and now she started to worry about that. The front door faced to the east, and Elsje could see that the shadows outside were getting longer. The air had a clear quality to it that was sometimes apparent at the end of a spring day when the final rays of the sun define everything more sharply, spotlighting in gold each object in creation before they all faded into the obscurity of the night, melting visually into everything else in the gathering dusk.

Where are you Gilles? Damn you, Gilles, hurry back! Elsje thought.

Gilles did not return before Suzanne returned, though. She was accompanied by her husband and her two boys when she entered the house again. The boys were very young, thin and pale, with large dark eyes like their father that seemed to greatly accentuate the thinness of their faces, both of them carrying unevenly distributed layers of dirt on their faces and hands. The youngest boy, who looked to be about six or maybe as old as a very small eight years of age, walked with a very pronounced limp. Suzanne's husband was a taller version of both of them, and he was also very dirty. Suzanne had apparently informed her husband of their guests.

"Bienvenue! Welcome!" Suzanne's husband cheerfully greeted Claire and Elsje. "Boys! This is your grand mere! Kisses for her! And welcome to you too, Madame …ah…?"

"Madame Jansen," Elsje acceded to their customs.

The boys obediently lined up and self-consciously kissed Claire on each cheek. She tried to embrace the two young strangers but all they shared with their family matriarch was her blood and the shape of her chin, so they resisted.

"Come boys, it's time to get washed now," Msr. LaFleur ordered.

The younger boy started to complain aloud, as if he was not at all used to such unreasonable demands but his father hit him swiftly on the back of the head.

"No complaining! Come *now*!"

The three farmers trouped back outside and Suzanne went over to stir the pot on the fire.

"I can't believe the size of Henri! And what is wrong with Louis' leg?" Claire inquired.

"He fell the wrong way on it when he was younger. I wrote to you about that. Didn't you get the letter? For months he cried when he tried to walk on it. It will never be the same, I guess," Suzanne said, shrugging her shoulders.

The strange voices in the room woke Bruinje. He slid off the bed and toddled over to his mother, his face still swollen with sleepiness, his eyes showing clearly that his mind was still somewhere far away but struggling to rejoin his body in the present time and place. He hadn't been asleep for very long at all but Elsje took no chances, leading her sleepy son outside to the privy after she asked for directions from Suzanne. Elsje was greatly relieved to find that Bruinje had *not* had an accident on the LaFleur's feather bed although she wondered if they would have even noticed, the bed being as dirty as it was. Elsje took advantage of the outhouse herself before they returned to the dwelling and the chair that they had been occupying. The boys and their father came back in from the river a short time afterwards, looking definitely wetter but only slightly cleaner.

"Everyone, sit down," Suzanne entreated them.

"Please, take your seat," Elsje offered Monsieur LaFleur his chair back. He would not hear of taking it from her, though, and the weak chairs all creaked loudly as everyone except Suzanne sat down. The chairs continued to squeak at odd times whenever anyone made the slightest movement. Suzanne pulled out wooden spoons from the sideboard and Claire insisted upon setting the table while Suzanne spooned the thin liquid from the fireplace cooking pot into her chipped china bowls. Elsje noticed that there wasn't very much in the dishes besides water and a few colored vegetables: carrots and turnips mostly. The bowls weren't even filled halfway but when the individual portions were consumed, more soup was not offered to anyone. A single piece of the bread was given to each person except for Bruinje, who got none at all. Ending a meal while she was still hungry was a new experience for Elsje and she began to worry again. She had to wonder if the entire settlement went hungry very often.

"Did you get enough, Dear?" Claire asked Elsje. "You need to keep your strength up."

"Oh, yes," Elsje lied, after she managed to comprehend the older woman's meaning. Even though the LaFleurs watched her as she did it, Elsje had pulled out all of the carrots in her soup for Bruinje and cooled them by blowing on the vegetables before she handed them over to her son. Bruinje tried to play with the little orange pieces and Elsje was greatly frustrated that he was wasting the little bit of food that they had to eat. She wanted the carrots for herself if he wasn't going to eat them but she patiently waited for him to chew each small piece into mush and then swallow it or spit it out. With a look of strong disapproval on her face, Suzanne watched as Bruinje spit the pieces into his mother's hand, but she said nothing aloud to Elsje.

"There are many Frenchmen going to the Netherlands now, yes?" Msr. LaFleur asked.

"Yes, *many* Frenchmen," Elsje replied, "in Amsterdam, Leiden *and* in Middelburg."

"I've heard that life is *very* difficult there for strangers. It's hard to find jobs or make a living if you aren't a Netherlander, that is, if you don't have the right papers," he continued, scraping his soup bowl, "or married to one," he added, an apparent reference to Gilles.

Elsje wasn't sure of his meaning, of what he was asking or implying. "My husband wanted to come here to be a farmer."

A strangled look crossed Suzanne's face and then a quick spasm of some sort but she had nothing to add to the conversation.

Her husband replied, "Well, that is *one* reason to come here. We also like the opportunity to worship God as He *should* be worshipped, and not be forced to worship some self-appointed god who places himself above humanity for the sole purpose of looting and bankrupting the country's treasuries and then surrounding himself with cardinals who are just as self-serving and corrupt as he is, while all of the *good* people of the earth suffer in silence."

He said these forceful words with such good humor that Elsje not only understood most of them, she had to smile in agreement. "We are *all* good Protestants in the Netherlands."

"That's *not* what I heard: I heard that you followers of Luther sing, dance, wager, drink bier and wine, and dress not simply immodestly but even ostentatiously. You *even* allow the Catholics to go on their way, not holding them accountable for *any* of their crimes against humanity, allowing them to continue worshiping as they please in spite of the horrors and miseries that they have visited upon the world. *Catholics in the Netherlands, oui?*" he asked, just to make sure that Elsje understood his question.

"Catholic Spain still occupies my country, Monsieur, but we don't bother our neighbors, no matter what their beliefs, and they don't bother us."

Elsje wasn't sure if she had the words right but she was getting angry. These French Calvinists were obviously a *very* different sort than her Protestant neighbors in Amsterdam, although barely a century had passed since there had been only the dichotomy of Catholics and heathens in the world, no Protestants at all.

"You tolerate other godless people there too, Jews and Muslims, isn't that right? Well, *all* is predestined anyway, and so it is, that many of us are *not* the Elect for salvation and are doomed from birth anyway. We are fortunate that our pastor is a man who *understands* the will of heaven. He has God's ear and *knows* what is in God's mind. He knows who among us was born into the Elect and who is a Reprobate. "

"We live in peace with *all* of our neighbors. We believe that complete faith as well as good works will bring God's miracles and salvation to *all* of us." Elsje was mixing in Dutch words with the French now but she could no longer hold her feelings back.

"You would place yourself on a level with *God Himself* then, believing that by your *actions* you will be saved, that a mere man or even a *woman* has *God's* power to change things?" Msr. LaFleur set his spoon down in total amazement of her audacity and her conceit.

"We are not ashamed of our faith *or* our country," Elsje said. "We do what we can to make life better for all, even when our leaders are misguided. We must show the way to our neighbors if they have strayed from the path."

"Well, we are *not* ashamed of being French! God forgive me for saying so, but it is our *government* that has gone astray, God, King and country being as one and sovereign to us."

Elsje said nothing more, having run out of vocabulary, no longer sure that she was understanding the subtleties of his meaning, if she had gotten *any* of her own words, let alone *all* of them correct in what she was attempting to say, and sensing that she was on very precarious footing with her neighbors already. She worried that if she said anything more, she would only be making matters much worse.

For herself, she didn't care. She could just stay in the house all the time and not talk with the neighbors, but Gilles would have to work alongside these men. Elsje smiled the most conciliatory smile that she could manage, the one that she reserved for her most important patrons who had some frivolous complaint about her inn's food, drink, or service, and in spite of her seething inner anger, she said no more.

Msr. LaFleur seemed to be considering further argument but he abandoned that idea. Perhaps he wondered why he was bothering to argue with an impertinent *woman*.

"Well, just as long as the Papists are in their place, preferably dead or at the very least, not here inflicting any more of their corruption or misery on us, eh? Now it is time for me to go and get my wife some water so she can wash the dishes."

Msr. LaFleur got up from the table and left the house for the river, seizing before he left a mold and moss-covered wooden bucket, while Suzanne sat looking down at her bowl. Elsje did not for a moment believe that he usually brought in the wash water, but she was pretty sure that he needed to leave the house for a time to cool down and they all allowed him this pretense. Suzanne at last rose from her place and started clearing the dishes. When the water finally arrived, courtesy of Msr. LaFleur, Claire insisted on washing the bowls and utensils and Suzanne did not protest. Elsje offered to help as well but there was not enough room near the bucket for *three* women, especially when there were so few dishes to do and no clean towels with which to dry them. Claire rinsed the dishes and utensils in the cold river water and then stacked them in a pile on a soiled towel that covered a small, roughly hewn and crude-looking table. The drainage soaked the towel immediately and the water dripped in a steady stream from the towel onto the dirt floor, enlarging an already-existing mud puddle and re-filling the outline where previous water had been standing in the past.

Claire engaged Elsje in conversation while she washed. "Well, if Gilles doesn't return soon, you will have to sleep here! I'm sure that we can find you a place to rest, though."

Suzanne gave her mother a sharp look that Elsje spied from the corner of her eye.

"My husband will be here *very* soon. I don't know what's keeping him but he said he would hurry back and he *will*," Elsje asserted, but fear in the dark inner reaches of her mind grabbed at Elsje.

What if he never came back? What if something has happened to him, if he had been killed by a robber or met with an accident or wild animal on the road? How would she and Bruinje be able to get back to Amsterdam? He couldn't be drinking at some tavern.

"Well, of course he will," Claire replied, patting Elsje's shoulder, "but if you are tired..."

The boys were hustled off with some blankets to a corner near the fire. They fluffed up a pile of hay on the floor that was not, in Elsje's opinion, far enough from the fire to be safe, but after chasing a large spider from their sleeping space, they were soon fast asleep. Bruinje, refreshed somewhat by his short nap, played at Elsje's feet, greatly enjoying, the mud and dirt he had never been allowed to play in before.

"This is your *first* child? You have no older sons to help your husband?" Suzanne asked.

"My younger brother may come from Amsterdam to help us work the fields," Elsje replied, although she shuddered involuntarily at the thought of little Heintje turning into one of Suzanne's boys.

"So will you live in Mannheim, but farm here?" Claire asked. "Is that why Gilles went?"

"We will stay there just until we get settled into one of the houses here."

Elsje didn't feel very much like talking. It was too much of an effort to understand the foreign language and she was so *very* tired. She just wanted Gilles to come and get them so they could leave this place. Bruinje ran around the room in circles, visibly irritating Suzanne, but Elsje could only manage to keep him quiet for a few minutes at a time. She hoped that he might soon wear himself out enough to fall asleep again, but that didn't seem likely to happen. Elsje tried to stay awake but as she sat there, her head nodded toward a sleep that she could not resist, even with Bruinje still noisily capering around her. It had been a *very* long day's journey from the inn they had stayed in further down the river the night before, and a very, very long time since they had left Amsterdam, a lifetime ago.

Elsje thought that she only dreamed of Gilles' arrival but it really *was* him, there at last when she woke up. It seemed to be very late at night and her neck pained her as she straightened herself up in her chair and looked around the dark room, now only illuminated with a single smoky and sputtering goose oil lamp and the dying fire. She realized with a start that her hosts had gone to bed already, snoring away on the bed right next to them. Only Claire stayed up to keep her company although she must have been nearly as tired as Elsje. Bruinje was curled up on Claire's lap, asleep once again.

"Have I been sleeping for very long?" Elsje asked. "Has Bruinje been much trouble?"

"Non, non, pauvre Chere." Claire patted her arm. "You can stay here tonight if you want. I'll fix you a place on the floor with me." Claire turned to Gilles. "Poor thing, she is *so* tired!"

"I've brought a boat for us. There is a good moon out tonight so we'll be fine," Gilles said, noting the objection to Claire's offer in Elsje's tired eyes. He helped Elsje to her feet.

"Is it very far to the town?" Elsje asked Gilles.

"It's across the river but easier going *with* the current than it was coming back."

"Our things! What about our things?" she objected.

"I had a boy help me drag most of them up here by the house but we'll take the one with our clothes in it with us. You'll watch the others for us, won't you, Mme. Montserrat?"

"Please! Call me Claire!" she insisted. "I'll be happy to watch your things for you."

"You'd better go to the privy first," Gilles smiled at Elsje, "and take Bruinje, too. It's a long trip over."

Elsje and Gilles said good night to Claire at the door and Gilles waited at the corner of the house while Elsje went to the privy with Bruinje. She struggled with their clothing ties and buttons in the dark but eventually they accomplished what they set out to do.

When she and Bruinje returned to him, Gilles was waiting outside the La Fleur's door and he delivered a request to her in a low voice.

"Put my money purse in Bruinje's clothes. I have kept some money out in case we need it but if we get robbed, this is *all* we will lose."

"What took you so long?" Elsje hissed at him, now wide awake and feeling much more like her irascible old self.

"Well, I had to find a boat to get across the river, make it across the current, find a safe place to leave it in the city, get a place for us to stay for the night…."

Gilles was getting short-tempered himself, thinking of *everything* that he had already attempted, endured, and accomplished today, much more than she could *ever* know while she sat there in safety and comfort, yet here was Elsje questioning him once again, expecting him to make it *all* fall into place immediately, to make it right for her without effort. Perhaps she had never been away from her home before and had no idea of how hard it could be. Maybe Gilles *had* been able to make everything better for her in the familiar confines of Amsterdam, but she seemed wholly unable at the moment to adjust her expectations down to their current reality and further, she appeared to be *completely* without gratitude for his struggles. He might have drowned on the way over, been set upon by thieves, even *died* in the effort of securing comfort for her: It was always a possibility and even more so now in this wild place.

Perhaps he had just not *explained* it well enough to her, that pioneering in a new land was *not* romance; that at best it was difficulty and struggle as well as tiring, dirty and perpetually discouraging work, day after day, without *any* respite or opportunity to rest. It was only *la fin*, only leaving a *worse* past behind and securing the prize of some measure of comfort after years of this difficult kind of life that made it worth attempting at all. Perhaps Elsje did not possess the kind of temperament that would encourage a man to bring such a partner into new and uncertain circumstances. Had he misjudged the woman that he had married? He hoped not. The mistake could be tragic, especially now that they were already here and return was impossible.

They were both so tired that Gilles could have quite happily stayed for the night on Suzanne's floor but he had seen with great clarity that *neither* woman was agreeable to that arrangement. Gilles hoped that his wife might be more reasonable tomorrow and would better comprehend the circumstances of their new situation. It would be hard, yes. It would be frustrating at every turn, yes, probably, but it was the *outcome* that they worked toward; his plantation and vineyards would make all of the misery between here and there worth while. Gilles had to have faith and believe that they would find peace, freedom, and prosperity here, as well as ownership of their own land, which was something to which *every* man aspired but only the very wealthy ever attained.

The trunk took up the entire stern of the small water craft and the weight of it had given Gilles some pause; if it wasn't for the current going *with* them, Gilles was not at all certain that he could have handled the additional burden, but he took heart that it was only *one* more trip over and his arms had not yet begun to ache too badly, although he was certain that the pain would be there with a vengeance before the morning light. He had left the chest at the waterfront and managed to get it into the boat by himself before he went back for Elsje. The boat reeked of fish but there was not much to be done about that, even if Elsje chose to complain about it, which she didn't. After Gilles helped Elsje and Bruinje into the little skiff and settled them into their seats in the front, Gilles took in the lines and climbed in to take his place in the middle. He directed Elsje to be quiet but to watch for hazards in front of them and keep Bruinje inside the boat and as still as possible. Gilles pushed off from the landing and rowed as silently as possible across the gurgling black water, holding his breath occasionally to listen for any sound that would indicate danger. Along the way in the gathering darkness, Gilles marveled in silence at the great, dark river moving quietly beside and under them in the moonlight, the three of them riding to their destination astride a great, dark beast with a life of its own. Gilles was afraid that their voices would carry over greater distances on the water if they spoke, attracting river pirates, but the noise of the murmuring river along with the frogs and night birds, including a night heron and an owl seeking a mate, served to mask their presence well.

The moon glittered over patches of water that had been roughed up by occasional light breezes. It was still early in the spring, and Gilles had expected that it would be much cooler here, especially at night, but it was certainly not as cold as it was in Amsterdam at this time of year. This climate would be *excellent* for growing crops, especially grapes, and for the first time all night Gilles had a chance to think about the future, not just their immediate needs.

Luckily the journey to the town was short enough, direct enough, and it passed without incident of any kind. Gilles located the mooring that he had found earlier and he also found a boy, scavenging in some garbage nearby, that Gilles recruited to help him carry the trunk to the inn. The place was only a short distance away although Elsje complained that now their chest would have mud and manure all over it since the boy was small and had a difficult time keeping his end up off the ground completely. The innkeeper helped Gilles heave the trunk up the stairs to their room as Elsje looked around, rubbing her cold hands together. There was no fireplace in the chamber but it had a bed and would serve as a dry shelter for the night. She spied a cobweb on the ceiling and inspected the mattress closely.

"Elsje…" Gilles said.

"Ja, Gilles?" she looked at her husband to see what he wanted.

"It *isn't* home but it will have to do for a few days until I can get us settled in our own house at Nouvelle Rochelle."

She smiled a tired smile at him and got Bruinje ready for bed, removing his dirty clothes and sitting him on the chamber pot.

As quickly as they could get ready, they all climbed into the one bed, and exhausted from their day, they fell asleep quickly. It seemed to be only a moment later that Gilles was shaking Elsje awake. It was morning and he was already dressed.

"Before you ask me Elsje, this is what I am doing today: I'm going to find the man and talk to him about getting the house, then I need to find the ferry that I learned about last night and return the boat before I find out where we can buy our supplies. Here is a little money for your own use today. Take a little out and hide the rest in Bruinje's clothes. *Don't* leave it in the room or anywhere else! Take the boy out for some good food and to see the town but stick to the main streets, stay inside the city walls, and be safe! I may not be back until the end of the day."

He kissed her and then he was gone. Elsje got up to secure the door after him and then she fell back asleep again. She woke some time later to the sound of Bruinje doing something to the latch on the chest. He sat in front of it, making a loud rhythmic thumping noise as he lifted it up and banged it back down, over and over again.

"Bruinje, come over here to Mother," Elsje called to him.

Bruinje looked over at her and briefly smiled an angelic smile at his mother before he returned to banging the latch.

"Bruinje, *stop it!*"

With no success at getting the boy to stop the noise, Elsje sighed and heaved back the covers. She rolled out of the bed, the sudden weight of her own body taking her by surprise. She felt twenty pounds heavier than she had yesterday and now she checked the girth of her stomach as well as a mental calendar. It wasn't going to be very much longer now. Why hadn't she stayed near cousin Vroutje until after the baby was born? It was too late now. She went over to Bruinje and pulled him away from the chest as he squealed in protest.

Elsje ticked off the reasons to herself why they didn't want to wait in Amsterdam long enough for their second child to arrive: There was her marriage that was rapidly deteriorating, probably due to Gilles' long hours of work for Msr. Ste Germaine and Gilles' desperate wish to be away from Amsterdam, to be *here*, farming in the Palatinate. There was her father's interference in their marriage, and then there was what had passed between her and Jean Durie, although in retrospect, Jean did not now seem to be a very significant reason for their leaving. Their goodbye at the dock had been comfortable enough, and it was almost possible now to dismiss what had happened between them as something that was really not as bad as she thought it had been at the time; that is, if it had really happened *at all*, and had not been just a strange dream. Elsje thought about Tryntje, too, missing her and hoping that her sister was taking good care of the customers and behaving herself.

Hunger tore at Elsje's stomach this morning but it was finally starting to feel less queasy than it had at the start of every day for so many months past. She was ready for some food but discovered that Bruinje had an accident and soiled his clothing, maybe because Elsje had been asleep for so long. Elsje needed to wash some clothing out today or Bruinje would have nothing clean to wear. She had no idea how she was going to get their laundering done in this strange country, in this new place. She was just glad that she had not *already* put the money bag in Bruinje's underclothes before his mishap.

When Bruinje was cleaned up again, his only remaining clean clothes on him at last, and Elsje could finally take the time to dress herself, she looked forward to immediately indulging her empty, suffering stomach with food. She hid the money as Gilles had requested but as she did this and bent down to take Bruinje by the hand and lead him down the steep stairs, Elsje felt headachy as well as a little light-headed and dizzy.

It was very quiet here, not at all like her busy inn at home. Every corner of the place had a few cobwebs that gathered dust and little fly carcasses, all held fast in their sticky and invisible traps. The only people that Elsje saw were the very old owner and his wife, a woman too fat and too old to do much more than uselessly wade around the room, bringing a spoon here and a plate there, wheezing and gasping for breath as she completed simple tasks that would have taken healthier people much less time and effort.

Elsje wasn't used to being the customer but she waited as patiently as she could for their breakfast to be served. It took far too long, with Bruinje whimpering constantly from his hunger. Finally the old woman brought Elsje some warm, greasy sausage.

"You're fortunate that we have some of this today!" she told Elsje as she set it down in front of her. "We don't *usually* have women or children here, so it must be your lucky day."

The old meat had a strange, flat taste to it and many hard bits and hairs needed to be removed before she could swallow it, but Elsje was so hungry that she choked it down anyway. She tried the undercooked flour cakes, baked in the coals apparently, as bits of peat and ash still stuck to the burned outsides of them. Elsje found that they were nearly unpalatable as well, but they would fill her empty, aching stomach and so she ate those too. She had always served her customers wonderful breakfasts and now she wondered how her poor customers were faring this morning with Tryntje preparing their food. It suddenly occurred to Elsje that it had been *weeks* since they had left Amsterdam and surely by now Tryntje would have learned how to cook, turned it over to one of the other girls, or found some other way to get good food on the table for their patrons.

As hungry as he surely was, Bruinje just wouldn't touch the food and Elsje finally gave up on getting him to eat anything. She would need her strength for the day though, and so she finished his portion as well. Either from the grease or the unfamiliar food, her nausea had returned to her but she was determined not to lose the nourishment that she had just taken in. She had to turn her mind to the tasks that needed to be done and away from the strange food that brought on physical sickness as well as her homesickness.

Elsje asked the old woman how she might get her clothes cleaned and where she could find a midwife. The woman was not very helpful regarding the laundry, except to say that there was *always* the river, but she was able to give Elsje directions to the local midwife's house, a woman named Frau Geldorf.

Elsje went back up to their room and cleaned Bruinje up from his experimentation with the breakfast food, then tried to get him to use the chamber pot again. After a short time though, Elsje relented and stood him up from the pot, the red ring on his small bottom a visible vestige of the most recent battle in the war to get him fully trained.

They ventured outside into air that was already warm even though it was still early morning. Elsje noted that she must have been exhausted the night before because she would have been awake many hours earlier if she had been at home. The town, which had once been "a major trade center" as the innkeeper had told her proudly, seemed to have been nearly completely destroyed recently. The few people that Elsje saw were poorer, less industrious, and it seemed to her, more menacing, more inclined to criminal intent, than they had been in Amsterdam.

The streets occasionally had paved sections, indicating that once there had been real roadways but now they were little more than wide mud fields between the buildings. Greater and lesser craters along the way looked as though they had been excavated by someone, perhaps a person intent on stealing the paving stones, maybe to build or repair houses. The rubble from burned out and toppled buildings spilled over from their respective plots out onto the street. Grass and bushes forged up through the piles of broken bricks and debris, some of these even sprouting sturdy young trees, growing up through mountains of refuse that had probably once been dwellings. Everywhere the watery feces of animals and people were deposited liberally. Elsje tried not to step in them or to breathe in the smell that rose from these piles, threatening to obscure completely the sweet spring air.

A handsome bird sang in a nearby tree and Elsje wondered what it had to sing about. Bruinje pulled on Elsje's hand to go and play in the dirt and as he did so, she thought she felt the moneybag slipping from its hiding place underneath her skirts. She had to discretely secure it again while holding Bruinje in front of her to make sure that no passersby might be lurking closely enough to see what she was doing. She checked to make sure that Bruinje's portion of the money was secure, too.

A few men hung around the streets with nothing better to do than to stare at Elsje, although one cart did go by, forcing its four wheels through the mucky unpaved ruts between the buildings, carrying in the wagon bed what looked like a dead body.

"Major trade center!" Elsje muttered to herself under her breath. Cramps gripped her midsection as she clutched her gut underneath her bloated stomach but she forged on, following the directions she had been given to the midwife's house.

She found the ancient woman sitting on the front stoep, chewing on a piece of tall grass, her wrinkled face constantly changing with the motion of her jaw. The yard was littered with garbage, animal droppings, and a few chickens that were tied to nearby stakes with dirty strings affixed to their legs.

"Are you Frau Geldorf?" Elsje asked. She hoped that if she spoke Dutch and gestured a lot, the woman would understand her.

"Who is asking?" the old woman asked her without moving anything but her lips.

"I'm Elsje Hendricks and I'm new to the city. You are a midwife? I will need one soon."

Elsje flattered the woman by calling her "midwife" and the town a "city".

"So I see. I can help you. You have gold for me? I only take gold."

"My husband will have it when it is my time."

"It looks like it's time now! How much longer? At most, two months, I'd say."

A dirty cat appeared from behind the house and wound its way around the woman's legs. The creature's eyes ran with pus and there were matted feces in its fur. Not getting any acknowledgement of its presence from the midwife, it walked over to Elsje who pushed it away with her foot. Seeing that it would get no attention, the animal ran up the steps and right *into* the woman's house. Elsje held her breath and tried not to look as disgusted as she felt. She wondered if the woman also kept chickens and goats inside the house, too. She had heard that it was so here, that they kept all manner of animals safe from hungry thieves by keeping them *inside* the houses. Bruinje stared, wide-eyed, and pulled at his mother's hand so he could follow after the creature. To Elsje's knowledge, her son had never seen any cats up close before and he was very curious about this one.

"Yes, a couple of months," Elsje answered the woman. Her stomach rumbled loudly.

"Well, it's good you already have one healthy child. Did you have a hard time with him?"

"Nee, not so bad."

"Well, if you can say that about the *first* one, I guess the second one will be *very* easy." The old woman laughed at her own joke, showing a few remaining brown teeth. Another dirty cat, a white one with four kittens pouncing on her back, rounded the corner and stopped at the woman's feet.

"Go feed yourselves! Plenty of rats around! Damned cats!" The woman kicked at them but there was humor in her eyes as she said, "We should *all* give birth as easily as cats!"

"Can you come to Nouvelle Rochelle, across the river, when it is my time?" Elsje asked, although by now Elsje was not at all sure that she wanted the dirty woman with the devil animals to touch her *or* her newborn babe. Witches kept cats and were said to delight in taking newborn children's souls for delivery to their master. Although Elsje generally didn't believe in such nonsense, in this strange place everything seemed menacing to her and this dirty stranger who would have complete control over her naked body and her infant's, was definitely no exception. At the moment though, Elsje's need of reassurance that there was someone nearby who was experienced enough to help if the baby's delivery was difficult, was even greater than her revulsion and fears about the old woman.

"If you send a boat for me, I'll come. My pay is one gold piece *before* I do my work, two if the child is born alive," the midwife said. "So many are born dead, I should get a bonus for it, don't you think?"

"Hartelijk dank. I'll send my husband with the money." Elsje's cramps had become unbearable, cutting across her middle and causing her to quickly end the conversation. She needed to leave right away and she hoped that she wasn't going into labor now, *not* here. Gripping Bruinje's hand tightly but trying not to crush it, she turned to go, anxious to find a privy somewhere and anxious as well to leave the fetid yard, not reassured in the least to have secured a midwife's services. Elsje believed that she had a few more weeks to think about it, either to get comfortable with having Frau Geldorf deliver her baby or to find someone else.

There was no privy along the way and Elsje was forced to go behind the crumbled stone wall of an old building, relieving her intestines of their swelling and groaning burden. She would *definitely* have to wash out her own clothing as well as Bruinje's now. She held fast to Bruinje's hand so he wouldn't wander off while her intestines gripped her and when at last her stomach and her gut were cleared of the poison, she rearranged her clothes, thankful that no one had accosted her while she was so indisposed, for her money or for anything else that they might desire from a woman all alone in a strange place with only the companionship of a small child.

Elsje looked around for a marketplace on the way back and thought that she might have found one but there was very little to be purchased there except for used clothing, possibly taken recently from the dead, and a few vendors who appeared to be trying to sell the very paving blocks that they walked on, perhaps stolen just hours earlier from further up the street. She did find a tiny bakery, strangely enough with no customers although it was midmorning and prime time for huisvrous to be out doing their shopping. Elsje purchased two loaves of dark rye bread, in fact the *only* two loaves the bakery had, one of which she devoured completely with help from Bruinje who was now very fussy, and no doubt by this time very hungry. Elsje brushed the crumbs from her cheeks and chin and sternly told herself that wasting time and money was *no* way to get the laundry done. Her stomach had quieted a little and in spite of some hiccups and a headache, now she was better able to think.

Still feeling tired and disoriented, for the first time in her life the possibility of her *own* mortality, her own death occurred to Elsje. Due to her illness during these last few months, she had been completely exhausted much of the time and she knew that the road ahead would be a hard one for her, a farmer's wife, and would be made doubly so in this very difficult land. Elsje's thoughts turned to Suzanne, Claire's bitter and care-worn daughter, who had lost so many children. If continuing to nurse her new baby was no guarantee of preventing further pregnancies, then Elsje was going to have to make sure that there were *no* children after this next one for a while: She just wasn't sure if she could survive another pregnancy right away and she was fairly certain that the children wouldn't survive, either. Elsje wished now that she had Cousin Vroutje or even Tryntje around to help her out every day, and she wondered if there were any midwives living in the settlement or anyone else who might deliver her baby.

Elsje envied Suzanne in that she still had her mother, her loving, sweet mother, who was still alive, standing beside her, and eager to help. Letting the tension in her shoulders go, Elsje tried to relax as she smiled resolutely and reassuringly at Bruinje, deciding that from now on, she would try to be more hopeful and cheerful. Life would get better soon. She just needed to get settled into her own house and soon she would feel better.

As they made their way back to the Mannheim inn where they were staying, Elsje grew more and more nervous about her surroundings, for no reason in particular except that the men all stared at her and the women she saw along the way were pale, dark shadows, creeping nervously along the streets. What had done this to these people? What horrors had been visited on them to turn them from people into beaten animals?

A few women had gathered at one corner, a small commotion occupying this part of town, and when she heard the women saying something about a drowning, Elsje stopped for a moment to listen to the whispering and gossip, understanding from bits and portions of their conversation that apparently a child had been drowned. Elsje resolved on the spot to teach Bruinje to stay far away from the great and terrible river until she could teach him how to swim. She had never asked Gilles about this, but most of the world, sailors included, didn't care to learn this skill, feeling that it wasn't necessary, and worse, would wash away all of the body's protective oils. The residents of Amsterdam were the exception, teaching their young children to survive a fall into deep water and many of the children and perhaps a few adults too, even *enjoyed* it so much that they continued to indulge in it even after practice was no longer necessary. With her children growing up so far away in this strange land, perhaps there would be no community, no adults around who kept watch over the village children as they had done at home in Amsterdam.

Elsje found a group of women washing their clothing at the river's edge and she decided to bring her dirty clothes to the spot later while Gilles watched Bruinje. She worried that Gilles might not be back before sundown and then she would have to wait yet *another* day to clean their clothing and after that, wait for them to dry. Bruinje would just have to wear the same clothes he had on, dirty or clean, until the chore could get done.

Elsje indulged herself in a much-needed nap with Bruinje before Gilles arrived back at the inn, before she had the time to start worrying about whether he had wandered off again and was drinking the afternoon away. She reassured herself with thoughts of their new home and was feeling a little better, a little more rested, and a little more optimistic when Gilles returned. His face wasn't right though, and something weighed heavily on his mind; Elsje hoped that it was not bad news about their house.

"What's the matter, Gilles? What's wrong?"

He knew that he would not be able to hide from her *all* that troubled him today so he allowed himself to share a small portion of it.

"There was a drowning today, a child," he said to Elsje, taking off his hat and cloak and tossing them over on the trunk.

"I heard about it," Elsje replied sadly.

"What *kind* of people are these in this town?" Gilles demanded.

"What do you mean?" Elsje searched his face for his meaning.

"For a man to drown a *boy* because he suspected him of stealing food…" Gilles' voice broke off and much as he tried to avoid it, his eyes strayed over to Bruinje.

"I had not heard *that* part of it," Elsje replied and she felt her stomach sickness returning. They both fell silent, Gilles sorry to have been the one to relay that portion of the story and Elsje contemplating what she thought would be too much for *any* mother to bear, the death of a child, especially since it was not an accident.

"Elsje, I want us to move into our own home in Nouvelle Rochelle right away," Gilles said. "It will be *different* there. Cities are not good places for children, anyway. It was so in France and it was also that way in Amsterdam."

Elsje did not argue with her husband, but she had never thought of Amsterdam as being a *bad* place for anyone, children included. There were occasional murders there, to be sure, sometimes executions and public floggings in the Dam, but they were well deserved by the perpetrators even if they were sometimes difficult to watch. Mostly her city only had the *usual* dangers to look out for, but *always* there had been neighbors to watch over you and your children, even when you didn't *want* them to be watching.

Gilles' visage brightened a little. "Ah! But I *did* get back to Nouvelle Rochelle to look at the available houses there and I also found the man here in Mannheim that we need to speak with about leasing one of the houses. I had the devil of a time understanding his concoction of a language but I managed to struggle through."

"Is it all settled then?"

"Not yet: The house that interests me is in need of some repairs, but we should be able to have it for a year until I can find out about buying our *own* land. I want to get the work done as soon as possible so we can move in. I'll go and look at the house on Saturday."

"Why can't you go tomorrow?" Elsje asked, never being one to put off a chore, and also being anxious to leave the dirty little inn and the miserable town.

"He can't go out there tomorrow. One more day won't be so bad."

"Good, then you can help me with Bruinje and the laundry tomorrow."

"I suppose I can." Gilles smiled at Elsje. "Well, we are here! They have some of the *best* wine grapes in the world right here, did you know that? *Almost* as good as the grapes in France!"

"I will miss my Amsterdam ale," Elsje confided to her husband.

"Then we will just have to get some good local ale and bier and *always* have plenty of it in the house, just for my wife!"

"You'd better hide it from our God-fearing neighbors, then," Elsje said. "I got the *definite* impression from Suzanne and her husband that they don't drink anything but water there."

The promise of the ale put her in better spirits, though. Within the year they would be *exactly* where they wanted to be, where they should have been from the beginning of their lives together.

It was early on Saturday morning when Gilles traveled back across the river to Nouvelle Rochelle. He had made arrangements to lease a fine horse from the stable he had located in Mannheim, giving the stable keeper a hefty fee for the privilege, of course. He walked the animal to the ferry dock that he had discovered *after* he had made his first trip over to the city. The crossing wasn't directly to Nouvelle Rochelle, but it was close enough that he could go up from the landing on the west side of the river, along the path, to the settlement. He had just started feeling a little more comfortable in this, his third trip over there, and beginning to believe that all he had left to do was to work out the details of his new life, but he grumbled to himself about the outflow of funds all the way to his scheduled appointment.

The thought had occurred to Gilles, and rightly so, that the horse probably belonged to someone who had *not* been given the opportunity to approve the "loan" but Gilles just had to trust that he wouldn't be hanged as a horse thief before he had the chance to transact his business and return the animal. The horse was necessary, an integral part of his plan, though, and so he just put this worry out of his mind for the time being. He trusted that Nouvelle Rochelle was enough of a distance away from Mannheim and on the opposite side of the river as well, so the horse's owner would be unlikely to spot him astride the animal. Besides, Gilles had more immediate concerns to worry about than what *might* happen.

Gilles rode through Nouvelle Rochelle saluting his future neighbors that he saw there. He waited for some time at the church, the appointed meeting place, letting the horse graze until Heinrich Goeble arrived. Gilles noted from the sun's position in the sky that it was a good deal *later* than the agreed-upon time. The dark-suited little man climbed up out of his carriage, although only heaven and Goeble knew *how* he had managed to get a carriage with two horses across the river and up through the wilderness with no streets and no roads, only a root-entangled path to follow. Perhaps that was what had taken him so long.

Goeble walked briskly over to Gilles, looking this way and that, behind and to the side of him, perhaps checking for robbers as he strutted over to conduct his business. Herr Goeble was as dark and somber as his suit of clothes, all business, except for the single large gold pin that he wore pinned to his breast.

Gilles had made some inquiries in Mannheim and discovered that Goeble was the cat's paw, in charge of parceling out all of the local lands to the tenant farmers. Everyone had to wait for him and in his own good time, when he got around to it, Herr Goeble would grant them an audience to allocate the leased properties so they could go forward with their new lives. Gilles took in everything about the man from the worn hat on his head to the newly shined toes of his boots, looking with a critical eye that had been trained to precision by the most discerning of judges of men, Jean Durie.

Gilles noted the gold pin and thought to himself that Goeble's security could be *greatly* improved if he just kept his flashy jewelry off his person when he traveled into these remote areas and then he wouldn't *have* to be accompanied by the four armed guards.

After this thought though, Gilles smiled to himself in epiphany; enlightened now and comprehending Goeble's role, Gilles waited for the German to start his presentation, say his lines, give his theatrical performance. The little man was barely up to Gilles' shoulder and Gilles could feel Goeble's beady eyes sizing him up as well, sniffing the air all around him to see if Gilles really did have enough money to pay for one year's lease of the house and the land.

"Sir."

Gilles pulled his heels together and swept down in a low bow as he removed his aigrette, the heavy plumed hat, from his head. Gilles knew with certainty now that he had been fully vindicated in his purchase of the stylish chapeau over Elsje's objections, even though they had argued about the money Gilles had spent on it for a full week afterwards. Gilles, generally very tight-fisted with his money, had spent an outrageous sum on the hat when he had bought it from one of Amsterdam's better chapeliers just before they left the city, making the argument to Elsje that it was a *necessity* for a man of his stature to have one, and that just *having* it greatly increased his bargaining power.

Goeble grunted in reply, making a noise in his throat in response to the pretentious formality of this prospective French tenant farmer, probably come here to raise pigs, or maybe he was just amused by the sight of the ostentatious hat, but all the same, a return gesture was good for business and so the representative had taught himself how to make a bow in return, even if it was a slight, clumsy, and stiff one.

"Monsieur Jansen," he replied as he lowered himself into the bow.

"Herr Goeble, soon I would like to *buy* some land if that could be arranged, but right now I want to rent a house from you for a year. I would like to move my family into it right away if you have a good one available. I would need to look it over first to decide, of course."

"And I would *love* to have you do so!" Goeble replied with enthusiasm. "Empty houses do my pocket no good."

Gilles could now plainly see the light shining from the man's eyes, the anticipation of the gold that would soon fill his pocket. Goeble, Gilles, and the borrowed horse left the carriage and driver behind as they trudged along in silence into the heart of the settlement, followed at a short distance by Goeble's bodyguards. They came to a halt in front of a small half-timbered home.

Gilles had already known with some certainty where they were going: He had made the very same trip two days before when he had returned the skiff and located the ferry route over from Mannheim. It was then that he had made inquiries and examinations of *all* of the houses, both the vacant ones and those that were already occupied.

The structure's thatched roof had partially fallen in and the house was as rundown as the settlement itself, but in a pleasant way it reminded Gilles of the cottage on his father's estate in Rouen. He had often played in it when he was a small boy, spending many happy hours there with his best friend Claude, where they played at being knights and kings so many years ago. Goeble's bodyguards lounged together at a slight distance from the two businessmen, passing the time talking among themselves and seemingly taking no notice of Goeble's activities.

"This is it, Jansen. Five silver pieces a year, due at the end of the harvest, no extensions, and five due now to move in." Goeble rubbed his hands together in hungry anticipation. He clearly expected immediate payment, just as long as Gilles *had* it, but Gilles didn't reach into his pocket right away; instead he examined the outside walls closely and walked slowly around the building, leading the horse as he went.

"Could you hold my horse?" Gilles asked Herr Goeble as he

rounded the last corner and came back into sight. Without waiting for an answer, Gilles handed Goeble the reins. "I need to look at the inside and there is no place here to tie my horse."

Goeble frowned but said nothing. He looked the horse over as he waited for Gilles to come back outside, perhaps wondering *how* this man Jansen came to have such a fine horse and why he needed to inspect the house so closely when no one else had ever asked such a thing.

"I have another house with a new roof on the other side of Nouvelle Rochelle. It's a little more expensive though," Goeble offered when Gilles emerged from the interior of the house several minutes later.

Gilles still did not hand over the money and he noted with satisfaction that now Herr Goeble had started to shift his weight from foot to foot.

"The one with the big Chestnut tree in the front? I've seen that one and it *won't* do. Five now and five *again* in the fall, you say?" Gilles pulled on the whiskers of his chin, still looking this way and that at the front of the house.

Goeble looked irritated. "That's right, I thought *you* were the accountant," he sneered.

"That's ten silver pieces a year for the first year," Gilles said.

"It's *five* silver pieces to move in and *after that* it's five silver pieces a year. I can't change the calendar!" Goeble snarled.

Gilles was unperturbed by the man's sudden shift in temperament. "Well, I guess I could give you *two* pieces now since most of the planting season is already gone and I *could* give you five pieces *after* the harvest, assuming I can plant my crops in time to have a harvest this year," Gilles thought out loud.

"You don't have it? Then *why* am I wasting my time here?" Goeble's voice was higher and had a hard edge to it now. The bodyguards looked over and made straightening motions as if they were readying themselves to leave, but Gilles had not moved a muscle.

"Oh, I *have* the money. It's just that there was another house that we passed on our way up the river. It was a pretty place and I'm having a hard time making up my mind between the two. I don't know why, but my wife wants to be *here*, probably because there will be other women around to gossip with. You know how women are! I can't see spending the money here though, when they wanted *less* for that house and the land looked like it was better for farming."

"There is no better land than here!" Goeble glared at him.

"No, that's what my friends who want to join me from Amsterdam said, that there is no better land in *all* of the Rhineland than right here in Nouvelle Rochelle..." Gilles stood tipping his head from one side to the other as though he could not make up his mind. He did not move from the spot, though, and Goeble still held the reins of the borrowed horse.

"...but still, to risk the money I have saved in Amsterdam from the New World fur trade and with *no* crops in for a few months..." Gilles clicked his tongue against his teeth.

Goeble's eyes lit up again with the glow of avarice. Gilles had surmised correctly that due to the miserable economic conditions in the region, the man was in dire need of rents and was having a difficult time finding any tenants who could pay. How many refugees were there who were *able* to pay and would risk handing over two years of rent when the crops might *never* come in at all, even if the fighting in the region was at last over?

Gilles had already guessed the answer because Goeble had offered to *personally* come out from the city to look at the available lands with him and had not sent some underling, someone of an even lower status in his place. Gilles was completely cognizant of the fact that he had said the magic words "fur trade" and "friends who want to join me", and he had a prescient certainty that Goeble was eventually going to agree to his terms. Gilles waited a few more moments for Goeble to drink in the promise of ready money now and more to come later before he continued on with his part in the little drama.

"Well, I *suppose* I could look around here a little bit more, couldn't I? Just to help me make up my mind?"

Goeble growled which Gilles took as a "yes".

Gilles nodded and mumbled to himself at certain places. He took measurements of the walls with the span of his hands, which Goeble endured with ever-thinning patience. Gilles looked up at the roof with the holes in it and put a worried look on his face, moving his head back and forth as if to consider the pros and cons of something before he spoke to Goeble again.

"Well, if I had to fix that, it would take *so* much time that I would not have any time left to plant my crops. My wife will *hate* that we have to journey back down the river where the owner of the other property lives. Thank you, I am *so* sorry to have wasted your time. Here is a coin for your trouble."

Gilles tossed him a small gold coin, not worried in the least that he might be risking it. Goeble caught it with two hands, his empty one and the one that still held the reins to the horse. There was no mistaking the heft of the coin as it sailed through the air and landed solidly in Goeble's hands. Goeble looked at it.

"What *kind* of a coin is this? It's not a silver Thaler!"

"No, it's not," Gilles replied. "It's gold. It's *better*."

Goeble looked at it for some time before he surreptitiously dragged his nail across the face of it to make certain that it *was* gold. He put it into his pocket and then he cleared his throat.

"You are making a *big* mistake, Jansen! There is no finer soil in all of the Rhineland! Who owns this land that you saw anyway? Reinhart? He *lied* to you about the price! This house will be *gone* when you come back and you will have *lost* the opportunity to get it."

Gilles' carefully composed response was a long sigh. "This *has* been my dream for *so* long, to come here and live. I will absolutely *despair* of having to write everyone back in Amsterdam to tell them that I wasn't able to find a good house here. I will feel so foolish having come *all* this way! So many more want to come, you know, in spite of the political, er, *difficulties* here. It's too crowded in Amsterdam and there is no land left there for farming."

"The war here is *over*! I guess I *could* make an exception, just for you of course, Jansen, and take three pieces now and then collect seven later," Goeble said, his position softening just slightly.

"But still, there *is* the roof." Gilles jingled gold coins together in his pocket absentmindedly while he squinted up at the roof. His actions had the intended effect on Goeble.

"I could have the roof *fixed* for you for another three gold pieces," Goeble offered.

"Eh?" Gilles turned to him in mock surprise. "*Me* pay for *your* roof? When the other house I saw was perfectly fine? This *is* a lovely house, but no, not for us, I'm afraid."

"All right, two gold pieces now and *I* will fix the roof!" the desperate man cried.

"You *do* drive a hard bargain," Gilles flattered him. "Now if we can find a witness and sign this paper I have here…"

"What *for*?" Goeble roared. "Don't you accept my word? I *never* sign papers!"

"Well *of course* I take your word! A fine gentleman like you, I just want to be certain that we *understand* each other and that there is *no* confusion. My understanding of your language is not always

290

so good," Gilles said modestly, smiling and shrugging his shoulders apologetically.

"You understand well *enough!* You bargain like a God-damned Jew," Goeble muttered.

"What? I didn't catch that," Gilles asked.

"Come on then, we'll find your witness now," Goeble growled.

He set out in a hurry to find one of the church elders, the only men in the settlement that Herr Goeble believed he *might* trust, the few that were not always trying to cheat him.

The thatched roof was repaired in no time at all; Gilles made the journey to Nouvelle Rochelle once again and watched from a distance a few days later as the thatcher carried great bundles of river reeds up the ladder, then worked them into place, securing them with tarred cording. Herr Goeble was very eager to begin collecting the two gold pieces in rent but Gilles had inserted a clause in the agreement that the pro-rated rent would be paid *only* upon their moving into the house and not a minute before the house was ready for habitation. Gilles had also reduced Goeble's payments by a reasonable percentage because the gold was worth more than the silver. Although the rent collector was enraged by these deviations from the usual agreements he obtained, he checked with trade officials in Mannheim and discovered that it was *true;* the gold *was* worth more and was not as subject to value fluctuations in the market. The financiers not only advised him to accept the reduced terms, but they further stated that he would be wise to do as many deals as possible, as quickly as possible, with the man who had the gold. Although it must have bruised his ego, Goeble was not a complete fool and so he had the workmen move the repairs along at a rapid pace, even going out personally across the river every day so that he could see with his own eyes if the work had been done yet.

When by chance Gilles met up with Goeble on the street in Mannheim a week later, the little man insisted on giving Gilles a detailed explanation for the delay and a progress report. In truth, Gilles wasn't so very worried about the crops getting in although he didn't say this to Goeble; the harvest was for his family's own use and he had money enough to get him through the winter if necessary. All that Gilles really wanted for now was a temporary place to stay, one that was not too expensive, a home base from which to scout out the very best land to buy for his future vineyards. He had started by making inquiries as to what restrictions there might be on an *auslander* buying property, and then asking around about land that he might be able to buy.

"There were rotted sections of the frame of the house but I have fixed *all* of that for you and now there is only the last of the thatch work to be completed," Herr Goeble offered.

Gilles smiled and shrugged. "Herr Goeble, don't trouble yourself if it is not finished yet! My wife is very happy to be living here in town. If I can't get the crops in on time this year, we might simply have to wait until next year to move in. It *would* save me the one piece of gold as well as the four for the end of this year. I have other business interests here *besides* farming..."

"But, but, it costs *money* to live in town!" Goeble sputtered. "You could have your *own* comfortable home and I'm sure it would cost *less* than where you are staying!"

"It's not unreasonably priced where we are staying now, but thank you for looking out for my well-being," Gilles replied.

Goeble looked stunned and Gilles could plainly see that the man was getting *very* concerned as he had already lowered his expectations from the original ten pieces of silver down to five pieces of gold with only one of those being collected the following week. Reducing the total to only *four* gold pieces, and these not coming to him until the following spring, would make for a difficult winter as Goeble needed the money *now*. Even if Goeble could wait for another six months to collect the rent, his prospective tenant, his newly-found plump pigeon ripe for the plucking, might well be gone by then. Goeble offered to obtain horses and cattle for Gilles too, for a small commission of course, but Gilles refused all offers, saying that he had no need of these things yet since he had no place to keep them.

Gilles had observed that Goeble did not pay very close attention when they signed the papers and obviously he had not gone back to read them over again: Gilles made sure that he had worded the document so there would be no cost to him *at all* if the crops could not be planted in time. He had gambled, and successfully too, that Goeble would sign the document even if he *did* read and understand all of what it said. Gilles was only mildly surprised to find that the subtle but exact meaning of the document, written in the language of the law, had *completely* escaped Goeble, who seemed to Gilles to be either not very well educated, not very bright, or maybe both. Perhaps it was only because Gilles had been in the trade business in France and later had investments in the Netherlands, both places where no words or actions were *ever* wasted, where every effort and the precise and exacting words used were all utilized to attain and maximize an ever-better profit margin in *every* deal that was written, the stuff of story and legend in the taverns at the end of the day. *Truly* a man's wealth lay not in his beginnings, education, or even his luck, but in his sharp wits and precise words. It also helped that Goeble had only practiced his bullying financial schemes on unwitting and naïve refugees who had too many other concerns to worry about when they first arrived.

On his first day in Mannheim Gilles had located, after a great deal of searching, a monastery that had a bilingual cleric to help him write the contract up in French as Gilles dictated it and then to translate it into the local German language before Gilles even went to look at the house. Gilles had given the matter a great deal of thought on the voyage up the river and made absolutely certain that the meaning in the contract was *exactly* as he had intended with very little possibility of alternate translations or legal interpretation.

There was only the local legal system to be concerned about: It might not uphold such an agreement but Gilles reasoned that if the Germans were *anything* at all like the Dutch, they would probably honor the signed papers although Gilles clearly remembered his father's distrust of the Rhineland natives. The window of opportunity for planting some of the crops, the ones that took longer to reach maturity and harvest, was closing rapidly. Elsje might be impatient to leave the inn and was growing more so with each passing day, but Gilles had supreme confidence in human nature, knowing that Goeble's avarice would get them into the house just as soon as was humanly possible and Gilles was not mistaken in this assessment.

On the following Friday morning, Gilles loaded his small family and their trunk of belongings onto the ferry and crossed the Rhine again, landing for the final time, on the western shore. He had purchased a battered old hand cart in Mannheim, a small one to pull along the trunk and Bruinje too when the child got tired of walking. Gilles thought that maybe the cart would be of some use in moving stones from the fields and eventually could be used to harvest his crops. Gilles reasoned that if it *wasn't* useful to him, he could always lease it out to his neighbors or sell the cart later. It being a glorious spring day, the ride from Mannheim across the river was a pleasant interlude between the long journey from Amsterdam that they had just endured and the years of hard work on the farm that were certain to lie ahead of them. Elsje marveled at the new roof on the house but she was visibly nervous about it, too.

"How can we cook inside here with everything made of *wood* and *grass*?" she asked Gilles. "Where are the bricks? Where are the stones?"

"The roof is made of reeds and it's perfectly safe," Gilles told her. "You even have a *stone* chimney here and many of the other houses don't even have *that*. Just keep the fire away from things that burn. You had *plenty* of wooden things inside your home in Amsterdam: tables, chairs, beds."

"But *never* a *straw* roof..." Elsje gazed up at the roof in awe.

Gilles laughed at her. "It's *not* straw! It's reeds, but straw is an excellent material for roofs too, Elsje! These roofs shed the rain, insulate against the heat and the cold, and when properly constructed, they last much longer than a wooden roof."

"What about bugs?" Elsje asked. "Aren't there bugs living in it?"

"Oh, Elsje!" Gilles laughed again and she dared not say another word to him about it.

Once she got over her initial fears, Elsje would happily return to cooking her own food and running her own house, Gilles was certain of this. It was her milieu, the place where she found the most contentment. From Mannheim they had brought along what they had purchased there, cheese, bread and what few vegetables they could find in the town, along with a new broom, two new buckets, some rags and rope, all loaded into the little cart with their chest.

Gilles shook his head as he looked at his wife.

She was a wonder.

Elsje was *every* bit as pleased with her new cleaning implements as other women might be with new dresses or hats. She didn't even wait for Gilles to unload the trunk from the cart but started immediately to sweep away the dusty cobwebs from around the front door, with their older collections of spiders and bugs caught in the fine webbing that also held newer bits of reed and wood shavings deposited there from the repairs to the roof. She told Gilles to bring her two buckets of water from the river right away, before he got the other trunks from the LaFleurs, unless he wanted his pregnant wife to go and fetch it by herself. Gilles complied, but on his return, he quickly set the water down and then left immediately to retrieve their other belongings before Elsje could think up *any more* cleaning work for him to do.

She didn't need his help now, though: Cleaning and organization were her specialties. Elsje made a quick inspection of the little house, although there wasn't very much to see. Like almost all of the others in Nouvelle Rochelle, it was only one single story high although it was a little larger than the other houses and boasted a large room *and* a smaller room. Elsje moved along the walls with her broom, starting next to the front door after having tied Bruinje up to the trunk with the new rope. After the walls were free of cobwebs, Elsje used the rags and one bucket of water to wash everything she could find to clean inside the house, starting with some crude wooden shelves that had been permanently installed by a previous tenant. Elsje hadn't quite finished this task before Gilles returned with the cart lugging the first of the three other chests into the house. After the third trip, he made his escape by pleading that he needed to check on the condition of the fields. Elsje was happy to let him go about his business now and she hummed a church tune as she started unpacking the few wooden dishes they had brought, setting them out in perfectly stacked piles, in perfectly aligned rows on the newly cleaned shelving. She forgot completely about morning sickness for the first time in months and the work of cleaning left her happy and pleasantly fatigued.

Bruinje first whimpered, then howled for a time at his confinement to a fixed radius but Elsje just sang louder until Bruinje was worn out from crying and from exploring his new surroundings, even if his explorations were limited by the short length of the rope around his waist. Bruinje climbed inside the open chest of clothing and fell asleep there, as cozy as a cat. Elsje didn't even try to move him; it was better for her if he was sleeping and out of her way, just as long as he didn't have any accidents on all of their clothes that were stored in there.

Claire stopped in to see the house.

"Come in," Elsje said, beckoning to her. "You are my first guest!"

"I've brought you some coals to warm your new home and some bread starter, Elsje. Oh, what a *nice* big house this is," Claire exclaimed as she stepped inside and looked around, "and with *real* wooden floors too! It even has a chimney!"

She set down a scuttle that held some glowing embers in it.

"It *is* nice, isn't it?" Elsje asked softly as if she was just taking notice of this fact. "Thank you for the fire." She put a finger to her lips and pointed to Bruinje before she spoke again. "But where is Suzanne? We can have some tea to celebrate our moving in! I'm glad I brought some from Amsterdam because I couldn't find *any* in Mannheim."

Claire shook her head in amusement at Bruinje, peacefully sleeping away amidst the chaos of the room, before the brief smile faded from her face and she answered Elsje's question.

"She hardly *ever* leaves the house and I don't know what I will do with her. She seems to be always *so* angry...." the older woman's voice trailed off to silence.

Elsje had no chairs yet and so she offered Claire a seat on the top of the closed trunk next to Bruinje's open one. Claire perched on the high seat while Elsje swept up the remnants of the last fire that had been in the house, a fire that had warmed someone and cooked their food before they had left this place for another destination, in this world or quite possibly the next one. Roasted chicken bones were in there along with what looked like charred vegetables and a bit of burned fabric of some kind. Elsje wondered what it was that they had eaten and what they had lived on when they lived here inside this house. She dumped the bucket of old ashes just outside the door and returned to move the live coals from Claire's scuttle onto the hearth. Elsje would now make good use of the old firewood that had been left behind by the last occupants. Although there had not been a roof with good integrity for some time, the firewood was not damp; it was dry and had probably already been aged when it was stockpiled there so it would do nicely to start a fire quickly.

Elsje yelped and jumped back in surprise when she uncovered a large black beetle crawling out of the woodpile, but then laughing and holding her stomach, which had hardened into a contraction after her sudden surprise, she recovered enough composure to scoop the bug up with a rag and fling it out the door before she returned to building the fire.

"Ugh! How can you pick up such a thing?" Claire asked in disgust.

"I *always* pick them up with my bare hands at home but there I knew *what kinds* of kevers bite. It's bad luck to kill them, and besides, if I stomp on it, I would just make for myself another mess to clean!" Elsje grinned at Claire's squeamishness. She wasn't at all certain if her poor French was comprehensible to her new friend, but she kept trying, dropping Dutch words into the mix when her French failed her. It was only now, a few years later on, that she was beginning to have an appreciation of how difficult it must have been for Gilles to learn *her* language when he had first come to Amsterdam.

The fire blazed up, the flames making their way from Claire's coals to the rough bark, then eating along the outside and slowly advancing on the brown heart of the wood. Green and red sparks exploded from the wood as popping noises and a pleasant smell filled the house, confirming that the fuel was apple wood, not the best kind for a sustained cooking fire, but a *very* pleasant way to begin life in their new home. It would definitely put out enough heat to warm a small iron pot of water for tea. Elsje located the pot for boiling water in one of the chests and Claire went to the river to fill it while Elsje took out bowls and the dried leaves for the tea. Her new friend would simply have to understand that she did not have a proper cup and saucer for drinking the tea but someday they would have all of the necessary household items for every day life as well as for entertaining.

While the women waited for the pot of water on the fire to heat up, Elsje showed Claire around the house, what little there was of it, and she talked about how she wanted to fix it up in the coming weeks. There were curtains needed for the two windows, the one larger window in the little room and the bear window, the little one by the great room's front door that was too small for any large creatures to come in there. Maybe Gilles would let her get a floor covering or could kill an animal, the skin of which could be used as a rug. Just one next to the bed would be very fine to keep their feet a little warmer in the morning, and a privacy screen of some sort was needed in front of their bed, whenever they might get one and when Elsje gave birth there. The little room would be kept for storage and eventually for Bruinje and his new brother to sleep in. There wasn't much to be done with the walls except to lime them and brighten them up, if that was possible, but how much would it cost and where would one find a craftsman here? Could they do it themselves, Elsje wondered? When the water on the fire came to a boil at last, the tour of the little house had long been finished. Claire commented, in a diplomatic way, about the haphazard placement of the wooden cross pieces in the walls but neither woman could guess *why* there was not an even pattern to it. Elsje carefully ladled some of the hot water into the bowls that held the dried black tea leaves. The smell of the steeping tea was almost as much of a comfort as the taste of it, but Elsje waited patiently for the beverage to take on a darker color before she started drinking hers.

Perhaps not being very familiar with the beverage, how it was prepared or what it was supposed to look like, Claire began to sip the clear hot water right away, peering down into the rising brown cloud at the bottom of her drinking vessel.

"The first day we came here was the first time I *ever* had it. This is *such* a guilty pleasure. I'm sure that no one else here drinks tea," Claire said to Elsje.

"Probably not," Elsje replied before she added wickedly, "Our neighbors seem to be the kind to only drink water," even though she knew the Dutch expression would be lost on the Frenchwoman.

"How are you feeling?" Claire asked, pointing at Elsje's stomach.

"I'm feeling well enough," Elsje answered, only realizing the improvement in her health now, as she took her first taste of the steeped tea.

"I missed the birth of all of my daughter's children, except for the first one. They have been here for such a long time and I had hoped that when I came here I would at last be a *real grandmere*, not just a stranger who sends letters and cadeaux from far away. They still don't know me at all, or even *care* to know me, even now that I'm here. Perhaps I shouldn't have come. I *did* have a choice."

Claire's eyes welled up and she fixed them on her tea, blinking back tears.

Elsje touched her arm. "Non, it's never a mistake to *try*. It's too bad Suzanne doesn't know the true value of family. My own mother is dead and I would give *anything* to have her with me now, but she died when I was very young. Maybe you just have to give them a little more time to get to know you again."

Elsje hoped Claire understood what she was saying, even with her inadequate French.

"It is never the place that makes us a home, no matter how beautiful, no matter how comfortable it may be; home is being in the company of those we love. Eh bien," Claire said, straightening up from her perch on the trunk and pulling herself together emotionally at the same time, "Well, nothing you want *ever* comes fast enough, does it? And I, I have *never* learned the virtue of patience. I shouldn't have bothered you with this. Are you ready for the baby to come?"

Elsje understood the question and laughed a little. "I would like to get my house in order first," she said, "but then I will *surely* be ready and it will be hard to be patient much longer."

"Do you need any help with the cleaning?" Claire asked.

Suzanne's house could use a good cleaning, Elsje thought, but perhaps Suzanne wasn't interested and didn't want her mother's help.

"With the cleaning? Merci, non, not today, but could I ask you to be here when my baby comes?" Elsje gestured to her stomach and to Claire to be certain that she got her meaning across. Elsje *was* anxious to get back to the house cleaning soon but this was the first friend that she had here, perhaps the beginnings of a new social circle and she wanted just to sit and talk. She hadn't realized until now how much she missed Tryntje and the kitchen girls.

Claire smiled a broad smile at Elsje and replied, "I would be honored to be here when it is your time! New babies keep us all alive! Just *seeing* a child makes old people feel young again and it gives the poor and dispirited hope in the future, no matter how hard their lot in life."

Elsje didn't agree with this sappy sentiment but she didn't say so; children were fine to have but when they were small, they made more work for everyone. "We'll worry about cleaning tomorrow. Today it is *so* good just to sit with another woman and drink tea. We have been

301

on that smelly boat for so long, stuck down in that dark, miserable, floating sewer."

Elsje shuddered at the memory. She realized after she spoke that she had mixed quite a few of the words up, the French and the Dutch, but she was feeling comfortable enough with Claire now to try and express her feelings. Hendrick had always warned Elsje that the French were *all* overly sensitive, thin-skinned in the extreme and unjustifiably critical of others when it came to outsiders failing at their language. He had always advised Elsje and Tryntje to just pretend they didn't know it, but for the moment Elsje didn't heed his words. She was lonely and she missed her sister, craved friendship, and her instincts told her that Claire was not the type to hold anyone's shortcomings against them; besides, if Elsje had never even *tried* to speak French with Gilles, she would not be married to him today.

What was wrong with Suzanne that she could not appreciate Claire and all of her good qualities? Elsje could see plainly that Claire had a very good heart and Elsje realized once again how much she had been missing her *own* mother over the past fifteen years. Surely Suzanne could appreciate that her mother loved her and had come a very long way, given up a great deal, and gone through much hardship just to be here, to try and help her daughter.

Elsje thought briefly about what it would be like if her father were to come here and move in with them. Just for a fleeting second, she felt an unexpected surge of empathy with Suzanne. Her father being under the same roof with them here, much as Elsje loved him, would be nothing but trouble. Because her father was far away and at a safe distance though, Elsje wouldn't allow herself to think these uncharitable thoughts about him, even if they were true, and so she pushed them from her mind. She replaced them with the thought that she would write to her father very soon and find a way to get the letter to him, at least to let him know that they had arrived safely. Gilles could help her write the letter when he got the planting done. She realized that all of these thoughts of home and it being so far away were dampening her spirits and doing nothing to improve Claire's either, so Elsje changed her thinking and then the subject.

"Does Suzanne know if there is a market nearby? I need to find a market. I can't go across to Mannheim every time I need something."

"Suzanne keeps a store of dried food and wild honey for when there is no fresh food from the garden but she *did* mention that there is a place down the river where you can buy some food. The men here catch fish and set snares for rabbits, wild boars, or other game in the fields and woods. I think she mentioned deer and partridges, too. Suzanne said that I should be careful of the traps when I go out looking for mushrooms, berries, or walnuts."

It sounded as if there was a great plenty here to eat, even if it was all wild. Elsje thought about the miserable meal they had at Suzanne's when they had first arrived and she wondered if Suzanne had only been selfish that night, deliberately choosing not to share her food. Elsje didn't want to believe that food was in such short supply here but then if Suzanne had no difficulty in denying nourishment to a pregnant woman and a small child after such an arduous journey, then it was an *equally* troubling thought regarding the charitable dispositions of her new neighbors. Elsje chose to believe that there was a temporary shortage of food because it was still early in the spring, and with the exception of some very early carrots and beans, most of the crops weren't ready for harvest yet. Elsje wondered what *she* could do to add food to the family table and maybe even help the rest of the community as well. She might learn how to fish while Gilles farmed, go looking for wild food, or ask Gilles to plant some extra crops above and beyond what they would need. She would definitely get some chickens as soon as she could and maybe some sheep too, if the wolves were not too much of a problem here. Elsje didn't like to think much about the wolves, though, or the bears, either.

After Claire drank her tea and left Elsje to her cleaning, Elsje went outside to find the privy. She was grateful that there were enclosed outhouses here, considered a luxury in most of the frontier settlements as well as in many of the larger cities of the civilized world, but after following a rather nice path of slate slabs that led over to it, she discovered that their privy was a communal one, shared with two other houses. It was a crude shelter, with lots of spaces between the upright boards, offering the most minimal of privacy and shelter from the elements. It was not at all what Elsje had been used to in the Netherlands, but she knew that she should be grateful that there was one at all in this woestijna. On her way back to the house, Elsje could see Gilles in the distance at the far end of what looked to be their plot of land, talking with one of the men who rested momentarily from swinging his scythe, cutting down some harvested winter wheat perhaps or other grain grass. After first making sure that Bruinje was still sleeping, Elsje took the broom outside and cleaned up the privy as best she could.

She couldn't do very much about the smell inside though, and when Bruinje woke up and Elsje took him out there, he refused to go inside, splaying his legs out in front of him like a balking old goat. He spied a large brown spider crawling just outside the structure, and it was then that he started to scream loudly for several minutes, bringing Gilles in at a run from out in the fields. Elsje tried not to laugh when she told Gilles what had just happened. Bruinje refused to go inside so for the moment Elsje directed the boy to relieve himself outside in some nearby bushes, but she was not going to allow him to use that spot for very long. With such setbacks, she might not be able to get him trained to the outhouse and chamber pot for another year and with a new baby coming soon, that was a very disheartening thought.

Gilles stayed at the house just long enough to get some bread and cheese for his lunch.

"You should get to know the neighbors later," he suggested. "Maybe they have a good recipe for onion soup. There are wild onions growing near our field and they make a great soup. My grandmere used to make the *best* in all of France."

Elsje filed this bit of information away for later and then she continued unpacking the trunks after Gilles had returned to the fields. Her spice chest was the centerpiece of the rough shelves, indeed, of the entire house, and Elsje ran her hand over the polished wood, smiling to herself as she remembered their wedding day, the day she received the gift. She had restocked all of the spices in the little drawers before they left Amsterdam and now she was more than ready to start her cooking *and* their new lives here. She might try to cook Gilles some of his onion soup first, since all she would need was outside her door. Although it seemed like a great quantity of items that they had packed into the trunks, in actuality they had so *few* possessions that Elsje was done putting the house in order well before the end of the day, even with the distractions that Bruinje offered her. The rope around Bruinje's waist came undone more often now than could be attributed to mere chance and Elsje knew that this preventative measure to keep him securely in one place no longer stopped him, but only slowed Bruinje down.

The clothes from the trunks all smelled damp and mildewed from the long journey on the river so Elsje took them outside and spread them out over some low bushes to air. She decided that a meal of bread, cheese, and vegetables would have to do for their supper tonight but tomorrow they definitely needed to find something more substantial to eat.

Just as the sun was going down, sinking into the forest behind the house and the fields, Gilles came into the house carrying some firewood a contribution of fish for their supper.

"Where did you get those? They're *dead*." Elsje sniffed at them doubtfully.

"Well, ja, but they were alive when I got them," Gilles lied.

They had promised to be truthful with each other, but Gilles was getting worried about Elsje and he hoped this small exaggeration might encourage her to eat them and start regaining some of her lost health and strength. The neighbor who had given Gilles the fish, Mlle. De La Noye, had noted Elsje's condition and told Gilles more than he *ever* wanted to know about all of the people in Nouvelle Rochelle who had become sick and then died from St Anthony's fire the year before. She advised Gilles to eat more fish and avoid eating any bread if they wanted to stay alive and have a healthy baby.

Besides, the fish didn't smell so bad to him; they could use the donated food, just for tonight. Gilles reasoned that if his neighbor was eating them and *she* was still alive, then they should be all right. The Netherlanders always turned up their noses at dead fish, even when they were fresh within the day; they even rejected what they considered to be inferior *types* of fish, the same kinds that were considered perfectly fine for any gentleman's meal in France.

"I thought you would be happy to have something more substantial for our supper, Elsje."

"I *am*, Gilles, thank you, it's just..." She looked at them and sniffed at them again but she put a smile on her face. "How is the garden coming along?" she asked. She retrieved the big knife from its new storage place to clean the fish.

"Fine," Gilles lied again. "I borrowed a faux from our neighbor and cut most of the long grass down so now I can plow. When it is spread out and dried, we'll have our first hay."

The planting field was in very rough shape and it was going to take a lot more hard work to get it cleared, more than Gilles really wanted to even think about. For the past year or more, all had it produced were weeds and stray seedlings, these in abundance. Another neighbor had made some comment to that effect and Gilles thought that maybe it would have been a better idea to have looked more closely at the field and *less* at the house when he made his decision as to which plot of land he should choose for them to rent.

He told himself that it didn't matter so *very* much, though: Things would be different after his crops came in. They would have plenty of food to put away for the coming winter and in the spring Gilles would have already purchased his own land, just as soon as he discovered where he should buy it and what legal issues he would have to navigate to secure a clear title. He had decided to plant orchards on his future land too, and in the coming years the wine he made from the grapes and the apples, exported through Jean Durie to the Netherlands, would make him rich enough to buy many more acres of land. Eventually he would have to hire men to help him cultivate it, probably the local Rhinelanders, because Gilles knew now after speaking with his neighbors for just a few hours that these Frenchmen were perversely and adamantly opposed to alcoholic spirits of any kind, *even* hard cider and aqua vitae. It was no wonder that they all appeared to have weak constitutions here.

This land was almost within touching distance of the French border, so close that Gilles could almost feel it, and he had to grudgingly admit that the soil and climate appeared to be even *better* than Rouen's for growing anything, including grapes. He had seen this with his own eyes as they had journeyed up the river, at times winding their way in between great walls of feral grapevines that lined both sides of the waterway and occasionally, seeing a few long lines of cultivated vines that stretched out over the hills.

While Gilles daydreamed about the future, Elsje tried to bring Gilles back to the present by showing him how to clean the fish. "They always cleaned them out for me in the market in Amsterdam but this is how you do it. I can take them to the river and do this or you can do this *before* you bring them to me so I don't have to go out in the dark with the wolves while you watch Bruinje. If you don't do it for me, it will just take *more* time before I can start to cook them. If you wait *too* long to clean them, the fish will be no good at all," she informed him.

"What happens if you just throw them into the pan the way they are?" Gilles asked, "without cleaning them out of their insides?"

"Then you have a hot, stinking, dead, rotting animal," Elsje replied with a sweet smile for him before she got that look on her face that said *"Men! They never use their heads for anything besides transporting fancy hats around!"*

Gilles decided that it was best not to ask any more questions about food preparation.

"You had tea. Did you get the water?" Gilles asked, seeing tea leaves in the bowls.

"Claire got that, and I only got a half-bucket afterwards. I'm *pregnant*, not ill."

"I thought you were both," Gilles said, as he washed his fish-slimed hands in the washing bucket and then wiped them dry on a towel. He put his arms around his wife and kissed her on the cheek. "How are you feeling today, hmmm? Better I hope."

"I am well enough to cook you some dinner if you take Bruinje outside for me right now," she replied, putting an end to his romantic attentions, at least for the moment.

Gilles decided to approach her again later, after they went to bed.

When it was served, the fish tasted very good, even *better* than good: It had been cooked with Elsje's spices and once again the food tasted familiar. They ate their meal as they sat on two empty trunks and used a third for their table. Eventually, when Gilles got around to it, he would buy or make a *real* table and chairs for them, but too many things had to be done first before they could concern themselves with such luxuries.

"It's good to have our own home," Gilles smiled at Elsje and he took her hand in his. "There is *no* inn and *no* Ste Germaine tonight; there is only you and me."

"And Bruinje. I need to find some milk for Bruinje tomorrow, Gilles," Elsje said. "We can't drink tea all the time. Claire mentioned that there is some kind of market or something down the river, I guess somewhere along the path."

"There is? I haven't seen one and I didn't think Nouvelle Rochelle was so big that it could support a market. Well, I suppose it will take us some time to find all of these things. I didn't know that there was a ferry crossing until I stumbled upon it. Our good neighbor Suzanne might have mentioned that fact to me on the first day, when I was trying to get over to Mannheim and back to you before midnight."

"Yes, she *might* have," Elsje agreed.

"Well, I hired one of our neighbors to come and plow our field tomorrow and I will get us some more wood for our fire then, too. Do you want to take some money and go find the market yourself or do you need for me to go with you?"

"I'd like for you to go too, but will it take all day for you to plow?" Elsje asked. She had never been around a real farm before and didn't know how much time it might take.

"It's a small plot of land, Elsje. It shouldn't take too long if the plow is good and the ox is strong. They tell me the field was turned less than two years ago and so I *hope* we will be finished pretty quickly. I need to get the seed in right away if it's going to grow well and I have to go into Mannheim to buy it yet. If you need me though, I will take the time out to go with you to find the market. Do you feel safe enough to go alone?"

"If the other women go there, then I'm sure it's all right. Nee, the planting is *more* important, Gilles. I'll just see if I can find it myself or maybe Claire can go with me."

Elsje shook her head and smiled to herself. It *was* difficult getting used to the idea of *her* Gilles, her French dandy, being a farmer.

They made their bed that first night on the floor with only the comfort of their blankets and the bales of wool. It was strange and more than a little uncomfortable for both of them, sleeping on the hard surface without having their heads and backs propped up against a headboard. The walls of the house were too cold to give them the same feeling of comfort and they were both too tired to come up with any other solutions before they fell asleep. The next morning, Elsje was vaguely aware of Gilles moving around the room, trying unsuccessfully to be quiet as he dressed. She didn't realize that he had been rudely awakened by a field mouse that had run *right* over him that morning. The rough and splintery floor had very wide spaces between the boards and they could feel the cold drafts that occasionally pushed up from underneath the house. It creaked as Gilles shifted his weight from board to board. Elsje moved to get up too, but she was still too fatigued. Gilles knelt down beside her to kiss her cheek.

"Don't get up," he said. He put one hand on her hip, then moved it down her thigh, taking the memory of it with him for the day.

"Sleep as late as Bruinje will let you! I will amuse myself in the garden all day." He patted her thigh once more and then he was gone.

Elsje smiled, did not argue with him today, and rolled herself over to her other side. Her choices of sleeping positions were now limited to her left side, her right side, or flat on her back, which ached for hours afterwards whenever she tried the latter position for more than five minutes. Even though she was still very tired this morning, she couldn't get comfortable enough to get back to sleep, and so she just got up. There was still much to be done to turn this house into their home and Elsje was excited about it, looking forward to having a place that she could make over as she wanted.

Bruinje slept on and Elsje was happy to have enough time this morning to use the privy *alone* and to prepare some bread, cheese, and leftover fish for the child's breakfast without Bruinje's impatience making everything twice as difficult as it needed to be.

She would have to find that market today, though and find it soon: They were quickly running out of the few things they had brought with them from Mannheim and they needed more variety in their diets if their innards were ever going to get sorted out again. She had started her mental list for the day when Gilles unexpectedly came back into the house with an armload of clothes, the very ones that Elsje had set out on the bushes to air the day before. She had been so tired last night that she forgot to bring them back inside before they went to bed.

"Elsje, what are *these* doing outside?" he demanded sharply.

"They were all damp from the journey and I set them out to dry so they wouldn't get *schimmel*," she said. "Why? Is something wrong?"

"Yes, well, they're dry *enough* now and they *won't* be dry if it rains," Gilles barked as he tossed them all down on the top of a trunk.

"All right," Elsje shrugged.

She hoped that farming wasn't going to put Gilles in a bad mood *all* of the time. After all, he had chosen this life, *he* had said this was what would make him happy. "Did you leave me some money for marketing?" she asked.

Gilles opened the hidden drawer in the big trunk and gave her a handful of the smallest denomination of coins he had. "They'll take *half* of what things cost in Amsterdam. Don't give them any more and if they say it isn't Pfalzland money, tell them it's *better*, it's gold, but tell them that it's *all* you have. If they want to steal it, let them, but plead with them just a little that it is *all* the money you have in the world."

"Yes Gilles."

She was always amazed that he knew how to do these things, including how to bargain with people, but Gilles had always laughingly said to her that what his merchant father and Jean Durie didn't teach him, he had learned from living for six months with the Amsterdam Jews, a race that carried within the very fibers of their being, centuries of experience trading and bartering in the bazaars of the Middle East and after that, in the Diaspora. Gilles always said they wouldn't respect anyone who *didn't* bargain with them. She put the coins into her apron pocket.

"Gilles?"

"Ja?"

"Have fun playing in the dirt today, Gilles."

She couldn't resist saying it. Her husband usually had a much better temperament and was more easy going, except after particularly long and difficult days at Ste Germaine's. She knew that he was probably worried about the future and if she took the time to think about it right now, *she* might be very worried too, but she wasn't going to start that so early, not today.

After Bruinje finally woke up, Elsje took him to the privy and had a little more success since the child was not awake enough to know where he was before he left. His mother cleaned him up, got him his breakfast, and together they set out to find the market. Elsje held fast to Bruinje's hand and carried one of the empty water pails along with them to use as a shopping basket. Away out in the fields behind the house, Elsje saw Gilles hauling large rocks out of the way as a man with two emaciated oxen pulled up chunks of the rocky earth with a primitive-looking plow. The contraption behind the animals appeared to be ripping the pieces out of the ground although Elsje had always imagined that plowing would be more like the bow of a ship cleanly parting open waters as the implement smoothly turned over long, even rows of dirt.

Ah well. The field was her husband's business. She would attend to the house and the marketing and let *him* worry about the crops. Elsje and Bruinje walked on together, hand in hand through the settlement houses along the river, passing by their new neighbors who were busy cleaning their clothes at the riverbank, tending their herb gardens, sharpening farm implements, making repairs to their houses and constructing or mending furniture. Elsje was too shy to stop and have a *real* conversation yet: She was afraid her language skills were not up to the task of conversing in depth with these strangers. Some of her new neighbors returned her tentative and timid greeting but others gave Elsje and Bruinje a look of indifference before returning to their work without saying a word in reply. Elsje was dismayed to see that the children of the village almost all looked thin and dirty, in fact, every one of them looked like Suzanne's sons.

"So this is where the outlawed bourgeois class of France goes if they don't come to Amsterdam," Elsje muttered to herself.

She tried to picture her little brother here and Bruinje growing to manhood here, but the picture would not take sharp focus in her mind, although she tried more than once to accomplish this as they walked along. As they progressed along the river, Elsje looked for a farm or shopping stalls, anything that might fit the vague description Claire had given her. Elsje reached the end of the settlement before she realized it and still she had not seen anything resembling a market. Perhaps Claire had meant to say the *south*, not north, *up* the river and not downstream. Probably Elsje had misunderstood her new French friend. Elsje turned Bruinje around and they walked past the houses again, past their own and other houses, on to nothing more but the church and the minister's house. Just beyond that their progress was stopped at a tangle of river willows.

The only landmark besides the houses that she saw on this end of the settlement was the cemetery. It took her aback to see that the burial ground was at the water's *very* edge and she wondered if the spring floods on the river ever claimed any of the bodies along with the land. At home in Amsterdam the dead were tucked safely away in their churchyards, at a fair distance from the dykes and the sea walls where they would be no more threatened by floods than the living. Only a very few of the monuments to the dead were made of stone, and those were not full-sized; the rest of the burial ground consisting of wooden monuments, circles of stones, and marker stones, presumably placed at the head and foot of each occupant. The circumferences of the circles and the distance between the marker rocks at either end of the burials told her, too, that this was a cemetery filled with children.

Bruinje pulled at Elsje's hand and tried to run after a large butterfly that danced in the air over the early spring flowers covering the graves, small white and purple blossoms growing wild and winding their way among the stones.

"Nee, Bruinje, *nee!*"

He made whining noises and pulled harder at his mother's arm.

"I said '*No!*'"

314

Elsje didn't want him to be in there. It was too much of a bad omen. *Perhaps these are the only playmates he will ever find here in this place. Perhaps my coming child will join all of the others in here..*

Elsje refused to accept these thoughts as she turned Bruinje around and dragged him back in the direction of Claire's house; she pointed out other distractions to the child to keep him moving in the desired direction.

"Look at the sheep, Bruinje! Baaaaah! Schaap!"

The front door to Suzanne's house was ajar, as usual.

"Bonjour! Bonjour?" Elsje called inside Suzanne's house when she got there.

Suzanne came to the door in the same dress that she had been wearing on the day that Elsje had arrived in Nouvelle Rochelle. It appeared to be even shabbier and dirtier than it was then and Elsje wondered if the woman had changed any of her clothing since that time.

"Bonjour, Suzanne. Claire told me yesterday that there is a market somewhere here but I couldn't find it."

Suzanne sneered her reply. "Market isn't the word I'd use for it. Maman! Maman! Go show the *Neerlandais woman* where the "*market*" is."

Suzanne threw this over her shoulder to the interior of the house and then she disappeared back inside without inviting Elsje in or even asking that she wait for her mother at the front door. While Elsje stood waiting for Claire, she took a deep breath and reminded herself that people who had *not* worked with the public or in a business like her father's *often* had bad manners unless they were of the higher and more refined classes and had been able to take the time and make the effort to cultivate these abilities. Dealing with people like this required a little *more* understanding and patience than usual. Elsje told herself that she should not begrudge the additional investment and expenditure of energy toward this end if she wanted to get along with her neighbors in the future.

"Bonjour, Elsje and Bruinje! I could use some fresh air. I'll get my shawl," Claire said.

"Oh, you won't need it. It's going to be warm out today," Elsje replied.

"Ah Elsje, I can *tell* that you are from the north! To me it feels very cool out there."

Claire grabbed her wrap from where it hung just inside, on a peg by the door, and then she pulled hard on the old front door, scraping it across the dirt to close it as best she could although there was still a gap where it wouldn't close completely. She took a step out into the morning sunshine as she threw the woolen shawl over her shoulders. This created a nice memory that Elsje would always keep with her, the two friends setting out on an excursion as the Rhineland's morning light filtered down through the mists still clinging to the tops of the tall pine trees.

It was as Claire had explained, not *really* a market, but a house where an old man sold extra food that he had. Nicholas, the old German farmer, lived alone, his children grown and his wife gone to the earth behind the house many years before the first grave was dug in the new French settlement's cemetery. His house was set back away from the others and from the river, the broken down fences guarding the property now extending almost into the encroaching woods that were slowly winning their territorial war, sending more seedlings each year to lay claim to the farmer's fields.

Claire knocked harshly on his front door and after a few moments he came outside, leading them wordlessly to his barn where he offered them some hanging dried meat of an indeterminate species that was garnished with buzzing flies, fresh eggs, and milk from his goats and cows. His hungry French customers had apparently been coming by frequently for several years now and he had learned enough of their language to transact business with them but Elsje couldn't know that generally they did not care to hold long conversations, perhaps thinking him their spiritual inferior, so he just conducted his business in silence by pointing, gesturing, indicating price with his fingers, and holding his hand out to collect their payment.

Elsje smiled at him though, and tried to speak with him, struggling gamely along in French; it was only natural for her to make the attempt after years of being a friend, mother, and advisor to the guests at her father's tavern, both her long-time customers and newcomers, putting them all at their ease.

He smiled and added a few extra eggs to Elsje's bucket after she purchased a dozen. He pointed at Elsje's stomach and gestured for her to take them.

Elsje didn't know how to refuse, other than by taking them back *out* of her bucket, so she accepted them. This felt more like *begging* than shopping but this was apparently how it was done here.

"Merci. You have chickens or cows?" Elsje asked.

"For eggs and milk, or to eat?" Nicholas asked, venturing a few French words.

"Both," Elsje replied.

"Chickens, oui, cows, non." he said.

Elsje held out her hand with the money and he puzzled over the Netherland coins briefly before he smiled and selected just one of them, then stuffed three squawking chickens into a burlap sack for her.

Elsje smiled her most charming smile of thanks at him as he secured the neck of the bag with a loose thread from the bag's weaving before he handed it to her. He ambled over to a large bucket, pulled back a cloth covering from the top of the container and poured milk into a small pail of his own for Elsje to take home. Then he eyed Elsje a little more closely and he had a question for her.

"You are a *Netherlander*, ja?" and the question came to Elsje in a language that was *very* close to her own.

"Ja," Elsje smiled and nodded at him. "*How* did you know? The money?"

"Not just that: I traveled a little when I was a young man and I have been to the Netherlands. You live among these French people?"

"Ja, my husband is French."

Nicholas continued to talk to her and Elsje understood most of what he had to say but Claire was left completely out of this conversation due to the language barrier that left her standing all alone on the other side of the linguistic border.

"Ah," old Nicholas said, "I *remember* the bier in Amsterdam! No one here knows our little secret, that they have come upon the *one* place under heaven with the best wine and the best bier in all of the world." There was a twinkle of mischief in his eyes. "...but I suppose you can't miss what you have never known, can you? No one over in the settlement drinks bier, ale, or even wine, not *even* for sacraments."

"Nee," Elsje sighed. "I suppose they think ale interferes with God's work."

"They do? And what do *you* think? I have some here if you want to try it, just for *comparison* purposes, of course. And your French friend could try some as well," he offered. "I could go and bring some out for you right now."

Elsje was not going to say no.

She missed it too much and although Claire might be shocked at the idea of drinking alcohol with a stranger, and with a male stranger at that, Elsje had lifted a great many drinks in celebration with people she hardly knew over the years.

It was the neighborly thing to do and besides, she wanted the ale and she wanted it badly. It might help her to recover some of the vitality that she had lost after so many months of battling her morning sickness. The old man seemed harmless enough. He was probably just very lonely for human companionship and probably this was the real reason why he sold his food, not so much for the few coins that he received in payment from the homesteading pioneers, although they did not provide much at all in the way of conversation, let alone friendship. Elsje couldn't believe that he really needed the money or that he had so much extra food. Her years of sizing up customers at the inn had given her a justifiable confidence in her assessment of people and Elsje was rarely wrong. If Claire or Bruinje had not been with her, Elsje might have been more cautious and not considered taking the old man up on his offer, but that *not* being the case today, Elsje thought for a moment, choosing her words carefully before she spoke them to Claire.

"Claire, he is offering us refreshment and it would be very rude of us to refuse. 'Better bargains are made over bier' we always say at home! Will you come and sit with me?"

"Is *that* what he was saying? I..."

Claire seemed just as uncomfortable with entering a stranger's house as she was about the variety of the offered beverage but Elsje was already following Nicholas, pulling Bruinje with her toward the kitchen door. She set the bag of chickens down and the bucket of eggs and pail of milk next to them before the bag moved off on its own, still making clucking noises, lurching and traveling over the ground like a great wooly brown creature with no legs or head, thrashing around and around in a circle.

"The birds will be all right there for now," Nicholas said. "Come in, come in! I *never* get to have guests, not for these ten years past!"

The old man's house was filled with half-completed tasks that started with the half-woven rush seat of a chair next to the door and stretched around the room to broken buckets and cook pots with holes, a hammer and some nails on the floor for some unseen project, and an oil lamp in mid-repair, taken apart on the table and lying next to a newly woven wick that had not been installed yet.

Even with the clutter, it was still a grander residence than anything Elsje had seen in the rest of Nouvelle Rochelle. From her vantage point she could see *several* rooms, not just one, and all of them with wooden floors. A great stone fireplace and a real oven were in the kitchen.

In spite of there being so much to see in the room, Elsje's eyes were immediately drawn to the fireplace mantel, over which there hung a large Catholic crucifix. Elsje heard an audible gasp from Claire who had obviously set eyes on the icon as well, but Elsje caught her breath and calmed herself; she believed him to be a kind old man, a good man, even if he *was* a Catholic. After her initial shock passed, Elsje realized with a sudden pang of sorrow just how much she missed her oven at home. Nicholas did not seem the sort to do much cooking although he had all kinds of cooking pots and implements, both hanging from the ceiling and stacked on shelves and tables all around the room. None of them appeared to have been used recently, judging by the vigorous settlements of spiders that inhabited them. It was not really a dirty house, just the house of a man whose old eyes had seen much of life and no longer saw the spiders as his enemies, but more as companions.

Nicholas gestured to two chairs and Elsje sat down at the table, avoiding the other woman's eyes and straightening Bruinje's disheveled hair after she pulled the boy up onto her lap. Claire sat down too after a moment's hesitation and the old man said he would be right back before he left the room.

"Elsje, I don't think…" Claire began in a whisper but before she could decide on or finish what she was going to say, the old man had returned, balancing three steins of bier in one hand. He even gave Elsje a spoon so she could give some of the foam from her ale to Bruinje. Elsje barely waited for Nicholas to sit down and lift his mug before she took her first sip.

It was *just* close enough to the taste of home to bring a lump to Elsje's throat. Claire sat stiffly, looking around the room nervously, obviously trying to avoid looking at the crucifix, at least directly, although she seemed to be keeping it in her sights from the corner of her eye. She never made a move otherwise and especially not to place her hand anywhere near the handle of the mug that held her ale.

"My name is Nicholas, did you know that? And what is your name? I met your friend the other day when she was here with another woman." Nicholas smiled and nodded at Claire although she was not taking part in the conversation, either due to her inability to understand the language, or because she was so very uncomfortable with the circumstances.

"I'm Elsje Hendricks and this is my son, Bruinje Jansen."

The old man looked at Bruinje. "Hello, Bruinje. Can you say, 'Hello, Grandpa? Guten tag, Opa?'"

Elsje bit her lip as Bruinje looked at Nicholas with interest but, as usual, the child remained silent. Elsje took another sip of the ale and hoped that Nicholas wouldn't ask if Bruinje spoke any more. Unfortunately Claire was now taking a bit more interest in their conversation.

"So you are from Amsterdam! What part of Amsterdam did you live in?" Nicholas asked. Elsje was greatly relieved that he had moved on to another topic while he sliced and offered them some dark bread.

Elsje nodded acceptance of the bread even though she was not sure how long it might have been sitting there on the table. It didn't look too moldy though and she was just happy that he had dropped the subject of Bruinje. Claire shook her head at the offered bread with another look of disdain on her face that reminded Elsje greatly of Suzanne.

"The northwest side," Elsje replied as Nicholas sliced the bread "near the Herengracht."

"Amsterdam is a *fine* place for Lutherans and Calvinists and there are plenty of Frenchmen there, too. You didn't want to make your home *there* with your husband, with the rest of your family?"

Elsje thought of all the reasons that she could give him as to why they had come here, imaginary or real, but she decided to answer simply, "Nee. My husband is a farmer. He wanted to come here to farm."

"Ah, they *all* seem to be," Nicholas said with a mischievous twinkle in his eye, "farmers or craftsmen."

"He learned to farm in France," Elsje replied, then wondered if she was saying too much. She had never before in her life had to be on her guard about what she said to anyone. Unlike her husband, Elsje's life had always been an open book, on display for all to see, friends, family and customers as well.

"This place may not be the ideal one for someone to get away from… from anything they want to get away from." Nicholas said, but he didn't explain this odd comment further.

"We are running from nothing," Elsje said defensively and she hoped that Claire understood none of *this* conversation, although Claire would probably be very sympathetic to Gilles' legal troubles with the authorities in France.

"Of *course* you aren't," Nicholas said. "It's just that the French marauders and Spanish armies sometimes turn up where you least expect them. I don't have to tell you that though; I'm sure you have seen enough Spanish soldiers in your lifetime, their *conquistador* helmets moving through your city streets where they are wanted the least."

Elsje nodded. She didn't want to think about that right now. It was in the past and she was going to leave it there. She had already finished her ale and now she wondered if she could ask Claire for hers, but Claire offered it to Elsje first with an added, "I need to get back to Suzanne very *soon*, Elsje."

Elsje finished the second ale more quickly than the first. She was painfully aware of Claire's impatience and she certainly didn't want the neighbors to see her leaving Nicholas' house and walking back to Nouvelle Rochelle alone. Claire probably wouldn't say anything to anyone but if the neighbors thought that Elsje had been out here alone, drinking with a man, even with an old man, it would surely be fodder for the settlement's gossips and a very inauspicious way to start her new life here. Elsje thanked Nicholas and stood up, feeling for a short time just a little light-headed, but more pleasantly relaxed than she had been in many a month.

"Come back *any* time, even when you don't need to buy food and bring your husband for some ale, too! It's too bad your friend has to leave so soon. I haven't had a real conversation with anyone in a long time and I have *greatly* enjoyed it," Nicholas said to Elsje, his watery old eyes shining a little brighter.

Elsje retrieved Bruinje, who had been for the past fifteen minutes lying on the floor with Nicholas' old black dog. The dog lay sleeping on the kitchen floor, undisturbed by the child who had first lifted the dog's ears and tail and then finally used the animal for a large and warm pillow. Elsje led her son outside and picked up the bag of chickens that immediately began to move and squawk again. Elsje bid Nicholas good day and Claire helped by taking up the buckets of milk and eggs since her friend already had her hands full.

"Auf Wiedersehen, Elsje."

"Dank u, Herr Nicholas."

"You are most welcome. Auf Wiedersehen Bruinje! Can you say, 'Auf Wiedersehen, Opa'?" Then he added in broken French, "Au revoir, ladies, thank you both for coming. Come again soon."

Claire mumbled a quick farewell in his direction.

Elsje could feel Nicholas' eyes on her as he watched them go. Maybe he was still wondering what kind of trouble followed the young woman's husband, forcing them to take refuge with the French outcasts instead of living comfortably with her own family, among her *own* people. Maybe he was just feeling happy that he had someone to talk with today.

"That old man is a *Catholic* and he talks too much!" Claire said. "… and asking us to drink *alcohol* with him! You are *too* accommodating, Elsje, you must learn to say 'non!' It's not *decent* for a woman to go into a man's house and not good to drink *any* kind of spirits at all! What if Suzanne smells it? And how can you forgive what they did to us on St Bartholomew's Day? Fifty *thousand* men, women and children, all slaughtered like they were nothing of consequence, like they were flies! In the Netherlands too, I heard, the Spaniards left no one alive in some of the cities, all in the name of the *Pope!*"

Elsje managed an apologetic smile, but she held her tongue. The memories of what had been done in the name of God pained her *too,* but today, she wasn't sorry at all that she had lifted a stein of bier with Nicholas. She *loved* the visit: It was like having her father with her, like being back at the inn, only *better* because old Nicholas was so pleasant and likeable, and unlike her own father, this old man seemed disinclined to cause any kind of trouble.

Elsje was pleased with her purchase, too, because they would have chicken to eat very soon and then chicken broth and soup. If Gilles didn't know how to kill it, Elsje would have to do it herself, but that was all right; she had watched her father enough times. She doubted if Gilles even *owned* an ax and she wondered who among her neighbors might have one that could be borrowed for the execution. She preferred to ask someone *besides* Suzanne and her husband, though.

They walked along in silence, Claire perhaps fuming at Elsje's lack of propriety, and Elsje thinking about how she could get more vegetables for them to eat before the crops were harvested. Perhaps Gilles could find some early peas or carrots in town or for sale by their neighbors. Maybe there were some early berries in the fields or watercress growing in the nearby streams. Elsje still wanted to start her own market. She wouldn't be in competition with Nicholas because she would sell *only* vegetables and fruits. Elsje needed to talk to Gilles and see what he planned to plant; even though the garden was his responsibility, these decisions could not be left entirely up to a man, particularly one whose background had given him *no* idea of what foods were needed in a household, of how much would keep a family fed for a year, what would keep well over the winter without spoiling, and what crops were *always* abundant enough to count on selling the excess. Did anyone in Nouvelle Rochelle have the money to buy vegetables if she started this market? They would surely buy from her if they had the money and if Elsje had beautiful vegetables for sale at a reasonable price. They could always trade services or barter *their* excess goods for what they needed.

Elsje decided, too, that she was going to make some soup or stew to sell to the sailors the next time one of the boats came in. Maybe she would *give* it away at first so they would come to look forward to it. The men on the boat would certainly be appreciative of a good hot meal after so many days on the water. At the moment there was no place for the river men to eat or to stay in Nouvelle Rochelle so *of course* they weren't inclined to stop for any length of time or to leave any of their money behind.

Elsje wanted Gilles to buy a cow somewhere, too. She couldn't haul milk for Bruinje *every* day, all the way from Nicholas' home, and she wanted butter and cheese as well. Carrying it all that distance would leave her no time or energy to churn it, let alone to do all the other chores that she had to do in a day, washing the clothes in the river, housekeeping, feeding the livestock, sewing and mending their clothing, making candles and wicks for the lamps, keeping the fire going every hour of the day and night, not to mention the cooking.

"Elsje, I don't want us to part on bad terms," Claire said suddenly as they neared Elsje's house.

"Ah, non!" Elsje replied, realizing suddenly that Claire had mistaken her silence for something more than contemplation. "We *are* friends, oui?"

"Oui!" Claire affirmed.

Gilles laughed out loud when he saw her coming toward him, loaded down with her purchases, including the wobbling, squawking bag.

"Chickens, eh?! I'll ask our neighbor Msr. Philippe if I can keep them in his barn for a time until I can get a pen built for them," Gilles offered.

Elsje just smiled, then hiccupped in reply and Gilles gave her a strange look.

"If I didn't know better, I'd say you had been…" Gilles broke off his line of thought, at least out loud, and he smiled at Claire. "Well, I'm glad you found what you needed today."

"Yes, we did!" Elsje told him enthusiastically.

It being Sunday the next day, they attended their first church service in Nouvelle Rochelle on the following morning. The day was long and tedious for Gilles even though it was conducted entirely in French. Although she couldn't *hope* to understand it all, Elsje seemed not so much to share Gilles' misery and boredom. She was happy to be in church again, even if there was no music and no singing.

Gilles found it bizarre in the extreme to hear a church service that was *not* in Latin. He had been to Elsje's church in the Netherlands of course, and it had been odd enough to hear it in Nederlands, but on top of the language of delivery, these French Protestants had some *very* strange rituals. Gilles was ruminating on this when he suddenly realized that the readings from their bible, purported to be taken directly from the scriptures, were *so* badly translated that the meaning of the passages had either been completely changed or left with no comprehensible meaning at all. There were no statues of the Virgin to look at, no bells to listen to, other than the small one outside that called the village to worship, no incense to smell, and no organ music echoing off the walls, ceiling, and floor to send vibrations of heavenly communication and awe through the earthbound bodies in the sanctuary.

Gilles thought briefly of Rene, a fellow prisoner he had known during his incarceration in France. The man had probably been sentenced to death and then either burned at the stake or hanged, a zealous but kind sort who had been an avidly practicing Huguenot. Gilles had never had so much as a glimpse of Rene's face; there had only been the comforting voice drifting over to Gilles from the adjoining cell. Was this *all* there was to it? Was *this* what Rene gave up his life for, his entire being and the remainder of his short time allotted to him in this world? Did he die only for a change in the format of an old ritual?

When Gilles and Elsje had first stepped inside the church, no one had moved aside to share their seat even as the Jansens quite obviously looked around for a place to sit down. In fact, some of his neighbors (did he imagine it?) gave Elsje and Gilles *less* than friendly looks. The minister, apparent to Gilles both by his position at the front of the church as well as by his odd combination of accoutrements, a sourpeliz and Geneva bands, beckoned for them to come up and sit with his wife up in the front row. Gilles carried Bruinje and escorted his pregnant wife through the crowd up to the pew.

The very long services in the morning and the afternoon, taking up the entire day on the hard and crude backless benches, were difficult in the extreme for Elsje with her already-aching back, but they would have been almost too miserable for Gilles to bear at all had it not been for the distraction provided by the man of God's wife.

Gilles had never experienced such a thing before unless one counted the occasional attacks of lust that had overcome him in his earlier teenage years. It was a truly *foudroyant* experience even to look upon her, a fragile angel diametrically opposed to her lank, dark, and plain husband with his pockmarked face and long scars that crisscrossed his prematurely balding head. She was very short, tiny in fact, and of perfect proportions, from her smooth little hands to her diminutive feet that were tucked neatly into sweet little cloth shoes. With her doe's eyes of dark brown emphasizing all the more her light blonde hair, she was a gem on display in a velvety smooth, fawn-colored dress *so* simple and so completely *without* ornament, that the draped fabric only served to flatter her beauty all the more. She could have been any king's queen, Gilles thought, or at the very *least* a marquis' or a duke's lady, but she had accepted for her life partner the grave and serious clergyman whose slightly crossed eyes and lofty thoughts seemed to be always so far away, on his god, and never on his pretty wife. Indeed, it was obvious right away that they had no children and Gilles wondered whether it was a shortcoming on the part of the wife or her husband.

Surely it had to be the husband's fault.

In a good way, she reminded Gilles of Marie, the girl that he had been betrothed to and almost married in France, and although she sat in the same row as Gilles, with Elsje and Bruinje sitting between them, the young woman was a source of fascination that kept Gilles' thoughts and attention occupied throughout the long day as he wondered various things about her, if her family was from Montauban or Toulouse, why the couple had not been blessed with children yet, or if she knew that she resembled greatly the statue of a roman goddess that had for centuries looked down upon Rouen's town square.

After the morning church services, some of their new neighbors greeted them although they did so in what Gilles perceived to be a less-than-friendly and judgmental sort of way. Several noted, in a polite way of course, that Elsje's dress was rather a bright color and had *buttons*. Most of the congregants greeted the family genteelly, if not cordially, but others seemed oddly unfriendly, even going to great lengths to avoid talking to them. Antoine De Mare, one of their fellow townspeople, told Gilles that they had all been wondering who moved into the house with the newly repaired roof.

"Couldn't you find a house that was *already* fixed?" Yves Blois asked Gilles.

"I wanted *that* house," Gilles replied. "It was sturdier than the others I saw."

"It's a little *too* pretentious, we all thought, so none of us wanted it. Which Church in Amsterdam did you belong to? Did you belong to the Westerkerk or a French Church? Did you know my cousin, Francois Motier, who lives there?" Christian DeiJos barraged Gilles with information and questions.

"We didn't attend the *French* church," Gilles changed the subject, just barely managing *not* to say that they wouldn't have gone anywhere near the Calvinist churches in Amsterdam for any reason. He did have a few questions of his own for them, though.

"Do you know Jacques Pierre? He should have arrived here a few weeks ago."

"The Palatinate is a large place; did he go to another town?" Gilbert Moser asked.

"I thought he was coming here, to Nouvelle Rochelle. He left Amsterdam over a month ago," Gilles said. "He brought grapevines with him."

"There was a crazy man on our boat whose wife and children died on the trip. He was always mumbling about grapes," David Tavernier said. "I think he said he was going to Mainz."

"We have no use for grapes here!" one stout woman with a red and angry face declared. "They were given to man by the devil!"

Gilles' first thought was to wonder just how badly the Protestant translations of the bible had been mashed up from the original if the woman didn't even know *which* fruit the serpent had offered to Eve. He then decided that his neighbors had just appended the list and he made a mental note not to talk to his neighbors about *any* kind of fruit from then on.

Perhaps it was just as well that Jacques Pierre was not there; Gilles had been a little concerned about living near a man who had known his family so well back in France. The Montroville name and their Catholic sympathies were known throughout Normandie and just having a neighbor nearby who knew all about Gilles' past might have made for a situation that was even more uncomfortable that it already was; still, if Jacques Pierre's entire family had died on the journey, it was a terrible thing. Where was the poor man now, and what was he doing? Was he still alive?

Even Gilles, who didn't always take note of such inconsequential things, noticed that most of the congregation appeared to be staring at their clothing. It was a little more stylish, oui, and it had a *little* more color to it, his suit being dark blue and Elsje's dark green with a lace collar, but it did not seem so greatly different to him except that Elsje kept their clothing cleaner. What *was* their fascination with her buttons?

Their neighbors all wore clothing that was solid brown, black, or dark gray, and the only unifying characteristics of these garments besides their bleak color were the holes and worn parts that had never been repaired or were poorly mended with great puckers of fabric and clumps of mismatched thread all bunched together, over-sewing these spots, or occasionally patching them with different material to close the larger gaps, seemingly half-hearted attempts to hide the damage from rips or burn holes. One woman asked Elsje quite pointedly if her ears deceived her when she thought she had heard *singing* coming from their home. Gilles made a mental note to himself that he would have to remember *not* to sing or hum out loud when he was happy. He didn't say anything to Elsje about his growing list of "thou shalt nots" and she seemed strangely quiet for the rest of the day too, even when the last service was finally over and they were able to go home for the evening.

On Monday afternoon the farmer who had helped Gilles plow his field brought several loads of manure over in an ox cart. Gilles worked each small mountain of it into the soil, turning load after load of the stuff with his new pitchfork and shovel. He had purchased the implements that morning in Mannheim along with a supply of vegetable seeds and by the end of the day, the seed was in. Gilles had asked some of his neighbors if he might borrow *their* tools and avoid the trip across the river, but the men he asked all said they needed them that day.

Every day after that, Gilles hauled water up from the river for his fields, sprinkling the water on by hand at first so as not to dislodge and disturb the tiny beginnings of their future food supply. At night Gilles braced himself before he removed most of his clothes and bathed himself in the cold river, as much to clean off the dirt as to cool the burning blisters on his hands and feet. His less-than-fastidious neighbors no doubt looked on in shock and disapproval but probably with some suppressed amusement too. Gilles' efforts paid off though, when tiny green plants popped up very quickly in the Jansen fields and soon caught up with their neighbors' crops.

Their house was made into a home, comfortable due to Elsje's daily efforts and Gilles and Elsje together managed to kill their first chicken. Elsje showed Gilles how to dress and clean it while he impatiently watched. He told her that it was *women's* work and as such, was something that he should never have to do. Elsje made no verbal reply but Gilles knew what her thoughts were on the matter as they were evident on her face

The two feathered survivors were housed in a small but secure pen attached to the house that Gilles built for them as his first construction project, after he had the crops started. He built it so that the wolves wouldn't be able to get at them very easily in their new surroundings, even if the pack dared to come that close to the houses. The chickens settled in and not long after there were eggs, then even more eggs after the chickens started eating the grain that Gilles brought back for them from town, feeding this sustenance and nourishment to them a few times a week. Gilles had often observed his father's chickens in France gathering eagerly around the spilled remains where the grain wagons were unloaded. He had *also* noted that those chickens were all the more plump and delicious for their indulgence. A few of their neighbors laughed uncontrollably at his *purchasing* food for chickens, sometimes even mocking Gilles to his face, while others made known their disgust at this waste of good food on livestock, but after a few weeks and a few more chickens, the Jansens had the best egg producers in the village. Soon there were fewer snickers and comments but there *were* more stares and whispers.

Gilles observed that his neighbors often spent more time praying for their little green plants than in carrying buckets of water to them and they spent even *less* time removing the weeds from the fields. Gilles worked very hard, throwing in a prayer here and there while he worked, since that couldn't hurt; he cursed the plowman while he was at it though, being convinced that the man had brought loads of *horse* manure, not cow dung as Gilles had specifically requested, as evidenced by the prolific number of strange weeds that came up along with the planted crops.

Even though it was springtime, the leaves of the oaks were reluctant to reach their full size and flopped over limply on their branches, maybe because there was very little help from the heavens with rainfall. His neighbors prayed and waited while Gilles hauled water, day after day. The neighbors that talked with Gilles told him that he should have more faith, that God would take care of watering the crops while they spent their days making furniture and patching up their decaying homes.

Elsje went to Herr Nicholas' house every day for the first week to get a fresh bucket of milk for herself and Bruinje. She always had a mug of bier with the old man and when Gilles ran out of excuses, reasons why he couldn't go with her and things that he needed to get done in the garden, at last he accompanied his wife on a visit to the old man. He told himself that he *really* should have gone long before this: The man could be dangerous, or even worse, he could be young and handsome and having an affair with his wife.

Gilles was pleasantly surprised to discover that Nicholas was the very same old man from whom Gilles had borrowed the little boat on their first day in Nouvelle Rochelle, when they had just arrived here, and Gilles was equally glad that he had *insisted* on being generous with his recompense although Nicholas had tried to refuse taking his money. Gilles was reassured completely as to the man's good character after spending an hour with him and when Gilles tasted his bier, he made a bargain with Herr Nicholas: It was agreed that in exchange for a bucket of milk and a jug of bier a day, as well as a little wine if he had any, Nicholas would receive butter made by Elsje and she could bake bread for him in his oven. Gilles also promised to help Nicholas with any heavy work that needed to be done around his farm. Gilles knew that he would have to be *very* careful while he was transporting his commodities though, so his neighbors did not see him with the contraband goods.

This arrangement worked out very well because the old man hated to bake or churn but he loved his bread and butter. Nicholas was happy to give Elsje full use of his oven for baking and Elsje once again had the best bread in town, just as long as she had enough flour. Elsje's health was much improved by her daily consumption of both the milk and the bier and she felt much stronger now, her pregnancy sickness finally behind her. Gilles and Elsje settled into their new routine. Both of them knew that their future security depended greatly upon both the success of the first year's crops and then finding good land to buy for Gilles' vineyards and other agricultural ventures.

"Will it be all right?" Elsje whispered anxiously to Gilles one night when they were settling into their newly built bed. Msr. Philippe from the next farm showed Gilles how to build the bed, then lent him the tools, and even complimented him on the job he had done, even though not all of the legs were the same length.

"Yes," he said definitively, "It *will* be all right. We will buy a large farm of our own once I know where the land is best, before the yearly rent comes due, and we will leave this settlement behind. You will be a great landowner's wife and your *only* job will be to oversee all of our children and all of our servants."

Gilles had squeezed her tightly and kissed her after he said this, but he wished that he had someone to reassure him: In the last few years his fortunes had gone through great reversals, his going from being the wealthy heir of a great estate to working as a stable boy, then to being a servant of the public, waiting on people in a tavern. Now he was a simple tenant farmer and although his personal fortunes had improved, progressing from Gilles' being in danger of losing his life and being constantly cold and hungry to finding relative security and comfort, still his status in society had not changed very much. It frequently seemed to Gilles that if he was not going backwards, then his forward progress in building a successful life was far too slow.

And yet, he was not working for anyone besides himself now, and no matter how long it took, he would not give up on his dream of owning land and of one day regaining his wealth and worldly status. He was *not* like the rest of the masses: He was a Montroville and they had always been landowners, never tenant farmers, as far back as Roman times. This new venture into farming was his chance and he would take it now, following it all the way to the final conclusion of his wager with fate, whether that was to his desired goal of great financial comfort or if God and fate willed it, to complete and utter failure.

Gilles had some good healthy crops coming up and he also had the savings and investments in Amsterdam. He reminded himself that he was still a young man although he didn't always feel this way in his bones at night after a long day in the fields. He did believe that eventually life would get easier and he would become more affluent as time went on, but right now poverty clung to him like ticks in the springtime, much as the smell of the stable had once permeated his clothing, his hair, and his very skin during that miserable time in his life when he had worked there. By constant reinforcement of optimism, a little self-righteous anger, and a lot of hard work, life would take them to that better place soon. Gilles held on to these thoughts and every day they kept him going forward, to haul another two buckets of water out to his fields.

When the first peas and beans came in, and the other vegetables were coming along at a good rate, at last Gilles came to the realization that the climate was quite mild here and he stopped having nightmares about the crops being destroyed by snow or hailstorms. He agreed to buy a cow for Elsje who had been nagging him about buying one ever since their arrival. She wouldn't even consider goats, complaining that the animals *and* the milk smelled bad.

If Elsje had many moments of doubt, she never mentioned them to Gilles. Maybe she did not want to appear to doubt her husband or maybe she feared that his answer might not always be an optimistic one, one that she wanted to hear. She missed her family, her city, and her country terribly and even the long church services on Sunday did little to bring her the comfort of the companionship that she no longer had. The settlement's services were rigid and dogmatic, as well as conducted in French, and though the visits with Nicholas and Claire eased her loneliness a little, it was not as it had been before, with family and friends all around her, people that she was happy to see, and people who were happy to see her. She took comfort in the tales Gilles told her at night of how it would be when the crops came in, when they bought their own land and built their own little house. She begged him over and over again to tell her, and Gilles did, as much to tell himself again as to tell her. She told Gilles about her future dreams for Bruinje and the coming child and Gilles enthusiastically told her about how the new farm would not fail to prosper with their two sons and Elsje's brother helping to work it. Gilles and Elsje would buy their land very early in the spring and send for Heintje before that so he could arrive in time to help with the planting and building the new house.

Gilles found the times when he dropped into bed and fell asleep right away from exhaustion disturbing.

"Are you getting old? What if you can't keep up with the work?" a fearful voice inside Gilles asked.

"I *have* to. *There is no other choice*," he would tell himself sternly, *"and there is so very much that still has to be done. My sons will soon be able to help me."*

Elsje occasionally had doubts, although she never told anyone, not even Gilles, *especially* not Gilles. She sometimes thought of going back to Amsterdam. Her family would be there to greet them and would welcome them back with kisses and hugs. Her father would be *so* happy to see them that he would welcome Gilles with open arms and the two men would get along as well as *brothers* from that point onward. Always at this point in the fantasy, Elsje knew that these were dreams that were beyond any possibility of reality. If they ever did return to Amsterdam, it would be with their crawling back in defeat and her father deriding her husband forever afterwards for being a dreamer as well as a complete and utter failure. She didn't think she could bear to see her husband suffer this fate and so it seemed that they could not quit, they could not return to Amsterdam, not ever.

There was an excited buzz in the settlement one morning as the unusually dry spring was turning into a very hot summer. A boat had arrived with a few new settlers and it also brought word that the King of France was dead.

"Louis XIII is dead, long live Louis XIV!" the cry went up.

"But the new king is only five years old!" Jean-Louis Cresson objected. "What will change, *really*, if there are the same old advisors and if Cardinal Mazarin is in charge?"

"Louis XIII was only nine years old when he became king; it is too soon to go home yet until we see who is *really* ruling France," Jacques Philippe said, remembering tales of the dead king's battles with his own mother, Marie de Medici.

"One would have thought that the King's father being assassinated by a crazy Catholic would have earned us an ally these many years past, *mais non*! He was *no* friend to us and he didn't even live six months after his dearest ami, Cardinal Richelieu died! That is past now, and we will see what a new King will bring to our homeland," David Tavernier declared.

"*Cardinal Mazarin*! He's not even a Frenchman! He was never ordained a priest and everyone has heard about his gambling problems; that his *greatest* love is money. Now that the King is dead though, we'll see if he openly shares the widowed queen's bed! He's been the Queen's lover for years now and we all know that the Dauphin is *Mazarin's* child. What a diplomat! Portraying himself to be a *modest* man, a holy man! He probably killed the King himself!" Suzanne LaFleur fumed, with more vigor and energy than she had shown in months.

"I don't know what the French soul is like now; I don't even recognize my own countrymen anymore," Charles DuBois spoke up.

"The Frenchmen we left behind at home are all evil, and *we* are the aberration; we are the only ones left of our kind who still have hearts and souls," lamented Jean-Paul Haener.

"Mais *non*! It is only France's misguided and greedy leaders who are at fault! It was Richelieu and his minions who *really* ran the government and all *he* cared about was power, breaking the nobles and the Protestant city centers, fighting the Spanish and the Austrians, then finding ways of refilling the coffers that he had been *so good* at emptying!" Alain Gagner declared.

"Then why did everyone follow him so *eagerly*? Why did they shout from bended knee that Richelieu purged the country of a spreading gangrene? And the Jansenists were no better! ... Er- no offense meant, Jansen," Daniel DeVall said.

"None taken," Gilles replied, although he had no idea who or what the Jansenists were.

"I always said the *same* thing myself, made excuses for them, until they took my niece and her husband. They were burned in the square in front of her children. The Kings of France have *nothing* of God in them anymore although they protest to the contrary!" another man said.

There were gasps of horror at this, both at the brutality of the punishment *and* the open heresy of this statement, as it had always been believed without doubt that King, God, and Country were *as one* in France, a holy union, just as inseparable as the holy trinity or as smoke from fire.

Gilles took notice that *none* of them had criticized the Pope yet, and he recalled with amusement some of the more ridiculous papal pronunciations, including the declaration that *any* man who smoked tobacco, and presumably any woman as well, would be excommunicated because the stuff was known to make one sneeze, to lose control, and as such, it was too close to being an erotic experience.

"How bravely these men *all* give their opinions! It was *not* so at home, when we needed *someone* to speak out, to speak the truth!" Rachel DuBois noted.

"I would *love* to go home again," Suzanne sighed to Jacques Philippe. "Do you think they will offer any kind of amnesty for us?"

"It is possible! *Anything* is possible now!"

339

Gilles wondered if the entire settlement might soon be disbanded on a moment's notice, leaving him alone there in the wilderness with his wife and child. He would have to wait and see.

There were the requisite prayers for the deceased and even a few moments of sincere and heart-felt mourning for the old king, for whom a few of the residents still harbored some affection, as everyone regrouped and tried to determine which direction their lives should take in the future. The atmosphere was one of renewed hope, no matter which way individuals or families were inclined, to consider a return to France or to stay in Nouvelle Rochelle. At this time the residents were *especially* mindful of the bittersweet fact that their tiny settlement was named to honor the spirit and resistance of the city of La Rochelle in France.

Some fifteen years earlier, their fellow Protestant countrymen's final rebellion had taken place there during the last of the many sieges of the city. There were few survivors afterwards, less than twenty percent of the original population, after all of the residents including those who were *not* Huguenots, had taken a stand against the eternally changing, ever-constricting, and unreasonable dictates of Cardinal Richelieu's Catholic Church. The city of La Rochelle had stood defiant, alone, and had resisted until her citizens had seen most of their women and children starve to death, until there was no more to eat, nothing that might in any way pass for food, including their leather belts and shoes. Not her fortified harbor, towers, lighthouse, or Huguenot prayers, not even the intervention on their behalf of the English naval fleet could save the city and the rebels, although the besieged and hungry population held off the attackers for thirteen months. Cardinal Richelieu himself had become the lieutenant general of the army, taking great pleasure in sending out the daily sorties and personally overseeing the starvation of some fourteen thousand citizens, using hired Dutch ships to finally bring the remaining citizens to surrender.

Those citizens of Nouvelle Rochelle, who had personal ties to La Rochelle, were considered to be a kind of royalty and they occupied a higher social position than the others in the settlement. There were a few families among them who had welcomed German spouses for their grown children, but it was not a common occurrence even though these new converts were frequently the most zealous in their renunciation of the Catholic faith. There was definitely a hierarchy but Gilles did not understand this new social order. For reasons that were not completely clear to him, most of their neighbors *rarely* came by to converse with Gilles and Elsje. Both of them had taken note of this but neither one felt comfortable enough to discuss it with the other, each thinking that it might be their fault.

Gilles wondered if they had sensed some deficiency in his anti-Catholic zeal. Elsje believed that it was due to her being from the liberal Netherlands, having the wrong kind of Protestantism and the wrong kind of clothing to suit a demanding French God, as well as being descended from the very people who had sent ships to help murder the residents of La Rochelle. Elsje knew enough about her government to know that it had probably only been a *business* decision, the hiring out of a few ships for an unspecified task to make a few guilders. Only Claire came by to visit with Elsje and Gilles although occasionally the minister's wife would come by after church to make polite inquiries about Elsje's health.

Perhaps it was simply that there was too much work to be done all the time although it was obvious that the other pioneers looked on Gilles' successes with suspicion. Jacques Philippe was more charitable than most and he pointed out to his neighbors that it was *God* who had blessed Gilles with better crops and healthy children, and that Gilles and John Calvin *both* were gifted from birth with an understanding of several languages.

For his part, Gilles ignored the neighbors, watering his fields every day and on Sundays too, surreptitiously of course, before sunrise and after dark, but his neighbors soon discovered these sinful activities, these failings of his faith, and viewed it not only as a lack of trust in the Lord, but perhaps also as an outright sin.

Gilles' Netherlander wife with her pushy ways and immodest dresses were another source of local gossip. Although Gilles did not know all of it, he knew enough about his neighbors to know that he couldn't wait to leave the confines of Nouvelle Rochelle for a homestead that was more remote from this kind of civilization and to stop attending their church; he also knew, though, that for the time being he would have to be patient and diplomatic. He could be magnanimous for a time, if that was what was required for the next few months until the harvest, until after Michaelmas Day, when the rents came due, although no one, not his neighbors or Herr Goeble, mentioned this day by name or spoke these Catholic words aloud.

It happened on a Sunday morning when the late summer crops were halfway up and the leggy yellow vines and lacy green cabbage leaves also gave notice that the pale aubergines, malformed beets and crooked carrots were nearly ready for harvest. There had been much-needed heavy rains the night before, a *deluge* compared to the drought that had plagued them for the previous weeks and months, the storm preceded by thunder that had rolled down through the valley, echoing off the hillsides and scattering lightning strikes in its wake, one of which hit a tall pine tree that was growing behind the settlement, leaving a burned smell of tar in the air. The morning was sunny though, and the air was colder, crisp and clear. A very loud noise sounded as if it came from close by, perhaps no more than a few houses away, waking Elsje from a sound sleep in her comfortable bed. She thought at first that she might have dreamed it, but other loud noises followed immediately after the first one, the screech of wood against wood, someone screaming, and the sound of a few footsteps and then many more, running through the settlement, right past Gilles and Elsje's front door. The Sunday morning peace was shattered into a commotion of cries and wails before Elsje could get herself out of bed and go to the door to look out and discover what might be happening. Just as Elsje got there, Claire was at Elsje's door, her wrap just barely covering her under dress.

"What is it?" Elsje asked her friend. "What has happened?"

"The Philippe's barn has just collapsed!"

"Let me get Gilles up," Elsje said and she closed the door again as Claire hurried off in the direction of the uproar.

Elsje shook a groggy Gilles awake, then wrapped her cloak around her while Gilles pulled his boots on. They joined the men and women from all over the settlement who were at the Philippe's land, gathering at the rubble where the barn had been standing until a few minutes before. Mme. Philippe and her children stood there, wailing and crying, wringing their hands as they stood next to the collapsed structure. Claire was holding the family all at once, trying to both keep them back and to comfort them at the same time while some of the men gingerly explored the perimeter of the wreckage that had previously been a barn.

"What is it?" Elsje asked Claire, "Why are they all standing around?"

"Msr. Philippe was *inside* the barn," Claire explained to her over the din.

Denis Moser was certain that Jacques Philippe had been working on this Sabbath morning and he offered his opinion that it was God's judgment for the barn to collapse on Msr. Philippe. Denis was of the opinion that they should just leave him there. Mme. Philippe cried out pitifully that he had merely left his cloak in there the day before and was retrieving it to wear to morning church services.

"God would not abandon Jacques! He has brought us all here to help him!" Alain Gagner said over his shoulder as he joined the men who were digging through the broken pile of boards. They discarded the planks that had snapped into smaller pieces, tossing them over their shoulders and dragged the larger ones away from the immediate site.

Denis Mosier and a few of the other men turned and walked away, either because they believed that they should not interfere with God's judgment or perhaps because they were afraid of being caught in a further collapse of the building since all four sides of the building were not down completely, only two of them with a third side slowly groaning toward the ground.

The rescuers pulled the boards up with their bare hands and one man even ran to get hammers and saws as well as long sticks to pry up the boards, even though it *was* the Sabbath and this kind of work was surely forbidden, although no one had yet stopped to consult the scriptures or even the minister, who was not even on the scene yet. Because the minister's recently built home was further up the river and beyond the church and cemetery, he and his wife had probably not yet heard the commotion.

Horrible screams of pain pierced the air, not from Msr. Philippe, but from the horse that was also stuck under the debris. There was no sound from or sight of Msr. Philippe. The back of the barn was still standing for the moment but the collapsed front and sides were leaning precariously against the arching back wall. It proved fortunate that Msr. Philippe could only afford to build a single storied structure, because it did not take very long for the frantically digging neighbors to find the missing man. There was still no sound from him while the rescuing men pulled boards up furiously, savaging the building materials while they tried at the same time to be as gentle as possible with the injured man. The women gathering there looked on in dismay and some others tried to shoo the settlement children away though they all stood fixated at the spot, gazing with fascination upon the horrific scene. There were great groans and squeaks still coming occasionally from the twisted pile of wood and the rear of the barn wobbled uncertainly, threatening to take down the rest of the structure. Two men grabbed Msr. Philippe under the arms and pulled hard but his legs were still stuck fast.

"Elsje, go stay with Bruinje; it's not a sight for pregnant women," Gilles warned.

Elsje nodded and complied; it was best to avoid any shocks at this critical time.

"Is he alive?" one woman screamed. No one answered her.

"Is he alive?" she cried out again.

Alain Gagner hissed, "We don't *know* that yet! Just *be still*, Woman!"

The men continued to dig and pull until at last they freed the rest of Msr. Philippe's body. A loud cheer went up from a few observers when he moaned, as four men dragged him from the rubble and hauled him home to his bed.

"Does anyone have any doctoring skills?" Catherine DuBois called out.

"I nursed my sister's children through the fevers," Elysabet Haener offered.

"My husband hurt his leg once in a riding accident," Jeanette Brochau volunteered.

"Is there a physician in town?" Giselle LaFountaine asked.

One of the older boys, Michel Guitton, the boy who had run

out onto the boat landing on Gilles and Elsje's first day in Nouvelle
Rochelle, was known to be the fastest runner in the settlement and he
was dispatched to run up the path to the ferry landing and see if he
could find a doctor in Mannheim who might be of help.

Msr. Philippe uttered no more noises as they put him on his bed
although he appeared to still be breathing. Claire ran to the river with
a bucket to get some water to wipe the man's face and wounds. His
face, arms, and legs were covered with scrapes, splinters and blood that
trickled down from the top of him onto the bedclothes, small red rivers
of his life slowly ebbing away. All of his limbs looked to be broken and
the wounded man's chest resembled more a piece of cast off clothing
that had been run over again and again in the wheel rut of a wagon path
than part of a man's body. Jacques Philippe was breathing erratically,
with gasping breaths coming in and jagged whistling sighs going out,
all the while his face was turning a deeper and more unnatural shade
of gray.

As Gilles stood at the Philippe's front door, he heard the
unmistakable sound of a gun shot outside as someone shot the dying
horse, mercifully stopping those terrible sounds that had continued on
in the background of the man's crisis. Although he had rarely heard it
before, Gilles knew *immediately* what the noise was, and he thought it
rather odd to hear it here in the peaceful wilderness of the Palatinate.
While it was certain that no one here in the religious community would
admit to the ownership of a firearm, a very sophisticated weapon of
violence, not even for the sake of hunting food to keep them alive,
when the time had come to use it in an act of mercy, there was at least
one person in the settlement who possessed one, *someone* who knew
when they must use it. Gilles wondered if it might not be a mercy
to use it on Msr. Philippe as well, with the terrible state that he was
in, and the obvious misery and pain that he *must* be enduring, even

though he had lost consciousness, but Gilles kept these unchristian thoughts to himself.

The Philippe's house was *very* small, the standard size of a cabin, confining too many of the neighbors too close to the suffering injured man and his frantic family, but it was almost time for church, so most of the neighbors left, not knowing what more they could say or do for the family. Gilles watched them go and he tried to escort Claire outside the house to leave the Philippes to their personal anguish. Claire asked Mme. Philippe if she could take the Philippe children with her to church. The distressed woman nodded in thanks and agreement.

"Go with Mme. Montserrat, I will come for you later," their mother told them sternly and the three little girls reluctantly obeyed.

They said nothing but they sniffed a lot.

"Bring them over to our house first if you want," Gilles offered, "just to clean them up a little and to use the privy."

"I will do that, merci," Claire replied.

When the sad little troop walked inside the house, Elsje was fully dressed for church and so was Bruinje. Gilles took Elsje aside and explained the situation quickly, while the oldest of the Philippe girls walked over to touch Bruinje's curly blond hair.

"He's like a little doll, isn't he?" Claire asked the girl, trying to make conversation.

The child looked at Claire with wide eyes but she didn't answer. She just turned back to touch Bruinje again.

"What's a doll?" the middle sister asked.

"It's like a baby, a toy baby," Claire informed her.

Bruinje was remarkably good-tempered and soon all three girls were touching and playing with his hair. Bruinje made a few noises of protest, but on the whole he seemed just as interested in the slightly larger little people as they were in him.

"He has fat arms," the middle girl observed.

The oldest girl's eyes suddenly welled up with tears and she started to sniff again.

"Here's a handkerchief," Claire offered.

"All of you need to come outside with me and then come right back here to wash for church," Elsje sternly directed the group to the back yard. "The services will start soon and we *don't* want to be late!"

Elsje took all of the children with her and then made sure that they were well washed after they had returned to the house but instead of leaving with them, Elsje said to Claire, "You take Bruinje with you, too. You and Gilles can handle them all? I'm going to stay with Mme. Philippe."

Claire started to protest that Elsje *couldn't* miss church and that her soul would be in mortal peril if she missed any services, but Elsje would not be moved on her decision.

"I will *personally* speak with God. He will understand or I will accept his judgment."

"I'm going with Elsje as well to see if I can help," Gilles said. "You can handle all the children?"

"*Oui*, but *what* shall I tell them?" Claire asked. She seemed to be greatly and genuinely distressed over Gilles' and Elsje's not attending church.

"Tell them that our neighbors come *first*," Gilles replied.

Reluctantly Claire left with the children. Gilles and Elsje didn't say anything to each other as they hurried over to the Philippe house. Mme. Philippe sat quietly by her husband's bedside watching him sleep. The boy who had been sent to find medical help had not returned from Mannheim yet and there was nothing more to be done for the wounded man. As all of his wounds had been cleaned and he was still unconscious, they had nothing to do now but wait. Elsje couldn't get the woman to leave her husband's bedside, even for some food or rest, so Elsje set about making some soup with what little she could find in the house.

After a time, Michel Guitton returned with a physick from Mannheim and it was fortunate that Gilles and Elsje were there as the man spoke not a word of French but could converse with Elsje and Gilles in a mélange of German dialects. When even these attempts at communication failed, at the last he spoke with Gilles in Latin. The doctor examined Msr. Philippe but told them that there was not much more he could do with such serious wounds. He prescribed Adder's Tongue juice if they had any, explaining that the flowers needed to be gathered in the spring, left for a few days in water that had been covering unripe olives if anyone could find any of those, infused with an extraction of balsam oil, and then applied to the wounds hourly. Gilles was fairly certain that the Philippes had *none* of those things but he gave the man a coin for his trouble anyway. The physick returned to Mannheim and Michel went on to the church services that were already in progress.

Gilles left Elsje alone with Mme. Philippe and he walked outside to the collapsed barn, staying well away from the weight-burdened back wall that was now the only one still standing. The chickens that had been penned in for the night to keep them safe from the wolves were most certainly all gone, crushed beneath the rubble, but the pigs were still safe in their stone pen a short distance from the site of the wreckage.

They can't waste the food, Gilles thought: That would certainly turn tragedy into misery with the scarcity of sustenance that *already* existed in Nouvelle Rochelle. Gilles returned home for his long knife and then he carefully dug the dead animals out from Msr. Philippe's barn, the ones that he could safely reach, which was most of the chickens and even the horse. He gutted them on the spot but the feathers and skin would have to be removed from the carcasses later on. Gilles ran out of rope while he was stringing up the meat, putting it inside the Philippe's smokehouse to keep it safe from scavengers and to let the blood drain out, so he went back to his own house to get some more as he could find nothing at the Philippe's suitable to this purpose.

On his way back to the house, he passed by the barn, and taking a last look around for anything else that he might salvage, he spied an incongruous object, the corner of a dark cloth protruding from the pile of lumber. Gilles pulled on it, ripping the fabric as the piled debris would not relinquish it right away into his hands, the rubble holding it fast and tearing at it with multiple protruding nails and splinters. Gilles saw immediately that he held the bloodied remains of Msr. Philippe's fateful cloak and suddenly a memory came to him, that of a man he had known in Amsterdam, a Jewish man, rending his clothing upon hearing the news of his son's death.

Taking up the cloak and his knife, Gilles went down to the river and washed the blood from his hands, his clothes, his face, his knife, and the cloak. A cloud of animate essence, the life serum so recently lost and transferred from living beings to landscape, red blood, billowed up in the water's currents then curled around like liquid smoke, winding away from Gilles' hands and on down the river, the blood of the chickens, the horse, and probably a great deal of Msr. Philippe's blood as well. Gilles rinsed it out as best he could, then spread the cursed cloak over the bushes beside the river to dry in the midday sun.

He returned to the house and advised Mme. Philippe to salt the meat or cook it up as soon as possible, then keep it in a cool place, burying it in the ground if necessary. Gilles asked her if she had enough salt laid by to preserve it. The woman just looked at him in a vague and stunned way: Of *course* she would not have any extra salt. Gilles realized then that she was in shock and probably had not comprehended *any* of what he said to her. He looked over at Elsje who had just finished washing off the knife from her preparation of the soup. She shook her head at Gilles as if to say that the woman was not hearing *anything* that anyone said. For now, his advice was wasted on the grief-stricken woman.

The church services were over shortly thereafter and Claire returned to the Philippe home with the three Philippe girls and Bruinje.

"I need to go talk with Suzanne now," Claire told Elsje in a low voice. "There was a great deal of discussion at the church services and some of the neighbors said some very *bad* things about people who miss church services, Michel Guitton, you and Gilles, and Mme. Philippe."

"*Bad things*?!" Gilles exploded with anger. "We were taking care of our *neighbors*, something that they were *not* doing!"

Claire put her finger to her lips and cast a glance at Bruinje. She did not say anything more to Gilles but on her way out she nearly collided with the minister's wife who had come to the Philippe's door. Elsje invited the woman in and Gilles wondered if she was there to help or to bring more misery and a lecture. Where was her husband, the minister who should be *ministering* to his congregation, particularly to those so *greatly* in need of comfort?

"I didn't know about what had happened until after the service started," she said to Mme. Philippe. "I brought you some bread and cheese. I didn't know what else to do for you."

"Thank you," Mme Philippe replied.

"That's very kind of you," Gilles said to her.

"It's not so much; the bread is a little burned on the bottom but you can slice it off." She lowered her eyes and blushed.

351

"I'm sure it will be just fine." Gilles took the bread from her, his hands contacting hers.

"Come along, Gilles! We'll come back *later*," Elsje said, "when her other company has gone." She took Bruinje by the hand and led Gilles out of the door by his elbow. "Let *her* tend to her flock for a time," Elsje fumed.

At home Gilles checked on the welfare of his own animals before he went inside the house and it was the first chance that he had to do so today. Gilles had no barn to worry about, only the little chicken coop. Elsje put another log on the fire and then put their midday meal, some soup, back over the heat. She had prepared it the night before for today's meals, thinking that it would be a nice thing to have on a Sunday between the two church services, having absolutely no idea last night that their Sabbath day would turn out to be like this, one so terrible that she would never be able to forget it. She stirred the soup occasionally so that it wouldn't burn, in between doing all of the other things she had to do, taking Bruinje to the privy and getting the bowls and spoons out. When the soup was at last hot enough, she gave Bruinje some and had a little herself. They were nearly finished with their meal before Gilles returned at last to the house.

"You've been outside for quite some time," Elsje observed. "Bruinje was *very* hungry and was getting fussy so we ate without you."

"I fed the chickens and then I looked over our crops. I saw the minister's wife leaving the Philippe house," Gilles said.

"Her work is *done* then?" Elsje asked with an edge of sarcasm to her voice. "I hope you won't be forever *damned* for feeding our animals on the Sabbath. Have some soup and watch Bruinje for a few minutes while I go to check on the Philippes."

Elsje wasn't gone for very long, just long enough for Gilles to finish one bowl of soup, and when she returned to the house she had the three Philippe daughters with her.

"Mme. Philippe said she can take care of her husband if I can watch her girls for the rest of the day," she told Gilles.

"Can you manage three *more*?" Gilles asked, frowning at Bruinje who had become increasingly more difficult to handle over the past few weeks.

"Oh yes, you can go and do whatever you need to do," Elsje encouraged Gilles.

"We can get ready for church and go see what all of our neighbors are saying about us."

"I don't care to go there today but *you* can do as you please." Elsje pressed her lips together and said no more but there was a scowl on her face.

Gilles was very much surprised to hear Elsje say this: She would never have missed church in Amsterdam, not even if she was on her deathbed.

Claire called in to Elsje from the front door. "Ah! The girls are here and ready to go, too! We can *all* walk to church together."

"You go with Gilles. I'll stay here with the girls for the afternoon. They don't need to hear what might be said there."

Gilles didn't say anything. He only offered his arm to her but Claire shook her head. "I'll stay and help Elsje with the children today," she said.

"What about Suzanne?" Elsje asked. "What will Suzanne *say* if you miss church?"

"I'll just tell her that the children's mother is caring for their injured father and one pregnant woman can't handle *four* small children by herself all day long."

Elsje didn't present an argument to this so Gilles made his escape out the front door.

"I have to go outside," the littlest girl said, her hands clutching at her crotch.

"I'll take her," said the oldest girl, "It's my job."

The middle girl, who stayed behind with Elsje and Claire, watched as Elsje cleaned Bruinje's hands and face. She spoke to Elsje. "He has pretty clothes. We don't have a brother."

"He *is* a beautiful baby, isn't he?" Claire asked her.

"Why doesn't he talk?" the little girl asked. "Isn't he old enough?"

"He can talk," Elsje defended her son. "He just doesn't say much."

"Say 'cow'," the little girl said to Bruinje. "Vache! Mooooo! Vache!"

Elsje made mooing noises, more to amuse the little girl than to encourage Bruinje. She doubted that Bruinje would say anything: He never did.

"Moo! Koe!" Bruinje suddenly replied.

"*Good boy*!" Elsje beamed. "That was *Nederlands* for cow," she explained to the girl and not coincidently, to Claire as well.

"He can't speak the way we do?" the little girl puzzled over how such a thing could be.

"He doesn't speak much *French*," Elsje said, "Maybe you can teach him."

Elsje *still* wondered what it was that she had done wrong and why Bruinje was this way. Maybe she had worked too hard when she carried him, maybe she drank too much ale, or maybe she had been frightened by something. When he was an infant, maybe she had hurt him in some unintentional way that she didn't remember. He *had* come down with a fever when he was only six months old and maybe that was reason for his silence. It was mainly because of the way that Bruinje was now, that

Elsje obeyed Gilles when he admonished his wife *not* to lift or carry things during this pregnancy, not to work too hard, or expose herself to fearsome sights, such as Msr. Philippe's injuries as frights were known to cause pregnant women to deliver deformed children. Even though it must have been more of a French belief and not a Netherlands one, that a woman shouldn't do any work when she was carrying a child, Elsje wasn't going to take any chances at all with her unborn child. Why was it then, that all of the women in Amsterdam that Elsje knew carried heavy water buckets, lifted their children and carried life on as usual during their pregnancies and most of their children were healthy? Their children were *all* talking before they were Bruinje's age.

"Parles-tu le Francais aussi?" Claire asked Bruinje.

Bruinje said nothing. He just reached out to grab the little girl's hair as the two other children returned to the house from their trip outside.

Elsje set the bowls of soup down for the children, giving the two youngest a cup since she had no more bowls. She ladled a bowl for herself, more for an example than because she was hungry, for she had already had one bowl, felt sick from the events of the morning, and was not feeling inclined to eat much of anything. She offered soup to Claire who refused, saying that she had already had her dinner although she admitted that she had not been very hungry, either.

"We must *all* finish our soup, every drop of it, and then we can go outside," Elsje said.

"It's such a nice day. Let's walk by the river and make some flower chains," Claire suggested, "but everyone has to promise to hold hands and *not* fall into the water."

The church bell sounded while the children ate their soup but Elsje said nothing regarding this and neither did Claire. Obediently they finished all of their midday dinner although Elsje could plainly see that the eldest sister struggled to get it all down. Claire got a fresh bucket of wash water and she helped the children clean up after they had finished eating.

They went outside with the smallest Philippe girl holding on to Claire's hand and Elsje holding Bruinje's while the oldest and middle Philippe girls held hands and ran ahead of them on the path.

"Suzanne is so bitter now," Claire confided in Elsje. "She wanted a daughter *so* badly and then when she had them, they were taken away from her. I think she is angry with everyone including her husband and God. It tortures her to even *see* someone else's baby or to hear a child crying."

"Has she no hope of having another?" Elsje didn't mean to pry but she wanted to explore all of the possibilities.

"Probably. Maybe. I don't know, she won't even speak to me of these things but a mother knows what is in her daughter's heart."

It was a fine day even if it was turning a little hot. Elsje found it a welcome relief to get away from the hot fire on the hearth and the usual toil of each day or it *would* have been, except that her mind kept returning to the reason that they were there on that beautiful day, walking along the river. Being the Sabbath, there were no sounds at all coming from the settlement and the silence was more than a little strange. There were no sounds of shovels hitting rock, no homes being repaired with hammers hitting pegs, and no sawing wood for ox yokes or furniture. There were only the sounds of the birds and the tenor of the preacher's voice today as they passed by the open door of the church.

"It's *not* too late. You can make it in time to go to church services," Elsje told Claire. "They will be *very* angry with you, too, if you don't go."

"Non, non! But if *you* want to go, *I* can manage the girls," the older woman replied.

"I get no comfort from the services here," Elsje told to her friend as she shook her head. "I cannot seem to find God in this church."

"Churches aren't for *finding* God," Claire said. "They are for celebrating and joining with the community of others who *also* seek Him. He will never be found in a crowd, or with the help of a crowd, only by someone alone who seeks him."

"We don't feel much like a part of this community," Elsje confessed.

"That is why it might be a good idea for you to go and sit with your husband. He understands this and is trying to become a part of this place."

Elsje snorted. "That's not why he goes! He doesn't care for our neighbors either, but he is afraid of their criticism and *that* is why he attends church. For myself, I don't care *what* they think."

Claire did not respond to this and Elsje felt that she should not have said this, even to her friend. They continued to walk on in silence, walking a very long way and taking plenty of time to examine every flower, butterfly, and insect along the way. After they had walked as far as they could, until a pile of driftwood completely blocked the river path, they had to make a decision as to whether they would go around it through a swampy spot, climb over it, or turn back.

Elsje asked for Claire's opinion. "Should we go back? Should we take the children back to see how things are at their house?"

"I suppose so. Maybe you could walk back with them slowly and I will run on ahead to check with their mother, just in case..."

Elsje wanted to be certain that the children didn't drown in the river on the very same day that their father was so badly hurt, so she called them all over to hold hands with each other on the way back.

Claire set out at a pace that was very fast for a grandmother as Elsje walked slowly back with the children, a very pregnant Madonna surrounded by children, not thinking serene and heavenly thoughts on this glorious day, but thinking about the Philippes and about Claire and her family. Elsje walked on, wondering if Suzanne's kind of insanity was a common thing here among the settlers, caused by too many physical and emotional trials spaced too closely together, with not enough time to heal from each assault before the next misfortune beset them or if it was simply an *inherited* madness, a weakness in Suzanne. Elsje was nearly at the Philippe house and wondering what she should do next, whether she should continue forward or delay their progress when she saw Claire coming toward her. The older woman drew Elsje aside.

"Their father is not dead but he just *lies* there. I don't know *what* we should do. It will be supper time soon."

Elsje saw people walking toward them now, including Gilles, and she knew that the church services were over.

"How is Msr. Philippe?" Gilles asked her.

"The same. How was church?" Elsje asked him. "Aren't you out a little *early*?"

"We need to attend a meeting there tonight," he answered and his face was as serious as Elsje had ever seen it. "There is no change in him *at all* then?"

"There is nothing to be done, Gilles," Claire replied, "nothing except to pray. The man will either get better or die, as God wishes. He can't even take nourishment so the only thing we can do right now is to wait."

"Gilles, I'm going to take the little girls in, to live with us for a time, if it is all right with their mother. Please take Bruinje and the girls to our house while I speak privately to her."

Before Gilles could open his mouth, Elsje had turned away and was striding off in determination toward the Philippe's door, her fists clenched at her sides and her back as straight as a sailing mast.

"Did she discuss this at all with you?" Gilles asked Claire. He asked this aloud before he had the time to think about it, and immediately afterwards felt like a complete fool for asking. Maybe the men at the church were right: Maybe he *should* have better control over his wife and her actions. She certainly wasn't like any of the women in Nouvelle Rochelle *or* in France.

"Non," Claire shook her head as she looked after Elsje.

"I should have known that the old Elsje would come back to me sometime, just as soon as she felt better; I should have known that she wouldn't stay away *forever*," Gilles muttered.

"What?" Claire asked him.

"Rien," Gilles replied, "I was just thinking out loud."

Mme. Philippe was not disagreeable to the girls staying with Elsje for the night. She was too distraught to think of anything except her husband but Elsje told her not to worry, that she would keep the girls safe for their mother and that the woman was *not* to concern herself with their care, no matter how long it was needed.

Elsje had never taken in any children before. It was always the men from the sea that she had adopted at home in Amsterdam and their needs were very basic: some food, some ale, a warm and dry place to sleep, directions to a destination and a friendly smile. Now that she had a little experience with Bruinje, Elsje felt confident that she could handle this, too. She set about finding enough food for them all for supper. With a little of everything and a lot of nothing, she put it all into the leftover soup, even though they had already eaten one hot meal that day. Elsje's creation was very tasty after she had finished adding her spices and it would be enough to take them through until the following morning but then something would have to be done to find them some more food.

Probably fish, Elsje thought.

The rabbit snares were unpredictable at best but Gilles should be able to catch enough fish to feed them all and Elsje could cook them up quickly. Tomorrow Gilles would just have to leave his garden for the morning or until he caught enough for them to eat. It was true enough what Gilles had once said to her: They would never starve as long as they lived near the river.

The oldest of the Philippe girls helped Elsje by entertaining the younger children, telling stories to Bruinje and her younger sisters. When everything was in the kettle and cooking, Elsje dried her hands on her apron, told the girl to stir the soup occasionally, being careful when she did so *not* to catch her dress on fire or fall into the flames, and Elsje went outside to find Gilles and tell him that dinner was ready. She thought she might find him in the fields, where he always was, even though he shouldn't be there on the Sabbath, but today she found him just sitting in front of the house, perched on the big rock and looking out over the river.

"What are you doing here, Gilles? Do you feel all right?" She had never seen him just sitting there like that before.

"I'm well enough, Elsje. Sit down with me for a minute and look at how beautiful it is here. Do you remember when I first met you and we would walk in Amsterdam, then sit together on the church steps and talk?"

"You mean before I had all these children and you waiting for supper and when I had help in the kitchen? I remember, although it seems like it was a very *long* time ago."

"Maybe having the time to sit down and enjoy life is the *greatest* wealth of all, and more available to every one of us than money," Gilles said to her.

Elsje sat down beside Gilles for a few minutes even though she had a good many things to do. How could she resist such an invitation from her husband? The sun still had not gone down behind the house completely yet but the deepening purple shadows highlighted a valley across the way that Elsje had never noticed before. Soft pastel colors touched the tops of the few clouds in the sky, bringing a peaceful feeling to her eyes and to her soul. Far away on the other side of the river a young doe took a graceful drink at the water's edge and a wading bird briefly broke the peace by making a fast splash into the water to retrieve a fish. A short distance away a small green lizard stretched lazily in the last of the afternoon sunshine, looking up at Elsje and blinking, sharing the contentment of the moment.

"It *is* lovely here, isn't it? I never noticed that valley pass through the hills before. Is it a stream coming down over there?" Elsje asked Gilles as she took in the panorama. She supposed now that Gilles must have been coming here to sit at other times but she had never seen him out here before.

"Probably, when there is more water, it is. Right now it's just a path along an empty streambed, wherever it comes from, maybe all the way from the great mountains, who knows?"

"Well, supper is ready," she said to him.

"I guess we'll need some more food if the children are going to be here for a while."

"There is no telling *how* long they might be with us," Elsje agreed. "I have to go back in now to make sure the girl is stirring the soup. You can get us some fish tomorrow and we'll find out what else we need to get for food. It's more mouths to feed but we *can't* let them go hungry."

"Nee, you're right. We can't."

Elsje got up from her space on the rock but before she went inside, she paused long enough to kiss Gilles on the forehead in just the same way that she always kissed Bruinje.

"Danks, Gilles."

"For what?"

"For being a *goed* man."

Gilles got up and followed her inside. The large group sat down to supper, sharing chairs and seats on the chests around their new table. The church bell sounding during suppertime was an odd thing to hear, and the sound of it startled Elsje.

"The meeting," Gilles reminded her.

"I'm *not* going; I'm too busy here." Elsje nodded in the direction of the Philippe children.

"They asked that we *both* attend," Gilles reminded her.

"Then you can just go and tell them that *I* decline their invitation," Elsje replied and she would not be moved from this position, even when Claire came to the door and told Elsje that she *had* to go with Gilles, and that she had come to watch the children for her.

"Non, I am needed here and my work is here, I have no time for meetings!" was Elsje's curt reply, so Gilles left without her, accompanying Claire to the church.

Elsje finished feeding the children and got them all ready for bed. She went through the chests to find something to use for bedding for the children to sleep on. She pulled out all of the winter cloaks she could find and made a bed of these for their three little guests in the corner of the room, a short distance from the fire. The children fell asleep quickly, being tired from the long day, the eldest child holding the younger two close to her. Elsje thought that it wasn't *really* so bad, taking care of all of them, especially with the oldest girl helping. It was reassuring to know that she would be able to handle this many children when she and Gilles had four children of their own, especially if they were blessed with an older daughter to help out. Elsje had very little energy these days, especially after the sun went down, and she knew that her time was coming soon to deliver her baby. She pushed herself to finish washing the supper dishes and then she decided to rest on the bed for a little while until Gilles returned. She quickly fell fast asleep though, so soundly that she awoke fully clothed and with one shoe still on when Gilles and Claire returned from the church meeting. Their faces were both very somber.

"What is it? What has happened?" Elsje asked them.

"They all voted on it and they have excommunicated us from the church," Gilles said.

"Does that mean that we can't attend services?" Elsje asked, not quite comprehending the full meaning of the decision.

"Yes, and no baptism for the little one, either."

"So," was all that Elsje said out loud. "*So.*"

"They demanded that we leave Nouvelle Rochelle *right away* but I told them that our rent was paid and our crops are in so we are going *nowhere* until our crops are harvested and our lease agreement for the year is up."

"It doesn't matter," Elsje said. "We will be moving out soon, anyway."

"I suppose," Gilles replied. "I just thought that you…" he stopped talking and perhaps just remembering that she was still there, he looked over at Claire.

"I-I'm so sorry Elsje!" Claire stammered, her tearful eyes cast down toward the floor and in the direction of the sleeping children in the corner.

Gilles saw the line that Claire's averted eyes had taken, and with a shock, he realized *what* it was that the children were sleeping under. He didn't know if Claire was looking at the children or at the brown robe; more specifically, Gilles wondered if Claire knew that it was a Catholic priest's robe. His first feeling was one of anger directed at Elsje for her carelessness, but she didn't know, of course she had *no* idea, and he hadn't taken the time to explain it to her after she had left the thing outside to air just after their arrival in Nouvelle Rochelle. Gilles granted Elsje absolution and removed his angry feelings directed at his wife, transferring them to his neighbors who had forced him for so many weeks to watch his every breath and his every move.

The children's wool blanket had no allegiance, no ill intent of its own. It knew no history of the murders that had been committed under this standard, in the name of God and religion over the past centuries. It only kept the children warm and gave them comfort in the midst of their uncertainty about their father and their future, in the very same manner that the garment had once served Gilles, during his escape from France.

Gilles thought that the damned thing should serve *some* good and useful purpose during its existence, as too often the robes were used as magic shields for men with evil purposes and agendas. He would burn it when they no longer had need of it, perhaps tomorrow, and now he thought that he should have burned the cursed thing a long time ago. Gilles said nothing out loud though: What could he say that would make the situation any better if Claire realized what it was? That it was just a piece of cloth with no other purpose than to provide warmth? Msr. Philippe's cloth coat came to mind and it was an odd juxtaposition, thinking about both of the garments at once and the parts they had played in the lives and the deaths of men.

Obviously not knowing what to say or how to act, Claire bid them a clumsy and uncomfortable farewell as she backed out of their home and their doorway until she was outside, where she turned and ran off into the dark of the night, her footfalls traveling rapidly in the direction of Suzanne's house. Gilles attempted to convince himself that she was upset over the distressing situation and not by anything that she had seen inside the Jansen's house.

"Ah well," he thought, *"what is going to happen will happen in the coming days and there is nothing to be accomplished by worrying about it."*

Gilles' second excommunication, this time from the Protestant Church, was only slightly less painful than the first, the one from the Catholic Church, even though he didn't know why he should care about either one. He rationalized that he was concerned about it for Elsje's sake, and for the sake of the new baby, but they would be leaving this place soon after the harvest anyway. They might be able to join up with another church in another town by claiming to be refugees if the new church pressed very hard for the usual requested letters of introduction from their old church.

If anyone was made uncomfortable by their continuing to live here, Gilles reasoned that it should be his neighbors. Most of them would have to walk right by the Jansen house to get to the cemetery and to the church. At least this time there were no plans, none that Gilles was aware of, to hang them or burn them at the stake. Gilles thought at first that it was more civilized behavior on the part of the Protestants not to kill people, but then he decided that it was a very clever strategy, this ostracism, to bring everyone into a single line and make them act as everyone else acted, to make them believe just as everyone else believed, and eventually to make them *think* as everyone else thought.

Alain Gagner alone had spoken up in their defense at the meeting, saying that Elsje was a *Netherlander*, a stranger to their ways, and ignorant, that reeducation was what was needed in her case, not punishment, but he could give no excuse or explanation for Gilles' conduct. Claire and the minister's wife had begged to be heard by the assembly, perhaps in Gilles' and Elsje's defense or perhaps not, but their request to speak had been denied, as women were never allowed to speak. No other men had asked to speak in the Jansen's defense and it seemed to Gilles as though the council of elders had their minds made up even before the meeting. Gilles decided that he would just forget about his neighbors and concentrate on his crops, even on Sundays. They could all just go to hell, or to church, either one being fine with Gilles, while he tended his fields.

Gilles had already left the house the next day when a red-eyed Mme. Philippe came to Elsje's door and requested her girls back. She didn't say anything about the church meeting and Elsje couldn't be sure if that was the reason *why* she wanted her children with her.

"Their father is gone, dead, but it's *really* a blessing. He might have gone on forever in that state," Mme. Philippe sobbed.

Elsje doubted that Msr. Philippe could have lasted very much longer, being as badly injured as he was, and she was surprised to hear that he had lived through nearly half of the night. She offered her arms and shoulder to Mme. Philippe but the offer was not accepted.

Msr. Philippe was buried on the following day in a crude wooden box that Gilles recognized as being the one that Alain Gagner had once used for keeping his tools in, until he built himself a new tool chest. Until recently Alain had kept dirt and worms in it, using them for fishing bait after he had painstakingly scavenged the squirming things at night under the glow of his lantern, moving slowly across his lot in the darkness. His new tool box, being more square than oblong, did not lend itself to the task at hand and there was no other lumber available for building a coffin, save for the collapsed barn. Apparently the use of the barn scraps had been rejected by the widow Philippe, for reasons that Gilles could easily guess: Building a coffin from the boards would have taken some time and effort, as well as valuable nails that no one had available, and then there was the peculiar thought of Msr. Philippe's going through eternity with these same boards that had occasioned his death. Alain Gagner could spare the donated the box, perhaps in exchange for the boards from the barn, which could be used again for something else in the future. There being no mill of any kind in Nouvelle Rochelle, lumber was much more valuable and infinitely more *useful* than a sack of gold in this outpost of civilization.

The widow Philippe cried silently while clinging to her children, her hair and clothing whipping around her throughout the ceremony by the gusty winds coming off the river today. Gilles, Elsje, and Bruinje, no longer allowed inside the cemetery on the sacred burial ground, stood outside, paying their respects from a distance, well away from the rest of the congregation. Elsje waited for the widow Philippe afterward and offered to take the children for a few more days if needed until the widow felt up to caring for them again.

"Non, I want them *with* me!" she sobbed. "I just don't know *what* I am going to do now!"

Elsje talked it over with Gilles during their midday dinner. "Could you not buy out her husband's share and bring in the crops for her? Or could she stay there in her house and try to find someone else to work the fields for her?"

"Elsje, there is no money coming in for us yet and too much going *out*. I don't know if I could find the time to work both my land *and* the Philippe's. Every day there are *more* weeds than there were the night before and even with the rainstorm, the crops are *still* brown and dry although I haul buckets and *more* buckets from sunup to sundown. We are having almost *no* help from the heavens here, having either no rain or too much at once. Even if I sent for your little brother *today*, it might be after harvest by the time he got here."

Not satisfied with this answer though, the next day Elsje took it upon herself to go over to the widow's house. The children looked hungry and Elsje saw no food around.

"What will you do now?" Elsje asked Mme. Philippe.

"I don't know," the woman replied with her head in her hands. "I guess I could give my children away. Will you take them?"

The children had been playing quietly in the corner but the oldest child heard what her mother said. She turned frightened eyes to her mother. Elsje knew that the woman had not made the offer lightly; that she was quickly running out of ideas and out of options.

"**W**ell, *it is the measure of a civilized place as to how we take care of our sister's misfortunes*, my Cousin Vroutje always said that to me. You bring your children and come to my house for supper," Elsje said, "that is, if you want to: You know we have had some trouble with the church. I will see what I can do for you. If you don't want to be seen with us, I can bring you some food here after dark."

Mme. Philippe accepted the invitation with gratitude though, and said that she would be honored to go to their home. Perhaps she had had no other invitations.

Gilles had only made three chairs so far to go with the new table so the Philippe children and Bruinje all sat on the chests. As Elsje told Gilles before supper though, at least there *was* a table and there *was* some food to put on it.

"Is there nothing more we can do for her?" Elsje whispered to her husband so that Mme. Philippe would not overhear their conversation.

"If this was Amsterdam, the *charities* would help her and if it was in France and she was a good Catholic, the *church* would take in the children, but here there is no one to help, no one at all, except her neighbors and the church. You forget that we have your little sisters and brother to care for if Cousin Vroutje can no longer keep them. It's just too much for us right now, Elsje."

Elsje sighed. "Of course you are right, Gilles. I just wish... perhaps there are some people *here* who could take the children in."

"And what about *her*? Should she stay on and work the farm by herself, like a man? Has she no family of hers or his that she can go to? Did her husband have a brother that can marry her?" Gilles asked.

"Neither her family nor his in France will have anything to do with them unless it is to turn them over to the authorities. They are all *good Catholics*." Elsje shook her head sadly, remembering the gossip that she had heard from Claire.

"Then she is *truly* all alone. I don't have any answers, Elsje. I wish I did."

"I have been thinking about it: How could such a thing have happened? How could the barn just collapse like that?" Elsje demanded.

"I saw the inside of the building before it fell and it was *very* poorly constructed. These people don't know how to build things at all! There was too great a distance between the posts that formed the framework of the barn walls. The supports were just stuck into the dirt without *any* stone foundation and they rotted away. The roof had about five layers of wood on it and the rain we had the night before soaked the roof, making it *very* heavy, collapsing and snapping off the rotting wood supports. "

"But Gilles, how..."

"A *great many* of the buildings here are like that, Elsje, and you *can't* build them that way and expect them to stay standing for very long. These men never built anything in their lives before and they are learning the hard way, without the benefit of carpenters or joiners among them. They have only *experience* to teach them and that is a cruel and harsh teacher. They are *not* tradesmen; they are mostly from well-to-do families who did not farm or concern themselves with such things and now they try to survive by doing the *very* things they know the *least* about."

Elsje shuddered and involuntarily looked up at the ceiling. Gilles knew what she was thinking and he quickly tried to put her mind at ease.

"Nee, *this* one is all right or I would *not* have agreed to take it. It is probably the strongest house in the settlement, which is *why* I took it, even when it had no roof and the field was such an overgrown mess. In France my sisters used to laugh at me for helping our workmen on the farm but I learned a great deal about construction from them. The other houses here though..." Gilles' voice trailed off as he shook his head in dismissal once more.

"We need to warn them!" Elsje said.

"And tell them *what*? That the houses they have so proudly constructed are ready to come down on their heads? It would only make them *more* angry with us than they already are."

"But it would save their lives!"

"I have *already* told some of the men; they think that I am either a great meddler or have the intention of causing them harm. They no longer wish to speak with me *at all* on the subject and this was *before* our difficulties with their church. They tell me that *God* will protect them, that I am *not* one of God's chosen ones, and because I dare to question those who *know* that they are destined for heaven, I will *not* have salvation and will burn in hell. How can I argue with *that*? I'm afraid I will bring more anger down on our family by saying another *word* to them. Their belief is that they have nothing to learn from anyone who is their spiritual inferior. I *know* I could help them, but they are just not willing to listen or learn. They have made a *choice* between God and man, although one has *not* been demanded, not that I can see."

Elsje sighed in resignation. Although she dismissed her husband too quickly at times, he *was* a very smart man. Wiping her hands on her apron, she put a smile back on her face before she turned around to the table and back to her dinner guests. She got the bowls and cups out and ladled the hutspot into them, hoping that they liked it, since she did not know if the French had anything similar in their cuisine. Elsje insisted that they *all* eat as much as they wanted, as much as they could. The children were quiet but ate eagerly until their stomachs seemed to pain them.

Even if she had *not* been feeling so upset by the Philippe's situation, Elsje could only eat a little at a sitting: Her stomach was greatly reduced in capacity by the expansion of her coming child into her midsection. For his reason Elsje sent the Philippe family home with nearly all of the leftovers ladled into her great bread bowl, all except for a small amount that she set aside for breakfast, feeling that it was little enough that she could do for the widow and her children. She still wondered if the other neighbors had done anything *at all* for the Philippes since the terrible accident, but she didn't ask. Perhaps the neighbors felt that God had a hand in the event and if it was His will, the Philippes would starve to death.

Elsje lay in bed that night rubbing her stomach and thinking about Mme. Philippe, wondering if she could give up Bruinje or the child inside her under *any* circumstances while she still had a breath left in her body. Perhaps for some women, worn down by the miseries of what was behind them and the challenges that lay ahead, it didn't matter so much, and as long as a good home was found for them, as one would do for a faithful milk cow that was no longer needed, that was all right, but Elsje's lifework was the caretaking of her own family and of others. Not to ever have taught Bruinje the *right* values, the wisdom of the world, the everyday civility that was *so* important when it came to getting along with all kinds of people, or the little songs that Elsje sang when *she* was a child, was unthinkable to her. Not to ever share with Bruinie the family stories about those living or dead, the memories of her own mother who had left the earth too soon, when Elsje herself was only a child, not to teach him to love and protect his coming little sister, not to hold his chubby little hand ever again, these were unbearable thoughts to her. Before she realized it, tears ran down her face in the dark

"Mother's Insanity!" Elsje chided herself, *"twill be gone after the child is born!"*

She had heard of it but had never had it with Bruinje and so she had believed that it was either an old wives' tale or a malady experienced only by the feeble-minded members of her sex. She tried to blame all of her runaway emotions on her pregnancy, but she knew that even a strong-minded woman would have been greatly moved by the events of the last few days and horrified at the dismal prospects that lay ahead of her neighbor. It was tragic, the mother losing her husband *and* her children, all within the space of a week, but such was everyday life for most of the world, as children were frequently passed from hand to hand of necessity. In the end it all came down to one *single* determination: the ability or inability of the mother alone to feed them, and so more frequently than not, they were given away like a litter of puppies to those who had the money, and so it followed, the luxury and wealth of keeping their families intact. Elsje knew this woman personally, and she was a good woman, but Mme. Philippe was no different than the millions of other women who faced the same miserable choice daily.

There were never enough families to take in *all* of the children who needed homes, even when the orphants brought inherited livestock with them, not even when the guardian of the child was entitled to the *increase* of the livestock in compensation for the care of these waifs, the value of cattle generally being greater than the cost of feeding a child. The children who had lost parents through disease, war, abandonment, or other catastrophe, natural or unnatural, frequently had no way of knowing if the home they were going to was one of love, harsh labor, or abuse. The children could be treated as well as their new master's children or as poorly as the master's barn cats; it was usually a great unknown. Elsje thought perhaps that she might be able to take *one* of the girls as she could use the extra help right now, but she knew in her heart that Gilles was right: She had only temporarily left her other three responsibilities behind in Amsterdam. Her father and Cousin Vroutje were not getting any younger and she was the only member of the family in a position to care for the little ones if something should happen to Cousin Vroutje.

"Are you all right, Elsje?" Gilles asked sleepily. "It's not time for the baby yet, is it?"

"Nee, Gilles. I was just thinking about how unbearably *hard* life can be sometimes."

"That's true," he mumbled, "but if you believe that, then you must *also* believe that it can be unbelievably good sometimes, too." He stroked her hair once and fell back asleep as soon as he had finished speaking the words.

"...and this from a man who claims to have *no* faith," she said to herself with a smile. She kissed his forehead, wiped her final tears away, and settled back into the bed's warmth.

Claire stopped by Elsje's house at midmorning when all of the men were in the fields and when all of the women were busy cooking the midday dinner. She stepped inside the house quickly.

"I can't stay," she said, looking around nervously. "I just wanted to let you know that we are taking in one or two of the Philippe babes."

The thought of the little girls living with Suzanne and Claire both consoled and horrified Elsje at the same time; Suzanne had wanted daughters desperately and yet with her sour disposition, it would most certainly be a difficult life for the little girls. When Claire left, Elsje took Bruinje with her to go speak with Mme. Philippe at her home.

"Where will you go?" Elsje asked the grief-stricken woman.

"We will go and work as household help in Amsterdam," the widow said. "My oldest girl is old enough to help and God willing, we will be all right and I won't have to bond her out as an indentured servant. At least we will have each other."

Elsje later told Gilles of the woman's plan and Gilles wrote down Jean Durie's name, address, and a brief letter of introduction for her, telling Mme. Philippe that Jean Durie could probably help them. Gilles also promised the widow Philippe that he would try to work the land and send her half of the profit from the crop when it came in.

"Half?" Elsje had cried out later when Gilles relayed the conversation to his wife. "And you call yourself a *businessman*?!"

But Gilles observed that the crops were *already* up and it was just a matter of keeping them watered, weeded as best he could, harvesting them, and getting them to a market in Mannheim. Perhaps he *was* too soft-hearted but what if it had been Elsje in the same position? He hoped that there might be someone who would deal thus with Elsje if it was ever her misfortune to find herself in a similar situation. Besides, no one else in the settlement had offered to bring Msr. Philippe's crop to harvest.

Mme. Philippe and her girls placed flowers on Msr. Philippe's grave just before they left for the boat that was tethered to the wobbling dock at the riverbank. Reluctantly, Mme. Philippe handed over her two youngest girls to Suzanne just before she and her oldest daughter made ready to board the ship that was headed down the river, bound for Amsterdam. Between a collection that had been taken up at the church and selling her few possessions to neighbors that could afford to buy them, Mme. Philippe had just enough for the boat fare.

As they climbed onto the walkway, the oldest daughter bit her lip. She knew that she should not cry but her eyes filled with tears as she hugged her younger sisters goodbye.

"We *will* come back for you! *Don't* give up hope!" Elsje heard her whisper to them. The little girls, also under orders from their mother not to cry, did very well following this directive until their mother turned to go out to the waiting boat. The baby cried and screamed "Maman! Maman!"

The only thing the poor woman could do was to keep her feet going forward and not slow down. It took *far* too long for the boat to pull out and the two little girls left behind in the settlement could be heard crying for most of the next three days. The two Philippe orphans clung to each other from that time on, rarely going anywhere, not even to the privy, without the other.

Gilles had been giving more thought to his coming child after Msr. Philippe's death, and he realized that very soon it would be two years since Bruinje had been born. Gilles thought back to the day of his birth recalling well that day and the visiting savages who had given him the name "*Speaks with all creatures*". Perhaps it had been a curse or a joke. It would be *such* sadness for Gilles if the boy did not have a good mind, but as he observed his young son, happily digging in the dirt at the end of the garden row as Gilles took a short break from weeding, it was obvious to him that the child was *not* an idiot, that in fact he was very bright. Bruinje took things apart and occasionally he even managed to put them back together again. The boy found a dozen clever ways to get exactly what he wanted without saying too much about it, from just helping himself to making motions with his hands that his mother understood.

Elsje and Gilles no longer needed to buy the farmer's eggs or milk from Nicholas now that Elsje's chickens had grown into a small flock and the cow they purchased was giving milk, but Elsje took Bruinje to Nicholas's farm anyway. Bruinje liked seeing *all* the animals every day and Elsje needed the break, especially on the days that Bruinje was fussy from the new teeth that were now coming in at a rapid rate. The old farmer had a few goats, sheep, wild barn cats, and the old dog too, which were certainly much better diversions and much more entertaining to a small child than just one placid cow and a few aloof chickens that kept their distance. Elsje and Nicholas would drink ale and pass the time in conversation while Bruinje played with the dog. Every week Gilles brought his bier and wine home from Nicholas' house in the little cart and occasionally Gilles would help the old man with repairs to the house and the sagging old fences.

Elsje's baby arrived long before Gilles could even set out for Mannheim to find the midwife, but in spite of their excommunication and their strained relations with the community, Claire kept her promise, staying with Elsje until she delivered a baby girl who appeared to be healthy in spite of a rather bluish tint to the infant's complexion. They named the baby Cornelia Jacomina after Elsje's mother and Gilles' mother, but even now, years after her mother's passing, Elsje still grieved for her mother so much that she couldn't bear to call the child by her mother's name. Perhaps too, she felt it might be a bad omen, that God might take both Cornelias *too soon,* and so she was called Jacomina. Elsje's initial relief and joy at having given birth to a healthy daughter was quickly superseded with anger now that her infant would not be accorded the privilege of a baptism through what Elsje considered to be no fault or transgression of her own, but Gilles was becoming quite comfortable with the idea that there would be no church of any kind in their lives: Churches only seemed to bring misery and trouble into his life.

They both worried when the child took on even more of a yellowish cast to her skin during her first few days, crying more than Bruinje had when he was a newborn. The neighbors, who heard the incessant cries of the fussy baby, were emphatic in their opinions: It just confirmed to them that God was punishing the Jansens. Elsje couldn't bear to think about finding a place to bury her new baby girl since the infant would not be allowed a space in the church's burial ground and Elsje was also loathe to leave her behind in the leased house's yard or way back in the woods with the wolves and the wild pigs, but after confronting her initial fears, Elsje made up her mind that she was simply *not* going to accept a bad outcome. She decided that she would pray until her baby daughter's health was restored. Elsje stayed close to the house, not going very far, not even to visit Nicholas and this strategy seemed to work. After taking the child out in the fresh air for a few days, Jacomina's health started to improve at last.

Gilles told his wife that it was superstitious nonsense when Elsje told him of the miracle of her prayers, that the child would have lived and thrived *anyway*, especially after being taken out in the fresh air. Elsje didn't argue with him, but Gilles noted that she did take the child out for longer periods of time every day after they had their discussion.

Of all of their neighbors, only Claire continued to associate with Elsje and Gilles, although this was only when no one else was around to observe this. She would suddenly appear at Elsje's door, come inside and stay for a very short time, and then abruptly take her leave, looking each way at the door to be sure that no one saw her going out. Elsje couldn't very well blame her, as Claire would have been thrown out of the church too, if anyone had seen her associating with the excommunicates. Sometimes Claire would walk by with the Philippe girls and it was during one of these passes that Elsje first noticed the bruises on the children. She normally took no notice of such things as children's small scrapes and bumps but the little girls both had identical bruises on each cheek. Later on that week Elsje spied identical marks on their bare arms as they walked by the house on their way to church. She mentioned her observations to Gilles but the orphans seemed hale enough to him, so Gilles reassured Elsje that Claire would *surely* keep watch over the Philippe girls and no serious harm would come to them while the good woman lived in the same house with them.

Very soon though, the bruises were not the main topic of interest or conversation in Nouvelle Rochelle; they were almost completely forgotten in the following days when so many in the village, the little girls included, began to fall ill. The pestilence didn't have the sudden onset associated with the fevers or the great swollen medallions on the skin associated with the plague, the Black Death.

There were no marks on the skin at all.

At first it was just the very young, very old, and those of more fragile health among them suffering from minor intestinal complaints but then the sickness began to slowly spread, and most of the village, even once vibrant and healthy people, became ill with fever, sharp pains, vomiting, and cramps. It was an insidious disease that crept slowly up on its victims, grasping them tentatively at first and then slowly pulling them down farther and farther into bad health, starting with the intestinal gripes and progressing to the flux, not abating or improving over time, but continuing to take a toll on each victim as what nourishment they did take in passed quickly through their systems. Only the Jansens and a very few others in the settlement remained healthy. Out in the garden with Gilles one day, while a few of their neighbors were nearby, Elsje speculated loudly that the Jansen's health was robust because they did not share the *foul air* that was inside the church, although she could not explain those who attended church services regularly but were escaping the epidemic, too.

An emissary for the Elector rode through the settlement that same afternoon, calling them all together and creating a brief diversion in the midst of their misery. He wished to speak publicly with all of the people of Nouvelle Rochelle and the official made a fine speech in German, translated into French for the assembly by one of the German sons-in-law, imploring the settlers to bring more family and friends to settle there. He assured them that everyone was welcome and that there were plans to rebuild the once great city of Mannheim. Gilles and Elsje listened from a distance while the sick residents of Nouvelle Rochelle struggled to stay on and listen until the end, all the while clutching at their cramping midsections and from time to time, in spite of their most heroic efforts, hurrying away to the privy vaults.

"The war will be over soon and we can look forward to greater prosperity now, as we turn our efforts together toward rebuilding our cities. While Mannheim is being rebuilt, if you wish to live in town, we will help you find work *and* a place to live."

After he delivered his message, the man bid them good day and spurred his horse on to the next settlement along the river. When the man was out of hearing range, Suzanne's response was loud enough for everyone to hear.

"Well, that's nice! An *official* 'Welcome' to hell on earth! The air is poison, the work is hard, and the crops won't grow! Come here and *die*, our cemeteries need to be filled up!"

She roughly jerked her newly adopted daughters off their feet and dragged them back toward their house, perhaps angry that she had wasted *any* of her time listening to what the man had to say.

Elsje said nothing out loud but she followed Suzanne and Claire with her eyes as they passed her by. Suzanne ignored her of course but Claire whispered to Elsje.

"Life is just *too* hard for her right now," she said in defense of her daughter.

Before the people of the settlement gathered together for the official's speech, Claire had been the only person outside of Gilles and Bruinje who had seen Elsje's new baby. Not being able to show the child off at church and there being no visitors to their home either, Elsje had received no gifts, and no offers of help as there had been when Bruinje was born. What bothered Elsje the most was that no one saw how beautiful her new child was, and Jacomina *was* becoming a very beautiful baby as her sallow color subsided and a rosy complexion appeared on the child's cheeks with none of the red, wrinkled blotchiness of most newborns. Not being content to sit at home alone with her pretty new baby, Elsje decided that the child was now well enough to take out and show her off to Nicholas.

Although several of the residents of Nouvelle Rochelle had died from the sickness already, Nicholas seemed healthy enough. He, too, had watched the sad processions to the cemetery from the vantage point of his front door. Elsje and Nicholas discussed the sickness, how it had made so many of them deathly ill but strangely enough did not even *touch* others, leading to great speculation among the Huguenots as to who among them had been chosen for death and whether this choice had been made by God or by the devil.

Elsje felt comfortable enough with him now to tell Nicholas all about the Jansen's trouble with the church, Claire's secret visits, and how on one of these, Claire had advised Elsje to drink more milk because it seemed to ward off the disease. They had made this discovery when the women exchanged gossip while washing their clothing at the river and found that the children whose families had cows and drank milk were *not* sick, but every child in the families without cows were all ill. Elsje had laughed when she heard this notion and she had replied that she should remain the *healthiest* person in the entire settlement with all of the milk that she drank daily just to keep her milk supply up enough for baby Jacomina's considerable appetite. Elsje decided that it might not do any harm to have more milk than ale, though, just to be safe. Gilles refused Elsje's suggestion to drink the milk, saying that it was for *infants* and that he would stick to his wine and the occasional ale. He would just have to take his chances and oddly enough, he did not get sick either.

It was late summer now and many of the crops were ready for harvest but few people besides Elsje and Gilles were well enough to walk even the short distance into their own fields, not even to get enough food for their next meal. The settlement's gardens, all except for Gilles', were overrun with weeds, and when the winds were westerly, Elsje could smell the precious food rotting away in her neighbors' gardens. She wondered how they were ever going to survive the coming winter if everyone was too sick to go outside and bring it in; even if they managed to harvest it, there remained the work of drying the beans and other produce that could be preserved for use over the winter.

Elsje knew that Gilles *must* have noticed this but he said nothing to her about it at all. He continued to work alone on his own plot of land and on the Philippes, both of which were now far and away the most successful gardens in the entire settlement. While Elsje was very pleased with his gardening success and with their abundance of food, *still* it bothered her, especially at night, to think of her neighbor's children going hungry. When she mentioned this to Gilles one day, he grew short-tempered with her.

"Why do you concern yourself with *them*? You have just had a baby! Don't you have *enough* to worry about? These are the *very* people who *deny* our child a baptism! They can do as they damn well please and it doesn't concern me in the least! We will be gone from this cursed place soon enough and then we won't have to look upon their vindictive, starving faces!"

Gilles said this as he sat eating a fine midday dinner of carrots, peas, bread, and rabbit while Elsje sat next to him at the table, managing to eat a bite here and there while she nursed Jacomina. They usually had Nicholas' ale with their meals but today Gilles brought out some wine just to celebrate his having *finally* caught a rabbit in one of his snares.

It had been very early in the morning hours a few days earlier when Gilles had made a most interesting discovery, quite by accident: The night before, Gilles had accidentally dropped some of the grain that he had been feeding to the chickens and in the early morning light he observed that the rabbits had a great fondness for the stuff. Gilles scattered some grain in the immediate area around their home and not coincidently, placed it within a circle of rabbit snares.

"Perhaps the neighbors will think that the snares are for them," Gilles had joked to Elsje. "It makes no difference to me if they think that; I will be quite happy if it keeps all of them far away from us."

"God sends us food and good health," Elsje observed as she looked at the roasted rabbit carcass in front of Gilles, "so we should *try* to help our neighbors. How they conduct themselves is their business, but I sleep better when I know that their children have had something to eat."

Gilles said nothing in response. He just told Bruinje to eat *all* of his dinner and then he gave his son a sip of the wine, laughing out loud when Bruinje wrinkled his nose, spit out the drink, and hastily returned to his cup of milk. Elsje scolded Gilles for giving the child the wine and making the mess on the front of his clothes but Gilles told her not to worry, that a few wine stains didn't matter. Who was there to care about the boy's stained clothes here? Gilles gave his conversation with Elsje regarding the neighbors no further thought, but he should have known that she wouldn't just let it go: Elsje was not one to let anything go.

She waited until the following Sunday morning when Gilles was outside in the garden digging up ground apples. It had been her idea to bring a few of them from Amsterdam and plant them here. Having grown fond of the foreign delicacy in Amsterdam, they seemed well suited to growing in this climate and they discovered that a few of their neighbors were already acquainted with them. They filled the belly marvelously and could be added to any dish. Not only did they have the advantage of being somewhat protected from the adversities of the weather, growing under the ground as they did, but they had the added benefit for Elsje this morning of taking *more* time to harvest, having to carefully spade them all up, thus keeping Gilles occupied for a longer time than he would be with any of the other vegetables. She fortified herself with a large mug of bier, picked up Jacomina and marched over to the church with Bruinje in hand. They were all inside, even those who could barely drag themselves from their beds, as she *knew* they would be, and the worship service stopped abruptly when she appeared at the door.

"I want to speak with all of you!"

Elsje's voice seemed to echo through the little building, maybe because there were a few more empty seats that day, or perhaps because her voice was just a little louder than she had intended for it to be. She only felt shaky for a moment until the years of calling out orders to a tavern room filled with loud, rude, and unruly patrons came back to her.

"She's *drunk* and she's brought this curse on all of us! We should just *kill* her now!" Gilbert Cyr cried, jumping to his feet. "Should we hang her or stone her? Woman, you need to *learn* your place and if your husband *won't* teach you, then we *will!*"

Elsje glared at him and when no one else got up behind him to support his aggressive stance, he stopped advancing toward her. Elsje took a step forward and continued speaking, a little more quietly but still firmly, just as she would to Bruinje, all the while holding her children tightly to her.

"I won't take much of your time. You can believe what you want to about us but I *still* care that my neighbors are hungry and that the rents will be coming due soon. Many of our neighbors are too sick to work and their food is going to ruin in the fields. If all of you work together, you can harvest everyone's crops together and *no one* will be hungry, no one will lose their home. You can send your produce into Mannheim to sell at market for a *better* price instead of just *giving* everything to Herr Goeble and taking his word as to the value of your crops."

"What if the prices in Mannheim are *lower?*" someone called out.

"That's all I have to say."

Elsje held Jacomina all the more tightly to her breast, turned, and left, dragging Bruinje along with her. Let them work out the details; it was men's work, anyway.

The French! What did they know? They were *all* stupid, sheep-like people, all except for her Gilles. They would all just lay there in their beds and starve if it was left up to them.

As she walked back to the house, she felt shaky from the encounter, but she hoped that she had done *some* good, that they would wake up and that at least one child would have more to eat as a result of her actions. In passing, she wondered if she would have done it at all without having had the bier first. She shrugged, went back to her cook pots, and nearly forgot about what she had done that morning as she set about finding something to cook for Gilles' midday dinner.

A short time later a dumbfounded Gilles strode into the house and confronted Elsje.

"Are you *insane*? Alain Gagner stopped on the way home and *told* me what you did this morning! What if they had taken you out and killed you on the spot? At the very *least* they might have pierced your tongue, branded you with a hot iron, or hurt the children!"

Gilles had never spoken to her in that manner before: Her actions had touched a raw nerve in him and she was fairly certain that it had *everything* to do with his past miseries in France. She was equally certain that he wouldn't ever talk about these past experiences with her, even if she had ever asked him directly about it. She had already done what she needed to do and so she meekly promised Gilles that from now on she would attend to her *own* house and to her *own* business and he didn't have to worry about her any more.

Alain did not tell Gilles, and Elsje could not have known either, that her appearance in church had completely disrupted the morning services and sharply divided the congregation. The discussion had continued for more than an hour before services could be resumed. No one bothered to take the time to speak against Elsje, possibly because it seemed pointless to further deride someone they all despised for so many different reasons, or maybe they were finally coming to the understanding that they had all held out for as long as they could *individually* and now starvation was becoming a distinct possibility. Several people rose to speak, including Jean-Louis LaFountaine.

"I have *never* been a man to keep my mouth closed or I suppose I would not now be living here, so far away from my home in France.

This Netherlander woman looks to our welfare but we haven't seen this from our *own* leadership, our pastor and our elders! The only thing we have thought to do is to pray, which is of course a good and necessary thing, but could it be that God has sent this woman to us to remind us that we need to help ourselves too?"

"Why should we follow the lead of this heathen woman?" Gilbert Cyr cried out. "God will save us *or not*, according to *His* will!"

Alain Gagner spoke next. "I have given a great deal of thought as to how she cared for the Philippe family when I myself had not the courage to do what I thought was right and neighborly at the time. Now I feel that I should do what I *can* for my neighbors although I fear I am too sick to help anyone else very much. God will *surely* see to it that we succeed or fail, as He wishes, but we must do our part as well."

Some of the women asked to speak, which was of course denied, and so many of them whispered in their husband's ears and nudged them in the ribs.

It was an immutable fact, Jean-Louis LaFountaine pointed out, that winter would come this year as it came *every* year, and though winters were generally milder here than they were where he had come from in France, something must be done very soon or they would all perish from hunger even if they managed to survive the disease that was slowly but surely decimating them. The rents would be coming due soon, too, and they all needed the crops or money from selling the crops to pay the lords of the land if they were to be allowed to remain in their houses.

Although many in the congregation felt that excommunication had not been *enough* of a punishment for Gilles' working in the fields on the Sabbath and his wife's *many* transgressions, at the moment they needed every able-bodied man and Gilles Jansen was certainly that, able-bodied; he also seemed to have some knowledge on the subject as he had been *very* successful in raising some good crops. They could always insist later that the Jansens leave Nouvelle Rochelle right away, just as soon as he was finished helping them get their harvest in.

It was decided that Jean-Louis LaFountaine, being an elder of the church and a skilled diplomat, would go to speak with Gilles and come up with a plan to bring in all of the crops for the entire settlement. The earliest crops had been harvested already of course. The peas, beans, carrots and even some early beets had been brought in many weeks earlier, but the second crop of carrots, the ground apples, onions, turnips, cabbage, and most importantly, the second crop of wheat and other grains had not been harvested yet.

Gilles and Elsje had only just come to an agreement that they would speak of their neighbors no more as it only led to arguments between them, when Jean-Louis LaFountaine knocked at their door.

After an uncomfortable beginning, their visitor got around to explaining why he had come to see Gilles. The two men declared a truce and agreed that there was no time to lose: They would start the very next morning. After they estimated how many healthy men there were, they devised a plan to divide up the labor and determine what might be the fastest way to harvest all of the crops. Elsje cooked while the two men planned, peeling her carrots and starting a stew with the leftover rabbit bones. She said nothing at first so that she would not be criticized by the men, but after the initial plan was set she cleared her throat and interjected that the women and the children would have to work as well.

Gilles argued that no one expected the women, and in particular the mothers of newborns to work, but Jean-Louis had to agree with Elsje: Because so many people were so sick, everyone over the age of six would probably have to help. The fields were just too large, the crops too extensive, and there were too few healthy people for them to succeed in their plan without having everyone working together. Gilles and Jean-Louis embraced to seal the agreement, Jean-Louis thanking Gilles once again and before he left, he complimented Elsje on how beautiful Jacomina looked, sleeping so peacefully in her cradle.

The lamps were extinguished early throughout Nouvelle Rochelle in preparation for the next day's harvest but certainly before most of the citizens fell asleep, they heard the sound of rain, blessed rain, that had been in such short supply all summer, but had *finally* come to their fields after months of drought. Gilles once again told Elsje that as a new mother, she should *not* have to work at all, but Elsje would not listen to him and she insisted that a little work in just *one* of the fields or bringing the men a little water to drink now and then would help them out greatly and do her no lasting harm; besides, had he not seen with his *own* eyes how grateful Jean Louis LaFountaine had been? Certainly the citizens of Nouvelle Rochelle would have a change of heart towards them after they all worked together out in the fields.

Gilles doubted this in the extreme, not being a great believer in the generosity and magnanimity of mankind, but this time he held his tongue. He needed to get some sleep and he was not going to spend half of the night arguing with her.

S ome of the harvesters had already started working the fields before
the sun came up. Gilles and Elsje began the day as they always did,
with a glass or two of bier, bread with butter, and cheese. There were
tentative plans for a communal midday dinner but Gilles and Elsje had
already decided that they would *only* share the food if they were invited
to do so, and would return to their own house for more bier when they
got thirsty, making up some pretense if necessary. Gilles left to join the
other men before Elsje had readied herself and the children for the day.
She brought Bruinje and Jacomina over to Herr Nicholas' house to
leave them there for a few hours, giving the old man an extra measure
of her butter for his watching them for her, and although he protested
that payment was not necessary, Elsje left it for him anyway.

"Do you want some kuchen from Opa, Bruinje? Your mother made
some the other day and you *always* like to have kuchen with me when
your mother comes to visit."

Nicholas tried to distract the child but Bruinje suspiciously eyed
his mother as she moved toward the door.

"He'll be all right with me, Elsje, just go on,"

"I'll be back to feed Jacomina in a few hours. Hartelijk dank, Nicholas," she said as her son began to cry and miss his mother, even before she was gone from the house.

"Niets te danken," he replied.

Bruinje protested out loud when Elsje opened the door but she shut out his screams behind her, knowing that her absence from him was needed to help feed the settlement; their collective survival depended on it. Although she was careful never to give any outward indication, it always pained Elsje to hear her son crying for her whenever she left her child. This morning though, her sympathies were for more for Nicholas, with Bruinje first and then Jacomina joining in, both children wailing loudly for Elsje as she left.

The men of Nouvelle Rochelle had started their work at the southwestern corner of the crops, at the back boundary of Jean-Louis LaFountaine's land, working from the edge of the woods, sweeping to the east and the north, out toward the river and the other neighboring fields. A brook ran through the forest at this point, flanked on either side by a mucky depression of swamp where only a grove of cedar trees thrived, cutting the great pine forest behind the settlement in two for a brief time. Jean-Louis had probably chosen this land for the availability of the water from the little stream although this summer the streambed had been frequently dry.

The women and children began harvesting the smaller and lighter crops, starting at the opposite end of the settlement, on the De Mare lands just south of Nicholas' farm. The two groups would work their way toward each other, the men spading up the potatoes, cutting down the grain that was ready and chopping the heavy and somewhat worm-eaten cabbages from their anchorage in the ground. The women, some of them with their babies deposited nearby under a shade tree and being watched by their older children, pulled up carrots, onions, and turnips as other children picked peas, beans, and squash. The children then hauled the produce over to small stockpiles on each lot and after the crops had all been picked and sorted, carts would be dispatched to haul the produce in to the individual houses.

There were those among them who had argued stridently that the minister and his wife should be exempted from doing such work but they were both healthy enough and, according to the women working near Elsje, they had both stated their intention to help their flock the night before, although Elsje had yet to see either one of them out in the fields.

Every pair of hands and every strong back was needed for the effort as an inordinate number of the residents were still in their beds, too sick to work, or confined to the privies, too stricken with the intestinal gripes to leave there even though they may have wanted to help. A few of the women had already prepared some food for the midday meal and others were drawing buckets of water from the river for the harvesters to drink, hauling it up to the field laborers on wooden yokes slung across their shoulders.

The morning was warm but the fields were still wet and muddy from the rain showers the night before. Their shoes, most of them being made of wood, bogged down in the mud and the brown soil clung to their shoes and to the hems of the women's skirts, caking on in ever-thicker and heavier layers as they worked throughout the morning. The scent of moist pine needles baking in the sun grew stronger as the sun climbed higher and the day got progressively hotter.

Elsje took up her position near Claire, although she knew that they probably wouldn't be able to converse with each other. There was no sign of Suzanne anywhere either, but Elsje didn't ask anyone about her, she just kept her questions and thoughts to herself as she started pulling carrots up, tossing them into lopsided piles at regular intervals.

"How do you work so hard and *never* get sick?" Madame Brochau asked Elsje, steadying herself on the fence rail, her porcine face wrinkled up in accusatory wonder, her sunken eyes staring at Elsje in disbelief. The woman had been very sick lately but it seemed to Elsje that she worked little enough when she *was* fit for work.

Elsje felt a little faint herself but she wasn't going to admit to it: It had not been so many weeks since Jacomina's birth. There was little enough sleep every night in the Jansen house and precious little rest during the day with two very young children to care for. She had started out this morning in good faith, hoping that working hard together for the good of all and a common goal might make peace and forge new bonds between them, but now Elsje was growing more and more irritated with the French women who talked too much among themselves, wasting their energy on gossip but not including her in any of the conversation at all until this moment. She was hot and tired, working hard to bring in food for her neighbors who returned not a shred of kindness or charity to her. Her temper got increasingly shorter as the morning grew hotter.

"I fortify myself with bier," Elsje said defiantly. "You should try it sometime!"

"It's *sinful* to drink alcohol," Giselle LaFountaine said sternly to Elsje.

"It's the devil's drink," Jeanette Brochau muttered in agreement as she sat down.

"Just rest yourself, Jeanette. We *know* that you are not feeling well," Claire offered.

Elsje found it difficult to have *any* charity left in her heart for someone who was not only lazy, but so blind that she could not see the *obvious* medicinal benefits of bier when the evidence was standing right in front of her. She pressed her lips together and worked on, though.

Biting flies that had not been so much in evidence before the rain made the work all the more difficult and most of the women were unaccustomed to working in the fields, some even having to ask which plants were the tops of vegetables and which were weeds.

The harvesters had planned to take a break together for the mid-day dinner, which Elsje *supposed* that she might be included in, but they never got that far. Annette Ferrier, coming up from the river and just arriving at the fields with the heavy water buckets swinging from the yoke over her thin shoulders, was the first to hear the noise in the distance. There were flickers of movement in the forest pathways and something was coming down through the wooded hills in the southwest, behind the men as they worked in the garden rows, accompanied by a rumbling sound, not of another thunderstorm, but the noise of many horses approaching.

"What *is* that?" Annette asked the women who carried buckets next to her and the women who were bent over, picking the vegetables. They all stopped their work, straightened up, and strained their eyes to see more clearly what it was out there in the distance.

"I don't know, what is it?" Elsje asked.

"Oh Mon Dieu, *non*! Mon Dieu!" Mme. Brochau shrieked as the sound of the hooves reached them, the sound coinciding with their first sight of the small army emerging from the woods, uniformly dark horses with men astride, sweeping toward the settlement, reaching first the minister's house. In the forefront of the horsemen were two riders bearing banners, one a standard with three gold figures on a field of white, the banner of the King of France, and on the other a large gold cross on a field of crimson; torch bearers and musketeers followed these.

The women water carriers as a group had already dropped their buckets and started to run before the first plumes of smoke rose from the minister's newly-built house. The other women dropped what they were doing and ran across the fields as the main force of the equine wave turned in their direction. The women and children of Nouvelle Rochelle shrieked and ran as fast as they could, some to gather up nearby infants, others toward the men and the safety of their homes, and the rest of them toward the woods that lay at a distance on the far end of the very long fields. The men, perhaps deafened by the sound of their own shovels and hoes, were still unaware of the approaching intruders although they were almost upon them now.

Elsje did not know exactly who it was that they ran from, but all of the other women seemed to know, and they seemed to fear them *greatly*; her first thoughts were to reach her children. The front wave of women, the fastest runners among them, had reached the men and the houses, raising the alarm just as the church bell clanged once before it was silenced, just as the standard bearer on horseback crossed over into the cemetery, urging his horse onward in the shortest distance to the settlement, through the churchyard, over the graves and in between the standing stones.

The women who had run to their homes to protect their family members, the children, the sick, or the elderly, perhaps thought they might safely barricade themselves inside. The men of Nouvelle Rochelle had by now seen the unfolding events and were running too, not in a few directions like the women, but in a completely scattered pattern, like the contents of a cup that had been carelessly dropped to the floor, the liquid spattering and disbursing in every direction. Some men ran back toward the houses, some ran into the nearby woods, and some ran diagonally across the fields, trying to make it to the muddy bottom lands by the river, headed toward the path to the Mannheim ferry since the southern escape route had been almost completely cut off.

The thundering herd of horsemen, perhaps fifty French soldiers on their black mounts, had planned and executed the sortie with precision: Some carried lit pine torches and others had swords drawn. They seemed not inclined to bother with their modern firearms that remained holstered at their sides, but bore down upon the village with the ancient weapons they had in hand. They all wore sky blue tunics, each one with a giant gold cross emblazoned on the front. Their stockings were trimmed in crimson as were their sashes, cuffs and breeches, the uniform identifying them as brethren of some sort. They wore their uniforms proudly and desired no confusion or uncertainty as to *who* they were or under whose orders they were acting. The approaching force drove their mounts across the consecrated ground of the cemetery, jumping stone-covered burial sites and churning up dirt on others, trampling most of the wildflowers that had been transplanted there by grieving relatives. The army rode on to the houses, stopping at each one, the fire bearers pulling their running horses up short to reach over and torch the wooden walls and roofs. As the combustible portions of the homes flamed up, the fires spread and screams came from the people within.

The response from the soldiers outside was laughter.

"Just a little foretaste of what waits for you *after* death!" one soldier shouted.

"Pour Dieu et pour Roi!" another cried.

The soldiers efficiently completed setting fire to *all* of the houses in the settlement and the victims that ran outside to escape the burning buildings met death by sword instead of fire.

"My sword is God's sword!" one soldier shouted, hacking away at a small boy.

"By fire and sword…! another quoted, dismounting quickly so that he had better leverage to run his weapon through an old woman.

"Justice is mine!" cried another.

The soldiers might have passed completely by the outhouses on their way to ride down the villagers who were still escaping through the fields and into the woods, but unfortunately one man opened the door of his privy to see what was going on and then foolishly ran outside. Two of the raiders spied him and one of them kicked him in the face, stunning him momentarily until another raider jumped off his horse to drag the screaming man back to the privy. Stuffing him inside with his one free hand, he latched the door shut from the outside and then set it ablaze with the torch he held in his other hand.

Upon observing this, a few of the trailing horsemen detached themselves from the main unit and searched *all* of the outhouses. Finding most of them containing fearful and sick occupants, they took great delight in securing the doors and then burning those.

"*The men*! Go after the men!" one soldier cried after they had burned everything that they could in the village. They turned from their sport at the privies to recoup their mounts and pursue what appeared to be their main objective, hunting down all of the *men* of the settlement, those rebellious Frenchmen who had led their wives and children here and even influenced their neighbors to turn away from The Church, from Catholicism.

The women, having been the first to see the King's soldiers coming, had a head start but with their weakened constitutions and their skirts made heavier with the dampness and mud that had accumulated on their skirts during the morning, they could not outrun the horses.

Gilles had looked around for Elsje when the melee began, but panicking, he couldn't stand there for *very* long, no more than a few seconds anyway, and seeing nothing but confusion all around him and no sign of his wife anywhere, he dropped his shovel and started to run. Gilles reached the edge of the woods ahead of the others, well before the first wave of soldiers, and he still had just enough presence of mind to pull up abruptly and stop to look around for the best plan of escape. The ground in the woods was marshy after the rain and he knew that he would not be able to run very fast through the muck. A horse would make very fast work of any distance he could put between himself and them, and even if he could run fast enough in his wooden shoes, his tracks would be plainly visible for anyone to follow. The others ran on, now running past Gilles, deeper into the forest, but Gilles made a sharp turn to the left, through brambles and up a wooded knoll, taking shelter by diving inside a large hollow tree trunk on the crest of the hill.

He had found the tree one day during a walk to look for berries so Elsje could make him a pie. He had been greatly disappointed at the time, thinking that he might find a store of honey inside but there had just been the cavernous empty hole.

Some of the loose fungus-encrusted wood fell onto his head and shoulders as he tried to remain perfectly quiet and not breathe too loudly after his terrified flight from the fields. The biting flies quickly found him but he dared not shoo them away although they bit him ferociously on his bare and sweaty arms, his hands and his face.

Only moments later Gilles heard the attacking horsemen plunge into the woods shouting, "We have some! We have some!" He heard screams nearby and one woman's voice sounded like Jeannette Brochau's. He heard more distant cries from several others, men as well as women, and he heard the sucking sound of hooves pulling out of the mud as the killing went on and on for far too long. He tried to shut the noise from his ears without moving, without putting his hands up to cover his ears, fearful that *any* motion could alert the enemy although that was ridiculous; he was safely tucked away inside the tree and no one could see him at this angle.

"Heavenly Father," he prayed, *silently* to the outside world, but shouting the words as loudly as he could inside his head, saying the Lord's Prayer and Hail Mary along with other nonsense prayers that were never a part of any service, not Protestant, and not Catholic. The blood in his chest and his ears pounded and the flies continued to bite him mercilessly, a tiny attack and taking of blood within the world of the tall stump, mirroring the larger assault that was going on outside. His entire body resonated with a fear that he remembered to the very core of his being now, a fear that he thought he had forever left behind him years ago in another time and place.

A prayer, a chant, came to him in words and then repeated in his head, a chant that followed the duration of his trial by fear inside the wooden sanctuary, the church of the tree: *Kyrie eleison, Christe eleison, Kyrie eleison, Lord have mercy, Christ have mercy, Lord have mercy.*

After a very, very, long time, the screams and triumphant cries grew softer than the prayer until they finally died away completely. The sound of the horses' hooves slowed and then slowly distanced themselves from Gilles. Only then did he calm himself enough to have the presence of mind to think about Elsje and his children.

He was ashamed of himself for running away and just leaving them.

He began to wonder how long he had been hiding inside the dark old tree but his senses had failed him completely; he couldn't begin to make a guess as to how much time had passed.

Hours perhaps.

He asked himself if the echoing screams he thought he heard might actually have stopped a very long time before: It was possible that he only *thought* he heard them long after they had ended, echoing on and on through his head. Now new thoughts came to him, rushing in too fast for his mind to rationally sort through them. He was bedeviled by the fear that one of the screams he had heard was that of his wife or Bruinje. He cursed himself for *all* of the things he had done wrong in his life, for bringing them here to this place, for abandoning Elsje and his children when the soldiers came, for not having been a better husband and father over the past few years. What would he do without them? Where would he go? Gilles made a bargain with God that if he survived this and if ever saw his family again, then he would live his life *very* differently.

Even inside the tree, Gilles could tell that darkness was gathering outside but it *couldn't* be night falling yet; it had to be approaching rain clouds. Gilles pushed the rotten wood off his shoulders and tilted his head back, moving it just enough to look straight up through the opening above him toward the heavens, but the canopy of leaves and pine needles was too thick for Gilles to clearly observe the sky.

The peculiar thought occurred to Gilles now that he was standing where the *heart* of the ancient tree had been, possibly for hundreds of years, where sap had once been coursing through the tree's veins on the very spot where he stood now. The timing of the tree's demise had been most fortunate for the preservation of his own life and he felt that he should give thanks to someone, to God or the tree or to whatever forces had brought about this conjunction of lives and deaths for his salvation, inside the dead body of another. It was only in death that the tree had performed its greatest accomplishment: It had saved a man's life.

He realized too that foxes, bears, wild boars and ravens would be coming into the forest soon after the sun went down, seeking to finish off the bodies, to eat the carrion, the remains of those neighbors that Gilles had been speaking with just hours earlier, and he needed to go somewhere safe, to be away from having to see it or hear the crunching and ripping sounds of it.

He was quite sure that by now he had been in his hiding place for a very long time as he no longer heard any sounds of humanity at all. He was becoming aware of his body again, now that his fear was subsiding, aware that his face and one eye were badly swollen from insect bites, that his legs and back ached from standing absolutely still for so long, and that his bladder was full. He still could not bring himself to leave the safety of his cache right away though, so he relieved himself inside the trunk, incurring still more insect bites on the newly exposed places.

Although he continued to shake from fear, he made his first rational decision since the attack began, and he forced himself to take a single step outside of his hiding place. It was very quiet now except for the singing of the birds and the chirping of the frogs, the grasshoppers and the crickets, these creatures seemingly unaware that anything unusual had happened here today.

Gilles' senses had not failed him completely; it *was* getting darker. Cautiously he stepped forward another single step and then stopped to listen again. He could smell smoke on the wind, now that the pungent smell of the dead tree's fungus was beginning to clear from his nostrils. It was the smoke of burning wood but it also had the distinctive quality about it that Rouen's soul-fed fires always had. He took another step and felt that he might be just too frightened to go on any further but he couldn't stay there all night, and by now the voice in his head had begun to nag at him that he *had* to find Elsje and discover what had happened to her. He pushed his feet forward, taking first one step and then another. Over the last few hours he had become a child again, just learning to walk, walking into a new world where he might very well be *all* alone, the last survivor of his family. Where had Elsje left Bruinje and Jacomina? She had said something to him about the children but he hadn't been listening to her: He had had the crops on his mind at the time, the goddamned crops. She wouldn't have left them with Suzanne. Was she with them now?

He came upon the two women's bodies just inside the woods, almost within sight of the fields, ripped apart as if by wild animals, flies still crawling and buzzing around the dark red stains that soaked the hair and familiar dresses. Their arms reached forward toward a safety that they had not been able to attain and the foot of one of the victims was tangled up in a rabbit's snare. Gilles sank to his knees, reached out and gently touched a strand of the familiar blonde hair that had come loose from the cap. The hair was matted with drying blood from the wounds on the head, deep gashes inflicted by the swords, the flow finally having been stanched by the hair when the woman's heart no longer kept the blood flowing freely.

He didn't want to leave her behind in the woods but he just didn't feel right about taking one out with him and not the other. It was better that they should be left together in death as they were in the last moments of their life. He touched a fold of the fawn-colored fabric and then rubbed it between his fingers, feeling the softness of it for a moment before he said the Lord's Prayer for her. Gilles thought that her soul might not object *too* much to this small act of reverence, even if it did come from him, an excommunicate, and he hoped that God would forgive him for *not* saying a Hail Mary, the requisite prayer at the time of death, but he knew that the minister's young wife would not have wanted this.

Giles was still shaking as he rose from his muddied knees to his feet again. There was an aching feeling in his stomach and he remembered now that they had not had the promised midday meal. He would have been *very* hungry by this time if it had been any other day but he still didn't feel much like eating; he was more inclined to vomit, but there was nothing left in his stomach, nothing there to dispose of. He needed to take his mind off his aching stomach and his fear, needed to find the strength of will to continue on to the settlement to find out what had become of his family. The pain of uncertainty, terrible now, would become unbearable if he was unable to find out for days, weeks, *or ever*, what had become of them, and he knew that if he didn't find them, he would forever after picture the very worst scenes, real and imagined, every time he closed his eyes, for the rest of his life.

With one hand clutching his aching midsection, Gilles made his way back in the direction of Nouvelle Rochelle and stopped at the edge of the forest. He stood on his toes and looked around, trying to sense what was happening over there, just as he had seen the doe across the river do so often at eventide. He now felt the weight of the animal's nightly fear and thought he would almost rather die right now than have to live with this kind of terror for the rest of his life.

He couldn't bring himself to walk down into the settlement yet, though: He could see that there was very little left of what had been there just hours before. Smoke and fire still rose from the remains of the houses although a couple of them looked untouched, but Gilles could see, even at this distance and even in the gathering darkness, that his house was *not* one of the ones that had survived. Elsje would not be in there, not alive anyway. A flash of lightning briefly lit up the sky and for a few brief seconds Gilles could better see the bodies littering the landscape before him, the remnants of a perverse battle where one side had not been apprised of the conflict beforehand, had been mostly women, children, and sick people, and had had no weapons of self defense other than farm implements. He saw no survivors.

Once upon a time Gilles had been thrilled whenever he saw the King's soldiers passing by, and had *dreamed* about riding with them someday, until his father discovered this secret wish Gilles harbored and explained to his small son, in the way that *only* Jean Montroville could, that the men were "just soldiers", and despite the pretty uniforms, they were the lowest of men, down there next to tenant farmers and beggars. Gilles had never really accepted this assessment, rejecting this notion of his father's along with many others but at this moment Gilles wondered if his father might not have been correct in his judgment and categorization of these beings. The French army had come upon the Palatine colonists this day, not like loyal and honored servants carrying out the will of God and King, but more like swarming ants brought forth from a disturbance in a great rotting tree. On the field of battle today no great decisions had been made as to the next path history would take and no major world questions had been answered. There was no battle waged to determine the successor to a throne. Where was the honor? Where was the sense in killing the poor, sick, and completely *inconsequential* residents of Nouvelle Rochelle?

Gilles moved silently along the edge of the woods although he was quite certain that by now the soldiers were gone. He thought that he might walk completely around the ruined village at a distance first before going in any closer to look through the corpses for those of his wife and children.

He had never walked along the woods like this before and it was a beautiful place, one that he would have liked to show to Elsje. It would be a peaceful place to bury them if it came to that in the next few hours. There were no houses here in the far reaches beyond the fields, none until he came to the house belonging to Nicholas. The old man's house was not only still standing, but it looked as it always had. What had happened to Nicholas? Had they killed him too or had they left him alone?

Gilles eased into the old man's back yard, skirting Nicholas' wife's grave and he tried to be silent so as not to alarm the old dog or any of the farmer's other animals, just in case the soldiers were still close enough to hear any commotion and return. Gilles moved up close to the house and looked inside the kitchen's window where a single lamp was burning. Nicholas sat with his arm around Elsje who sat crying, her face blotchy red, twisted in distress, her dress in muddy tatters as she rocked back and forth while she nursed Jacomina. Bruinje clung to his mother's knee, looking very pale and his great wide eyes were as frightened as Gilles had ever seen them.

More than anything else right now, Gilles hated the men for having put that look of fear into his son's eyes. Gilles looked quickly around to be sure that no one was watching him as he entered the house without knocking, quickly shutting the door behind him.

Elsje jumped to her feet and ran over to him, the emotional buildup of the day spilling over as she burst into fresh tears, crying "Danks be to Gott! Danks be to Gott!"

Nicholas got up and offered Gilles his chair, saying "Sit, sit! It's all right, now. The soldiers have gone and your family is safe. God's army has returned to their promised land."

Perhaps as much to leave them alone with each other as to get them some fortification, which was his stated mission, Nicholas went out of the room for some bier while Gilles tried to calm a sobbing Elsje and to assure himself that she was all right. Her dress was stained with blood and dirt but she seemed otherwise unhurt except for scratches on her face. Gilles couldn't stand to hear her cry anymore and so he begged Elsje's forgiveness, telling her that he was sorry that he had not been there to protect her and the children. Elsje calmed herself enough to reply that he could not have known what would happen that morning and even if he had, he would *not* have been able to reach them in time or perhaps it all would have ended very differently and *not* so well.

"She's right," Nicholas said to Gilles as he came back into the room. "The soldiers came here and they took most of my food but I understood them to say that they had no interest in Germans. They saw the cru… uh, they looked around and couldn't understand what these young children were doing here with an old man but I guess they took the children for Rhinelanders, too, since Bruinje asked them in Nederlands where his father was."

Gilles couldn't believe what his ears were hearing: Bruinje might just as easily have come out with French words and in all probability both of his children, as well as Nicholas, would be dead now. Gilles gave silent thanks to the heavens for whatever angel had whispered into his little son's ear to use the right language at the right time.

The old man urged them both to drink some bier and then he gave them all some dark bread. "It's not much for a meal but it's all they left behind. I'm just thankful that they didn't find my bier! You stay here tonight with me. I'll get you some vinegar for those insect bites."

Gilles did not argue. He didn't feel completely safe here but he felt less so outside.

The four of them slept together on the floor that night, refusing the offer of the bed from Nicholas. For reasons that Gilles could not explain, even to himself, he wanted the reassurance of being with his wife, but she was still too upset, refusing his physical advances and crying quietly for a time until there was only silence and Gilles assumed that she had fallen asleep. Gilles slept with a knife from Nicholas' kitchen at his side even though he knew that the invading soldiers were most likely billeted comfortably somewhere far away, perhaps even in France by now, and a kitchen implement was no match for the guns and swords of a professional army.

Nightmares, thunder, and occasional downpours of rain that sounded like returning horsemen interrupted Gilles' sleep throughout the night, as did the terrible itching all over his body from the insect bites he had incurred during the day. At times he thought he could hear Elsje lying awake beside him but he said nothing to her. He had already made his apologies to her and he didn't know what else he could say that would make either of them feel any better. The morning light would bring new challenges and they both needed to get as much sleep as they could. He relaxed his body as much as he could, endeavoring to sleep for just a little longer until it was morning.

When at last it was nearly daylight, old Nicholas tiptoed out from his bedroom but Gilles and Elsje were already awake, being unable to sleep any longer. Nicholas gave them more bread and bier and he even had some milk for Bruinje and Elsje left over from the day before. "I'll get you some fresh milk while you're drinking that. They took all of my chickens but I guess they couldn't easily carry away the cow," he said to Gilles with a smile. "Maybe they were kind enough *not* to kill it because they saw the children here."

"Or maybe yesterday was a *fish* day," Gilles said sarcastically.

Nicholas smiled at this but Elsje surely did not comprehend this joke or the reference to the Catholic calendar of feasts and fasts, with fish or meat prohibited or allowed.

"I need to go now and see what is left of our house," Gilles said, running his hands through his hair, still pulling out remnants of bark and dead bugs, souvenirs from the old tree in which he had taken refuge.

"It's not good to go out there now. I think the soldiers are far away but there is much sadness and anger that they have left behind them," Nicholas said.

Elsje was in agreement with her husband, though. "We *have* to go and see," she said to Nicholas, "waiting *won't* make it any better. Can you watch Bruinje and Jacomina again?"

"Oh no, you are *not* going with me!" Gilles said. "Your place is here, with the children."

"I'm *going*." Elsje glared at her husband.

Gilles thought about asserting himself, of being the head of the family and just telling her "non!", but for some reason, maybe it was something in her eyes, he believed that today there might be more to her obstinacy than their usual battle of wills. It seemed like Elsje needed to go, perhaps to find some resolution or to feel like she was taking control of the situation. He closed his mouth and nodded acquiescence.

"Be *very* careful, then," Nicholas advised. "I will watch your children for you until you return for them. Be safe!"

Elsje gave both of her children a fierce hug and Bruinje started to protest as he saw her leaving again but Elsje resolutely went out the door, *almost angrily*, Gilles thought.

The morning was overcast, gray, foggy and damp and they could not see very far ahead of them. As they got closer to what had once been Nouvelle Rochelle, they could see that there were no outhouses left and that there were odd, rounded piles of charred timber where the angular houses used to be. In spite of the soaking rains of the night before, steam still rose from some of the burned debris.

"*Now* we get rain, after all the hundreds and hundreds of heavy buckets I carried all summer long!" Gilles complained to Elsje as he scratched at a swollen bite on his arm.

She pointed out bits of things on the ground to him: a single wooden shoe, bits of hair, chicken feathers, thatch that might have come from someone's roof, perhaps even from their own, some small bits of singed fabric. The fields were no longer demarcated into individual plots of land, individual territories, but had been united into a single battlefield. Although Gilles had hoped that a *little* something might be salvaged to feed them at least for the day today, he could see that all of the crops had been badly trampled by horses, pigs, and people alike, all having as their only objective fleeing and surviving, priorities all greater than respecting the preservation of mere plants.

They were almost at their house when both Gilles and Elsje heard low voices on the wind and they stopped to listen. The sounds came from the far end of the settlement, near where the church had been. There was nothing particularly unusual about these murmurs but their human quality had a very disquieting effect on Gilles; he almost felt safer in the isolation of the woods, far from mankind, where animals had never taken up arms against them, had never gone out of their way to harm him. Together Gilles and Elsje crept forward to see who was talking and what they could find out about the current situation or the heinous acts that had been visited upon their village the day before.

"...but no one knows *where* the rest of our families are now or what has become of them!" someone said.

"I know where *mine* are." Suzanne's acid voice cut through the stillness. "*Dead.* They are *all* dead with the exception of myself and my oldest boy."

The survivors espied Gilles and Elsje walking toward them and there was a sudden and soggy silence as they approached their neighbors and the mountain of ashes that had once been a place of worship. The twisted and melted bell was perched atop some charred lumber but there was nothing else that was recognizable. Gilles noted that his neighbors all looked tired, wet, and more bedraggled than usual. He did not expect to be greeted with enthusiasm but Gilles thought that he would be civil to them. Before he could say a word though, Suzanne called out to him.

"The devil arrived here with *you*, Jansen! We have had *nothing* but bad luck since you got here, you and that *witch* woman of yours. Oui, you think we don't *know* what you are, drinking wine and bier, both of you, *mocking* God. *You* brought this curse down on us!"

"You are a crazy woman and someone should beat that out of you; either that, or have you locked up away forever, far away from good and decent people."

Gilles couldn't stop himself from saying it. He was tired and he had been through too much in the last twenty four hours to have any patience or charity left for the miserable woman.

"You wouldn't talk to me that way if my husband was still here! You're a damned secret *Catholic*! We have all *seen* your priest's cloak! You just came here to spy on us and tell them where we were!" she snarled.

"Your luck was bad *before* we came, you said so yourself, and if your life is bad, then it is God's judgment on *you*," Gilles retorted.

Elsje stepped forward. "We have to stop this, right now! There are bodies in the woods that need Christian burials, bodies here that we need to collect and we *still* have to complete the harvest work that we started yesterday! We need to find food so we can feed ourselves!"

These words did not have the calming and uniting effect that was intended; far from it, and then Suzanne turned on Elsje.

"I *told* you as much," she said over her shoulder to the others. "They are *both* evil. We have all lost so many people in our families and yet they, in the middle of it all, are *completely* untouched! I'm surprised that the soldiers didn't leave their house standing too, but maybe they just set fire to the wrong one."

Suzanne's voice was chillingly calm but laced with hate. Her oldest son, her only surviving relative, stood behind her saying nothing at all, perhaps still being in shock, too devastated by what he had lived through to say anything at all.

"Your other children died before we came here and then you started to kill those little girls yourself with the beatings you gave them! *Who is the evil one here?*" Elsje fired back, Suzanne's personal attack at last bringing up her temper.

"God has cursed *you* with a mute imbecile child! It's a sign!" Suzanne retorted.

Gilles saw it coming and he made a grab for his wife's arm but he was not fast enough and could not catch her before Elsje swung her fist around and hit Suzanne squarely in the face. Streams of blood came down from her nose as Suzanne lifted her filthy apron to her face to stop the flow. Elsje looked like she was about to apologize but Suzanne spoke first, recharging the emotions of both women once again.

"Take my blood, *take it!*" She screamed in a muffled voice from behind the apron that covered her face. "You *need* it for your blood rituals, don't you? You aren't even *familiar* with our church services so you could not have *been* to any in the Netherlands! Maybe you just wanted our infants for your sacrifices!"

Gilles realized with sudden clarity and shock that the crowd was with *Suzanne,* and not with Elsje. Perhaps they were too aggrieved to listen to reason yet or perhaps it was simply that their fundamental beliefs embraced these same ideas. This reality had escaped him until now. They were unable to open their eyes and minds. He shook his head in a resigned way and led a struggling Elsje from the group, although she struggled to get back at Suzanne.

"You *can't* argue with crazy people," Gilles told his angry wife. "You *tried* to help them with nothing but good intentions in your heart and they attacked you for it *every* time you tried. They can *all* just go to hell."

Elsje was not listening to the voice of reason that was her husband's. She was still struggling, still furious.

"My son is not an imbecile!" she shouted back over her shoulder at the small crowd as Gilles summoned all of his strength to haul Elsje farther away from them.

Suzanne replied with something that he did not hear.

"Of *course* he's not an imbecile," Gilles comforted Elsje. "Bruinie will talk soon enough, when he's ready."

"How can you take that?" Elsje sputtered, still looking like she wanted more than anything else in the world to return to fight Suzanne.

"*Forget* Suzanne! I need you and your strength for the *other* battles that we will need to fight for ourselves, for our own survival right now, today!"

Gilles dragged her over to where their house had been standing the day before. It was a smoldering wreck now but two walls were still somewhat intact and a few of their things were recognizable inside the debris. The animal shed was burned and one chicken carcass was all that was left, lying dead in the pen. Their cow was nowhere to be found. Giles couldn't guess why the house had not burned fully although the rains soaking the thatched roof the night before the soldiers arrived might have had something to do with it.

"All of our things are gone, Gilles." Elsje looked like she was about to cry again.

Gilles didn't want to see any more of her tears so he said the only thing that he could think of. "It's all right, Elsje. We are all safe."

It sounded trivial and hollow to his ears, stupid, but he could think of nothing else to say to stop her from crying. He thought he would go *mad* if he had to listen to her crying any more.

"You aren't going to talk about rebuilding are you?" Elsje looked up through tearful eyes.

Gilles laughed grimly, "Nee, not here. Not unless you really want to."

Elsje managed a smile for him through her watery eyes. "I want to go *home*, Gilles. I *tried*. I'm sorry about your dream and the farm and the vineyards and..." She drew a gasping breath and stopped for a moment before she could go on. "I just want to go home!"

"It's all right," he said, putting his arms around her. "It never worked out here. The neighbors were terrible, the soil was bad for farming; it wasn't meant for us."

"I thought I would be buying crystal and lace all the time and living on a fine farm with great vineyards. It was my dream, *too*," Elsje volunteered. Then she looked at her husband more intently and asked, "You won't mind going home to my father? It will be hard for you, I know."

Gilles sighed and rolled his eyes. "He wouldn't be your father if he *wasn't* difficult. I can get my old job back at Ste Germaine's and I know that you have missed the inn. Everyone will love to see Bruinje and Jacomina and they will be the most spoiled children in all of Amsterdam. Maybe we'll see what we can do about getting your brother and sisters back under our roof, too."

Elsje smiled at him, a small wavering smile, but Gilles knew that he had found the right words, exactly the right ones, that made all the difference in moving her focus from the miserable present to a more hopeful future. He picked up a long pole that had been lying in front of their house, something that might have been part of someone's bucket yoke once and then after that, used as a weapon by either an attacker or a defender. Carefully Gilles made his way into the warm wreckage and poked and pried at the charred remains with the stick. He kicked the smaller debris aside and climbed over everything else.

"I wonder why the *whole* house didn't burn?" Gilles mused aloud. His feet were hot, even through the soles of his wooden shoes, and his skin felt like it was roasting now, too. He hoped that his shoes weren't going to start smoldering before he could get back outside again.

"It must have been my witches' spell," Elsje said sarcastically.

"Don't even say that out loud!" Gilles stopped long enough to glare over at her as she stood peering inside the shell of the house, watching his progress. "They will have you put to the water test and then drown you in the river if you give them *any* such ideas."

"Hmph! I'd like to see her try it!" Elsje said, folding her arms in defiance, but she cast a quick glance over her shoulder.

After a few minutes of silence Elsje called out to him again. "Never mind, Gilles, we don't need *any* of it! Father can pay our fares when we reach Amsterdam if we take one boat all the way in. Besides, if I know you, you already have enough money somewhere in your pockets to pay our way back."

"I'm *not* leaving without it. We put our sweat and blood into this place and I'm not leaving *anything* behind for those bastards!"

"It doesn't exist anymore, it's melted!" She knew he was looking for his money.

"Melted or not, it's in there somewhere and I'm going to get it."

Gilles angrily shoved away a charred board that had come down from a wall, and taking a large step over some indeterminate twisted black rubble, at last he reached the area of the house that he had been targeting. Gingerly he dug through the still-warm ashes, the topmost layer being cooler but sticky from being wet with the rain, searching for the trunk with the secret drawer where he hid his money. The trunk was still there and although it was still hot, especially the metal bands around the base, it was only charred on one side, as it had been in the part of the house that had not been completely burned.

"Can't we just leave now? Gilles, there is *nothing* here to take. Let's just *go* before the soldiers or our neighbors come back."

414

"No."

"You are one *stubborn* man."

"Yes, I am, and you are one stubborn woman. We make a *fine* pair." Gilles progressed to the bottom corner of the chest. "Aha!" he said as he dug out his large knife. He tore a section of cloth from the hem of his shirt to use as a potholder. "Hot, but serviceable."

With a frown of concentration on his face, he wrapped the cloth around the handle and used the knife to start working the locked drawer open, but then, growing impatient with his slow progress, he finished by kicking it in, smashing it open the rest of the way. He might have used the key in his pocket to open it but the latch was still too hot to touch and Gilles no longer cared if the lock was broken out of the wood or not. He pulled out the leather moneybag which had survived but having been baked at a high temperature by the intense heat, it now had a harder, more parchment-like quality to it. The coins had melted slightly into each other and into the bag, but it was all there and could still be broken apart into useable pieces of currency. He wrapped the warm golden mass in the rag and stuck it in one of his pockets.

"Are my pearls in there too?"

"I don't see them... Oh, here they are! They will need to be restrung."

He lifted handfuls of them out and put them in his pocket, too, the weakened horsehair no longer serving the purpose of holding them all together in a single string.

"*It is just too bad that they weren't lost in the fire too,*" Gilles thought as he picked out the last remaining pearls from the drawer. It was strange that the mere sight of them still disturbed Gilles, even after all this time, but he *did* understand that the cursed necklace meant a lot to Elsje, so he didn't waste any more time in thinking or talking about it; he just scooped up all of the pieces for her.

Gilles dug a little deeper into the chest to see what else might be salvaged. "I never asked you, how did you, I mean what did you do, when they came?" He *had* to ask her.

"I…I hid under a stoep. It's too smoky in here, Gilles. I'm tired and I can't breathe."

"Step back a little, then. Go sit down and rest yourself. I just wanted to make sure that we got everything that survived the fire."

Gilles kept digging. The rosary was in there too, in better condition than the pearls for whatever reason and Gilles put that in his other pocket: He could always use the extra protection.

Back in Amsterdam, before they had set out for their sojourn in the Palatinate but after Elsje had packed everything for them to go, Gilles had gone through the things that she meant to leave behind, finding the knife and the Montroville family rosary. Since there was only one key and Gilles kept that in his pocket, he tucked these into the secret compartment. He wanted to take these items along into the future with him but moreover, he didn't want Hendrick finding them after Gilles and Elsje left, even if Gilles was quite certain that he would never see Hendrick again. Whatever else it represented, the rosary was one of the few things that Gilles had left of his family and his old life in France. From time to time in recent months, Gilles had entertained the thought that he might tell Elsje a little about his life before he met her, but they had been so busy here that the subject had never come up between them. He might have brought it up that night when they sat on the rock, looking out over the river, but Elsje had gone back inside before he had the chance.

Maybe he hadn't been ready to talk about it yet, though.

After rummaging around a little more, at last Gilles finally found what it was that he had *really* been looking for and he was glad that Elsje had retreated to a distance so she could not see what he was doing.

She surely would have thought him a madman if she could see *why* he stayed in the choking smoke that was still drifting up slowly from the cinders and hot ashes, why he endured the still-hot embers under his feet: Poking at them with his stick, Gilles discovered that the priest's robe had burned up almost completely and a scorched and disintegrated bundle of stinking woolen fibers, smelling like burned hair, was all that remained of his old cloak that he had brought with him from France. Gilles didn't care about the rest of his clothing or about anything else that might have survived, just his old mantel.

Jean Durie had teased him mercilessly about it, saying often that *surely* by now Msr. Ste Germaine was paying him enough to afford a new one. There was not enough left of it to take even a small square of it with him so Gilles pulled the still warm gold and mother-of-pearl button off the disintegrated neck of it and stuck that into his pocket with the rosary.

On reflection, it seemed a fortuitous thing now that Gilles had *not* had the long knife with him: He might have been more disposed toward taking a stand and fighting off the invaders if he had been armed.

Ah well, it was over and in the past now. There was no sense in reliving the horrific event and the outcome being what it was, it had turned out well enough.

Gilles started to make his way back outside, climbing over the remnants of a chair when he spied what looked like a stone with a leather string wrapped around it, lying all alone in a clearing in the middle of the ash and soot-covered floor. For a moment he puzzled over what it could be and then he stepped over some more debris to get a better look at it. When he got closer, Gilles realized that it was the red stone, essonite or garnet the jeweler in Amsterdam had called it, when Gilles had taken it in to be examined and appraised. In fact, it was the *very* stone that Francois had given to Bruinje on the day he was born.

"To protect him," the savage had said.

Gilles picked it up and cleaned it off by rubbing the stone against his pants.

Where had that come from?

Elsje must have brought it with them from Amsterdam, and during the fire it had fallen to the open spot on the floor from high atop one of the shelves after they had burned and collapsed. The shelving had been almost completely consumed by the fire, as had Elsje's spice box that once used to sit safely on the top shelf, well out of Bruinje's curious reach.

"Protection?!" Gilles asked out loud. He shook his head in doubt, but almost as an afterthought, he tossed the stone necklace into the air, then caught it and put the stone into his pocket with the rosary and the button. Maybe it *was* protection.

He pried opened the only other trunk that was not totally consumed by the fire, perhaps only escaping total destruction because it had been under the part of the ceiling that had not burned and was later drenched thoroughly by the night's hard rains. Inside he found a dress that Elsje might be able to wear after washing it out in the river to get rid of the smoky smell. He picked up some other slightly damp and damaged clothing that might be salvaged or cut up with his knife to use for cloths for Jacomina. It was too hot inside and the destruction was too thorough, so abandoning the search, he left the destroyed dwelling, climbing out to where Elsje waited for him.

She was sitting on an old tree stump a short distance away, her chin cradled in her hands, staring dejectedly down at the ground.

"I *am* sorry Elsje, but your spice box didn't make it, and I can't find any clothing *at all* for Bruinje."

"It's all right, I suppose I can always get another box and collect some more spices," Elsje said, "but it *was* a beautiful box and it *was* from our wedding."

"Well, when do we leave?" Gilles asked her.

"Let's go today," she replied without hesitation. "Right now. We'll find what food we can in the fields, take it all back to Nicholas', and if there is a little left for us to eat without having to cook it, we will bring that with us. We can take the ferry boat over to Mannheim, and then find a ship heading down the river for Amsterdam."

"I'll go with that plan." Gilles smiled at her and it was the first time in the last twenty four hours that he had used those facial muscles.

Elsje replied, "Well, we don't have many preparations to make this time, do we?"

They brought the trampled and dead chicken along with them, Gilles picking it up and carrying it by a broken foot as they combed over their field, looking for more undestroyed food. Among a few bodies, they found enough in their garden and in the Philippe's to fill both Elsje's apron and the dress that Gilles had found in the trunk. Elsje wanted to bury the dead that they found on their land but Gilles refused her this wish, and not just because it would take them a long time and be very hard work.

"Let the congregation bury them where they will. They don't want *us* touching them."

Elsje reluctantly admitted that he was right. She admonished Gilles to get as much mud off the vegetables as possible and Gilles obliged by wiping the muddy vegetables off on the weeds and on Msr. Philippe's trampled wheat.

Gilles no longer cared about the wheat. Before it could be consumed, it had to be threshed, separating the grain from the chaff, ground into flour, mixed with starter, water, and eggs, left to rise for a day, baked for an hour, and then cooled. Wheat was a crop that was planted for the *future* and as such, it was of no immediate use to Gilles and Elsje: Their tomorrows would not be here, not in this place. Gilles endeavored to pick up every vegetable that he could find, though; he didn't say this out loud to Elsje, but after months of backbreaking and miserable work, hauling buckets of water and pulling weeds, it infuriated him to find so *little* food and he was not going to leave any of it behind for the people who had treated them so poorly. They might have the wheat and make of it what they would if Nicholas didn't want it. Perhaps as they ate it later they might remember that it was Msr. Philippe's wheat, tended all summer by Gilles, that was keeping them alive for a time after the French army's devastation.

At Nicholas' house, Elsje put together a quick soup with the salvaged vegetables and the roasted chicken. There was no time for this simple dinner to thicken, but Nicholas gave thanks for the food before they ate, a Catholic prayer. When they had finished eating , Elsje and Gilles thanked Nicholas for everything that he had done for them over the previous months, in no way coming close to expressing the full measure of their gratitude, not the least of which was saving the lives of their two children.

"You are leaving here then?" Nicholas asked.

"Ja, we are finished with this place," Gilles affirmed. "We want to leave *now*."

"It's too bad that it didn't work out," Nicholas commiserated, "but there was *not* what you needed here to make a good life."

"What is that?" Gilles asked. "More rain? More fertile land?"

"Nein! People that *care* about each other. I'm sure you don't know this, but many of their building stones came from the stone foundations of an old village that stood here once. Our church was off in the woods but there is little trace of it now, only the two large trees that used to be small saplings on either side of the entrance. The houses of my neighbors, and even their grave markers, have been gone many years now, grown over with thickets, but I am too old to tend all of their graves. They died out of the pox a long time ago but before we were gone, we had comfortable homes, plenty of food, loving neighbors and the most beautiful land that ever God made."

"It's easier to understand the cruelty of disease than of our fellow men. How could they *do* this to us, to their *own* countrymen? We are *all* Frenchmen!" Gilles said.

"It's a mystery, isn't it? Once I met a very great man. He was a man of *peace*, although he was the king of a savage country and the general of his invading army. His love for his fellow men, *even* his enemies, was only surpassed by his love for his little daughter that he left behind at home, naming her no simple queen but the country's Girl King. His sworn blood enemies were impressed with his military skills but they were *in awe* of his insistence upon treating them well, even to the extent of killing his own men if they displayed any cruelty to their captives. He rode through our town one day with his army, requested food and drink and then he *compensated* us for what he and his men consumed, although it is usually customary for invading armies to repay a man for his kindness with the point of a sword. He was the great Lion of the North, was Gustavus Adolphus of Sweden, and though he came to us as our enemy, he earned our respect, our trust, and our friendship. He was killed by his own kind too, and sadly, I fear the world will never see another like him."

"If everything here is gone, then come down the river with us," Gilles said impulsively.

Elsje looked surprised but she raised no objection.

"Nein, nein, my place is here beside my Ana. What was, was. This is my home and I will meet my end here, no matter when or how it comes; besides, my time is nearly finished. Don't grieve for me, I have

421

had everything I could have wanted, and my wonderful Ana too. I would not trade five minutes of the good life I have had for a hundred more years of life. You need to go on to a new life now too and I hope that you will find such a place before the end of *your* time. I will miss you all, especially dear Elsje and Bruinje. When you find that place, *invest* in it. Take the time for your neighbors and family, and don't let *anyone*, not a government, invading armies, or even your own dreams and hard work take it away from you. It *is* worth dying for."

Nicholas insisted that they take some milk and some of the green apples from his trees, too. The fruit wasn't completely ripe yet and would give them stomach aches if eaten in great quantity, but as he said, it would fill them up for at least a part of the long journey home. Elsje took both children outside to Nicholas' well to wash them after their modest meal and to ready Bruinje for the journey. While she was there, Gilles gathered up their meager belongings, the extra clothes and the food, tying it all up in a bundle made from Elsje's spare dress. He spoke with Nicholas for the last time.

"I want to thank you for protecting Elsje and my children," Gilles said. "It's not enough to just say it but I don't ..."

"It was nothing. I did what I could, which *wasn't* very much. She didn't come across the fields to my house until just before you did."

Gilles would have to ask Elsje more about it later: He had assumed that it had been Nicholas' stoep that she hid under and that she had been with the old man for some time before Gilles made it back to the farm.

After Elsje and the children returned to the house, Gilles shook Nicholas' hand and embraced him. Elsje kissed Nicholas goodbye, knowing that she would never see him again and that she would miss him greatly, but she knew that she would never forget him or his kindness. The Jansen family set out on their journey back to Amsterdam by walking the familiar path down alongside the river, passing through the very small bit of local scenery that had remained unchanged over the last few days. In front of them there was the journey on the river and behind them lay burned ruins, missing houses, and a greatly altered landscape.

At the ferry crossing, they would have to wait an indeterminate amount of time for the ferryman on the opposite shore to come across from Mannheim for them. Elsje surprised Gilles by handing Jacomina over to him and then, after hiking up her skirts, she waded into the water right up to her waist. She said she would be cooler that way if the afternoon got very hot.

Gilles observed that she might be right: The clouds *were* lifting completely now, leaving only tiny wisps of dissipating white and gray in the blue sky above them. The water looked good to him too, and when Elsje left the water, he turned the care of the children back to her, took his shoes off, and he waded into the river. He didn't care that the water was cold. He rinsed off the last of the sweat and soot that clung to his body and to his hair. He even smiled outright when the thought passed through his mind that he would no longer have to work in any damned hot garden, not today and not any *other* day in the foreseeable future. The cold water helped soothe his blotchy insect bites and he brought his wet shirt up to his swollen eye for a few moments to see if he could reduce the swelling a little more.

It would have been very tranquil there by the water except for a persistent noise that was coming down the river from the south, at first only on the periphery of his consciousness, but after a time it grew louder until it was unrelenting. The farm implements that had survived the conflagration were being put to a different use now as the sound of digging shovels traveled on the wind from the settlement's graveyard down to their ears. Gilles wondered if the community had finally learned to work as one, to accomplish more as a group than they ever could as individuals, coming together at last for the purpose of burying their dead when they could not agree about feeding the living. Maybe the survivors and the dead could *finally* find peace in this place.

Struggling out of the river in his heavy water-logged clothing and over the slippery rocks, back up the bank to Elsje, he saw the distraught look on her face and Gilles thought that she must be trying to block out the noise by singing quietly to Jacomina and Bruinje. Claire and Elsje had been close friends, perhaps Elsje's best friend ever, besides her sister Tryntje. Was Claire gone now, or was she trapped here, her spirit still walking along the river path with the two little Philippe girls?

Gilles supposed that it depended upon a man's perspective and beliefs. Elsje might have been thinking about her own dead mother at this moment too, and maybe reliving that loss. Someday Elsje might talk with Gilles about it, reminiscing about her friendship with Claire. Gilles had lost someone here too, but he would never be able to share his sorrow with his wife or with anyone else. He left Nouvelle Rochelle with absolutely no regrets about doing so, leaving nothing behind to tie him to this terrible place. It was his profound hope that they would all quickly forget that they had *ever* come here at all.

Luckily they waited for only a short time, maybe an hour, until the ferry came across the river. A lone stranger disembarked and called out to Gilles as the ferry docked at the little wharf.

"Have I *finally* found Nouvelle Rochelle?" he called out to Gilles in French.

"Oui, what is left of it!" Gilles called back to him.

"Is it much further?"

"Not so far. Up the path. Are you *sure* you want to go there?" Gilles asked the fellow.

"*Absolutement*! I leave *nothing* of importance behind me!" came the reply.

"There has been much trouble there. Maybe we can wait here for you to go see for yourself. You can return to Mannheim with us," Gilles offered as he looked back toward the wisps of black smoke that were still rising up into the air from the burned houses.

"Ca ne fait rien," the man replied. "I will go *anyway*." He hauled up a canvas bag, a carpenter's drawknife and froe from the bottom of the ferry boat, slinging these up on the landing first before he climbed out.

Gilles shrugged. If someone had told him *not* to go there only a few months earlier, he would not have listened, either. The man would have to find out for himself whether this was the place for him or not. Perhaps the survivors would treat this newcomer better, especially since his arrival was timely, his carrying with him some rather providential tools. Most of the survivors of Nouvelle Rochelle had nowhere else to go and so there was little choice *but* to stay here. Their descendants might very well populate this valley for generations to come

Gilles could not have known it at this moment in time, but within a generation many of the surviving Palatine settlers would be homeless again, leaving the valley and scattering across the seas and seeking refuge in many foreign lands. Gilles refused to look back, only looking ahead to his future as the ferryman rowed them across the Rhine to Mannheim.

Having convinced Elsje that it might be a very long time before they found a *real* ship heading to Amsterdam and that they should just get transportation of any sort heading in that direction as quickly as possible, Gilles secured passage for them on a produce barge. Elsje was not pleased with this arrangement at all since it was already loaded down with vegetables and grain that the boat's master planned to sell for a better price at more active and prosperous markets down the river. She acquiesced though, realizing that passage on another vessel might be difficult to secure before the end of the day.

With a single step, Gilles crossed from the soil of the Rhineland to their conveyance on the river. He helped his family aboard the floating platform, all the while feeling like a beggar as he could feel the eyes of the crew on him as they stared at the Jansen's ragged clothing and their pathetic little bundle of goods. Gilles was alive though, on a ship going in the right direction, toward Amsterdam, and leaving this failed part of his life behind him. For the moment, that was enough for him.

The vessel's small crew appeared to consist of farm boys, perhaps all brothers, all strong German youths. They maneuvered the vessel out into the current and then before very much time had passed at all, they worked the rudder, some crude oars, and the long poles to bring the barge in to the shore again, stopping at a desolate spot on the water for the night. On the second day, it seemed that they had barely started to pick up speed down the river again when they were headed in toward the docks that demarcated the port area of the city of Worms.

Elsje was not in the *least* happy to learn that they were tying up there for the night when they had barely gone a few miles during the day. It was all that Gilles could do to prevent her from taking the matter up *directly* with the barge's master. If they were put off this boat, Gilles couldn't be sure that they would find another one right away that was willing to take them further down the river: They certainly didn't look like they had the money to pay for passage and what was even more of a concern to the freighters, the extra weight of passengers just slowed the river vessels down, cutting into their time and their profits while the produce sat on the deck, spoiling in the hot sun. Waiting for a day or even a few hours for another boat would do nothing to improve Elsje's black mood either, Gilles was certain of that.

Elsje didn't keep her complaints to herself though, and she angrily told Gilles in a loud voice that they would *never* reach home if they stopped at every bend in the river that boasted of a few customers. Gilles tried to reason with her, telling her the truth, that there were too many hazards, both under the waters of the river and lying in wait for them on the banks, for them to safely continue their journey after darkness. Elsje's retort, of course, was that there was more than enough daylight left to travel on a little further, to get a little bit closer to Amsterdam.

She was unhappy enough about their circumstances but even more so when Gilles told her that he would have to leave her and the children in the captain's care while he went into town to get some provisions.

She understood that they needed to eat something other than the carrots and green apples that they had been living on, understood that someone should stay behind to keep their place on the boat, understood that the strange city might *not* be safe for the children, and she knew that it was out of the question for her to go into a strange town alone, leaving Gilles behind on the barge with Bruinje and Jacomina, but even knowing *all* of these rational facts, even being as sensible as she usually was, Elsje was still very unhappy that Gilles had to be the one to go and leave her behind.

Gilles slid his big knife into his waistband, hiding it under his shirt before he disembarked. He tried not to look *too* pleased about leaving the cramped barge and his cranky wife, but he noticed that he was fairly skipping along by the time he reached the end of the wooden dock and the beginning of the roughly-paved stone streets, which were obviously more for the convenience and comfort of the horse-drawn wagons than for any aesthetic appearance or nod toward abetting travel by the human foot. Just being alive and with a new adventure in front of him, albeit a *small* one, was a good thing; what more could Gilles ask from life on this afternoon?

He quickly found the marketplace where he purchased five loaves of bread, knowing full well that the baker asked a little more for it because the merchant could plainly see that Gilles was one of those strangers who came up from the river, desperate for food and not knowing the going price of things here in this place.

Today Gilles didn't mind; it was the price of admission, the cost of his entertainment, and if things had turned out any differently, on this day he might just as easily have been lying dead back in Nouvelle Rochelle. In fact, Gilles would have bought more bread, even at the inflated price, if it was not for the certainty that it would go moldy after a day out on the river, two days at most. Gilles tore great hunks of bread from one of the loaves, eating it right away as he walked up the street, then bought four bottles of wine, pleading with the man selling it to throw in a burlap sack so he could carry his purchases along with him.

Gilles also purchased a large wheel of cheese that had a color and an aroma that were not familiar to him. The fromage was different than anything Gilles had ever seen, but it was not unpleasant and so he decided to buy it anyway, even if Elsje refused to eat it. It mattered not at all to Gilles if it went moldy on their journey; they would just slice the mold off and throw that portion out to the fish. The provisions would be enough to sustain them for the next several days and by the time they had been consumed, the Jansens would be closer to Amsterdam and hopefully passing larger and more civilized towns along the way.

The bread that he had so quickly devoured stuck halfway down his gullet. Gilles quickly and carelessly broke the cork and wax seal from one of the wine bottles with the point of his knife, not caring at the moment if he ruined the wine with the broken cork. He dislodged the bread in his throat with a few sips, and noticing that the wine *was* very tasty, he consumed a third if the bottle before he stoppered it back up again with the largest remaining piece of the cork. The sun had not gone down behind the buildings yet and Gilles took just a few moments to look around him at the local sights near the market. In a few hours he would be gone from here forever and now it seemed a pity to him *not* to see the city, a lost opportunity. His eye was immediately drawn to the towers of a great cathedral nearby and he told himself that a very slight detour for just a few minutes would not make any difference. It *was* possible that having a little more time away from her husband and very soon, a little more food to eat, would improve Elsje's mood.

Ever since they had left Nouvelle Rochelle, Elsje had been in the *worst* mood that Gilles had ever seen her in, and this observation took into account all of the time he had known her, including both of her pregnancies. She had said next to nothing aloud, and Gilles, being afraid that in some way she might be blaming him for the events that had happened back there, wasn't going to ask what was on her mind. Putting time and miles between them and their past horror in Nouvelle Rochelle had not helped, not yet.

He knew that she was grieving for Claire, but what could he say to her? Claire was dead and gone; nothing was going to change that sad truth. He, too, regretted all of the hardship they had endured during their wasted and errant summer but at least they had not thrown away any more time and being young yet, they still had many good years ahead of them.

Gilles stood outside, looking up at the magnificent exterior of the cathedral. He had seen nothing like this in a very long time and he stayed fixed to the spot, taking in every detail of the stone exterior that had been brought into being at the hands of some long ago and long dead craftsmen. Their creation had carried their work, and in a sense, a part of themselves, forward into the future. They may have started out as very young apprentices to the original stone masons, perhaps clumsy children of not even sixteen years of age when they began to work on it several centuries earlier, but at some point while building this great cathedral, they must have passed through a strong and vigorous youth, a precise and efficient maturity, grown old and then feeble, eyes dimming and joints beginning to ache as they took on apprentices and journeymen of their own. They must have realized eventually that they would not be there to see it themselves, but that their work would be around for future generations, as their children and the descendants of the people they had known would pass by these *same* walls each and every day on their way to the market or their work.

Feeling a little foolish because he just stood there with his mouth open, probably looking like a complete country bumpkin to the passing residents who had already relegated the architectural masterpiece to a mere backdrop of their everyday lives, Gilles decided that he needed to either keep walking or go inside. Curiosity was the deciding factor and he ventured in through the great doors. When he saw that he had not been struck down and killed by a vengeful god right away, both for his past sins and for not availing himself of the confessional recently, he walked all the more boldly forward into the echoing stone interior, past magnificent sculptures that he would have liked to linger over, had he not had to return to Elsje so soon. He walked beside and over the entombed bodies of great citizens in the city's past, now lying in repose under the marble slabs on the floor and in vaults in the walls, the words carved into the stone defining and summarizing a life that may have spanned as much as a century, the distilled total of milestones in the life of the deceased. In the great main chamber, Gilles picked out a spot, knelt down with his sack of goods, and crossed himself.

The feeling was still there for him, the sensation of awe and that he was in the presence of something far greater than himself, greater than any *one* king or any single emperor, greater than all of mankind put together, even after every accomplishment, every good deed, and every good intention in all of history had been tallied up on the human side of the ledger. Gilles opened up his mind, unwrapping it from the protective envelope that generally surrounded it and he requested a full accounting from all of his senses to determine if it was a threatening force that inhabited this place, a jealous or spiteful force, as had been written and *promised* by the priests and the ancients, or if it might be a kindly, helpful, and beneficent power. Gilles would never have had the audacity to ask this kind of question before he suffered through the terrible events that made him leave France, and probably not even while he was living in Amsterdam either, but now he cleared his mind of his own thoughts and he listened for the answer.

Gilles was certain that there was *something* here, and now he believed that it was waiting for him; he even thought for a few moments that he heard it *breathing*, but he felt no malevolence coming from it, no tinge of anger, no great hunger for revenge or retribution. Gilles only felt peace and calm acceptance emanating from it, even when he summoned recent memories of *all* of the misery that he had just left behind him, a short distance up the river from this place, the evil of so many men that he had known and all of the past difficulties in his life, a sort of presentation of *his* evidence for divine review by a heavenly pontiff or judge.

"WHY? WHY?" he screamed silently.

Gilles stayed where he was for some moments, pretending to say the prayers associated with *this* kind of church, the prayers prescribed by the priests and proscribed by the reformees. His attempt to get an audible reply to his question in human language was futile though, and he simply could not reconcile in his own mind what he had lived through and witnessed at the hands of man and the existence of such a feeling, the serene force that he felt was here, residing not only in this place, but in many other places where there were no walls.

The thought occurred to him then that perhaps one had nothing at all to do with the other and eventually Gilles gave up on trying to make any sense out of it; he just stayed there, trying to relax for a few moments, to let the tension and misery of the past flow away from him. He let the peaceful feeling seep into his being and then he constructed beautiful images of his future, of his family's future together, hoping that his desires would somehow take flight on his prayers, going up to heaven and coming back down to him in some concrete form in the future. Gilles would work and grow grapes, live in his own comfortable home, have whatever he needed, be surrounded by good neighbors, friends, and family. His wife and his children would all be healthy and very happy.

When Gilles felt that the feeling had finally permeated him completely, he unclasped his hands, said a remnant of a prayer he remembered from somewhere that seemed applicable to the moment, and then he crossed himself. It had been a long time since he had given this outward sign of his devotion to God and it felt strange to him now. He got up from his knees and took up his sack of goods, but as he lifted it over his shoulder and turned to leave, his eyes were drawn to a shaft of sunlight that came through the colored glass and fell on one of the pews, in fact, in the very *same* location in the sanctuary where Gilles' family had their reserved seats in their cathedral at home in Rouen. As he hesitated for a moment there, wondering if it was a sign from God or just an interesting coincidence, an old man approached him, not begging for money as Gilles anticipated, but muttering something about St. Nicholas.

Gilles supposed that the man was a drunk and had taken him for a drunken sailor as well, in search of a statue of the patron saint of sailors and travelers to bless the next leg of his journey. Gilles turned away from the man. Whatever he was trying to say, Gilles wasn't interested: He was finished with saints. Their stone ears never heard his prayers and their stone lips never dispensed any helpful advice. Gilles' eyes fell on the confessional as he turned to leave. When he was young, he *never* left without stopping to make confession. He was in accord with Father Victor, sure that he was through with that now, too. He would not confess to any man who walked on human feet over the face of the earth, not now, and not *ever* again. The men of the church had squandered Gilles' precious trust, had lost their status as caretaker of his soul forever. Gilles would keep his own secrets or share them, as *he* wished, and some of his secrets would surely go with Gilles to his grave.

Afterwards maybe he could square things with God.

The Huguenot ways made as little sense to him as the Catholic ways. What did *either* method of categorizing existence have to do with that presence that he had just felt in this place?

Rien, nothing at all.

Gilles should have felt confused by these conflicting and mutually exclusive ideologies but in fact, he felt *better* now, better than he had felt in years. Everything in the world that he had to fear was behind him and he resolved that he was going to leave it here in this place and was *not* going to take that fear along with him into his future.

Gilles left the church and attempted to walk back along the same route that he had taken to the cathedral from the market place but he missed a turn somewhere and as the realization came to him that nothing looked familiar and that he should have already been within sight of the river, he knew that he had lost his way. It was getting late and the sun was going down quickly now. Gilles knew that he had to find his way back to the boat before the night people came out and relieved him of his provisions and his money. Another turn in what Gilles thought *might* be the right direction did not bring him back to the river either; instead it took him to a place that he had never been to before and yet it was oddly familiar.

Yes, he remembered every detail: the two candles in every window, the peculiar script on some of the shop doors, every man with a hat and a beard, every woman with her head and arms completely covered, even before the heat of a hot summer afternoon had fully dissipated. The passers-by in this place openly stared at him as he walked on, and now Gilles realized that he might be getting even *further* away from his destination. He came to a very ancient cemetery with six sided stars adorning the tops of the stones and the markers confirmed without a doubt what he already *knew*, that he had ventured into the city's local place of the Hebrews. Any Christian man without Gilles' particular history of living among these people would have been terrified, panicked, and backtracked as quickly as was humanly possible, but Gilles was not in the least concerned: In fact he was quite *relieved* to be here and it only reinforced the ideas that had just passed through his head, that he should go forward trusting in that greater force.

He was safe here. He took a quick inventory and was confident that he remembered enough of the words in their language and that he *could* do this, and do it with ease. He just wished that he had a hat of some kind to put on his head but he had not had one to wear since he lost his during the attack at Nouvelle Rochelle.

Gilles stopped walking when he came to the cemetery gate but he did not go inside. He put a pleasant look on his face and simply waited for the next people to come walking by. First in German and then in the language of the Spanish Jews, Gilles greeted the two men who had been engaged in some deep discussion with each other before they saw the stranger who was just standing there. Gilles asked them which way it was back to the river, in a mix of three languages that he wagered they *might* be able to decipher and eventually point him in the right direction.

The men looked him over, unable to hide their surprise and perplexity regarding the outsider. Gilles could see the inner struggle on their faces as they tried to make sense of *what* Gilles might be, even as they pointed the way back to the docks and gave him more precise directions in their own language. Gilles understood enough of what they said to get his bearings right, realizing that he had been going in the wrong direction for some time now. It was probable that Gilles had come out of the wrong door when he left the cathedral. He thanked the men and bid them good evening before he started back, his sack of goods slung over his shoulder.

As Gilles was walking away, one of the men ran after him and pressed several coins into his hand. Did he look like a beggar to them? Gilles tried to refuse the money but the man closed Gilles' fingers around it with his own, smiled at him, and made shooing motions.

"*Take it, take it!*" he seemed to be saying.

Puzzled but grateful, and being unable to explain fully that he didn't *need* any money, Gilles thanked him again and walked away, hearing excited chatter behind him and only catching two words that he understood, "…*shaygets?*" asked as a question by the other man and the name "Aylija!", spoken with more emphasis and possibly some fear and awe by the man who had just given Gilles the strange coins.

That night Gilles, Elsje, and the children slept again on the open deck of the little barge, between barrels of wine vinegar, bales of hops, and piles of newly loaded cabbages, covering themselves and the children with a single blanket that smelled of old perspiration. The covering was all that they had but it had been generously donated to them by one of the crew so they made good use of it. Gilles had not given a thought to blankets while he was in the city, as it had been a very warm day. It served not only to keep them warm but also to keep the flying insects from biting them and the worms in the produce from crawling over them. Gilles knew that Elsje was disgusted and frustrated with their living conditions and he *was* genuinely sorry for her lack of comfort and present humble circumstances, but he refused to feel very guilty about it because there was not much that he could do about it, and in truth, he was in no *real* hurry to end this adventure and get back to Amsterdam, back to Elsje's father and work at Ste Germaine's. *Of course* it would be very pleasant when they were in the city again with all of its civilized comforts, but here on the water it was serene: There was no hard work in the fields, no Ste Germaine barking at him, nipping at his heels all day, and best of all, no Hendrick, sniping and snipping at him with his daily barrage of insults, both large and small. This might be the last opportunity Gilles would *ever* have to travel in his lifetime and so he decided that he was just going to relax and drink it all in, every bit of it, so he could commit it to his memory forever: the peaceful river, the patient hills, the ancient castles, the great wading birds, the schools of fish, even the people that he saw every day on the river during their journey. It was beautiful here and finally, for the first time in his life, he felt at peace; he appreciated the luxury that this acquired patience offered. Ahead of him was a whole lifetime of dull and tedious work and so he gathered up his mental souvenirs to save for the future. *"I will remember,"* he told himself. *"I will always remember."*

The crew cast off very early the next morning after loading some timber, flax for sails, pitch and tar for repairing ship's hulls and copper onto the little ship to continue its way down the Rhine toward the

Netherlands. The little barge was loaded down completely and had just pushed off when a cry came up from the shore.

"*Stop!* Come back! I have an urgent message!"

The cry was repeated in French by a youth on horseback who called out to them, jumping off his horse and running full speed out to the end of the dock, stopping just short of falling over the edge and into the water. It was too late for the vessel to go back now, though, and in spite of the sailors' best efforts to hold the boat's position, they were still moving slowly, further and further out into the river. The boy wasted no more time in delivering his message from the riverbank.

"Is Gilles Jansen of Amsterdam and Nouvelle Rochelle on this boat?"

The young rider didn't *look* like one of the French king's soldiers and he was too young and fresh-faced to be a bounty hunter. He was also too far away to be much of a threat so Gilles called back to him.

"*I* am Gilles Jansen. What news do you have for me?"

"Jean Durie sends an urgent message: He is sending Elsje's brother and sisters to you!"

"We can't take them! We are returning to Amsterdam! Send that reply! How did you find us?" Gilles called back, having to shout louder to be heard on the shore as the boat was now entering the noisy main current in the river.

"You had already left Nouvelle Rochelle when I got there!"

The youth's voice just barely carried over the noise of the nearby rapids and the distance between the boat and shore was increasing quickly. The crew was unwilling to invest any more effort to stop the boat's progress downstream, even if it had been possible for them to do so.

"What other news have you?" Gilles roared his last question.

"I can't hear you!" the young man called back.

The distance from shore, the babble of the river, and even the light breeze over the water, all conspired to carry Gilles' question away and to disperse it into the air with the spray from the river. The rider turned away from the pier, walked back to the riverbank and collected his horse, moving forward now at a leisurely walk, his message delivered, his mission accomplished. Gilles and Elsje could do nothing more but stand there and watch him go.

"Oh, no! Cousin Vroutje and my father are *dead!*" Elsje wailed.

"Shhh, shhhh, *nee Elsje*, Jean would *not* have held back that news, I'm sure."

Gilles wasn't *really* certain of this but he wasn't going to tell *her* that: She had been through so much lately and it was still a *very* long way back to the Netherlands on a very *small* boat with no escape from her if she was going to be distraught all the way home.

"What *else* could it be then?" she demanded of Gilles.

"I don't know, but Jean will take care of things, as he *always* does, at least until we can get back there, and we will just have to find out when we reach Amsterdam."

The hot sun beating down on them reflected off the water and had already burned their exposed skins to a bright color the day before, even with Elsje's attempts to protect the children, so Gilles rigged up a covering using borrowed bits of rope and the old blanket to shade and shelter his family. Later on, while the children slept under their makeshift tent as it sailed on down the Rhine, Elsje washed out their few articles of clothing in the rushing river currents. Gilles overheard a few of the crew complain to the boat's master that the drag of the clothing being washed was slowing their progress and if the Netherlander woman fell overboard, they were *not* going to go in after her.

Gilles wondered if he should speak to Elsje but it seemed to him that the clothing might actually be *helping* their progress, working as a sort of underwater sail and not as a sea anchor to slow their progress. Before Gilles could do or say anything though, the skipper strolled over, nodding at Gilles as he passed, but saying nothing until he had made a complete circle of the barge. Gilles could hear the man's voice well enough as it carried downwind while he addressed his crew; the captain had observed that the precious *few* items that the family had left in their possession consisted mainly of Jacomina's diaper cloths and that losing a few minutes a day was *greatly* preferable to living on the small boat with the stink of an unchanged infant. Besides, the family had paid for their passage and did not beg to travel with them at no cost as was the case with so many of the other impoverished people wishing to travel up and down the river valley. Gilles silently agreed with this assessment of the situation and he flashed the barge captain a smile of gratitude.

Elsje's extra dress that Gilles had found in the ashes of their home was also washed out and it dried quickly after being set out in the sun, the breezes coming off the river also speeding up the process. She changed into the clean dress, taking advantage of the privacy under the blanket. When she had finished dressing, she went to wash out the soiled dress that she had been wearing through all of the misery of the last few days, the dress that she had put on to harvest the crops on that terrible morning. The water's current was too much for her though, and the dress was snatched out of her hands by the driving force of the river. The dress floated on, dancing away on a different path down the swiftly moving waters of the Rhine. Gilles thought that this bit of bad luck might bring at the very *least* a curse to her lips, if not an angry outburst, but Elsje said nothing at all about it. She just stood up and silently watched it go.

Gilles was aware that Elsje slept very little that night, and very little every *other* night afterwards, alternately worrying silently and then worrying aloud all the way into the Netherlands that something terrible had happened to her family while Gilles told her over and over again what words he could think of to ease her relentlessly worrying mind. Only during the day did Elsje nod off, exhausted, as she leaned against the cargo or against Gilles with Jacomina still in her arms and Bruinje next to her.

Many weeks and two boats later they arrived in Amsterdam just as night was coming down and moving across the face of the city. Even Gilles was happy for the journey to be over. He would not have believed that just being on a boat for several weeks could be *so* tiresome but their slow mode of transport, barely floating planks for the most part, fresh air, hot sun, limited diet and previous trauma had all taken a toll on their energies. They were physically and emotionally exhausted *before* they left Nouvelle Rochelle and they fared only slightly better at their journey's end. The crew had just tied the vessel down and Gilles was helping Elsje and the children out, making ready for the final leg of their journey, the walk home to Hendrick's inn, when another boy, this one younger than the one they had seen at the dock in Worms, called out to them from the quay.

"Do you have a Gilles Jansen on board?" the boy called out to them, a French accent much in evidence in his Dutch speech.

"Who asks?" Gilles replied.

"I have a message for him from Jean Durie."

"What is it then?" Gilles asked, getting Elsje and the children to the dock safely while the boy delivered his message.

"Jean Durie wants to see you *right away* when you get in. He asks that you make *no* stops and take no detours but go directly to his house *first*."

The boy didn't leave after he delivered his message but stood there waiting expectantly.

"Je comprends," Gilles answered the boy and flipped him one of the lumpy, melted coins.

The boy caught it expertly, made a small sound of satisfaction at the weight of it, and then disappeared into the twilight. Gilles picked up their small bundle of belongings, even smaller now than it had been when they left the Palatinate, as it no longer held the carrots, apples, or Elsje's extra dress, and took Bruinje by the hand, leaving Elsje to handle Jacomina. They walked over the landing's boards to the terra firma of the shore which had a peculiarly hard and unyielding feel to it after all of the time they had spent floating on the river. Gilles flagged down an empty produce wagon that was grinding along by the docks, the farmer heading home after a long day of selling his goods in the marketplace. For another coin, Gilles convinced the farmer to take a small side trip and carry his tired family to Jean Durie's house.

"I don't *want* to go to Jean's! I want to go *home*, Gilles! We are all so tired and I just want to see my father and Tryntje and sleep in our own bed! Maybe Father is dead and Jean just didn't want to tell us!" Elsje objected.

"Nee, he can't be dead." Gilles told her, for what seemed to be the four hundredth time since they had left Worms. *The old bastard's too miserable to die*, Gilles thought, but of course he didn't say that out loud to her. Instead he said in his most reasonable voice, "Jean *must* have had a good reason for stationing the boy here at the docks all day and all night and telling us not to go to the inn first. We will see what news Jean has first, and then, I promise you, we will continue on to the inn if it is safe. I must trust Jean on this if he has gone to so much trouble to send not one, but *two* messengers to intercept us."

Gilles didn't want to alarm his wife, but now he was concerned as well, thinking that Jean's message might in some way be connected to the French army's attack on Nouvelle Rochelle. It was also possible that someone had managed to trace Gilles to Amsterdam from France and they might now be lying in wait for Gilles at Hendrick's inn. Even if Gilles was so inclined, just to keep her from constantly complaining every step of the way, Gilles could not, under any circumstances, give in to Elsje's wishes tonight or his entire family might be put in harm's way.

Elsje didn't argue with him, though. She remained silent as they made themselves as comfortable as possible on the old straw in the farmer's wagon bed. As they jolted over the stone streets, the first paved streets they had traveled over in quite some time, Elsje stretched her neck out to look in the direction of the inn. There was nothing to be seen in the twilight, especially at this distance, and Gilles directed the driver well away from the inn, just in case there was anything to be avoided there, giving the location a wide berth as he gave the driver somewhat roundabout directions to Jean Durie's house.

Gilles couldn't see what coin he handed to the driver when they got there, but it no longer mattered very much: Although Gilles had been very generous with the messenger boy, he held the rest of the guilders back, knowing that one gold piece was too much money to pay for a short ride, no matter how greatly it was needed and appreciated. Gilles had an assortment of money in his pocket, guilders, stuivers and various French and German coins, but here in Amsterdam all of it could be converted to Dutch currency at the exchange house. Gilles thanked the farmer and helped Elsje down from the back of the wagon first. He climbed back up and handed baby Jacomina to his wife before he set their belongings at the edge and then returned one last time to hoist a soundly sleeping Bruinje up over his shoulder. Gilles climbed down from the wagon bed with his son slung over his shoulder like a full sack of grain before he took up their belongings with his other hand. Only then did Bruinje rouse himself for a few moments.

"Home?" the little boy asked in French, his eyes fluttering open slightly and then closing in sleep again right away.

Gilles looked at Elsjc and shrugged his eyebrows. *Someone* would have to try to explain it to him tomorrow: It was fairly certain that the only home the child would remember now was far behind them in the Rhine Valley and the house that had stood on that land was gone now. The farmer's wagon moved forward, off into the dark shadows and Gilles led his tired family over to Jean Durie's door.

"Ah, the boy *told* me that you had made it safely back!" Jean said, throwing open the door after Gilles' knock. He dragged them all inside and kissed Gilles and Elsje enthusiastically, maneuvering his embraces around the two sleeping children that they still held in their arms.

"You can just put the little ones down on the floor over there. I'll bring some bedding out for them. Make yourselves comfortable!"

Jean left the room before they could say or ask him anything more.

"Jean, is my father all right?" Elsje called after him and then she searched his face for the answer as soon as he returned, carrying two blankets out from his adjoining bedroom.

Jean replied as he spread one blanket out on the floor. "Hendrick is well enough, Elsje."

Gilles and Elsje slowly lowered the children down so as not to wake them, and Elsje covered them with the second blanket while Jean continued to talk in a muted voice.

"I didn't mean to take you away from your new life but there are things going on here that... well, I felt that you needed to know. I didn't take the time to put it all down in a letter; I just sent the messenger. Let me pour you both a drink."

Elsje looked up at her husband in puzzlement but Gilles shook his head to indicate that he had *no* idea of what Jean was going to say either. They remained standing there while Jean poured a glass of Port for Gilles but Elsje refused the offer. Gilles remembered the Port from his father's business meetings and the smell of it brought back to him in one whiff, the debates about trade strategy and future market position, the camaraderie, and the *good* memories, but the offered drink instead of just wine also told Gilles that something very serious had happened here in their absence. He readied himself for it and he just hoped that Elsje was ready for it, too, whatever it might be.

"We were on our way back to Amsterdam when your first messenger found us," Gilles said, not waiting any longer but taking a fortifying sip and savoring the taste of civilization.

"Yes, he told me as much." Jean said. "It was very *good* news to hear that you were coming back as I have missed you greatly. Sit! Both of you; don't just stand there!"

Jean pulled a third chair over to his card table, not to his business desk, and Gilles wondered if this choice of location was to put Elsje at her ease. Jean generally had a strategy and a reason for *everything* that he did. Mercifully Jean didn't wait any longer but plunged headlong into what he had to say to them.

"It's probably just as well that you are here: Recently I received information from some of my connections in France that the King's soldiers were probably going to be making raids into the Palatinate to forcibly remove the French settlements that have been established there. It might not have been safe for you to continue living there."

"*Really?*" Gilles asked mockingly, but he let Jean finish saying what he had to say. Just because Jean's *timing* was imperfect, at least they might now have some answers as to why it had happened, why they had been so viciously attacked in the Palatinate.

"It seems that the French King, or should I say his *advisors*, since the new King is only an infant and probably without a strong personal opinion on this particular subject as yet, have had *another* change of heart. They were not too concerned that they were ridding the country of these agitators, these *fleas* as they have called them, but having lost so many of the merchant class, the *best* of France's intellect and tradesmen to the ranks of the fleeing Reformees, they discovered that it has had a most *drastic* affect on the tax collections, much more so than they had at first realized. If they could not have the revenue of these people for themselves, then they wanted no one else, especially the Habsburgs or the Electors, to receive profit from the talents and labor of France's escaping middle class."

"They did *indeed* send us that clear message, Jean. They harrowed us there and it was bestial, what they did to us. We managed to survive but many of our neighbors did not; the settlement was almost completely burned," Gilles verified.

"Hmm," Jean answered, looking rather more closely at each of them as he continued talking. "I'm sorry to hear that, but you *do* look well enough, thank God. There is more that I have to tell you, though. There have been some recent developments here. You asked about your father, Elsje, and he is well enough, as I said, but I'm afraid that your inn has not fared so well. I know this will be a shock to you, but the inn has been completely destroyed; it is a total loss. There was a fire there too, and your father was injured but he has been nursed back to health at your cousin Vroutje's home."

"And my sister Tryntje?" Elsje asked meekly, her hands clenched rather tightly together in her lap.

"Don't trouble yourself for a *moment* about Tryntje, Elsje; she is *very* well!" Jean laughed.

Gilles reached over to take Elsje's hand in his but she did not respond to his touch so he put his one hand on top of both of hers.

"I'll have that drink now, Jean. You don't have bier or ale, do you?" Elsje asked him.

"Sorry, no. I have wine or I can offer you something stronger," Jean said.

"I'll take the wine. What about all of our things? All we have left in the world is what we are wearing now and what we have carried out with us!" Elsje pointed to the small burlap bundle next to the children.

Jean smiled at her. "Ah, that may be a *little* bit of good news among the bad, then! It is my understanding that the things you left behind had already been removed to your cousin Vroutje's upper story for storage *before* the fire, so strangely enough, more of your things than your father's survived the disaster."

Elsje nodded in understanding of his words and Gilles gave her a little time to pull herself back together emotionally. Jean excused himself and went out to the other side of the house, the side inhabited by the owners of the building.

"Are you all right?" Gilles asked Elsje when he had gone.

"Ja, ja! It's just *so much* and all at once!"

"Your father and Tryntje are fine and we are fine. It is a lot to bear but we will go on, we will be all right," Gilles told her.

Jean returned with a drinking glass that had been blown into an elaborate rounded shape and from his spirits cabinet he pulled out a bottle containing a red-gold liquid.

"Try some of this, Elsje. It's the greatest contribution Portugal has made yet to the civilized world."

"What *exactly* happened to the inn, Jean?" Gilles was impatient now. He was ready for more facts, more information. He had the distinct feeling that Jean was still holding something back from them.

447

"Well, I suppose I should start from the very beginning. Just after you left, Tryntje was married to a very fine gentleman with a good position in the West India Company, Adriaen Ver Hulst. Do you remember him, Willem's nephew? You didn't get the letter? Oh, well... It *was* rather a sudden decision, but your father made a fine match one night over a few drinks and the wedding was on. Tryntje is quite wealthy now, or I should say, her husband is. Adriaen would not allow her to work of course, and so Tryntje left the running of the inn completely up to the servants and your father. That was probably fortunate because she was already gone from the city, not even there on that night, safely out of harms way and secure in the arms of her new husband. Hendrick got involved in an altercation between some Spanish soldiers and some French bounty hunters who showed up at the inn at the same time. As you know, your father isn't *always* the most diplomatic of souls. Hendrick told me later that he thought they might just go outside and fight with each other, leaving everyone else out of it, but they were all drunk, all armed, and they ended up setting fire to the inn after attacking one of the kitchen maids. Your father was injured slightly in the fight but due to the good medical care of Doctor Tulp, he is recovering nicely now."

Elsje looked stunned and stared into her glass after she took a very large sip of the liquid, holding it in her mouth for a time until she swallowed. One rivulet moved slowly back down the inside of the glass and Gilles watched it as it rejoined the main body of the drink.

"I *should* have been here, with Father. I *never* should have left," Elsje murmured.

Jean cleared his throat. "Yes, well, if you *had* been here at the time, Elsje, they might have killed you both, and the children too."

"Those bastards!" Gilles exploded. The accumulated stress of the past few months was too much for him and now Gilles could no longer contain his anger. He was tired and hungry, weary of fighting just to claim a small piece of earth for himself, a little space in which to just *live* his life. Mere survival was taking all of his energy, leaving him with no strength to accomplish anything more than that.

Elsje put her finger to her lips and nodded in the direction of the little ones sleeping peacefully in the corner, warning Gilles not to wake them, but he could see that his wife's face reflected the same battle fatigue that he was feeling.

Gilles drew a deep breath and calmed himself before he went on, firing a volley of questions and thoughts in Jean's direction, albeit at a lower volume.

"Even if I *could* go to Ste Germaine and borrow the money from him to rebuild the inn, is it safe? We have our investments, I suppose. I could use some of that money. We *do* still have those investments, don't we? Is it safe for us to be here in the city now?"

Jean hesitated. It seemed as if he was deciding which one of Gilles' questions to answer first, and that all of his replies required some longer answers than a simple 'yes' or 'no'. Jean replied to the financial questions first, of course; discussing pure business had *always* been easier for both of them.

"Our investments are safe but it has been a very bad year over in New Netherland as far as trade goes. They say there have been difficulties with the savages although not much news has been coming out of New Amsterdam for reasons that we don't fully understand yet. You *can't* go back to Ste Germaine's though, Gilles. He is gone."

A flicker of sadness crossed Jean's eyes, a shadow passing so quickly across his face that only Gilles would see it. Gilles had a bad feeling about this, too. He wasn't going to ask in front of his wife but Elsje asked the question first.

"What happened to Ste Germaine? Did they burn his place down too?"

"No, his place is fine but he is dead."

"Dead? How?"

"Garroted and drowned. La Rue filed a complaint with the officials and then left town right after the trial, which itself did not last very long. The execution was at the Dam and then they took his body to the Ij in irons with a weight…" Jean stopped speaking while he poured himself another full drink.

"Oh my God," Elsje murmured.

Jean cleared his throat and went on with the story. "He was charged with, and convicted of, Unnatural Vice. He made little attempt to defend himself and besides, how he lived his life was not *exactly* a secret. No one had bothered him about it before and there were no complaints about him because everyone knew him to be a good and decent man."

"Why wasn't LaRue executed with him?" Gilles asked.

"He claimed *complete* innocence; claimed that he had only been Ste Germaine's friend and had been shocked when he was assaulted one night by Ste Germaine. LaRue even went so far as to show up for the trial with an alibi and a *fiancée*, some prostitute he hired just for the occasion, no doubt. No, your being here would not have changed a single thing. It would not have saved the inn nor would it have saved Ste Germaine. *I know.* I went to his trial, I tried, but I could not save him."

Jean took another drink and his face suddenly relaxed, as if he was leaving the events behind that he had just been so intensely reliving.

Gilles wondered how so much could have changed so fast, in just the few months that he was gone; he also wondered how difficult it had been for Jean to bring himself to attend the trial.

Gilles remembered only too vividly when his own death sentence had been pronounced, his and Jean Durie's, during their trial for heresy in France. It was still a fresh wound even though years had passed. Gilles didn't know if he could stand to be in a courtroom again, even to go to the defense of another man as Jean had done, even for as good a friend as Ste Germaine had been to him. Gilles hadn't permitted his mind to go back to that terrifying place since their escape from the fires in Rouen, but now that he allowed himself to think about it, even just a little bit, he remembered only too clearly the disbelief of what his senses relayed to his mind and the debilitating, sickening fear that spread through his limbs and his innards as he stood before the French judge.

"*Why* did he do it? What did LaRue have to gain from Ste Germaine's death?" Gilles asked Jean, not ready to leave the subject behind yet.

"That is a *complete* mystery to everyone," Jean replied. "The inn sits vacant and LaRue has no claim to it. That was all that I could think of, that LaRue had thought he would be named Ste Germaine's heir at law and inherit his home and business."

Gilles wasn't sure if he should ask his next question in front of Elsje but he decided to ask it anyway. He had to know and he had to know now.

"You didn't answer my *other* question, Jean. Is it safe for us to be here in Amsterdam?"

Jean smiled a little. "The French bounty hunters *always* ask and always poke around everywhere, since they are unable to come up with any productive avenues for finding their quarry. The Spanish soldiers have all been gone for weeks except for the regular patrols, so sleep peacefully, Gilles." Jean looked over at Elsje and placed a wider smile on his face. "Life goes on, and if it can get worse, it can also get better, *n'est-ce pas?* I am *so* happy to see all of you here again though, to know that you are all in good health, and to see your beautiful new little one."

The initial look of pride on Elsje's face in response to Jean's praise of her little daughter was quickly overtaken by a frown. She was not to be distracted by flattery, not tonight.

"What will we do now? Where will we go?"

Elsje looked at her husband when she asked the question but Gilles was lost in his thoughts, too busy thinking about what he would like to do to LaRue when he saw him again. The cook had been right about the nature of LaRue's character all along. What else had Gilles *not* known about LaRue? He remembered the alias LaRue used and he was beginning to suspect that there was a lot more to the man's personal history.

It may not have been his place, but nevertheless, Jean attempted to answer Elsje's question. "*This* is the reason that I sent word to you and tried to send your sisters and brother to the Palatinate: Right now your family needs your help. Cousin Vroutje and her husband just can't handle them all, even though they have tried, to the very *utmost* of their abilities. One man working in the ceramic tile and brick production just can't earn enough money to feed and clothe six people properly, even with all of the city's new construction going on. Your sister Jennetje has gone to work with him, although she is quite young yet, but her talents with a paintbrush have not gone unnoticed, and she has turned her natural talents to painting unique tile creations for some of Amsterdam's nouveau riche to help feed the family. She is *quite* the artist, a regular Judith Leyster of the tiles, and she is making a name for herself too, at least among the masons and carpenters in the guilds. There has been some pressure to put little Heintje to work as an apprentice somewhere, perhaps at the printers since there is *great* demand for that service, but Vroutje is adamant that he is too young as yet, has already been farmed out too much since your mother died, and she will not hear of his running messages at the docks for fear he will, either willingly or unwillingly, be taken away to sea as a deck hand. Heintje and Corretje sweep the steps of some of the businesses in the city to earn extra money for the family. I have tried to help them out, but they are *very* proud people and will not take more than an occasional gift of food which I always have to get them to accept from me under false pretenses. Perhaps you can get their situation sorted out and then go back to a safer region of the Palatinate. Or not," Jean added quickly, seeing a panicked look on both faces. "A good many people from Amsterdam are going in the *other* direction, over to New Netherland. Tryntje and her husband left for there right after the ceremony and they must *surely* have made port by now. I am leaving for there myself within the next few days."

Gilles looked around the room and noticed now for the first time that Jean's things were in the process of being packed up.

"There are just too many people from France and Spain still looking for me here and besides, I hear that they are in desperate need of a good negotiations and accounts man over there. The useless bureaucrats that have already gone over could use some practical help in setting up trade agreements with the English settlements to the south and the east, the Savages everywhere, and if I can overcome their *extreme* distrust of each other, with the Swedes as well."

"You're joking of course. *You*? In the New World?" Gilles looked at Jean in disbelief but there was no jest in his friend's eyes.

"It will only be for a short time, a few years at most. When things calm down here, the Spanish soldiers will have nothing more to fight over. They will all go home and at that time I will come back, a rich man from the New Amsterdam trade, and pick up here where I left off."

Jean was perfectly serious but Gilles *still* could not accept this scenario as future reality.

Jean smiled sympathetically at Elsje. "I can see that this is all too much of a shock for one night and perhaps I should not have burdened you with *all* of it right away after your long journey, but I wanted you to know; I did *not* want you to come upon the inn unprepared for what you would see there. It's late. Rest here tonight and don't worry. It's not so bad; you will see that for yourselves in the morning."

Jean offered to get them some food but even though they had not eaten very much lately, Elsje and Gilles did not want to eat, they only wanted to sleep, a dreamless sleep if they could have it.

Jean went out into the hall and returned with a servant that belonged to the main household. "Go with Neeltje. She can put you in the guest bedroom in the main house for the night. You can leave the children to sleep on my floor if you want; they will be fine here."

Elsje wanted the children with her and Gilles was certain that it was not just to feed Jacomina during the night as Elsje insisted; he knew that she needed the reassuring presence of her entire family near her now, even when she slept. Once more Gilles and Elsje gathered the children up and then followed Neeltje out of Jean's chambers to the other side of the house.

When they were alone in the guest bedroom at last, Gilles took his pants off and climbed into the clean and sweet-smelling bed. It was softer than he remembered beds could be, and if he wanted to say anything or do anything more before he closed his eyes, it did not happen because he was fast asleep even before Elsje had the children settled, even before she blew out the lamp. Gilles did not remember another thing until he woke suddenly from his deep sleep, hearing Elsje up and getting dressed in the darkness.

"Elsje, come back to bed, it's the middle of the night!" he called out to her. "I had to get up to feed and change Jacomina. The sun is coming up, Gilles. I have to go and see what has happened to our inn."

"Elsje, it is the lantern light from the alehouses and the warehouses that work all through the night. You aren't used to seeing them because they had *neither* in Nouvelle Rochelle."

She pulled the curtains aside and looked out the window for a moment before she answered, "I'm *sure* it's the sun and I haven't slept all night for the nightmares I've had. We should have just gone straight to Cousin Vroutje's last night."

Gilles got out of bed, walked over to her and put his arms around her. "What could you have done so late at night? Besides, the children were *so* tired. You are tired, too. Come back to sleep."

"I have to go *now*, Gilles. I *have* to see the inn."

"I will *not* let you go out at night by yourself. Wait for the morning light and we'll go together."

He climbed back into the bed and loudly patted the spot next to him. He hadn't been with his wife in a *very* long time, not since before the attack on Nouvelle Rochelle, although he had tried his very best to talk her into it while they were on the boat on the river. It would be a very pleasant way to pass a little time until the dawn, particularly in this *very* comfortable bed.

Elsje was not relaxing though. She perched on the edge of the bed, not going back to sleep and not receptive in the least to Gilles' overtures of intimacy.

Gilles tried again. "I *promise* you, Elsje, just as soon as the morning light comes, we will go. Now come back to bed. Please. For me."

Elsje didn't move, though; she was being very stubborn. At length Gilles finally gave up, heaved a sigh at the same time he heaved the covers back, and got up to put his pants on.

"We will go to Cousin Vroutje's first even though they are *certainly* still sleeping and then we will see to the inn. After that we will go by Ste Germaine's and then on to the churchyard to your mother's grave. Does that plan meet with your approval?" he asked her.

Elsje turned to him and even in the darkness he could feel her smile. He knew *exactly* what it was that she wanted and needed to hear. He kept talking.

"…then we will need to find some clean clothes and cloths for Jacomina and *sometime*, sometime before we sleep again, we will find a little time for you and I to be alone together, eh? Do I sound like *you* yet?"

Elsje said nothing in reply but Gilles heard her lacing up her dress and walking over to the wash basin. He heard the water pouring into it from the pitcher, heard it stop and the pitcher being clumsily set back down on the table. A few splashes told him that she had found the water and managed to wash and dry her face and hands, even in the darkness.

There was a light knock on the door and some lamplight came underneath it from the other side. Gilles pushed aside his initial fears as he knew it was a woman's hand upon the door.

"Enter!" he responded. The door swung open and the young girl, the one who always tended the fire in the mornings, came into the room, carrying a lamp.

"Excuse me, I *thought* I heard voices. I wasn't told that there would be guests last night."

Gilles smiled at the girl. "We arrived late and are guests of Jean Durie's. He told us that it would be all right for us to stay the night here."

She pulled her wrap tighter around herself and tried not to look at Gilles' open shirt. "So it is. Any guest of Jean Durie's is always welcome in our home. Can I get you some tea now or something to eat?"

"Nee, danks," Elsje replied as Gilles simultaneously said, "Ja, that would be wonderful."

"Elsje, please let the children sleep just a *little* longer," Gilles urged her, "while we have some tea. You haven't eaten in so long; you will have *no* milk for Jacomina."

Elsje glared at him impatiently but the servant yawned and replied, "I can get you some tea. It won't take me very long. The water has been kept warm over the coals all night. Some tea cakes, too," she added, as if she had just thought of it. "I'll leave the lamp here for you."

Gilles hoped that his mind would start to clear and that some solutions to their current and future challenges would present themselves more readily to him after he had some morning tea. So many complex problems lay in a jumble in front of him with only untried and inexact formulae to help him find his way through to safety, material comfort, and future prosperity.

Elsje used the chamber pot, not a mere porcelain vessel in this house, but a wooden throne, much like the one that Gilles had purchased for her. When she finished, she washed her hands again and then alternately paced the room and tapped her foot until the tea was brought in to them. She nibbled impatiently at a little cake while Gilles savored the taste of the dark Chinese brew. It had been so many, many, weeks without any tea.

"We probably smell like cheese and cabbage," Gilles said to Elsje, trying to elicit a smile.

"Hmph," Elsje replied. "You have some dirt on your face. Wash before we leave."

"Your cousin will still be asleep. We shouldn't wake them up so early."

"Hmph," Elsje said again.

She was quiet for a few minutes but finally she could stand it no longer and she exclaimed, "Please Gilles! You carry Bruinje and I will carry Jacomina, or just let me go there *without* you right now. I can't wait any longer!"

Gilles knew that it was no good to argue or to try to stall any more. He had hoped to keep her in the house, at least until the sun had started to come up, but that just wasn't going to happen. He nodded acquiescence and Elsje waited no longer but picked up Jacomina, their bundle of belongings, and a leftover breakfast cake as she headed toward the door. Gilles did get her to wait just a few moments longer, only just long enough for him to pick up Bruinje but the boy woke up, rubbed his eyes and told his father that he needed to use the chamber pot. Gilles didn't mind this extra delay at all, but Elsje stood by the door with Jacomina in her arms, fuming and telling Bruinje to hurry.

They couldn't make very fast progress over the misty morning streets, having to carefully pick their way over the damp and slippery pavers leading to Cousin Vroutje's house. Just as they started out, Elsje handed Gilles the leftover cake and told him *not* to eat it, that it was for Bruinje's breakfast. Gilles always wondered how women managed to do that, to hold a child, another bundle, *and* a cake, all at the same time without dropping or crushing any one of the multiple items, even while their minds spun around through other things, marketing and cleaning and gossip.

As they walked along, Gilles looked around and he was struck with how strangely familiar it was to be back here in this place. He wondered if Bruinje remembered Amsterdam or the rest of the family at all, even though they had not been away for such a very long time, only a season. When they got to the little stone house with the corbie-stepped gables, Elsje unlatched the door and they all went inside.

Gilles was right, it *was* too early: The family was still asleep and Gilles wondered what they should do next. Elsje, with her arms full and her line of sight to the floor obscured, nearly tripped over her younger brother Heintje who was sleeping on a little makeshift bed near the front door, his soft little snores remaining rhythmic even as they all walked as quietly as possible around him, the plank floor creaking and squeaking as they went. Once they were in the kitchen, Elsje directed Gilles to open up the little settle bench, and dropping her cloak into the box with one hand, she lowered Jacomina into the cozy space that she herself had slept in as a child. Bruinje didn't need a place to sleep as he was wide awake now, just as he had been on the walk over, kicking now and struggling, protesting until Gilles set him down to wander around the room, exploring everything that caught his eye and his interest. Elsje rekindled the fire and put the water on, rubbing her chilled hands briskly over the small flames before she sat down wearily in a chair at the table, one hand cupping her chin and the other draped across her lap, as she kept a watchful eye on Bruinje.

"J'ai faim!" he said, turning to his mother.

"Yes, Bruinje. Mother will find you some more food." Elsje wearily pulled herself back up onto her feet.

"Ik heb honger!"

"I know, *I know*, be patient!" Elsje admonished her son.

"Does your cousin have some tea somewhere?" Gilles asked Elsje.

"I gave her some a long time ago and unless she has learned to drink it since we left, she probably *still* has it somewhere," Elsje replied.

Gilles didn't find the tea, but Elsje found a little piece of cheese in the cupboard and she sliced some of it for Bruinje and for Gilles.

A door in the kitchen closed off the steep stairs leading to the upper story, shutting out the cold drafts that swept down those stairs in the wintertime. Now footsteps descended the staircase behind the door, coming down toward the kitchen as Gilles and Elsje watched and waited. Cousin Vroutje jumped in surprise after she reached the last step, lifted the latch and swung the door open into the kitchen, only to find several unexpected visitors staring back at her.

"Elsje!" she cried as she scurried over and hugged Elsje tightly. "God in Heaven, I have missed you *so* much!"

She kissed both of her niece's cheeks and her mouth. The women wrapped their arms around each other and tears ran down Vroutje's cheeks as Gilles looked on uncomfortably. Women were *always* far too emotional and he could expect a lot more tears today: They would certainly revel in the misery of what had befallen them in the Pfalzland when that tale was told and it was probable that Vroutje's family would blame him for that *and* for the things that had happened in Amsterdam, too, while they were away.

"We have lost *everything!*" Elsje exclaimed, not breaking this news gently at all, but letting the full measure of it fall like a hammer on a discordant chime.

"No, we haven't, Elsje," Gilles interjected defensively from the post he had taken up by the fireplace. "We are all safe and we still have our savings. We haven't lost anything, really, nothing that can't be replaced."

"What about the inn?" Elsje demanded. "What about all of our things?"

"Nee, nee, shush, child! Your husband is *quite* right," Vroutje smoothed Elsje's hair back as if she was still a small child. "We are all well and your savings are safe with the Westindische Compagnie. Jean Durie has been a godsend to us and anything that we might have needed, he has taken care of for us."

"What about Father?" Elsje asked. "Is Father all right? We talked with Jean Durie before we came here and he said that Father had been hurt."

"He didn't explain?" Vroutje asked, a little anxiously, looking from Elsje to Gilles.

"Nee." Elsje looked in her aunt's eyes, ready for whatever was to come next.

"That night, when the soldiers went to the inn, your father put up a fight and was injured. The wound became infected and..."

"Is he still sick?" Elsje asked.

"He no longer has his left arm, Little One. They cleaned it and bandaged it up right away but infection *still* set in. He started to lose the arm and his health was failing so they took it off and now he lives. He was lucky enough not to get the lock-jaw."

Elsje said nothing in reply to this. She was pale and suddenly she had to sit down again.

"Elsje, you need some food! Have you eaten yet today?" Vroutje asked her.

"She hasn't eaten much *lately*," Gilles offered, not being happy to admit this, but hoping that Vroutje would have a little more success in convincing his wife to eat something. Now that he took a good look at Elsje through Vroutje's eyes, Gilles could tell that she had lost some weight recently.

"You need to keep up your strength, Child! Don't worry about your father; he is well enough and just as feisty as ever; it's only that he is missing one arm."

Gilles wished that he had some medicinal spirits to give to his wife for her mental state. He wondered if it would be out of line to ask Vroutje for something stronger than tea, even though it was very early in the morning. He decided not to make the request at the moment but Vroutje must have been thinking somewhat along the same lines because she said, "Sit, both of you. I can see that you are *very* tired from your journey. I will give you bread, butter, cheese and herring and you will have some ale, too. Can you drink a little ale, Elsje?"

"Yes, ale," Elsje said, receptive to this suggestion.

"So Jean Durie's message brought you back home to us?" Vroutje asked.

"Ja," Elsje said and Gilles was glad that she took this shortcut to a full reply.

"He *said* he would send word that Heintje and Corretje were anxious to join you very soon, although I'm not sure *exactly* what he was going to say. The children have missed you so much! I'm just sorry that you came all the way back here for nothing. We are *fine*, really, you can just see for yourself and then, after a nice visit with us, you can go back, with or without the children." Vroutje took a momentary break before she chatted on breezily while slicing some bread to put on a plate for her guests. "Is someone taking care of your farm for you?"

"Nee, we are home *to stay*! We should *never* have left our family!" Elsje cried.

Gilles could tell from the strain in her voice that his wife was becoming emotional and he cringed: Now that she had a chance to take in all of the family's combined misery, Elsje would *surely* blame him for the greater share of their misfortunes. His thoughts were interrupted as the water in the iron pot started to hiss and then boil over onto the fire.

"Now, now, you can stay here as long as you like. See for yourself that your father is all right and then you can decide what you want to do next," Vroutje said soothingly to Elsje as she pushed the iron arm holding the water pot over to the side of the fireplace. "I *know* that Gilles is going to want some tea and I still have the tea you gave me, somewhere in here..."

Vroutje went over to the cupboard, and stepping up on a little stool that was kept nearby, she dug around for a moment at the back of the top shelf before she produced the box. She removed the top from the wooden container, putting a clump of dried leaves in the bottom of each cup.

"Is that enough?" she asked as she handed a cup to Gilles. "I never know…"

He nodded. The tea was very dry and pale-looking. It barely smelled like tea anymore but Gilles decided that it would have to do for now and he would forego the stronger beverage that he craved, at least until a little later on, in the interest of keeping peace with his wife and her family.

Vroutje's husband came down the stairs and into the kitchen with Hendrick following close behind him. Gilles noted that Hendrick didn't look different at all except that his left sleeve was oddly flat, folded up at the halfway point, the bottom of the sleeve pinned up to the top of his shoulder.

"Father!" Elsje rushed over to him and threw her arms around his neck.

"What the devil is the matter with her?" Hendrick asked Gilles. "What did you do to her? She's so *thin*! Were you starved out of *farm* country?"

Elsje took a step back to look at her father as Gilles shrugged in reply. He had expected this kind of greeting and truth be told, it was somewhat of a relief to have it over and done with, out of the way for the time being. The old man had lost none of his irritating and unpleasant manner during their absence.

"Oh, my damned arm!" Hendrick said in response to Elsje's attentions. "There is nothing to be done about it. The bastards got it but they didn't get the rest of me and they didn't get my daughter's husband."

Gilles had to stop for a moment to catch his breath: Did the old man *mean* to say that he had lost his arm in defense of his son-in-law? Gilles had to ask him the question.

"Were they looking for *me*, Hendrick?"

"Ja, it was the second time that they came in to ask, but maybe they *finally* understood that you were not here and that is why they got angry. I told them I knew no such person, that my daughter's husband was named *Jansen*, not Montroville, and anyway, he lives far away in the German Palatinate. They asked me about Jean Durie, too but I didn't tell Jean that: It's not important. They don't know what you look like."

Gilles wondered if those who sought him had been at his family's home in France, too. Perhaps the French authorities no longer believed that Gilles' body was interred in the family burial grounds. Could they return to Amsterdam again at any moment to look for him here and might they make threats against Cousin Vroutje's family? These thoughts buzzed around Gilles' head and would not go away although he tried to dismiss them with arrows of logic. While he tried to straighten out in his thoughts which threats were real and which ones were obfuscated by fear and fatigue, Gilles took a sip of the tea that had finally turned a slightly darker color than boiled water, drinking it as he strained out the floating black specs of tea with his teeth. The blazing fire had made it uncomfortably hot in the little kitchen already this morning and Cousin Vroutje opened the back door wide, letting the cooler air swirl into the room, settling in around their legs and ankles.

"This summer has been *so* hot! I'll be so much happier when it's cooler outside!" Vroutje declared as she fanned her red face with the bottom half of her apron. "Klaas, you'd better have something to eat before you go to work. I'll go up and wake Jennetje now or you will *both* be late! Elsje, all of your things are up in the girls' room, your mother's chests of linen too, that is, what Tryntje didn't take with her. Let's go and find you some clean clothes to wear. You will feel like a *new* person when you bathe and put some clean clothes on."

Vroutje led Elsje up the stairs and Gilles marveled that Elsje was so meek and accepting of all of Cousin Vroutje's directions. Gilles stayed where he was, drinking his tea, and wondering how long he could avoid talking with Hendrick.

"It did not go well there?" Hendrick asked him, answering Gilles' query very quickly.

"Nee," Gilles replied, not wanting to go into any more detail than he had to. The less he said to the old man, the better.

"You brought my daughter back alive though, and with a new baby."

Hendrick nodded his head in the direction of the sleeping child.

"Ja. We named her Cornelia Jacomina."

Hendrick said nothing in response to this but Gilles could see that the old man was pleased to have the child named for Elsje's dead mother. He didn't say so out loud, but Gilles hoped that his father-in-law would notice that neither of his grandchildren had been wanting for food.

"And there is my old friend Bruinje!" Hendrick called out to his grandson, holding his arms open wide.

Bruinje had been exploring the kitchen and looked up at Hendrick but he didn't go over to him: It was clear to Gilles that Bruinje either did not remember Hendrick or just was not very comfortable with him now, even though they had only been away for a few months. Perhaps the child was only preoccupied with the new and interesting house to explore.

A small commotion upstairs told Gilles that other members of the family were awake and welcoming Elsje home. Jennetje was the first to come down the stairs and the tall and thin young girl they had left behind now looked more like a young woman, a younger version of Tryntje. The change in Jennetje impressed upon Gilles that things *had* changed, and time had indeed passed while they were gone, time that could never be recovered.

"Go say 'Goede Morgan' to Elsje's husband," Klaas prompted and Jennetje complied with a shy embrace and kisses before she joined Klaas at the table, helping herself to the bread, dried herring, and cheese that Vroutje had left there for their breakfast.

Bruinje was now playing with a bed warming pan, opening and closing it, over and over, each time with a loud clatter as he sang a tuneless song to himself. It wasn't until he repeated it a few times, like a songbird, that Gilles realized what the child was saying.

"Opaopaopaopaopa."

"I think Bruinje *does* remember you, Hendrick. He is saying 'Opa'," Gilles said.

Hendrick smiled at this and Gilles hoped that he might have found a bridge, the way to improving relations with his father-in-law, through the old man's grandchildren.

Elsje and Vroutje came back down the stairs, followed by Corretje, all three of them carrying armloads of clothing. Some of Heintje's old clothing would fit Bruinje well enough and they even found some clean diaper cloths for Jacomina, packed away and saved after Corretje and Heintje no longer had any use for them. Corretje had to be pried away from Elsje's side to go say hello to Gilles but she quickly returned to following her older sister around just as soon as she had delivered a proper greeting to Gilles.

Vroutje offered the privacy of her bedroom for Gilles and Elsje to change their clothing and to bathe, but first Vroutje insisted that Elsje eat some more food. Gilles selected some pants and a shirt from the pile of clean clothes that Elsje had brought down with her. He seized the opportunity to go upstairs and clean up, fully aware that there was the added bonus of leaving Hendrick and the weepy women behind him as he escaped the room.

The washing cloth and the water were both brown by the time Gilles finished washing. He had been wearing the same pants ever since that fateful morning in the Palatinate, the very ones that he had ordered from the Jewish tailor's shop in Amsterdam so long ago. The dark color did not completely hide all of the stains, the dirt from the fields of Nouvelle Rochelle, soot from their burned out house, blood from someone, animal or human that Gilles had come into contact with on that day, and a lighter-colored smear of cheese that he had acquired during their trip down the river. Gilles left his filthy pants on the floor next to his tattered and dirty shirt. As he pulled the clean shirt on, Gilles observed that very soon he would have to get some new shirts made: He had noted that the styles had changed a little in his absence, but the main issue was that his shirts no longer fit him comfortably in the shoulders, his muscles having greatly increased in size and bulk over the past months due to his intensive laboring in the fields. The one pair of stockings that he had worn since the attack had been washed out frequently by Elsje while Gilles went barefoot on the barge taking them downriver, but with the great number of holes in them now, they were little better than fishermen's nets and Gilles wondered if they were worth darning at all or if they should just be unraveled and the yarn reused again in a fresh pair.

Gilles had washed himself slowly, waiting for Elsje to come up the stairs and join him in his ablutions, but she never did. Eventually he had no choice but to go back down the stairs to the kitchen, carrying his dirty clothing with him, all of it rolled up into a ball. He found Elsje still in the kitchen, listening to Vroutje's recounting all of the city's gossip for the past few months: Who had new babies, who had died, who had been married, who was in prison, who went to New Amsterdam, and who had been promoted or lost favor at the India Companies.

Klaas and Jennetje had already left for their work for the day and Vroutje seemed less distracted now by the demands of the household's daily routine. She directed Gilles to leave his dirty clothing outside in the back yard for washing later. Elsje took the opportunity to go upstairs to bathe, taking a large pitcher of clean bath water up with her. Gilles was still hungry and maybe Vroutje sensed this because she urged Gilles to have some more to eat. He didn't refuse the offer, sitting down at the table and eating a little more breakfast although he wondered with each bite if he was consuming someone else's meal. He heard the sound of the dirty water that he had left behind in the upstairs basin landing with a great splash out in the back yard of the house as Elsje disposed of it through the open upstairs window.

Hendrick reached up on the fireplace mantel and pulled down a wooden box that held his tobacco and pipe. Gilles thought briefly about offering to help the old man but Hendrick had already mastered the art of filling and lighting his pipe with his one remaining hand. He listened too, as Vroutje recounted to Gilles all of the business news that she had told Elsje, all that she could remember hearing ever since Gilles and Elsje had left the city. Hendrick took in Vroutje's narrative of the events and added comments and corrections here and there.

If there was any subject that had not been discussed in as much detail as Gilles expected that morning, it was Tryntje's wedding. Hendrick had talked about Elsje's wedding incessantly for months and even *years* afterwards, boring his acquaintances to distraction with the telling and retelling of every detail, even the most minute and trivial information about the food, right down to how the oysters had been arranged on the platters. Surely the wedding of his second daughter to a groom as important as Adriaen Ver Hulst would require much *more* information on what a wonderful marriage Hendrick had secured for Tryntje. Gilles wasn't interested at all in the usual details about the festivities: He was more interested in how the family's new ties to the Ver Hulst family might help his own future fortunes than he was in what color flowers Tryntje wore in her hair. Maybe later, when Elsje joined them again in the kitchen, Gilles might be able to bring the conversation back around to Tryntje's wedding.

Just as Vroutje was finishing up with telling Gilles all of the news and starting to repeat stories that she had already told him, the younger Hendrick finally woke up, having slept through all of the commotion of the morning. He came into the kitchen looking for his breakfast and greeted Gilles enthusiastically, with a handshake and a hug, and Gilles felt for the first time as though he had truly been welcomed back home. Gilles wondered guiltily if he had eaten all of Heintje's breakfast but he was relieved to see that Vroutje had set aside some food for the child.

It appeared to Gilles to be rather a small portion on Heintje's plate for a growing boy and upon taking a closer look around the kitchen, Gilles noted that there was not a lot of food to be seen and no fresh fruit or vegetables at all. He knew that Vroutje and her husband had never had a great deal of money but with so many more mouths to feed, especially with their unexpected guests this morning, it must have been too much. Hendrick must have been giving Vroutje some money to care for his other two children over the years. Why had Gilles not known this when he lived in Amsterdam before?

It may have been because he had never spent very much time at this house back then, but it could also have been because Gilles had never given hunger much thought before he went away to Nouvelle Rochelle, except where it concerned *him*. The family would certainly be looking to Gilles for help now, expecting him to go to work somewhere and help feed them all. His job with Ste Germaine was gone though, and Hendrick's inn was in ruins. Gilles had his savings and investments but that would be used up quickly if he did not find another source of income and find it very soon. To top off these concerns, Gilles had spent more money than he thought he would in the Palatinate, for the rent, for food, drink, seed and farm implements, as well as for the trip back, all with no income from his crops to offset the debits and replenish his funds. These thoughts threatened to bury Gilles under the rubble of worry if he did not find an immediate plan for success, one that would reassure him, as well as the rest of the family, that survival was more of a probability than a mere possibility.

After Vroutje had sent the two youngest children out to their work and had told Gilles all of the gossip that he cared to hear and then even a little *more* than that, Gilles asked Hendrick again about the night that the inn had been burned. Hendrick obliged, reveling in some of the more gruesome details, Gilles thought, but then he reminded himself that it would, in all likelihood be the greatest single event of the old man's entire life, and worth recounting again and again, even if it had been a terrifying experience at the time.

Gilles was annoyed, then incensed as Hendrick told the story.

"Can they *still* be looking for me? How *long* is their memory? I have been gone from France for years now, *years*! *Surely* they have someone *more* important to look for by now! This city is *full* of fugitives! Who am I? I am *nobody* now!"

Hendrick said nothing in response to this bit of *colere* from his son-in-law, puffing silently on his pipe and for once Vroutje was strangely silent too, perhaps uncomfortable with Gilles' uncharacteristic outburst. He calmed himself and took a few moments to pull himself back together; surely it was the combined strain of the last few months and hours that had taken a toll on his temper and his nerves.

Jacomina whimpered, then she started to cry. Vroutje picked the child up to console her but the baby cried even harder until Elsje hurried down the stairs to her daughter, her long hair still loose and wet, with Elsje looking to Gilles very much as if she had just fallen into the canal. Elsje took Jacomina from Vroutje's arms and immediately put her to nurse.

"My but she's *noisy*! Is she *always* so hungry?" Vroutje asked ten minutes later, after watching the child's relentlessly loud and vigorous sucking.

"Oh yes, she has a wonderful appetite," Elsje replied.

"Its no surprise then, that you're so thin!" Vroutje said to Elsje before she looked over at Hendrick and gave him a meaningful look that Gilles took to be in his own defense.

When the chubby baby had finally had enough to be satisfied, Jacomina turned her head away and smacked her lips. Elsje cleaned the infant's sticky cheeks with a damp washing cloth and gave the baby a kiss on each freshly-cleaned cheek before she changed the infant's wet diaper cloth.

"She's getting a rash," Elsje noted. "We'll have to take her outside in the sun later."

"Such a pretty child she is!" Vroutje observed.

"She looks like Gilles," Elsje replied as she finished closing up the front of her bodice.

"Nee, she looks *just* like your mother! I would know; I used to change your mother's cloths. It's *Bruinje* who looks like you now, Elsje."

Vroutje looked over at Bruinje and talked a little louder. "I'll bet

Bruinje is such a *big* help to his mother. Does he sing his baby sister songs?"

"Nee," Elsje answered for him.

"Well, I'm sure he will *very* soon," Vroutje said. "They just start talking one day and after that you can't *get* them to stop, at least until they get older. Little boys never talk as early or as much as little girls."

"Gilles, I want to go see the inn now. It's light enough outside," Elsje said, suddenly changing the subject.

"I'll watch the children for you," Vroutje volunteered. "You go ahead now if you want to. Did you get enough to eat for breakfast?"

"Ja, ja," Elsje said impatiently, "Thank you. We'll go and then we'll come back very soon. We won't be too long."

Elsje waited not a moment longer but left Jacomina in Vroutje's arms and Bruinje struggling to free himself from his grandfather's one-handed grip. She hurried out the door with Gilles running along behind her, trying to keep up with his wife who was trotting up the street.

"My God, *my God*!" Elsje moaned after they were out of ear shot, the pleasant social smile that had been firmly set into to her face all morning quickly falling away. "I can't *believe* that all this has *happened*!"

She twisted her wet hair up on top of her head, even as she ran, pinning it in place with one long hairpin and then pulling her cap over the whole mess as her feet continued to race swiftly toward the inn.

Elsje's hysteria and her drama only served to irritate Gilles all the more this morning: He had enough to concern him without worrying about her state of mind too. Everyone in Amsterdam was as well as they had been when Gilles and Elsje had left with the possible exception of Hendrick who was fine enough since he had never done any work in his life that he needed his arm for anyway. The inn had only been a place for them to sleep and it really had been far more misery than it was worth most of the time. Elsje didn't *have* to work; she only needed to care for the children.

Really, what did *she* have to worry about? Gilles had all of the members of his family, and now Hendrick's family also, to feed and shelter and this with no employment prospects in sight. As the man in the family who was the youngest and the healthiest, they would all be looking to Gilles now. Yes, things had happened while they were away, but what was done was done, at least for the others. Gilles' troubles were just beginning, though. He was overwhelmed by the number of mouths that he would need to feed in the coming weeks, mouths that he needed to be feeding *right away*, and this without his previous income from Ste Germaine's. If anything happened to Vroutje's husband and *his* income, Gilles would have *nine* people besides himself to support.

It was all just too much.

After less than a minute of their walking so quickly, what was left of the inn came into view. The brick and stone exterior had held up to the fire well enough and Gilles and Elsje were able to climb the stairs and walk inside the front door just as they always had before.

"Mind the weakened parts of the floor," Gilles said, pointing over at the charred and scorched parts after they were inside. The smell of burned wood had not disappeared entirely from the air yet.

A patch of blue sky was visible as they looked straight up through all three stories from their vantage point at the entrance to the dining room. The wreckage of tables, chairs, crockery, and dinnerware littered the sooty floor and although many of the ceiling beams were darkened now, mostly they were still intact.

Elsje turned to her left and pushed open the door to the private back dining room. The door's working was hindered now by debris on either side of it and a new unevenness in the planks on the floor caused it to scrape and bind, but Elsje got it open far enough for them to squeeze inside. The oil lamps were strewn about the floor and the room seemed a ghostly and charred mockery of what it had been, with its elegant but blackened draperies still hanging neatly at the window. Gilles recalled that Pieter Stuyvesant had dined here and that their wedding feast had been here, in this very same room. That all seemed like such a long time ago.

They squeezed back through the door again, back into the main dining room, past the table where Hendrick used to hold court and the fireplace that was as blackened on the outside now as it had once been on the inside, past a great sculpture of delicate charcoal pieces that had started out as whole tables and chairs, the stacked up elements of a bonfire used in an attempt to burn the entire inn to the ground. In this one area of the structure, the upper floors had collapsed all around this tower of rubble. Looking behind the collapsed timbers toward the kitchen, Gilles could see more broken bowls and some utensils littering the floor.

"They must have wrecked it *first* before they burned it!" Elsje declared as she bent down to pick up a piece of a crockery bowl with a blue design on the rim. "What did we ever do to them? We welcomed *everyone* at our inn, friend or stranger, sailor and soldier! I hope there is a *greater* judgment and punishment after death for those who destroy people's homes!"

Gilles didn't know what to say so he didn't answer her.

She wandered a little further along the perimeter of the room and into the kitchen. "This was *my mother's* bread bowl," she said, picking up the broken pieces and Gilles saw a tear slide down her cheek.

Gilles wanted nothing more than to take her away from here. Looking at all of the damage and destruction was painful but she did look, she had to look, and she couldn't seem to pull herself away from any detail. Together they gazed at the disarray in the kitchen and then beyond, through the little window into the back lot. The animal shed was untouched and Gilles was relieved that he saw no decaying animal carcasses there.

"I didn't think to ask what happened to our chickens and cow," Elsje said, turning back to Gilles and the inside of the inn. The steps leading upstairs to the apartment were navigable and that portion of the building was eerily untouched except for the black powdery residue that covered everything. Gilles noted that there was definitely an advantage to living in a civilized place where city neighbors organized themselves to come and help put out house fires. He had no doubt that his neighbors' efforts with buckets of water had saved the parts of the inn that were still there. He didn't know enough about construction, though, to know if it had saved the building from being a total loss.

They continued up to the family quarters on the third floor, now empty except for some broken remnants of chairs and a ripped and sooty featherbed on the floor, too far out on the other side of the damaged floor to safely retrieve. The great bed that Gilles had recovered in once, after his being attacked in an alley, was gone, perhaps having fallen through to the floors below or maybe someone had been able to salvage it and remove it to Vroutje's house. Gilles and Elsje could not venture into the living quarters or their former bedroom at all because of the questionable safety of the floor.

"So," Elsje breathed, looking around from where she stood at the top of the stairs. She looked up at the damaged roof and then down through the hole that had been drilled through the heart of the house by the pillar of fire, through a second story chamber and all the way back down into the main dining room.

"Come on, Elsje." Gilles tried to lead her back down the stairs but she wasn't leaving.

"*So,*" she said once again.

"Elsje, let's go now."

She nodded in acquiescence but her feet didn't move. "Well, we will just have to rebuild it," she said at last, a little hoarsely.

Gilles looked doubtfully at the destruction in front of him. Once again he made no reply.

"We can use your investments and we can make it better! Father can't do much now but you ran Ste Germaine's and you can run our inn here. The kitchen girls can help; Grietje said she would stop working and live with her daughter's family when she left us but I *know* we could get her to come back for a time, at least until we could train someone else. We can find out what happened to Ste Germaine's things. There will probably be an auction where we can buy his furnishings and then we can use them in *our* inn."

Elsje was often at her best in a crisis and she now had an energy that Gilles had not seen in her for months. It heartened him and frightened him at the same time: He could almost share her dream of creating a new inn together, but it was the soldiers, the French and Spanish soldiers, lurking in the shadows, that tainted this bright vision. Gilles said nothing about that now, as much to keep the peace with her as to keep that part of his wife, the hopeful and strong part, with him for just a little while longer. He couldn't stand to see her when she was so crushed, so beaten down, as she had been lately.

"Let's go to Ste Germaine's now," Gilles suggested, although he was afraid that he was going to see destruction there similar to what he was seeing here. His offer was the impetus that Elsje needed to leave this scene though, and as they left, Elsje started to talk, slowly at first, and then nonstop, to Gilles and to herself, about how they would need to go about rebuilding and refurbishing the inn.

Ste Germaine's establishment stood looking out over the canal as it always had, and this was almost harder for Gilles to bear, knowing that inside nothing at all had changed except for the missing people. At the front door he paused. He thought he still heard the great clock that stood in the entry way but that was ridiculous: There was no longer anyone inside to wind it. The magnificent oak front door had boards nailed across it and a municipal notice had been posted there saying that a public sale of the property and goods would take place within the week. All Gilles could think about was that Ste Germaine would have had an apoplectic *fit* if he could have seen the ugly nails and boards covering the glorious polished wood and brass entrance to his superior establishment.

"There, you see?" Elsje said brightly, pointing at the notice. "*What* did I tell you? They *always* have an auction when a criminal leaves no heirs!"

Gilles said nothing in reply. He was trying to get used to the idea of Ste Germaine's name and the word "criminal" being used in the same breath.

Elsje hadn't noticed that she had said anything wrong or out of place though. Walking around the outside of Ste Germaine's, Gilles noted that the building seemed secure enough but that the cave had been broken into and the door was completely off its hinges. Either the authorities did not know that it was back there, or more likely, they had no idea as to what the odd mound of dirt in the back lot could be. The temperature and humidity balance had been seriously compromised but when Gilles peered inside, he could see that it no longer mattered: The cellar had been cleaned out completely and all of the fine wines had been consumed, probably by the city's drunks and vagrants. Gilles was quite certain that the looters had *not* paused to consider the dry summers and the wet ones, and the differences *between* the bottles as they consumed it all, every drop of it, the wine that had been so carefully and lovingly collected over the years by Ste

Germaine. Only a small pile of broken bottles off to one side gave any indication of what had previously been stored in there.

Gilles looked out toward the sea and he shuddered. Were they *really* so civilized here? Was the Netherlands any better than France, the German states or even Italy? What kind of people put a man to death simply because he had the poor judgment to associate with one such as LaRue? Where was LaRue now? Nothing bad had happened to *him*. If Ste Germaine had died for his sins, then LaRue should have been put to death, too.

"Please, Gilles, can we go to the churchyard now?" Elsje asked him, breaking into his thoughts.

"Of course."

Gilles was in shock himself, but now he was worried about Elsje too; he knew that she needed his understanding now if she was to maintain her ability to cope with all that they had just seen and been through as well as all that was yet to come. As happy as Gilles had been to leave Ste Germaine's employ and his finicky ways, he had never wanted anything bad to happen to him. Gilles took in a deep breath, an inside-out sigh that his body took in to recharge, the events of recent weeks being entirely too much for him to deal with in their entirety at the moment.

"Are you all right?" Elsje asked. "You've been awfully quiet this morning."

"It's just a lot to take in."

"Yes, it is."

Gilles put a smile on for her, took Elsje's arm and walked her forward, away from the inn. His feet were leaden and suddenly he realized that he was *so* tired. Along the way they passed neighbors and acquaintances that they knew very well, but neither Gilles nor Elsje was inclined to stop long enough to engage in a lengthy conversation:

It would have required more energy than either of them had at their disposal.

"Welcome back, Gilles!"

"Thank you."

"Elsje! You are home! We will see you on Sunday in church!"

"Yes, it's good to be home."

"You've come home! Sorry about your father, Elsje."

"Thank you. Bless you."

After making their way past all of the people that they knew, witnesses to their pain and their misery, they reached the churchyard. Elsje went directly to her mother's stone and prayed, standing there with her head bowed and her fingers laced together. Gilles prayed also, a quick and silent prayer to whatever power that was out there, to have mercy on them and to help him meet his many future responsibilities. He wasn't sure if praying would help at all but he hoped that the sensation of comfort and well-being that had come to him in the cathedral in Worms was a valid indication of what the future held for them and that the feeling would return to him here. He couldn't accept that he had lost every bit of hard-earned security that he had gained over the previous few years.

And yet, he felt a small piece of it, even in this *other* place, this place that was so far away from the cathedral at Worms and so full of Protestants. He wondered if he might *even* feel it in the Jews' holy places.

Now *that* was an interesting thought to ponder.

Elsje prayed silently for a few more moments before she turned back to Gilles. "I always feel *so* much better after I talk to my mother. It will be all right. We will rebuild our life as it was and things will be good for all of us once again."

She hugged Gilles and kissed him on the cheek. Perhaps the gesture was meant to comfort or reassure him but it had the opposite effect and he worried now that his wife might be losing her mind completely. Elsje took his hand and together they walked back to Cousin Vroutje's house in silence.

They were not even fully inside the door when Bruinje ran to his mother, having been disconsolate since she had left.

"Maman! Maman!" he cried and threw his arms around her. "Ou vas-tu?"

"Oh, Bruinje speaks French?" Vroutje asked, her eyebrows flying up in surprise.

"Yes, sometimes." Elsje said. She didn't mention that he also spoke a little Nederlands sometimes, often throwing in some German words, mixing and mashing the words all up together like a hutspot, frequently using odd tenses and unusual combinations in his communications, that is, when he deigned to communicate verbally with them *at all*.

Gilles wasn't ready to spend the rest of his day at Cousin Vroutje's house. He needed to find some wine somewhere so he could get away and take a brief respite from it all, just for a little while.

"Elsje, I need to go find out about my investments now, to see what I have available for rebuilding the inn. Can you manage without me for a short time?" Gilles asked his wife.

"Of course, but when will you be back?" Elsje demanded. "It's nearly dinnertime."

"I'll have midday dinner with Jean and be back later this afternoon. I won't be too long."

Elsje gave him a warning look that said, *"You'd better not be going off to get drunk for the day!"*

Gilles just kissed her in reply and gave her what he thought was a reassuring look. He couldn't get to Jean's house fast enough, and in spite of the intimidating look that he had received from Elsje, he would not be turning down any drinks that were offered.

"Ah, there you are, Gilles! It's a good thing that you are back! I have so much that I need to *tell* you before I go! I did tell you that I am leaving tomorrow at the morning tide? I leave my affairs here in your capable hands until I reach New Amsterdam safely. The proper documents and authorizations as well as my will have been drawn up and are in the care of the WIC's legal people. I had to change my beneficiary to *you* on all of the paperwork this morning! See Cornelius De Vries if you have any questions about it."

Jean said all of this before he finished letting Gilles inside the front door. "Listen, I have told the Van Vrankens that you need a place to stay and they are fine with letting you stay here in my apartment for another week until their new tenant comes in. Pour yourself some Sherry! I leave most of my stock of refreshment for your use, too, except for a few bottles of *very* special vintage that I have packed for my trip."

Gilles nodded "yes" to the Sherry and "yes" to the legacy of Jean's supply of spirits. The little apartment was almost completely packed up now; Jean only had the few rooms, and so there was not a lot of packing that needed to be done. He had always lived a frugal, uncluttered life and perhaps that was one of the reasons why he was still without a wife: Jean had never really needed one.

"I am leaving my bed here for you, too, and you can take it with you if you like, or not. I found a smaller bed to ship over since they charge more for taking the bigger, heavier one and I can't take all of my furniture with me, so you can just sell it or use it, do as you wish. I have leased a very small cottage over there which will suit my needs very well. If you decide to join me there later, I am sure that you can get a job in *some* capacity with the West India Company and we can

481

continue our trade business together on the side! The WIC can't find enough warm bodies to go and they need every man they can get to hold the territory, what with the English, French, and Swedes *all* trying to move in on them, making their ridiculous claims to the land. You can get a Patroonship and they will just *give* you the land! Oh, and your investments are safe, on deposit with the WIC. You can get it there, at the offices, as much or as little as you want at any time, and they can transfer your account easily to New Amsterdam if you *do* decide to go there. I've already engaged Henri Greenleaf to run the Amsterdam end of the fur business but with a stroke of a pen you can have full control again if he doesn't meet with your approval. He's a good man though, knows Van Curler, and has connections everywhere but you should meet with him in person... "

"Jean!"

"What is it Gilles?"

"Jean, this is too much, too fast! Were you planning to just *go* and then write me a letter in the Palatinate to let me know that you had *already* left?"

"Well, yes, I did. I had already posted the letter to the Palatinate but you aren't there to get it, now are you? Spanish soldiers have been here in the city twice, looking for me and to be *absolutely* honest with you, every day that I am here, I feel that I may be pushing my luck to the limits. I waited just a *little* too long before I left France, didn't I? And look what almost happened there."

"So you were not honest with me when you said it was safe for us to remain here? Was it because Elsje was in the room or because we were so tired from our journey that you neglected to tell us this? They could come for us at *any* time, take me into custody and send me back to France in irons!"

"Oh, non, non, non! *Calm* yourself, Gilles! You should be fine!

Spain's soldiers are not interested in *you*; they are looking for me, some trumped up nonsense about helping army deserters and enemies of the Church and King! There aren't many French bounty hunters around now and I think they really *do* believe that you are in the Palatinate and that I am dead, that is what my sources tell me."

"And what if the French bounty hunters come back and talk to the Spanish soldiers on regular patrol who have seen me walking in the streets every day?" Gilles demanded.

Jean sighed. "They aren't the *best* of friends, you know, even if they do share a love of Pope Urban VIII and Barberini's *eloquent* poetry." Jean smiled, hoping that Gilles would enjoy the little joke. "Anyway, I don't think they know what you look like and it's doubtful that your name would come up in casual conversation between them, but I can't know that for certain, can I, Gilles? You will have to make your *own* decision as to what is the best course of action for you to take. We can only live our lives to the best of our abilities, within the realm of probability, as our conscience dictates. I have *no* idea why I still have armies from two countries looking for me! Perhaps in New Amsterdam I can just live my life for a time, making my wagers *only* on future wealth, not on present safety as well, and no one will ask me who I *was* or where I came from before I got there. One very *good* thing about the new world is that it is big enough to start over again whenever you need to, for whatever reason. Who knows *where* I might end up eventually, Brazil? Malaysia? India? Ah, but that is *ridiculous*. I talk too much today! I *do* wish that you were going with me, my friend, and I shall miss you *greatly*, Gilles. Even if you don't stay here again tonight, at the very least, come around to wish me a *bon voyage* early tomorrow morning."

"I'll do that, Jean."

"Ah! I forgot to tell you last night! Your Mme Philippe that you

483

sent with your letter of introduction made it safely here and found me. There are so many refugees here in the city now that she *never* would have found a decent position so I sent her and her daughter to New Amsterdam. Reynier Van Dusen's wife died in childbirth leaving him with *five* children, including the surviving infant and he needs another wife. I assured her that he was a *good* man, a kind man, and she seemed receptive to the idea, so I sent her over to him."

"But they don't speak the same language!"

"That's not important: He needs a wife and mother for the children and she needs a husband to care for her and her daughter."

"But they've never met and they aren't the same religion!"

"That doesn't matter; trust me Gilles, they *will* work it out. Oh, and I must make my apologies to you: I only found out after you left Amsterdam, that in Nouvelle Rochelle they were a *very* strict bunch, more like England's so-called *"Puritans"* than many of the Huguenots who are excellent vignerons, some of them even distilling their own Aqua Vitae and selling it to support themselves and their colonies. I should have made more extensive inquiries as to the *nature* of the settlement before I sent you there. Anyway, you haven't told me yet what happened to you in Nouvelle Rochelle. Was there *more* that you were *going* to tell me when Elsje was not around?" Jean peered closely at Gilles.

"Not much," Gilles replied, not really wanting to explain in great detail to his best friend that he had hidden himself in a tree stump like a coward, at the mercy of French soldiers and flies alike, while his wife and children had somehow managed to save themselves from being savaged by the vicious two-legged beasts that swept through the place in Gilles' absence. "The French soldiers attacked and we were able to hide from them, but the farms and our neighbors were not so fortunate."

"And is that how Elsje got the scar on her shoulder?" Jean asked. "I saw it when her dress slipped last night. She *has* lost a good bit of weight."

Gilles did not recall seeing any scar and he did not know of any injury that Elsje had sustained on the boat during their return trip. She had said nothing to Gilles about an injury.

"I suppose," Gilles replied, shrugging. He didn't want to talk any more about his failed venture; he wanted to sit and drink with his friend throughout the afternoon, talking and reminiscing about their past successes and future investments.

Jean couldn't seem to sit still long enough to talk about the past though, and they were not going to have any *immediate* future together. He was in no state of mind to reminisce leisurely as he scurried around, packing his remaining belongings and scratching frantic notes on a sheet of paper with his quill, alternately slopping ink from the inkpot across the leather top of the escritoire and then mopping it up again with a rag, the paper a ready receptacle to capture his racing thoughts.

Two porters came to the house, further disrupting the day while Gilles sat there, trying to have a peaceful drink of wine and talk with his friend. Jean told the duo what baggage was to be taken away in their cart and the men dragged it out noisily, scratching the polished floor as Jean cursed at them under his breath in French. The upheaval in the household was too much for Gilles to bear any longer and he sighed in resignation.

"*Eh bien*, I suppose I should let you finish your preparations and I should get back to Elsje now. I don't know if she will want to stay at Vroutje's tonight, but I will be *certain* to be here early tomorrow to say farewell to you."

"I'll see you tomorrow then!" Jean said and he clapped Gilles on the arm. "Oh! I almost forgot this, too! You have a horse here. I got him from Ste Germaine's before the authorities seized everything at his country house. He's stabled with my landlord's horses up the street and his keep is paid up until the end of the month. A fine horse he is, Gilles! I rode him a few times while you were gone, just to keep us both in shape."

"Yes, *only the best* from Ste Germaine," Gilles said.

"Well, go on home then, Gilles. Elsje will wonder where you are and you will be in trouble once again."

Gilles didn't want to go back to Vroutje's house yet so he decided to go check on his investments at the West India Company offices first. He *had* told Elsje that he was going there. He advanced himself a quantity of guilders from his savings and they adjusted his account balance, handing him a statement, with interest, which Gilles noticed had not grown much at all over the past few months while he had been away. Profits were indeed down and Gilles wondered why there had been so little income for the company to divide among the shareholders.

"It's trouble with the Wilden," Cornelius De Vries explained. "Oh, and welcome back to Amsterdam, Gilles."

"Thank you, it's good to be home," Gilles replied.

He started back across the Dam but remembering some errands that he could do now that would keep him away from Cousin Vroutje's for just a little while longer, Gilles stopped in at a jeweler's shop. He pulled all of the pearls out of his pocket, in handfuls at first and then one by one, until he was sure that he had all of them out on the counter. He asked if the jeweler could restring them for him and the jeweler replied that there would be no problem; they would be ready for him to pick up any time after the coming Saturday. Gilles made a purchase, too, and he left the shop with the small packet tucked into his pocket, that and the satisfaction that he could tell Elsje when she asked him about her pearls, that he had *already* taken care of it before she had to remind him.

An ache in his stomach made him realize that it was now past dinner time and he eaten very little today. Gilles stopped at the Dam and bought himself some gauffres from the man who sold them in the street. He had never cared for them much before but now the funny little cakes gave him comfort, reassuring him that he was indeed safely back in Amsterdam, the city that had protected him and kept him from harm for the past few years. He nodded a greeting as he passed the rat catcher and his helper and then he passed an aging Rembrandt Van Rijn, now even more disheveled and disagreeable an old man since he had lost his wife the year before. Nothing ever seemed to change very much here in the city, and yet in Gilles' life, *everything* had changed, and it had changed very quickly.

The only meat he had in the Palatinate had been rabbit and chicken, and expenses be damned, just for tonight they were *all* going to eat well for a change. As he was trying to decide between buying some pork or some venison, he saw a woman on the other side of the stall with her back to him. He thought that it *must* be her and yet he knew that it couldn't be: She was dead. It was not the same dress, but the hair, the slight shoulders, they were the same, *exactly* the same. He couldn't let her pass without seeing her face though. He had to satisfy his own curiosity and *know* that it was not her. He left the meat vendor in mid sentence. Catching up to the woman, he still couldn't see her face as her head was down and she was struggling with some bundles she carried.

"Here, let me help you," he offered.

"Danks," the woman replied, lifting her head, and looking Gilles fully in the face, a little suspiciously perhaps.

Of course it was not her. He knew it wouldn't be. The woman

thanked him and then she went on her way. Gilles returned to the market table, shaken, but ready to resume his shopping.

Gilles hauled the heavy slab of pork back to the house and put it on the table in the kitchen while Cousin Vroutje protested that he should not have spent so much of his money on them, and that he didn't *really* need to buy them any food, but the delighted looks on the children's faces told Gilles that they had not seen meat for some time. There was plenty of bier and ale, though, and the spirits of the adults were high due to the unrestricted consumption of the beverages as well as the joy of the family reunion. Cousin Vroutje put the meat on to cook right away and Corretje amused Bruinje with singing and tickling games while Elsje bounced Jacomina on her lap. It would have been a very happy family gathering if there had not been the uncertainty of the future that lay before them.

"What are your plans now?" Gilles heard Vroutje ask Elsje.

"We are going to rebuild and stay here. We found out that we are city people and have had enough of farming!" Elsje declared.

"Do you think that is such a good idea? The soldiers..." Vroutje asked uncertainly as she looked over at Gilles to see what *his* opinion might be. Gilles was not going to be drawn into this conversation so he pretended not to hear them and for the time being, Cousin Vroutje let the matter drop.

Jean was still awake when they returned to his house that night. Gilles finally succeeded in convincing Elsje that they would be more comfortable over there and so would Cousin Vroutje if the Jansen family slept at Jean Durie's for the time being.

"Take some wine over to the room with you," Jean said to Gilles. "Sleep in the guest room again tonight and move over here tomorrow morning when I have gone. It's all arranged."

"Wake me up tomorrow morning, Jean. I want to see you off at the docks," Gilles told his friend.

Gilles took a wine bottle and two glasses with him across the hall to rejoin Elsje who was getting the children ready for bed. There had been so much excitement during the day that Bruinje took a little longer than usual to fall asleep. Gilles waited patiently though, emptying his third glass of wine before Elsje joined him in bed.

"I've missed you," he said to her as he pushed her hair back from her face.

"That servant isn't going to come in, is she?" Elsje asked him.

"No, they are trained not to just come in without knocking first. You remember our wedding night here? Hmm?" He put his glass down on the bedside table and kissed her cheek first, then her lips.

As Gilles' hands passed over her shoulders, he felt the cut that Jean had mentioned.

"How did you do that?" he asked her.

"I got caught on a nail when I was hiding under the Lanphier's stoep," she told him.

Gilles pulled her closer. "Ah, well, that's all over and in the past now. We won't *ever* think of it or speak of that place again. I'm sorry that we ever went there," Gilles said. It was his way of apologizing to her and Elsje seemed to understand this.

"You couldn't know…" she murmured before Gilles kissed her again, stopping her from saying any more.

Elsje thrashed around in her sleep, even hitting Gilles in the face with a flailing arm during the night but at least she slept. Gilles did not sleep well at all and he woke several times after dreaming about the WIC losing all of his money and the family facing starvation, all of them being reduced to begging for money in the streets. It was true enough that his trading and frugality had left him with a tidy sum of money that would support them all for a short time if absolutely necessary, but if he had to tap into his capital for rebuilding the family inn, he would need to build a viable business that produced income quickly. The inn keeping business could be deadly slow in the wintertime and now autumn was nearly upon them. Even if the inn was rebuilt completely tomorrow, it could be *months* before any real income flowed back into Gilles' pocket. It was Gilles who climbed out of the bed early the next morning after a nearly sleepless night. What was he going to do?

He didn't know.

He pulled his pants on and ran his hands through his hair. He thought briefly about getting his hair and beard trimmed later on and then seeing if he could find a position somewhere as an accountant. Thinking he heard rain outside, he got up and went over to the window, moving the drapes aside to look out.

There were always lights on somewhere here. This city never went completely to sleep and Gilles could see up beyond the bend in the street that the usual lanterns burned near the waterfront but there was no rain; it had only been the noise of a passing breeze. He had almost forgotten the sounds that were Amsterdam.

"You're my city now," he thought. *"We will stay and we will make a stand here. This is my home and I won't be forced to leave."*

He hadn't given much thought to France lately. Rouen had been his place of birth and of course it had been his home when he had lived there: It was light shining out of the dining room windows illuminating the winter darkness, even on a moonless night, the warmth inside the house welcoming him back as he walked his horse up the drive.

This city, Amsterdam, had taken him in, had not just adopted him, but treated him like a true son. Gilles knew every street in every section, the merchant's section, the artist's section, the Jewish section, the

Marrano section, and the growing French section. He knew every shop and stall in the Dam, all of the bridges, canals, dykes, and windmills, and of course, the houses, as well as every cracked stone paver in the streets. Knowing the birds and the trees too, Gilles had a great affection for the city. He knew that he could never just walk away from this place and leave Amsterdam to her fate at the hands of whichever world power felt they could just come in and take it over for their own nefarious purposes at the moment: He cared *too* deeply about what happened here. Gilles felt as though the city itself had protected him and now he needed to stay and protect *her* from the impertinent and disrespectful Spanish soldiers.

Nouvelle Rochelle had not been like that: It had *never* been a home to him although Gilles had tried his best to familiarize himself with all of the people, all of the wild flowers, the animals, and even the trees. It could just burn up completely with the collective ashes blowing away on the next gust of wind down the Rhine, and Gilles wouldn't mind in the least, wouldn't have given it a second thought. Nicholas had said something to that effect, that it was *community* that mattered, the hearts of the people that made a home.

Gilles looked over at his sleeping wife and it surprised him a little to realize that he cared deeply for her as well. He had been brought up to think of marriage in terms of alliances and successful financial combinations but he knew now that he had to be where Elsje was, and if Amsterdam was the place that made her happy, then here they would stay. If there was a force out there that watched over them and protected them, then they would continue to survive, no matter where they chose to live their lives, or what difficulties the future held for them.

Now his thoughts turned to Jean Durie and it was painful to think that *just* as he had found his true place in the world, he was losing his best friend, at least for the next several years. Seeing Jean again had been *the* major reason that Gilles wanted to return to Amsterdam. Gilles would still have Elsje to talk to when Jean was gone of course, but it was not the same thing.

For so long Gilles had urged Jean to take a lover, if not a wife, had even told his friend, as if Jean couldn't see it for himself, that women from every quarter of Amsterdam took a great interest in him, some of them even with their father's blessings. Remembering these past suggestions to his friend, poorly received though they had been, brought a smile to his lips even as he heard Jean's steps coming for him from across the hall. Gilles met him at the door before Jean could knock and wake Elsje or the children. Gilles walked out with his friend, closing the door gently behind him and crossing the hall to Jean's apartment.

"Elsje has been *so* exhausted lately that I thought I'd just let her sleep late this morning," Gilles explained.

"Then you will say good-bye to her for me and tell her…" Jean said but he left the sentence unfinished as the kitchen maid entered the room with a tray of pastries and tea.

"We will miss you, Msr. Jean," she said to him.

"And I'll miss you too, Katrina."

"Your other things are ready, too. Shall I bring them over now?" she asked.

"Yes, this is a good time."

Jean poured the tea and Gilles helped himself to the French pastry. He hadn't seen any food like this in many months, let alone tasted it. He savored it, letting the buttery crust melt in his mouth before he swallowed and washed it down with his tea. Very soon the girl returned to the room with a large wicker box and set it down on the desk where Jean indicated it should go. She looked over in surprise at the nearly empty pastry tray before she left again.

"What's in there?" Gilles asked, gesturing with pastry in hand at the box.

"Provisions for the journey. You don't expect me to live on bug-infested biscuits, salted meat of indeterminate origin, and aqua vitae for three or four months at sea, do you? If *only* I had some of Elsje's famous bread to bring along with me too…Oh well, too late to ask for it now."

Gilles reached for the last pastry on the tray, holding his hand under his chin to spare his shirt any accidental stains and he noticed for the first time that Jean was dressed in some very plain clothes that did not seem like something that he would normally wear. There was no ornamentation and the wool, although light enough for summer wear, was a very drab color. Well, the ship's long journey would not be a pleasant one, Gilles knew that well enough. It was good to be as comfortable as possible. They did look a great deal like the clothes Gilles had purchased from the Jewish tailor shop, only lighter. Upon seeing the direction of Gilles' stare and the expression on his face, Jean laughed out loud at him.

"Do you like them? Do I look *average* and provincial enough? Like any other traveler?"

"It looks like something the *English* or the *Swedes* would wear!" Gilles teased him. Actually the Puritans came more to his mind: Gilles had seen the roundheads in town waiting around the docks before, the cult originating in England, shutting down all the Shakespearean theaters and other amusements deemed in their eyes to be immoral, some of them settling for a time in Leiden before they headed on to some other place that was more tolerant of them and their strident demands to change existing governments and cultures to suit their *own* ideas. They were intolerant of anyone else who was *not* like them and it was almost amusing to see the severely-dressed men cordoning off the homely and much put-upon women, and the dour little children all dressed in black, looking more like somber crowds of miniature adults in mourning or corbies gathered around a discarded piece of bread but without any of the raucous good humor usually associated with flocks of crows.

"Oh *stop*! They aren't *that* bad!" Jean said, smiling briefly at Gilles before his face took on a more serious air. "I *shall* miss this place, Gilles. I have enjoyed living here."

Gilles had some things that he needed to say to Jean too, although he wasn't sure how he would say them: Ships *did* go down occasionally, and although that surely wasn't going to happen to Jean, it was best to part company having said everything that should be said if circumstances conspired to keep them apart for more than just a few years.

"I don't know what I will do without your help, Jean. You helped me with anything and everything, all of my needs and requests, both the reasonable ones and the unreasonable ones. You even lectured and scolded me when I needed it, and aside from Elsje, you have been my *only* family here these past few years. I just wanted to say '*merci*' once again."

Jean straightened his band collar. "You always thanked me for my help and that *is* sufficient. Ah, Gilles, it's just too bad that you won't be on this new adventure with me or waiting at the dock when I get there, but if I am eaten by the sea monsters, I guess you will be the only one to mourn my passing, just as long as you get word of my demise! Dying at sea is better than burning, though, just as long as I don't go down *inside* the ship." Jean shuddered at the thought, his old fear of enclosed places obviously returning to him.

Gilles wondered how his friend was going to stand being shut inside the ship's hold for several weeks at a time. Jean must have had very good reasons and strong motivation to go on this long voyage.

"You *won't* drown. I'm sure that you have thoroughly researched the boat *and* the captain, haven't you?"

Jean grinned at this comment. "You know me *too* well, Gilles! I have indeed found a good captain who can navigate the seas as well as the pirates at Dunkerque and I believe that I have the *best* chances of arriving safely on this ship or I wouldn't be going on this voyage at all. Believing in the good outcome of a venture and keeping your mind on what you want is always just as important than anything else, maybe *more* so, except for doing the preliminary work in finding out all there is to know about your chosen subject. Remember that, Gilles. But we will write to each other and I will be back here again in just a few short years. By then you and Elsje will have a large brood of children and you will have turned the old inn into a successful business, I'm certain of that."

"Thank you, Jean. I appreciate your confidence in me and I *won't* let you down. I won't be the only one here who will miss you: There are many in Amsterdam who feel the same way."

Jean gave Gilles an odd look over the top of his tea saucer. "I doubt that! One man can't change anything in this world, not really. Do all you can and still, *ca ne fait rien*! Good men die and evil men prosper, that's just the way of the world. I only try to do what *little* I can to help others along on my way through this life. It just seems that things are put in my way sometimes."

"Providence?" Gilles asked him with a smile.

"I don't believe in such things and I didn't think that *you* did, either. What in the name of heaven happened to you over in the Palatinate?"

"I'll write to you and tell you all about it sometime; it will give me something to say in my letters. You will have to write and tell *me* all about the savages in the New World."

"You have made up your mind to stay here in Amsterdam permanently then?"

"Oui. We'll name our next son after you."

Gilles thought that Jean would be pleased with this gesture of affection but Jean seemed a little uncomfortable with it as he answered, "Yes, well, you'd better ask Elsje about that *first,* before you make promises to me that you can't keep. If you are staying here in the city, be sensible and stay safe, but go ahead, dream and plan again. Nothing is accomplished without plans and if we don't do that, we might as well perish right now."

"I plan to stay out of sight as much as possible but it *does* seem as though something always comes along in time to save us from death."

Jean snickered at this. "The desire to save our own miserable hides coupled with our own *quick wits* is what preserves us! Well, we will be a little early, but let's go to the ship now so I can find a good spot on board. I want to be gone from here before sunup, long before the Spanish soldiers are awake and come looking for me. I think I hear the porter outside the door now."

Gilles was glad to see that Jean was in high spirits: Their parting would have been even more difficult if Jean had been unhappy about the path that he was being forced to take. In all probability it *was* contra coeur, as Gilles had no doubt that Jean's decision to leave Amsterdam had been more or less thrust upon him. A very dark young man dressed in bright clothes and a turban stood outside of Jean's door. Jean hastily stoppered his ink bottle, wiped his quill off with a rag, and tossed both items into the one small chest that remained in the room, slamming it shut even as the boy came across the room to get it.

"Do I take that too?" the boy asked, pointing at the little provision box.

"Nee," Jean answered, "I have it. You can get that one all right? *De Trouw* is the ship."

"Ja, ja," was the impatient answer from the boy.

Jean gave the youth a coin and the boy hoisted the chest onto his back and shuffled out the door. Jean pulled on his over coat and straightened the sleeves.

"Ready?" Jean asked Gilles, "Do you still want to walk me to the ship?"

"It s the *least* I can do for you, to make sure that you get off safely. I'll take the other side of the provision basket."

They walked out of the apartment and Jean closed the door behind him for the last time. One final time they walked together down the dark street to the docks. The boy who had taken the little trunk was moving quickly up the street with other boxes and barrels piled high in his overflowing little tumbrel that rumbled over the stones behind him as he pulled it along.

"We should *all* be like the Moors," Jean commented, nodding in the porter's direction. "That boy works very hard day and night, always cheerful, and I have *never* seen him trouble anyone else about the merits of his *own* religion over theirs or the shortcomings of others."

"Which ship did you say that you were taking?" Gilles asked. The harbor was so full of ships this morning that Gilles believed he might easily walk across the decks if he wanted to, from ship to ship, all the way to the North Sea, not straining very much to do so and never having his feet touch the water.

"*De Trouw*, The Faith. I think I can travel more safely through the seas under the flag of the Netherlands if I am in the company of Reformees and stacks of Bibles. Not that the Bibles will protect me, you understand; its just that the waters through the Pas de Calais are fast becoming infested with pirates who are more likely to attack merchant ships for their cargo and treasure on board or for the superior ships and their guns. The modest little church ships are seaworthy enough for travel but not a prize of enough significance for anyone to attack and seize."

Gilles laughed a scornful laugh. "I don't know how safe you'll be traveling along in a nest of rats! I'll tell you sometime about the *good* God-fearing Reformees of France that we came to know *so well* in the Palatinate. Just try not to anger them during the trip or they will throw you overboard to be eaten by the fishes!"

"So you are nominating Richelieu for sainthood, now that he's gone?" Jean grinned.

"I have no use for *any* religion now," Gilles declared, "not any more."

"*Shhhh*, they'll hear you! Here's the launch boat, Gilles. If there *is* a God and if He *does* watch over us, then God be with you and your family, Gilles!"

Gilles knew that Jean only said the last part a little louder for the benefit of any of his fellow travelers who might have been within earshot, but it was still a nice sentiment.

"...and you too, Jean."

They set the provision box down long enough to embrace one last time before Jean climbed into the small boat that was already filling up quickly with passengers to be ferried out to the larger ships. Gilles could just make out The Faith as she sat at anchor in the outer harbor, her white sails draped over the giant crosses formed by her masts and spars.

"Oh wait! I almost forgot!" Gilles ran forward and handed Jean the jeweler's package from his pocket.

"What is this?" Jean asked him.

"Open it and see. I promised it to you on the *last* sea voyage we took together."

Jean tore the brown paper and string off. "A watch on a neck chain! Isn't that a *thoughtful* gift! Then I will know *exactly* what time I leave and *exactly* when I arrive, even if I have absolutely *no idea* what day, month, or year it might be! But thank you, all the same, Gilles. I *did* bring your knife and some wood with me to pass the time. I will carve you something."

Gilles was glad that Jean was able to see the humor in his gift and he didn't for one moment regret spending some of his money on the frivolous bauble: The watch would be a keepsake for his best friend until the next time he saw him. It cheered Gilles to find out that Jean had taken up his wood carving again as Gilles suspected that Jean's knife was more than just an idle pastime; it was something akin to Jennetje's paintbrush or Elsje's spices, a tool that made him more complete in some incomprehensible, maybe even spiritual way.

"Don't have mal de mer!" Gilles called out to him as the packed ferry boat pushed off from the dock.

"I won't! I will be on the deck for the full three months helping the crew if they will let me!" Jean called back. "Tell Elsje and Hendrick 'goodbye' for me."

Jean waved a final farewell to his friend and Gilles waved back. The moon was still out this morning, just starting to set now, and to his great relief Gilles saw that the moon was a full first quarter now, the danger of the new moon being safely behind the travelers. The early morning light arrived before the sun, layering varied shades of orange over the eastern horizon. Three small and flat dark clouds appeared to be bidding Jean *Godspeed* rather than offering a threat. It looked like Jean's ship would make it out to sea well in advance of any approaching bad weather.

The full load of passengers caused the little ferry to sit very low in the water as it elbowed its way through the tangle of seagoing vessels this morning, slipping between the tall ships as the rowers carefully made their way out this way and that in the general direction of Jean's ocean-going vessel, stopping to discharge a passenger here and a passenger there at other ships along the way. Gilles watched for a time until the little launch disappeared behind the real ships and then there was nothing more for him to see unless he wanted to stand there for another hour watching them get the sails ready.

It was time to say goodbye, time to acknowledge that Jean was really going. Gilles turned around, feeling very much alone now except for the reassuring thought that he had Elsje waiting for him at home, or rather where home was located today. Jean Durie had been Gilles' last link to Rouen, his last link to his childhood and his past and now he was gone. Without Jean or Ste Germaine around, if Gilles wanted to speak French at all, if he needed to express himself in a fit of temper, a burst of enthusiasm, or to run his full range of verbal expletives at some indignation in his native language, Gilles would have to schedule these emotions into a trip to the French quarter of Amsterdam and exchange a few words with the merchants there in the same way that he went there to indulge himself in the food of his childhood.

Gilles arrived back at Jean's house to find most of the household, Elsje included, still sleeping. She was *so* tired that Gilles began to wonder if she would ever get her strength back. Gilles would let her sleep but he didn't feel like going back to bed himself. He went over to Jean's apartment where the young maid was sweeping and dusting.

"I can't believe he's *really* gone," she said, but being aware of her duties too, she asked, "Can I bring you some tea?"

"Yes, thank you." Gilles looked over at the Sherry, wines and Port that Jean had left behind but it was still too early for a drink. It was just as well: He would need all of his wits about him today. He would have to get workmen to go to the inn and estimate how much it would cost to restore or rebuild it. He would go to the town hall and make sure that there was no problem with the city laws and regulations regarding rebuilding the structure. He had to draw up a contract with workmen, track down the servants they would need to work at the inn when it was finally rebuilt, and make long lists of what was needed just to run the place before he even *thought* about buying food and beverages. He would have to find out the exact time and date of the auction for Ste Germaine's belongings and go buy the furnishings for the inn there, being sure that he bought *only* what was needed for Elsje's inn and resisting buying up faux frais, sentimental things like the entrance clock or the paintings. It would be wonderful to have Ste Germaine's belongings and in a sense, to continue the business for the dead man. It was as if it *was* an inheritance, continuing a family business and tradition.

"He thinks of you as a son you know," LaRue had told Gilles once. It would be Ste Germaine's legacy to Gilles and for a few minutes Gilles allowed himself to imagine owning and running Ste Germaine's *and* Hendrick's inn, but he knew that he did not have enough money to buy Ste Germaine's in light of all of the capital that would be needed to rebuild and refurbish Hendrick's inn. Gilles would have loved to hire the cook from Ste Germaine's, temper notwithstanding, but he *knew* that Elsje would not hear of it, even if Gilles was somehow able to find out what had become of him. That was probably just as well: Gilles knew that he must not try to go too far or too fast with too few resources.

Perhaps they could make do without much of what they had before in Hendrick's inn and salvage some of the pieces that would just need repair or a good cleaning. Gilles would also have to make discreet inquiries into his family's safety here, a task made even more difficult now that Jean Durie was gone.

What would Jean have done? Jean knew so many people and he always told Gilles the same thing: *"Don't worry; I will take care of it for you,"* and he never failed to follow through on his promises. Whenever Gilles needed anything he always asked Jean about it first.

Gilles wondered if Jean's ship had pulled up anchor yet. He couldn't see the harbor from here. Walking around the room, he looked at everything that Jean had left behind. There was only the bed and a chest of drawers remaining in the bedroom. The nicer paintings were all gone from their frames, probably rolled up and sealed into a water-tight container for the journey, but there were still a few small canvases that Jean had left behind. In Jean's sitting room, the little table with the axe from the New World was still there along with two chairs, a console table and the escritoire with Jean's packing list still on it, the ink barely dry. The axe table was small and quite nice; Gilles wondered why Jean had not taken the table with him but the axe *was* rather an ugly object; still, it was a little surprising that Jean would leave it behind, curious item and important part of his collection that it was.

Maybe he had just forgotten to take it.

Gilles picked it up. It was comfortable in his hand and rather *heavier* than he thought it would be but the heft took nothing away from the balance of the thing. It lent itself to comfort of use and Gilles made chopping motions with the thing. It didn't seem very well suited to that function, though, being rather lighter than what would be helpful in clearing any large trees. Gilles heard a noise behind him and he turned, gripping the axe, with disconcerting thoughts of Spanish or French soldiers racing into the room for a fleeting moment. It was only the little maid who stood there, looking up at him in a frightened way, but she had the presence of mind not to drop the full tea tray that she held in her hands.

"Your tea," she squeaked, standing there with her eyes fixed upon the axe in his hand.

"Thank you." Gilles smiled at her and she dipped her head, quickly set the tray down and scurried away.

Gilles looked back at the axe in his hand with new eyes.

So *that* was what it was used for.

It had not been fashioned at all for the purpose of felling trees. He looked more closely at the brown stains where the head of it met the handle. Gilles put it down quickly and stared at it, wiping his sweaty hand on his pants. Whose blood was dried there and still upon it? A civilized man's or a savage's? Jean *must* have known about this and yet still he kept the grisly thing here. And Jean was going off to live in that place *anyway*, knowing what horrors were there?

It was true that a sentence of deportation to the colonies was a cruel punishment, a slower and more painful death inflicted upon a person, no matter how it came, and worse by far than the swifter mercies of the executioner's axe. Most men, if given a choice, chose execution here rather than exile there. Jean would *surely* have known this and Gilles could not believe that he would go there anyway.

Until this moment Gilles had completely forgotten about the land in New Amsterdam that Jean had deeded to him on his wedding day but he was quite sure that Jean Durie had not overlooked it: Jean never seemed to forget anything. Jean had secured a renter for the property, handled the accounts and had the rents deposited directly into Gilles' account at the Westindische Compagnie. If Gilles had been thinking clearly over the last couple of days, he might have remembered the house and offered to let Jean live rent-free on his land but being too tired and too overwhelmed with recent events, it had not even entered Gilles' mind. Why hadn't Jean just asked him outright for his permission to live there? Gilles would have *gladly* evicted the tenant without hesitation so that Jean could move in. Jean was certainly shrewd enough to save more than just pennies when an opportunity presented itself. Perhaps Jean believed that Gilles needed the money from the rent or maybe he hoped that Gilles would need the house when he joined Jean on the other continent.

Leases!

They were *such* a headache. Gilles was glad that he had driven as hard a bargain as he had with that chiseling little flea over in the German state, the little man Goeble.

"Gilles?" Elsje stood in the doorway. "Has Jean left already? I wanted to say 'Goodbye' to him before he left."

"Yes, he's gone, on to new adventures." Gilles straightened his back and smiled a tired smile at his wife.

"I would not have believed that he would *ever* go there." Elsje pushed her hair back out of her sleepy eyes and scratched her arm.

The maid came into the doorway behind her. "Would you like some tea, as well, Madame?"

"Yes, thank you." Elsje seemed very tired and subdued this morning but a little more relaxed than she had been the day before.

"We might be able to get the upstairs at the inn livable. Has your father done *anything* to look into repairing it?"

"Nee, Gilles, he has been too sick! Can't you do it for him? For us?"

"I guess I could; I have no work to go to. We would need to *at least* fix the roof and close it to the weather before any more damage is done. That might be done within a week if the structure is strong enough and if I can find some good workmen. The downstairs is going to take some time, though. Maybe the younger Claussen can do the work."

"Do you think the soldiers will come back?" Elsje asked Gilles, taking him by surprise.

"Jean thought not, but I don't know. I will make some inquiries about that too, today.

"How will we live like this, in hiding while we try to run an inn?" she asked him.

"I am *so* sorry. I should have *explained* to you in more detail *before* you agreed to marry me what it is to be married to a *fugitive.*"

Gilles was irritated with her, that she asked so *many* questions, asked so much, and offered so *few* answers. He had expected that she might be a *little* more helpful and have offered *some* solutions. After all, she had been living here her entire life and her family had run a business in the city long before Gilles had come to Amsterdam.

An annoyed look replaced the sleepy one on her face and Gilles knew that he should never have given her such a curt reply: It was probably going to be a *very* long day now that it had gotten off to such a bad start with her.

The maid came to the door with a cup and saucer for Elsje's tea. She set it down on the tray, not giving any indication as to whether she had heard any part of the contentious exchange.

Gilles and Elsje fell silent as they watched the girl pour Elsje's cup before she took the teapot away, presumably to heat it up or to bring them some more. The maids in this house must have heard *many* interesting things with the kind of business that Jean Durie had conducted here, international and local trade. That Jean had stayed in this house for so long told Gilles that they could trust all of the members of the household, the servants included, and that they were secure here, but after Gilles and Elsje left this refuge, who knew if they would be safe? They only had a week to find another safe haven.

"Are the children still asleep, Elsje?" Gilles softened his tone when he spoke to her again.

"Yes, they are still so *very* tired. Can we not start the day off a little better, Gilles? I look at Cousin Vroutje and my father and I feel like there is so little that we can do for them and so *much* that needs to be done. We can't waste our energies in arguing with each other."

"I know," Gilles replied sympathetically, "but we will have to fix the inn *first* or we will not be in a position to help anyone, including ourselves."

"There is just so much, so much to do…" she stopped speaking and shook her head.

"Well, if you have any better ideas, you can just tell me what you think we should do."

If Gilles had learned one thing over the past few years, it was that Elsje could not argue for very long with someone who *insisted* upon agreeing with her.

Gilles left on his many missions before the children woke up and in spite of the enormous task that lay before him, he was glad to get started on this work and glad, too, to be out of the house. A headache threatened to go from vague pressure to something more severe this morning and his discussion with Elsje had done nothing to improve it.

Gilles found Andries Claussen first. The young timmerman, the fifth generation in his family to work as a carpenter, was already an excellent craftsman but still only a journeyman apprentice when Gilles and Elsje had left for the Palatinate. He was now a master craftsman, a full-fledged member of the guild in his own right. He told Gilles that he would only be able to go by the inn today to make an estimate, being very busy with other repair work, including damage resulting from the same Spanish soldiers destroying other property on the night that Hendrick's inn had been burned. He also had a few chests and some furniture that he was finishing, a side business that he dabbled in only for his friends and family and his own pleasure, as he was not skilled enough in the more exacting and demanding finishing work, and not qualified to join the furniture maker's guild either. In addition to this work, due to a temporary shortage in ship's carpenters, he had been pressed into service to help the shipbuilder's guild with building one of the new East India's galleons over at the shipyard, the scheduled delivery already falling behind the agreed-upon date that had been promised to the investors.

Andries explained to Gilles that ordinarily no one would *care* if they were late with delivering a sea-ready ship but cash penalties had been written into this contract, fines to the guild for *each* day that the ship was not ready to sail. Added to this already formidable backlog of work were Andries' everyday requests that came in for urgently needed home or ship repairs ("It's only a *piece* of the railing; you can finish *that* in a few hours!"), a cracked aft mast on the Eyckenboom that he promised to help with, and Andries had *more* work than he could finish in a year. These demands did not even take into consideration the enormous number of new buildings going up in Amsterdam, just as fast as they could fill in the land and reclaim it from the sea to accommodate the rapidly multiplying city population. Andries estimated that he could not even *begin* to start work on Hendrick's inn for several weeks at the earliest, and even then, only as a favor to Gilles.

Gilles understood. Andries was one of those rare men who was not only skilled in many different types of wood construction, but he always did such a good job, no matter how long it took and no matter the abuse that his patron of the day heaped on him, that he was the first man his fellow tradesmen thought of whenever a man working with lumber or wood needed help. Andries was skilled enough and diplomatic enough for them to farm their work out to him without having to worry about the quality of the job or it being completed in a timely fashion.

"What did they do, come through and try to destroy the whole town?" Gilles asked Andries in response to this bit of bad news. Gilles hoped that he might try to get some sense as to whether the inn had been singled out or if the damage was more widespread throughout the city, the result of a narrowly targeted attack or merely a drunken frolic.

"Two large boatloads of Spain's finest came ashore with their guns loaded, already drunk and talking loudly about teaching the "*intractable damned Netherlanders*" a lesson, according to men at the docks," Andries offered. "Mostly they just wrecked whatever things they came across and looked for people to fight with or dogs to shoot. I heard that they did the *most* damage over in the Jewish section and Marrano area. I haven't been there myself for any repairs, but I understand that it is *very* bad, much worse than over here."

"Maybe all of Europe will be burned to the ground before there is finally peace."

"Maybe," Claussen replied. "It's good for my business though!" He grinned at Gilles.

The men at the town hall were not very helpful to Gilles, either.

"Does anyone know if this will be a regular occurrence, if the soldiers will be coming back very soon?" Gilles asked Joris Jansen, after he had made inquiries inside the town hall about the legal requirements for rebuilding the inn.

"No one knows *anything* for certain," Joris Jansen told him. "It could have been just a few drunken soldiers who took it on themselves to look for an evening of entertainment or it might be the start of a new military campaign to take back control of *all* of the Netherlands.

We can't just sit around and think about it, though. We must defy them by living our lives as we always have."

"That *does* seem to be the only reasonable course of action, doesn't it?" Gilles sighed.

"…unless you want to go to New Amsterdam with everyone else. If you ever *do* decide to do that, the West India Company has a position for you, Jansen. We had no idea that you were such a calculated risk-taker and a shrewd trader. You certainly made some money in that trading deal with your father-in-law and now there is even a distinct and specific market for 'Hendrick's Furs'. It seems they are much thicker and finer quality than what we usually see. Why is that?" he asked Gilles, peering curiously at him.

Gilles smiled mysteriously back and replied, "It's our trade secret."

Joris laughed a hearty laugh at this response. "You come to my house in the country on Saturday night, Gilles. Bring your wife for supper at six o'clock. You know where it is?"

Gilles started to make an excuse but the idea of going to a fine house for a big dinner and discussing business with cultured people was *very* appealing. He wasn't sure where he would find a carriage to get him there, or even if he had the proper clothing, but he would think of something.

"Just come over, Gilles! We will have a fine dinner and talk about opportunities here and in the New World." Joris clapped him on the back.

Gilles agreed to go and they parted company. The "opportunities here" part sounded *particularly* good to him. Maybe he could get hired by one of the big companies to do accounting work that paid well. Greatly encouraged, and thinking that perhaps there was a greater power that would bail him out once again, Gilles headed back to Cousin Vroutje's after he stopped to buy some vegetables in the Dam.

He would have to give Elsje some money so she could go there soon to do the shopping but for right now, he liked hanging onto his money: He liked the sound of the coins in his pocket and he liked the way the family greeted him when he walked in the door with food for their meals.

"I brought you some Swedish turnips," Gilles announced.

"Oh! We'll have that tomorrow, then," Vroutje smiled at him. "Tonight's supper is ready but take just a minute to come out here with me and see my roses before we eat. I haven't had five minutes to talk with you alone since you came back to Amsterdam, Gilles."

"She had to show all of us her rosebushes so why should you be left out?" Elsje asked good-naturedly as she finished measuring out the yarn to make new winter stockings for Bruinje.

Gilles didn't seem to have much of a choice in the matter so obediently he went outside into the little back lot with Cousin Vroutje. His thoughts went back to his childhood home in Rouen where long ago he used to walk after supper with his fiancée Marie among the great rose garden that was a part of the estate. In Normandie the rose bushes alone had taken up at least a full morgen of land behind his family's manse, and the plantings required the services of three full-time gardeners just to care for them all. Vroutje had two pathetically small rosebushes with leaves made lacy from the bugs feeding on them and a few flowers that were similarly ragged.

Gilles remembered his manners, and that he was a guest in her house, so he obligingly smelled them, even though he still hated the smell of roses. Roses always took him back, unwillingly, to that night when the dining room was filled with them, when the air was heavy with the scent of summer, when the soldiers came and took him away from his old life. He didn't know what else to say to her and so he said, "They smell very nice. The beetles like them too, don't they?"

Vroutje sighed. "Yes, they *won't* leave them alone; and it seems that trouble will not leave Amsterdam alone, either. I don't know if you have had the opportunity to talk with anyone at the Westindische Compagnie but the news is *not* good here, Gilles. Our own Governor grows increasingly jealous of the Amsterdam merchants' trade success and wealth; he can't be relied upon to protect his own people and there are those that say he *invites* France and Spain to help him remove his enemies from the city, meaning those who seek refuge here. Alliances are shifting under our very feet and the Bickers family has even allied itself with *Spain* as they say that at least the Spanish King can be trusted to keep his word, more so than our *Dutch* leaders! The Elector will stop at nothing, possibly even ordering the destruction of our city to make our rich and powerful trade families bow to him in the same way that the ignorant people do in those backward and dark countries across the water. It will be even *worse* when Willem finally becomes the new Stadtholder: The Catholics will join forces with him. They haven't been this stirred up since Marie De Medici came here a few years ago and everyone made such a fuss over her! The Spanish soldiers strain at their leashes like dogs on the scent of a rabbit, and there are those that say more fighting, and maybe even war with England, is inevitable. My father told me stories about the misery the last time the Spaniards sent their full force to our shores, the murders in the street, the bodies frozen where they lay, the great starvation. If that is not *enough* to worry about, there are also the French spies here in town who will surely ally themselves with their Catholic brothers in Spain. If they find you... well, I worry about the future here for *all* of you. I know that our Elsje is a very headstrong girl but she will listen to you, Gilles. You have to find a way to make her see reason, to take her away from here to where you both will be safe. You have to take her away to New Amsterdam."

Gilles thought that perhaps Cousin Vroutje had gone mad or maybe his ears had heard wrong: No one else had cried as much or protested more when Gilles and Elsje had left for the Palatinate.

"I love my niece and I will miss her greatly but my heart's desire, above all else, is for you to be safe. Elsje told me a little about what happened in the Palatinate and I can understand your feelings about trying another venture but there's something more that you should know: I think it was *not* a coincidence that French soldiers went to the inn that night looking for you."

"In the Rijn Valley, the King's men were only after the Reformees, the Huguenots. If they find me here, they would probably not bother Elsje, they would just take me away."

"And Elsje is going to run an inn all by herself, with her crippled father? Cornelia, Elsje's mother, would have wanted her daughter to be safely *away* from all of this. I know that life is *very* hard over in New Amsterdam but at least there she would be away from that damned inn! It worked Cornelia to her early death and if you stay, it will kill Elsje, working her to her death in just a few years, too. You have proved yourself to be a reliable man and a good provider, Gilles. You would be able to feed your family all right over there, wouldn't you?"

"Ja, but Elsje has *already* made up her mind. She wants to stay *here* and rebuild the inn. You have heard, too, that things are not so peaceful there either, and that there are murdering savages that inhabit the New World? Right now things are very unsettled there."

"Yes, yes," Vroutje dismissed his last question *too* quickly and *too* easily in Gilles' opinion, "but the people I have talked to, those who know, they *all* tell me that the residents are safe within the city walls. You would be safer in New Amsterdam than you would be here. Above all, even above *happiness*, I want my Elsje and her family to be out of danger. What is the difference, really? *Our* lands are full of murdering savages, too; just because they dress in velvet and hang art on their walls, it does not make them any *more* civilized than the Wilden that live in the woods over there. Will you think about it?"

"Of course," Gilles replied, but he had absolutely no intention of it. The idea was ludicrous. He was not going off into the wilderness to live inside a stockade, a flimsy bit of wood that imprisoned him and kept him away from the rest of the civilized world while he died a slow death of starvation. Besides, Elsje had *already* made up her mind and there would be no changing it now.

"I know that you have a house there, Jean Durie to help you, and an entire sea between you and France. What is here for you?"

"Home?" Gilles asked, although he was careful to ask this in a respectful tone of voice.

"It *was* home. Look around you, Gilles! What *was* is gone now and we don't know when or if it will be restored to us. Although we love our country, it is under assault from inside and out. We may or may not survive it." Vroutje pinched off a flower and scattered spent rose petals on the ground, putting the bulb of the flower into her apron pocket. "Rose hip tea," she explained to him, "They say it cures anything."

"Then maybe you should make me some," Gilles said. "I need a cure for a great many things right now."

"You are a good man, Gilles. I must tell you that I was opposed to your marrying Elsje when Hendrick told us but the great storms that you have taken my Elsje through are those that only the best captain could have managed."

"These are difficult times for many of us and I'm sure that in time ..." Gilles began with some half-thought out platitude to placate the older woman before his speech was cut off.

"I am *not* talking of just the country's troubles which would be *quite* enough for anyone to deal with! I mean her *father*! I want you to know that I *do* understand what you have had to put up with, and

Elsje, as much as I love that child, I know that she is *not* always easy to live with. You have to take Elsje and go away before she gets too comfortable with the idea of staying here, before *I* get too comfortable with the idea of you staying."

Without another word to him Vroutje picked up her skirts and went back into the house, leaving Gilles alone to look at the roses.

It was impossible to even *consider* such a thing, but Jean Durie had said to him only hours before, *"I can find you a job if you decide to come."* *"Opportunities in the new world"* were Joris Jansen's words on the subject.

Gilles reviewed the ledger in hopes that the optimal solution would become apparent to him as it usually did in his accounting work. There was Joris Jansen's offer and there was Vroutje's opinion. She was not a worldly woman, but she was not a stupid woman, either, and Elsje's trust in Vroutje's ability to raise the three younger children had been well-placed. The New World had a house, some land to farm, a probable job, no soldiers looking for him, and Jean Durie. The Old World was the repository of all of his old dreams though, a still-life painting of the good life that still existed somewhere nearby, and all that had *ever* been familiar to him, hanging just a little too high up on the wall, just out of his reach.

The New World had savages and a world full of unknowns. The Old World had the definite reality of soldiers who hunted men, setting snares for Gilles just as deliberately as Gilles had set traps in the Palatinate for wild rabbits. The past lay in ruins here and years of toil were ahead of them to get back even a *small* piece of what had been before, even with a very *large* investment of capital and hard work for many years to come.

Even if he *did* come to the conclusion that it was best for them to go, how would he ever convince Elsje? How would he ever get her to walk with him back up a gangplank and onto a ship, sailing off into another unknown like the one that had just ended *so badly* for them in the Palatinate? He had wanted *so* much to be her champion, her hero, but after that miserable failure, perhaps she no longer had any trust at all in her husband's judgment, and rightly so.

It was not only their prosperity and security that had been shaken by the experience: Their relationship with each other was suffering also. They seemed always now to be alternately silent and then short-tempered with each other, and Gilles could feel that Elsje had had no real interest in his attentions to her in bed the night before. He worried that this might be a permanent state of affairs and he had no idea when or how this had happened, just that *something* had changed drastically between them after the attack in Nouvelle Rochelle. Gilles ran both of his hands through his sweaty hair. It gained him nothing to think about it; both paths appeared to be equally dangerous and perhaps only imminent death waited for him in both directions.

Screams from inside the house brought his attention back to the present. What folly was this? He had no weapon on him. He seized this opportunity to avenge himself, to defend his family this time as he ran into the house with fear gripping him, wondering which country's soldiers he would have the opportunity to battle first. He only realized when he reached the doorway that the screams and shouts were happy ones.

"A letter! A letter from Tryntje!" Elsje cried out to him.

"I can't live my life with the fear of invading soldiers all the time!" Gilles told himself sternly as his racing and pounding heart gradually slowed again to a normal rhythm.

Vroutje had the letter, the seal bearing the arms of the West India Company, and it seemed for a time that she was much more interested in waiving it around than she was in reading it.

"Well? Read it!" Elsje cried. "It's the very *first* one they've received from her," she explained excitedly to Gilles.

Vroutje finally obliged and ripped it open, accidentally tearing part of the letter before she flipped it open and started to read it to the rest of the family, paraphrasing as her eyes skimmed quickly over the document.

"They made good time and arrived safely, she's well...she has a lovely big house...a wood and brick house! She can't find enough servants and...has *seen* savages and even *has one as a servant in her home!* Oh my!" Vroutje clutched at her chest and seemed to need a rest at this bit of news as Elsje tried to grab the letter from her cousin's hand.

"You read it, Gilles!" Elsje prodded.

"No, no, I'll finish, I'll finish!" Vroutje said, recovering her composure as hysteria threatened to break out among her listeners too.

"She's having new dresses made for *every* day of the month and says it is much too hot to wear furs there just now...she wishes she had bought more Amsterdam diamonds as there aren't *any* jewelers there... there is some sickness in the village from the heat but not too much... the food and bier are *different* but taste good and even the *water* is delicious...she is busy dining and entertaining newcomers and officers in the West India Company...and there are a lot of black slaves and... That's all. *All my love dearest family, Your Tryntje.*"

"Is there any more, Cousin Vroutje? You look sad," Elsje said, studying the older woman's face. Vroutje shook her head. "Well, there is no mention of babies yet," Vroutje replied.

"*Babies?* Give her time!" Elsje cried. "She hasn't been married for very long and she has just had a very difficult journey on the sea, I know *all about* that!"

Cousin Vroutje handed the letter to Elsje who looked at it briefly, passed her hands over the lettering with a smile and then handed it to Gilles without further comment.

The older woman seemed to be startled by this unexpected action and Gilles didn't really *want* to read someone's personal letter addressed to their family and not to him, but to be polite, he pretended to do so. Just as he was about to hand the letter back, his eye caught his own name as well as Hendrick's and he noticed the last paragraph which Vroutje had not read aloud, the part advising Vroutje *not* to send the letter along to Elsje in the Rhineland, just in case Gilles should read the whole thing to Elsje, and not to tell Hendrick either, but that Tryntje was *very* lonesome being so far away from the rest of the family and that she wished with all of her heart that Elsje and Gilles could join her, life being so good over there except for her desperate homesickness. Gilles' eyes caught Vroutje's as he raised them from the letter and she shook her head to indicate to him that he shouldn't say anything to Elsje, not just yet.

Gilles complied with her silent request, handing the letter back to Vroutje without a word.

"Do you want to see the letter?" Vroutje asked Hendrick and her husband perfunctorily as she prepared to fold it and put it into her apron pocket. Her husband shook his head but Hendrick took it and studied it carefully for a long time. Vroutje shifted uncomfortably as Hendrick reached the last paragraph and puzzled over it while the rest of the family excitedly started to tell each other bits of stories about Tryntje as a child, speculate as to her adventures in the New World, and remind each other again how wealthy Tryntje's new husband was. Elsje joined in these stories until Hendrick handed the letter back to Vroutje with a serious look on his face.

"What is it, Father?" Elsje asked him.

"I'm just tired. I think I'll go lie down." He patted her arm and left the room but gave Gilles a peculiar look on his way out. Gilles knew that the old man understood what was in the letter and what it would mean to Hendrick if both of his daughters went away to live far across the ocean.

"Dinner is ready and Elsje is going to dish it up! Everyone come and sit down now!" Vroutje called out. She pulled Gilles aside while everyone else moved over to the table, still chattering excitedly among themselves about the letter. Vroutje spoke to Gilles in a low voice.

"It would be good for the girls, to be together. It doesn't sound so bad there, I think."

Gilles didn't know what to say to this, except to tell her very quickly that he had been invited to supper on Saturday night at Joris Jansen's and that they might talk about opportunities in New Amsterdam.

"I will watch your babies for you while you go. Elsje will change her mind about going there." Vroutje smiled a self-assured smile as she nodded in Elsje's direction but Gilles felt that it was still not even *remotely* a possibility, even if Vroutje were to tell Elsje what was in her sister's letter.

"Oh Husband, you should have *seen* Tryntje when she was little!" Elsje said as Vroutje and Gilles joined the group already gathered around the table. "She drove Mother mad, chasing the little boys and throwing rocks into the canals. She was the *worst* seamstress you could imagine and the only thing worse than her sewing was her baking, even when mother measured it out and mixed all of it up for her! It's a good thing she married a rich man and has servants to do that for her and it is just lucky for *you* that you married *me* and that I am such a good cook!" Elsje winked at him. She was in extremely good humor now, due entirely to the letter.

The merry conversation continued throughout dinner and afterwards Elsje and her two younger sisters washed, dried and put away the dishes. Vroutje straightened up the house and Hendrick and Gilles managed a polite exchange of business news without getting into an argument. When everything from the meal was cleaned up, the women and girls all took up their needlework again but Gilles had a private conversation with Elsje in one corner of the kitchen. Perhaps she thought he wanted to talk about the children or to steal a kiss; she stood against the kitchen wall as Gilles stood very close to her.

"Why didn't you tell me that you couldn't read?" he asked her quietly.

Her face clouded slightly when she did not hear what she had been expecting him to say.

"I can read well enough! Does it matter? I didn't know if it would make a difference to you when we first met. I don't need it to handle women's things, anyway. Is it so different for women in France?"

"For many women in France and here in Amsterdam too, it *is* different. It's all right, it's just, well, just that I didn't *know*. Your father and Vroutje read well enough. Can Tryntje write? Was it her handwriting?" Gilles wondered if the words in the letter were Tryntje's true thoughts.

"Oh yes, it was written in her hand. She reads and writes better than any of us. Mother knew how to write, too. I knew my letters and a few words but I just got too busy and after Mother died I didn't bother with it any more."

"It's all right," Gilles said and he smiled at his wife. "As you said, you are a wonderful cook." He pulled a strand of her hair out from under her cap.

"Who told you that I couldn't read? How did you *know*?" Elsje asked him as she pushed his hand away and took her hair back from his hand, tucking it back into place.

Gilles considered avoiding the answer but he decided that it might be a good time to bring it up, particularly since he couldn't think quickly enough of a lie that was believable.

"There was a part of the letter that Cousin Vroutje didn't read out loud. I read it and I know your father read it, too."

"She's not sick?"

"No, she just misses the family very much and wishes that we lived closer."

"Why didn't Cousin Vroutje read that part of it? That would be *wonderful*," Elsje sighed, "to live next door to my sister and to raise our children together. If *only* they would return soon."

"It doesn't sound like they are coming back at all. She wants us to go live there."

"Well, *that* is out of the question. We have father to take care of, as well as the little ones, and an inn to rebuild."

Gilles didn't answer this directly but instead he said to her, "I forgot to tell you! Joris Jansen has invited us to supper on Saturday."

"Well, we can't go; we have too much to do."

"He could tell us more about New Amsterdam, more about where Tryntje is. It might be well to go and develop some future business for the inn, too. When it is ready to reopen, we want to notify *everyone* and make sure that we have our *best* customers coming back in. Remember Ste Germaine's grand reopening?"

"What would I wear? What about a carriage? Who would watch Bruinje and Jacomina?"

"How about the blue silk, a hired carriage, and Cousin Vroutje?"

Elsje was silent for a moment but when she started musing that the dress might need some alterations, Gilles knew that she would go. She had felt cut off from the world too, missing greatly all of the excitement and daily activity of the inn. Even though she sometimes might feel ill at ease while conversing with the wealthier citizens of Amsterdam, getting out to talk with other people proved to be an irresistible lure.

"It should still be in good condition in the chest. I hope it still fits but if not I'll just have to take it in. We can borrow Cousin Teunis' carriage; it's not much, but it will get us there. Maybe Cousin Vroutje can ask him for me. He can't say 'nee' to her! We should ask Joris Jansen about the savages over there."

Elsje sailed off to plan the evening leaving Gilles behind in her wake. He knew that he would just have to find something to wear on Saturday night and be ready to leave on time. Elsje would take care of every *other* detail, just as she always did.

The supper at Joris Jansen's house was held on a perfect late summer evening. The sun was still high in the sky as Gilles drove out of the city, toward what he hoped would be a pleasant and successful evening. He maneuvered the old horse around the worst of the ruts in the lanes and mused to himself that it was *just like* the financially secure to be so exacting on a time for them to be there.

What did it matter what time they arrived?

The rest of the world ate when they were hungry, as their means on each day allowed, and slept when they could no longer keep on working, forever trying to find a tolerable balance between their relentless needs and the constant outflow of labor and money to meet those demands, putting their best efforts forth each day to bring in as much income as they possibly could before the sun went down, but rarely attaining enough comfort or sleep for complete satisfaction. It was no great wonder to Gilles that when people lost patience with the unending daily demands of just staying alive, they frequently gave up on trying to make it all work out evenly and instead turned to strong drink or to a life of crime, caring no longer about *any* requests that might be placed on them by creditors. Neither demands for rent nor taxes due were respected or acknowledged by a poor man's income.

Gilles' father had *never* understood this, could not see it from his privileged vantage point far above the masses. In his world, one with great abundance and plenty all around him, money was always there even if one objected to spending any of it, but Gilles saw the dissonance of debtor and claim holder clearly now that he had been for a time on the other side of fortune's wheel. To Jean Montroville's way of thinking, poverty was the inevitable result of laziness and unfortunate breeding practices but Gilles had come to the conclusion that these had very little, if anything, to do with success in life: He had come to the conclusion that it was more mental determination along with hard work and *who* you got to know, along with a small dollop of luck on top of that.

Over on the other side of life's balance sheet, the financially fortunate Westindische Compagnie's senior officers and wealthier shareholders seemed to have an obsession with time, perhaps because they were no longer internally driven to meet their own basic needs, but only strived to break their old records by amassing a certain amount of money within a set amount of time, or achieving new "firsts", a gambling game that they indulged in daily to pass the time, to pass away their boring lives and seek some satisfaction from somewhere. Most of the WIC members had accumulated more than enough riches for any conceivable need or whim of their own, and in a way that was highly *uncharacteristic* of most of the Dutch population, some had even ceased to worry about what their neighbors thought of their eccentricities and excesses pertaining to their increasingly ostentatious spending habits.

A tall, magnificently carved oak clock was the centerpiece of the WIC's splendid front reception office, and it was nestled in among lavish oil paintings of ships and the sea that created a varied and glorious pictorial frame around it. These items mainly gave visitors the impression that the company's single greatest ambition was to bring the exotic and delightful back to their dreary lives in Amsterdam from every corner of the globe. From this elaborate clock in the front to the rough old single-handed tidal clock hidden away in the back planning office, the greatest company in the world seemed to have been built entirely around the concept of time.

The old clock in the back offices never had any of its many layers of dust and cobwebs removed, except by accident when the boy who checked the clock against the sea levels, then wound and adjusted the clock daily, accidentally brushed up against some of the accumulated grime. The contraption was more of an ugly curiosity, an experiment, a crude attempt to map the timing of the tides just as surely as the land masses of the ever-expanding reaches of the known world were now being mapped in the chart makers' offices in Amsterdam. The machine was not *completely* accurate though, and as such, it was disrespected in spite of all of the critical information that it attempted to deliver, which was of course only as successful as its maker's inexact design and the boy's daily adjustment allowed. It was certainly never polished with lemon oil every day as was the ornate clock in the front, the one with the carved acorn-adorned pediment on top of a similarly ornate entablature. The visiting public, the unwashed masses, never failed to be impressed by the clock in the front and they always admired it as they waited impatiently out there for official responses from company representatives.

The private clock in the back was not surrounded by any kind of publicly acclaimed or appreciated art, but only by greasy finger-smeared charts of the currently known ocean currents, completed and then updated with inked-in recent discoveries of navigational hazards, and several years of calendar pages that all overlapped and crowded each other, posted in layers across much of the remaining wall space, showing each ship's departure and arrival times for the previous five years and the anticipated destination arrival times for ships sailing within the next three months. There were charts of sales figures, past, present, and hoped for, organized by month and week, condensed to the quick reference of a jagged line across the page, the visual information sourced from the accounting books and smaller charts that detailed imports of each one of hundreds of items from dozens of countries: exactly how many Ming vases had been imported by the company over the last five years, how many tons of New Amsterdam beaver pelts, Swedish iron ore and so on, with the trajectory of profit for each item they dealt in, past, present, and future projected out into the foreseeable future. In the inner sanctum of the WIC, in that back war room that the public never, ever, got to see, there was no space left at all for even a single tiny Van Rijn sketch, one Venetian blown glass bud vase, or anything else that might speak of beauty to them other than the numbers, the glorious numbers, that so enthralled and titillated the company's directors in the fellowship of the worship of the guilder.

Gilles had gained a brief entrance into their sanctuary once, about a year earlier, while he was looking for Jean Durie one day and some lower level clerk, newly installed in the outer office, had accidentally gestured for him to go on to the back before the breach of security was discovered, before Gilles was escorted quickly back out to the reception area again. Standing inside the back room alone for just a few moments, Gilles felt bewildered and as though he had been suddenly transported to a strange and alien land, far from either France or the Netherlands, to a place where the inhabitants spoke to each other not in words but only in numbers.

Even though he was an accountant by training, Gilles was not one of them, but tonight he would not think of his host as one of those number lovers or of the other differences between his everyday life and his host's, not tonight. He would only think of their *common* bonds: a love of good food, pleasant company, and profitable trade alliances.

As they jolted down the country road, Gilles' initial nervousness over driving a carriage after all these years slowly eased away. He hadn't taken up the reins to a wagon since the servants in Rouen had allowed him to briefly take a turn, a thrill for a young and sheltered boy who was expected to always sit comfortably and sedately in the passenger seat while the servants drove him everywhere, that is, unless his papa wasn't there. Gilles couldn't be seen arriving at the Jansen's house tonight with Elsje driving, though: It was a matter of personal pride as well as presentation of the image that he wanted, nee, that he *needed* to project tonight; that he was a man in charge of *every* aspect of his world.

Gilles was perfectly at home in the saddle, any excellent rider's match or better, but the thought of driving a wagon tonight had initially given him some pause. He thought at first that Elsje might drive tonight but very soon he realized that his wife knew even less of driving. In fact, Gilles had nothing to worry about: The horse that they had borrowed from Vroutje's grown son was very well behaved, too old to try any nonsense, and knew the rules of the Netherland byways much better than Gilles did, even when they had to get around other carts and carriages that they met coming the other way on the narrow road. Not having to think about the horse too much and only having to locate the estate where they were going to dinner tonight, Gilles now had the luxury of time to think about the future, that is, in between Elsje's trying to engage him in some banal conversation regarding whether it was too early for Jacomina to be getting her first tooth or if the other women at the dinner tonight would be pleasant to her or no.

Gilles didn't know *what* he was going to do if he couldn't secure some promise of gainful employment tonight before the end of the evening. He did not believe that there was anyone in the world like Ste Germaine, for better *or* for worse, and Gilles knew that it was highly unlikely that he would be able to find another job anywhere that would pay him so well to just stand around and act as a host. He might be a *manager* and manage something for someone, but he had no idea what. A warehouse? A counting house?

No, it was far more likely that he would have to *ask* for a job in accounts somewhere and then take whatever he was offered, no matter how menial or boring, no matter how bad the pay, just to keep his family's finances flowing in the right direction, *in*, and not out. If he had to, he might try his hand at carpentry. There was plenty of need for that skill in shipping, furniture, and house building. His table and chairs that he made in the Palatinate had been serviceable and he had a little bit of experience with repairs although he had none of Andries Claussen's knowledge or Jean Durie's natural talent for creating anything beautiful with a knife and some wood. How much more could there be to know about it, though? Just draw the shape, carve it out, and join the pieces together.

As they drove on through and past the purlieus of Amsterdam, Gilles could plainly see that they had entered an area in the province where there was seamless wealth, the beauty of the countryside unmarred by any visible poverty; even the little farms were picturesque, this in spite of the fact that the countryside was just a short distance beyond the bustle and interwoven good and bad fortunes of the city of Amsterdam. Joris Jansen's house was just up the road, past the entrance to Ste Germaine's country home that Gilles had visited on several occasions when he went there to ride his horse. It was a shock for Gilles to see Ste Germaine's fine house sitting dark and deserted across the fields with no people or living creatures anywhere around it. The horses in the fine stable were already gone, having already been auctioned off and Gilles supposed the other livestock had been sold at the same time. The unoccupied house waited miserably for a new owner, unwanted, like an aging slave on the block that had neared the end of his useful life, perhaps to be passed on to some less than enthusiastic new owner.

If the opportunity presented itself to bring the subject up in polite conversation, Gilles might ask Jansen why no one had made a deal with the local authorities and moved into the beautiful house yet. Did they think it was tainted in some way because it had belonged to a criminal or to a man with perverse and unchristian tendencies?

Maybe it would be best for Gilles to pretend that he hadn't even *known* Ste Germaine, although everyone in the city who knew anything about Amsterdam society would certainly know that Gilles had been not just Ste Germaine's employee, but also his right hand in running the business, as well as his friend. Everyone present at the dinner party tonight would surely know this and there would likely be questions, perhaps unspoken ones, but there nonetheless.

Gilles found the place and turned the horse up the lane, well marked as Joris said it would be with stone statues of dolphins, the artifacts probably illicitly removed and brought back to Amsterdam by the West India Company's men from some distant and ancient civilization. Just behind the dolphins were two large brass plaques bearing the name Jansen, the plaques affixed to stone pillars situated on either side of the drive. Gilles wondered at the choice of dolphins: Were they just an amusing bit of nautical statuary that Jansen happened across, relating to his business which was dealing with matters of the sea, or were they meant also to convey a sense of royalty, a faint echo of Le Dauphin, French royal heritage? Now that Gilles had for all practical purposes changed his last name to the more common name of Jansen, he shared a surname with his host this evening and the amusing thought occurred to Gilles that perhaps Joris might *also* be the son of a man named Jean in France, and perhaps he, *too,* was a fugitive. Gilles had to smile at this fanciful notion.

The house was grand enough, a small-scale castle attempting the guise of a bastion of excellent but modest taste. Gilles successfully brought the horse and carriage to a halt in front of the imposing stone home. After two of Joris Jansen's servants helped Gilles and Elsje out of their vehicle and led them inside, another servant drove their carriage off to the stables. A fourth servant took responsibility for their cloaks as Gilles and Elsje stood in the foyer, listening to a group of musicians playing elegant music in the great marble entry hall while a fireplace took the early evening chill from them as soon as they entered. The reredos of the fireplace boasted a tiled sailing ship, setting a course right through the flames. Gilles had little time to admire that *or* the gilt leafed Spanish figureheads on either side of the fireplace, probably reproductions or new creations as they were identical to each other and much too small to be used on actual sailing ships. Gilles and Elsje were escorted into a very large reception room where Joris Jansen and his wife greeted them just inside the door.

Joris introduced everyone, starting with his wife, and reminded each one of them that Gilles preferred having his name pronounced in the French way, *Jeel,* and not *Yellas.*

Joris Jansen's wife was a portly woman, her embonpoint a manifestation of good health, a testimony to a rich diet and easy life for at least these ten years past, somewhat loud, but extremely good-natured and very pleasant to talk with. She might have been mistaken for a motherly fishwife who bellowed out her wares for sale at market were it not for the crisp and perfect little brown curls that framed her face and chins, the matching beaver fur trim on the bosom, sleeves, and hem of her dress and the abundance of diamonds on every exposed part of her body. She *did* seem in an odd way to complement her husband's worldly but no-nonsense and plain-spoken manner. Gilles had no doubt that the two of them could get along well with any guest at all, from the King of France to a beggar in the streets, and together they would be able to find some conversational topic of mutual interest to make a visitor feel at his ease. Gilles was relieved that he and Elsje were neither the first guests to arrive nor the last, and he hoped that this would make Elsje feel a little more relaxed. Elsje was the perfect hostess in her own milieu, at Hendrick's inn, but Gilles could tell that she acutely felt the difference in their status here among Amsterdam's wealthier citizens.

Eventually there were five other couples who joined them for the evening, not including their hosts. Gilles vowed to be thankful tonight for any small favors, even just having a night of good and abundant food, and he was not going to let the embarrassment of the old carriage or concern over Elsje's comfort level bother him for the entire evening. The Jansen house *was* very elegant and Elsje was more than a little bit intimidated by its grandeur.

"I wish I had my pearls!" Elsje whispered to Gilles, confirming what he knew she must be thinking, as she adjusted the gold locket at her neck, an adornment on loan to her for the night from her younger sister, Jennetje. "The jeweler didn't have them ready today as he had promised?"

"Nee, I *told* you that. He said they would be ready on Tuesday, at the latest," Gilles replied. He was certainly not going to let these fat Netherlanders make *him* feel inferior. He was after all, a Montroville by birth. *Of course* they would recognize his good family background and superior class status, *of course* they were going to offer him a position tonight that was fitting for someone of his social standing.

"Your family's house was like *this*? I don't even know what kind of food this is that they serve me!" Elsje confided to Gilles after they were offered their choice of different appetizers piled high on silver plates, placed around the room on tables and at intervals brought back around to the guests by the servants. Gilles didn't bother to tell her that the Montroville lands were *much* more extensive than this little piece of real estate, that his family's manse could comfortably hold at least *four* of these houses and that the wing that *he alone* was supposed to have occupied would have had more living area than this house. He wouldn't even get into the vast tracts of land his family held in France: the vineyards, the orchards, the other cottages on the property, the gardens, sheep pastures, and cattle fields.

There was much more to see here tonight though, much of interest to *both* Gilles and Elsje. The Jansens even had an African slave, a very black-skinned man whose midnight face was covered with red tattoos and scars, with frightful piercings in various places on his head. He seemed to be more of a novelty that they kept mainly for conversational purposes as he didn't appear to have a very large role assigned to him in caring for the guests.

Gilles whispered a constant flow of information to Elsje. "That is *caviar* and surely you have seen *dates* for sale at the market in the Dam? I believe that might be dried *pineapple*, as I have heard of it but never tasted it before. It will be all right, Elsje, just watch me and do what I do or watch the other ladies. You don't have to eat *anything* you don't want to, and you don't have to impress anyone. It is not a matter of great importance to me."

He said this to put Elsje at her ease but in truth it *did* matter: The offer of a position tonight was something Gilles needed badly given the family's current hardships and future financial uncertainty. His mother's words came back to him from long ago, that a wife could make or break her husband's business fortunes and now Gilles looked Elsje over carefully, appraising her with the critical eye of a stranger. Elsje *did* look good tonight, even with her rough hands and her face still a little ruddy from the journey down the Rhine on the produce boat. She was not a bad looking woman at all, and she could be *very* sociable and *very* charming when she was in the mood, just as long as she was relaxed and happy, and as long as her temper was under control. It was that temper that Gilles worried about more than anything else but maybe she would be intimidated enough by tonight's upper-echelon companions to keep her manner mild and her tongue civil for the entire evening.

Elsje smiled an uncertain smile at her husband's encouragement but a few minutes later she gamely jumped into the conversation when one of the ladies spoke to her, asking Elsje if she had any children. Elsje's practiced hostess skills served her in good stead and Gilles relaxed a little more as she carried on an appropriate conversation with the woman, thankfully not using any of the coarse words that sometimes peppered her lively conversations with Hendrick's kitchen help.

The ladies were all very nice and very attentive to Elsje and it was then that it *first* occurred to Gilles, that a special effort was being made to be nice to his wife in spite of the fact that the other guests had social positions that were all far above that of an alehouse owner's daughter. In spite of the fact that the Dutch were famous for their hospitality and greatly tolerant of social status differences, Gilles' suspicions were aroused now and he wondered if something else might be afoot tonight: He paid very close attention to every question, every reply, every comment, and every private glance to find out what more there might be to the night's invitation. Everyone in the room, even the other guests, all pressed Gilles and Elsje to eat more, drink more, and enjoy their evening.

When supper was announced, the guests passed from the reception room back through the entry hall and into the dining room, passing by the musicians as they played, and the sweet music followed after them, lingering softly in the background like the scent of perfume.

They sat down to dinner at a linen and lace covered table that had been set with silver, polished to the light of the sun's radiance, and a profusion of crystal dishes and glasses that sent little rainbows of light everywhere after the individual prisms had processed the input of the late day sunlight and the multitude of little fires from candelabrum candles burning on the perimeter serving tables in the great dining room. Gilles was a little surprised to realize that he had very nearly forgotten what an elegant table could look like: The crockery and wooden utensils that Elsje and Hendrick had used in the inn always took *away* from the light, absorbed it, and always seemed to make the dining room there even darker than it was already with so few windows and the smoky air from the fireplace and the tobacco pipes. Ste Germaine's utensils had been marvelous but were not as magnificent as these. Gilles wondered if Elsje had ever had the opportunity before to hold a piece of *real* silverware or crystal in her hands before. All of the men were debonair and all of the women were gracious.

Asparagus shoots, endive, four varieties of fresh vegetables, large portions of juicy beef and salmon, lamb with mint sauce, spiced tongue, lemon butter, duck with orange sauce, hutspot, eel salade and orange compote were served first. It might not have been too much for a large wedding celebration or a christening, but it was far *too much* food given the small number of people in attendance and the everyday occasion of the meal. It was also a very odd and peculiar mélange of French delights and commonplace Dutch cuisine, as if it had been prepared for *every* palate from the most plebian Dutch taste to the most discerning of French tastes.

"What shall I do?" Elsje whispered to Gilles, overwhelmed by it all.

"Take some of two dishes that look the best to you, all the vegetables you want, and eat what you can but eat *very slowly*," Gilles replied, whispering in her ear and kissing her cheek as if he had been whispering words of endearment to her.

His gesture did not escape their hostess' eye and she smiled a warm smile at Gilles, to show her approval of a man who was so obviously fond of his wife.

Now Gilles wondered if this night's invitation might be some kind of a test for himself and for Elsje. There was enough polite conversation throughout dinner about the weather, recent harvests and generalities of trade, but no difficult questions were asked of them or queries that required any serious thought before giving a reply.

Gilles was almost completely off his guard by the end of the main meal but his suspicions were heightened once again when a dozen enormous trays of desserts were brought in and placed on the serving tables. There were almond tarts, lemon puddings, cream rolls, white peaches, cherries and apple slices in brandy, krullers, klets koekjes, hernhutters, makronen, appel beignets, apple puddings with cream and several plates of marzipan, all crowded together in indecent amounts on great platters that were so large that they required two menservants to carry each one of them into the room. It was *not* a pleasing arrangement at all and Gilles thought that if he had been there, Ste Germaine would have been quite disgusted by the stockpiles, by the lack of presentation or any central theme around the dinner. Servants attired in crisp uniform clothing, white shirts and black velvet pantaloons, stood by, at the ready to jump into action in an almost comical way to serve the desserts to the guests should they express any curiosity or interest in any or all of the dishes.

The entire meal from start to finish had been a production worthy of Caesar. Was there some *other* guest present tonight, someone of much *greater* social status whose importance Gilles had not realized, someone who might be the focus of all of this excess, or did they always serve food in this way at their gatherings, *un repas sans gout*, heaping up every dish that came to mind in a most unattractive and tasteless way along the periphery of their dining room?

If that was the case, Gilles thought that perhaps they should have a warehouse built, complete with troughs to serve their dinner guests instead of a dining room with a table. He wondered if the Jansens knew that there was hunger in the city, hunger even among people who frequently came face to face with the WIC crowd, people who were *not* so very different than Gilles and Elsje. Gilles decided that it was quite possible that the Jansens did *not* know and it was also quite possible that if they *did* know, they did not care. Such shortsightedness seemed to be the natural consequence of holding such a highly paid position for so long and Gilles reminded himself that hunger's pains were generally forgotten quite soon after eating consecutively good meals for just a few weeks.

He reminded himself that he should not be overly critical if the Dutch people were all just too ignorant to know how to have a proper dinner party, what good taste entailed, and what proper decorum was required. After all, *their* culture was not one that valued highly, or aspired to, great ideals of civilization. As a people though, they were quickly succumbing these past few years to diseases that were the consequence of too many excesses in consumption; indeed, the very *idea* of moderation was disappearing in the tidal wave of wealth that threatened to drown Amsterdam.

"I understand that you know some people who are already over in New Amsterdam, is that right, Gilles? I haven't been over there myself but I have heard that it is *impossible* to imagine all of the great wealth that is there. Mere men become kings overnight!" Joris Jansen winked at him. "We would book passage ourselves *tomorrow* if I wasn't needed so desperately here at the company, and if my dear wife could manage to live without her old mother and father for a year or two."

His wife did not take offense in the least at this teasing from her husband but responded good naturedly. "Joris! You well know that I would miss *all* of my family far too much if we went, most especially my *dear* sister! And did I hear that you have a sister over there *too*, Elsje? Ah, my dear, I'm certain that you must miss her so very, very, much." She tsk-tsked and shook her stiff brown curls in sympathy.

Gilles thought to himself that they *must* know all about Elsje's family over there: They probably had been in attendance at Tryntje's wedding, but even if they had *not* been there, everyone at *both* India companies and every other trade company would surely know who Adriaen Ver Hulst was, even if they didn't know him personally. The wedding of that very rich and very eligible bachelor to Hendrick's daughter must have been the sole talk of the city for many weeks after the actual event.

Gilles was greatly relieved to see that Elsje remembered to swallow her food first before she opened her mouth to answer Mme. Jansen. Elsje was even looking a little bit more relaxed. Maybe it was the wine; Gilles had urged Elsje to have at least one sip with dinner and he noted that she had taken him up on his advice.

"I *do* miss my sister; she was married and left for New Amsterdam while we were away and living in the Palatinate. I didn't get to congratulate her after she married Adriaen Ver Hulst, and didn't get to say 'goodbye' to her before she left for New Amsterdam." Elsje smiled in gratitude at their kind and heartfelt understanding.

"Oh!" all of the ladies exclaimed, looking much more attentive to the conversation after Elsje had said aloud the sacred name of "Ver Hulst".

"You were not even at the wedding then?" one of the other women asked. "Have you been away for so long?"

"Not so *very* long, but long enough to miss the ceremony. I only knew her husband slightly, mostly from gatherings at my father's."

"Elsje's father is Hendrick Hendrickson, who owns the alehouse over by the water," Joris Jansen's wife explained to the other guests, "the one that was so badly burned last month."

Since Elsje had already mentioned her father's place of business, Jansen's wife probably felt that it was safe to mention it again and to elaborate a little.

"Oh!" said the ladies again, clucking and shaking their heads in sympathy over the fire.

"*Inn*," Elsje corrected Jansen's wife, bristling at the terminology used. "He owns an *inn*, not an alehouse."

Gilles held his breath but Elsje had not lost her temper, not yet.

"You know Adriaen Ver Hulst is a *very* rich man," one of the other ladies said to Elsje.

Gilles wondered if this was the man's sole distinguishing feature or if there was anything, anything else *at all*, that might set him apart from the rest of humanity.

"Is he?" Elsje asked politely and all of the ladies giggled.

"Oh, yes!" another one of them assured her.

"Joris, did you men want us to retire to the reception room so you can talk business now?" Jansen's wife suddenly asked. "Elsje can come with us and we can have some more of that delightful marzipan that she is enjoying so much."

"Not this evening, My Dear. I understand that Elsje *runs* the family business and might enjoy our small talk about New Amsterdam business, particularly since her sister is over there now," Jansen explained, rejecting his wife's suggestion. "That is, if we don't talk too much for some of you other ladies who have no interest in matters of commerce or the colony," he added with a patronizing smile at the women who were assembled there.

"Not at all!" the ladies all assured him, perhaps happy and pleased to be included for once. Not one of the women made any excuse to leave the table; instead they all looked at Elsje with even greater interest, all except for Joris' wife who looked as though she might have known all of this about Elsje already. The Jansen's social circle certainly wouldn't mix very much with the kind of women who ran their own businesses, although Amsterdam was unique in that unlike any other part of the civilized world, the city had a good number of businesswomen, and not just the widows and prostitutes who had no other choice *but* to work if they were to survive.

"I hear from everyone who has been there, that New Amsterdam is a wonderful place, Elsje!" Jansen leaned up the table in her direction, resting his elbows on either side of his oversized dinner plate that still held large quantities of uneaten food. "Has your sister sent back her initial impressions of the place yet?" he asked.

"We just received our *first* letter and she seems to like it very much," Elsje responded.

"The only difficulty that we at the company have, is in getting enough *good* people to go there. Imagine, not being able to get people to go to paradise! It *is* a long journey and most people don't want to leave any of their family behind, even for the opportunity to make a great deal of money in a *very* short period of time. Gilles, I hear that you have done very well with your investments in the fur trade there, especially for someone so young with little experience in that market. In fact, you made *more* at that last year than you did wasting your time working in that high-priced meeting house, isn't that right?"

Gilles was certain that Joris probably knew *exactly* how much money he had made from his investments because most of his money was on deposit with the West India Company, open to observation by Jansen, as well as any other high-ranking company officer who might regularly peruse the books. Gilles found Joris Jansen's oblique reference to Ste Germaine interesting, even amusing: The WIC men had once frequented Ste Germaine's dining room regularly, but now, after his conviction and execution for unnatural vice, it was surely an embarrassment to them and perhaps they still looked askance at each other, wondering… Gilles recalled a time when they had been only too willing, even eager, to be seen by the general public there, back when it was to their social advantage.

Gilles smiled amiably at his host. "Between my deposits at the West India Company and at the Wisselbank, I suppose that I *have* done all right."

Gilles knew that mentioning the added bank account would impress Jansen and he also knew that Jansen probably wouldn't have any idea at all of how much money was in his other account. This was a good thing because the account did not have a great deal of money in it.

Jansen smiled at Gilles before he spoke again. "Gilles, there are men who go alone across the ocean for a time and they *do* come back with a tidy profit but we have found, in our experience, that if their wives go along too, then these men are less inclined to leave before they have realized a more substantial fortune, one that will ensure security for the *rest* of their lives. When their wives accompany them, we have the benefit of keeping good men in place longer without constantly having to rebuild relationships all over again with our overseas counterparts and with our trade partners. I understand that you already have put some trade agreements in place with the Wilden, ja? And you *did* know that members of the WIC who go over to New Netherland with five other souls above the age of fifteen are entitled to the gift of a

Patroonship, your own little kingdom? An outright gift of two hundred acres, sixteen miles of river frontage, is a *lot* of land to farm and trap on! All you have to do is get fifty other families to join you within four years and you can *certainly* do that! We at the WIC had no idea that you, Gilles, had such a talent for business, a gift for turning a profit, or that you, Elsje, were so adventurous that you would follow your husband to the Palatinate. Had we known that, we would have made Gilles an offer and conscripted him much *earlier*, sent him to where we need him, where there is *real* profit to be made. We need many more men like you, Gilles, and that is why we want to offer you a position in New Amsterdam."

The ladies around the table were now looking politely bored at the effusive praise heaped on him but Gilles was not to be distracted by this flattery: He now believed that *every one* of the other guests was complicit in Joris Jansen's recruitment of Gilles and Elsje to go to New Amsterdam, and *that* was why the other guests were suddenly silent and no longer made any real verbal contributions. They were letting Joris Jansen take the lead as they extended their appropriate little exclamations and quiet support to his position.

Was that it?

Were relations with the Wilden worsening to the point where now they were scouring the city, looking for *anyone* who had any trading relationships already in place to go over and get the fur trade back on track?

Possibly.

Gilles smiled at his host but he held his tongue. He would let Joris Jansen talk on and give more details, say what he was going to say, but the word "offer" *had* piqued Gilles' curiosity and gotten his full attention.

"It would be *very* worth your while to go, Gilles. We will guarantee your income though it is but a modest position there in accounts at the New Amsterdam shipping office, giving you five shares of the company as an outright *gift* just for coming to work for us and you would, as a member of course, have the option to purchase *more* shares in the future. You could work in the office while you do some trading and your farm gets established. The planting and harvesting could be done by your slaves or tenant farmers, say for the first five years, or if you preferred, you could just work your own farm and not work *at all* in the office; that is *entirely* up to you. As an additional bonus, a nest egg if you will, we are prepared to buy the land in Amsterdam where the fire was. It is well suited for us to use as a warehouse, it being located on the other side of the Dam but still so close to the water. I can offer you five thousand guilders for the place right now, just the way it is, and that money could buy you a great deal of future security! I am certain that you would have no trouble at all in getting three other adults to go over with you both, as we would relax the requirements just for you, and count your friend, Jean Durie, who is *already* over there, as one of the five others for the Patroonship. What do you say to that, Gilles?"

It was a breathtaking proposal and Gilles was completely at a loss as to what he *could* say. This had been entirely unexpected and he wasn't used to conducting business in front of a room full of guests that he barely knew, especially *women* guests. He had hoped that he might ask Joris later on, in private, for a modest accounting position here in the Amsterdam office of the Westindische Compagnie. The extended offer could add up to a great deal of money when one considered that New Netherland was probably full of fur pelts, valuable timber and other natural resources. *All* that they asked for in return was that Gilles go across the sea and lay claim to it. It was too much to turn it down out of hand, even with some substantial personal considerations and limitations on his ability to accept.

Gilles decided quickly that he might as well bring those reservations and difficulties up right away, even if it *had* to be in front of everyone. If this was the way they conducted business here, it was best to bring these impediments to the fore rather than to waste Joris' time and get his own hopes up for nothing. Besides, they might even offer *a little more* if he seemed hesitant, although he could not desire anything more.

"The inn is not mine to sell, but thank you, it is a *most* generous offer," Gilles answered and he felt his face turning red.

Not deterred in the least, and seeming not to take great notice of Gilles' discomfiture, Jansen turned immediately to Elsje.

"What do *you* say then, Elsje? Will you sell us your alehouse property?"

"It is an *inn*, not an alehouse, and I don't know how my father would make a living if he was to sell his *inn*," she replied, with an unmistakably sharp edge to her voice.

Gilles hoped that she wasn't going to lose her temper now: He might *still* try to negotiate, turning Joris' original offer across the sea into a local job. Maybe Elsje and Hendrick could take the money for the sale of the inn and they could buy Ste Germaine's or some other inn. Was Jansen's offer contingent upon Gilles' going to New Amsterdam?

But Gilles knew that Elsje was just not going to sell the inn's property at *any* price or under any circumstances: The wonderful opportunity was not meant to be. She was not going to go to New Amsterdam and quite frankly, Gilles couldn't blame her at all for flatly refusing to get on a boat with him again and taking another chance on the unknown after the last misadventure that had just recently ended *so* badly. Gilles wondered now how he could ask Joris for a job in the city instead of in New Amsterdam without it seeming like he was begging.

Joris Jansen was not acting like a man whose offer had been rebuffed, though. He was not finished and he spoke again to Elsje, breaking into Gilles' ruminations.

"Perhaps your father would go with you to New Netherlands to help make up the six adult requirement? That would make four adults right there. As an employee and shareholder of the WIC and a Patroon as well, we would of course pay *all* of the fares for Gilles' party, even if you had many more adults and children accompanying you. The entire family could be reunited with your sister, Elsje! Now I have heard that you are *very* good at accounts, Gilles. The accountant's position on the island wouldn't be very much, I'm afraid, but it *would* get you started. I'm sure that you would want to spend more time on your land than in the office anyway, planting lucrative crops like tobacco, but you could be a *great* help to them in getting their books back in order. I would consider it a personal favor to me, and to the WIC, if you accepted the accounting position, Gilles, and I would be very much in your debt. They are in a terrible mess over there, and in need of some good organization. If you wanted to, you could leave the position just as soon as it was straightened out."

Joris had addressed Gilles and Elsje at the same time, and he had fired off so many ideas and questions that Gilles found it difficult to reply to *any one* of the specifics. He was sure that Elsje was having similar difficulty in formulating her response.

Gilles could have asked for nothing more: It was *everything* that he could ever have asked for. The only difficulty was that the job and the land were so far away, that, and the immutable fact that it *all* seemed to depend on Elsje's and Hendrick's approval and they were just *not* going to go along with it. Gilles tried to ascertain what Elsje might be thinking now. Whatever it was, from the look on her face, he was reasonably sure that she was quite conflicted about it.

Elsje said to Joris Jansen, "That *is* very generous of you, but what would we *do* in New Netherland? What would *I* do? What would my father do?"

"I guess you could build another alehouse!"

There were giggles around the table, responses to Joris' humor as well as a release of tension. Gilles was beginning to feel uncomfortable now. He began to plan his excuses for a quick exit from the dinner party in case things started to get any worse. Perhaps the evening *was* going to end badly after all: He could sense the irritation rising in Elsje; the red flush across her face and neck was one that he recognized as anger although the other guests in the room might take it to be the warmth of the gathering or the effects of the wine.

"*Inn*, not an alehouse," Elsje said, omitting any response other than the correction.

Jansen now seemed to sense her annoyance as well and he quickly diffused the situation, demonstrating how he came to be so highly placed in the company, displaying his excellent diplomatic skills.

"I *like* your spirit Elsje! Don't take offense, dear lady, an inn would be an even *better* investment there, what with the comings and goings of so many traders and company officers, and with *no* decent place to eat or sleep there now. You would have no competition to speak of and I have no doubt that you could bring new standards of civility to the island of Ma na hatta."

He smiled a charming smile at Elsje and to Gilles' amazement, Elsje even smiled back at him a little. She even appeared to be *thinking* about something. Could she be considering the offer or was she just thinking about doing the laundry?

It was *always* a source of great frustration to Gilles: All women, and that included his own wife, were *such* a mystery with their frequent and sudden flights of thought. He had absolutely *no* idea what his wife was thinking and right now, he was desperate, frantic even, to know what her thoughts were. He felt as though he was free-falling through space, over a cliff, out of control, his entire future at stake and he did not know if he should take hope in his wife's sudden restored calm and questions or just give up right now on any hope for a good outcome. Perhaps Elsje had suddenly become calmer because she had *already* rejected the offer and that was the end of it.

Joris addressed Gilles now. "There is *great* opportunity there, Gilles, and you don't have to make up your mind right now. It's just that there is another more senior position that might have to be filled very soon and you might be *almost* qualified for it. With the junior position to start with and some recommendations from the right people, you would be *nearly* as well off in a few years as Ver Hulst himself."

"Well, perhaps not that rich!" one of the men interjected and there was laughter all around the table once again.

"Would you think about what a great offer this would be for your husband, Elsje? You are a *very* influential woman, both in the family and around the city, as we well know. You can think about it, talk it over for a while, and let me know in a few days. I would consider it a personal favor if you would both give this matter your most *serious* consideration."

"I will think about it but we couldn't sell the inn. Not even for five thousand guilders," Elsje said, taking another bite of an apple dessert. She put her fork back down suddenly as if deciding that she really didn't like this dessert that much or perhaps she was no longer hungry and was wondering if they would have to stay here very much longer.

"All right then, eight thousand guilders. Your wife drives as hard a bargain as you do, Gilles."

Gilles and Elsje both nearly gasped out loud and exchanged glances. Even though the location of the inn was good and there was almost no property to be found in the city at *any* price due to the rapidly growing

545

population, even with the municipality putting up new buildings in the city at outrageous prices as quickly as they could push back the sea, eight thousand guilders for a burned-out shell of a building was an unheard-of offering.

"Talk to Elsje's father, Gilles. See how he feels about it and see if he could manage to start over again or consider retirement on that sum. Does he *really* want to keep working so hard now that he is a cripple? When you are ready, call me to sign the final papers this week. We won't talk business any more this evening, dear lady. Here, have some more of the marzipan."

Jansen called for his pipe and offered a pipe to both Gilles and Elsje. They politely refused the tobacco offering but Gilles accepted Jansen's suggestion of French brandy. A couple of the other men lit pipes and in the smoke-wreathed room there was a return to small talk about the New Amsterdam colony, mainly about the idea of starting a school there for the growing number of children in residence. Gilles listened closely but there was no mention of savages or difficulties with trade; there was only talk of births, marriages, and which ships had come into port with treasures from the Brazil colonies or from the Western Indies islands lying far to the south of New Amsterdam.

Elsje must have been thinking along the same lines as Gilles, because she asked her host directly about the Wilden, in particular the Mahikanders that she had heard so much about. Her knowledge of the *name* must have impressed the attending company greatly because everyone stopped talking to hear his reply. Joris Jansen quickly dismissed Elsje's query by stating that *his* understanding of the situation was that the aboriginal savages were never around at all except when they came into the settlement to trade peacefully.

After Elsje had listened politely to his assessment of the situation, she pleaded that she had to go home to her children, having left a very small baby in the care of her cousin this evening. Even though Gilles tried to get her to stay just a little longer, she flatly refused. Gilles had been hoping to be the *last* one to leave this evening so that he might inquire privately about securing a job at the WIC offices in Amsterdam, but Elsje would not have any of it. She asked Joris Jansen outright if someone could go and get her cape for her right away.

Although Gilles insisted that the servants could see them outside, as much to save himself the embarrassment of revealing his old and decrepit mode of transport as to leave his host to his other guests, Joris Jansen walked Gilles and Elsje out to their carriage. Gilles was further discomfited when Mynert Schermerhorn and a servant followed along too, the servant bringing portable steps for Elsje to climb into their conveyance, Schermerhorn and Jansen bringing nothing more than their presence and wishes for a safe journey back.

In France, it had *always* been preferable for one man alone to escort a guest out, to bid him adieu, and any private conversations were always finished well in advance of a departure, as the coach drivers might overhear something that was not meant for their ears. Having additional servants or other guests around only increased the risk of inadvertently including and informing spies for the King. Gilles well understood from an early age, that even though one's politics might be correct, the accusers and testifiers who said otherwise were not *always* bent on the destruction of their perceived enemies per se; more often than not they were simply kites, sailing on the currents of the ill winds that blew across the landscape of France, taking in an easy pocketful of coins here and there, inadvertently taking away any lives that happened to be holding fast to the other end of the string.

While it was true that Gilles had no driver tonight, and he suspected Joris Jansen of nothing more than being *overly* solicitous, it was an old habit, deeply ingrained in him, to walk out alone and it was awkward to have all three men still standing there and watching him as he and Elsje silently made their departure. Gilles offered his thanks for a good dinner, shook hands with Joris and Mynert, and Elsje did the same before they were helped into their driverless old buggy by the servant.

So the entire evening had been about getting their hands on Hendrick's property. That's what it *always* seemed to be about, the immoral coercion, if not illegal seizure, of someone *else's* possessions. It had been so in France, and Gilles was certain after having had the opportunity to think about it for a few years now, that it had been the *only* reason the authorities had accused him of consorting with the Huguenots, a treasonable offense punishable by death, with the final objective of seizing some of his father's property, ostensibly to defray the court costs or to call it a fine or penalty to settle the matter since they could not break Jean Montroville financially or pry the land from him by any other means.

Here in the Netherlands avaricious men were probably not so very different. All that a man asked of life was a little patch of dirt on which to place a house and grow some crops, but the great landholders *never* wanted to share any of it, not unless they could take it away from someone else for free before selling it again for a profit or making a gift of it to someone else in exchange for some act of loyalty, fighting in a war, or staking a claim to a disputed territory.

Gilles was glad that this matter was out of his hands. The land in question belonged to Hendrick, so Gilles had nothing to say about it at all, but maybe Gilles could drop by the Westindische Compagnie and thank Joris personally for the fine evening later on in the week, taking with him the family's official rejection of the offer for the inn's land, and then somehow bring the conversation around to local employment opportunities for himself.

Maybe it was just as well that they were leaving the dinner party now because Gilles was getting concerned about any thieving Spanish soldiers who might be out on the roads, looking for plunder just as soon as the sun went down. The sun sat on the horizon now and it would be dark before they reached the city. All of Joris Jansen's other guests probably had country homes nearby and certainly they would have drivers, possibly even armed bodyguards too, to protect them even if they *did* have to drive back into Amsterdam this evening.

Certainly *they* didn't have to worry about being seized for extradition back to France and subsequent execution. Gilles had to suppress a smile at this thought though: Joris Jansen and his other guests *surely* didn't know that they had been socializing with a wanted felon, someone who had been a guest In the French King's jails.

Joris directed his servant back inside the house but he and his associate lingered for a few moments longer on the portico, watching as Gilles and Elsje drove down the tree-lined lane, back toward the city of Amsterdam.

"Do you really think they will accept your offer?" Schermerhorn asked Jansen.

"They will. I know they need the money and we will make certain that they accept it, even if they don't willingly come around to it on their own right away. If we don't get Ver Hulst's wife's sister over there to stabilize things, it will just get worse. It's not *just* that though: We need every man over there that we can get right now. It's in a hellacious mess. Young Gilles is bright, hardworking, multilingual, and intensely loyal, a characteristic found frequently in those with Gallic blood; he proved that by staying in Ste Germaine's employ, although I'm sure he was not *completely* ignorant of what was going on there. I am convinced, as are the other company members that I have conferred with, that he has no such bizarre tendencies himself, but we wouldn't be sweetening the pot so much if it wasn't for his wife, tough chicken though she is. We could use a hundred more men like young Gilles, men like Van Den Bogaert, good with the languages and trade, but not overly ambitious or conniving like that *knave* Van Der Donck.

I think I can share this with *you*, Mynert, and you will keep my confidence: I don't trust that Van Der Donck bastard for a minute, but the board of directors has given him free rein for far too long. Yes, young Gilles will take the bait of the Patroonship, with the added incentive of a minor position in accounts over there, although we really have no need of another accountant with business so far off the mark this year. He'll take it and he'll stay there in spite of the mess. He'll do a little trading, a little translating, a little farming, and his wife will do what she has to do; it's only *natural* that she would."

"But *she's* the one who is holding back, I can see that. Are you sure she'll change her mind and accept?"

"Oh yes. I *always* get what I want, don't I?" Joris Jansen took his eyes from the lane, now that the wagon had disappeared behind a grove of oak trees, and looking over at his friend he smiled, a sly one-sided smile.

"Ja, you always do," Schermerhorn had to agree, as the two men turned around to go back inside to the other guests.

The ride back to the city was silent for a short time but Gilles knew that it couldn't last: Elsje was only silent when she was in great mental turmoil, angry or upset about something. A financial offer that could change their lives was not as concrete and as serious a matter to her as burning the day's soup, but still, she must have had *some* inkling of what it could mean to them. It could be the beginning of a great fortune and an incredible future.

Or not.

As the sun settled down securely below the horizon, a multitude of pale stars started to appear in the darkening sky through the clear and cool night air. There were so many of the little stars sprinkled across the firmament that they might have been able to drive back to Amsterdam entirely by starlight, even without the light of the moon that was just starting to rise over the horizon.

Elsje was so quiet for so long that Gilles began to suspect that she was angry about something, either something that he had done or maybe about Joris' continual references to her burned home as an "ale house". Gilles' greatest wish at the moment was to make it all the way home without getting into an argument with her.

Elsje found her voice though, and she spoke to him, as Gilles *knew* that she would eventually. It seemed that she *always* found something that was just too pressing to keep to herself, something that she simply *had* to share with Gilles, whether he was interested or not.

"My bodice is soaked through and through from my breast milk! I *had* to get my wrap to cover it up and I knew that Jacomina will be getting very hungry soon if she isn't already starving! I don't even know if she took the milk I left for Cousin Vroutje or if she has finished it all *hours* ago with her big appetite. All I could think of, all night long, was my *poor* hungry baby that I left at home."

"Ah," Gilles replied, understanding *now* about her sudden request to leave and her slightly distracted manner all evening.

"That was a lot of money that they offered for the inn," Elsje remarked offhandedly.

Gilles wanted to discuss it with her *sometime* but he didn't feel that now was the best time: She hadn't had a chance to think about it and the drive back would be too long and miserable if she harangued him all the way there. Gilles decided that, for the time being, he would keep

551

her completely in the dark as to his feelings about Joris' offer, as well as the other pertinent conversations that he had that week regarding moving to Nieuw Nederland, those with both Jean Durie and with Cousin Vroutje to name just two of them. If Gilles was too enthusiastic about encouraging Elsje and her father to accept the money, she would reject it out of hand, just to be contrary, just as she *always* did, but if he was too dismissive of the idea, she might well be persuaded not to give it a second thought.

"Yes, a lot of money," he replied, trying only to repeat what she said, trying to stay well away from any developing emotional waterspout of hers.

"I don't know how I would even *begin* to tell my father about it! They should have invited him tonight if they wanted to talk about selling his inn. It wasn't respectful of them to do that."

Gilles heart leapt in his chest. She had actually been listening to the offer and she hadn't disregarded it completely or forgotten about it already. Somewhere in the back of her mind, could she be considering the proposition at all?

"They probably don't understand who *actually* has ownership of the inn," Gilles offered cautiously. Perhaps Elsje was thinking that she might buy another inn in the city with money from the sale, perhaps even Ste Germaine's if the auctioned price was within their means, but she wouldn't want to do that, would she? Even if that was her intention, Gilles had been under the impression that the money for the ruined inn had been offered *only* on the condition that he go over to New Netherland with the company.

"Oh, yes they do!" Elsje insisted. "They know *full well* that my father is the sole owner and has complete and total say over what is done with it. They just *knew* that he wouldn't ever consider it! Either that or he isn't *good enough* to sit at the same dining table with *their* kind."

Gilles shut his mouth and kept it shut tightly. He tried to look like he was thinking, while in reality he was trying to discern her thoughts and feelings on the matter by listening very carefully to her words and to the tone of her voice. Jean Durie was *so* much better at this mind-reading thing than he *ever* was. After just a few moments of silence she shared a few more of her thoughts on the matter with him.

"It was *rude* and it was stupid of them to think that I needed my *husband's* permission to sell my *father's* inn! If we had that money, we could *easily* get the inn rebuilt, but we can't put the money into the inn if we have already sold it, now can we?"

"No."

"If I *could* build our inn all over again, in *any* way that I wanted to, I would make the kitchen bigger. It has *never* been big enough for three women, and when you or the children are downstairs eating, we are packed in like mackerels in a basket at the market. Yes, I'd make the kitchen *bigger*. If I could have anything that I wanted, I would have *two* ovens in it as well."

"*Two*? Mm-hm," Gilles agreed, "two ovens." He *was* shocked at this extravagance.

"You know, everyone thinks that the location is *so* wonderful, but if I *could* pick it up and move it anywhere, I would move it *closer* to the two India Companies: It was in a good location when the whaling company was going strong a few years ago, but the other side of the Dam and closer to the water would be even *better* now, with fewer prostitutes and thieves on the streets at night, I think. Of course I would *not* want to be so close to the sea that I would worry when the storms come up and threaten the dikes."

"No, you wouldn't," Gilles agreed, "but is there *any* inn over there that your father might buy with money from a sale?" Gilles cautiously tested the waters of these thoughts that swirled and eddied around in her mind, muddying the streambed far and away too much for him to see the bottom yet or to gain any firm footing

"Nee, there is nothing even *offered* for sale there, at *any* price."

"Is there any other place then, like a house that could be made over into an inn, if your father had the money to do it?"

"It's not even worth *thinking* about, Gilles! Father has his mind set on rebuilding *our* inn. He started it up with his father, you know. Even if he had the money, he wouldn't go anywhere else and start over, certainly not without me, especially if you and I were far away in New Amsterdam with Tryntje."

Gilles wondered if he should take any hope in her mentioning New Amsterdam or if it was merely a slip of her tongue, a meandering of her mind, but the full content of her statement took any germinating optimism away from him and did so very quickly: He simply *hadn't* realized before this moment how deeply the roots of the partnership between father and daughter were entwined, although he should have seen it before, should have known it from the beginning.

Elsje and Hendrick were *more* than parent and child, not simply family: They were lifelong partners, a single package of two, a left glove and a right one, in all probability bound together for as long as they both lived. Gilles' blind spot on this reality was assuredly due to the fact that he could *never* have envisioned working with his own father in this way, although that promise had been held out to him and reiterated aloud frequently since the day he was born. It had been Jean Montroville's plan to have all three of his sons in a "partnership" with him, just as long as the senior Msr. Montroville ran things the way that he wanted them run.

"…and then there is my husband to consider." Elsje finished some other parallel or adjoining track of thought out loud that had been started silently.

"Oh, no, leave me out of this! I will have *none* of the blame for any decision that you make on this! As you yourself said, it is not *my* inn to bargain with," Gilles argued. "This is your decision. But if you are talking about going to New Netherland, that is a separate issue entirely."

"They are *not* separate issues! They are joined together as we are!" Elsje insisted. "Gilles, I have never said so before, but it has been *very* hard on me these past few years." She clutched her cloak closer to her throat to keep out the cold evening air and she turned her head to look directly at her husband.

"What has?" Gilles asked, knowing now that she had something more to tell him, but panicking a little too, as he had absolutely *no* idea what she was talking about or where the conversation was headed now. For the past few years, she had been living as she always had; the *only* thing that had changed was having a husband who shared her bed at night and not so incidentally, contributing to the support of the household.

"I don't worry at all for myself or even for the children, Gilles, but every time that you are away, every time that you are late in coming home, even when I left you sleeping soundly upstairs in our own bed while I was working downstairs, I wondered if *today* was the day that they would come for you, if today was the day that you might be taken away and I would never see you again. They could come for you at any time and always, always, I *know* this. It never leaves me when I am awake and it never leaves me when I sleep. I sometimes dream that they have come for you and I am all alone."

Gilles hadn't realized that she had been anxious about this *at all*, hadn't believed that she had ever given it a moment's thought during her busy days. After all, he had been in the Netherlands for a couple of years now and *he* no longer gave it a great deal of thought. It served no practical purpose to squander his time and energies worrying.

"Well, if anything ever *does* happen to me, you could always marry Jean Durie, that is, if you wanted to," Gilles added hastily, covering himself just in case she took exception to this suggestion for any of the many reasons that she might: His Jewish beginnings, his being more like a father figure to her, his finicky tastes.

"I *don't* want to! I can take care of myself but it's not about that, it's about losing *you*. I know Jean is a good man but when you are gone, there will be no one else. Anyway, Jean is far away in New Amsterdam now, that is, *if* he has made it there alive, and he is too far away to help us now, even if we did need him." Elsje paused for a moment and then continued in a sharper tone of voice. "You haven't *already* spoken with Jean about this, have you? If you *have* reached some agreement concerning me, you can just *cancel* it and release him from any promise because this is *not* France where women are passed around from man to man like a plate of herring! We make our *own* decisions about our own lives here!"

"I admire your fortitude, Elsje, but women *need* to be taken care of by men; that's just the way it is. It is simple human decency and consideration for a husband to appoint someone ahead of his time to look after his widow, just as he names a godparent or a guardian for his children. I suppose I could find *another* one for you if you object to my first choice, but I certainly would *not* appoint my brother in France."

Elsje snorted and disregarded most of what Gilles said, including the reference to the brother that she had never heard Gilles mention before. "There are *twice* as many bounty hunters who seek Jean Durie than seek you! It would gain me *nothing* to marry Jean, except to bring down on me even more trouble! I managed to live well enough before I met you, without your help, and I will continue to take care of myself and our children when you are gone. If God is willing, and I believe that He is, then you and I will live to be very old together, and then our son can take care of *both* of us, so I'm *not* going to worry about our old age just yet. What I *want* to know, and what I *don't* know, is what we are going to do *right* now. What will we do for the next few days and the next few months and years? I don't know."

This discussion was moving closer to the heated kind that Gilles had been hoping to avoid but he did wonder if this might not be a good time to ask Elsje to consider accepting the offer to move to New Amsterdam, at least for a few years, to think about all of their options, or at the very least, not to reject the idea of moving to New Amsterdam completely until she thought about it some more, but he was not bold enough to ask her this, not yet.

She had suddenly stopped talking and fell silent again but Gilles didn't want her to be quiet now; he was impatient to find out her thoughts on the matter and finally he gathered up his courage and asked her a more direct question.

"Well, where do you *want* to end up?" Gilles asked her, "I mean, when you and I are *very* old together? We can start going toward that place right now."

Elsje only thought for a moment before she delivered a ready reply. "When my time is up, I want to end my life with my very large and very healthy family living all around me, in a peaceful Amsterdam with no Spanish soldiers, with plenty of food in our cozy warm home, surrounded by our good neighbors that we have known all of our lives and of course, to be healthy enough to go to my church every Sunday too," she replied. "That is *all* that I ask of life and of the Almighty. I don't ask for, or need, a large fortune, many servants, or any great adventures."

"Then we will make it so," Gilles told her, although he had grave doubts that the soldiers would ever leave the city in his lifetime and a great many of their neighbors had already left Amsterdam on ships sailing to the far corners of the earth, probably never to return home again.

There were no mercenary soldiers waiting in the bushes on the sides of the road home. None were out this evening, even though the weather was fair. They might have all been off somewhere out of the night air, drinking warm bier together after a long day of standing in the streets, harassing innocent citizens and pinching passing girls. Gilles was grateful now that they had the old horse and wagon with them tonight: Even though they were dressed in finer clothing, they didn't look rich enough from a distance to attract any harrowers and Gilles wondered if Joris Jansen might have believed that Gilles cleverly and purposely used this ploy to avoid becoming the target of villains on the highway. Gilles still felt the warmth of Joris Jansen's praise, delivered in front of the other guests *and* Elsje, that he was a great businessman and risk-taker, *very* high praise coming from a Netherlander and a member of the West India Company. It seemed like it had been a very long time since anyone had sent any kind words his way or recognized him for his hard work and talents, his successes more than his failures. These lauds made Gilles want all the more to please Jansen and to grant *any* request of the man's, no matter how large or how small, especially when the request was something that Gilles already wanted to do for himself.

Gilles regretted that he had found no opportunity tonight to ask Joris for a local position of employment, even though truth be told, going to New Amsterdam was a much more attractive alternative to him. Gilles did know, and only too well, that there were innumerable members of the WIC who sought Joris out to ask him for paying positions anywhere in the world for impoverished nephews and hungry cousins from the surrounding countryside.

If it had been *entirely* up to him to decide and with no family to think of or other considerations, Gilles would have unhesitatingly accepted the position in the New Amsterdam colony and asked Joris when the next ship would be going out. He couldn't blame Elsje, though, for not wanting to risk her life and the lives of their children, enduring a miserable, perilous, and frequently deadly sea voyage lasting months, just for the sole purpose of trying to stay alive on a tiny forsaken island on the far side of the known reaches of the world, an island that was plagued by disease, great extremes of weather, poor management, and blood-lusting savages who surrounded and greatly outnumbered the settlers. The dark thought came to him now though, that until his dying day, Gilles would have to carry around inside him the guilt resulting from his persuading Elsje to go to the Palatinate with him and the terrible things that had happened to them there. It was this memory more than anything else that held him back from pressing her to accept Jansen's proposition and asking her to talk her father into taking the money and selling the remains of the old inn.

Maybe she was right, though. Maybe it *was* too dangerous for them to go.

Gilles might simply have to reconcile himself to the fact that they weren't going to go anywhere and that he probably wasn't going to get any offer of local employment from Joris, especially if they rejected the offer to go to New Netherland for the Westindische Compagnie. Gilles would have to find a way to graciously turn down the proposal and then he would have to find a way to bring in money to feed them all. If Elsje chose not to worry about savages in her future, that was fine; she would simply have to live the rest of her life without bothering him too much with her fears of bounty hunters or being hungry.

Gilles wasn't sure how much he should worry about *himself*. Cousin Vroutje thought that the French mercenaries had been looking for him at Hendrick's inn before they burned it but they had gone away empty-handed and Jean Durie's opinion was that Gilles shouldn't be overly concerned with the French. Gilles had already made the firm decision, and he was going to stick to it, that he couldn't and wouldn't live the rest of his life looking over his shoulder. He was going to go out and live his life without fear no matter how little or how much time was left to him on this earth. After all, he might be safe enough from the soldiers only to have the plague take him or a scratch develop into a mortal infection next week. It was impossible to know what the future held.

Maybe the old inn could be repaired, pulled together just enough to provide them all with shelter for the winter and they could serve just bier, ale, and soup while Gilles found other employment in the city as an accountant or in carpentry.

"We *do* need the money, don't we?" Elsje suddenly asked him. "From the inn, I mean."

"Claussen is supposed to get me an estimate on repairs tomorrow morning but if we have to, we will find a way to get by without it," Gilles told her magnanimously.

"God will show us the way," Elsje offered, more positively, more decisively.

"Maybe He had Jansen make us the offer," Gilles joked, "to show us that we should go and be with Tryntje in New Amsterdam. Oh well, don't bother yourself too much about it, Elsje. It will all work out in *some* way; it *always* does: Life is never anything more than a daily turn of the dice, anyway. All that matters is where you place your bets."

Elsje looked askance at Gilles and this time he saw surprise on her pale face, the expression of her features accentuated even more by the contrasts of light and shadow in the moonlight that had taken over illumination of the world from the retreating sun.

"You don't believe that, Gilles! We Netherlanders are the *masters* of games of chance and we know that it *is* sometimes possible to influence the dice with your will and your faith. *You* may not be aware of it, but you are one of the most religious persons I know."

Gilles laughed out loud at this, so loudly in fact that the old horse leaped in surprise at the noise, jumping like a startled stag until Gilles' soothing and calming voice eased the animal's nervousness and reassured it back into its steady, ambling pace in the rut it had been following back to town since leaving Joris Jansen's house.

"There, there, it's all right. Easy, Horse! Elsje, you must be thinking of some *other* husband, not me! I spend no more time in church than I have to, no more than you *make* me go anyway, and you must know that I only do that to keep you happy."

"I know you carried your prayer beads with you into the Palatinate," she replied flatly.

"A family memento, a good luck charm, nothing more than a pocket full of herbs."

"…and I also know that you never lose faith or doubt the power of the Almighty," she said, and with such conviction in her voice that it was Gilles' turn to look at her, and his turn to be astonished.

"The *All-mighty*, if He exists at all, doesn't enter my mind, not *ever*," Gilles said to her. "I am too busy with *real* concerns to waste my time on thoughts of some imaginary being, some great faerie or elf who has nothing better to do than look down and make our lives better or worse depending on His whim for the moment."

It was a very peculiar kind of conversation to be having on this night when they could be talking about the food, the music, being back at home in Amsterdam from the German state, the offer of a

Patroonship, *anything* but this ridiculous subject. Gilles supposed that he should be grateful that the inane discussion wasn't an argument about something else, although it held the promise of turning into a disagreement now that he had thumbed his nose at her religion.

Elsje didn't seem to be upset though. She even had a little smile for him. "Maybe you are just not aware of it, but I see that you are *always* trusting, always certain of His mercy and grace. Otherwise, why would you just go forward *every* time with such a surety that you are always right, that it is going to *be* all right? You *usually* are, too. I always need to check over every detail of everything and agonize over every one of my decisions, what might be the *one* best plan of action, the *right* plan, whether it is a big decision or a small one, which recipe I should cook for the day or how many loaves of bread to make so that I have enough, but not too many left over that will go bad."

Gilles shook his head at her. "Sometimes I just don't think *enough* first, and you know only too well that things don't always turn out right for me. Look at the misery that we just returned from, look at my having to leave France! No, it seems that nothing in my life *ever* goes right."

"If you had not left France where would you be today? Dead? In prison? Not married to me! If we had not been out of Amsterdam when the inn was burned, what would have happened to us all here? Nee, Gilles, it was *God's* will that we be here together now, alive, healthy, and with a future in front of us."

"You tell *me* then, what does God want us to do now? The offer from Joris Jansen was a fine thing, but as you indicated, you will not accept it and your father will not accept it either, so it makes *no difference* that he even made us an offer *at all*. We are right back to where we were before the evening started."

"What would you decide for the family, Gilles? I have no experience with making such great decisions. I usually only have worrying little things to deal with, too little flour, not enough chicken, being out of carrots."

"Oh, no," Gilles objected again, "as I said before, I will *not* make *any* decision for our future, only to have you tell me later, and to tell me *every* day for the rest of my life, that you didn't like what *I* decided. No, I will not decide alone what we should do or what to do with the inn but I *will* tell you an easy way to make a decision: Which choice will make you the most money?"

"I will have to think about this some more, Gilles. I always have to take some time for myself and pray for the right answer until I feel calm about it and then I know that it is right."

Elsje was calm for the moment but now Gilles was in a state of agitation: A great door had been opened for him tonight, leading to unbelievable opportunity, only to have Elsje and her father slam it shut on his fingers, on the very hands that had worked so hard to find that door and to pry it open for all of them to walk through to greater prosperity. It was not an easy thing for an outsider, *especially* one who was not born a Netherlander, to make it into the India Companies' inner circles, let alone to become a share-holding member *and* a land owner. They just had *no* comprehension, no appreciation of Gilles' hard-earned successes.

He gritted his teeth and sighed. Elsje and her father would *inevitably* choose the safety of Amsterdam, the path that they knew so well, throwing away future opportunity with both hands just in order to embrace the familiar, even if what was familiar was hardship. Elsje was leaving Gilles with no option but to find yet *another* solution to their financial difficulties and certainly none would be as appealing as Jansen's offer. How many offers could he expect in a week?

Gilles was more than a little aggravated with her right now: Elsje wasn't the one who had to take full responsibility for feeding them all, although she might have to give it a little *more* thought if every single member of the family had to go out and work just to keep everyone fed. Even if Gilles could find a job in Amsterdam with a very good accountant's salary, even if he could tolerate the misery of this kind of work, there would be no refuge for him at home with all of them living under one roof in Vroutje's cramped little house.

It was *incredibly* frustrating to him: They had an excellent offer on the inn's land that Elsje and her father wouldn't accept, the offer of a great deal of land and a job that would just be *given* to him without cost but it seemed that he could not even accept the job without leaving Elsje and the rest of the family behind on another continent. Gilles did, for a few moments briefly consider taking the position and leaving them all there in Amsterdam, then sending for them later if they would come, but he just didn't think he could stand to live alone without her for any time at all, especially not for years and years the way some of the company men and soldiers did; it would be *too* lonely for him, even if he had Jean Durie living nearby.

Cousin Vroutje was on his side, his one ally, but Elsje could be more than just a *little* stubborn and Gilles held out scant hope that even together, he and Vroutje could persuade Elsje and Hendrick to open their minds enough to consider a different path to a new future. These were very depressing thoughts to him and now Gilles just wanted to forget about everything for the rest of the night. If it hadn't been so late and if he hadn't been so tired, he might have found an excuse to go out somewhere and have a few more drinks even though Joris had been most attentive in keeping the wine glasses filled. There was precious little money to be wasted on taverns now anyway, so Gilles would just have to take advantage of Jean's cabinet of spirits when they got back to the city. He would have that drink, maybe a couple of drinks, before he slept.

Complete darkness was coming on quickly but now they had reached the first clusters of houses in Amsterdam's outer environs. In the sky above them, the stars grew brighter, shining with more assurance down upon them. The faraway lights of the universe glittered behind several rows of clouds that had just rolled in, a school of silvery fish peeking out from under the frothy waves of a celestial ocean. Gilles saw one star that was much brighter than all the rest, maybe a flame from some heavenly lighthouse bonfire on a distant rocky shore or perhaps a very bright gleaming pearl that had escaped from an oyster shell of a cloud. He didn't mention what he saw to Elsje, and he wasn't sure if she saw it too; it was a magical kind of thing and Gilles couldn't be sure that he wasn't imagining it. Speaking of it aloud to her might break the spell.

That night Gilles dreamed of walking along the docks in New Amsterdam, a great abundance of beaver furs and garden produce stacked up high all around him. He had money in his pocket every time he reached in to pull some out, whenever he had the slightest inclination or whim to buy one of the many exotic things that were sold there. When he woke in the morning, he was sad at first when he remembered that it was not to be, but he had been left with a feeling of well-being, a pleasant enjoyment of the dream, and what was even better, an underlying feeling that there was nothing at all that he needed to do about it right now to get to that place of contentment, that things would all somehow work out the way they were supposed to, and in the timeframe that was meant to be. Perhaps it would come to pass in the distant future, in some later years, when his son would go over across the sea and send for his aging parents later. Maybe Gilles would get to see the new world in his old age or maybe the plenty that Gilles saw had really been sitting on the docks of *old* Amsterdam all along.

The matter seemed settled at last. They were not going to go anywhere even though there would be many years of hard work ahead of them. Gilles assumed that his lack of impatience and his peaceful state of mind were due to his having finally and completely lost all of his senses, and he settled down into his familial responsibilities. Contrary to Elsje's convictions, her belief in God, and her belief in her husband, Gilles had no ready ideas or plan of action, let alone any assurances, but he took away such comfort from the dream that he thought perhaps he should have lost his mind a long time ago.

Elsje was very quiet this morning but Gilles knew that she was not angry about anything; she was just pre-occupied with her thoughts of their conversation from the night before. She was probably wondering if she should tell her father about the offer or not, and soon some changes would need to be made in their living arrangements, as they would have to move into Cousin Vroutje's tiny house with the rest of the family in a week's time.

Any other husband, and certainly any self-respecting Frenchman, would have just told his wife that he had already made his decision, decreed what she had to do next, ordered her to pack up the family belongings, and just gone ahead with his own plans, even if it meant leaving an angry storm to rage on for years to come, but not Gilles. While his reluctance to relate to his wife in the customary way of the world was certainly seen by most men, and truth be told by most women too as a sign of personal weakness, having peace in his home was more important to him than anything else. The daily battles were just not worth fighting and so Gilles did not issue any demands or ultimatums. He would suffer the assault to his ego even though everyone, the men at the WIC included, would probably also lose any respect they ever had for him. All Gilles could do was to try and present it to them as his *own* decision, his own idea.

"Do you really think that we should consider it at all?" Elsje asked Gilles as she dressed Bruinje in preparation for their going from Jean Durie's apartment to Vroutje's for the day. Before Gilles got his racing heart to calm back down again, she clarified her query, dashing his hopes once more.

"Taking the money for the inn, I mean, and starting over in another part of the city?"

"I think we need to consider *everything* now," he answered her honestly and the neutrality, objectivity, and common sense of his statement pleased his own ears, "but I think they *only* offered the money on the condition that I go to the colony for the company."

"Can you ask them if that is true? Can you find out?" Elsje asked him.

Gilles nodded but he said nothing in reply to this. He was fairly certain of the answer but he didn't want to think about it right now. He would think about it later. He had a few days left before he had to give Joris Jansen an answer, before he had to tell him "no".

Gilles accompanied his wife and children along the street until they neared their old neighborhood and then he parted company with the rest of his family to go look over the battered inn while Elsje took the children on to Cousin Vroutje's house. True to his word, young Claussen was already there, listing needed repairs and what he would charge for making them. He had an estimate ready for Gilles, written with charcoal from the fire on a smooth piece of scrap wood.

The numbers were not good.

After Claussen was gone, Gilles went inside the structure and drew numbers from Claussen's board in the sooty dust on one of the dining room tables.

First of all there were the renovations; add to that refurbishing or buying new tables, chairs, and beds. They would have to buy dishes, utensils, pots and pans. All this was needed *before* the cost of buying food and drink. Even without any wages, the list was extensive and so was the cost. Gilles totaled the column of figures again to make sure that he had made no mistakes in getting his *best* estimate on how much they would have to pay to get the inn up and running again.

He wrote on another table in the fresh, undisturbed dust there. About fifteen tables plus the back room, an average of three men at each table and ten men in the back room, an ale every half-hour for each, ten dinners every forty-five minutes times the price they charged for the ale and the food....

The numbers were just not coming up right.

Maybe he was short on the income estimate. Maybe they could charge *more* than five stuivers for a meal although that was a pretty high price. Maybe they could get by without buying so many new dishes or hiring the kitchen help, although it would be a lot on Elsje who already had her hands full with two small children. He ran the numbers all over again charging ten stuivers for a full meal but unfortunately came up with all too similar numbers.

His accountant's mind had been trained for precision, damn it. The estimates just *had* to be off, though. Had there been *more* tables in the room? Did men drink *more* than one ale or bier every half hour? Gilles had no choice now but to ask Elsje or Hendrick exactly how much money they made at the inn on an average day. He couldn't imagine asking Hendrick outright but if they expected Gilles to liquidate all of his investments and turn over his life savings for them to rebuild and save the inn, he was going to have to treat this venture just like any other investment.

And if Gilles had to say "No" to them, what then?

He didn't even want to think about it.

He didn't have Jean Durie around to ask for a second opinion on the matter. Gilles wondered idly if the inn were to burn again, to burn completely to ashes, if Elsje would still want to go ahead and rebuild. The thought occurred to him that even under those circumstances, it might not be *enough* of a deterrent to her: She was determined to save the family inn and he had to admire her for that, even if it wasn't what he wanted to do.

Gilles dropped his thoughts for the moment and just let his eyes wander over the charred rubble near the front door. It seemed that he could see the future clearly and he saw Bruinje, a young man now, welcoming people inside and then taking up his place and his pipe at Hendrick's old table. Gilles looked over to the kitchen door. He could see Jacomina as a grown young woman, looking a bit like both Elsje and Gilles, young but already tired and work-worn, bringing steaming plates of food out to the patrons. He could see both of his children, illiterate and struggling to read something that was handed to them. Gilles winced and turned his mind back to the problems at hand, the problems of the present, not the future.

He looked again at the numbers that he had written in the soot. Hendrick had been so adept at drawing up the figures for the fur trade proposal and their partnership had given Gilles such a good return, that the old man *had* to have worked out the profit margins for the inn too. Gilles didn't know how much his father-in-law might have invested in other ventures over the years but he hoped that it had been a healthy sum. Gilles was going to have to ask Hendrick for exact figures: There was just no other way around it.

As he returned to his family, Gilles' thoughts turned to France after he heard two men speaking French as they passed him by. He hoped that things might be better there now that the old King and Cardinal

Richelieu were dead and gone. There were still those men who hunted others down for the offered rewards, rat catchers of men who did not worry themselves for a moment over lives ruined, the veracity of the testimonies, or any extenuating circumstances of convictions. Had the fires burned out in France yet? Gilles wondered if life there would ever return to what was good, or good enough in his lifetime for him to go back home again.

It was strange that he thought about going back at all, or perhaps it was *why* he thought about it, just now when his future path seemed so completely open but was still leading him so far away from the place where he had been born. Gilles envisioned presenting his wife and children to his parents and then he thought about his children growing up with Charles' and Marie's children, the children of his brother and his ex-fiancée. As badly as Gilles wanted to sit in that dining room in France once again, if it might ever be safe to do that once more someday, he knew that his parents would never, under any circumstances, accept Elsje or her children into the family nor could Gilles reconcile himself to Marie and Charles' children having what *his* children should have had as their rightful inheritance. No, it seemed to him now that he could never go back home again.

Cousin Vroutje and Elsje had made a large hutspot for the family's hot midday dinner and it had all of the ingredients including the ones that Elsje had been unable to get in Nouvelle Rochelle while they were living there. The dish had the same aroma that it used to have when Elsje made it in the old inn and she had even baked some of her famous bread that was loved by everyone who had ever dined at Hendrick's. There was still some time before dinner was ready, time until the places were set at the table, time until the bread cooled enough to be sliced evenly without tearing, and time until the tough carrots were completely cooked to a consistency that Hendrick could manage with so many of his teeth missing. Gilles seized the opportunity, steeling himself by rationalizing that waiting any longer would *not* make it any easier. He said to Elsje, "I need to talk to you, alone, about the inn. Can you talk with me for a few minutes now, before dinner, so I can tell you what Claussen found?"

"Sure," she said as she dried her hands on her apron and followed him outside.

Gilles turned to her, took a breath and then dove right in to what he had to say.

"Elsje, I have been *trying* to work the numbers but I am having a hard time seeing how we can rebuild the inn and how we can all keep fed at the same time. I need to know much more about your father's business although you know that I have *never* asked you about it before. I need to know for all of us, if I should spend what little money I have saved in my lifetime on rebuilding the inn, putting all of my efforts there or if I need to find other work for a time."

"We *have* to rebuild! What other choice do we have?" Elsje asked him.

"I'm sorry to say that there *are* other choices; It might be just *too much* money that is needed for too little return of profit. We need a minimum percentage of profit to survive. It is necessary for me to use what talents and experience I have, to think with my *head* and not my heart on this, to make sure that I can take care of us all. Do you *know* how much profit you made on the inn every week?"

"We always had enough to buy supplies but all the money we made was turned over to my father. He handled it all and invested it all so I don't really know how much it was. I just know that there was always enough for anything I needed although he insisted that we not waste anything. Maybe he saved enough so we won't even *need* any of your money to rebuild!"

"I need to know with *certainty*, Elsje, before I can make a commitment, give my word to Claussen, and sign a contract to have him make the repairs. Can we ask your father? Should I ask him alone or would he cooperate more if we asked him about it together?"

Elsje immediately understood the gravity of the situation. She pursed her lips and frowned, wrinkling her brow but nodding her assent. "After dinner," she said. "We will ask him together. It's just possible that he has enough saved up to rebuild it without your money."

Gilles gave Elsje an encouraging smile but he was not too sure about this: If Hendrick had any savings put away, then Vroutje would *surely* have more food on the table unless Hendrick was being too selfish and Vroutje's husband was too proud to ask him for any more. Gilles needed to know how much of Hendrick's money had come from profits *solely* from the inn and how much had come from his other ventures: There probably wouldn't be as much money coming in from trade in New Amsterdam for the foreseeable future and Gilles knew that to be safe, he should not count on that income at all for the present.

Dinner took far too long to finish. Gilles cleaned his plate and impatiently tapped his fingers while everyone else finished eating and exchanging small talk. Since their return from the Palatinate, he had been holding back on eating as much as he would have liked, leaving food on the table for the others, but tonight he wasn't hungry for more food: Gilles wanted information. When Hendrick at last rose from the table, retrieved his tobacco and took up his pipe, dinner was officially over. Cousin Vroutje had banned Hendrick's smoking inside the house, saying that it was not healthy for the new baby. Although Hendrick disagreed heartily, saying that the tobacco was a well-known health restorative, he respected Vroutje's wishes, taking his filled pipe and a lighted candle with him out into the back garden. Rising from the table too, Gilles beckoned to Elsje, indicating that she go outside with him now to talk to her father.

Gilles stepped outside the house and jumped onto the subject without waiting a moment longer, ignoring the sharp look that Elsje gave him. "Hendrick, we need to talk about the inn."

"Eh? What is there to talk about with the inn? Color? It's your money, just paint it any color you want!"

"Hendrick, I need to go over your records to find out how much profit you made so that I will know how much money we can safely risk." Gilles softened his tone so as not to anger him but it made no difference: Hendrick was already on the defensive.

"You talk nonsense! Just fix it up and I will pay you back. When I die the inn will be yours and Elsje's anyway, so what does it matter?"

"It *matters*, Hendrick! Did all of your accounting records burn too?"

"Father, do you have the book where you kept the records?" Elsje asked gently, intervening between the two men and trying to placate her father with gentle words before he got too upset with her husband.

"I had a book of money that people owed me! The bastards are all in New Amsterdam now, hard as hell to collect on them across an ocean, even if the book *hadn't* burned in the fire!"

"No other records, Father? Nothing at all that you could remember?" Elsje wheedled.

"No! I had no records! What did I need *records* for? I took the money every night and put it away for safekeeping or I invested it!"

Elsje put a gentle smile on her face just for her father and waited for a moment before she gently pressed on. "So you kept it somewhere?" she asked softly. "Invested it? With the East or West India Company?"

"Somewhere. Or invested it," the old man returned crankily, evasively.

"Do you have any of those investments now?" Gilles asked.

"What damned business is it of *yours*? You can't have my money! I worked too hard my whole life for it!"

"Now Father, we may need *some* of the money, just a little of it, to rebuild the inn the way it was," Elsje interjected in her most diplomatic way. "Where are your investments, Father? Can we use just *a little* of it?" Elsje persisted.

The old man's jaw jutted out, then shook visibly, shaking the loose folds of skin on his wrinkled old neck as he shouted at them, "I don't *have* any money except for a few guilders! If I ever had some, I would have invested it, but I *never* did! I saved a dowry for you girls to have a nice wedding but that was *all* I could manage! The inn and your husbands were my investments in the future and now the inn is gone!"

"And the fur trade? The venture that we went in on with the savages who were here?" Gilles asked him calmly, trying as much as he could to keep all temperaments, his own included, under control and on an even keel.

"It was my *idea*, wasn't it? That was *enough* of an investment, wasn't it? I was *going* to put more money into it but I never got around to it and trade has been *terrible* this year! You can ask anyone!"

The old man threw his pipe to the ground and slammed out of the wooden gate that opened out into the street, striding along at a summer thunderstorm's pace toward the Dam.

Elsje gave Gilles a helpless kind of a look, a panicked look, picked her skirts up and ran after her father.

Gilles didn't know what to do so he just sat down wearily on the weathered old wooden chair that Vroutje kept out there to sit on while she shelled peas. He felt like the wind had been knocked out of him and he wondered if this was what having a heart attack felt like.

Elsje had been *so* hopeful and truth be told, he had taken encouragement from that, much more than he should have, and it had all come to naught: There *was* no family money. Gilles knew that now.

Cousin Vroutje came outside, wiping her hands on her apron and pulling up stray wisps of her graying hair, tucking it back behind her ear and inside her cap as she approached him.

"I couldn't help overhearing, Gilles. We *all* thought that Hendrick had money put away."

Gilles said nothing to her. There was nothing to be said. Vroutje touched his shoulder gently but Gilles was still in shock, and could think of no reply at all for her. Vroutje gave up, turned away from him, and went back inside the house.

Gilles blew out the abandoned candle and sat there, staring at Hendrick's still-smoking pipe lying on the ground and the wilting roses for a very long time.

There was really nothing that he could do.

He could not bring himself to risk all of his savings on a failing venture, or at least on a venture that had so many holes in it that it barely kept afloat above the waterline. He had a greater question now: Would his refusal to try to save the family inn cost him his marriage too?

No.

There was a time when he would not have been too sure about this, but he knew now that *somehow* they would be able to weather this storm, too. He had more confidence in his relationship with Elsje and he knew that she would understand eventually, even if that day was not today. She wouldn't like it, but somewhere down the road she would come to understand his decision. They were both very different people now than they had been when they first met, different even from the people they had been before they left for the Palatinate just a few months earlier. A long time ago it would have made a terrible difference to Gilles that his wife had no family money and no higher position in the world, that she had not enough education to read a simple sentence. These facts no longer mattered to him, though: He had changed, too.

The emotional price of moving forward with their lives would be a high one for Elsje as well as for her aging father but she would have to get over it in time. She had her husband, her children, the rest of her family around her, and she would have good things coming into her life in the future.

No, Gilles could not spend all of his money to rebuild the inn, not even to spare Elsje the pain of losing her home, and now it suddenly seemed that they could not stay in Amsterdam either. All of the opportunities presenting themselves were in the new world and all of the misery and challenges belonged to the old one. The balance of his life seemed suddenly like the great scales that stood outside the West India Company's offices for weighing the incoming furs, suddenly tipped completely to one side, the side of New Netherland.

Hendrick came back after an absence of several hours. He didn't speak to anyone on his return but went directly inside, up the stairs to his room and closed the door behind him with a click of the latch. Elsje wasn't with him though, and she *still* wasn't back when it was suppertime. The hutspot from midday dinner would be served again for supper, supplemented with some cold bread and cheese. Vroutje started to dish it up even though only the children seemed to be very hungry today. Jacomina was crying now, probably famished, looking all around the room for a glimpse of her missing mother. The infant was passed from Vroutje's hip to Corretje and back again but Jacomina was no longer being comforted or distracted by singing or rocking.

Now Gilles was getting worried: Elsje had never abandoned her children before, not even during the soldiers' attack on Nouvelle Rochelle.

"Maybe you'd better go find her," Cousin Vroutje said to Gilles as she swung Jacomina back and forth, up and down, still trying everything she could think of to distract and soothe the baby. "I'll give her some cow's milk and bier and hopefully Elsje will come back *very* soon. I'll save you some supper, too."

Gilles set off in the direction of the Dam. The square was still busy although it was very late in the day and the sky was overcast. He thought he saw one of his father's ships in the harbor but it was just a Spanish trader that looked like the Venture. Another great ship anchored out in the water looked like it might be headed to the New World very soon. In the distance he could just make out the name, *Den Eycken Boom*, The Oak Tree, on her side.

Elsje wouldn't be near the ships though: she would be in the market place, talking with the vendors, sizing up the quality of their vegetables and arguing with the farmers over their prices as she always did. Gilles continued on, scanning the square and the little alleys and the side streets as well as he passed each one.

Elsje wasn't there.

The one place that he should have checked *first* came to mind and he cut diagonally back across the square to the churchyard. He almost missed her, sitting on the bench with her head bowed down, hands on either side of her face, holding her head as if it ached.

"Elsje, it's time to come home now," he said gently as he walked up to her.

"We have nothing left, Gilles, and now you will leave me, too. Take your money and find yourself a French woman! Go to New Amsterdam! I will release you from your vows."

"You speak nonsense!" he said sharply to her, seriously worrying now that she might be losing her sanity. Then he added more kindly, "You have been through too much lately, Elsje. Come home with me now."

He didn't dare to touch her yet, even though he moved closer and stood right next to her. Her temper might boil over at any time and if that happened, then he wouldn't be able to get her to come home *at all* until her anger was spent and she was good and ready to return.

"It doesn't matter. Father and I will find a way. We *always* have before. I thought we had some money saved but it's all right if we don't. I can go to work for some of the West India people as a cook or something and we will save up enough to rebuild the inn someday."

"Are you finished yet? You *must* listen to reason, Elsje! I need my wife and children with me and although we might run another inn here *someday*, right now our place is across the sea in New Amsterdam. Did you think that I *only* married you because I thought your father had some money?"

His question was met with silence and momentarily, Gilles was dumbfounded. It was ludicrous, the very *idea* of a Montroville marrying a tavern keeper's daughter for their money, although he had to admit that the security aspects of the marriage had played a role initially in his interest.

Perhaps Elsje had been the victim of *too many* schemes and the target of too many fortune seekers before she met Gilles. She would have had no knowledge and probably no comprehension of the *size* of the fortune Gilles had been born into as he had never shared much with her on this subject. Elsje had never asked, though. Maybe they didn't know each other as well as he thought they did, even though they had been married for a few years and had two children together.

"I need a partner for my newest venture, Elsje. I'm offering it to you *first,* and *exclusively* to you, as I greatly value both your cooking and organizing abilities as well as your feminine charms. We will build a new inn for you but it will have to be relocated across a *little* stretch of water. We can sell it or leave it in the care of someone else for an investment over there when we return to Amsterdam in a few years. It will be *very* hard work but we could make a great deal of money and buy a grand inn here when we come back. Will you accept my offer or no?"

Her eyes were red and swollen; Gilles could see that she was making an effort not to cry.

"What about Father? And the old inn here? And the little ones? And Cousin Vroutje? And my mother? I *can't* leave my home! I *can't* leave them all behind! Don't ask me to do it, Gilles! I just *can't* make that choice, even if you *are* my husband!"

"We'll make a *new* home, Elsje. We'll bring *all* of your family with us, every last one of them, if they will go. Except for your mother; I'm afraid she'll have to stay here."

Elsje looked over to the grave and her eyes welled up. "How can I leave her? She will be *all alone* here in the city then!"

"Cousin Teunis or his wife can take care of her while we are gone. I think maybe your mother watches over you anyway, *wherever* you are."

"Yes, but...." Elsje stopped talking and heaved a great heavy-hearted sigh of confusion.

Gilles remained calm and spoke to her again. "Elsje, it's time that we started over, got a fresh start and got away from everything, settled into a good life, far away from the old miseries and the old hatreds.

We could do that together over there. It would be *different* than it was in the Pfalz Land. They are all Dutchmen over there, they are all like us and it is far enough away to be safe for me. We already know *good* people who are living there and this city is no place for us to be right now." Gilles held out his hand to her. "Come away with me Elsje," he said. "*Please.*"

"No one ever made me feel like you do, Gilles Montroville," she said, brushing back newly formed tears with the back of her hand.

"What, exhausted and confused?" He decided to try a little humor and he hoped that the outcome would be a good one, reconciliation, and not more tears or an angry outburst. He had no assurance of this for a few long moments.

"Sometimes," Elsje sighed, but then she let him take her hand and lead her away.

He hadn't been able to sleep very late for the past few mornings, and not just because of the hard floor that they shared every night with Heintje in Vroutje's hallway. There really wasn't a good reason for him to get up early, as the bulk of the preparation was behind them and there was only the final packing of food left to do. The contents of the barrels and chests had been left mostly up to Elsje and for the first time in recent years, with the exception of their journeys up and down the Rhine, Gilles had nothing more to do than sleep. Even nature seemed to be in accord with him as high tide had been only a few hours earlier and they sailed on the next one, very late in the morning. When he opened his eyes, he stretched a slightly stiff back, luxuriating in the warm and cozy featherbed, thinking that he might even go back to sleep for a little longer, as he listened to the sound of Elsje's breathing and directed his thoughts toward the anticipation of a happier future.

Gilles knew very well that this morning would be the last morning in his life that he would wake up hearing the sounds of Amsterdam although he breathed not a word of this conviction to Elsje: He knew what he had told her and he also knew that she needed to hold fast to the belief that they would be returning to the city in a few years.

Maybe they *would*; anything was possible now.

Gilles knew every sound here, man made and natural, and he listened for a few minutes but very soon he gave up on the idea of sleeping any more, even though he had told Elsje over and over that *she* should be as rested as possible before the long voyage started. He was too excited to close his eyes again and besides, he had months on the ship to catch up on his rest. He eased himself out of the covers then pulled on his pants and boots that had been sitting in a pile over against the wall. Carefully he climbed over Elsje and the children, nearly losing his balance once and stepping on them, maneuvering around Heintje, and after grabbing his coat from the nail by the door, he went outside into the morning chill and fog. The late summer morning mists had begun to creep heavily into the streets overnight with the cooler air, the condensation already collecting in shallow, paper-thin puddles, presaging autumn and inevitably, another Netherlands winter.

Gilles didn't bother going by the inn: He had seen the remains of it enough times already, had said his good-byes, and he was done with it. Elsje would want to do that later and he knew that she would also go to her mother's grave to say a final farewell. Gilles went to the Dam. There was something more that he had wanted to do there, or get there, something left over from his preparation lists that nagged at him, but now he couldn't remember what it was.

It was probably some kind of dried food that Elsje had requested, her thinking up more and more things for him to do than he could *ever* remember to write down or find, but they had more than enough provisions for the journey and with the ever-exacting Dutch regulators recently establishing minimum standards for food supplies *per person* on long voyages, they certainly weren't going to starve unless the ship was blown many weeks off course.

His feet took him beyond the square and on into the French quarter. He had already had the company transfer most of his funds to New Amsterdam's Westindische Compagnie accounts, in Jean Durie's care, or if Jean had not made it to the new world alive, Gilles' recently drawn-up will would ensure that all of his possessions that survived him would go to his remaining family members or if they, too, failed to outlive him, to Cousin Vroutje. Gilles was practical in the extreme but he was not a pessimist, and so he had kept a little cash out for his own pocket, more than enough to buy one last French pastry from the only shop that was open at this early hour, the *boulangerie*. After all, he might never get to taste another one again. As he walked on, he read all of the shop signs as he passed them by, noting that some of them were new and a few had been repainted. Except for a few books that he was bringing along, Gilles wondered if he would ever see another word printed in his own language or hear it spoken again.

Of course he *would*: There would be documents to translate for the West India Company and possibly even the occasional French ship bound for New France or Barbados that would make port in the New Amsterdam colony's harbor.

In many ways, it was very like other mornings that Gilles had gone down to the sea, with excitement permeating the air, as perceptible to him as the morning mists, anticipation of the future, and the knowledge that very soon there would be that pure joy that always washed over him when they were underway, the sensation of traveling like a free bird on the canvas wings of a ship gliding over the sea, flying without earthbound tethers through the salt air.

This trip would be different from all of the other trips, though: He would probably have to spend much of the voyage below deck and this journey would not be a short one. He wouldn't be returning any time soon, but neither would it be a sad trip with too many final good-byes.

No, this time Gilles was leaving and he was taking most of his life with him, leaving the old city of Amsterdam with little trace left behind that he had *ever* lived here, had taken a wife here, had baptized both of his children here, had worked until his back and feet ached here, and fell asleep here listening to the sounds of the ships and the ocean just a few streets away. There were only the already-fading inked church records that would be around until the next great city fire took them or until the scraps of paper were relegated to a misplaced box and then forgotten completely in some dusty and mildewed crate in a back storage room. They would be the only tangible things, besides living people's memories, to note Gilles' life and his passing through this place, unless the people that Gilles had left behind found some tale about him to be interesting enough that they would remember it and then pass it on, telling it to their own children, thus allowing those descendants to obtain from their elders a sort of second-hand memory, a remnant of a man they might not ever have actually known in their lifetimes.

But what was there to tell about Gilles?

He hoped that it wasn't the not-so-good things about him, his mistakes, his shortcomings, his foolish youthful dreams that had not been realized, might *never* be realized in a world where social conventions and the order of things were changing rapidly. In a way, it was as if Gilles had *already* died while he was still alive. Ste Germaine had left his ghost behind here and with it, a good tale that would surely outlive *any* story about Gilles Montroville, no matter how many more years Gilles walked the face of the earth.

There was no more time for Gilles to leave a legacy here though, for good or for bad. Gilles was leaving and his story here was finished. The only people of great importance that he was saying goodbye to today were cousin Vroutje, Vroutje's husband, and Hendrick's middle child, the third oldest or third youngest of Hendrick's five, depending on your point of view. Vroutje needed Jennetje's financial and culinary contributions to the household, especially with her old age fast approaching, and Jennetje Hendricks had grown very close to her mother's cousin, adopting her as a surrogate mother in every way after her own mother had died when she was only five. It was a sad fact that Jennetje no longer really remembered her own mother clearly, as she said she had only a faint memory of rustling skirts and the smell of buttered bread, all that was left of her mother's entire life.

Gilles noted a conversation taking place on the docks this morning between Grietje Simonsze and Tiedeman Pels. Gilles wondered if Tiedeman would be on their ship going over.

He hoped so.

Everyone in the city knew about Tiedeman's two or more wives, probably including the wives themselves, and almost everyone wondered why Tiedeman hadn't gone *completely* over to piracy yet, considering the many promotions that had been passed over his head, on to others far beneath his rank and experience, but everyone *also* knew that Tiedeman was a good man to have on a ship. He was roguish and outspoken, particularly when he had been drinking, and he had a definite proclivity for flouting the WIC's rules that he considered mainly for window dressing or for *other* people to follow. He generally secured his objective of the moment in any way that he could, whether it was with women, his job, or his own survival, forever earning him larger demotions in the immediate and frequently turbulent wake of any of his small advancements. He could be the hardest working member of the crew, as long as he wasn't missing, off somewhere on the ship where the captain couldn't find him, possibly checking that the cargo was properly secured in advance of an approaching storm before the captain even *thought* to ask anyone to do so, or more likely, having a tot of rum or a pull on a pipe when he should have been working.

In short, he was excellent with the larger picture of getting the ship into port in one piece no matter how he managed to do it and *in spite* of some of the captains that he had the misfortune to work under. Tiedeman was familiar with the mechanics of nearly every type of seagoing vessel on the water, but not overly concerned with following through on any of the formalities, that is to say the proper and recommended ways of doing things. In spite of his creativity and shrewd assessments of sailing conditions as well as his great usefulness, he was passed from master to master, from captain to captain, never finding a permanent home or permanent employment on any one ship.

It looked to Gilles like Tiedeman was now back at sea after a long recovery, having broken some ribs and possibly his back too a few months earlier while saving a slave child from being washed over the side of a ship during a journey back from the African coast.

The child had come loose and *shouldn't* have been up on the deck during the storm. The spar shouldn't have snapped the way it did, and Tiedeman shouldn't have even *tried* to salvage the small bit of cargo, as he told everyone later during his three month drunken convalescence. Tiedeman shouldn't have lived to tell the tale, given the extent of his injuries, but since he never followed any of the expected rules anyway, he was just young enough, tough enough, and contrary enough to survive. His money and friends had been running thin of late, though. Both of his wives had kicked him out again, probably only temporarily as he always managed to get back into their good graces eventually, and he surely needed the duty pay, although Gilles could see from the way that he stood and the way that he gingerly shifted his weight, that he was an older Tiedeman, aging now and still in some pain although he had had a seriously good run of things during his thirty-three or so years of life.

It now looked like Tiedeman was going to stick with sailing as his vocation. His previous attempts at learning the carpentry and glass businesses had been dismal failures with each master, as had been expected and even predicted by the gamers who had put wagers on it, collecting only a little when the master craftsmen both eventually turned Tiedeman out into the street again.

Grietje was the daughter of one of the West India Company's highest-ranking officers and had married as she was expected to, a man believed by all to be a rising star in the company. Her husband was to have risen up in the ranks, inspecting the company ships one last time before giving them his final clearance to pull up anchor by signing off on the papers. He was expected to quickly work his way up through the company, each position on the way up being little more than a formality really, after he had mastered the details of the final inspection job. It was supposed to take only a few months time, but Grietje's husband never mastered the job and he didn't work out as expected, either as a company man *or* as a husband; instead he proved himself to be an excellent drunk. Grietje didn't leave him but neither did she let him face the consequences of his own actions, or more accurately, his inactions; instead Grietje had borne him a child and at the same time taken it upon herself to do the work that she had learned how to do, mostly from following her father around, but a little from her husband, too. She inspected the ships herself when her husband was too drunk or too hung over to do his duty, which was most of the time, making up the rest of the job as she went along and then signing her husband's name to the certification document.

The interesting and intriguing thing about this arrangement was that no one to Gilles' knowledge, none of the sailors, and none of the captains, not a *single* official in the WIC, all of whom greatly respected and feared her father, ever made a direct reference to this state of things or said a word about it. They simply pretended that it hadn't happened and it wasn't happening, and if the clerks noted a difference in the handwriting of the same name that was on the papers from day to day, they didn't mention it either. It might have been very different if one of the ships that had been cleared for sailing by Grietje had ever gone down, but none ever had, not yet, and so everyone in the Amsterdam shipping business, from the very top to the very bottom, looked the other way. Established crew members elbowed new-to-the-ship mariners into silence if they exclaimed out loud that there was a *woman* on board. Far from being bad luck though, it was believed that having this particular woman on board before sailing was *good* luck, even if she did always find just one more thing, and sometimes more than that, to find fault with, frequently nothing of any importance whatsoever, and then insisting that the item be repaired or changed before she would sign the papers, in short, doing her husband's job but without the alcoholic component.

Gilles noted that she was not an unattractive young woman, having dark chestnut hair, dark eyes and a remnant of childhood freckles still on her nose. Gilles dismissed the thought that there might have been something *more* between Grietje and Tiedeman, even with her looking up into his eyes with the trace of a shy, girlish smile on her lips, and him grinning down at her as he took her hand and helped her up from the dock onto the launch boat. Gilles wondered if they both might be on their way out to *Den Eyckenboom*, the ship that Gilles would board in a few short hours.

It was still very early in the morning, perhaps not even five-thirty yet, and on his return to the house, Gilles expected to find everyone still sleeping, even Elsje, but the little dwelling was already filled with noise, activity, excitement, uproar, and more than just a little panic on Elsje's part. Only Heintje still slept through the din.

"*Where* have you been?" Elsje demanded, one hand on her hip as she met Gilles at the kitchen door with a nursing Jacomina cradled in her other arm.

"Only saying 'goodbye' to Amsterdam," he replied.

"You can say 'goodbye' from the ship's deck! You need to start *helping* me!" she snapped as she turned on her heel, nearly separating Jacomina's mouth from her breast as she turned away. "I have *much* more to do and I'm not sure if there is enough time to do it all!" she called over her shoulder to him.

He had heard this refrain of hers before; Hendrick hadn't done very much at all to help Elsje, but Vroutje, and yes, even Gilles, had worked *very* hard to organize everything that they could *possibly* think of during the past couple of weeks, every single item from readying for shipment two beds, the new trunks and barrels with all of their contents, and anything else that they could conceivably need for their new lives, right down to packets of sewing needles, salt, spices, and washed lamb's wool. The bales of warm fluff would be used to make stockings, mittens, and chest warmers for the coming winter after they had first served as headrests or backrests for the travelers during their voyage. Countless times they went over the lists that Gilles had written down for them, Elsje now learning to recognize many of the words on the paper or drawing little pictures next to the string of characters to remind herself of what the squiggles and lines represented. They had succeeded in putting a mark of completion next to every item on the list, but Gilles still couldn't escape the feeling that he was forgetting something.

He walked the house from the far end of the very top floor through to the bottom floor and outside to the very end of the downstairs back garden. Every item that belonged to them had already been sent to be loaded on the ship yesterday afternoon or was neatly piled by the front door, ready to go to the ship with them, everything except for the passengers. All of their possessions that were not being left to Vroutje, the little that remained after the French soldier's destruction in the Palatinate and the fire that burned Hendrick's inn, had been accounted for, the shipped items either to be used by them across the sea or, if fate was less than kind, going down with them at sea on the voyage over.

Perhaps it was only Elsje's increased nagging that was making Gilles so uneasy, that and the many choices that he was being forced to make in a very short time. He had finally made the difficult decision to leave his horse with Vroutje, feeling more than a little guilty that he was not in a position to help the old couple out a little bit more, but there *was* the reduced burden of the three extra mouths to feed, the two youngest children and old Hendrick, who were all going to New Amsterdam with Gilles and Elsje. Gilles had left the horse's fate entirely in their hands, telling them to do as they wished, keep it or sell it, suggesting a minimum acceptable price and giving Vroutje the names of two possible buyers. Gilles did initially think about bringing the animal with him but he just couldn't see keeping the poor creature confined on a boat for three or four months and putting it through the torture of a sea journey, even if the animal managed *not* to break a leg and end its life as dinner's main course one day on the way over. The trip would be hard enough on the human passengers who had the great advantage of self-comforting thoughts to pull them through whenever they got to the breaking point of sanity, as Gilles was quite certain would happen more than once, when they could no longer tolerate the weeks of ongoing misery: constant cold, damp, discomfort, stench, and bad food, not to mention being confined in such close quarters with each other for such a long time.

They had just barely made it onto the Eyckenboom's passenger list, even with the intervention and help of Joris Jansen, as it had filled up quickly with many passengers trying to get the last ship out to the colony before the winter storm season arrived. In spite of the news of "difficulties" and "hardships" over in the colony, euphemisms for the purest forms of human hell that were so prevalent over there, there were many families wishing desperately to be reunited with loved ones and individuals whose luck had run out in the old world, passengers ready to take a chance and step willingly into the ship's murky hold to travel to an uncertain future.

After Elsje and Gilles had jointly come to the conclusion that there was only one choice they could make, and after a very brief period of a few hours of stunned disbelief as they gradually realized that they were actually going to do this, there had been the crushing awareness that there was much that needed to be done before they left, and they would have to leave almost immediately. Among these last-minute tasks was the ordering of chests from the timmerman and barrels from the cooper and then the hasty baptism of Jacomina in Elsje's church.

Gilles had announced to Elsje that he was not leaving without first getting the additional two adults that he needed to secure his Patroonship, even if he had to stand on a street corner for the next week asking passers-by to come with him.

Gilles had not realized how difficult it would be to find just *two* more adults in the whole of the city who would be willing to take a calculated gamble on the future, although he initially thought that he would have an army of eager would-be traders, planters, and fortune seekers begging to go with him. It soon became obvious that he was going to have some difficulty in finding *anyone* who was willing to join up with his party. Gilles felt betrayed by the many people that he had lent a few stuivers to when they were a little short on funds or down on their luck, had bought drinks for with no reciprocation expected and none given, and the unfortunates for whom he had put in a friendly word to the right people to help them find employment so they could feed themselves and their families.

Gilles had never expected any repayment for his good deeds but their rebuffs of his generous offer for a new life and their complete lack of interest in his future plans hurt his feelings. Gilles put aside his pride for the moment, even though he must have looked the fool, searching everywhere, asking everyone, even those people that he knew even slightly, if they knew of anyone at all who might be willing to become a part of his new company.

Young Claussen had even laughed outright at him when asked, and Gilles was angered by this response, this humiliating rebuke to his own aspirations and dreams, and his only satisfaction was in knowing that he had not given the young man the lucrative contract for rebuilding the inn. Every man that Gilles asked was either too fearful of the dangers or too reluctant to leave what little he had acquired over his lifetime. There were a few who expressed some interest, either being faintly interested or maybe just polite, but they all refused to make a commitment, perhaps fearing that making the crossing as a member of Gilles' Patroonship would require them to reside *outside* the stockade walls over there, subjecting them to even greater danger from the savages.

With just days to go before the deadline, Gilles was still two adults short of meeting the conditions of the agreement and receiving his land grant. As for those in his group who would actually be working his farm when they got there, Gilles was painfully aware that his father-in-law was missing one arm, Jean was no farmer, and his wife was a woman too busy with babies to be of much help to him. This did not bode well at all for their collective survival. If it had not been for the house that he already had over there and the promised salary from the company accounting position, Gilles might have been completely disheartened. He knew only too well that his final list of six names had to be in to the WIC no later than the day before they sailed to give the clerks enough time to draw up the papers, sending the signed copies out with Gilles after recording the transaction in the Amsterdam offices.

Gilles rejected one old man, something which he came to subsequently regret when it seemed unlikely that he would find *anyone* else to go, talking him out of going with his elderly wife as they were too old and infirm. The voyage alone might kill them. Gilles had to wonder what would motivate an old couple to leave their present circumstances for certain death but he didn't ask. He promised to let them join up with his group in the springtime when Gilles would take actual possession of the land, after the snows in New Amsterdam had melted.

As eager as Gilles was to see the place right away, to pace off his new land, to blaze the trees along his lot lines and demarcate the outer boundaries of his new kingdom, they would be making landfall on the other shore just as winter was coming on and it would be much too hazardous to attempt to start a settlement at that time of year. Without exception, every one of the West India people and anyone else who had ever been over there, had advised him most strenuously on this point: The winters there were severe and not to be trifled with. It was definitely *not* the time to go off into the wilderness.

Gilles really didn't want to just find warm bodies to fulfill the requirements as some of the other Patroons did. He seriously wanted to make a go of his planned farms, orchards, and vineyards, using every last bit of the acreage for production, right down to the strawberries he wanted to plant around the houses. With time running out though, Gilles began to seriously reconsider taking the old couple or taking someone out drinking and illicitly getting them to sign up. He confided his concerns to Elsje on their final shopping trip into the Dam, perhaps complaining somewhat loudly, when he got interest and results from an unexpected quarter.

The girl who sold Elsje her ground apples and carrots overheard them talking and she begged Gilles to be one of the settlers.

He was more than a *little* doubtful about this: Although she was over sixteen and as big and strong as a Belgian workhorse, she *was* a woman. Gilles wondered what her husband would say, or if they might have already been considering the move but couldn't save up enough to pay for the passage over. When he found out that she wasn't married, Gilles refused to even consider taking her. She made her case to Gilles first, telling him that her father could find no husband for her, being the youngest of six girls, except some other farmer whose primary interest was in securing another farm hand to work his fields for free and then offer her the added misery and insult of cooking, cleaning, and bearing his children while she was expected to continue laboring in the fields. Being passed over for marriage so many times due to her lack of dowry had at first made her more desperate for a good husband and then had hardened her and made her much *more* selective as she contemplated her future. She decided that if she was destined to be alone and destined to be a farmer, then she wanted only to farm her own piece of land, for her own income and profit, without the added burden of a husband and children. If Gilles would *only* give her a very small piece of land of her own on which to grow her cabbages and other produce to sell in the local market, she would go with them and work as hard for him as any man.

There was no denying it; Gilles was put off by this strange creature.

Although he knew that her unfortunate plain appearance was not her fault, he found it difficult to look at her as she was *not* pleasing to his eye and so he resisted taking her along. The girl tried a different tactic though, directing her second appeal to Elsje as a fellow businesswoman, and after a few minutes Elsje took up her cause. In spite of his reservations and doubts, Gilles soon realized that he could not fight both women and in the end he agreed that the girl, Aafje Van Der Cloot, could be one of the six if she got written permission from her father.

A peculiar look on the girl's face and very quick compliance the next day, providing a written statement that his daughter could go and just a mark for the father's signature, made Gilles suspicious as to whether the girl had actually secured her father's permission at all, but by now Gilles knew that he needed her and with only three days left before they sailed, he was more concerned with being one person short of the Patroonship requirement than he was about Aafje's taking shortcuts around her father.

Although he had just one more person that he needed to convince to go with him, Gilles thought he had *already* asked everyone in Amsterdam, so the remaining task seemed impossible to him. He was *so* desperate that now he even considered the pirates, the criminals, and the homeless, although he knew that these miscreants would be living *with* his family, under one roof, at least through the winter and probably well into the spring, until they could get separate dwellings built on the Patroon lands.

The thought had occurred to Gilles that he might look in the orphanage, but the boys as well as the girls were usually all apprenticed out well before the age of sixteen. Still, the people who ran the orphanage might know of some apprentice who *wasn't* working out well for their master and so Gilles made his inquiries there, too.

There were no orphans of the right age available and now Gilles worried over the exact terms of the contract, the fine print. When he found his sixth person, he wanted someone robust enough to help him farm. If that person was sickly or had only a tentative grip on life, they might let their hold on it slip through their fingers, dying on board the ship during passage. Being so close to the required number, Gilles didn't want to be short of his quota upon arrival as he wasn't sure if the death of one of his company *before* reaching New Netherland would invalidate the contract. Gilles had seen the document and there was nothing specific in there about this but still he worried. He could always argue that he *had* his full number when the agreement was signed, before he sailed. Was there anyone who would be there to check when he got to the other side?

Probably not.

Gilles had stood at the harbor, painfully aware that there were only *two* days left before the ship was to leave, only twenty-four hours before he had to get his final list of names in to the WIC. He looked into all of the faces of passers by, thinking that he might find some newcomer to Amsterdam here at the quay, maybe a traveler like Jacques Pierre, or a refugee like Gilles had been a few years earlier, although he was pretty sure that whoever he took with him would have to be a citizen of the Netherlands.

Gilles told himself that he *would* have the six and he would have them today: He just couldn't come this close and then miss this opportunity. He wanted the land desperately but he *also* believed that there were fortunes enough over there for everyone to make one in the new world. As long as a man was willing to work hard, prosperity would come to him. Gilles sought a worthy person with whom he could share his dream and this gift but at the end of the day he returned to the house alone, tired and hungry, with precious few hours to go before the deadline was gone and with it, his dreams.

The next morning he tried to change his thinking back to hope, to believing that a reprieve would come. The first order of business on this, the day before their departure, and before he could get back to the problem of finding his final colonist, was to send the barrel of house wares and all but one chest out to be loaded onto the ship. Gilles asked the Moorish porter, too, as he asked everyone else, if the young man knew of *anyone* who might be willing to join up with his new company and his new venture.

To Gilles' delight and astonishment, the young man replied that *he* would be willing to go. After establishing that he was of a majority age and that the man's father had been born in the city, Gilles took out pen, paper, and ink and wrote down the man's information. The Moor had a most unusual name and the pronunciation was difficult, even for Gilles, but after some minor difficulty in writing it down, Gilles raced to the WIC with the information in hand to secure his precious document. There was at first a question as to whether the foreigner fulfilled the terms of the agreement and a clerk was sent to fetch Joris Jansen. Gilles waited impatiently, nervously, for Joris to come and sort the matter out, but only his acquiescence was sent in his stead and at last Gilles was officially a *Patroon*, now in the company of other Gentlemen of great stature, including the wealthy pearl merchant Kiliaen Van Rensselaer and Cornelis Melyn, a Flemish farmer of no modest means.

Those final hectic days before their departure had passed quickly and now it was here, the day that they were to sail away. Elsje went out briefly to say her goodbyes, taking Bruinje and Jacomina with her, although they were too young to retain the memory of the ruined inn or their grandmother's grave. When at last they all reached the wharf, the voyagers said their last goodbyes to cousin Vroutje under the great old oak tree that had stood near the harbor for as long as anyone alive could remember, "Wolfert's Tree", as Elsje called it. Vroutje's husband

and Jennetje had already gone to their work and they had said their farewells earlier that morning. The golden leaves were brilliant today against a cloudless cerulean sky.

Gilles told Vroutje not to tarry there: She would not be able to see anything of the ship beyond the many masts in the harbor, even with most of the fishing fleet already having left for the day and they could not be certain exactly when *Den Eyckenboom* might pull up anchor, although they had been given a boarding time. Their departure could be minutes or even hours away. Gilles stood at the quay this morning with his right hand in his pocket, rubbing his fingers over the red stone that Francois had given Bruinje. There would be more stones like that over there, the red claret-colored rocks, "garnet" Joris Jansen had called it, when Gilles described it to him. The charm had a place in Gilles' pocket along with his rosary and some money for their immediate needs when they landed. His mind briefly strayed back to the Palatinate and a momentary wave of panic came over him.

What made him think that this next venture would be any different, any *better*?

What if something went wrong and he did not get his Patroon lands? What if the savages tried to wipe out the settlement and everyone in it, just as deliberately as the French had tried in Nouvelle Rochelle? Gilles put his hand on his chest over where the Patroonship paper was sealed in a small waxed packet, nestled securely inside an inner breast pocket. He longed to take it out, to rip it open, and read it again and again, to check that the signatures were in order, but he would force himself *not* to do that until his feet touched land again, some three or four months hence, in the new lands. He would have to content himself with the memory of the details until that time: the location, the size of it, the neatly labeled river branches, the hills and other landmarks.

One very auspicious omen reassured Gilles and gave him great hope: He discovered that their departure had been scheduled for St Gilles' Feast Day, *his* day. The future could very well be just as bad for them over in New Amsterdam, and yet, he felt that it *would* be better, that he had to try again, just one more time, if only because he was getting older and felt that his opportunities were drying up and his bridges were burning ferociously behind him.

Elsje stooped down and picked up one of the acorns that had dropped from the great old tree. Large and ripe and perfect, the acorn had not yet been trampled under the feet of travelers or merchants, nor had the foraging squirrels come to take it away as yet. Gilles saw her put it in her pocket, taking a little piece of her homeland, the fatherland, away with her. With great relief Gilles noted too that the farm girl and the baggage boy were both already there, waiting for him. The sailors would all be witnesses to this and there could be no accusations later that the terms of Gilles' contract with the WIC had not been met.

Their small company and their few belongings were loaded into the little launch boat headed out to the big ship and Gilles finally relaxed just enough to notice for the first time that Elsje and the children were dressed in their very *best* clothing, rather a poor choice for the voyage, considering how miserable conditions were going to be for the next few months. Did Elsje pay him no mind at all when Gilles told her that she should dress with practicality and comfort uppermost in her mind, and what conditions on the ship would be like?

Now he recalled that she had retorted with something about her being "a company man's wife" and perhaps this was the rationale for their inappropriate dress, although being the wife of a man who did a few accounts for the company was *very* different than being married to a Joris Jansen or an Adriaen Ver Hulst. Perhaps Elsje meant that she was the wife of a Patroon now, a *landholder*, and in spite of the small company of forty five or so other simple folk that would comprise their floating village for the next few months, Gilles allowed his breast to swell just a little with the realization of this and pride in it too, his first major accomplishment due entirely to his own efforts and not bestowed upon him by right of birth.

Gilles thought for a moment that Elsje might turn around and go right back to the city when she was confronted with climbing up the long ladder on the side of the ship but she managed it. Bruinje and Jacomina were carried up and handed to her by two strong young sailors and Hendrick managed the ladder all right too, even with his one arm, hooking the stump through the rungs and holding fast before his feet gained each temporary placement. Corretje and Heintje both seemed to thoroughly enjoy the experience, bouncing a little more than was necessary on the way up, much to the amusement of the sailors who followed closely behind them to ensure their safe arrival on the open deck.

In truth Gilles was excited by the thought of being at sea for so long and the stories of sea monsters didn't worry him in the least: He had never believed most of them anyway. He only hoped that they would all be allowed out on the deck frequently and would not be held captive down in the dark hold of the middle deck for the entire journey.

Several official West India chests, conspicuous by their unique design as well as by the company seals, were hoisted on board from another launch boat and were later rumored to contain gold pieces to pay the company officers in New Amsterdam, mainly because they were accompanied on board and for the duration of the trip by several burly-looking soldiers carrying guns and other weaponry. The chests were taken far away from the passenger deck though, probably to the Captain's quarters or possibly to another area where the soldiers would watch the chests day and night until their arrival in the new land. Trade items including barrels of flour, a box of clay tobacco pipes, bolts of fabric, crates of Swedish iron cooking pots, and barrels of nails had already been loaded onto the ship and secured on the lowest deck with most of the other baggage before the passengers with their carried-on belongings were permitted to come aboard.

Provisions for the passengers, supplied by the Philipse Company of the grocer's guild, were also taken on: Dried and salted fish, ham, lamb, pork, peas, beans, apples, cheese, herring and of course, bier. The ship was scheduled to arrive just before the onset of winter, the captain having decided *not* to take the longer West Indies route which went down the coast along Spain to Africa and across to the Caribbean before heading north again to New Amsterdam, but to use the more *direct* route that was finally starting to gain acceptance in spite of the greater expanse of sea it had to cross, making a run for it straight across the wide Atlantic and hopefully not straying with the storms too far down into the Virginia Colonies or too far north into the French claimed territories. Joris Jansen had reassured Gilles that the ship would be equipped with all of the most modern and trusted equipment: the sextant, astrolabe, cross staff, telescoping lenses and even a Davis Quadrant. The ship's navigator, identifiable by his attitude as well as the equipment he carried, had come up the ladder behind them, hauling along a bulky wooden case on a shoulder strap. It was purported to be filled with the tools of his trade, as well as prisms and mirrors, items that he had used in experiments, guarded jealously, and refused to let anyone touch, even to help him bring them up the long and unsteady ladder.

Only a few days ago the *Wapen Van Rensselaerwyck* had set sail for Van Rensselaer's patroonship, located further up Hudson's River from the islands where New Netherland's first and principal settlements had been established. She would make a stop in New Amsterdam to take on new food supplies and to deliver a few items, including letters from Gilles to the tenant in his house, requesting the man's immediate removal from the premises, and to Jean Durie, who had departed Amsterdam only a few weeks earlier. It was not reasonable to expect that Jean would be there yet, or to expect any kind of reply, but Gilles wanted to let them know that he was coming. He hoped that Jean might take the initiative and evict the tenant if necessary, making sure that the house was still habitable and ready for Gilles and his flock upon their arrival. It would be a tight fit over the winter in a small house, what with Gilles' large family and the two others who were not quite strangers, but not quite friends yet, either.

Gilles didn't know *what* he would do if he decided during the voyage on the way over that he didn't want one of them living under his roof but he would certainly get to know his two tenant farmers much better in the coming months. Aafje Van der Cloot and the Moorish porter, who told everyone now that his name was Garrett Van Amsterdam, were on board the sailing ship with them and they both seemed excited and ready for the adventure, too. Gilles' company, including his family, totaled nine souls.

Hendrick muttered to himself, just loud enough for Gilles to hear, that they were *all* crazy for taking this voyage, would die en route, and complained that he would not have enough tobacco to last the whole trip even if he *could* manage to keep his pipe lit from the cook's fire. Gilles would have dearly loved to leave Hendrick far behind him in old Amsterdam but there were too many reasons for taking him: Gilles needed every man for his contract, Elsje would never consider leaving her father behind, Vroutje didn't need the extra burden of feeding the old man, and Hendrick, not wanting his oldest daughter to go anywhere without him, might have succeeded in either talking Elsje into staying behind or in making her completely miserable about her choice to be with her husband.

Gilles had resigned himself very early on to Hendrick's accompanying them. He hoped that it would be less trouble in the long run to just bring him along and if Hendrick didn't die on the way over, the old geezer might go to live there or at least spend all of his time with his other daughter, who was already there and living in a fine big house with plenty of extra room. Getting old Hendrick married off to some rich widow might not be an impossibility either: His financial prospects were not good but some lonely widow of independent means might still take him off their hands, in spite of his missing arm. At the very least, he could make himself useful by watching the children for Elsje while she did her chores.

Hendrick had irritated Gilles a great deal during the preceding weeks by telling him that he would *never* find two people foolish enough to go over with them and then by mumbling about how he had been unable to find a *suitable* husband for his oldest daughter, only a crazy French one with krankzinnig ideas about traveling around the world all the time. The old man had received an *enormous* sum of money for the sale of his inn though, and luckily Elsje had enough influence over her father to make him deposit all of it, every single stuiver, with the West India Company for safekeeping until they reached New Amsterdam. No longer blindly trusting in her father's financial acumen, her plan was to somehow find a way to transfer it over to Gilles for *him* to invest before Hendrick spent it all, gambled it away, or was robbed of it.

Hendrick believed that he would most certainly die on the ship, long before he ever got to spend any of it anyway, and that Gilles had been after his money all along, but Elsje managed to convince her father that there was no place to spend the money on the way over. She was not going to allow her father's savings for his old age to be lost with dice or in a card game and she advised Hendrick that the *least* he could do was to leave something for Jennetje's future if they all died at sea and his daughter left in Amsterdam turned out to be the family's sole survivor.

Gilles had seen to it that his will was updated and he had Hendrick draw one up as well. In addition to the clerk's copies, one copy of each was left for safe keeping with Cousin Vroutje and one was sent to be kept on file for a few months at the Westindische Compagnie offices. Vroutje and her husband were named guardians for Jennetje until she came of age, and both documents were very strange ones for Gilles to witness in that he was unaccustomed to seeing a *woman* given any responsibilities in the execution of a legal agreement or to inherit anything beyond a bed to sleep in. Elsje insisted that it was frequently done that way in Amsterdam, and the lawyer who had drawn up the papers made no comment about these instructions so Gilles assumed that Elsje was right. As a witness only, it was not his place to ask questions or make comments so he just closed his mouth and signed the documents with his full legal name so there could be no doubt as to which Gilles Jansen had signed it, *Gilles Jansen de Montroville,* the final "e" in his signature ending in a flourish..

"Do you think we will ever see home and Cousin Vroutje again?" Elsje asked Gilles as they stood at the rail, looking out at Amsterdam for one last time before they went below, watching the last of the passengers and their belongings come aboard.

"Oh, I'm sure we will," Gilles said cheerfully, but he had his doubts in the extreme. "We thought we had left forever when we went to the Palatinate!"

Elsje shivered and Gilles pulled her closer to him. "Are you cold?"

"A little bit."

"Nervous?"

"A little," she admitted to him.

She called to Bruinje to stay close to her, even though she already had a rope tied around him and for once he came over to her, perhaps hoping that she would give him some koekjes or other treats that Cousin Vroutje told Elsje to put in her pocket for Bruinje to have on the trip.

"Elsje, it *will* be all right, you know," Gilles tried to reassure her.

"I'm not so much concerned for myself, but for Father. He has never been on a ship, never been out of sight of land before."

"Well, having lived on the water for practically all of your lives and being surrounded by it, I'm sure he'll get used to it soon enough. He knows the Widow Bradt who is going over to join her son. They can *amuse* each other." Gilles winked at Elsje.

He stayed cheerful for Elsje's sake and refused to allow doubts any quarter at all in his mind but *still* he had that feeling...

Gilles hoped that he wasn't just transporting them all to a worse fate. He resolved that he would increase his chances of success by recruiting more men for his Patroonship once he reached New Amsterdam, men who understood more clearly the opportunity that he offered them, able-bodied men who would ensure the Patroonship's success. It was up to a man to make what he would of himself, wasn't he proof of that?

Anything that had been left behind or left undone could either be sent to them later by Vroutje, or disregarded, as it probably was no longer of any consequence. Vroutje's family would do well enough on the two incomes, Vroutje's husband Klaas' and Jennetje's.

"You are very quiet," Elsje observed, with a sharp look at Gilles.

"I can't help but get the feeling that I have forgotten something," Gilles confessed to her. "There has been so much going on with the packing and Jacomina's baptism and the Patroon papers that I just have the feeling that I am missing something."

He touched the stiff packet of papers again. Yes, they were safely in his breast pocket, along with his wedding and family baptismal certificates. Elsje's family bible and a few books had been packed up in the first trunk.

"I *always* have that feeling when we are doing something out of the ordinary, something other than what our usual days were but it has been so long now since we had a regular day and a settled life that I'm surprised you aren't well *over* it! It's just all of the changes that we have been through lately and that's all it is," Elsje told Gilles with a reassuring pat on his arm. "We don't *need* anything besides what we have here: our family, a few things to wear, a shelter when we get there, and food to eat. I'm glad you told me what Jean advised us to pack for food and drink for our trip. We will have apples, dried fruit, and some wine for you, for a few weeks anyway. I have those right here, so don't worry, I didn't forget."

"They *will* feed us on the ship but don't expect a lot from the food," Gilles told her. "It will be mostly salted and dried fish, with some beans if the water and the cook's fire hold out."

"Well, what else is important besides family and our basic necessities? We have your new aigrette of course; you and your *hats*! We have Father's pipe, Bruinje's blanket that he can't go to sleep without, Jacomina's baptismal record, Heintje's knife and Corretje's gold locket. If it's something like a farming tool that you wanted to bring with you, it is no matter of great importance," Elsje reassured him, "*surely* they have smiths over there that can make you one."

Gilles had a smile for his wife's generosity. "You didn't say what is important to *you*."

"My family is my most prized possession, of course! My family, and my string of pearls that you gave me just before our marriage."

Gilles couldn't believe that he forgot the *one* thing that Elsje wanted to bring with her; no doubt he would hear about this misstep of his, probably nonstop, for the next three months.

It was not his fault!

The pearls had been on a very *long* list of items to get at the Dam in a very *short* period of time yesterday while Gilles was trying to complete final preparations for the trip. Somehow picking them up at the jeweler's had gotten lost among his many errands as he said his goodbyes in the street to old acquaintances and juggled item priority to complete his list using the most efficient route possible for gathering in all of the extra items that Elsje had thought up for him to get at the *last* minute, in addition to all of the items that *he* had suddenly remembered as he piled up his purchases, barely able to lug them all home in one trip, even after hiring a boy with a cart.

"You *did* get my pearls?" Elsje asked sharply, searching his face for his reply and tapping her foot *ever* so slightly, the way she always did when she was waiting longer than she cared to for his response, the *only* response that she wanted to hear.

"I...I...there was so much to take care of yesterday," he stammered.

Elsje said nothing but her face was a thundercloud, a breaking storm just barely held in check for the moment.

"We can write to Cousin Vroutje and she can send them over with someone in the spring. You will have them by next summer, *I promise*," Gilles offered.

This was a perfectly reasonable plan as she probably wouldn't be able to wear them much over there anyway, not in a frontier cabin in the winter time, or on board the ship going over, but Elsje's right

eye had a twitch in it, and that eye appeared to be falling upon Gilles'
brand new hat with the jaunty white plume. He didn't have to guess
about what she might be thinking.

"All right, Elsje, they probably won't pull up anchor for some time
yet. I will just go back over to the jewel smith's and get them right now
for you. Will that make you happy?"

"You'll miss the boat!" she shouted, still glaring at him.

"I *won't* miss the boat. It will take me thirty minutes at the most,
even with full ferry boats. We still have *at least* an hour before we sail.
Look, the tide isn't even *near* the high water mark on the big rock."

"Well, just make sure that you *don't* miss the boat then," she
admonished him, "Or we will go without you!" She did look just a
little bit happier, though.

Gilles checked with the captain first, of course.

"You have enough time," the captain told him, confirming that
they probably wouldn't leave for another hour. "I ring the ship's bell
three times, wait about another ten or fifteen minutes and then sound
another six rings for the last call to board, to signal that we are pulling
out. You should be able to get back well within that amount of time."
He pulled the lanyard on the ship's bell once to show Gilles the tone,
what the ship's bell sounded like, and the entire crew stopped in unison,
in mid-motion of whatever it was that they were doing, from below the
deck, from the main deck, and from up on the mast and rigging, they
all looked and listened to see what the communication was that the
captain had for them. The captain held up his hand and waved it to
convey that he was only demonstrating the sound for someone, and
that they should all go back to their work.

"It *is* a good distance from the shore and there are other sounds and
other bells, but if you are listening for it, it can be heard quite plainly
on the shore. When I hear it, I can't *possibly* mistake it for any another

ship's bell," the captain assured Gilles. "It has a tone that is just a *little* different from the others, perhaps because it is an English bell made with inferior metals, liberated by us from one of her freighters."

Gilles was not convinced or reassured by this assertion but he had little choice at this juncture but to go forward. He nodded at the captain, kissed Elsje quickly on the cheek, promised he would hurry back with the pearls, would *not* miss the boat, and then hailed one of the small passing launch boats in the harbor. Gilles clambered down the ladder and seated himself quickly.

"Were you just out saying goodbye to your family?" the man at the oars asked him.

"Nee, I *forgot* something and I need to *hurry back* so I don't *miss* my boat," Gilles said as he handed the man double the fare to ensure his speedy return to the shore.

The astute ferryman took the hint, and the boat, being nearly full by now anyway, made straight for the docks. The ferryman even told the other passengers to sit where they were until Gilles climbed over them and got out first. Gilles still had plenty of time but even so, he walked briskly to the jewelers, barely noting the execution of a murderer that was currently underway in the Dam as he strode through, wondering idly who it was, if he knew them or not. He lost no time in his thoughts though, and continued without stopping to retrieve Elsje's pearls.

Gilles waited impatiently for them although he remembered to voice his admiration for the quality of the work as the craftsman took his time, pointing out first the superiority of the workmanship, the replaced gold on the clasp, the fine color of the white horse hair used to string them, and *finally* the overall excellent quality of the pearls, worthy of even Kiliaen Van Rensselaer's wares, the knowledge and the skill that set this one jewel smith apart from all of the other artisans in Amsterdam.

"Yes, yes, I can see that," Gilles said as he closed them up in the case, stuck the case in his pocket, shook hands with the man quickly, gave him the money and then hurried back outside to return to the ship.

He didn't *need* to be so impatient, so impolite, Gilles told himself. He had been gone no more than twenty minutes at the most and he still had plenty of time to make it back, but Elsje was surely going to grouse *anyway* about how long it took him and how distressed she had been all the while she had been waiting for his return. She would probably grumble all the way to the Pas de Calais if he didn't hurry back just as soon as he possibly could, but then again, she might grumble anyway, no matter how much or how little time it took him. Gilles told himself that he should probably just resign himself to hearing about it for the next few days or even weeks.

He was preoccupied with these thoughts and only vaguely aware of the steps behind him before he felt the knife at his back.

"Slow down, Montroville. You walk too fast. You wouldn't want to trip and injure yourself."

The French voice was somehow familiar to Gilles but he could not immediately place it. Gilles did not reply, putting all of his energy into using his ears as a substitute for his eyes. He did not dare to turn around and look, because he was fairly sure that it *was* a knife and not any other piece of metal at his back and while he keenly felt the point of the blade, he also felt a softer pressure, the tug of a hand gripping his coat as well.

"A slip of my hand *just here* and you will probably *not* live to see tomorrow. For myself, I don't really care if this is how it ends or not. I will *still* get the reward for bringing in your hide, providing of course that they can still identify your pretty face, so be assured, I will be *most* careful not to damage that. We will take a little stroll along the Dam here and keep right on going until we get to the Town Hall where I can properly register my prize with the authorities and collect my reward."

Gilles looked ahead and wondered what he would do now. Could he jerk away from the man's clutches and outrun him? Was the man behind him a faster runner? Would the commotion lead to his capture and a result that he *didn't* want, Gilles' being handed over to the French authorities anyway? What would happen when they finally reached the Town Hall?

Surely his friends, neighbors, and associates who knew him as Gilles Jansen would be doubtful at first, but then disappointed to learn the truth about his past. The documents he had signed during the past week had the name "Montroville" all over them and would surely lead to his deportation. The authorities *might* be sympathetic enough to postpone or delay the eventual outcome, but in the end they would probably have no choice but to cooperate with the French unless they wanted to drag the Spanish occupying army into it too and eventually bring a great deal of trouble down upon themselves. No, it just wouldn't be worth their while to protect a French fugitive and put the citizens of Amsterdam, not to mention their own high positions, at risk.

Perhaps they would not be *so* surprised, though, to learn about his past. Gilles could just say goodbye right now to the job in New Netherlands, goodbye to the Patroonship, goodbye to his family, and goodbye to his life in the most literal sense. He would probably not be able to escape the flames in France a *second* time unless he made the decision to die now by the knife. He was not yet twenty five years old and he really didn't want to die, not just yet: There were too many things that he still wanted to do.

Gilles made a fast and firm decision: He was not going to go to the Town Hall, not willingly. As he thought about his situation a little bit more, in rapid-fire motion because there was little enough distance left for him to come up with a plan of action, he became angry. Like some stupid animal or a compliant child, he had *willingly* let them lead him right up to the slaughterhouse gate in France the last time. He no longer was that person, that child, and never again would he be a willing party, an accomplice to his own murder, no matter by *whose* authority judgment had been passed, whether it was the King, The Church, or even God Almighty himself. Gilles decided that he would be the master of his own fate until the very end, until his life was over and completely extinguished.

These angry thoughts gave him a new strength and assurance, a new determination, and he made a pact with himself, deciding that he would rather die here and now if he had to, rather than to die there and later. If he died here, perhaps his grave would be next to Elsje's mother's, in the old church yard. The family would receive the news of his death, get off the ship before it sailed, and manage somehow to live the rest of their lives out in Amsterdam with cousin Vroutje, although Gilles was sorry that he would be letting them down, his family *and* the farm girl and the porter, too.

Gilles forced himself to be calm; he couldn't make a scene in the street or make an attempt at freedom in the open or a crowd would gather, attracting the authorities. Why had no one yet noticed Gilles walking along with a knife-wielding stranger at his back? Were people *so* busy and wrapped up in their own lives or was the weapon somehow concealed? It didn't *feel* concealed.

Gilles espied the carpenter's and the cooper's shops up ahead, standing side by side next to each other, the places where he had purchased the barrels and chests for their journey. Now it seemed like *such* a long time ago, ordering those chests for the trip that would not happen now, a chest full of items that belonged to Gilles, items that

Gilles would no longer have any need of in this lifetime except for the clothes that he might be buried in.

Gilles did know that there was a long, narrow alley between the shops where the two businesses stored the wood and iron, the raw materials for making their chests and barrels, and some extra finished products, the inventory of containers that had not been special ordered, were available for purchase on the spur of the moment for less-than-particular customers, or those that had been ordered and constructed but for whatever reason, had never been picked up.

Gilles realized why Jean Durie suddenly came to mind now: His friend had been his strength, not because he was so clever or so determined, although he was both of those things too, but no matter what the situation, Jean had *never* given up, not even in the hopelessness of the dark and stinking prison in Rouen. He had remained calm enough and focused enough, taking enough time to consider *every* possible option that was still open to him, every opportunity, every chance that there *might* be, and had, as a result, found a few options that might well have succeeded on their own, had they been in prison any longer and if Gilles' father had not succeeded in his attempt to free them first.

The magic was not in Jean's physical attributes, it was all in how Jean *looked* at things. Nothing was ever an obstacle to him; new situations and circumstances were just curious and interesting puzzles, challenges and opportunities, each one with its own advantages and disadvantages, a buffet of life's choices uncontaminated by the distraction of fear or the perception of threat. The jailers had tried to frighten and then beat the optimism out of him prior to Jean's going before the magistrate in France but he had refused to relinquish it, holding fast to the only weapon that he would *not* surrender and it had served him very well.

In the end it had been the *only* weapon he needed and infinitely more valuable than a sword; somehow, Jean must have known this.

What had Jean said to Gilles just before he left and often in the past?

"If things can get worse, they can also get better."

If an alley could cause Gilles trouble, then perhaps it might also help him out of a bad situation. Gilles surmised that there were probably no thieves or criminals lurking there today: It was a short alley, no more than two coach lengths long and just as wide. There was no outlet, either, except through the two shops. The kuyper and his helpers made too many trips into the alley, making them all too frequently and everyone who had been here would know this; Gilles might keep his abductor at bay until the cooper or his apprentices walked onto the scene and then Gilles would simply explain that it was a robbery attempt by a madman. Gilles would then have to convince the shopkeeper and his helpers to hold the man there while he went to notify the authorities, which of course he was not going to do; Gilles would just keep on going and board the ship that would then sail out into the safety of the Atlantic.

His first thought was that LaRue had come back but no one in this city, including LaRue, knew Gilles by the name of Montroville, no one except his Dutch family on board Den Eyckenboom, only them and the man, whoever he was, that followed so closely at his heels with the knife at Gilles' back. It was simply a case of mistaken identity, Gilles would tell the cooper and his apprentices before he ran for freedom, hoping that the ship's crew could let out the sails quickly and the prevailing winds would take them out of the harbor before the men in the alley grew tired of waiting for Gilles' return, before the officials could discover the truth.

Gilles walked slowly and calmly, waiting until he was right next to the alley before he wrenched his coat out of the man's clutches and veered in, breaking into a run and going directly to where he recalled seeing a pile of oak barrel staves, and not being fatally disappointed, Gilles snatched one up from the pile as he whirled around to face his abductor and fend off the man and his knife.

Gilles' only thoughts so far were that he had gambled and won, at least up to this point, outdistancing the man, gaining freedom from his clutches and also gaining a weapon of defense, inadequate though it might prove to be in the coming minutes, but he didn't know that yet with any certainty. It would have to serve as his wooden rapier, even though it would not cut or inflict great harm, but it might defend him adequately enough to gain the desired result. There was no one else in the alley with them just now, neither friend nor foe. Gilles stayed well away from the knife with his wooden response at the ready, and having gained some space at last, he was finally able to move his eyes briefly up to the face of the man who had abducted him, the face of Captain LeBlanc.

He had been the trusted captain of one of his father's ships, a man that Gilles had held in *such* high esteem, had so revered, that once Gilles had even wished desperately that LeBlanc had been his own father instead of the man who had sired him.

Le Blanc's appearance had changed greatly and the captain had obviously been through at least one ordeal since Gilles had set eyes on him last: His visage was more browned, more lined, with a trail of open sores across it, but the most surprising new feature was a bright red scar running in a long line from the man's forehead, underneath a dark eye patch and across the bridge of his nose to a portion of the man's cheek. A chunk of flesh was missing from his formerly square chin too.

"Oui, it's *me*, Boy! I'll bet you a *year's* wages that you never thought you'd see *me* again! For some time I thought that I would never see *you* again, either, but a little bird, or should I say, a little *priest*, whispered his own dying confession into my ear, that you were still alive! Now your family can greatly increase my fortunes when I collect the reward money the King offers for your return. Your father never would pay me more than a *pittance* for all of my hard, back-breaking work for him over these many long years, even with *all* of his money, but it doesn't matter now. I have the prize that I have sought for so long, my ticket to better fortune!"

Gilles didn't know what to say to this. Briefly it crossed his mind to wonder if his best friend in France, Claude, could be dead, if *he* could have been the priest who had betrayed Gilles. Whoever he was, Claude, the Amsterdam blacksmith or another one, Gilles sincerely doubted that the unnamed clergyman's death had been entirely of natural causes, considering the open malevolence on the face of the twisted creature who stood before him now.

Gilles had no time to think any more about that because he had other more immediate concerns, including his own survival, and he wondered, too, if there was much time left before his ship sailed without him. He couldn't stand here *talking* all day and he thought about making the first move, attacking LeBlanc first. The knife that LeBlanc held was very long and very thin, almost a miniature epee. It was not as long as the barrel stave in Gilles' hand, but it *was* a great deal sharper and Gilles had no doubt that LeBlanc was an experienced fighter who knew how to use it. What did Gilles know about hand to hand combat?

The answer was nothing, nothing at all, except for some gentleman's lessons that he had as a boy but he had never actually fought a man before and this fight would be to the death, he had no doubts about that.

Gilles might just be able to defend himself, holding LeBlanc at a distance but then that would mean facing inquiries by the authorities into the reason for the fight. No matter what the outcome, there was still more than a good chance that he would miss the boat.

Where was the damned kuyper? Where were his apprentices? They were Gilles' best hope. Was it midday dinner time and were they *all* away from the shop for an hour?

When they came out, *if* they came out in time, Gilles would have to tell them, as calmly and persuasively as he could, that this Frenchman was a madman. The only difficulty with adopting this strategy was that Gilles was a terrible liar and the truth was generally evident on his face whenever he made any attempt to prevaricate. If he had much more practice, as his brother Charles had, Gilles was sure that he could get *better* at it, but this was not the best time to try and develop new skills.

It *was* possible that LeBlanc didn't know enough Nederlands to communicate intelligibly with them and perhaps Gilles could find a way to walk away and just leave on the ship while they attempted to sort out what LeBlanc was trying to say to them.

LeBlanc smiled at Gilles now, in a chilling way.

"Now *wouldn't* you like to see France and your dear Papa and Mama just once more before you die? It makes no difference to me if I turn over a live person or a dead body to the King. I'm no expert on anatomy as the Dutch physicians here are, but I have seen many men die and I do know *a little* something about wounds, that some are usually deadly, and others are not always. Ah, but you are wondering *how* I found you! The priest told me that you had come to Amsterdam, and I learned from a man who lived on the streets here that you were *still* around. Sadly, he died before he could tell me *exactly* where you could be found. Greedy Botte! He *wouldn't* tell me where you were, not before I gave him more money. Maybe his greed was what did him in.

Maybe *you* killed him. The authorities could look into that as well and add that to your list of crimes. I don't think so though: You do not have it in you to kill *anyone*, I can see that in your eyes. Put the little stick down, Boy, and come along with me. You must face up to your fate and take your punishment now like a man."

Gilles didn't believe him when LeBlanc claimed not to know who killed Msr. Botte: Gilles believed now that Captain LeBlanc had killed Botte, a Gentleman who had lived an easy life of abundance in France but ended his life as a homeless vagrant in Amsterdam. He had recognized Gilles one night outside Ste Germaine's establishment and the next morning Botte had been found dead, beaten to death with his own gold-headed cane. Gilles' money, an attempt at charity and not bribery, was still clenched in his cold fist when they found his body.

Gilles was adamantine in his resolve to survive and he gripped his wooden weapon harder. Still he said nothing to LeBlanc but the captain was in a talkative mood and Gilles wondered if the man had been drinking. That could be helpful too, if the man was even the *smallest* bit inebriated.

"Ah, but now you are worried about your *wife*! Which one of Hendrick's daughters was it that you married? I never *could* get them straight. But knowing the Montrovilles, it would be the *oldest* daughter, wouldn't it? It would be the oldest, so that you could inherit anything that there is to get from Old Hendrick. I heard about the fire at the inn and that is *just* too bad. There isn't anything left to inherit here now so that is surely why you were just about to take the ship out to the New Amsterdam colony. It's just a shame that you will not be on it, Montroville.

I came back here to have another look around some weeks ago when I was finally certain enough of your whereabouts to bring the authorities over to Hendrick's tavern but you had escaped me again,

Petit Renard! I thought I might have lost you once more but it's a good thing that I came back one more time to this miserable city. What a stroke of luck! You have come *right* into my hands again here in the French Quarter, an answer to my prayers. Now you can see for yourself that God is on *my* side.

Oh, and you needn't trouble yourself about your wife's fate: I travel quite widely now across the open world and I promise you this: I will visit her *faithfully* in New Amsterdam where I will inform her that I am an old and dear friend of yours and will make frequent contributions to her upkeep. I'll see to it that her derriere is kept quite warm in the winter. I'm sure that I will have a great deal of assistance in that, when I'm not around to see to it personally. There is a great need there for the services of a white woman on the shipping lanes' ports of call and being as young and attractive as she is, there will be plenty of demand for her. She will be able to make quite enough money to keep on feeding that small brood of yours."

Gilles was very angry now. He gripped the wood harder, trying to control his emotions. It looked as though there would be no help for him in this fight and he would have to take care of LeBlanc himself, would have to *succeed*, and so he calmed himself and started to form his plan.

A quick blow to the hand that held the knife, moving quickly to LeBlanc's blind side and a well-aimed punch or two landed before LeBlanc could recover. Gilles would have to finish him off, though, before anyone heard the noise and came onto the scene; he would have to *kill* LeBlanc and kill him quickly if he wanted to live.

So intent was Gilles on these thoughts and in forming his plan of action that he almost didn't see the form moving just beyond LeBlanc, behind a tower of very large barrels stacked there. The movement was not the flickering shadow of people passing by the entrance to the alley:

It was too close for that. There was *someone* there who was listening to their conversation but for whatever reason, he was not making his presence known, not to Gilles or to LeBlanc. Gilles had no way of knowing if it was the kuyper, his apprentices, or someone else, friend, foe, or curiosity seeker. LeBlanc gave no sign that he had noticed this movement behind him.

"Not talking, eh Montroville? Well, you don't *have* to say another word! Mute or not, your face is your conviction. All you have to do is relax and be yourself. It's time for us to go now. Don't make me kill you first: I'd have to haul your heavy carcass all that way across the square and I *hate* dragging heavy loads. It bothers my poor old back these days and you would just be *dead* weight." LeBlanc grinned at him.

Far in the distance a sound carried over the water and reached Gilles' ears, breaking into his concentration briefly. It was the sound of three bells. Gilles was *certain* that it was the sound of the bell that the captain had rung for him, sure that it was *his* ship that was making ready to leave. He readied and steadied himself: There was no more time for talk or thought. Gilles would have to make his stand now and die here in this alley or live long enough to make the ship, hopefully without wounds that would prove fatal to him before he reached New Amsterdam's harbor across the sea. Even if he was badly wounded in his attempt at freedom, Gilles couldn't take the chance of staying behind in Amsterdam to seek medical attention: It might take just enough time for the local authorities to discover his secret, his previous identity.

"Don't be so *foolish*, Montroville! I have won many, many fights with this very weapon and with much greater opponents, all of whom were better armed and better fighters than *you*. In point of fact, I have won *all* of my battles or I would not be standing here today. I would wager that you, Boy, have never even *seen* a real fight in your sheltered little life. I'll wager five guilders. What will you wager against me? I'll even let *you* tell *me* if you have seen one or not, and knowing that you *are* a Gentleman, I will take your word on it as to who wins the bet. I could always tell when you were lying to me, you know. You never *were* any good at hiding the truth. You never had very much luck either, so it's probably best for you if you stay away from games of chance altogether, especially since you have such a short time left on this earth. It doesn't matter who wins *this* bet though; I will have more than enough money from the reward I will get for turning you in, so I can spare it. Your parents could put your winnings on the bet toward your burial or leave it for your wife. Or do they even know about your alliance with a *tavern girl?*"

LeBlanc took a step toward Gilles, still controlling the passing time.

A long time ago, Gilles had thought LeBlanc a fearsomely strong man, a formidable man, when he had first sailed with him into Amsterdam, but as menacing as the man was now, Gilles also thought that now he looked old and tired, especially with his missing eye. Gilles vaguely recalled overhearing the artists in Amsterdam talking among themselves about losing an eye.

What had they said?

Something about their art and this thing they called *perspective*, saying that it was better to lose a leg, that those without *two* good eyes were unable to paint, unable to accurately judge distances very well. The captain's old body was still wiry and strong but Gilles had changed, too, in the years since he had last seen LeBlanc, especially after working long days in the fields of the Palatinate. Gilles had accumulated a sizable mass of muscle and he was no longer a tall, thin, gangling boy facing an athletic adult, but a large man himself, at least by French standards. If he could overcome the fear that he had of his adversary, rationally and objectively Gilles *knew* that he stood more than a good chance of victory, just as long as he was not defeated by his lack of experience and skill in fighting. Gilles gripped the wooden stave, readying himself.

He still could not make out who it was who lurked behind LeBlanc but perhaps it didn't matter: Gilles could wait no longer: The ship would sail without him and his future would be lost so he resolved to fight *now*, taking his chances that he would win and also taking the chance that the intruder was a friendly presence, or at least neutral, and not a foe that would help LeBlanc since the hidden spectator had not made any move so far to show himself or to reveal his identity.

LeBlanc advanced slowly, moving the epee around in a circular motion. "Ah, Montroville! I *knew* that you were spying on me when we used to sail together, telling your dear *Papa* all kinds of terrible stories about me, but this works out very nicely, a reward for my patience and the misery that you put me through by dogging my every move, you and Jean Durie. It's unfortunate that he will not be here to share your fate this time but I imagine I will catch up with him soon enough, over in New Amsterdam."

Gilles spoke for the first time, thinking to bring the other person out from behind the barrels, especially if it was the cooper, frightened and in hiding there. Gilles wasn't sure how long the resolution of his current predicament would take or how this vignette would play out until *one* of them made the first move, starting them both toward an irrevocable outcome.

"If it's money that you need, I can get you some, enough to help you buy back your ship," Gilles offered, hopeful, and trying one last time to talk his way out of a physical fight.

"Ah, the ship. You *know* that I lost my ship in a rigged card game? Your father bought the ship from the miserable buccaneer who stole it from me but then your *papa* made me work for next to *nothing* for him while I tried to save up enough to redeem it or buy myself another one

It would have taken me a *lifetime* with the trifling pittance that bastard paid me. Why should I wait any longer? It's easier to just take what you want when you are out at sea and it's easier to take my *just* rewards; it is simply what I deserve for having found and captured you."

"It doesn't look so easy," Gilles observed, looking at LeBlanc's missing eye, "To just *take* things."

"It's easier than working for your father for the next fifty years!" the older man growled.

"I can get you the money, just let me go now."

Gilles thought of the pearls in his pocket. If he gave them up, he would have to make up some story to tell Elsje about what had happened to them. He wouldn't want to worry her with the truth and he would rather take her berating him for years to come than to cause her any more worry, about someone tracking him, tracking all of them, across the ocean and on into the future. They would never be free of fear if that happened. But what assurance did Gilles have that giving up his pearls would make LeBlanc leave them alone? They might come face to face again in the future, somewhere across a wide ocean.

"You know, Gilles," LeBlanc started in a conversational tone, still approaching him with the weapon pointed at his quarry, "for a long time I thought it was about the money, too, but then when I heard that you were still alive, still living and living *very well* here in Amsterdam, something in me changed. It was like I was *alive* again. I contacted your father and delivered my news to him. He *has* been paying me a little bit better for my silence than he did for my superior sailing skills, but it's *just* not enough for me anymore. Arrogant *little shit* that you are! I just want to see you *dead* and your father suffer as I have suffered and *only then* will I be happy. Ah, what the hell! I'll just kill you now and be done with it. It doesn't matter any more. We have wasted enough time here."

With less than ten feet between them and the distance closing, Gilles knew that he had to take his chances now and before LeBlanc was within striking distance, but at this moment the shadow, the third person in the alley stepped forward from behind the wall of stacked barrels. Gilles was astonished to see that it was not the kuyper at all; it was Claes Van Zeelandt. LeBlanc saw the movement from the corner of his good eye and stepped quickly to the side of the alley, the brick wall at his back with his weapon raised and prepared for battle, against both Gilles and Claes if necessary, both men in the line of sight of his good eye.

"Claes!" LeBlanc greeted him with such enthusiasm and insouciance that Gilles' heart immediately sank. "Well, well, well, it *is* good to see my old partner once again!"

Gilles had never trusted Claes, although it had turned out that Claes was the nephew of Jacob, Gilles' employer at the time. It seemed now that Gilles' suspicions were justified and the nightmare had come full circle: The attempt on Gilles' life had not succeeded a few years earlier but now they were both here in *this* alley to finish him off.

"You there, Claes! Help me to subdue this insolent boy!"

LeBlanc called out to Claes in Nederlands that was so poorly constructed and with such a bad accent, that it was difficult to understand what the Frenchman was trying to say.

"Is it true that there is a *reward* for him? You didn't *tell* me that there was a *reward!*" Claes objected.

"You listen? Ja, he is a reward but I keep it!"

"I could watch him while you go get the authorities, but then you will have to give *me* a share of the reward," Claes offered.

LeBlanc understood this and he laughed. He abandoned his attempts at the Dutch language for a short time and spoke only French, perhaps for Gilles' benefit, but he addressed Claes in a mordant way that an imbecile could understand, even if Claes could not speak a word of LeBlanc's native language.

"Nederlander salaud! You think I give you my reward? You think I let him out of my sight until I get the reward in my hands? I piss in my breeches *first* before I lose sight of him!" Then in Nederlands LeBlanc said, "*You* go get help and we talk *later* about rewards, *maybe!*"

"I don't know who is looking for him. Where should I go? Who should I tell?" Claes asked, either ignoring the insult, or more probably, not understanding what the words meant.

"Stupid pig farmer! Let me explain it to you: Ecoute! This man is *wanted* in France. You simply go to the authorities, to the Town Hall, and find out how we go about extraditing wanted French fugitives. You have *some* experience with this, n'est-ce pas? Ah, just look at him, will you Claes? Gilles here looks *just like* a Netherlander and he even *speaks* like one, too. It's no surprise that he passed as one of you for so long. He probably told everyone that he was from Leiden or Walcherin and they probably took him for a *born* Netherlander. *Look at him!*"

At LeBlanc's insistence, Claes looked Gilles up and down, then he simply shrugged in response. Perhaps he was not comprehending very much of this. Perhaps he just didn't care.

LeBlanc continued on with his rambling speech, making just enough sense for Gilles to understand him. Gilles was convinced now that the captain was either drunk or feverish and the years of hatred that had been pent up and simmering over the years bubbled over, spilling out and finding release, LeBlanc neither stopping to observe nor caring whether Gilles or Claes was interested in the least in what he had to say. It was all about *his* sufferings.

"There are so many, many things, but I really do think that what I despise *the most* about this little turd and his entire family is their *pretense*. He *pretends* to know about ships and the sea, he and his father, but they know *nothing,* except how to count their money, each single little piece of gold and silver! His father *pretends* to be a good and kindly man bestowing his favors and helping others but he cares nothing for anyone except himself! He exploits the weakness of others to make *slaves* of them for his own benefit. They all pretend to be so cultured and so superior to us all in *every* way, ah but they have their dirty little secrets! *This* secret has already made me some money and it is about to make me *even more.* If hard work won't make you rich, then finding a man's secrets will, and every man has at least one that he will pay *dearly* to hide, each according to the maximum of his means, and then maybe even a little bit *more* if it is important enough to keep it hidden away. Did you know his friend, Jean Durie? Ah, my dear Claes, that one has a *boatload* of secrets and a boatload of money just waiting to be plucked from his greasy little hands. When I finish with young Gilles here, I'll be on my way to track him down across the ocean. Maybe I'll even take Gilles' place on the ship that he meant to sail out on and keep his dear wife company, consoling her all along the way. If Durie won't pay me, but I am quite sure that he *will,* then I will tell *everyone* over there what he is, *the Jew,* and that will be the end of him and of his fortune! The rest of the world thinks *very* differently about his kind: The Dutch here in Amsterdam are stupid and lazy when it comes to lancing out that kind of creeping infection in their midst. *Sheep* they are! But enough talk! You! Claes! Go and get the authorities since young Gilles here isn't cooperating with me."

When Claes continued to stand where he was for a few more moments with an empty expression on his face, LeBlanc addressed Gilles. "Ah, the stupid boy doesn't understand me! I will probably just have to kill you right now."

Gilles assumed that Claes did not understand most of what LeBlanc said, although the reprieve proved to be short-lived as Claes slowly moved off toward the street. It seemed that Claes was going to comply with LeBlanc's directive and now Gilles would have to take on the captain and do so just as soon as Claes was gone from sight.

From near the mouth of the alley there came a deep rumbling sound as two tall towers of heavy oak barrels, each container three feet high and weighing nearly as much as a yearling pig, toppled over onto LeBlanc from the direction in which Claes had just taken his leave, coming down with a thundering crash on top of the captain and sending Gilles leaping to the safety of the innermost reaches of the alley.

The kuyper and his apprentices now came out at a run, into the alley through the door from their shop and Gilles recovered his composure quickly enough to remember his plan, to tell them that there had been a robbery attempt. It would be Gilles' word against Claes' and a drunken French pirate's, and if Claes didn't stand in Gilles' way or put up too much of a fight, Gilles *might* convince them to let him go. The kuyper had known, of course, that Gilles planned to leave Amsterdam and if the WIC people were brought into it, they would know that Elsje was already on board the ship in the harbor, waiting for her husband.

The cooper was shocked and upset that someone had been injured by his stack of barrels, and after the disarray and broken barrels were quickly cleared away, LeBlanc lay still, his hand still wrapped tightly around his long knife. The side of his face that was showing was scraped and looked oddly compressed and elongated. His neck appeared to be at an unnatural angle too, and a small but steadily increasing trickle of blood came out from under his head, spreading across and through the brown dust of the alley.

"Was he trying to rob you?" the kuyper asked.

"Ja," Claes answered before Gilles had the chance to speak.

"Weren't you just in here last week buying barrels from me?" the kuyper asked Gilles.

"Ja, my wife waits for me on the ship and it's about to sail *without* me," he replied.

"Go ahead then, I'll tell the authorities what happened," Claes told Gilles.

For the moment Gilles wasn't sure what was happening. Perhaps he had lost an old blackmailer and had gained a new one, or perhaps Claes had saved Gilles in repayment for Gilles' help in getting Claes some new business contacts and a new life. Gilles had no time to think about that now: His more immediate worry was to make for the ship before it sailed. He had not heard the second set of bells yet but he was getting concerned about the amount of time that had elapsed; with all of the excitement that had just passed, Gilles had no idea how long he might have been in the alleyway. The barrel makers were all talking excitedly, arguing with each other about the incident, whether one of them was to blame for stacking the barrels in an unsafe way, and whether they had seen this man lurking around here before. Gilles made his way from the depths of the alley, around the arguing coopers and the body, out toward the freedom of the street.

As he passed by Claes there was no acknowledgement from him and a look of stunned surprise on the other man's face told Gilles that the outcome was *not* what he had expected. While the craftsmen talked loudly about the incident among themselves, Gilles saw Claes surreptitiously give the captain's lifeless body a hard and swift kick in the ribs and he also saw a quick flash of unmistakable anger cross Claes' features before it was gone. Perhaps Claes had understood all of what LeBlanc said, or at least enough of it.

Maybe there was more to it: Maybe Gilles' father had not been LeBlanc's only blackmail victim or perhaps Claes had a sense of justice that coincided with Gilles' own. Did Le Blanc know, as Gilles did, that Claes' family had Jewish origins? Claes looked up at Gilles who had not as yet left the alley.

"Go! Hurry! I will tell them," Claes urged Gilles. "You'll miss the ship!"

Not knowing what else to do, Gilles offered Claes his hand. "Thank you, Claes. Maybe we'll meet again in New Amsterdam."

"I think not; I've decided to return to Zeelandt for now," Claes said, accepting the handshake and returning it. "God go with you."

"And with you. Good luck to you, Van Rosenvelt."

"And to you, Jansen."

Gilles pushed his way out of the gathering crowd, leaving the body, Claes, the kuyper and his apprentices all in the alley as he made haste back toward the harbor, all the while hoping that he would make it to the ship in time and that LeBlanc was really dead or at least too badly injured to talk to anyone until Gilles was very far away.

At the same time though, Gilles hoped that the vile and evil man was not really as badly hurt as he appeared to be: Gilles didn't want the responsibility of being involved in the commission of a mortal sin, even if the man's death was not at his own hands. He had wished the man dead and perhaps that was enough to merit condemnation and eternal damnation from the Almighty.

As quickly as Gilles needed to get back to Elsje, he was still fearful of attracting the attention of the authorities and so he was careful not to break into a run until he rounded the corner, well away from the incident. He strained his ears to hear the bells, and he thought he heard them just then, six bells pealing from across the water, at the same pitch that he heard when the captain had demonstrated the sound of the bell. Gilles pleaded with the ferryman to take him out to the boat right away, as fast as he could row, and the last bells *did* sound just as

Gilles came into sight of the Eyckenboom's crew, proving that his ears had played tricks on him just moments before.

"Wait!" Gilles shouted frantically to the sailors who waved an acknowledgement of their hearing his plea. Gilles grabbed the ladder just as the crew started pulling the anchor up and two sailors on the deck glared down at him.

"They have *days and days* to get here and at least *one* of them is *always* late," one sailor muttered to another, loud enough for Gilles to hear the remark.

Elsje, waiting for him down below in the hold with Aafje Van Der Cloot, Garrett Van Amsterdam and the rest of the family, was greatly agitated and angry with Gilles, as was her father, but she was also greatly relieved.

"The devil delayed me," Gilles said. "The jeweler couldn't find the necklace," he lied.

The explanation was *half* true. The devil had *indeed* held him up, but today Gilles had won the round.

Now he began to wonder if the necklace could be cursed. It certainly seemed to have brought him no *end* of trouble ever since he bought the damned thing. Every time he touched it, bad things happened.

Just after he had purchased the pearls in France, he had lost his fiancée and was taken away to be executed for treason. When he brought them with him to the Palatinate, they were attacked by French soldiers, and when he went to retrieve them from the jewelers in Amsterdam, he met up with Captain LeBlanc. So it was with some trepidation that he watched as Elsje immediately pulled the pearls out of the box and put them around her neck, asking Gilles to fasten them for her.

It was all quite ridiculous: Ridiculous for her to *wear* the jewels down in the dank and dark hold for several months and ridiculous for Gilles to think that mere things like a string of pearls could bring a person bad luck. It was *medieval*; it was backwards superstition that only the ignorant would believe. *Of course* they would all be fine on this voyage, now that Gilles was on board the ship, regardless of whether Elsje was wearing the pearls.

"Bruinje has been busy *talking* with everyone on board," Elsje informed Gilles, losing a little of the edge in her voice. "In Nederlands, in German, and I think while you were gone, he was learning English from those people over there." Elsje pointed to a few Puritans in ugly brown garb who must have been separated from their group and now traveled with the Dutch to join up later with their own kind in the English colony at Plymouth.

"*Talking?* Has our son suddenly made the decision to speak?" Gilles was incredulous.

He saw the joy and excitement in Elsje's face and he felt it breaking out on his own, too. Their son was not a mute or an idiot after all, and perhaps now Bruinje would begin to talk as other children did. Jacomina suddenly reached up and grasped a handful of Elsje's hair with a grip so strong that Elsje was obliged to reach up and try to free it from the infant's sticky hand.

While his wife struggled to free her tresses from their daughter's chubby grip, Gilles looked down at Bruinje as his eyes adjusted to the dim light in the hold. He muttered under his breath, in French of course so Elsje wouldn't be as inclined to pick up on it, "It's just a pity that he speaks everything *but* French."

Bruinje looked up at his father with his wide blue eyes, his blond curls moving slightly in the early afternoon breeze that swept in off the sea, down the hatch and into the hold, bringing them all a temporary and much appreciated breath of fresh air.

"Francais aussi, Papa!" the little boy proclaimed.

Gilles laughed out loud and Elsje, who had been preoccupied with extricating Jacomina's fingers from her hair, had heard neither Gilles' quiet comment nor the boy's reply and so she turned back around questioningly to Gilles.

"What? What is so funny, Gilles?"

"Rien! Pas du tout!"

Gilles smiled and shook his head as Bruinje smiled up at his father. Gilles would have a few months on board the ship with nothing more pressing to do than to start teaching Bruinje *all* of the languages that he knew before they arrived at their new home.

Elsje smiled at her husband too, the best smile that Gilles had seen in a very long time, one that took him back to the time before she had become his wife, a time when he knew for certain, without her saying a word, that she was genuinely happy to see his face at her door.

Cries from the captain above to make ready and then to let out the sails led to the sensation of forward motion and Gilles heard the sound of the sea moving beneath them. The vessel made her way slowly out of the pack of ship's masts, sashaying between her sisters and then picking up speed as she headed out across the Zuider Zee toward the open ocean, out to the new world, leaving home and hearth and the fires of Europe far behind them.

LaVergne, TN USA
10 September 2009
157376LV00002B/1/P